PANIC SWITCH

MICHAEL DiMERCURIO

Dedicated to U.S. Navy Admiral Hyman G. Rickover
Father of the Nuclear Navy
The Kindly Old Gentleman

"How can you call yourself a well-rounded engineer if you've never read Shakespeare? Get out. *Get out!* GET THE HELL OUT OF MY OFFICE!"

Admiral Hyman G. Rickover to
then-Midshipman Michael DiMercurio
Nuclear program interview, 1980

"Holy Mary, Mother of God, pray for us sinners now and at the hour of our death."

Luke 1:28, Luke 1:42

"The KGB is more than a secret police organization, more than an intelligence and counter-intelligence organization. It is an instrument for subversion, manipulation, and violence, for secret intervention in the affairs of other countries."

Allen Dulles
USA's first CIA director
The Craft of Intelligence: America's Legendary Spy Master on the Fundamentals of Intelligence Gathering for a Free World, 1962

"Confrontation between intelligence organs never ended but with the end of the Cold War, contrary to expectations, actually intensified."

Vyacheslav Ivanovich Trubnikov
Former Director of the Foreign Intelligence Service (KGB First Chief Directorate, now the SVR) and currently First Deputy Foreign Minister of Russia

"When in October 1991 Gorbachev decided to break up the KGB, his intention was to de-fang it. The most radical change was the severing of counterintelligence (Second Chief Directorate) from foreign intelligence (First Chief Directorate). The Second would eventually be renamed the FSB and the First the SVR. On paper, the KGB should have been cut down to size, a shadow of its former self. But it's not the way things turned out."

Robert Baer, *The Fourth Man: The Hunt for a KGB Spy at the Top of the CIA and the Rise of Putin's Russia*, 2022

"I was the CIA director. We lied, we cheated, we stole. We had entire training courses. It reminds you of the glory of the American experiment."

U.S. Secretary of State Mike Pompeo
Addressing Texas A&M University, April 2019

"Pompeo's 'confession' is only a glimpse of the gigantic U.S. intelligence system's ingloriousness, from the production of unsubstantiated intelligence that gave Washington pretexts to invade others to the engagement of assassinations, abuse of prisoners, wiretapping, and public opinion manipulation, among other things. The shameful and deplorable record, while having long since shattered the credibility of the intelligence community a long time ago, has also laid bare its nature of serving at the pleasure of U.S. decision makers, regardless of truth, facts, and human conscience, as Washington plays power politics and seeks to preserve a hegemonic position in the world."

Xinhua Global Service
August 2021

"Endless revelations concerning warrantless wiretapping, the use of torture, and extrajudicial killing have done little to enhance the prestige or the moral standing of America's defense and intelligence establishment."

Patrick Radden Keefe, "The Surreal Case of a CIA Hacker's Revenge,"
The New Yorker, 2022

"The emergence of autonomous weapons systems and the prospect of losing meaningful human control over the use of force are grave threats that demand urgent action."

Report by Human Rights Watch and the Harvard Law School
International Human Rights Clinic, 2021

"The prospect of a future where the decision to take a human life is delegated to machines is abhorrent."

Phil Twyford
New Zealand Minister of Disarmament and Arms Control

"Pentagon Confirms Russia Has a Submarine Nuke Delivery Drone.

This is very bad news.

The existence of Status-6 was originally greeted with some skepticism—the weapon sounds so horrible, so devastating, so completely over the top it is difficult to process that someone would actually want to build such a thing. Unfortunately for all of mankind, it appears that it is very real."

Kyle Mizokami, *Popular Mechanics*, December 2016

"*You* find a leak. Flooding finds *you*."

Submarine Force wisdom

"Save the mission, save the ship, save the reactor, *then* save the crew—in that order."

Submarine Force directive

"I still have one torpedo and two main engines."

Commander Michael Pacino, Captain of SSN-21 USS *Seawolf*

Operation *Jailbreak*
Bo Hai Bay, surrounded by attacking
Red Chinese destroyers and aircraft

"If I have to die on this mission, I intend to die with an empty torpedo room."

Lieutenant Anthony Pacino, Arabian Sea, Operation *Panther*

PROLOGUE

NOW: 2:45 pm local time

The panicked communication that a fire had broken out in the middle level of the forward compartment came over his headphones, since the boat was rigged-for-ultraquiet with the 1MC general announcing speakers disabled.

Lieutenant Anthony Pacino felt the hard shot of adrenalin hit his system as he selected the ship-wide circuit and barked into his boom microphone. *"Fire in forward compartment middle level, fire in forward compartment middle level, casualty assistance team muster in the torpedo room! All hands, don EABs!"* He could feel his thinking becoming intensely focused, one track of his mind responding automatically to repeated training for this emergency, another wondering what started the fire and how bad it was, a third thinking ahead to what this meant to the mission. The submarine force's directive rang in his mind — *save the mission, save the ship, save the reactor,* then *save the crew, in that order.* If the fire were severe, there would be no saving this mission, he thought, glancing at the chart display for an escape route.

Pacino hurriedly pulled on his emergency air breathing mask with the fireproof hood, took an experimental breath of the dry, hot air and frowned through the mask's faceplate at the navigator. The control room they stood in was on the widest deck of the boat, straddling the centerline of the cylindrical hull of the submarine. In the forward compartment. In the forward compartment's middle level. The very same level as the fire.

1

"Navigator," Pacino ordered, "get the fuck to the scene and see what the hell is going on."

ONE HOUR AGO: 1:45 pm local time

The rigged-for-ultraquiet submarine *Vermont* hovered a hundred yards north of the twin islands of the deep channel of the Zapadnaya Litsa Fjord, less than 1500 yards from the Russian Federation's Zapadnaya Litsa Submarine Base.

U.S. Navy Lieutenant Anthony Pacino stood from where he'd been leaning over the navigation chart display along with the navigator, the Nav stationed due to the restricted waters the ship had entered, supplementing the section tracking party. The chart showed their present position, just northeast of the turn an emerging submarine would take to get to the fjord's channel. The expected outbound transit of the colossal, modified Omega II-class Russian submarine *Belgorod* was expected to start any minute.

Pacino walked to the port forward large flat panel display, which showed a real-time image taken from an orbiting Apex drone high overhead, the drone's data beamed down to their floating wire antenna, the picture showing the eight piers of the submarine base. Pacino shook his head—that the Russians had chosen this godforsaken ground for a sub base showed how differently they thought than westerners. The base was in one of the harshest climates on the planet, 175 nautical miles north of the Arctic Circle, with scant vegetation growing on the rocky mountains that rose suddenly from the deep cracks in the earth's crust that formed the fjord. It was August, and even so, the control room felt cold, the fjord's water temperature barely climbing above freezing. He imagined that in winter, it would take constant patrols from icebreaking ships to keep the fjord open, and the piers would be piled high with snow and ice. The satellite image showed the same status as an hour ago, when they'd arrived on station, five miles deep into the length of the fjord.

Pacino called to the navigator, "Zoom in closer to the Omega's pier." The navigator sidestepped to the command console and manipulated the panel and the image slowly zoomed in until the length of the pier took up half of the large widescreen display.

Tied to the pier was a huge black submarine. It wasn't apparent from the view how enormous and wide the sub was, but the small figures of four long-haul trucks on the pier lent a clue. Two tugboats were tied up on the outboard side of the sub, and if Pacino's guess were correct, each tug would be at least 80 feet long. That made the Russian's sub's length over 700 feet, 55 feet in beam, matching the secret-level intelligence estimate that claimed she displaced a whopping 35,000 tons. That was bigger than the largest World War II aircraft carriers. By comparison, their own submarine, the Block IV Virginia-class USS *Vermont*, was tiny, only 8000 tons submerged, 377 feet long and 34 feet in beam. And if its size were not impressive enough, the Omega II could act as a mother ship to a smaller nuclear powered deep submergence submarine, the Omega built to host a deep-diver called *Losharik*. The op-brief insisted *Losharik* could dive to a mile deep or even deeper.

"You're right," Pacino said, smirking at the navigator. "They *should* have named it *the 'BUFF.'*"

The navigator nodded back without smiling, glancing between the overhead drone intel display and the chart table. "Big ugly fat fucker, it definitely is."

"You know, Nav, I still think it's odd that *Belgorod* is tied up at Zapadnaya Litsa instead of Olenya Guba outside of Polyarny. Olenya Guba's their usual base, where they pick up the *Losharik*."

"Who knows what the crazy-ass Russians are thinking at any given moment," the navigator said, frowning down at the chart display, laying in a red dotted line for the expected track of the *Belgorod* when it departed the fjord for the open seas of the Barents. "They must be leaving without the deep-diver being docked to the underside of the hull."

The navigator, Lieutenant Commander Rachel Romanov, looked up from the chart at Lieutenant Anthony "Patch" Pacino, fifty thoughts about him flashing through her mind. The youth had walked back to the command console and leaned over it, wearing his black coveralls with the gold embroidered submariner's dolphins over his name patch on his left pocket, the U.S. flag patch on his left shoulder, the emblem of the USS *Vermont* on his right. He was tall, just over six feet, and trim without being bulky, as if he were a swimmer or a runner. He had straight, thick, longer-than-regulation chestnut hair that reflected the red of the overhead lamps, all of them turned red under the rig-for-ultraquiet as a reminder for absolute noise quieting. His face at first gave the impression of being rugged, as if it would seem natural to see him in a sheepskin coat on horseback, but on closer examination, his individual features were smoothly refined, almost feminine, his face narrow with strong cheekbones, a sculpted nose over puffy lips that a vain woman would pay a plastic surgeon a fortune for, but the feature that stood out the most were his almond-shaped eyes colored a deep emerald green. There was no doubt that on looks alone, if he desired, he could stop a woman's heart. Romanov had noticed him on his first day and constantly had to remind herself not to stare at him, hoping he didn't notice how attracted to him she was. Yet it was clear from his demeanor that Pacino had no idea of his good looks. There was a deep humility to the kid, she thought.

Which was another oddity about Pacino. Only twenty-three-years-old, the sonar officer of the *Vermont* had a chest of ribbons that twenty-year veterans would envy, one of them the Navy Cross itself. When Romanov had first heard about the medal, she'd dismissed it. It was a fluke from his senior year midshipman cruise disaster, when acting on instinct alone, he'd managed to save three crewmen of the ill-fated submarine *Piranha*, one of them a VIP admiral who had put Pacino up for the medal, in addition to Pacino being the son of the former Chief of Naval Operations, the admiral in command of the entire Navy, so a green junior officer wearing the Navy Cross could be explained away from a freak occurrence combined with nepotism and office politics. But then the lad had done it again, displaying the same dagger-in-the-teeth courage on the last operation, hijacking an Iranian submarine equipped with a Russian fast nuclear reactor and sailing it halfway around the world, evading the Russian submarines hunting it with search-and-destroy orders, even facing down a front-line Russian attack submarine. The result of the operation was Pacino winning the Silver Star and being granted his submarine dolphin emblem early, the dolphins indicating that he was "qualified in submarines," only months after being assigned to the *Vermont*, most of that time spent on the Iranian submarine. The officer cadre of *Vermont* had at first teased Pacino relentlessly that he hadn't truly earned his dolphins, but in the month after Operation *Panther*, Pacino had proved himself an able and competent officer, and the teasing died out.

And that led to today's operation, in which Lieutenant Pacino had the captain's confidence to trail and conduct an underhull of the Russian super-sub *Belgorod* as leader of the section tracking party, which was just a few watchstanders short of full battlestations.

Romanov felt her mind fill with other thoughts about Pacino. Operation *Panther* had led to the final confrontation with her soon-to-be ex-husband Bruno Romanov, the commanding officer of the missile cruiser *Javelin*. In early May, *Vermont* had suddenly been ordered to sea with all communications locked down, and for two months the crew had no contact with the outside world. The Navy had called it a *dark transit*. Romanov called it a marriage-killer. In the brutal aftermath of the breakup of her marriage, she'd leaned hard on Anthony Pacino, their friendship the only thing that seemed to keep her sane. She'd moved out of the two-story colonial house in Virginia Beach she'd shared with Bruno and had crashed at Pacino's dark, dreary, nearly windowless apartment. They'd taken turns sleeping on the couch, joking with each other that the crew could tell who'd had the queen bed and who'd had the couch the night before, as that couch was distinctly uncomfortable and useless for allowing a good night's sleep.

At Romanov's insistence, Pacino had terminated his lease and gone in with Romanov and three other of *Vermont*'s officers on a four-bedroom house near the beach, their roommates Dieter Dankleff, Mohammed Varney, and Duke Vevera. Romanov had claimed the master bedroom by virtue of being the senior officer, Pacino taking the room next door that shared the common master bathroom, Vevera and Dankleff down the hall, with Varney taking the makeshift bedroom in the basement. Vevera had christened the house "The Snake Ranch," the time-honored term for a Navy bachelor pad, presumably due to lonely "snakes" inhabiting boxer shorts. Romanov had objected, what with a female as one of the roommates, but the name had stuck so hard that even the captain and executive officer—the XO—had taken to referring to the house as the Snake Ranch.

There had undoubtedly been speculation as to the relationship between Pacino and Romanov, but they remained platonic friends. At least she told herself that. There had been a drunken ship's party after Operation *Panther* wrapped, and the two had shared a momentary embrace that led to a short but intense affair, but Romanov had recovered, realizing that she was on the rebound from Bruno and her jangling nerves only now calming from the *Panther* run. She'd already lost her marriage, and she'd be damned if she'd also lose her career for having a romantic relationship with a fellow officer on her submarine, a more junior officer at that. Besides, she was eight years older than Pacino, and any fling they would have would eventually, inevitably end. She'd go on to the next assignment, hopefully as an executive officer of a submarine, Anthony would go on to be a department head, and there was no guarantee they'd even be on the same coast on those future assignments. The certainty was that if a relationship ever started, its ending would be embedded within it, and that was no way for either of them to live, she thought.

It occurred to her that since she was his roommate, she might have to suffer seeing him meet and date another woman, and she knew that would bother her. She reminded herself that there were even bigger issues. Even in the oddball fantasy that they started a relationship, and for the sake of argument, it became serious to the point that she'd quit the Navy to be a wife, she couldn't become a mother. Her sterility had stressed her marriage with Bruno, who had desperately wanted a son, and had wanted her to stay home to take care of the baby. Old-fashioned, she knew. She'd actually agreed with Bruno, but nature had had different plans. Two years of fertility treatment had gone nowhere. So it was hard to believe young Pacino would want to end up with a barren woman who couldn't give him children.

Pacino's voice startled her out of her thoughts.

"Training run, maybe," Pacino said.

"Say again?" Romanov said, bringing herself back to the mission.

"Maybe *Belgorod* is just going out for training without the deep-diver sub. Maybe he'll shoot some exercise torpedoes or conduct maneuvers with the surface fleet."

"Maybe he's headed out to rendezvous with *Losharik* to see if they can dock submerged, undetected. The op-brief mentioned that they haven't tried that yet."

"Could be," Pacino said.

Pacino stole a glance at the navigator. Lieutenant Commander Rachel "Dominatrix Navigatrix" Romanov was tall and slender, only a few inches shorter than he was. She was compellingly beautiful, with nearly perfect features. She had wide brown eyes that could peer all the way into someone's soul, he thought. Her shining long dirty-blonde hair came down past the middle of her chest, although today she'd put it in a ponytail. He'd met her at a ship's party the day he'd reported aboard *Vermont*, and in that moment he'd been so stunned by her that he could barely speak. People always talked about the lightning bolt striking when meeting a soulmate and he'd always maintained that was ridiculous. There *were* no lightning bolts and there was no such thing as a soulmate. But after laying eyes on Rachel Romanov, Pacino began to understand.

During his first days on the submarine, he had had trouble reminding himself that she was a senior officer. A happily married senior officer. He had caught himself staring at her and would bite the inside of his lip to stop himself. Romanov, thankfully, was unaware of how he felt about her until just before he locked out of the submarine in scuba gear to invade the *Panther*, when he'd become so convinced that it was a suicide mission that he'd decided hiding

7

his feelings no longer mattered. But despite their short liaison after the Operation *Panther* victory party, and despite her separating from Bruno Romanov and filing for divorce, Rachel had insisted they keep their relationship platonic and official because anything between them would probably end badly, and that would impact their careers. Reluctantly, Pacino had agreed, and they had gone on as close friends, but nothing more. There were times at the Snake Ranch, when he'd lie awake at three in the morning staring at the ceiling, or standing officer of the deck watch during the midwatch, when he couldn't help but imagine him and Rachel being together, and in those moments, he was positive he would be much happier than he was just being her friend.

"Officer of the Deck, look," Romanov said to Pacino.

Something was happening on the pier. There were no longer lines connecting her stern to the jetty, and the gangway had been pulled off by a crane.

"Here we go." Pacino stepped over to the port side, where the number one sonar stack was glowing in green stripes and graphs. "Senior, you ready?" Senior Chief Tom Whale Albanese manned the main sonar display stack with its triple screens, the upper one selected to broadband waterfall noise, the middle to time-frequency graphs of tonals, the bottom screen showing transient noise detection.

"Sonar is ready, Officer of the Deck," Albanese said over his shoulder. Pacino walked to the starboard side, where Vevera stood watch at the BYG-1 attack center of the battlecontrol console as the firecontrol officer of the watch.

"You all set up, Firecontrol?" Pacino asked Vevera, clapping his shoulder. Vevera wore his leather motorcycle jacket over his coveralls, the one with gold embroidery of the Indian Motorcycle Company logo on the back. Vevera insisted on wearing wrap-around sunglasses while on watch at the console. "And can you even see your displays with those shades?"

"I hold that BUFF in the palm of my hand, Officer of the Deck," Vevera said. "And these glasses help me see the displays better. Plus, it has the distinct advantage of making me look cool."

Pacino laughed and returned to the forward port corner to peer at the drone image. The aft tugboat had pulled the massive hull slowly away from the pier, an angle forming in the dark water of the slip between piers.

"Forward lines are cast off," Romanov said. "The BUFF is underway."

Pacino returned to the command console and picked up a phone and buzzed the captain's stateroom, the earpiece of the phone put to his ear opposite his one-eared comms headset.

"Captain," the baritone voice of Commander Tim Seagraves came calmly over the phone.

"Officer of the Deck, sir," Pacino said, "*Belgorod* has shoved off. She'll be in the channel momentarily. We're ready to trail and perform the underhull."

"Very well, Officer of the Deck," Seagraves said, sounding almost bored.

"Do you want to station battlestations for the underhull, sir?" Pacino asked.

"No, Mr. Pacino. I'm sure you and your section tracking party can handle it. But call me if something unexpected happens."

"Aye aye, sir," Pacino acknowledged, but the captain had already hung up.

"Tugs are maneuvering his hull into the twin island channel," Romanov called. On the drone display, the tug on the Omega's starboard side was tied up, pulling the submarine backward into the wide channel. Once he cleared the pier, the second tug cast off from the starboard side and repositioned himself to take station on the sub's port side, the two tugs carefully moving the ship slowly and steadily westward into the fjord's basin, clearing the islands and spinning the hull counter-clockwise so that it would point northeast along the fjord's deep channel.

9

"Quite a contrast to your 'back-emergency-ahead-flank-without-tugs' underway you pulled off from Norfolk," Vevera said to Pacino.

"Hey," Pacino said, smiling to himself, "not everyone can be a natural born ship handler."

"Ouch," Vevera said. Vevera had famously tried the same maneuver himself and had ended up putting the *Vermont* into a complete 270 degree out-of-control spin in the Elizabeth River Harbor Reach.

"Let's not forget what Admiral King said about ship handling," Romanov said absently. *"The mark of a great shiphandler is never getting into situations that require great shiphandling."*

"That's probably what the captain of the BUFF is thinking right now," Pacino said. "Sonar, do you hold narrowband contact on the BUFF on the wide aperture hull arrays?"

"No, not yet, Officer of the Deck, and broadband is a complete acoustic shitshow with the tug engines and screws."

"An *acoustic shitshow*—I like that. We'll put that in the patrol report," Pacino said, grinning.

"Once the tugs bug out," Albanese said, "and he's under his own power, I'll have his broadband trace called out as 'Sierra One.' When the underhull is complete, as long as he's doing more than five knots, we can stream the towed array and I'll get a wealth of tonals."

"We can't wait for the tugs to shove off before the underhull," Pacino said. "Let's hope he heads down the channel nice and slow so we can get this underhull done and back off."

"We're going to have to underhull him here in the fjord," Romanov said. "Fortunately it's deep enough that the BUFF could have just vertical dived right by the pier if he'd wanted to. I suspect that once he reaches the mouth of the fjord and the Barents Sea, he'll dive and start hauling ass to wherever he's headed."

"That'll be the easy part of the mission," Pacino said quietly to Romanov, his hand covering his boom microphone. "Trailing him when he's making flank turns will be cake. This underhull maneuver will be a bitch."

Romanov nodded at him in understanding. "He's in the center of channel now," Romanov said, "and he's casting off the tug lines. Looks like the tugs are escorting him out."

"Attention in the section tracking party," Pacino called to the room. "The BUFF is headed right for us. We'll let him pass overhead, then put on turns to match his speed and add revolutions until we close the distance with the number two periscope up and get close to his screws to get a good video shot and a sound pressure level trace. Then we'll maneuver farther under his hull and check out his cold water injection scoops and then forward until we can see his ventral docking bay and docking hatch. The op-brief wants a glance at his bow to look at the size and configuration of his torpedo tube doors, but by then he may already be ready to dive, and doing that would put us very close to his spherical sonar array in his nosecone, and getting counterdetected by the Omega would be bad for business. So we'll see what happens. As you were."

"Officer of the Deck," Albanese called, "I have reliable broadband contact on the BUFF, bearing two one zero, designate contact Sierra One."

"Sonar, designate Sierra One, the BUFF, as Master One. Firecontrol," Pacino called to Vevera, "can you infer a range based on own-ship's position and Master One's position on the drone image?"

"OOD, it's rough, but I show Master One's range at one thousand yards."

"Speed?"

"Also rough," Vevera reported, "but it looks like he's doing about eight knots. He'll be on top of us in about four minutes."

"Pilot, mark your depth," Pacino called to Lieutenant U-Boat Dankleff who stood watch at the pilot's station on the forward port side of the room.

"OOD, depth one hundred feet."

"Pilot, take us down to one one five feet."

"Make my depth one one five feet, Pilot, aye," Dankleff acknowledged.

"Look-around number two scope," Pacino called, awaiting Dankleff's speed and depth report.

"Depth one one two feet, speed zero," Dankleff reported.

"Up scope," Pacino said, opening a switch cover and selecting the number two periscope's switch to raise the optronic unit out of the sail. The ultrahigh definition widescreen display on the command console came alive, the view looking a dark blue. With the scope controller, a unit that looked like it had been stolen from a kid's gaming setup, Pacino raised the optics to look almost straight up at the waves high above. From this depth, with the keel 115 feet beneath the surface, the periscope optics were forty feet deep. The surface above looked silvery, a wrinkled mirror, rays of sunlight streaming down here and there.

"Sonar, report bearing to Master One," Pacino called.

"OOD, Master One bears two zero eight."

Pacino trained the view to bearing 208, then rotated the view downward so he was looking up at a forty-five degree angle to the vertical, the deeper water darkening the view, the surface no longer visible at this angle.

It was then he heard the noises. The sound of the Omega's screws could be heard faintly through the hull, the whooshing noise becoming louder every second. And then it came slowly out of the blue haze into view, the enormous bow of the *Belgorod* coming toward them. The bottom of the hull was coming straight toward the optic's view. The BUFF's draft was deeper than estimated by five feet. Pacino lunged for the periscope hydraulics switch and dropped the scope to keep it from being snapped off by the Omega's deep draft hull.

"*Down scope!* Pilot, make your depth one two five feet smartly," Pacino ordered, his voice louder than normal. The noise of the Omega's screws was louder now, almost the volume of conversation.

"One two five feet, aye, sir, and my depth is one two five feet."

Pacino glanced at Navigator Romanov, giving her a half head shake, as if to say, *that was a close one.* She returned his gaze, responding with a half nod.

12

"Raising number two scope," Pacino called, muttering under his breath, "let's try this again."

The scope came out of the well and the display lit up a second time. Pacino trained the unit to look straight up and saw the massive hull of the Omega submarine passing slowly overhead. It kept steaming by, the noise of the screws getting louder now. He'd have to yell to be heard over the din of it.

"Master One is passing overhead," Pacino said, although it was more for entering the news into the record of the "conn open mike," a sort of blackbox video and audio recording system set up in the control room to preserve the actions of the crew for later examination. "Nav, what course do you recommend to maintain center of channel?"

Romanov looked at her chart display. "Course zero two eight, sir."

"Pilot, make your depth one two zero feet, all ahead one third, turns for eight knots, steer course zero two eight," Pacino ordered.

Dankleff acknowledged. They were putting on turns to match the Omega's speed, but it would take time to accelerate up to eight knots, and by then Master One's twin screws would pass overhead of the scope optics, at least they would if Pacino timed this right. Pacino trained his view flatter to look aft along the Omega's hull. The Russian submarine's hull began to narrow, the bottom of it becoming shallower. As it tapered at the rudder, the wide-diameter double screws could be seen, both of them churning up bubbles and foam from the power of their revolutions.

"Pilot, mark speed."

"OOD, speed seven knots."

"Pilot, make turns for nine." Pacino would need to speed up or the Omega would vanish down the channel. He must be going faster than their calculated eight knots, or he'd sped up.

The churning screws got closer but were still a bit too distant. *Vermont*'s speed seemed matched to that of the Russian.

"Pilot, add five turns," Pacino ordered. "Come up to one one five feet."

The view of the screws grew closer. Pacino stared hard at them, trying to see if he could tell the number of blades. At least the first data the op-brief had wanted was in—the Omega was not using ducted pump-jet propulsors, but conventional brass screws, the blades in a scimitar shape, but counting blades was tough at their present speed.

"Sonar, you have a turn count and a blade count?"

"OOD, Master One is making six zero RPM on two seven-bladed screws."

"Very well." Pacino would leave the visual blade-counting to the people who later would examine the high-def video frame-by-frame. It was time to move the view forward. "Pilot, add two turns, make your depth one two zero feet."

The view slowly moved along the hull until two structures came into the optics, both on the starboard side, a similar set on the port side. They looked like jet engines, but angled downward by forty-five degrees. "I have the cold water injection scoops," Pacino reported. "Dear God, those are huge. You could drive a car into those scoops and not touch the sides."

The view moved farther forward. Pacino turned his view aft as *Vermont* sped forward relative to the hull of the *Belgorod*, trying to get a view down the throats of the scoops, then trained the view forward again. Forward of the quadruple scoops would be the flat hull until the mechanism for docking the deep-diving submarine appeared. The view was moving forward until Pacino could just barely see a dark opening in the hull. It looked rectangular, its long axis along the centerline of the hull. Inside the opening it was too dark to make out anything. Pacino was just starting to think about activating the sail's underice lights to illuminate the Omega hull opening when a breathless voice suddenly crackled over the shipwide phone circuit.

"*Fire, fire, fire! Fire in forward compartment middle level! We've got a bad fire—*" The transmission continued, but became unintelligible, then went ominously quiet.

NOW: 2:45 pm local time

Without conscious thought, Pacino clicked into the shipwide phone circuit and shouted into it, reminding himself to speak slowly and clearly despite the adrenalin slamming into his system.

"Fire in forward compartment middle level, fire in forward compartment middle level, casualty assistance team muster in the torpedo room! All hands, don EABs!"

He pulled on his emergency breathing air mask, tugging at the fireproof hood and tightening the straps behind his head. The air was hot and dry, but seemed otherwise normal. The ventilation system suddenly stopped blowing air into the room as the rig for fire was executed, and the room immediately soared in temperature. Pacino could feel himself start to sweat all over, perhaps from the heat in the room or the fear. He shot a hard look at Romanov. With no more information coming over the phones, he'd need an officer to take charge at the scene and report what was happening to the control room.

"Navigator," Pacino ordered, "get the fuck to the scene and see what the hell is going on." She waved at him as she unplugged her air hose and dashed forward to the door leading to the combat equipment room and the ladderway to the lower level torpedo room. She'd have to make her way aft through the lower level, link up with the casualty assistance team and help fight the fire. Odds were, the fire was happening in the galley. If they were lucky, it was just a grease fire and would be out in a few minutes, but if it were more serious, fighting the fire could make tremendous noise and alert the Russians.

He glanced at the chart, realizing he'd have to break contact with the Omega and escape the fjord undetected, all the while having to fight a goddamned fire.

"Pilot, all stop! Make your depth one five zero feet and hover!"

As Dankleff acknowledged, Pacino lowered the periscope and stepped to the chart table. As the *Vermont* slowed to a stop, the noise of the huge screws of the Omega came closer, thrashing the water directly over them now. The channel turned northward here, so that the outbound course would change to 015. If Pacino hovered while they put out the fire, the Omega would sail on away from them, but it would still be a disaster if they had to put up the snorkel mast and ventilate the smoke out of the ship. They were far inside the twelve-mile territorial limit of Russian waters, which was a violation of international law, and if detected, the Russians would be justified in taking them all prisoner or even firing upon them. This miserable situation could come down to the agonizing decision between being captured or suffocating. Or even worse, being burned alive.

Romanov's voice came over his headset, her voice iron hard, but he knew her well enough to know when she was afraid.

"Conn, Torpedo Room, Navigator, the fire is in the wardroom and is extremely severe and spreading forward to officers country."

"Nav, did you say the wardroom?" Pacino asked, not believing his ears. Why would a fire break out in the officers' mess and conference room?

"Conn, it's an oxygen fire. There is an O2 line running into the wardroom for when it doubles as a surgical suite and it—it must be a double-ended shear and oxygen is blowing into the room and the room is engulfed in flames. We can't get anywhere close to it!"

"Can you isolate it upstream? Cut off the O2 flow?"

"We're working on it now but the fire has spread to the crews' mess where the forward isolation valve is. I've got Chief Nygard getting into a steam suit now. He's going to attempt to get to the valve."

It was then that the casualty grew far worse. The air feeding Pacino's mask suddenly cut off, and as he tried to inhale, he just drew a vacuum on the mask. He pulled it off, thinking something must have happened to the EAB manifold. He looked up to find the other control room watchstanders dumping their masks. The air of the control room smelled awful, like burning insulation. And now black smoke was pouring into the room from the aft door, the foul-smelling smoke in mere seconds filling the room.

"Navigator, Control, we've lost emergency breathing air up here. What's your status?"

16

"Conn, Navigator, Chief Nygard is in the middle level crews' mess trying to get to the O2 valve now, but we've lost emergency breathing air throughout the compartment. We've got a few OBAs and a few air-packs, but not enough to go around. OOD, you know what this means."

The smoke continued filling the room, making it even hotter, while visibility was shrinking. Pacino could barely make out the sonar console from the command console. He stepped aft and shut the aft control room door, but the smoke was still getting worse, pouring in from the aft bulkhead despite the shut door. Vevera stood up from his panel as it went dark. "Loss of battlecontrol," he said to Pacino.

The sonar consoles on the port side blacked out. "Loss of sonar," Albanese said.

The smoke had completely filled the room. Visibility was near zero. Pacino coughed desperately, sinking down to his knees, hoping that the air would be breathable near the deck, but it seemed no improvement. He could feel dizziness start to overtake him as the overhead red lights clicked off, leaving the room in the darkness of a coal mine.

And now the decision he'd feared was here. There were only two options—surfacing the boat and abandoning ship, or scuttling the vessel in the deep water of the fjord to avoid capture by the Russians. In the first case, they'd be taken captive, held as criminals, interrogated, and tortured, and certainly used as a propaganda win for the Russians, with the top-secret project submarine *Vermont* in their hands. In the second, every crewman aboard would die and the USS *Vermont* would sink below crush depth in the deep fjord and scatter wreckage on the sea bottom, all to be harvested by the Russian deep-diving machinery. If the boat still had propulsion, and it were clear that all was truly lost, Pacino could order full speed and a steep angle to crush depth and get all this over with fast, and maybe that way the hull breakup would be violent enough that it would spoil any Russian salvage attempts.

"Maneuvering, Conn, report your status," Pacino ordered over the tactical circuit.

But there was no reply. The circuit was silent.

"Navigator, Control, report." No reply. "*Navigator, Officer of the Deck, report!*" But there was nothing.

By then, the room was so filled with smoke that there seemed no way to breathe. Without remembering how he got there, he found himself lying prone on the deck, coughing so hard it felt like he'd toss up a lung, and it was then that the strangeness began.

He saw a beam of light attempting to shine through dark smoke, rotating around to shine on the other crewmembers.

A second light beam came into view and then a third, a fourth, and more. One of the lamps shone in his face, blinding him, and when it moved from his face, he could see the dim outline of a masked figure oddly wearing a fireman's helmet.

Everything went black then, but while he couldn't see or hear anything, he felt a sense of time.

Then he could see and hear again, but only for a brief moment, and while he could see, he couldn't move. He saw a circle of bright light, half obscured by smoke, and if he didn't know better, he could swear it was an open hatch, and he felt himself incline from lying flat to being vertical, but he wasn't standing, he was just...floating.

The world went black again, and again he had that strange sense of time passing.

And like a cosmic strobe light, the world returned once more, this time the light around him so bright he became convinced he'd passed on to the other side like he had in his near death experience aboard the *Piranha*, but then he saw a flash of something. His head was turned to the side and he could see the outside of the hull of the *Vermont*, but she wasn't in a Russian fjord, she was lying in a drydock, drenched with the afternoon Virginia sunshine. A short trailer or container box was placed on the top of her deck aft of the plug trunk hatch, block letters on the trailer reading *TRACON*, with the emblem of Submarine Development Group 12 next to the letters.

Pacino couldn't move his head, or anything else, with the exception of his eyes. He looked up and saw a hovering helicopter overhead, its blades rotating in slow motion. He scanned the chopper to see if it had markings of the Russian Navy, but it was painted red with a large white cross painted on it. He could make out the word *MEDEVAC* on its side just before the blackness came again.

This time the blackness seemed to last longer, and when it ended, the white room around him came into focus. He could see machinery around him, medical machines, and someone in a white outfit starting to rush into the room, but then the universe went black again.

Still that odd sense of time passing. He waited for the world to light up again, but other than waiting, he was unable to think or process what he'd experienced and seen.

When the curtain lifted again, Pacino looked up to see his father, former Admiral Michael Pacino, who was now the National Security Advisor to the president. The elder Pacino leaned over him. Pacino noticed his father's dark tailored suit and red patterned tie. He blinked and saw his father try to say words, but no sound emerged. Then the blackness came back for him, but this time, there was no sense of time.

It was just a black nothingness.

THREE WEEKS LATER

BOOK I
OPERATION *POSEIDON*

1

Lieutenant Anthony Pacino waited impatiently on the wood bench outside the hearing room, wearing his starched dress white uniform—the outfit given the name "choker whites" due to the stiff, high collar. The formal uniform made it even more uncomfortable in the hot, airless corridor. Per Navy regulations, Pacino wore full medals with the uniform, feeling his usual discomfort at the Navy Cross, but at least proud to wear the Silver Star—that at least he *knew* he had earned without people claiming that he'd only acted mindlessly on animal instinct like they alleged after the *Piranha* incident. Above his ribbons were the polished, solid gold dolphins awarded him by the commander of the submarine force, Vice Admiral Catardi. Anthony felt his father's palm on his shoulderboard, the old man attempting to comfort him.

"I can't come into the room with you, Son," the older Pacino said quietly in his baritone voice.

Anthony looked over at his father, who was wearing a dark suit and dark black tie. It still felt strange not seeing him in his Navy uniform. Even though the senior Pacino was older now, in his mid-sixties, he still looked the same as he always had. Tall and gaunt, with a deeply tanned face, crow's feet at the corners of his bright green eyes. His white hair had started to thin just a little, but it would take a close look to confirm.

"I know, Dad." Anthony's voice was still just a hoarse croak from the damage from the smoke inhalation.

"Look, it's not for me to tell you your business," Michael Pacino said gently, "but I've been through four of these boards of inquiry. One for the original *Devilfish*, one for *Seawolf*, one for the War of the East China Sea and one for the SSNX. And if there's one thing that seems to work best in this situation, it's this—just look them in the eye, leave all feelings of guilt aside, and tell them the straight, honest damned truth. Make them understand you'll take whatever judgment is coming to you. Take responsibility, but *never* condemn your own actions. Make them see that at all times, you did what you thought was right."

"I know, Dad," Anthony said, his croaking voice dull and dead. "But people got hurt. Torpedoman Chief Blacky Nygard got third degree burns. And my friend Rachel—the navigator—is still in a coma, on life support, with some serious burns. They don't even know whether she'll come out of it. And on the conn open mike video they showed me, one of my last orders was directing her right into the goddamned fire." Anthony clamped his eyes shut, sniffing back his emotions.

"Has any of your memory returned?"

The younger Pacino shook his head sullenly. "The last thing I remember was the underhull. Looking into the Omega's giant cold water scoops."

Michael Pacino nodded. "Son, the physicians testified that smoke inhalation—particularly toxic smoke from cable insulation, hull insulation, paint, laminate wall coverings, amines, lube oil, and a thousand other chemical compounds that caught fire in that hull—combined with the low oxygen levels and the high concentration of carbon monoxide and carbon dioxide—could have led to severe changes in the crew's mental states. Confusion, fainting, seizures, and coma, I'm afraid, are all on the menu. I have to believe partial memory loss is possible as well, and especially hallucinations."

"They have the video, Dad. They don't need me to testify to what I remembered."

"Son, your mental state at that time is *important*. They're going to ask you that one question that's on everyone's mind."

"Yeah, I know," Anthony said, staring at the deck as he twirled his hat in his hands, "when the fire started, why didn't I just terminate the exercise and evacuate the hull, get everyone out of there and let the shipyard fire brigade fight the fire?"

"Right. But given the altered mental state that the toxic smoke caused, leading to hallucinations," the older Pacino said, "it's possible you no longer recognized you were in a training drill. In your mind, you could have actually *been* in the Zapadnaya Litsa Fjord with a raging oxygen fire and the emergency air system failing. Hell, Anthony, the doctors said that cocktail of smoke may as well have been a super-dose of LSD. You weren't responsible for your actions from the moment you had to dump your EAB."

"I guess it's possible," Anthony said. "I don't know if they'll accept that answer, though. And if they do, they're saying that they believe I was crazy at the time."

"Don't think like that. Keep your thoughts positive. Now, assuming you get through that, they might ask the follow-up question."

"What's that?" Anthony looked up at his father. No follow-up question had occurred to him. The main question was difficult enough to consider.

"Simple. Had it been a real fire while you were trailing the Omega, what would you have done? Surface the boat, admitting to the Russians you were illegally trespassing in their territorial waters and surrendering to capture, or scuttling the ship with the loss of all hands aboard, including yourself?"

"God, Dad, what a question. How the hell should I know? What would *you* have done?"

"Anthony, despite what people think, no man can truly say what he would do in *any* given situation until he's actually *in* it. That decision, coming at that particular time, could be influenced by a thousand things. If they ask that question, I recommend you stick with that answer. But I want to share something relevant with you. It's still codeword top secret, so this stays between us."

27

Anthony looked up from the cap he was twirling and sat up straight on the wooden bench and looked at his father.

"The situation we're discussing, getting caught deep in enemy waters, actually happened to my Academy roommate, Sean Murphy. You knew Sean."

Anthony nodded, thinking sadly that Murphy had been the Superintendent of the Naval Academy when Pacino had attended, but who was now gone from lung cancer.

"I remember Admiral Murphy. He called me into his office when your cruise ship went down." Anthony remembered the moment that the Supe had told him his father was missing and presumed dead in the terrorist attack on the Navy's stand-down cruise. "But you said Murphy was in hostile waters—and caught?"

The elder Pacino nodded. "His submarine *Tampa* was captured by the Red Chinese spying in the Bo Hai Bay during their civil war. The crew was impounded aboard, tied up at a Chinese PLA Navy pier at Tianjin outside Beijing, with destroyers tied up on either side."

"Wow," Anthony said. "What happened?"

"You remember Uncle Dick Donchez?" Donchez had commanded the submarine force back in the day. "Dick pulled me out of retirement to command the rescue mission. I took over *Seawolf* and went in with a platoon of SEALs. My dad used to talk about projects around the house, grumbling that a particular chore took every tool in the toolbox. Well, this particular chore used every SEAL, torpedo, and cruise missile in the inventory and we still came up short."

Anthony looked at his father, his eyes wide. "Is this where your cryptic 'famous naval saying' comes from, the one engraved in brass on the wall of the Naval Academy's Memorial Hall? *I still have one torpedo and two main engines.* I always wondered what that was all about."

Admiral Pacino nodded. "There were multiple Chinese frigates and destroyers attacking us. They had our position nailed down and were depth charging us to Hell. I was preparing to surface the boat and wave a white flag, and that's when the SEAL commander put a loaded .45 to my temple and threatened to blow my brains all over the periscope if I surrendered. Gun to my head, I looked him in the eye and said, 'I still have one torpedo and two main engines.' I surfaced and sent a junior officer to the bridge to wave that white flag, and while the Chinese surface task force prepared to board us, I shot my last torpedo and sank one destroyer and rammed the other with the sail while half re-submerged, and I cut it cleanly in half and it sank on the spot, but the other surface forces gathered around us like angry hornets. If not for the fighter wing aboard the *Ronald Reagan*, which shot that surface force into splinters, *Seawolf* would have been lost. The fighter that blew away the destroyer that was sending down depth charges right over my head was flown by one Lieutenant Commander Paul Carlucci. I don't know your politics, Son, but at the next election, you might want to consider voting for him."

Anthony stared at his father, not knowing what to say or how to react. Finally he managed to croak, in his hoarse voice, "What happened to *Tampa*? Did she make it out?"

"*Tampa* made it out. They lost most of her officers and chiefs to Chinese executions or torture, but we got her out. And made it out ourselves. So I guess the moral of the story, Son, is even if you and your ship get captured in enemy waters, you will never be forgotten. America will come for you. Guns blazing."

Anthony shook his head. He'd heard his father's career was a storied one, but he'd never heard about any of this.

The door to the hearing room opened and a female lieutenant in tropical whites motioned to Anthony.

"They're ready for you, Lieutenant Pacino."

"Good luck, Son."

Anthony stood, looked into his father's eyes, and nodded dejectedly.

————————————

Lieutenant Anthony Pacino nodded a solemn farewell at his father after begging off the old man's offer of dinner. The elder Pacino would undoubtedly want to talk more about the accident and the inquest, but that was the last thing the younger man wanted. He walked slowly out to his old '69 Corvette, climbed in, tossed his officer's cap onto the passenger seat and turned over the engine, the more modern LS-2 power plant he'd installed himself with the low profile supercharger. The engine throbbed with power, but Pacino's mind was too far away to enjoy it.

The words of the inquest commander still rang in his mind.

We find Lieutenant Pacino blameless in the fire that broke out on the middle level of the USS Vermont's *forward compartment due to the extenuating circumstances arising from him and his crew being immersed in a completely realistic training drill scenario, so real, in fact, that none of the participants recognized the fire as being a separate event from the drill's script, and as the fire progressed, with no rescue coming from the shipyard's force, and with smoke blowing mind-altering chemicals into the control room, the drill participants all came to truly believe that the drill's simulated reality was the actual reality, and they acted accordingly until such point as the shipyard rescue forces finally entered the hull. In fact, up to the point of his losing consciousness, this Board of Inquiry finds Lieutenant Pacino's actions to be in keeping with the highest traditions of the U.S. Submarine Force and the U.S. Navy. Accordingly, this Board of Inquiry is concluded with no punitive findings for Lieutenant Pacino or any member of ship's force. Mr. Pacino, you're free to go, with my best regards to you, sir, and please convey our very best wishes to Navigator Romanov and Senior Chief Nygard, with this board's hopes that they both make a full recovery.*

Of course, the question was, did the board's findings arise from them being leaned on by Pacino's father, or Vice Admiral Catardi, or even the president himself? And even if not, in his own mind, was he truly blameless for what had happened? When he had screened the conn open mike video, he'd searched for signs of incompetence or wrongful action, and although he still had no memory of anything that happened after the underhull of the cold water scoops, the actions taken by the figure of himself in the control room all seemed appropriate, although having unfortunate consequences for Rachel Romanov and Senior Chief Nygard. The answer to his father's second question nagged at him, though — *if it had been a real fire in that scenario, what would you have done? Surface the boat, admitting to the Russians you were illegally trespassing in their territorial waters and surrendering to capture, or scuttling the ship with the loss of all hands aboard? Including yourself?*

He couldn't answer the question without regaining his memory, but the fact that he'd demanded to know propulsion plant status from the reactor plant watchstanders made him think he had been getting ready to sail the boat down below crush depth. And that would make him a suicidal mass murderer, certainly one with exigent circumstances — to keep the top secret, front line attack submarine and crew out of Russian hands — but could he really have given orders that would kill the whole crew? And himself? To avoid capture by the Russians? Thinking about this was madness, he thought.

Without conscious thought, he realized he'd driven to the parking lot of Naval Medical Center Portsmouth, the hospital that was part of Norfolk Naval Station. He cut the engine, engaged the parking brake, grabbed his cap and walked slowly toward the entrance, realizing he must look absolutely foolish still wearing his starched choker whites with full medals, but he honestly didn't care. Almost as if in a dream he watched himself ride the elevator to the eighth floor, the burn unit ICU. Pacino found himself in the hospital room and saw Rachel lying there, completely helpless, with burn dressings on her abdomen and legs. She was fed oxygen by a ventilator, multiple IVs snaking into her forearms. He became aware of a second person in the room, the man solid and at least four inches taller than Pacino, dressed in jeans and a golf shirt, with a shaved head and a square jaw, looking like a middle-aged boxer. Slowly Pacino realized he was staring into the face of Commander Bruno Romanov, Rachel's soon-to-be ex-husband.

"Bruno," he stammered in his hoarse voice, not knowing what else to say. "Commander Romanov." An intense stab of guilt sliced into him then as he glanced at Rachel, then at Bruno. He was forming the words to apologize to Bruno for almost getting Rachel killed.

But Bruno smiled down on him kindly, almost in a fatherly way, and put his arm around Pacino's shoulders. "It wasn't your fault, Patch," he said in a gentle but booming deep voice with a slight Eastern European accent. "You did what you thought was right. I heard about the Board of Inquiry. They cleared you, so you're cleared in my book."

Pacino looked at Commander Romanov. Was Bruno here to reclaim his relationship with Rachel? Then more guilt came, because that assumed she'd wake up, and no one knew whether she would.

"How is she?" Pacino asked. "What are the doctors saying?"

Bruno Romanov's expression fell. "Physically, the doctors are not worried about her burns or the skin grafts, but her lungs and heart were damaged by the smoke inhalation. But what's worse is that her brain activity is not good, Patch. There's not a lot the staff will share with me, but the fact they look away when I ask? I don't like it."

Pacino shook his head sadly, looking at Rachel. He'd wanted to spend a moment with her alone, but the guilt came through him like a blast of cold water. Perhaps, he thought, it would be best to leave.

"Well," Bruno said, "I'd like to stay with her, but you know— you must know by now—we're not married any longer. The divorce was final the day of the accident. Keep that to yourself, or the hospital will kick me out of most of the visiting hours. Even with this, though, I've got ship's business to attend to. Time, tide, formation and Big Navy wait for no man. Or no family emergency. I'll leave you to sit with Rachel."

"Thanks, Bruno," Pacino said, unsure what else he could say.

Romanov clapped Pacino on the shoulderboard and walked out. Pacino stared after him, then turned to look at Rachel. Her long shining hair was spread smoothly over the pillow, as if someone had lovingly brushed it—Bruno, maybe? Pacino sat on her bed and took her hand in his, and when he spoke, emphatic words came from somewhere deep inside him, without conscious thought.

"Rachel, it's me, Patch. Listen, when you get better—and you *will* get better, I swear you will—I won't take 'no' for an answer. I don't care what you say. I'm in love with you and I know you have feelings for me. So we're starting a relationship, dammit. You read me, Madam Navigator?" He felt her hand carefully to see if she'd squeeze his, but her hand was as asleep as when he'd first held it. But he looked over at the vital signs monitor.

Was it his imagination, or had Rachel's pulse rate suddenly jumped?

2

National Security Director Michael Pacino stepped quickly into the large jet helicopter with the presidential seal on the outside flank. The president's rig, he thought. President Carlucci had called shortly after the younger Pacino left the base, asking the admiral to come to D.C., adding that the presidential helicopter would be waiting. Pacino strapped himself into the plush leather seat and looked across the row at CIA Director Margo Allende.

Allende was in her mid-forties and had a habit of dressing frumpy, keeping her sleek copper auburn hair in a bun, avoiding makeup and hiding her deep blue eyes behind large-lensed red-framed 80s glasses, as if doing that would make men take her more seriously, or perhaps keep them from finding and expressing interest in her, but today Director Allende wore her gleaming hair straight and down below her shoulders, the glasses gone, her face and eyes made up, and she wore a tight cashmere dress hugging her almost perfect figure. Pacino looked at her appreciatively, winked and said, "What's a nice girl like *you* doing in a place like *this*?"

"Why, Admiral Pacino," she said in her honey-smooth Atlanta Southern accent, smiling brightly at him, "if I didn't know better I'd swear you were hitting on me."

Pacino smiled back. "Guilty as charged."

He and Allende had been dating since the end of the *Panther* mission. He spent at least three nights a week at her Georgetown townhouse, but they were careful to take separate cars to the West Wing to avoid interoffice gossip. Pacino never said it aloud, but sometimes he thought being with her was like a wartime romance, all the drama and intrigue of their jobs making them comrades as well as paramours, and he hated to think about it, but he knew that eventually he'd retire from Carlucci's administration and she'd still be in the thick of the intelligence business, and it wouldn't be the same. But if he ever made any noises like that, Allende became possessive and swore that the only way she'd ever let him leave her would be in a box. She smiled when she said it, probably realizing it sounded psychopathic, but he had to admit he liked how fierce and passionate her feelings were for him. He had to admit, when he thought about it, his affair with Allende was the best relationship of his life.

"Patch," she said, her expression serious, "how did Anthony do? Is he okay?"

"The inquest acquitted him, or more accurately, found him without fault, but he's pretty badly rattled. His navigator and buddy, a pretty young thing named Rachel Romanov, got burned and is in a coma. The *Vermont's* torpedoman chief got badly burned fighting the fire. Anthony feels tremendous guilt about what happened to them."

"I saw the video, Patch. He did nothing wrong."

"I know. But now *he* has to know."

Allende looked out the window. "God, life absolutely sucks sometimes."

The two were quiet for some time as the lush Virginia countryside sped by out the windows.

"What were you doing down in Norfolk, Margo? I didn't expect you on this ride."

She gave him a half smile. "I wanted to see you. I made up an excuse that I needed to prepare you for the Situation Room briefing."

"Okay, so what's up?"

"There's a Russian super sub, called the *Belgorod*. An old and refurbished Omega-II class."

Pacino puffed out his lips. "I know the Omega class," he said, barely audible over the roar of the helicopter's rotors and engines.

35

"You'll remember, Omega unit one and my *Devilfish* had it out under the polar icecap. It didn't end well, for either of us."

Pacino knew Allende knew the story. He'd shown her the top secret file in her office SCIF conference room. His attack sub, back when he was a Navy commander, had been sent under the icecap to counter the original Omega when the Russian super sub had been tasked with being a command platform for the launch of a tactical nuclear strike on the U.S. east coast. His *Devilfish* and the Omega had fought it out to a draw, killing most of their crews.

"*This* Omega, Patch, is modernized far beyond the old Omega's technology. It carries multiple very large torpedoes called 'Status-6' weapons. They're really more like autonomous mini-subs than torpedoes. The Russians renamed them 'Poseidon' torpedoes. They can swim to a programmed area and loiter on station for months — they're nuclear powered. And they pack a ten megaton punch. We think the Russians are either going to use *Belgorod* to deploy these Poseidons or their ride-along deep-diving sub will deploy them."

"That isn't good, Margo, but it doesn't sound particularly urgent. After all, they aren't on the way now, are they?"

Allende shook her head.

"So, why the sudden call to Washington?"

"We think the *Belgorod* is preparing to leave port with orders to deploy these weapons. Think of this as the launch of a Russian intercontinental ballistic missile—or three or four—but with the missile speed slowed down to ten knots."

"When will the *Belgorod* sail?"

"Unknown, but they may be waiting for President Vostov's visit. He's got tentative plans to visit the Sevmash Shipyard to tour the Poseidon factory and the *Belgorod*. And you know from experience how presidential plans constantly change. Scheduling something a month out? It could move ninety days further out. Or it could happen tomorrow."

"We'll need the submarine force to get a unit in position to trail *Belgorod* out," Pacino said.

"They've already deployed two subs. But they've been on station about eighty days and are running out of food and spare parts."

Food, Pacino thought. The seemingly inconsequential thing that almost lost Operation *Panther*.

The stairs of the helicopter were flanked by uniformed Marines, and both saluted Pacino, who returned the gesture. He and Allende walked quickly to the West Wing entrance, the president's chief of staff's aides escorting them. Pacino's own deputy should have been here, he thought, glancing at his Rolex.

At the West Wing portal entrance, a Navy official staff truck pulled up, and out emerged Vice Admiral Rob Catardi, the head of the Submarine Force, but Pacino noticed something immediately. Catardi was no longer a vice admiral. He sported a new star on his shoulderboards, apparently having been promoted to full admiral, a four-star position.

Pacino smiled at his old friend. Rob Catardi had been one of then-Commander Pacino's junior officers on the original *Devilfish*, having temporarily detached from the submarine to go to chief engineer school just before the boat's orders to the polar icecap. Years later, as captain of the Seawolf-class submarine *Piranha*, Catardi had played host to young Anthony on his first class midshipman cruise, when a nuclear-powered, unmanned U.S. Navy drone submarine—having been hijacked and hacked—came after *Piranha* and put her on the bottom. If not for Anthony Pacino's instinctive and brave action, Catardi would have died in the wreck of the *Piranha*. Two years later, Pacino and Catardi had suffered through the two month mission of the *Vermont* when she sailed into the Gulf of Oman to commandeer the Iranian submarine *Panther*, both of them watching in disbelief and horror as *Vermont*'s skipper Scotch Seagraves had assigned young and inexperienced Anthony Pacino to the *Panther* boarding party as assistant-officer-in-charge. But despite terrible odds, Anthony and the boarding party had prevailed and the older Pacino and Catardi had celebrated with a steak dinner and thirty year old scotch.

"Four stars, now, Rob?" Pacino said, shaking Catardi's hand and pulling the younger man into a bear hug.

Catardi nodded. "They made me Vice CNO. And as of now, I'm acting CNO." The admiral-in-command of the U.S. Navy was called the chief of naval operations, so Catardi was now the deputy to Admiral Grayson Rand, but if Catardi had been appointed "acting CNO," something was wrong with Rand.

"What's up with Admiral Rand?" Pacino asked. "And who's minding the shop at SubForce?"

Catardi followed Pacino into the double doors of the West Wing entrance. As he produced his identification, he looked over sadly. "Rand was diagnosed with a glioblastoma. The kind of brain cancer that takes you in two or three or four months and has you screaming at your family and urinating in your desk drawers. Inoperable. He was trying stem cell therapy and a newfangled vaccine but he got complications. Water on the brain. They took him to surgery to ease the pressure, but it was just a band-aid. Looks like he's retired to spend his last weeks with his people. I'm filling in for him until the SecNav and the president decide on the appointment of Rand's replacement."

Pacino shook his head. "Goddamned hard to hear that, Robby. Grayson Rand is a good man and doesn't deserve all that. But who stepped in for you at SubCom?"

"You remember John Patton?"

"Sure. He took over for me as CNO after I was out after the *Princess Dragon* incident. Amazing guy. He put me in charge of the mission to avenge the sinking of the *Piranha*. But Patton left the Navy years ago."

"His younger brother, Wally 'Stiletto' Patton, came up through the ranks and now he's got the baton. He should be in our little conference today."

"Small world, ain't it, Rob?"

The security forces cleared them, and Catardi, Allende and Pacino walked down to the lower level and the Situation Room. It only had a few aides sitting in wall chairs, but there were pad computers and notepads on the table.

"Looks like the crew is in the mess," Allende said. "Buy you boys a cup of coffee?"

In the mess, a group of people were gathered around Allende's deputy director for operations, Angel Menendez. Menendez was a compact, shorter man, wearing a sport jacket over a brightly colored Hawaiian shirt, a black fedora in one hand, a cup of coffee in the other. He saw Allende and burst into a smile.

"Boss," he said, nodding and smiling at Allende. He looked at Pacino and shook his hand. "Admiral Pacino, good to see you again, sir, although the circumstances aren't ideal."

Pacino nodded, looking over at three general officers he didn't know.

"This is the new head of NSA," Menendez said to Pacino, indicating an Army general with a chest full of medals and airborne wings with a combat star. "General Foster 'Nick' Nickerson. He's an old paratrooper from West Point, but we don't hold that against him."

The National Security Agency chief grinned with a mouth stuffed with white teeth, his mustache bushy for a general officer. "Never listen to CIA," Nickerson said to Pacino, shaking his hand. "They lie. Just ask Ms. Allende's predecessor."

Allende smirked. "Just because the Chinese accused him of lying, doesn't mean it's true."

Nickerson laughed. "Hey, sometimes lying is our business. Just not within the family, right?"

Menendez pulled over an Air Force general, a stocky older officer with grey hair cut into a flattop, a similar bouquet of ribbons on his chest, with pilot's wings with a combat star above them. "Admiral Pacino, this is Lieutenant General George 'Buck' Rogers. The recently appointed boss of the Defense Intelligence Agency. We pretend to like him, but he's actually a son of a bitch."

Rogers guffawed and shook Pacino's hand. "Don't listen to 'Fedora' Menendez. I and my boys know the *real* no-shit intelligence. Fedora's just mad because we don't always share it with *him*."

A solidly built man came into the room, flanked by two of his aides. The chairman of the joint chiefs of staff, Air Force General Abdul Zaka, was the senior statesman of the military, older by far than any general officer Pacino had met, surviving in active duty well into his late sixties. He'd come to the Pentagon after commanding the strategic command that controlled the country's nuclear weapons, and before that, several bomber groups. Despite his background being vastly different than Pacino's, they'd gotten along famously since they'd met at a seminar fifteen years before. Zaka had invited Pacino to his hunting compound a few years later, an impressive lodge far from civilization in the deep woods of western Virginia, and they'd stayed up late into the night discussing military strategy. Zaka was perpetually curious about naval strategy and tactics, a parallel universe to him, and he considered Pacino the world's expert after the end of the War of the East China Sea. Pacino always scoffed at that, telling Zaka that in a thousand ways, he and his fleet had gotten very lucky.

Zaka came up to greet Pacino first, grinning his characteristic smile, with what seemed two dozen straight white teeth. He was gray-haired, his hair cut into a crewcut, his face still retaining its youthful shape, although rumors abounded that he'd had plastic surgery several times. He gripped Pacino's hand in an iron grip. The general outweighed Pacino by at least fifty pounds, all of it seemingly muscle.

"I heard about Little Patch getting exonerated by the board," Zaka said. "I was glad to hear. Damned shame what happened."

"I'm just glad he's okay, but his friends are hospitalized, one with burns, the other in a coma that she may not come out of."

Zaka shook his head in sympathy.

Pacino looked over at a shorter, slender officer who wore the shoulderboards of a two-star admiral, who seemed too young for his rank and appeared almost lost in this crowd. He wore submarine dolphins over his ribbons, so he must be the head of the sub force, Pacino guessed.

"You must be Wally Patton," Pacino said, scanning the man's face for signs of resemblance to John "Blood-and-Guts" Patton, but there were none. Patton nodded respectfully and shook Pacino's hand.

"Your brother and I go way back," Pacino said, regretting that he hadn't stayed in touch with the older Patton. "But he never mentioned you, or maybe I wasn't listening."

"I was just the humble chief engineer on the new construction *Bunker Hill* when John was CNO," Patton said. "We'd had some words between us back then, but we're okay now."

Pacino nodded as a slender blonde woman walked up, wearing Navy tropical whites with a skirt, her hair pulled back into a severe bun, wearing black-framed glasses, her shoulderboards indicating her rank as a rear admiral. She came up confidently to the group and addressed the male generals and admirals. "Gentlemen, as usual, wonderful to see you."

Pacino reached out to shake her hand. "I'm Pacino, the new National Security Advisor."

"Frieda Sutton, head of ONI. And it's great to meet you, Admiral. Your predecessor was—well, none of us thought she understood military force."

"Do any of us?" Pacino quipped. ONI was the Office of Naval Intelligence.

He saw Allende with her phone to her ear. She hung up and addressed the crowd. "Everyone, the president is on his way. Let's get to the room."

Pacino took his seat, two chairs down from the end seat of the president, the other seats reserved for the Secretary of War and the Secretary of the Navy. To his right sat General Zaka, Admiral Catardi, and next to him, Admiral Patton. Across from them sat Allende, Menendez next to her, then NSA Director Nickerson, with Defense Intelligence chief Rogers on Nickerson's left, and to his left,

ONI's Admiral Sutton. The seats at the periphery of the room were occupied by various military and civilian aides.

They waited expectantly for the arrival of the president. Pacino checked his phone, scanning for any new texts or news files alerts, but everything seemed routine. He looked up to see Secretary of War Bret Hogshead walking in, his face flushed, whether from exertion or emotion, Pacino couldn't tell. Hogshead was one of the cabinet members whom VP Karen Chushi had labeled a "silver spoon," the super-rich who controlled much of the world. Hogshead's people had come over on the *Mayflower* and owned most of Massachusetts.

Behind Hogshead was the Secretary of the Navy, former test pilot and Space Shuttle astronaut Jeremy Shingles, who Pacino considered an ally and friend. And walking in behind Shingles was Vice President Karen Chushi, the former Senator from Texas with the grating west Texas accent to go with it. This seemed odd, Pacino thought, since Chushi and President Carlucci did not come anywhere close to getting along, and Carlucci had broken precedent by briefing her into the *Panther* operation, but then shutting her out of his day-to-day administration immediately after, yet here she was, a dark frown on her face. Pacino looked at Chushi, who looked like she'd aged ten years since he'd seen her last—perhaps some difficult crisis in her life weighing heavily on her.

While the occupants awaited the arrival of the president, Pacino shivered despite it being one of the hotter late summer days in Washington. The air conditioning was blowing intensely in the Situation Room at the president's insistence. Despite being a career politician, and while he enjoyed being surrounded by his subordinates in the Oval Office, he hated gatherings in stuffy confined quarters like his office on Air Force One or down here in the Situation Room. In fact, he'd taken the PEOC—the Presidential Emergency Operations Center—out of service for a long construction overhaul, the complex buried deep beneath the East Wing of the White House, equipped for use as a nuclear bunker in the event of a full-scale nuclear attack, but by virtue of being carved out of the bedrock, it was small, cramped and nearly airless. Carlucci had insisted on a dramatic expansion of it. Pacino wondered whether that were the real reason for the construction, or if Carlucci just wanted it out of commission for the rest of his term so he'd never have to go down there. Odds were, Pacino thought, no one would be able to convince Carlucci to descend into any of half a dozen other presidential evacuation bunkers within six hours of Washington.

Pacino heard President Carlucci's smooth tenor voice greeting them all. Carlucci stepped into the room and flashed his usual politician's smile as he took his seat at the end of the table, his Secret Service agents behind him. Pacino knew the president well enough to know he was anxious despite his confident expression. Carlucci was in his fifties, a tall, slender, athletic man almost never seen out of a several-thousand dollar suit, with a swooping head of salt-and-pepper hair. Pacino and the president went back to the days when Carlucci was running for the U.S. Senate seat for the state of Ohio after being the mayor of Cleveland.

Carlucci had called on Pacino to be his National Security Advisor at the start of the *Panther* operation, and Pacino had almost quit when the operation wrapped, but Margo Allende had talked him into staying. At the time, Pacino had felt resentment that Carlucci had played fast and loose with the submarine force—and with Anthony's life—risking their lives over an objective that seemingly had limited utility. But in the month since, he and Carlucci had gotten along well, the younger man leaning heavily on Pacino for advice.

Rear Admiral Frieda Sutton, head of Naval Intelligence, stood in front of a large display screen at the end of the room. Carlucci frowned at it, his arms crossed over his chest. On the display was a torpedo-shaped object. The figure of a man stood near it for scale. The torpedo was gigantic.

"Sir," Sutton began, "you've heard before from us on the Russian 2M39 Ocean Multipurpose System that NATO code-named 'Kanyon,' before we heard that the Russians called it the 'Status-6.' President Vostov put it out to the public in a press release and asked for the Russian population to give it a name. The Russians operate much differently now than in the Soviet era, when we had no idea what they called their weapon systems, leaving us and NATO to name things. The weapon was renamed 'Poseidon.' Regardless of the name, the unit is a deadly weapon designed to get nuclear warheads on target while circumventing our ballistic missile defenses.

"The unit is launched from a large host submarine such as the modified Omega-II class *Belgorod*, which we think can hold three of these, or from *Belgorod*'s deep-diving submarine, *Losharik*." Sutton clicked her slide deck and a 3D cutaway view appeared of the Omega-II submarine *Belgorod*. To show its scale, the right side of the slide showed the sub oriented vertically next to an image of the Empire State Building, the sub climbing to three-quarters of the skyscraper's height, the point being that *Belgorod* was enormous.

"What is this?" Karen Chushi asked impatiently. "Why are we worried about a torpedo? You worried about our aircraft carriers?"

"No, ma'am," Sutton said. "This is an autonomous weapon with a nuclear power plant and a range of up to seven thousand nautical miles. It can travel at up to fifty-four knots. It's two meters in diameter and twenty-four meters long and can dive to a thousand meters. It has enough nuclear fuel to loiter on station—that is, lie on the bottom—for years. It has a nuclear payload of between two and ten megatons, with some sources claiming it could be as big as a hundred megatons. We've refined our estimates in the last months to put its yield at ten megatons, one of the biggest hydrogen bombs in military use. As you know, most of our nukes are now in the hundreds or mere tens of kilotons. It's been years since we used yields in the megaton range."

"Why is that?" the VP asked.

"Our weapons have dramatically improved in accuracy," Sutton said. "The smaller yields get to all those hard-to-reach places despite being kilotons rather than megatons. The other reason is that our revised targeting is almost all military targets. And by and large, we no longer target civilian cities, which is the only thing a megaton-range nuke does for you now, which is city-killing.

"The NATO name 'Kanyon,'" Sutton continued, "was appropriate, because this weapon was designed to drive itself into a coastal port and wait. At the time to detonate, this unit would make a crater that would form a brand new bay. The displaced water would form a tsunami that would cause even more damage inland. Worse, there is speculation these bombs might have warheads doped with Cobalt-60, which would leave the radioactive areas downwind uninhabitable for a hundred years or more. So we modeled what a ten megaton blast would do to the Port of New York—" Sutton moved to click to the next slide, but Carlucci cut her off.

"Don't show that slide, Admiral," he snapped. "It's inflammatory. We *get* it. A ten megaton nuke would be bad for business. But big deal. So the Russians have a big scary torpedo. So what?"

Sutton glanced at CIA Director Margo Allende and sat down. Margo looked over at the president, glanced at the heads of NSA and DIA and then back at Carlucci.

"Sir, Russian President Vostov and his staff have been sending memoranda about the possibility of deploying Poseidons from the *Belgorod* at several target harbors on the U.S. east coast. Then yesterday Vostov's calendar was changed, inserting in the upcoming month a tour of the shipyard factory that assembles these weapons, and of the *Belgorod* itself. This and other intercepts hint that Vostov's actually committing to sending these to American shores."

For a long moment, Carlucci leaned back in his seat, his face hard, his arms crossed. "Well," he finally said, his voice deep and furious. "Obviously that's goddamned *unacceptable*. Ms. Allende, I want a meeting with you and your deputy ops director in my study in one hour." Carlucci looked at Pacino. "You too, Admiral Pacino." There was no doubt. Carlucci had definite ideas about how to respond to the Russian president.

3

Monday mornings were always brutal, Anthony Pacino thought, but never so much as when it was Monday in the shipyard. He rolled up to an empty parking space at Norfolk Naval Shipyard's Admin Building 1182 just as the sun rose over the horizon, the old red brick building a short walk from Graving Dock Number One, where the burned-out hulk of the USS *Vermont* lay helplessly on the blocks, black smoke still wafting out of her hatches while shipyard engineers and technicians swarmed over her, trying to assess when she'd be seaworthy again, if ever. And what the plan would be to repair her. Odds were they would have to rip out most of the forward compartment and start over at the bare hoop steel. It could be years before the boat would be refloated. And what, in the meantime, Pacino thought, would he and the crew do until then? Babysit the shipyard shitcanning the interior structures?

He cut the Corvette's engine and grabbed his briefcase and cover from the passenger seat, got out and locked the door, putting on his *Vermont* ball cap. He wore the shapeless, baggy, awful khaki two-piece fire-resistant working uniform that resembled pajamas, hating the uniform. He swore, if he ever rose to a high enough rank in the Navy, he'd bring back the uniforms that made the enlisted and officers proud to wear them. *Goddamned Big Navy*, he thought, out of touch, more concerned with political correctness than warfighting. If it ever came to combat, he thought, they'd be in sad shape indeed. He clenched his jaw, forced himself to stand up straight and walked to the entrance to the admin building, wondering if the crew would be blaming him for the fire on the submarine.

He climbed the stairs to the second deck, already starting to sweat from the sweltering August morning in a building with substandard air conditioning. Down the hallway, he stuck his head into the department head bullpen, where the engineer, navigator, weapons officer and supply officer had desks, each pushed against the outer wall of the room. He glanced mournfully at Rachel's desk, which had been piled high with "get well" cards. The weapons officer and supply officer were absent this early, but the chief engineer sat at his desk, reading glasses perched on his nose.

The engineer, Lieutenant Commander Elvis "Feng" Lewinsky peered at his tablet computer, reading some memo from the shipyard about the health of his reactor plant. The engineer had no problems, Pacino thought, with the exception of his auxiliary machinery room forward of the reactor compartment, which had experienced some measure of fire damage. The emergency diesel engine, rumor had it, had been unscathed.

Pacino stepped all the way into the room.

"Hey, Feng," Pacino said to his old friend. The "Feng" callsign acknowledged that Lewinsky wasn't just the engineer, he was the *fucking* engineer.

Lewinsky looked over, tossed his tablet and reading glasses to the desk, and stood up, an expression of deep sympathy coming to his face. He walked up, shook Pacino's hand, and clapped his shoulder. Lewinsky was Pacino's height, but muscle-bound, taking his frustrations out on a heavy bag and his bench press rig. He had a close-cropped blonde crewcut, a strong jawline, and usually an intimidating expression unless he were smiling, or like now, when he looked concerned.

"Patch. How are you bearing up?"

Pacino found himself blinking back moisture in his eyes, embarrassed at his show of weakness.

"I'm okay, Feng. I just got back from the hospital."

"The Nav—any change?"

47

Pacino shook his head. "She's not good. Doctors won't say she's brain dead, but her brain activity is not good and the coma continues. I suppose her burns are healing. They used this new artificial skin for a skin graft and it's looking good. But I'm worried for her."

"Yeah," Lewinsky said.

Pacino supposed there was nothing more to say about Rachel. "Are you hearing anything from the yard birds about the boat? Repair schedules?"

Lewinsky glanced back at his pad computer and turned to Pacino. "It's not good. In fact, it's so bad that they're thinking about cutting off the forward compartment of the *Vermont* and replacing it with the bow of the new construction boat, the 798 *Massachusetts*, then rebuilding *Vermont*'s forward compartment and welding it onto the ass end of the 798. But a maneuver like that—imagine a head transplant on a human being. Every single cable, fiber optic line, duct and pipe has to be cut off at frame one-oh-seven and then re-spliced into place in the new location, and then you'd have to sprinkle holy water on it and pray that it will all work when things are said and done."

"You're kidding."

"That's the easy part. The *Vermont* forward compartment has to be moved to a floating drydock while they move the 798 from Electric Boat in Groton down here into Graving Dock Number Two and rip off its forward compartment, then float the 798's forward compartment over to Dock Number One to weld onto *Vermont*'s reactor compartment bulkhead, then Frankenstein the 798's hull together with our old forward compartment while they try to bring it back to life."

"Fuck's sake, Feng, you're talking about a year of work."

"More like two, Patch. Maybe three."

"That's insane. What the hell are we going to do while all that's going on?"

"I heard the XO has plans for you junior officers. I don't want to steal his thunder, though. You'll hear the news soon enough."

"Thanks, Feng. I guess I'd better report to my goddamned desk for a day of paper-pushing."

"Hey Patch," Lewinsky said, "Chin up. It'll be okay."

"I hope you're right, Feng," Pacino said, and walked farther down the passageway to the junior officers' bullpen office. He found his desk and dejectedly tossed his bag and cap onto it. He was alone in the room. He pulled out his laptop and plugged it into the docking station and scanned his email, but it was all routine.

Lieutenant Duke "Squirt Gun" Vevera entered the room, tossing his backpack onto his seat. He looked at Pacino sadly and shook his hand, looking into Pacino's eyes. "You okay? Any of that smoke stuff cause permanent damage?"

Pacino shook his head. "I coughed all through the nights the first week, but I think I coughed it all up."

Vevera was, like Pacino, an Academy grad, Pacino later learning that Vevera had been a classmate, although Pacino hadn't known him at Annapolis. He was stocky, barrel-chested and built like a refrigerator, his physique earning him the initial nickname of "Man Mountain." The "Squirt Gun" nickname came later, from him ill-advisedly remarking to the executive officer at midnight rations one night that his pretty young girlfriend was a "squirter," and ever since the crew would regularly greet Vevera by tossing towels at him. Vevera had missed the *Panther* run to fight off a rabidly aggressive form of cancer, and against the odds he'd beaten the disease with an experimental treatment when everyone was certain they would be burying him when the *Vermont* returned, but he seemed as healthy as before the cancer struck. He owned an enormous motorcycle, an Indian Chieftain, in a turquoise and beige two-tone paint scheme with brown leather and leather tassels sprouting out everywhere, which earned him even more teasing from the enlisted men, who jokingly insisted no straight male would ever drive a motorcycle like that. Vevera was perhaps most famous for attempting to pull *Vermont* out of Norfolk when she'd been tied up bow-in, and during the reversal the stern had gone north instead of south, and to line up

49

the boat to point northward, Vevera had just kept going in a backward circle, making a 270 degree turn instead of a simple 90.

Vevera had taken over for former mechanical officer Lieutenant Kyle Lomax, who'd left the ship to go to shore duty after the *Panther* mission. Vevera regularly complained about working for Lewinsky, but Pacino knew he secretly loved his job and revered the chief engineer.

"So, Patch, any news about the Nav?"

Pacino filled Vevera in, as he had the engineer.

Vevera just shook his head sadly. It was then Don "Easy" Eisenhart walked into the room. Another Academy grad, Easy was the ship's communications officer, and Pacino was still getting to know him. He looked at Pacino with a half-smile.

"I hear you royally fucked up the boat, Lipstick," he said.

Pacino's other callsign, "Lipstick," had arisen from an unfortunate drunken night of liberty in a foreign port when he'd awakened in the bed of a woman he barely knew, then reported to the ship with his lower face completely smeared in her lipstick, his appearance causing paroxysms of laughter from both officers and enlisted alike. Pacino waited for the memory of that morning to fade, but regrettably, it still lived on.

"Actually, it wasn't—"

"I know, Lipstick," Eisenhart said quickly, sensing Pacino's sore spot. "Tough break. So, let me ask. How realistic was the simulation when it was done in-hull?"

"Easy, you have no idea how fucking realistic it was. When the fire broke out, I thought it was part of the scenario, and then when the smoke came in something happened. It must have fucked me up and I totally lost the bubble—I forgot it was a drill. I was so convinced I was actually at Zapadnaya Litsa that the Board of Inquiry must have thought I'd gone around the bend. It's safe to say, they'll never train *that* way again."

"Wow. Well, better you than me. I'd have never survived that Board of Inquiry. *You*, with your admiral father working for the president and all, hell, one phone call and you were off the hook."

"I thought that too, but Dad swears no one said anything."

"Still, they did know they were dealing with a Pacino."

"The thing I love about you, Easy? You definitely keep me humble."

Eisenhart laughed. "Hey, *someone* has to." He pointed his thumb at Pacino. "Fuckin' guy gets the Navy Cross and steals an enemy nuclear submarine to earn the Silver Star—how you gonna keep *his* feet on the ground?"

Pacino laughed. "Fuck you, Easy."

Eisenhart returned the verbal salute with, "And your mother too."

Lieutenant Dieter "U-Boat" Dankleff, the damage control assistant, slouched into the room, his eyes still half shut, a coffee cup in one hand and his backpack in the other. He looked up and grunted at Vevera, Eisenhart and Pacino. The DCA was half a head shorter than Pacino, stocky, going bald, with a pockmarked face from adolescent acne, his thick black glasses his trademark. Despite his ordinary looks, Dankleff had always been almost irresistible to women, a fact he had always been cocky about. But today he seemed deflated, his usual laughing and joking replaced by a dour depression.

"Morning, U-Boat," Vevera said loudly, suspecting that Dankleff might be hungover.

"Quiet, please," Dankleff said, his voice a croak.

"Good weekend?"

Dankleff waved off the grinning mechanical officer and made his way to his desk and plugged in. He wandered off to get a coffee refill, then came back in again, quiet at his desk. Pacino could almost tell the moment the DCA's coffee kicked in. Dankleff's eyes opened wider and he swiveled in his chair and seemed only then to recognize that Vevera and Pacino were there.

"Well, fuck, Lipstick," he said to Pacino. "I heard you burned the boat down all the way to the drydock blocks and we're fucked for two years."

"I didn't start the—"

"Two *years*?" Vevera said in shock.

"Yeah," Pacino said. "They're going to Frankenstein the ship's ass end with the 798 *Massachusetts'* forward end and take our burned-up bow and stitch it up to the aft end of 798. Eng says at least two years. Or more."

"Oh, fuck me," Vevera said. "Two years in this goddamned shipyard?"

"Another good deal from Big Navy," Dankleff said, sipping his coffee.

U-Boat Dankleff got his callsign from his great grandfather, who'd commanded the Nazi U-boat *U-767* that went down in the English Channel in World War II, but not before taking down thousands of tons of allied shipping. Dankleff had been the OIC, officer-in-charge, of the Operation *Panther* hijacking mission, with Pacino as his second-in-command. The two of them had privately admitted that they were certain they were going to die on that mission, but had put on a brave face for their small crew. Somehow fortune had favored them, and they'd survived against astronomical odds. But now this, Pacino thought. Two years of his life would go down the drain, this drydock disaster putting them all in the miserable boring routine of shipyard life.

While the four junior officers sat there in silence, a procession of enlisted men walked down the corridor outside the room, each one ceremoniously sticking his hand through the door and lighting a disposable lighter, then moving on, the next hand coming in and lighting a lighter, then the next. Vevera and Eisenhart started laughing and Dankleff clapped, both glancing at Pacino's red face.

"For fuck's sake, dammit," Pacino said quietly, "I didn't start the—"

After the last enlisted man walked on, the executive officer stuck his head in the doorway. Commander Jeremiah Seamus "Bullfrog" Quinnivan was on loan from the Royal Navy as part of a U.S. Navy / Royal Navy exchange program, and had been second-in-command to Captain Seagraves during the *Panther* run. Quinnivan was an Irishman with the thick-as-Irish-stew brogue to go with it. A medium-height, slightly built officer, Quinnivan sported a tightly trimmed beard streaked with gray, his ultra-short haircut attempting to hide the fact that he was half bald. In contrast to the American officers' shapeless working uniforms, Quinnivan wore a tailored dark blue shirt tucked into dark blue pants, his rank worn in the center of his chest, the dark emblem showing three horizontal gold stripes, the top one making a loop in the middle. He grinned at the junior officers with unnaturally white teeth, who some said had been capped after he'd been in a bar brawl that he insisted he'd won.

"Pacino! You *arsehole!* You fookin' burned my boat!" Quinnivan's voice rattled the windows.

"Sir, I—"

"Yeah, yeah, yeah, we've all watched the fookin' video, yeah? And we all know you only had seconds before the EAB system shit the bed, so I'm not *really* blamin' ye, lad, but you coulda given us better *luck*, don't ya know? Like some of that fookin' Operation *Panther* luck, yeah?"

"Sir, um…" Pacino's voice trailed off.

Quinnivan addressed the room. "Now listen, all you half-witted scurvy junior officers, I want you all early to officers' call. Your United States Navy has new plans of all of ye."

The four lieutenants glanced at each other, then back at Quinnivan.

"Sir, may I ask," Pacino started, but Quinnivan had just waved and disappeared down the corridor.

"New plans?" Dankleff asked.

"Sounds like TDY to some other boat," Vevera said. TDY meant temporary duty. Maybe sea duty, Pacino thought, thinking maybe they'd augment another attack submarine's crew.

Ten minutes later the four junior officers were joined by the rest of the boat's officer cadre, the other younger officers showing up directly to the conference room, placing their briefcases and backpacks against the outside wall. The seat at the end of the long table would be reserved for the captain, but he almost never attended officers' call, leaving that to the XO. The executive officer would hold court from the seat immediately to the right of the captain's chair. Next to him, the seat was empty, reserved for the navigator. Across from the navigator's seat sat the engineer, and next to the navigator's seat, the engineer's direct reports would sit so they could look across the table at their boss. Damage Control Assistant Dankleff sat next to the navigator's seat, since he was the senior officer of the engineering department—and in fact, he was also the "Bull Lieutenant," the most senior of the junior officers aboard, although that title remained disputed by Vevera—and next to him sat Main Propulsion Assistant Vevera. The seat to Vevera's right was taken by Electrical Officer Muhammad "Boozy" Varney. On the other side of the table, next to Lewinsky, sat Weapons Officer Al Spichovich, then Eisenhart, then Pacino, then Torpedo Officer Li No. Finally, at the other end of the table from the captain's chair sat Supply Officer Anik "Gangbanger" Ganghadharan.

Quinnivan frowned at the assembled officers. "Well, lads, I suppose you've all heard the bad news that our beloved navigator is hurt and in hospital and in a deep coma. And that Senior Chief Nygard is still in the burn unit and will be for some time. Since Lipstick here burned up the entire forward compartment to the ground and hosed the *Vermont*, she'll be stuck here for at least two years while the shipyard tries to figure out what to do to fix it."

Pacino bit his lip, realizing that for the next week, at least, every crewmember he'd run into would be casually mentioning that he'd burned the ship to the ground. They all knew, of course, that he didn't, but in keeping with submariners' tradition, any weak spot would be pounded away at. It would seem ruthlessly cruel to outsiders, but it was actually a twisted form of showing affection, as strange as that sounded.

Just then the captain stuck his head in the door. Captain Seagraves was tall, with a full head of what Quinnivan called "politician hair," his chiseled face looking like it belonged to a soap opera actor or a senator. He frowned as he said, in his booming baritone voice, "Good going, Mr. Pacino, for burning my boat down.

Nice work." Before Pacino could react, he disappeared down the passageway.

Pacino looked dejectedly down at the table. "Fuck me," he said quietly. He felt Eisenhart's hand clapping him on the shoulder, as if to encourage him to take heart.

"Don't worry," Eisenhart whispered. "In two years, she'll be good as new."

"Okay, next order of business," the XO said, opening a folder and tossing papers across to the officers. "All of you junior officers are going TDY to another boat until the shipyard un-fucks the *Vermont*. I'm passing out your orders now."

"What boat, XO?" Dankleff asked as Quinnivan slid a sheaf of papers to him.

"The 796 *New Jersey*, newest Block IV Virginia-class attack sub coming freshly out of new construction. Her alpha sea trials and commissioning shakedown runs are complete, and there's a long laundry list of things that are hosed on the boat, but she's putting to sea anyway. All repairs and post-repair sea trials are postponed for an urgent spec-op. She's being officially placed in commission today, as I speak."

Pacino scanned his orders. The 796 *New Jersey* was moored at DynaCorp Electric Boat Division in Groton, Connecticut.

Vevera caught it first, having consulted his pad computer. "XO, *New Jersey* was built at the McDermott Aerospace and Shipbuilding facility at Newport News, a half mile from where we sit. Why is it at Electric Boat in Groton?"

"Ah," Quinnivan said. "The post-sea-trials list of shit to fix, yeah? The deal is the Electric Boat ships are repaired by the McDermott shop and vice versa. The cost of repairs is backcharged from one shop to the other, as an incentive to build in quality the first time. It's also more efficient. But I'm guessing. Maybe there's another reason."

"Sir," Pacino asked, "if the *Jersey* is in Groton—maybe she's going to go to ComSubDevRon Twelve up there instead of SubRon Six down here."

"Jersey was originally destined to be a DevRon Twelve boat," Quinnivan replied, "but since she's the direct replacement for *Vermont,* she'll be in-chopping to Squadron Six here in Norfolk. When *Vermont* is repaired, the bosses will make a decision then whether to have the rebuilt *Vermont* go to Groton and leave *Jersey* in Norfolk. That decision is TBD, people."

"XO," Dankleff asked, "What about the chiefs? Are they staying here with the *Vermont* or going with us to the *New Jersey?"*

"We're handling that on a case-by-case basis. Tactical divisions will probably take their chief petty officers and leading petty officers with you junior officers to the *New Jersey.* Obviously, torpedo division will need a new chief, since Blacky Nygard is laid up for some time. Supply and engineering chiefs will most likely stay with *Vermont* to aid in her rebuild. But that's still to be determined."

Quinnivan concluded officers' call, telling them to pack their seabags and report to the pier at Groton Submarine Base in forty-eight hours, and to be ready to disappear for a while. A long while.

Back in the junior officer bullpen, Vevera whispered to Pacino. "A spec-op? What do you think is going on?"

A "spec-op" was short for special operation, the kind that the USS *Vermont* had done before going into the drydock. The kind that couldn't be spoken of outside of a SCIF, a special compartmented information facility, or inside the hull of the submarine.

"Who knows?" Pacino said. "Are we all keeping our present jobs? Am I still sonar officer and you main propulsion assistant?"

"It would seem logical," Vevera said. "The fastest way to staff the new boat with minimal disruptions."

"What about the present crew and officers of the *New Jersey?* What happens to them?"

Vevera shrugged. "They're a bunch of drydock rats and have been building the *Jersey* for four years. I suppose they'll cross-deck them onto the *Vermont* so *they* can fix her."

"And what about our department heads? And the XO and captain?"

"I suppose we'll find out soon enough," Vevera said as he packed his backpack and headed for the door. "I'll see you at the Snake Ranch."

Commander Jeremiah Quinnivan, Royal Navy, knocked on the open door jamb of Commander Seagraves' temporary office on the admin building's third floor.

"Come on in, XO," Seagraves said, rolling his high-backed chair away from the desk and putting his steel-toed boots on the spread-out printouts on top. "Have a seat. Something on your mind?"

Quinnivan settled into one of the chairs in front of the captain's desk, leaning forward, his tense body language a contrast to Seagrave's relaxed pose.

"I'm a bit worried about that wee lad, Lipstick Pacino, yeah? All this seems to have taken the wind from the boy's sails, if you know what I mean, Skipper. And I'm still convinced he's our good luck charm. So, frankly, sir, we need him cocky and full of himself again, ya know?"

Seagraves shrugged. "That should come soon enough, XO." Seagraves never called Jeremiah Seamus Quinnivan by his given names or his "Bullfrog" callsign—taken from some forgotten 1960s rock and roll song lyric—but always simply "XO," perhaps to keep reminding the Irishman that while they were friends, good friends, they still were in command of a high-stakes weapon system and the people who ran it. Seagraves had seen excessive informality hurt military discipline in the past, and he swore it wouldn't happen on his command.

"You think we'll be able to bring him back to life in the next assignment?"

"Let's hope so, XO. All we can do is give the young man time."

Quinnivan stroked his beard, the way he did when weighing his words carefully.

"I suppose so, Cap'n. Did you decide yet whether to tell the lads about where *we're* going?"

Seagraves looked for a moment out the window, frowning to himself. "I'm thinking we should let that be a surprise to the boys," he finally said.

"Yeah, a big surprise, sir."

"Hopefully, they'll see it as a good sign."

"I don't know, Skip. They may see it as the gravestone for the USS *Vermont*."

"Don't say that, XO. The spirit of the project submarine *Vermont* is immortal. She shall return in all her glory, and when she does, we and our wardroom and goat locker of pirates, misfits and cutthroats will be right there with her."

"I don't know, sir. Two years in a dock? A lot can happen in two years."

Seagraves smiled, took his boots off the desk and rifled through a pile of disorganized papers until he found what he was looking for. He handed the stapled package over to Quinnivan and waited for the exec to skim it. Quinnivan looked up, stunned.

"Six months? They'll repair her in *six months*?"

"Crash program. Admiral Stiletto Patton came down hard on the Navy shipyard personnel and on McDermott Aerospace and Shipbuilding. He told both organizations that heads will roll unless *Vermont* sails the seven seas on her own power by the first of March."

"Wow. I suppose, sir, it's nice that we command a project boat. President needs her back in service."

"Nothing like a phone call from the White House to get things rolling," Seagraves said, taking back the sheave of papers from Quinnivan. "Now we just have to get through our own TDY assignment."

"That we do, Cap'n, that we do."

4

Mid-August, and the weather in Murmansk, Russia, was only a few degrees above freezing, a cold rain beating down, making a drum-beat noise on the metal roof over the bar's outside porch. Georgy Alexeyev looked up at the lit sign above the door, the sign showing a graphic of a wolf ripping off the head of a sheep, blood splashing onto the face of the wolf. The Lamb's Valhalla had been a popular hangout for the officers of the Northern Fleet before the brass came down and blackballed it for the practice of a backroom filled with friendly hookers. Ridiculous, Alexeyev thought, wondering if one of the senior female officers had insisted on the bar being made off limits.

Inside the solid wood door, the bar's atmosphere was steaming hot, the wave of heat a welcome feeling. Alexeyev pulled off his heavy sheepskin coat and hung it on one of the many hooks by the door. A smiling, large-breasted, tall blonde waved him to his usual booth. After he settled in, she returned with a bottle of Glenfiddich scotch and two glasses. She asked if he would want any food, but he waved her off. Tonight was for drinking, he thought.

Captain First Rank Georgy Alexeyev had a thick, full head of gray-streaked hair swooping over his forehead and ears, the mirror reminding him that he needed a haircut. He wore a black eyepatch over his right eye. He really didn't need the patch anymore, now that the surgery had been done to put in a glass eye, but he was self-conscious that the glass eye didn't look realistic, and he'd rather

59

people just realize he was half blind rather than try to guess why his face looked odd.

Alexeyev was tall, a bit over 185 centimeters, and he'd always been thin—even gaunt—although since the disaster in the South Atlantic, he'd gained a few kilograms he could stand to lose. But the weight was largely unnoticeable at his waist, his jawline still ruler straight.

Tonight he'd decided to dress in jeans and a denim shirt under an olive-drab submarine service pullover, forgoing his usual uniform. After all, showing up to an off-limits bar in uniform would seem to tempt the bosses. He was halfway into a glass of the scotch, which was cold despite being unrefrigerated, when his friend walked in, still wearing his coat, which was dripping wet.

"Take your coat off, Sergei," Alexeyev said.

"Oh," Sergei Kovalov said, shaking his head. "My mind is elsewhere. Pour one for me, will you?" Kovalov went back to the door, took off his jacket and returned as Alexeyev was corking the bottle. He slid over into the seat opposite Alexeyev. Captain First Rank Sergei Kovalov was a shorter man, built like a bear, everything about the man thick and hairy. He had a fleshy face with wide penetrating eyes, red hair, and a thick mustache. He was the son of a high-ranking government official, although Alexeyev had no idea what Kovalov's father had been, since Kovalov refused to speak about him. Alexeyev and Kovalov had been friends ever since their junior officer tours on the *Tambov* a million years ago. Kovalov had nursed many a drink with Alexeyev during the troubled times of Kovalov's divorce, the two of them convinced they could find the answers to life's problems at the bottom of a bottle. And while they'd proved that theory wrong on multiple occasions, that didn't stop them from continuing to try.

Kovalov raised his glass, and Alexeyev joined him. "To fallen comrades," Kovalov said, and Alexeyev thought for a sad moment about the personnel he'd lost in the South Atlantic when his K-561 *Kazan* went down, at the wrong end of a damned Russian supercavitating torpedo. Alexeyev shut his eyes and drank, saying a momentary prayer that wherever the souls he'd lost were, they were okay. When he opened his eyes, he noticed his friend was staring down at the table, seeming lost.

"Are you okay, Sergei?" Alexeyev asked.

"Wife and daughter are driving me crazy," Kovalov said, blinking. "Tonight they were screaming at each other so loud that not one, but two neighbors pounded on the apartment door to demand quiet. And then Ivana insisted that I remove Magna's door from her room. Somehow, Mommy thinks that destroying the girl's privacy is the cure to the trouble. And through all this, Magna's *still* not speaking to me. After, you know, the thing. So at home? Pure chaos."

"Removing a teenage girl's door? You'd be throwing gasoline onto a fire already burning," Alexeyev said.

"I know. So, Georgy, enough about my problems. You wanted to talk. Are there new sorrows to drown?"

Alexeyev poured more scotch for both of them. "You know, Sergei, the trouble with the attempt to drown sorrows in alcohol is that sorrows are such good swimmers."

Kovalov smiled and tilted his glass back, drained it, and called for more.

"My sorrows are the usual, I suppose," Alexeyev said. "Natalia was upset at living close to the base and insisted on us moving to Murmansk City. At least I'm close to your apartment now. But is she happy now? No. Now she's throwing a fit about my being away on the next mission. And I can't even tell her if we sail in a week or a month."

Kovalov waved his friend's complaint aside. "Please, Georgy, you have no problems. That woman loves you more than her next breath. It's obvious for anyone to see when they see you together. Count your blessings. You have a gorgeous female who thinks the sun rises and sets over your head. Of course she's going to bitch about you disappearing to the far reaches of the Atlantic Ocean for two months, maybe more."

"That's not all that's on my mind, Sergei. It's the new mission profile. It's not like anything we've seen before."

Kovalov nodded. He looked around the bar, but it was mostly empty and no one was near. "I know," he said quietly. "Deploying Status-6 units in enemy harbors. It's a terrible idea. If any of this stupid plan leaks out, well, it will be a disaster."

"If the American defenses are waiting for us, it might be a bad day."

"Yes, exactly," Kovalov replied. "Being depth-charged to death could ruin your entire week."

"Natalia doesn't know that she could have even bigger things to complain about."

Kovalov looked at his drink. "If we're lucky, the depth charges could be nuclear. I imagine dying in a nuclear explosion is a good way to go. It's over before you even realize something is wrong."

"No way I want to go out that way," Alexeyev said. "I'd like a minute or two to consider my own mortality. I always figured an airplane accident from high altitude would be the way to die. A short time of contemplation, then lights out in an instant."

"Either way," Kovalov said, "it beats dying in a flooding submarine."

Or one on fire, Alexeyev thought. "I'll drink to that."

In the morning, Georgy Alexeyev awakened to an empty bed. His wife Natalia was up early, presumably to make breakfast for him.

As he sat up in bed, he realized that what woke him up was a smell. A bad smell. It was a Belomorkanal cigarette, a bastard child of cigars and cigarettes, a *papirosa* with a cardboard tube instead of a filter, with cigar-type tobacco stuffed into it, the foul-smelling cigarette that had the characteristic stench of a dead wet dog tossed into a bonfire. The kind of cigarette that only one person in his life had ever smoked—Captain Third Rank Alesya Matveev, his dead chief engineer on K-561 *Kazan*.

He looked over at the table and chairs on the window side of the bedroom, and there Matveev was, sitting there at the table, her legs crossed, calmly smoking the cigarette, her big brown eyes fixed on him. She wore the powder-blue coveralls with the high-vis stripes on the sleeves, upper torso and ankles, the color she'd picked out for her engineering department. He'd never known her to wear makeup, and in life she would have had to strive to become plain, but as she sat there, her face radiated a tranquil, serene beauty. Alexeyev wasn't sure if it were the light from the low-on-the-horizon sun shining through the blinds or something from within her, but she seemed to be backlit by a kind of aura made of white light.

Twenty emotions ran through him like the current from a high voltage short circuit, and instinctively he backed away from the apparition, slinking back against the headboard, his mouth open. An acidic witch's brew of abject terror, intense sadness and dark guilt pumped through his veins. He tried to speak, but his voice wouldn't come. He felt like a fish dying on a pier, his lips moving, but no sound coming out, and he realized he couldn't breathe, a uncontrollable panic starting to bubble up in his mind.

It was then she spoke to him. It was Matveev's scratchy voice, but it came to him in his mind. Her lips never moved.

Hello, Captain. She smiled at him mysteriously, not showing her teeth, but her eyes making happy horizontal commas the way they did the rare times she'd smile when she was alive. The voice seemed to soothe his terrified and guilty spirit, and the fear drained from him, replaced with an odd, calm, intense focus.

Alexeyev finally found his voice. "Chief," he said, calling her by her former shipboard title, short for chief engineer, then thinking that sounded too formal. "Alesya."

She dipped her head in a half nod of respect, tamped out her cigarette in a large K-561 ashtray, reached for another, and lit it with a lighter with the colorful coat-of-arms of the K-561, the smoke curling toward the ceiling.

"Why are you here?" he asked. When she just looked at him, he got the feeling she would only answer if he asked her the right question. "*Ty v poryadke, gde ty?* Are you okay where you are? Are you safe there? Are the others okay?" He meant the other

63

engineering watchstanders who'd perished with her on that awful day. But Chief Engineer Matveev just kept looking at him, a seeming amusement in her eyes.

It occurred to Alexeyev that when a man saw dead relatives or friends, that was an omen that he was near his own death, and that the dead ones were there waiting to escort him to the next world. That thought made some of the fear return, and he became aware of his heart hammering in his chest.

Perhaps there was an exception to the appearance of the dead foreshadowing his own death, he thought. If the spirit were here to warn him, he might well live on. That is, if he heeded the warning.

"Did you come to warn me?" he asked Matveev.

She took a last puff of her foul-smelling cigarette and put it out in the ashtray, then looked over at him and nodded solemnly.

Distance, she said seriously without speaking, her thought coming into his mind, her lips not moving, her expression a frown of worry.

"Distance," he repeated dully. What did she mean? "Do you mean—?"

But before he could finish his thought, Matveev became transparent, then turned to mist, the mist turning to smoke that wafted toward the ceiling with the dying smoke of her cigarette, and then all traces of her were gone but for the smell of her smoke.

As he stared at the chair near the table, his mouth dropped open, and just then Natalia walked in, her face crumpled into disgust, fanning her face.

"Georgy, what's wrong? Dear man, you look like you've seen a ghost. And *what* have you been smoking? That is truly foul. Did you pick up a bad habit?"

What should he tell her, he wondered. That he had just seen a ghost, the apparition of his dead chief engineer, and it had been she who had been smoking? He felt his pulse still racing and his lungs bursting, trying to get in air, hoping Natalia wouldn't notice and suddenly make a fuss over him.

"It's Kovalov," he said haltingly, trying to bring his breathing back under control. "Sergei was trying a new cigarette brand, but it was even more foul than *he* could tolerate. It must have gotten on my clothes from when we were drinking at the Lamb's Valhalla."

"That *awful* place. But it's odd," she said, picking up clothing from the floor. "I didn't smell it last night when you came to bed late."

"You were fast asleep," he said. "I don't think you would have smelled a dead skunk the way you were snoring."

She smiled at him. "I don't snore," she said, smiling, their running joke since he'd spent his first night with her, the noise of her at first keeping him awake, but now it was somehow comforting. The first night aboard ship was always difficult without that sound.

"Woman, you snore loud enough to shatter windows," he said, reaching out to slap her hindquarters. He was starting to feel normal again, and the fact that Natalia hadn't noticed him turning blue from lack of oxygen, or noticed his trembling hands, encouraged him.

"Save my spanking for later and come eat your breakfast, smelly man," she laughed. "Hurry up, you'll be late for your conference with the admiral."

"Yes, ma'am," he said, trying to smile at her and wondering if she would see through him to his inner turmoil, but Natalia had already hurried back to the kitchen, her mind on preparing the food. He found his black eyepatch and put it on, then strapped on his submariner's watch.

As he got up to go to the kitchen, he noticed that there was no ashtray on the table, no K-561 lighter, nor any sign of a cigarette butt. But the smell lingered on.

―――――――――

As Captain First Rank Georgy Alexeyev waited for the admiral to arrive, his mind kept returning to Matveev. *What the hell did her appearance mean?* And what had she meant by saying *distance*?

He looked over at Kovalov, wondering if he dared tell his old friend about Matveev's manifestation.

Finally the secure conference room's inner door opened and Admiral Gennady Zhigunov hurried into the room, nodding at Alexeyev and Kovalov, who had stood and snapped to rigid attention.

"Seats, please, gentlemen," Zhigunov said. The admiral was in his sixties, a grizzled tall figure, still considered handsome by Alexeyev's female officers. He had a full head of completely gray hair and a chiseled face, time worn and beginning to sag. He took his seat at the end of the table opposite the large flatpanel display. He dropped his pad computer on the stainless steel table's surface and reached into his inner tunic pocket, withdrawing a blue pack of cigarettes and his lighter with the emblem of Northern Fleet Command. The unfiltered French brand Zhigunov favored, *Gauloises Brunes*, made noxious smoke, but nothing like Matveev's, Alexeyev thought. He offered the submarine commanders cigarettes. Alexeyev waved him off, but Kovalov took one, taking the admiral's lighter when he'd lit up. Kovalov smoked a different brand and had a general contempt for Western cigarettes, but he acted as if he smoked *Gauloises* every day.

"Have you both read the mission profile?" Zhigunov puffed hard on his cigarette, tapping out his ash on a tray he'd pulled over from the center of the table. When the officers nodded, he reached for a remote and projected on the screen, the display showing a detailed map of the globe taken from high over the north pole.

"So. The mission, then. At the time to be determined, Captain Alexeyev, your *Belgorod* will sortie from Zapadnaya Litsa Submarine Base and make your way north to the Barents Sea, where you will rendezvous with Captain Kovalov's *Losharik*, which will leave port from Olenya Guba and rendezvous with *Belgorod* here." A bright red dot lit up north of the Kola Peninsula. "You will take aboard *Losharik* while submerged."

"Admiral?" Kovalov said, hesitantly interrupting while stubbing out his half-smoked cigarette in the ash tray. "We've never docked *Losharik* to *Belgorod* at sea, and never while both units are submerged."

66

Zhigunov nodded, seeming distracted, while he put out his cigarette and lit a second. The room was becoming filled with smoke. Alexeyev had a momentary thought about his conversation with Kovalov the night before, about dying in a depth-charged submarine, and unbidden, a flash memory came to him, of the upper level of *Kazan* when the first compartment exploded and the passageway leading to the escape chamber had filled with flames and smoke. With a conscious effort, Alexeyev blinked away the waking nightmare.

"Something wrong, Georgy?" Zhigunov asked, flashing Alexeyev a penetrating gaze.

"No, sir," Alexeyev said, trying to keep his facial expression hard. "Please continue, Admiral."

"When *Belgorod* departs, you will be loaded with three Status-6 weapons. When you arrive on-station, you'll transfer them one at a time to *Losharik*, which will place them in their mission-determined locations."

Alexeyev bit his lip. Firing an exercise-shot Status-6, which his *Belgorod* had done a dozen times, was routine. Transferring a dummy mockup of a Status-6 to the deep-diver *Losharik* he'd only done once, and it had been a disaster. He was still smarting from the post-exercise critique of that endeavor.

"Sir, if I may," Alexeyev said slowly, "transferring a Status-6 to *Losharik* is problematic. We've never managed to do that well. Our only attempt—"

"I know, Captain Alexeyev," Zhigunov said. "I'm well aware of the exercise failure, but I am confident that this time you will be successful. Unlike the exercise you participated in, you will be in shallow water. A dropped weapon can easily be recovered by *Losharik* and the mission will continue."

"So, sir, the mission? We're actually deploying Status-6 weapons?"

Zhigunov nodded. Alexeyev could tell the admiral was passing along orders he didn't agree with. Zhigunov manipulated the display and the image of the globe turned to focus on the east coast of the United States. Three red dots appeared. The southern-most dot flashed brighter than the other two.

"The first unit will be placed here off the border between their provinces of Florida and Georgia, where their main strategic missile submarines are based." The red dot flashed for a moment and Zhigunov zoomed the display far in, the aerial view looking down on the Saint Marys Channel. "The weapon must be placed in the mid-point of the deep channel leading out of the submarine base. The water is too shallow for *Belgorod*, but not for *Losharik*. The weapons must be placed with absolute precision, which is why we are not relying on their internal navigation systems. The weapons will be in stand-by mode and asleep when you drop them.

"The second unit will be placed at the exit of Hampton Roads, the place where their naval ships leave their main base in Norfolk in the province of Virginia." Zhigunov zoomed the display image far out, then zoomed into the Virginia Beach area. "Weapon placement will be inside the channel exit of the bay near the Chesapeake Bay Bridge. Also in waters too shallow for *Belgorod* but not for *Losharik*."

"The third unit will go into the Long Island Sound, outside the submarine base the Americans use in their province of Connecticut, not far from New York City, at the mouth of the Thames River." Zhigunov navigated the display back to a vantage point above the north pole.

"Questions?"

Both captains began to speak at once. Zhigunov waved them to silence and pointed at Alexeyev.

"Yes, Admiral. *Why* are we doing this?"

"Orders from the president," Zhigunov said, as if it were obvious.

"Does he intend to detonate these?"

"I doubt it," Zhigunov said. "I imagine it is a demonstration of capability. For all I know, after these units are deployed, he may tell the Americans, then generously offer to remove them. But who can say what politicians think at any given moment?" There was silence in the room for a moment. "Speaking of the president, I know you'll

68

enjoy this next part. President Vostov is traveling north to tour Sevmash Shipyard and the Status-6 factory. He will then tour the *Belgorod*, then the *Losharik*. I suggest you both prepare your ships and crews for a presidential visit."

Zhigunov glanced at each submarine captain. Alexeyev tried to keep his expression neutral, but Kovalov looked like he'd just swallowed rotten caviar.

"I know a VIP visit is counterproductive to combat readiness," Zhigunov said, "but think of this as a way to show your crews just how important they are. It will raise their morale."

Fat chance of that, Alexeyev thought. *They'd be scrubbing and polishing the boat for weeks until Vostov showed up, all the while cursing him for their unnecessary labor.*

"When is he coming?" Kovalov asked.

"Next week or next month," Zhigunov said with a shrug. "To be determined. Exact itinerary to follow. Meanwhile, *Belgorod* will be loading out the weapons and stores for the voyage. You'll need enough for a four-month deployment."

"*Four months?*" Kovalov's eyes seemed to bulge from their sockets.

Alexeyev looked at Zhigunov. "Admiral, I think I *will* take that smoke now."

Zhigunov smiled and shook out a cigarette for Alexeyev. The smoke was strong but satisfying.

"There's still more good news, gentlemen. Your route to your destinations." With a few clicks, Zhigunov changed the display from a globe to a Mercator projection, showing all the continents. A flashing red dotted line emerged from the naval bases at Russia's Kola Peninsula, extending deep into the Arctic Ocean, not far from the pole, then descending between Siberia and Alaska into the Pacific, and from there around South America's Cape Horn and up the South American coast, traveling northward in the South Atlantic, past the equator and into the North Atlantic, finally arriving at the east coast of the United States.

Alexeyev glanced at Kovalov, whose face had turned as red as his hair. Zhigunov, anticipating their reaction, held up his palms.

"I know, I know. This is the long way."

"Long?" Kovalov said, his voice too loud for a briefing with a flag officer. "Instead of a five thousand nautical mile trip, you're sending us on a twenty-thousand-mile route."

"Twenty-one thousand five hundred, to be precise," Zhigunov said. "For several reasons. One of them is the NATO trip wire sonar systems set up between the United Kingdom, Greenland and Iceland. And because there may be waiting American or British submarines lurking outside our Kola bases. When you enter the Barents and turn *east* instead of west, any NATO submarine will assume you're going out to do exercises rather than going on an offensive mission. Third, you'll lose any trailing submarines in the polar icecap. The pressure ridges and icepack will make your sound signature indistinct. The noises of the icepack itself will be far louder than *Belgorod*."

Alexeyev frowned. The icepack shifting, creaking and grinding was transient noise, loud certainly, but nuclear submarines emitted bell tones—tonals—that could easily be picked up by sensitive sonars coupled to mighty computers with vast data-filtering power, able to discern needles from hay in the acoustic haystack. But he decided to move on to the next objection.

"Sir," Alexeyev said, "there is still the chokepoint between Russia and Alaska. The Bering Strait is, what, only fifty miles wide? If you think the GI-UK gap is problematic, it's nothing compared to the Bering Strait."

"No one will suspect you're coming," Zhigunov said, waving off the objection.

"But Admiral," Kovalov said, "*Belgorod*, with *Losharik* docked, is gigantic. We could get stuck in a thousand places under polar ice."

"It's summertime," Zhigunov said, as if that solved the problem. "The ice won't be a problem. And if it is, *Losharik* can undock until you can free yourself from whatever pressure ridge is troubling you, then re-dock on the other side of the obstacle. In the worst case, you can always fire a torpedo to clear the path. I know," Zhigunov said, anticipating yet another objection. "That would be loud. But again, no one is following you. And even if they are, they will believe the detonation of your torpedo to be part of an exercise."

Alexeyev glanced quickly at Kovalov, who was biting his lip as if trying to contain a further outburst.

"Sir, this route will take forever." Alexeyev looked at Zhigunov, but knew this issue would be ignored as the previous ones had.

"We're in no particular hurry, gentlemen," Zhigunov said.

"If I may be so bold to ask," Kovalov said, "whose idea was it to go this route?"

Zhigunov hesitated, but finally shook out another cigarette and lit it. "Our orders come directly from President Vostov himself."

So, there could be no further argument, Alexeyev thought.

"Any other questions?" Zhigunov asked. "Any other thoughts about your orders?"

"Not from me," Alexeyev said.

"Sergei?"

"None from me, Admiral," Kovalov said slowly. Alexeyev could tell his friend was furious.

"Normally I'd invite you both to dinner, but I've been called to Moscow to go over our plans with the president," Zhigunov said, standing and picking up his pad computer, then stubbing out his cigarette.

The meeting, obviously, was over, Alexeyev thought, standing and shaking Zhigunov's hand. The admiral shook Kovalov's hand and made a hasty exit from the room after turning off the display screen.

"Georgy," Kovalov began. Alexeyev waved him off.

"Not here. Not now."

"Lamb's Valhalla then," Kovalov said. Alexeyev nodded, then reached for his officers' cap and coat.

———————————

71

Alexeyev and Kovalov smoked in silence in the Northern Fleet staff car, then climbed out at the club, instructing the driver to wait for them.

Once comfortable in their booth, the customary toast to fallen comrades complete, Kovalov looked at Alexeyev and said, "Even before we talk about this madness, I have to ask you, Georgy. There's something wrong, perhaps even more troubling than these orders. Someone's walked on your grave, yes? There's something you're not telling me. What is it?"

Alexeyev looked at Kovalov and nodded solemnly. "Something happened this morning, but I'm not sure I have the courage to tell you about it."

"Courage? You? You were awarded the Medal for Military Valor First Class for the South Atlantic run."

Alexeyev scoffed. "That award is for those who are victorious, not those who lose their ships in battle. To this day, I still don't know the motivations of the admirals for giving me that."

"Perhaps to communicate into your thick one-eyed skull that you are a courageous *hero*, not the failure you think you are. So *what* if your sub went down? If you'd had two more torpedoes, you would have prevailed."

"Maybe I wasted two torpedoes early in the fight," he said.

"In countermeasure mode? Surely, had you not fired them, you would have gone down sooner. Georgy, what can I say to break your mood? This is a dangerous line of thinking."

"Wait until you hear what I'm about to tell you," Alexeyev said, draining his scotch and pouring more. Over the next few minutes, he told the tale of seeing Matveev in his apartment when he woke and the smell of her cigarettes. He tried to keep his voice level and even, but he could hear his voice trembling and his hands had started to shake, and by the end of the story he had that same shortness of breath he'd felt when Natalia came in. He concentrated on breathing deeply, trying to disguise his emotions by taking a deep pull of the scotch and refilling his glass, but his hand trembled and some of the liquid spilled on the table. Kovalov pretended not to notice.

The two men were silent for a long moment, Kovalov pouring out the remains of the bottle, then calling for the server to bring them a fresh one, two packs of his favorite cigarettes, and a new lighter. When she returned, Kovalov handed one pack and the lighter to Alexeyev. "Your bad habit is back, my friend. You'd best lay in a few cases of cigarettes before departure." He hadn't yet commented about the ghost from this morning.

"Sergei, do you think I'm crazy?"

Kovalov shook his head. "Crazy men have no self-doubts. The crazy ones are those who never question their own sanity. But let me tell you something, Georgy. My grandmother used to say, *never trust the first half hour after waking or the last half hour before sleeping, for that is the witching hour, when uninvited spirits and things-that-go-bump-in-the-night appear.* Most likely, you were having a dream that just seemed too real, and Matveev's mysterious warning about 'distance' could mean anything."

"Sergei, I would see things your way, but what about Natalia smelling the cigarette?"

Kovalov looked at him and shrugged. "Odds are, Natalia smelled the smoke on your clothes from one of your crew from your workday on the ship, and her emotions about not wanting you to smoke made that smell worse than it would smell to us."

Alexeyev narrowed his good eye at Kovalov. "Yes," he eventually said slowly, "I'm sure you are correct, Sergei," the doubt apparent in his speech. He'd not been around anyone who'd smoked the previous day.

As if trying to close the discussion about the dead engineer, Kovalov raised his glass. "A toast to Captain Third Rank Alesya Matveev, that wherever she is, it is warm and safe and beautiful."

Alexeyev raised his glass, shut his eyes, blinking back moisture, and drank.

5

He woke with a headache and a dry mouth. He sat up on the edge of the bed and forced himself to stand and walk to the ornate bedroom's enormous bathroom. Usually he was up at least four times during the night to urinate. Advancing years, and doctors who were idiots, no doubt contributed to *that* problem. But last night had been somewhat uninterrupted. It was the dreams that woke him up this time, not his bladder.

After washing his hands and drying them on a fresh white towel, he stared at himself for a moment, preparing to shave before showering, running his fingers over his face. For a sixty-four-year-old face, it was almost youthful, but certainly not good-looking. But then, he had never been what anyone would call handsome. His hair had been a rat's nest since he'd been a child, leading him to crop it all off since grade school. The short hair had helped, giving him a military air, which had gone a long way to helping his career, he thought. There was not much left of that military bearing now, nor the hair, for that matter. He'd added kilograms, most around his waist. He was told by people who sought his favor that he carried the weight well, that it made him resemble a bear, but in his own mind he was an older, overweight ghost of his former vigorous self.

He thought for a moment about the dreams. In the first, he was on a cross-continental train. His mother was in the window seat and she was old and sick, as she had been in her final year of life, some twenty years ago. He and his mother had stopped getting along after he had followed in his father's footsteps. But in the dream, his mother leaned against him, seeming affectionate. Her eyes were shut. Her forehead was deeply lined. Feeling regret for their angry words of the past, he put his forehead against hers, and her skin was warm at first, but then rapidly and alarmingly cooled. He had blinked, wondering if she had passed, but before he could do anything, he was standing at a podium in the amphitheater of the Lubyanka, the gigantic emblem of the KGB behind him. It was a blue and red shield with a vertical sword behind a red star emblazoned with the gold hammer-and-sickle. He was again a low-ranking officer, there to give a presentation to the entire leadership of the KGB and representatives of the Central Committee, and he had lost his slides. The projectionist shrugged, not knowing where the slides were. He felt a stabbing anxiety, bile rising into his throat. He was lost without the slides, and he began to babble about what little he remembered of the subject of his speech until his old boss pulled him off the stage. Before the old man could say a word, the dream dissolved into the pre-dawn bedroom.

As he lathered up his face and grabbed his razor, the image of his wife standing behind him appeared in the mirror. He looked up at her and nodded a solemn greeting, wondering what mood she would pick to start the day. For two weeks, her mood had been either stormy or disturbingly quiet. He much preferred her anger. God alone knew what she was thinking when she descended into a cold silence.

"You're up early," she said, her tone neutral.

He turned to look at her, trying to remember the night before. As usual, when he'd had too much to drink, the memories of the hour before he retired seemed to vanish.

"Are you okay?" he asked, not knowing what else to say to her.

She frowned. "Dimmi, do you realize it has been *three months* since you hate-fucked me?"

He blinked. Larisa Vostov's colorful expression for the rough sex she loved had always seemed shocking to him. A good Saturday night for her would involve him throwing her around the room, slapping her, choking her almost to the point of her losing

75

consciousness, and finishing off with a simulated—but damned realistic—sexual assault. Afterward, she'd smile blissfully at him through her new bruises. She had always worn heavy makeup, but he had worried that one day he'd break her jaw or cheekbone, and the world would think he was abusing his wife.

And that was the thing about marriage, he thought. A man marries the woman who suits him when they marry, but what if the man changes? When he'd met Larisa ten years ago, he was full of anger and bitterness about his divorce and hatred for his first wife. On the advice of friends, he'd taken up martial arts and had tried to exorcise his demons on a heavy bag or in the cage, but it hadn't helped. Then Larisa came, and what she wanted in bed *exactly* suited what he'd needed then. With her, back then, he'd been a raging animal, breaking furniture, ripping curtains, ruining the bed. Once, as Larisa showered after a particularly violent sex session, he'd found her bleeding in the shower. Panicked, he'd looked her over, but there were no visible wounds. And what had Larisa said? She'd smiled at him adoringly, her soft hand on his cheek, and said, *Don't worry, Dimmi, it's just blood from my anus, and you know what they say, if there's no blood, the orgasm wasn't strong enough.* She'd pulled him into the shower and kissed him, the blood wetting the shower floor, seeming not to stop until the water got cold.

A decade ago, he was the man for her and she was the woman for him. But today? The pressures of his advancing career took up more and more of his energy and time. And Father Time did his part, the lessening of testosterone and the physical changes of age had made him much less of a sexual beast. The rapprochement with his first wife and reconciliation with his older children had contributed to ease the former rage within his heart. Life had changed him, he thought. He was a kinder version of his former self.

Perhaps too kind, he thought. His political opponents had begun to point out what they considered weakness in his leadership. Their first bullet point was his so-called failure to retaliate against the American president when the U.S. Navy, in broad daylight, had stolen the Iranian submarine testing the new Russian fast reactor, then gone on to sink three of his frontline attack submarines in their escape with the test vessel. But there were damned good reasons for what he'd done—risking an escalated war with the Americans and NATO made no sense, not over an old Iranian sub with a reactor that was certainly revolutionary but nowhere near disclosing the deep secrets of the Russian Republic. And the three Russian subs lost, hell, one of them blew itself up from a design flaw, the second crew escaped, and the third had been taken down by, of all things, a Russian-designed torpedo, but with limited loss of life. He should attack the Americans for *that*? Plus, President Carlucci had made secret concessions to Russia that none of his opposition knew about, including a transfer of thirty billion Euro for the cost of the Russian submarines lost. So, while the Americans sank them, they paid for them, including the one they hadn't directly destroyed. It had ended up being a better deal for Russia than they'd started with before the whole Iranian fiasco. However, perception was reality. Which was one of the reasons for the upcoming deployment of the Status-6 weapons. Once they were in place, no one would accuse Dmitri Vostov of weakness before the Americans.

But even if that political problem got solved, his present personal problem was starting to become a more pressing crisis. He remembered the divorce, when his first wife, Evelina, had broadcast lies about him in order to gain advantage in the court system, and to ease her rage over his affair with Anastasia Inessa, his former aide. If Larisa decided to go down the road that Evelina had, it would not end well for him. Larisa would certainly out him for all that rough sex, omitting that she'd instigated it and loved it. He considered his options. He was at a rank and station now that with a few words and hand gestures, he could make Larisa disappear. He smirked—if only he'd had that power ten years ago. Evelina would lie in a forlorn, cold grave where no one would ever find her. But he couldn't do that to Larisa—Larisa was the mother of his six-year-old daughter Anya, and he would do *nothing* that would hurt Anya, no matter what. Of course, thinking like that is what gave women so much power in the combat theater of divorce, but so be it.

77

"Dimmi, what is it? Do you not find me attractive anymore? Don't you love me anymore?" She sounded pathetic for just a moment. She looked at him plaintively with her big brown eyes, tears forming in them. Vostov put down his towel and looked at her, opening his mouth to reassure her, but her mood changed instantly, from insecurity to accusing. *"You're fucking someone else*, that's what it is, *isn't it?* All your sexual energy, which you used to reserve exclusively for *me*, now you're giving it to someone else. Who is it? Is it that *whore* Tonya?"

Here we go, Vostov thought. Tonya Pasternak was his chief of staff, and had an impressive but cold beauty. For the last five years, Tonya had offered herself to him, and for five years he'd kept her at a distance. But saying that out loud would not help here. After all, what woman accusing her husband of infidelity would drop the matter on the mere basis of the husband's denial?

"Larisa, calm the fuck down," he said, his voice commanding. "I'm not fucking anyone else!" He made the denial despite his earlier thought. Perhaps it was a husband's reflex.

"Oh, *calm down*, is that it? You want me to calm down? Why don't you *make me*, you pussy?" And with that she slapped his cheek hard, shaving cream flying and hitting the mirror.

There was something about that slap that ignited a hot fury in Vostov. He dropped his towel and grabbed Larisa's wrists. "Shut up!" he roared at her.

"Make me!" she screamed at him. It made him even angrier, and to his surprise, he realized he had grown an erection unlike what he'd had for half a decade. He grabbed Larisa by the throat so hard he lifted her off her feet, threw her against the wall by the shower, the slightest awareness entering his mind of the small blood stain that appeared where Larisa's head had been, but it seemed to feed his fury anew. He picked her up under his arm, carried her into the bedroom, tossed her on the bed, slapped her face hard, and ripped off her nightgown. Without conscious thought, he climbed on top of her and entered her as hard as he could, and she was soaking wet. He drilled into her hard, his thrusts violent and fast, his hand still on her throat, choking her hard, only releasing his grip when he saw her eyes roll up, then continued for what had to be a quarter hour. When he saw tears start to stream out of her eyes and fall down her temples onto the bedsheets, he finally finished hard inside her, his orgasm seeming to roll through his entire body for more than a minute.

He rolled off, covered in sweat, breathing like he'd just sprinted two miles. He could feel his wet body soaking the sheets. He chanced a look over at Larisa, and she was giving him a languid happy look, the smile spreading slowly over her face.

"Oh my God," she gasped, "that was *great*. My big angry bear, you took me like the champion you are." Slowly she shut her eyes, and within a minute, she was fast asleep, snoring softly, a half-smile of contentment on her face.

Vostov clamped his fist against his forehead for a moment, thinking that he hated *himself* when sex was like this. Perhaps that was an alternate meaning of the term, *hate-fuck*. It occurred to him that this was the last time he would have sex with her. He made the decision in that split second. This marriage was over. And there was no telling what Larisa would do when she realized he would be leaving her. The only thing to do was to go away on business, he thought. Suddenly.

He kissed her cheek, rolled off the bed, finished shaving, showered quickly, and donned his dark brown suit with the dark red tie. He grabbed his phone and left the suite as fast as he could. He unlocked his phone and sent a quick text while he hurried down the hall to Anya's room and opened the door just as the first beams of sunshine streamed in. He'd tried to be quiet, but the six-year-old opened her eyes and sat up in bed in her pajamas with the pattern of the brave little girl cartoon character staring down a ferocious tiger. She smiled brightly at him.

"Daddy!"

He sat on her bed and hugged her, feeling a wetness rising in his eyes. What would Larisa do, he wondered. Keep little Anya from him as punishment for his filing for divorce? He released her and sat back to look at her, running his hands through her tousled brown hair.

"You're going away, Daddy?"

He was, he thought, but he couldn't tell Anya that, or she'd tell the news to Larisa.

"What makes you say that, little angel?"

"You're wearing a brown suit, Daddy. You always wear one of your brown suits when you're about to go."

"Well, we'll see," he said. "Daddy's schedule is very busy this week."

"Can you take me to school today?"

"Sorry, little one. I have a car waiting for me. I have to get going. I just came to give you a good morning kiss."

She wrapped her small arms around him again and kissed his cheek. He stroked her hair, trying mightily to keep his eyes dry. He sniffed and tried to smile at her.

"I'll see you soon, baby," he said.

"Tonight, Daddy?"

"We'll see. It might be late, after your bedtime. Now listen to Mommy and be good for Daddy, yes?"

She smiled and nodded. He stood and waved at her and she waved back.

He hurried from her room and down the hallway to the elevator. As he left her room, he was joined by two of his SBP *Sluzhba Bezopasnosti* Presidential Security Service guards.

"Good morning, Mr. President," the senior man said.

"Morning, gentlemen," Vostov replied without thinking. He hit the speed dial for his chief of staff, Tonya Pasternak. She answered on the first ring.

"Good morning, sir," she said alertly and formally.

"Tonya. Call off all the week's meetings. The trip we'd discussed, to Murmansk? Make it happen. Now. I'm having my driver bring me to the airstrip. Pack for a week and send a detail to my suite to get a week's worth of suits, plus clothes suitable for touring a factory and going into a submarine. Get the plane fueled, loaded, and staffed. We're leaving immediately."

Most aides, Vostov thought, would sputter and object to such a radical change in the schedule, especially with the itinerary the upcoming week held, but not Pasternak.

"I'm on it, sir. Who do you want to accompany us?"

Vostov thought for a minute as the elevator descended. "Get Sevastyan and his deputy, Ozols, and Mikhail and *his* deputy, Prokopiy." General Gennadi Sevastyan was head of the FSB—the internal security organization and half of what had been the KGB before its breakup in the 90s—and Colonel General Advey Ozols was his second-in-command. "Mikhail" was the nickname they called Marshal Radoslav Konstantinov, the minister of defense. General Osip Prokopiy was his deputy.

"No one from SVR, sir?" The SVR was the other half of the former KGB, the group responsible for foreign intelligence and covert operations.

"Not for this trip, Tonya."

"Understood, sir. I will see you at the jet."

The presidential motorcade was perhaps the riskiest portion of the trip. Tonya Pasternak always fretted that the opposition party would attempt an assassination or kidnapping. Vostov had no such fears. His opponents had a small but key portion of the journalists in their pockets and some foreign support. They'd most likely come at him head-on, he thought, in the upcoming election. It would be more dangerous for him after he won another term, he thought.

The motorcade arrived at the secure base, recently constructed close to the Kremlin after the condemnation and demolition of a dozen western hotels, to the protests of the corporations involved. The sleek supersonic Tupolev Tu-144 waited at the end of the 3000-meter runway, its loud jets already at idle. The previous Russian president had used a Sukhoi Superjet 100, a twin-engine subsonic passenger jet upgrade, but Vostov had had a Tu-144 rebuilt from scratch, the magnificent Russian-designed supersonic transport brought to the market even before the Concorde. The TU-144s had all been warehoused in 1999, but Vostov had commissioned the construction of a new, improved version based on the original plans, with more powerful jets, the interior modified for presidential use. It was louder and less comfortable than the Superjet, but much faster. Vostov used it for travel internal to the country—overseas trips were for the Superjet, the latter more civilized, not breaking the windows of a host country's buildings.

Vostov's limo rolled to the access stairs to the forward hatch. He ducked inside and greeted the two Air Force pilots, moved back through the communication and tactical compartment, which was able to conduct a nuclear war remotely, to the more luxurious staff accommodations and the galley. At the end of the plane was the soundproofed and heavily secured outer and inner office Vostov used for meetings and for when he wanted to be alone, with a small desk, conference table seating six, a private bathroom and a small bunk with a reading light. Computer flatpanel displays lined the bulkheads, leaving only one small window on either side of the office.

Vostov was accustomed to boarding his plane before the staff. As he waited, he and Pasternak took seats at the conference table, with Pasternak opening a pad computer for her to present to Vostov the daily briefing. He could see out the window as an Air Force staff car disgorged the four-person tactical and communications team, who would take their positions in the first compartment, ready for any emergency involving wartime operations. He could see the disgusted look on the face of the commanding colonel as he emerged from the car. Obviously, the Air Force staff disliked the supersonic transport, much preferring the Superjet, which allowed twice the number of officers and more redundant comms equipment.

Pasternak was almost done giving the daily brief when a gleaming black limo arrived and two men emerged, both wearing suits, both hurrying up the stairway, then a second staff SUV pull up, with another two men egressing and going to the stairs. The second pair were also wearing suits, but seemed to move much slower—both were much older.

The phone on the table trilled and Pasternak answered it. She said, "very well, send them back. You have permission to depart," and hung up. "Everyone's on board, sir."

"Anything else in the briefing?" Vostov asked.

"Two things, sir," Pasternak said, flashing up a satellite photo taken of a drydock with a submarine in it, the sub surrounded by scaffolding. "The GRU military intelligence people reported that a key U.S. Navy project submarine, the USS *Vermont*, has been destroyed in its drydock by a raging fire, injuring two crewmembers. If you'll remember, sir, the *Vermont* was the American submarine involved in stealing the Iranian sub with our test reactor earlier in the summer."

"Good," Vostov said, a tone of bitterness in his voice. "It was too bad their crew all survived. What was the second thing?"

"The GRU reports that they've picked up intelligence that American frogmen have placed nuclear mines in our major ports. They claim that the mines are two megaton hydrogen bombs. At least two dozen of them."

"Yeah, right," Vostov said, shaking his head. "Remind me to order Mikhail to find one of these and dredge it up as proof. This all has the ring of pipelined disinformation to me. Something to make us afraid, not something real."

Vostov looked up as a knock came at the door and four men entered the room, the first the defense minister, Marshal Radoslav Mikhail Konstantinov, the elder statesman of the military. He walked in slowly, with a quiet dignity. The man had to be in his late seventies, Vostov thought, his full head of hair completely gray, his face ruddy. Mikhail's hand shook with palsy as he reached to shake hands with Vostov, who stood to greet him. Rumor had it that Mikhail had Parkinson's disease, and that his treatments were starting to fail. Pasternak had wondered aloud about Vostov appointing a replacement for him, and they'd both toyed with the idea of Mikhail nominating his own successor, but the rising opposition to Vostov's governance made them both cautious, and they'd postponed the decision.

"Good morning, Mikhail," Vostov said, his voice deep and gravelly. "Sorry to roust you out so suddenly for this trip."

Konstantinov just smiled, his face lighting up when he smiled, his eyes shrinking to horizontal slits. "I'm glad to be with you on this trip, Mr. President. I was going to suggest we move this up in the schedule anyway, since the mission is vital."

The room grew louder as the aircraft's jets spooled up to full power. Vostov waved the men to their seats. Outside the windows, the runway and the Moscow surroundings blurred by, the plane shaking with vibrations as the aircraft sped up on the runway, but in a few seconds the cabin inclined upward and the vibrations disappeared, the groan of the landing gear retracting loud for a moment. When the cabin quieted, the deck seemed to get steeper for a few minutes with the engine noise easing somewhat as the plane flew over Moscow's center city and then over the outskirts, the jet throttling back up as it flew over Moscow Ring Road.

Vostov looked over at Mikhail's deputy, short and barrel-chested General Osip Prokopiy. Vostov had never approved of Prokopiy. He insisted on keeping his hair too long, a thick beard gracing his face, obscuring the knot of his necktie. He was an Orthodox Christian and insisted the beard and hairstyle were part of his religious practice. He was a quiet man, diffident and reserved, but—according to Mikhail—the smartest mind in the ministry. Vostov had his doubts, but he'd pay attention to what Prokopiy had to say on this voyage.

Vostov nodded over at the pair from FSB, Gennadi Sevastyan and Avdey Ozols. When the Soviet Union fell, the magnificent and successful KGB, the *Komitet Gosudarstvennoy Bezopasnosti* or Committee for State Security, was split in two. The mostly domestic functions of watching the population, tracking diplomats and foreign spies on Russian soil, and interior counterintelligence became those of the FSB, the *Federal'naya Sluzhba Bezopasnosti* or Federal Security Service. The foreign mission of spying abroad and black operations, formerly those of KGB's First Chief Directorate, became the tasks of the SVR, *Sluzhba Vneshney Razvedki Rossiyskoy Federatsii,* or the Foreign Intelligence Service.

Tonya Pasternak had once proposed the idea of reuniting the SVR and FSB back into a combined organization and giving it the traditional name of the KGB, but Vostov opposed the idea. That would concentrate entirely too much power in one organization. Many of the old Soviet bosses after Stalin had risen to prominence in the KGB, to the point that it could be inferred that the intelligence community ran the country. Despite Vostov being a former KGB officer in the decade before its split into the SVR and FSB, he deeply distrusted a reunited and integrated KGB. He'd prefer to deal with internal security separately from foreign operations. From a pragmatic aspect, each organization was jealous of the other and routinely devoted resources to spying on their opposite numbers, which could keep a coup from happening. And in the abstract, Vostov was convinced that an integrated KGB would be bad for the country and would be unpopular with the citizens, and anything unpopular with them could cause him to lose an election.

The Chairman of the FSB, General Gennadi Sevastyan, was tall and slender, with a handsome open face graced with bushy eyebrows and a full head of salt-and-pepper hair. His age was indeterminate, either late forties or mid-fifties. In working with Sevastyan over the past decade, Vostov had grown to trust the man, inviting him to the presidential offices for after-work drinks of the vodka that only politicians and diplomats could obtain. Sevastyan was a family man, like Vostov, with two children in grade school, with a pretty and friendly wife. His hobbies were rowing, his dacha on a river where he would row a one-man scull for hours while dictating memoranda on a waterproof recorder, his deputy the recipient of all of Sevastyan's memos and random thoughts.

"Gennadi," Vostov said, smiling at Sevastyan. "Good to have you with us."

Sevastyan smiled and nodded. "We almost lost Avdey from this trip. I caught him just as he was climbing into a plane."

"Oh?" Vostov looked at the FSB Deputy Chairman, Colonel General Avdey Ozols. Ozols was much older than Sevastyan by at least a decade, a trim man of medium height who had a rigid posture and a military bearing. He was a storied FSB operative, having been involved in the hostage rescue from the Chechen takeover of the Moscow Dubrovka Theater in 2002, when 850 hostages were taken. Most were rescued, with the forty terrorists killed, and despite the loss of 131 hostages during the counter-assault, Ozols had been credited with the public relations win. Ozols had gone on to half a dozen more high-profile successes, and was considered a viable successor to Sevastyan. As head of the presidential security detail in addition to his normal duties, he was a man Vostov trusted as deeply as Sevastyan. If only, Vostov thought, his trust for their opposite numbers in the SVR were as deep.

"I was headed to a trouble spot, but as it turned out," Ozols said, "my people took care of things before the door could shut on the plane."

"Well, I'm glad we got you here in any case," Vostov said. "So, Tonya, can you go over what our itinerary is for this trip one more time?"

For the next ninety minutes, Pasternak briefed the five men, the room's displays lit up with her presentation on the Status-6 torpedoes, the *Belgorod* and the *Losharik*. Early in her briefing, the Mach number indicator showed the Tu-144 reaching Mach 1.95. As she wrapped up, the plane slowed and the cabin tilted downward as the jet made its approach to Murmansk Airport. A few minutes later, the jet touched down and taxied to the military terminal. The FSB and defense officials stood. Vostov waved to Pasternak to stay.

"Gentlemen, go ahead. We will meet you at the Sevmash Shipyard. I have something to go over with my chief of staff."

Once the engines were shut down, the jet became ghostly quiet and the air inside cooled.

"You wanted to talk to me, sir?" Pasternak prompted.

"Yes, Tonya. Something serious is happening in my personal life."

"It's Larisa, isn't it?"

Vostov knew Pasternak had never liked Larisa, thinking her entitled and immature. Her dislike might have been fueled by her thinly disguised desire to have a more personal relationship with Vostov.

Vostov looked at his chief aide. She was tall, only a few centimeters shorter than he, slender, with long legs, a thin waist, and large breasts. She had long gleaming raven-black hair, puffy red lips in a model's face with high cheekbones and large almond-shaped dark eyes. She dressed professionally, but her beauty shone through any outfit she'd wear that attempted to mute her femme-fatale appearance. Her voice was deep for a woman, which helped in this mostly all-male group of officials, giving her a more authoritative air.

Vostov pursed his lips. "It's Larisa. The marriage is over. But you know Larisa. She's volatile and has a volcanic temper. Divorce proceedings will be a disaster. This could destroy my candidacy and the campaign."

Pasternak nodded solemnly. "Can your divorce wait until after the election?"

Vostov shook his head. "Larisa can see right through me that I'm done with her. I had to have a—well—emphatic 'session' with her this morning just to hold her off for a week. But she knows. What she'll trumpet to the press will be devastating. And if I know Larisa, she'll take off with little Anya and it could be a long time before I see my daughter again. It's like my first divorce, but with what Larisa will paint as misconduct on my part. She'll say I'm abusive."

Pasternak blew out her lips. "She's the one who's addicted to rough and violent sex, not you." She paused. "Sir, you should let me take care of this. I've gone through contingency plans for this with Ozols."

Vostov raised an eyebrow.

"You don't want to know, sir. You'll need deniability. But there will be, let's say, an incident. Larisa will no longer be a problem."

"Tonya, nothing can happen to Anya. I don't want her embroiled in any, let's call it a 'scenario.' I don't want her in any kind of harm's way. I don't want her to see anything that will scar her for life."

"Leave it in my hands, sir. Just do me a favor."

"What's that?"

"Promise me you'll stay with the staff in Murmansk for at least a week. If we wrap up these tours of the factory and submarines too early, that will cause complications. Try to linger here. Perhaps tour other military facilities in the region."

"A week?"

"A week, sir. If possible, it will happen sooner. But no later than a week. By the time we fly back, things will be well in hand. And I promise the result will paint you in a sympathetic light. And Anya will be fine. Well, as fine as she can be with her mother, you know." Her voice trailed off.

Vostov nodded. "Let's get to the motorcade. I don't want to keep the boys waiting."

6

President Dmitri Vostov felt self-conscious for the first time in five years, but that probably made sense, as he was walking through a world as foreign to him as the surface of the Moon, clad in ridiculous-looking avocado green coveralls, which were a half size too small for him, his girth stretching the fabric at his stomach.

He was in a group with the ship's commanding officer, a hard-looking tough man with black hair streaked with gray and an eye patch over his right eye, giving him the air of a eighteenth century pirate. With them was the Sevmash Shipyard's head of the engineering and design directorate, a slender and slight man in blue coveralls who had been introduced as Anatoly Voronin. The Defense Minister had decided to skip the tour, but his deputy, Prokopiy, was with them, as was the FSB deputy, Avdey Ozols. There was no sign of Pasternak, who had asked to do some work in the ship's crew's messroom.

They stood in what Captain Alexeyev had described as the first compartment, or the torpedo room. It was dimly lit, despite dozens of overhead LED lamps, which seemed only to cast shadows from all the space's tightly packed weapons on a triple-deck rack, with piping and cables and valves and junction boxes occupying seemingly every cubic centimeter of the volume of the room.

Alexeyev walked Vostov forward—although by this time, Vostov had lost all sense of direction—to the forward bulkhead of the room. To the left was a wall with an opened door, and inside, the space was jammed with control panels with glowing buttons and blinking lights, one cabinet door opened to reveal a rat's nest of wires and computer cards. To the right of this tight room were the torpedo tube doors. The tube's doors were wide enough to allow a man skinnier than Vostov to squeeze in.

Perhaps sensing Vostov was partly overwhelmed and partly bored, his guide, Captain First Rank Georgy Alexeyev, asked if Vostov were in the mood for the mid-day meal. Normally, on a tour of this kind, Vostov would look at his watch and beg off, citing schedule pressure, but Pasternak's words about extending the trip still rang in his ears. He smiled with what he hoped looked like genuine happiness and told Alexeyev that he was, indeed, famished. The smell of the meal cooking had been wafting through the entire ship, and if Vostov were honest with himself, it had been making him hungry ever since he'd stepped through the access hatch in the conning tower and descended the steep stairs to the submarine's central command post.

Alexeyev's tour of the central command post revealed a bafflingly complex space, looking like what a fighter jet cockpit would look like if it were expanded to the size of a house. Consoles, displays, lights, buttons, valves, switches, cables and panels everywhere. How any sane man could stay in this horrible, incomprehensible environment was beyond Vostov. No doubt, his nation owed these seafaring heroes a deep debt of gratitude.

That made him think about what Pasternak had read to him from Alexeyev's file, about the mission of the ill-fated *Kazan* and the battle the ship had had with that Iranian submarine. Usually Vostov could read people like a book, but Alexeyev was a mystery to him. Vostov couldn't tell whether mentioning the *Kazan* sinking would be negative or positive. As for negative, obviously, his ship sank. But for the positive—Captain Alexeyev and his crew had fought against impossible odds, fighting both that damned Virginia-class American sub, the *Vermont*, and the stolen Iranian. In what had to be some sort of freak accident, the boarding party of Americans on the Iranian sub had somehow figured out how to deploy a Russian supercavitating torpedo at the *Kazan*, and taken it down in seconds. *Kazan* had battled bravely, and most of the crew had lived to tell the tale, reality again becoming freakish when the very Americans who sank them came to their rescue.

But if Alexeyev were embarrassed about the incident, he gave nothing away. It was as if the *Kazan* incident had never happened. He toured Vostov through the spaces of his gigantic submarine *Belgorod* as if the president were a freshly minted officer from the Marshal Grechko School of Underwater Navigation. The other sub skipper, Sergei Kovalov, was nowhere near as steely-eyed as Alexeyev. Kovalov's tour of his boat, the *Losharik*, earlier that day, had been short and intense, and all through it, Vostov could sense Kovalov's extreme discomfort at having a VIP to take aboard that tiny sub. Quite a contrast between *Losharik* and *Belgorod*, Vostov thought. *Losharik* was an overgrown mini-sub, with seven small titanium spheres contained inside the outer hull, each capable of withstanding her 2500 meter dive depth, and of the seven, the rear four were all propulsion plant, ship controls, electronics, and atmospheric controls. The forward sphere could accommodate perhaps five crewmen in the control space. The two spheres farther aft were for hotel spaces, firefighting equipment, and spare parts. Touring *Losharik* was like going into a space capsule, Vostov thought. That tour had only taken an hour, since there was so little to see. Then the entourage had come to *Belgorod*. And the super-sub, though cramped inside, was absolutely vast compared to the mini-sub.

Alexeyev led them through the galley to the officers' mess, where Vostov spent twenty minutes shaking hands and chatting with the officers. It was a bit strange to Vostov, since Alexeyev's second-in-command and three department heads were women. The younger officers, who reported to the department heads, were mostly men, but they seemed so *young*. Perhaps that was just Vostov's impression from his getting older, but still, they all seemed like pimple-faced teenagers.

Alexeyev motioned them to seats at the large officers' messroom table, with him at the end seat. Vostov sat immediately to his right, apparently the seat-of-honor, with the other dignitaries at Alexeyev's end of the table, the more junior officers on the other end. The mess attendants served tea first, then what they called Kamchatka crab salad, which was amazing. The main course came out soon, a grilled zucchini with shrimp and sea scallops with broccoli, a side of poussin with vegetables. Despite his vow to eat little, Vostov found himself digging in, the food excellent. He was engrossed in conversation with Alexeyev, Voronin and Prokopiy, who were talking about how the *Losharik* could be docked to the underbelly of the *Belgorod* and how they would link up in the Barents Sea, and how *Losharik* would carry two of the Status-6 torpedoes if it had to. Alexeyev's officers were quiet but listening intently. Evidently, not many mission details had been discussed at their level.

"Have you seen the Status-6 factory floor yet, Mr. President?" Alexeyev said as he waved off the main course's dishes.

Vostov shook his head. "We revised the schedule to move that to later today if there's time. We'll need an hour or two to do some routine things. I have a teleconference with the Council of Ministers. I thought I'd take it in Mr. Voronin's offices at the shipyard."

Alexeyev nodded. "The Status-6 is quite a weapon," he said, his voice neutral.

"Some people consider it destabilizing, that it could lead to war. Perhaps even nuclear war." Vostov said. He looked at Alexeyev. "Do you agree with that, Captain?"

Alexeyev came as close to a smile as he had all day. "Sir, that's not for me to say. This is, after all, a combat submarine, not a think tank. We don't make policy, we simply execute it."

"Well said, Captain," Vostov said, smiling at Alexeyev.

The mess attendants brought in dessert, a berry and cream concoction over vanilla ice cream. Despite his watering mouth, Vostov waved off the dessert, wiping his mouth with a linen napkin.

"Mr. President," Alexeyev said, "we have a 2015 Chardonnay and a 2015 Western Slope Merlot." He winked at his officers. "We usually don't get a treat like that, whether in-port or at-sea, sir. Shall we pour some?"

Vostov considered and nodded. "How can I say no to that, Captain? As for me, the white wine, but just half a glass."

Once the meal was done, Vostov looked over at Captain Alexeyev. "Captain, why don't you and I go to your room — your sea cabin? — and talk for a moment, privately. I would ask my chief of staff to come with us, and naturally one of the SBP detail will come, but obviously won't listen or contribute."

"My pleasure, Mr. President. Please follow me." Alexeyev left the large officers' messroom through the forward door, down a wide passageway with walls laminated with a light birchwood pattern. At the end of the passageway were two doors, one with a small window at eye level, its glass red. Alexeyev opened the other door and motioned in the president, Tonya Pasternak, and the suit-clad SBP guard. Alexeyev sat at the end seat of the large conference table, which adjoined his large wooden desk, the table and the desk forming a "T" shape. Vostov took a seat next to him in a seat facing the door they'd entered, with Pasternak seated opposite him. The SBP man stood in the corner near the door.

The stateroom was large, the bulkheads lined with large flatpanel displays, the conference table and desk dominating the room otherwise. The captain's bed was tucked against the long wall of the room in an alcove. At the end of the bed was a large storage closet and next to that, the wall of the captain's head. At the aft end, where Alexeyev's end seat was, a door led aft, labeled "FOSR," which Alexeyev explained meant "first officer's stateroom."

"So, Captain," Vostov opened, "I assume you have questions about this upcoming operation. I figured you might want to air them out now, but away from your men."

"Thank you, Mr. President. My first question is, why are we doing this? Parking ten megaton hydrogen bombs in American ports? Understood, they are military ports, but still. This seems extremely aggressive."

"Yes. I understand that point of view," Vostov said. "Do you think you could call for some more of that white wine? That was pretty good."

Alexeyev reached under the table for a phone handset, pressed a button on it, and muttered a few words into it. Not a full minute from the call, the mess steward knocked and came in with a tray with the wine bottle in an ice bucket and three glasses. Pasternak waved off a glass. The steward poured for Vostov and Alexeyev, replaced the wine bottle and disappeared out the forward door.

"The defense minister would tend to agree with you, Captain," Vostov said. "In his words, we're launching three ICBMs, just missiles that travel at ten knots, not two thousand. My head of the SVR feels the same way, and even the top ranks of the Navy itself have objected to this idea. But I simply don't see it that way. These weapons are sleepers. They'll just sit on the bay bottom, inert. They won't even be in communication with antennae, so they can't be activated by remote."

"What? I'm confused," Alexeyev said. "What good is a loitering weapon if it can't be awakened in a, well, let's call it a 'tactical situation'?"

"It's not the same thing as an ICBM at all, you see. It's just a deep contingency. Back during the Cold War, the Spetsnaz GRU used to construct weapons caches and survival bunkers on enemy soil, for use, well, just in case. This is somewhat similar. If a world war were to break out against NATO and the Americans, we'd send diver commandos to activate the weapons. For that reason, it's important that you report back the exact location of these Status-6 units. They must be placed with precision and their positions noted with extreme accuracy, which is why your ship and *Losharik* are deploying them manually rather than simply firing them from the North Atlantic and letting them find their own way. I'm told their onboard navigation systems can lack accuracy. It would do no good for a ten megaton sleeper weapon to get confused and be lost to us. Or even worse, broach somewhere on a sandbar and be recovered by the Americans."

"If you say so, Mr. President. Let's leave the purpose of the Status-6 placement aside for a moment. Why the polar transit? And the months-long passage under the ice, through the Bering Strait around South America to get to the U.S. Atlantic coast? We could make that voyage from here at a patrol quiet speed of ten knots in a little over three weeks. The polar path will be much slower, due to the ice, and will take at least three-and-a-half months."

Vostov nodded. "This boat is old. Laid down in, what, 1993? It has only been modernized to be able to dock with the *Losharik* and carry Status-6 weapons. It's still as loud as a third-generation attack sub. If you transit past the U.K., Greenland, and Iceland, the sonar trip wire of NATO will pick you up. And odds are, there's an American or British attack submarine loitering off Severodvinsk waiting for you and *Losharik* to leave port, and they'd follow you all the way to your destination. If they see you headed north to the pole, they will assume you are simply conducting an exercise. Even if they follow you northward, it's not guaranteed they'd keep up with you. And say they do. You are loaded out for a four-month journey—you have food in almost every compartment and space—and any following enemy sub could never stay out that long without resupply, which means they'd have to surface. By then, you'd be long gone."

Alexeyev frowned. "Sir, the icecap, even in the summer, is treacherous. Deep pressure ridges close off what would seem a viable path. We might have to back up, retrace our path, and take another route. Our average speed might be near zero. It could take a month or even two just to clear the icecap. A smaller submarine could get by, but *Belgorod*, sir, this vessel is huge, and even bigger with *Losharik* docked."

"If it gets to be a problem, Captain, perhaps undock the *Losharik* and keep trying. It's been done before, with the first Omega submarine, the *Kaliningrad*. *Kaliningrad* surfaced at the North Pole."

"Sir, *Kaliningrad* didn't make it back from that mission."

"I know, Captain Alexeyev, but neither did the American sub hunting her."

"Understood, sir. How urgent is the delivery of these weapons?"

"We're in no hurry, Captain. If you can get them there by Christmas, it will be a nice present all around."

Alexeyev nodded and poured more wine for the president, then more for himself.

"One thing, though, Captain," Vostov said.

"What's that, Mr. President?"

Vostov sighed. "Evidently the Poseidon torpedoes are not quite ready. Engineer Voronin has requested another week to prepare them. Between you and me, I think it will take longer. I believe our comrades at Sevmash have over-promised on these weapons. But let us think in a positive frame of mind, yes?"

Vostov drained his wine and stood. "Perhaps we could return to your officers' messroom? I enjoy spending time with the troops. Maybe you could bring in some of the non-commissioned officers as well. We could have a sort of miniature town hall meeting."

"Absolutely, sir." Alexeyev grabbed the phone handset from under the table again and spoke into it, then motioned the entourage out of his stateroom.

Ten minutes later, Vostov was answering a question asked by a mechanical petty officer when the door to the room was suddenly smashed open by the chief of the SBP security detail, who waved a hand signal to his troops. Up until that moment, four of the SBP guards had been posted in the officers' messroom, standing calmly and almost invisibly in the corners, but then suddenly sprang into action and forcibly grabbed Vostov under his arms and dragged him out of the room and down the passageway. Vostov could barely feel his feet touching the deck plates as he was rushed to the central command post and forward to the ladderway to the access hatch. His heart was pounding in his throat. He had the slightest impression of the officers in the room staring at him with their eyes bulging out.

Outside the hatch, six more SBP agents waited, hustling Vostov into an idling utility truck, the other men of the entourage climbing into the trucks ahead of his and behind it. The convoy of trucks roared off down the long and wide concrete jetty, turning hard at the road at the end, speeding up to what had to be 120 kilometers per hour as they made a short trip to a huge military helicopter. Vostov looked at the SBP agents on either side of him in the back seat.

"What the hell is going on?"

"You'll be informed soon, sir," one said. "Let's just concentrate on getting you to your jet."

"Where's Pasternak? And Konstantinov? And Sevastyan?"

"They're being rushed to your aircraft, sir. But that's all I know."

The truck screeched to a halt at the helicopter, the rotors already beating loudly, the dust underneath the huge machine blowing in the wind it generated. Vostov climbed the steps to the chopper and was strapped in. He was handed a helmet with an intercom on it.

"Who's the senior man aboard?" he asked, trying to make his voice hard and demanding.

A man in olive drab coveralls up front, with the emblems of an Air Force lieutenant colonel raised his hand. "I am, sir," he said, his voice in Vostov's helmet's earphones.

"Can *you* tell me what's going on?"

"We don't know, sir. We got the orders from General Sevastyan just moments ago. It must be serious. All we know is this is not an exercise."

Vostov sat back in his seat, waiting impatiently. Eventually the chopper descended and settled at the airstrip near the Tu-144. The SBP agents rushed him into the plane. He was barely inside when the hatch shut and the jet's engines roared, the jet at full power on the runway before he could make his way into the back inner office.

He strapped himself into his chair at the desk and looked up at Pasternak. At the table's chairs were the same officials he'd arrived with. As the deck inclined for takeoff, he glared at Defense Minister Konstantinov and FSB Chairman Sevastyan. "One of you people care to tell me what the hell is going on?"

"Mr. President," Sevastyan said, "we have a live feed from the GUM shopping mall." Pasternak helped the FSB chairman project his pad computer on the large flatpanels on the forward bulkhead.

The view showed the plate glass windows fronting the Brunello Cucinelli shop, but the inside was obscured by smoke. A crowd of tactically-outfitted SBP agents and police were crowded in front of the store.

"Maybe the news," Pasternak said, switching on a flatpanel display to the RT Moscow local affiliate. The announcer was a woman standing somewhere in front of the black-clad police.

"Turn it up," Vostov said.

The announcer seemed to stumble through her words, seeming shaken by what was happening.

"...in front of the Brunello Cucinelli boutique, where we believe sixteen shoppers and four staff are being held hostage inside by elements of the United Islamic Front of God, who are—who are, apparently, terrorists. We have preliminary word that among the hostages is Larisa Vostov, the wife of the president. The UIF have communicated to the commander of the hostage rescue team that their demands are the release of six prisoners held in Tomsk Prison, each of them in maximum security, serving sentences for murder and terrorism. They have stated that they require an escort from the mall and a helicopter to a private jet, plus ten million Euro, failing which they will execute a hostage every hour until their demands are met."

"Mute it," Vostov barked. "Is Anya okay?"

The FSB deputy, Ozols, was speaking on a phone, one hand covering his ear. He looked up at Vostov. "Anya is safe, Mr. President. She's under SBP guard. She was removed from her school and is arriving at your north dacha now, sir. We have agents inside and outside with roadblocks set up on all roads in the vicinity, and the anti-aircraft units are stationed and ready. Any move against Anya will be met with deadly force."

Vostov breathed a sigh of relief.

"Mr. President, you have to make the decision," Deputy FSB Chairman Ozols said, looking at him expectantly.

Vostov looked at Ozols. "What decision?"

"Do we promise to release the prisoners and get the chopper, money and plane? Or do we storm the store and try to rescue the hostages?"

"Everyone leave this office except for Pasternak," Vostov ordered.

The staff bolted to their feet and hurried out of the room, shutting the door behind them.

"Can I get you a bottle of water, sir? You look white as a ghost."

"Tonya, what is this? Is this related to what we spoke about before?"

Pasternak didn't say anything, but just gave him a solemn half nod.

"So, how do the options break down?"

She took a deep breath. "We have to consider the right thing to do given the political situation and our opposition. If we accommodate the terrorists, we look weak to our constituents and the opposition. And to the world."

"But if I give the order to rush those criminals, it could result in all twenty of the hostages being killed," Vostov said.

"Correct, sir."

"I want the ages of every one of the hostages," Vostov said. "I want to know if children are inside."

"I'll be right back."

Pasternak hurried forward to consult with the FSB officers. While he waited, Vostov unmuted the news channel. There was not much new coming from RT. They were approaching the time when the first hostage would be executed, failing word on the prisoner release, the money, the helicopter and the private jet. Pasternak hurried back in, brushing her hair out of her face.

"Sir, of the sixteen people who aren't staff, fifteen of them are women between the ages of twenty-one and forty-seven. There is one male, a nineteen-year-old who is the son of the older woman. FSB thinks he will be the first hostage to be executed."

Vostov leaned back for a moment. "Call for the flight attendant to bring back a bottle of vodka and glasses. Get Sevastyan and Ozols back here. Then put me in touch with the man in tactical command at the scene."

It took a moment for Pasternak to set up the call. The FSB chairman and his deputy stepped back in and took seats at the

99

conference table. Vostov stood from his desk and joined them at the table.

"The tactical commander is on the speaker phone, sir," Pasternak said.

"This is the president," Vostov said to the speaker on the center of the table. "Who am I speaking with?"

"Sir, this Colonel Vanya Nika, GRU, assigned on duty to FSB."

The hostess arrived with the vodka and half a dozen glasses. Vostov motioned for her to pour four glasses. He grabbed one and downed it in one go. Pasternak refilled his glass.

"Colonel, what's your assessment of the scene? What are the chances you can get these hostages out? With minimal loss of innocent lives?"

"Sir, we have a good tactical plan," Nika said, his voice clipped and tough sounding. "We'll breach the ventilation system and deploy concentrated carfentanil gas. It's similar to the one we used in the Moscow Theater attack, but improved. It might cause one or two deaths of the twenty, but we believe within a minute, the terrorists will be unconscious. Then we'll use explosives on the plate glass and go in with a full platoon. We'll put a bullet in the heads of every terrorist. It will be over in five minutes. But sir?"

"Yes, Colonel?"

"Sir, I can't guarantee we won't have casualties or collateral damage. Mr. President, I can't guarantee your wife's safety."

"Colonel, give me two minutes. Stay on the line. I will mute my end."

Pasternak clicked the mute button and looked over at him.

"Well, Gennadi, what do you think?" Vostov asked.

"Sir, I say we go in," the FSB chairman said.

"And you, Avdey?"

The FSB deputy glanced at the vodka glass in front of him, then at Vostov. "I agree with General Sevastyan, sir. We can't give in to these people or else this will happen a dozen more times."

"We could promise to release the prisoners they want, or even release them," Vostov suggested. "That would buy time."

"Time is our enemy, Mr. President. The longer we wait, the more hostages they will execute. Perhaps one of them, your wife," Ozols said.

"No," Sevastyan said. "They'd save Larisa for last. She's their biggest bargaining chip."

"That assumes they know one of the women they hold is Larisa Vostov," Pasternak said.

"Of course they know," Sevastyan replied. "That's why they targeted this shop. And even if they didn't know, they know now." Sevastyan pointed to the RT news screen.

"Where the hell is her SBP detail?" Vostov asked sharply.

Sevastyan looked down at the table. "She's shaken off her detail twice before, Mr. President, intentionally. She doesn't like being followed around by men in suits holding guns. I sincerely apologize for the failure of my men on this, sir."

Vostov waved his apology away. "Recriminations are for later, people. Let's just get through this and do the right thing. The right thing, not just for me, but for Russia. So I'll ask again, do we storm the store or buy time? Sevastyan?"

"Breach the store, sir. It's our best option."

"Ozols? What do you say?"

"Rush the store, sir."

"Tonya?"

"I agree with the chairman and deputy, sir. Rush the store."

Vostov downed the second vodka and unmuted the speaker phone.

"Colonel? You there?"

"Yes, sir," Colonel Nika's voice said from the speaker.

"Colonel, I am ordering you to storm the store," Vostov said. "Keep this circuit open. I want a status report as soon as you have it."

"Understood, sir. We will commence the operation forthwith."

Vostov muted the phone and noticed that the other three finally drank their own vodkas. Vostov unmuted the news.

101

"...something is happening here," the announcer said. A tremendous explosion happened behind her and she fell to the floor, the camera shaking, the view tumbling. "The police have—there seems to be—the police have breached the store and are running into—" Vostov muted the news. There was nothing but confusion on the screen.

The next minutes seemed to last an hour. Finally the speaker phone squawked.

"Mr. President, we've secured the scene. The terrorists are dead, all except one from our bullets. One shot himself before we could get to him."

"The hostages?"

"None of them took any rounds from us or the terrorists, but they're all unconscious from the gas, sir. We're getting emergency medical teams in here immediately and evacuating the civilians."

"My wife?"

"Can't tell yet, Mr. President. It's in the hands of the medevac team now."

"Thank you, Colonel," Vostov said. "And good job." He clicked off the speaker phone.

"I guess now we wait, sir," Pasternak said.

7

Lieutenant Anthony Pacino climbed out of his car service's sleek, new electric sedan, missing his Corvette. He looked up at the huge building, a few blocks from State Pier, New London, Connecticut. It was called "The Power House," a refurbished power plant from 1897 that had been abandoned in 1955, then reclaimed in 2012 to be a brewery, pub, and pasta and steak joint. He half-smiled to himself—it might seem an odd business plan to reclaim an old power plant for this, but he liked the atmosphere already.

As he entered the antique wood entrance doors, he had a sense of stepping a hundred years into the past. The lighting looked exactly like old gas lamps—done with modern and safe LEDs, of course—but everything else within view was antique, with nineteenth century furnishings, even large ceiling fans turned by belts and pulleys. He saw the wrap-around bar, formed of timbers taken from upper floor supports when they'd been removed to allow a high ceiling and space for the brewery vessels. The bar was huge, tended by a half dozen bartenders and had multiple tap setups and a tall set of glass shelves displaying what seemed every alcoholic drink known to modern man. For a moment, Pacino regretted that Commander Bullfrog Quinnivan—*Vermont*'s exec—couldn't see this, as it would have put him in heaven. Over the shelves of bottles were huge flatpanel television screens displaying every sports game happening at that moment, except for the one screen tuned to a news channel. On the far side of the bar, Pacino could see Squirt Gun Vevera and U-Boat Dankleff waving him over.

Pacino had checked into the "Q" the night before with the rest of the boat's junior officers when their airport shuttle had arrived. "Q" was short for "BOQ," which itself was short for bachelor officer quarters. Now that there were almost as many female officers as there were males, he thought, the term "bachelor" seemed outdated, but he'd leave it to Big Navy to correct any politically incorrect nomenclature. At the Q, he'd slept fitfully, rising late on this Sunday morning to run a few miles around the hilly Groton Navy base overlooking the wide Thames River. After a shower, he logged in and went through his unclassified electronic mail, then tried to relax by reading a novel, but couldn't concentrate. He considered calling Vevera or Dankleff to see what they were up to, but odds were, they were sleeping off the previous evening's beer and tequila.

Around five o'clock, he got separate texts from Vevera and Dankleff instructing him to show up for a "command performance" at The Power House, where the attack sub *New Jersey*'s captain, executive officer, and department heads demanded to meet their new junior officers. Since Commander Quinnivan had given the *Vermont* junior officers their new orders, there had been no word, not even a whispered rumor, of who the *New Jersey*'s captain or exec would be. All anyone knew was that the "PCU" captain and XO would not be commanding *New Jersey*. PCU stood for "pre-commissioning unit," the designation for a ship not yet accepted by the Navy for combat service. The PCU crew were "drydock rats," experts at assisting in giving birth to the ship from the millions of components brought to McDermott Aerospace and Shipbuilding's Newport News assembly plant, but they weren't combat operators like the officers of *Vermont*. It was recognized throughout the fleet that *Vermont*'s crew were the most recent to fire torpedoes and depth charges in anger, and there was a definite prestige that went with that. It was natural that the PCU *New Jersey* crew wouldn't take her out on this upcoming special operation, but rather the *Vermont*-ers, as they began to call themselves. But the success of the crew depended on the success of the wardroom of officers, which was entirely dependent on who the captain and second-in-command were. Great junior officers and department heads were nothing with poor leadership from the skipper and the XO, Pacino thought.

He approached the crowded bar, where Vevera and Dankleff had saved him a barstool. Dankleff clapped Pacino on the shoulder.

"I see you're twenty minutes early, Lipstick," Dankleff said, beaming. "Good job."

Pacino grinned back at him while shaking Vevera's hand. "That was the first thing you taught me onboard *Vermont*, U-Boat," he said to Dankleff. He slumped to give an impression of Dankleff and made his voice sound deep and imbecilic and said, "*if you're early, you're on time, if you're on time, you're late and if you're late you're off the team.*"

"Fuck you, Lipstick," Dankleff snorted. "Anyway, Squirt Gun, as I was saying, *I'm* the bull lieutenant."

"No way," Vevera replied. "I got to *Vermont* two, maybe three months before you showed up as a nub non-qual. So *I'm* the bull lieutenant."

The "bull lieutenant" of the boat was the most senior of the junior officers assigned, a title which Pacino had assumed had gone to U-Boat Dankleff.

"Yeah, but you took, what, three? four? entire months off fighting your, well, your diagnosis. So when it comes to time served? *I'm* the fuckin' bull lieutenant."

"What do you say, Lipstick?" Vevera asked. This would not be a dogfight Pacino would involve himself in, he thought, since Vevera and Dankleff were his two best friends, but he and U-Boat had survived Operation *Panther*, and that counted for something. Pacino just laughed at them and waved over the bartender and ordered a double McAllen 12.

"So Lipstick, looks like you're not the junior man of the wardroom anymore," Dankleff said. "We have two new nub officers showing up here. They're the only hold-overs from the PCU *New Jersey* crew."

"We're keeping some of the *drydock rats*?" Vevera's face showed contempt. "So not only are they non-qual nubs, they've never been to sea?"

"Well, they must have been aboard to conduct sea trials," Pacino said, "without dying. There's something to be said for that." The bartender placed Pacino's scotch on a coaster in front of him. Pacino held his glass up for a toast. "Well, gents, to victory at sea."

Vevera hoisted his on-premises-made beer and Dankleff raised his Jack Daniels.

"So, guys, any word on who the skipper or exec will be?" Pacino asked.

"Nothing at all," Dankleff said.

"Department heads?"

"No word on that either."

"Damn," Pacino breathed. As sonar officer, he would report to the weapons officer. His upcoming life would depend greatly on who that officer would be, and on the XO, since the XO ran the wardroom and could easily make life miserable for all of them.

"The bar's getting full," Pacino observed, calling the bartender over for a refill. "All we have are these three stools. We've got all the other J.O.s coming."

"We have that big table over there," Dankleff waved with this glass, then traded the empty one for a refill from the bartender. Five tables had been pushed together in the center of the high-bay area to form a single large table.

"Let's go over there now before someone else decides to take it," Vevera said, dropping his credit card on the bar. "I'll meet you after I close out."

"Wait, *hold on*," Pacino said, noticing something on one of the large television screens over the bar, the only one not devoted to sports. It was tuned to SNN, Satellite News Network, a 24 -hour news channel, where a female announcer was making a report while standing in front of the Kremlin. The banner at the bottom of the screen read, "*MOSCOW TERRORIST HOSTAGE RESCUE SAVES ALL BUT 2...RUSSIAN PRESIDENT'S WIFE DIES AFTER POLICE RAID....*"

"Jimmy, turn that up, will you?" Dankleff shouted at the barman, who grabbed a remote and raised the volume.

"...police and elements of the FSB—the follow-on to the KGB—stormed the boutique shop inside Moscow's famous GUM shopping mall, the giant architectural wonder situated in Red Square itself. President Vostov's wife was one of the hostages taken, and reports have been received that Mrs. Vostov routinely evaded her SBP security detail, as she did on this occasion. A statement released by the police commander onsite indicated that Larisa Vostov was alive and unharmed by the barrage of gunfire during the raid, but the paralyzing gas used by the police and FSB led to her death and the death of a nineteen-year-old man who was one of the hostages. All of the terrorists were reportedly killed by the police units, and the other hostages were all rescued and are in stable condition in Moscow hospitals. The Kremlin released a short statement from President Vostov, which only indicated that a state funeral will be held for Larisa Vostov and the young man who died today. Meanwhile, there has been no sign of President Vostov, who is believed to have been whisked by his security detail to an undisclosed location. It's speculated that he is in one of the hardened presidential bunkers outside Moscow. I'm Monica Eddlestein reporting live from Red Square, Moscow, SNN News—"

"You can turn it back down now, Jimmy," Dankleff said. "Dear God. Well, come on, boys, let's hit the table."

Pacino stared at the now muted screen. "Man, the balls on those guys, taking the president's *wife* hostage. No wonder the Rooskies went in, guns blazing."

"Them Russians don't fuck around," Vevera said.

"I happen to know that from personal experience," Pacino said, walking toward the table.

BOOK II
TEST WIVES

8

Pacino, Vevera and Dankleff took seats in the middle of the table on one side, with a view of the main entrance so they could beckon over the new arrivals. Two of the other three "*Vermont*-ers," "Easy" Eisenhart and "Gangbanger" Ganghadharan, arrived together, bringing in two strangers with them.

"Easy! Gangbang!" Vevera called.

"Gang's almost all here," Lieutenant (junior grade) Anik Gangbanger Ganghadharan said. "No pun intended." Ganghadharan had been *Vermont*'s supply officer and presumably would retain the position onboard *New Jersey*. He was a shorter youth, dark-skinned, of northern Indian descent.

"And who are these guys, Gang?" Dankleff pointed to the strangers. One was short and stout, but built of all muscle, his blonde hair cut short, a pugnacious look about him. He looked like a boxer, Pacino thought, although he didn't have the height to pull it off. The other newcomer was tall and thin, his legs and arms long, as would well suit a basketball player, with dark hair, also cut short, with a young, innocent-looking face. A bit doe-eyed to be a combat submariner, Pacino thought. And at a half-head taller than Pacino, he looked too tall to be allowed to serve in submarines.

"Gentlemen," Gangbanger said, "Allow me to introduce our new nubs. By some strange twist of fate, the detailers sent two officers to *New Jersey* with the same fuckin' last name. They are *both* named Cooper. Apparently, to distinguish between the two, that tall one over there they call 'Long Hull' and of course, the shorter one who looks like he'd knock you out with one punch? That's 'Short Hull.'" The sub force had been known to take submarines and extend their length by adding compartments, leading to some being called long-hulls, as they were currently doing with the Block V Virginia-class, adding an entire compartment aft of the forward compartment just to hold cruise missile tubes. The Block IV sailors looked with disdain upon the Block Vs, considering them just big missile-carriers rather than true attack submarines.

Pacino shook Long Hull's hand, then Short Hull's. "Nice callsigns," he said. "I'm Patch Pacino, sonar officer. Some idiots have been known to call me 'Lipstick,' but don't you two dare ever call me that, or I won't sign your qual cards."

Long Hull Cooper made a sour face. "'Long Hull,' for fuck's sake. I guess it beats 'Wingspan,' which is what they called me at the Academy. But my first name is Ben."

"Oh, an *Academy* grad," Ganghadharan said. "So are these three morons." He nodded to Pacino, Vevera and Eisenhart.

"What about you, Short Hull?" Dankleff asked. "And call me U-Boat."

"My first name is Eli, believe it or not, but I was always just called 'Coop.' And no Naval Academy for me. My dad flunked out a decade before I was born, so I suppose they thought I'd screw up too. I ended up at Penn State. Electrical engineering."

"Ah yes, the great Penn State, my very own alma mater," Gangbanger said, looking pleased.

"Why 'U-Boat'?" Short Hull asked Dankleff. Dankleff pulled him close and spoke into his ear for a moment.

"Either of you guys married?" Vevera asked. The newcomers both shook their heads. "You know, we'd be an all-bachelor crew but for Gangbanger over here. That idiot got pulled into an arranged marriage. Can you believe that? In these modern times?"

Ganghadharan smirked. "Allow me to show you what you get in an arranged marriage, people." He pulled out his phone and drew up a photo of his wife. "Sonia, in all her glory."

"Holy shit," Pacino said, whistling. "I've never seen her picture or met her. She's gorgeous. You're kind of punching over your weight class with *her*, aren't you, Gangbanger?"

"Sonia may invite us all to dinner after this op," Ganghadharan said. "But not you, Lipstick. Arsonists are most certainly *not* invited. Pacino here burned the *Vermont* down to the drydock blocks," Ganghadharan explained to the new officers.

"Oh hell," Pacino muttered.

"We all heard the story," Short Hull said. "I managed to get to watch the video. I was pretty impressed, Mr. Pacino."

"Call me 'Patch,' Coop," Pacino said. "What jobs did you guys have on the PCU unit?"

Short Hull spoke first. "I was torpedo division officer. Not sure if they'll scramble up our jobs now with you *Vermont* guys cross-decking over."

"And you, Long Hull?"

"Reactor controls division," Ben Cooper said.

"Have you guys spoken to Easy Eisenhart over here? Easy, you're being awfully quiet tonight. What's up?" Pacino looked at Eisenhart, who seemed close to tears. Out of character for him, Pacino thought. He'd never seen Easy in any mood but jocular.

Lieutenant Don Eisenhart, *Vermont*'s communications officer, or "communicator," lifted his eyes from the floor. "Remember the girl I was seeing in Virginia Beach? She just decided she's had enough of dating a fast-attack sailor. Turns out, SSN does *not* stand for submersible ship nuclear. SSN stands for Saturdays, Sundays and Nights. Being at sea all the damned time doesn't make for much intimacy."

Dankleff clapped Eisenhart on the shoulder. "Hey, chin up, Easy, there's always another girl to romance, marry, divorce, and give half your stuff to."

"U-Boat here got divorced from Eurobitch," Vevera explained to the new officers. "His little feelings are still hurt from it. Hey, look, it's Boozy Varney. Boozy!" Vevera waved over a short, slender, black-haired, olive-skinned man to the table.

"Listen up, Hulls," Dankleff said to the younger officers. "This is Muhammad 'Boozy' Varney, our esteemed electrical officer."

"Boozy?" Short Hull asked, confused.

Varney shook the new officers' hands. "These alcoholics call me 'Boozy' because I drink—in moderation, unlike them—despite being a Muslim. The way I figure it, the USS *New Jersey* is damned lucky to have us aboard. Except you, Lipstick. Try not to burn up the *New Jersey*, will ya?"

"Dammit," Pacino said.

"Hey, as of now, we have all the J.O.s, right?" Vevera said.

"You're MPA, I'm DCA," Dankleff said, referring to Vevera's job as main propulsion assistant and his own job as damage control assistant. "Easy's commo, Lipstick's sonar, Boozy's E-div, Gang's supply. Short Hull Cooper is torpedo division officer and Long Hull is reactor controls officer. So yeah, we're all present."

"So now I guess we just wait for the department heads and the XO and skipper," Vevera replied. "Let's get a couple rounds of drinks here before they come."

"Kind of strange," Pacino said to Dankleff while Vevera went off to grab a server. "An all-male wardroom."

"Who knows? We haven't met the navigator, weapons officer, XO or captain. One or all could be female."

"A female captain. Hasn't been one since *Devilfish* went down," Pacino said.

"I'll be the next one," a female voice said, but a booming female voice that was an octave deeper than Pacino's. Pacino looked over to see a petite woman in tight jeans tucked into ugly sheepskin boots, with a black sweater that clung to her well-proportioned figure under a black sport jacket. She had full and shining black hair that was combed straight and reached below her shoulders. She had conventionally pretty features, but there was something about her eyes. Her dark brown eyes looked normal one second and eerily wide the next, and when they went wide, she looked frantic or even crazy.

Believing her to be one of the department heads, Pacino reached out and shook her hand. "Ma'am, you've arrived at the table for the USS *New Jersey* wardroom. I'm Patch Pacino, oncoming sonar officer."

She smiled at him. Her warm hand seemed strangely rough in his.

"I'm Lieutenant Commander Alyssa Kelly. Oncoming chief engineer of the *New Jersey*."

"*You're* the eng?" Vevera asked. "I'm Duke Vevera, MPA. This is Dieter Dankleff, DCA. Muhammad Varney, electrical officer. Over there is Don Eisenhart, communicator. These guys are the nubs, both named Cooper. That one's Long Hull and he's Short Hull. Short Hull is the PCU torpedo division officer and Long Hull is reactor controls officer."

Kelly greeted the officers with a smile, shaking their hands and learning their street names, and all the while, her eyes kept up that normal-then-wide-eyed thing, as if she were flashing messages with her eyes. After a moment, Vevera became brave enough to ask her what her callsign was.

"I've had a few," Kelly said. "Hated them all. *Machinegun Kelly.* *Moose*—that's the one that's seemed to stick the hardest, because of my stupid baritone voice. And my least favorite, *Crazy Eyes.* Any of you J.O.s ever call me Crazy Eyes, I swear I will write you up to the XO."

"Eng," Pacino said, feeling strange calling her 'Eng,' the usual name for the chief engineer of a submarine, since the Eng for him had been Elvis Feng Lewinsky back on the *Vermont.* He'd always think about Elvis every time someone said 'Eng.' "Do you know who is going to be the XO?"

"No idea," Kelly replied. "I guess I'll find out when you guys do. But I do know who the weapons officer is. River! We're over here!"

Kelly motioned over a tall, slender brunette woman who wore a gray cashmere form-fitting dress that came just above her knees with tall black high heels. As she walked over, Pacino felt his stomach descend several floors. The woman was Wanda "River" Styxx.

Before the *Panther* run, there had been a party for the *Vermont* officers at AUTEC—the Bahamas Atlantic Undersea Testing and Evaluation Center, the Navy's version of Area 51—when Pacino had been awarded his full lieutenant bars by Vice Admiral Catardi, the commander of the submarine force, and been ordered to "drink his bars" by downing a large glass filled with rotgut scotch with his new rank emblems at the bottom. The scotch had gotten to him and he'd gone into a full memory blackout. When he woke up the next morning, he found himself naked in the bed of a beautiful and similarly naked woman. And that woman had been the aide to Admiral Catardi, Wanda River Styxx. When Pacino had arrived back at the submarine, the crew had doubled over in laughter. His face was covered with Styxx's lipstick, from his nose to his chin and from ear-to-ear, earning him the ignominious nickname "Lipstick." And now here she was.

She walked up to Pacino first, acting as if he were a mere acquaintance. "Hello, Patch," she said. "I'm oncoming weapons officer, so you'll be working for me." She smiled brightly at Pacino and shook his hand, her hand warm and soft in his. He couldn't help thinking that this was the hand that had been draped over his chest when he woke up that awful morning.

Pacino blinked and swallowed hard, becoming aware of the bug-eyed expressions of the other *Vermont*-ers who knew his history. "Good to see you again, Commander."

"Please," she said, "Call me River. Or, of course, Weps."

"Yes, ma'am."

She laughed. "And definitely no ma'ams." She greeted the other officers, remembering them from meeting them during the party at AUTEC.

Fortunately, the next officer joined them at the table then, taking all the attention away from Pacino's embarrassment with Styxx.

"What the hell?" Dankleff said, breaking into a grin and pulling the newcomer into a bear hug. "What are *you* doing here?"

Lieutenant Commander Elvis Lewinsky had sneaked up on the gathering, a grin on his features. He shook the hands of the *Vermont*-ers and introduced himself to the nub officers.

"Elvis, for fuck's sake," Dankleff said to his old boss. "Really, what are you doing here?"

"Ladies and gentlemen," Lewinsky said, "you are looking at the USS *New Jersey*'s new navigator. Which reminds me, where the hell *are* we?"

"Great," Vevera said. "Lame navigation jokes already. Elvis, if you're navigator here, who's taking care of the repairs to the *Vermont*?"

"Turns out it was a pretty easy decision for Naval Personnel Command. After we turnover with the PCU crew, the PCU guys—except for the Hulls here—are taking on the *Vermont* repairs."

"It's going to take me a while to learn to *not* call you 'Feng,' Elvis," Dankleff said. "Man, a split tour as engineer and navigator. You're going to be heavy as hell for your upcoming XO tour." The term "heavy" in submarine lexicon meant knowledgeable.

"I'd half hoped you were showing up to *be* the XO," Eisenhart said. "You're heavy enough now."

"Oh no, that honor is reserved for a man I understand is a *real* bastard," Lewinsky said. "You J.O.s better stand the fuck by. The new XO is a killer. He reportedly eats junior officers for breakfast." Lewinsky looked at Styxx and Kelly. "And department heads for lunch."

"Great," Pacino muttered. "Elvis, do you know who he or the captain is?"

"I know," Lewinsky grinned, "but I ain't sayin'. But worry not, crew, because here comes the XO now."

The officers all turned their heads to see who was approaching the table, and the *Vermont*-ers' jaws all dropped when a man in falling-apart steel toed boots, ripped and stained jeans, a Grateful Dead T-shirt and an unbuttoned lumberjack fleece shirt over it walked up, smiling mischievously.

"Oh my God," Dankleff said. "*Bullfrog? You? You're XO?*"

Commander Jeremiah Seamus Quinnivan, Royal Navy, shook hands all around, looking quite pleased with himself.

"Well, of course, lads and lassies, I'm XO. Who did you think would be capable of running you scurvy, misbehaved and out-of-control misfits and pirates on a spec-op?"

"This is almost too good to be true," Pacino breathed to Dankleff. "Now we just need to know who the captain will be."

"If Quinnivan is XO, I can guess who the skipper is," Dankleff said.

As if on cue, Commander Timothy "Scotch" Seagraves, up to then *Vermont's* commanding officer, arrived at the table, nodding seriously at the crowd.

"Captain!" Vevera said, shaking Seagraves hand. "Just like old times."

Seagraves, a serious officer, and never much for partying, spoke up, his baritone voice commanding. "Let's grab seats, people, and get this dinner underway. We've all got an early day tomorrow. We'll be taking turnover from the *New Jersey* PCU crew. Change-of-command ceremony is at fifteen hundred. I hope you all brought your choker whites. By sunset, the *Jersey* is all ours."

"Sir, if you're able to answer, you know, in public," Vevera said as he stood next to the captain. "When do we shove off?"

Seagraves regarded Vevera seriously. "You'll be missing the change-of-command ceremony, Mr. Vevera, because you'll be starting the reactor."

Vevera grinned. "Outstanding, sir."

———————————

"And there she is," Pacino said, arriving at Pier 1 North.

Vevera, Pacino and Dankleff had decided to walk to the boat's pier from China Express, the passage into the builder's yard security gate quick compared to that of Squadron Six in Norfolk. Back at the parking lot across the street from the restaurant, a DynaCorp flatbed half-ton truck had loaded up their seabags and suitcases to transport them to the ship and bring them into the wardroom, where the officers would later relocate their stuff into their staterooms. So far, the XO hadn't assigned staterooms. Typically each of the three officer staterooms would be assigned to a department head, and his or her direct reports would bunk there. Which was somewhat miserable, Pacino thought, since there would be no getting away from the boss. Doubly awful, considering his boss was River Styxx.

They had walked by the massive submarine assembly building, which was currently assembling the 802 *Oklahoma*, then a jog south, then west to the jetty leading to the North Pier, eventually walking past a material storage yard and maintenance building to the end of Pier 1 North.

"Yes, thar she blows," Vevera said.

The three officers stopped and gazed at the USS *New Jersey*. The boat was mostly identical in appearance to the *Vermont*. A long, black cylinder, lying deep in the water so that the deck's curvature allowed walking on the top surface. The plug trunk hatch was open, as was the forward hatch. There were no dog-houses erected over the hatches since they would have gotten in the way of the wooden platform placed on the hull aft of the sail — the conning tower, which was a vertical fin rising out of the hull near the bow. The platform was painted white and had railing draped with red, white, and blue bunting. A lectern was located in the center of the platform. At the top of the sail, the periscopes and masts were all retracted. Unlike *Vermont*, her anechoic tile coating was fully intact and looked brand new, the hull shiny and black. The boat was tied up port-side-to, her stern facing north, her sonar dome facing south, down-river. Pacino looked northward, at the drydock and roll-out table.

"Well, there won't be a back-full-ahead-flank underway from here, not the way the *Jersey* is tied up," Pacino said. "Put on a backing bell and run right into the drydock."

"Damned shame," Vevera said. "I would have liked to see you do that back-full-ahead-flank thing."

"He made it look easy," Dankleff said, clapping Pacino on the shoulder. "Although it turned out to be a back-*emergency*-ahead-flank underway. Still, Lipstick here drove it like he stole it and we slipped right out of Norfolk. Not like the time *you* fucked it up, Squirt Gun."

"Hey, I showed him how *not* to do it. After that? Success was an easy day."

"You'll have to learn how to deal with tugboats and a harbor pilot this time, Lipstick," Dankleff said, grinning. "Assuming you're the one driving us out."

"Check out the other side of the assembly roll-out table," Pacino said. "Floating drydock." The dock was lined up with their pier. Inside was the bow of a submarine, the sonar dome removed, the internals covered with canvas draped over scaffolding, with more scaffolding in the dock, arranged so densely around the boat it could barely be made out to be a submarine. "I bet that's the north end of the 798 *Massachusetts* there. The future *Vermont*."

"All these names of states," Dankleff said in disgust. "At least Big Navy finally woke up and named the last four *Barb*, *Tang*, *Wahoo* and *Silversides*. So named for World War II combat submarines, decorated all."

"Much cooler," Vevera said. "Still, *New Jersey* is a tough state, and who can forget the fighting battleship *New Jersey*? Well, let's get aboard and get our stuff sorted."

Pacino and the others greeted the topside watchstander, a short and petite female sonarman third class, who wore a nametag ironically reading LONGFELLOW. Pacino wondered how much teasing she'd suffered on the boat from *that* name. She read their orders, since this was their first time reporting aboard, and scanned their retinae with her handheld biometric device, then returned their salutes as they formally requested permission to come aboard.

"Permission granted, gentlemen."

"That always sounds strange to my ears," Pacino remarked as they crossed the gangway to the plug trunk hatch. "Somehow, 'gentlemen' is something a more senior man would say to a group of junior guys."

"It's the plural of 'sir,' Lipstick," Vevera said. "She can't say 'permission granted, *sirs*.'"

120

"I suppose," Pacino said. He leaned over the gaping maw of the plug trunk hatch. *"Down ladder!"* he called, then stepped down the ladder into the cavernous plug trunk. The smell of the submarine invaded his nostrils then, identical to his father's old boats, as well as his own—the *Piranha* and the *Vermont*—a blend of atmo-control amines, ozone from the electrical equipment, cooking grease, lubrication oil, diesel fuel, diesel exhaust, seasoned with a slight tang of sewage. But there was something else—something cooking in the galley, something greasy.

He stepped through the side hatch and then to the steep stairway—called a ladder—to the middle level central passageway, ducking left into the wardroom, the conference room for officers, also used for their meal service, and in an emergency, a surgical suite. On the outboard bulkhead, a gigantic framed aerial photograph of the old battleship *New Jersey* was bolted, the massive warship firing her guns, huge plumes of flames emerging from the guns. The room was crowded with a pile of luggage at the forward end. At the aft end, the XO was muttering something to the supply chief, who vanished aft into the galley. Quinnivan looked up and saw the three junior officers. They were the first aboard.

"Hey! You scurvy lieutenants! Pick up your trash and stow it in your fookin' staterooms! This is the wardroom, not a luggage carousel."

"But XO," Dankleff said, "you haven't assigned us staterooms yet."

Quinnivan paused. "Okay, then, stateroom one, farthest forward, goes to the navigator, Elvis Lewinsky, with the communicator and supply officer bunking in with him. Stateroom two is for the engineer, Madam Moose Kelly. So you, Vevera, and you, Dankleff, will bunk in with her. Draw straws for bottom or top bunks, I don't care. Middle rack is the engineer's."

"Aye, sir," Dankleff said, finding a seabag he thought was his, but tossing it back on the mountainous pile.

"And as for you, Mr. Lipstick, you'll find yourself in stateroom three with the weapons officer, Ms. River Styxx, with electrical officer

Varney bunked in. Even though Short Hull Cooper is in Ms. Styxx's department, he's a fookin' nub, so he's going in the upper level forward half-sixpack along with Long Hull." The upper level forward half-sixpack room had belonged to Pacino on *Vermont*. It would feel odd to be in one of the three numbered staterooms, odder still to bunk in with River Styxx, who he had slept with before, although he had no memory of it other than waking up with her. At least she'd seemed happy and satisfied when the sun had risen. God help him now, he thought, if he'd disappointed her that night.

The three J.O.s found their bags and lugged them to their staterooms. Pacino was almost fully unpacked when Quinnivan poked his head in.

"No officers' call today, Mr. Lipstick. But find your opposite number from PCU *New Jersey* and get turned over. Change of command ceremony is at fifteen hundred. You got your choker whites?"

"Yes, XO." Pacino had packed them, but the ultra-starched service dress whites were probably as wrinkled as an unmade bed from being tossed into his seabag.

"Good. Pass that word on to your scurvy buddies, yeah?"

"Aye, sir."

"As soon as the command change is over, you're driving us out. Or I should say, Short Hull Cooper is driving as your under-instruction. See to it he doesn't fuck up, or it's *your* head."

"Understood, sir."

"And laddy, you'll be using tugs and a harbor pilot for this run. Think you can handle it?"

"It won't be a problem, XO."

"Good, lad. I'll see you topside at fourteen-forty-five, yeah?" With that, the Irishman vanished.

Pacino had stowed his things into one of the cubbyholes and the rest into the bed pan under the upper rack, then taken the ladder steps to the upper level to the sonar equipment space, or SES. Inside, he found two chief petty officers deep in conversation. They turned to look at him, and to Pacino's delight, one of them was Senior Chief Tom "Whale" Albanese, who had been his leading chief of sonar on *Vermont* and had gone with Pacino on the *Panther* run.

"Whale!" Pacino said, grinning and pulling the senior chief into a bear hug, the wiry redhead smiling back, his uniform smelling of the cigarettes that he chain-smoked when he could get away with it in the non-smoking universe of the submarine force.

"Mr. Patch!" Albanese exclaimed.

"I wasn't sure if the goat locker would embark on *New Jersey*," Pacino said.

"We were given a choice, but XO put pressure on me and a few others, but he needn't have bothered. I'm happy to be here."

"Aren't you married, Whale?"

Albanese made a sour face. "Newly separated. Yet another reason to get out of there."

"Kids?"

"Fortunately, no. Diane had a miscarriage, and we fought so much after that...well, it just didn't make sense to stay together."

"I'm sorry to hear, Senior Chief. Really. I haven't been through anything like that, but I feel for you."

"Thanks, Mr. Patch. Anyway, I was going through the turnover with Chief Carlyle-Smith here."

Pacino shook the PCU sonar chief's hand. "How is the turnover going? And where is the PCU sonar officer?"

"We're in great shape," Albanese said. "And the PCU sonar officer is in the hospital."

"What happened?"

The PCU sonar chief looked at Pacino. "Domestic dispute. His husband punched him hard enough to break his jaw."

"What?" Pacino said. "*His* husband?"

Albanese half-nodded at Pacino. "It's a brave new world, sir."

"It don't matter none," Chief Carlyle-Smith said. "Sonar is a hunnert percent. I ain't never seen a sonar suite this tuned up and perfect. Especially coming out of new-con."

"Hey, don't jinx it," Albanese said.

"Sprinkle some holy water on it, Whale," Carlyle-Smith said. "Anyway, it's all yours. I'm out of here."

The PCU sonar chief stepped out. "Is it as good as he claims?" Pacino asked.

Albanese nodded. "For once, the shipyard didn't hump the pooch."

Pacino nodded. "Well, okay then. I guess I'll jump into my choker whites for the change of command. I'll see you topside, Whale."

———————

Commander Timothy Talisker "Scotch" Seagraves was almost finished unpacking his gear into the captain's stateroom. He decided on a last-minute shave before he'd don the starched tunic of his dress whites. He glanced at his face in the mirror, somewhat encouraged that despite turning thirty-nine, his face hadn't really changed in fifteen years. He was fortunate that despite rich submarine food, he had retained his thin build, although he had gained perhaps ten pounds since Annapolis graduation, but it helped that he was over six feet tall, he thought. He could carry the weight easily. Seagraves' ex-wife—back before she'd decided she hated him—used to go off about how movie-star handsome he was, but he'd never seen it himself. His face seemed bony to his own eyes, with stark cheekbones, a pronounced brow, shallow cheeks, a cleft chin, ruler-straight jawline, and too-full lips. He shook off the internal debate, lathered up, shaved and was just toweling off when the 1MC general announcing circuit clicked, then boomed with the topside watchstander's soprano voice.

"ComSubDevRon Twelve, arriving!"

That would be the boss of the local squadron, Seagraves thought, Captain Liam "Twister" Flanagan. Which was odd, since word had come down from ComSubFor that New Jersey was to be a Norfolk-based Squadron Six boat, not a Groton-based Development Squadron Twelve unit, which was Flanagan's fiefdom. Seagraves had known Flanagan years in the past when Flanagan had been the navigator of the USS Newport News and Seagraves had been her MPA. They'd sailed Newport News for a year together before

Flanagan rotated off to be the XO of the *Topeka*. Soon, a knock came to the door and Seagraves opened it.

Captain Flanagan was short and slight, with a bushy head of brown hair and a well-trimmed goatee. He was dressed in starched dress whites, obviously for the change of command ceremony upcoming in the next hour. Seagraves had put on the pants and shoes, but he was still just wearing his white T-shirt tucked into his white pants, the starched high-collar whites with full medals on a hanger by the door to the stateroom. Seagraves shook Flanagan's hand and waved him to a seat at the small conference table. He sat in his high-backed command chair and looked over at Flanagan.

"Can I get us coffee, Commodore?"

"Coffee would be excellent, Captain."

Seagraves made a call to the wardroom, then made small talk with the commodore about his family and life on the base, and how well he knew the base commander, a Naval Academy firstie when Seagraves was a lowly plebe. Once the coffee service arrived and Seagraves had poured for them both, Flanagan got down to business, withdrawing a folded manila envelope he'd had in his back pocket under his choker white tunic.

"Your sealed orders," Flanagan said, smirking. "Top secret and very hush-hush."

Seagraves opened the envelope and spread the two pages on the table. He scanned the order, then reread it more carefully. He looked up at Flanagan.

"His Majesty's Naval Base, Clyde, Faslane, Scotland. U.K. submarine base. Way the hell up north."

Flanagan nodded.

"The orders seem to stop there," Seagraves noted. "Make all haste to UK SubBase Faslane, where *New Jersey* will load out weapons, gear and supplies for a hundred-and-forty day run. Then it stops." He frowned. "A hundred-and-forty days, Commodore? What the hell is going on?"

"Unknown, Scotch. But obviously, if you're going for your load-out at latitude fifty-six north, you're spec-op will be farther north to see our good friends from the Russian Republic."

"This loadout looks unusual," Seagraves noted.

"Arctic supplies," Flanagan said. "A dry-deck shelter. And a team of SEALs will be joining you. Same blokes you deployed to the Gulf of Oman with this summer."

Seagraves nodded. "Always good to operate with old friends."

Flanagan nodded. "The same reason you folks from the *Vermont* all cross-decked together over to the *New Jersey*." Flanagan stood. "I suppose I should get topside for your change of command."

"Thanks for coming over and delivering the orders personally, Commodore."

"It was good to see you again, Scotch." At the door leading to the passageway, Flanagan turned to Seagraves. "Oh, and Scotch, try not to burn *New Jersey* to smithereens, will ya?"

"Fuck you, Twister," Seagraves said, a crooked smile on his face.

He pulled on the starched choker whites and buttoned them up, then picked up the orders and reread them. Oddly, there was no code-name for whatever this operation would be. The orders were classified top secret but not code-word, which meant the real secrecy would begin in Faslane. Seagraves put the orders in his safe, locked it, then grabbed his white officer's cap with the scrambled egg embroidery on the brim, and left his stateroom to head to the plug trunk hatch.

9

Captain Seagraves stood at rigid attention, saluted the PCU commander of *New Jersey*, and said, "I relieve you, sir."

The PCU commander returned the salute and said, "I stand relieved."

Light applause broke out on the platform and on the pier. Lieutenant Anthony Pacino watched Seagraves shaking hands with the DevRon Twelve commodore. Ditching the after-ceremony conversations, Pacino stepped to the plug trunk hatch. The sooner he could dump these dress whites, the better. He hurried to stateroom three, hoping he would beat River Styxx to the room. Changing into his working uniform for the underway operation would be embarrassing if she charged into the room while he was in his boxers. He finished changing uniforms, grabbed his pad computer, his binoculars and his brand-new USS *New Jersey* ball cap and opened the door just as Styxx was reaching for the doorknob.

"Ma'am," Pacino said instinctively, coming to rigid attention. "Weps."

"There's no ma'ams onboard, Mr. Pacino," she said, smiling slightly. "Just Weps or River. Although, I propose if we're undressed in the same space at the same time, we're strictly on a first name basis."

Pacino smiled at her, relieved that she was being friendly.

"Any news about your navigator?" she asked. "Romanov?"

Pacino's smile vanished, his face drooping to sadness. "Last I heard, she was in bad shape. She may have lost brain function." It was easier to say that than the words *brain dead.*

Styxx put her hand on Pacino's shoulder. "I'm sorry, Patch. Maybe we'll hear an update when we're on the way to, well, wherever we're going."

"Any news on that? Where *are* we headed?"

"Your buddy Lewinsky plotted navigation points on the chart, but they only go to the dive point due east of Nantucket and then fifty miles beyond. After that, it's apparently top secret. Maybe he'll tell *you.*"

"Did you ask him?"

She nodded. "Predictably, he told me to go fuck myself." She grinned. "You know, in a totally professional way."

"Oh, of course," Pacino laughed. "Anyway. I'd better do a pre-watch tour."

"Have fun up there, Patch. I'll be your contact coordinator."

"Watch out for all that dangerous surface traffic."

"Yeah, sailboats and the occasional family fishing outing on a motorboat."

"And the inevitable Russian trawler."

Pacino turned and hurried aft to go to maneuvering to see Vevera and how the reactor plant was behaving.

Pacino climbed through the deck grating's hatch up to the cockpit of the sail, joining Ensign Short Hull Cooper on the bridge. The bridge was a recessed standing area cut into the top of the sail, the top surface of the conning tower retracted using segmented flaps called clamshells. The deck of the space was grating set over the bridge tunnel, the vertical accessway to the bridge from the upper level of the forward compartment. With the boat facing south, the way out of the river, the conning officer would start out on the port side to supervise their disconnection from the pier, and since Short Hull would be driving, Pacino put his pad computer on the receptacle on the starboard side. In the river basin, a large tugboat slowly approached them. Short Hull's VHF radio crackled to life.

"U.S. Navy Submarine Captain, this is Navy tug *Massapequa II*, requesting permission to tie up on your starboard side, over."

Short Hull looked over at Pacino. "What do I do, sir?"

Pacino shook his head. "The only 'sirs' onboard are the XO and the captain, Short Hull. Call down to the captain's stateroom and ask permission to bring aboard the tug. Hand me the VHF."

Short Hull picked up the 7MC, selected the captain's stateroom and clicked the microphone button. "Captain, Junior Officer of the Deck, sir."

Pacino clicked the VHF radio's transmit button. "Navy tug *Massapequa II*, this is U.S. Navy submarine, please stand by, over."

"Navy submarine Captain, roger, standing by," the VHF rasped. In the channel, the tug's engines grew quiet as she idled, only keeping up with the current in the Thames.

"How come you didn't answer up as the USS *New Jersey*?" Short Hull asked.

"We never self-identify," Pacino explained. "In case our good Russian or Chinese friends are loitering out in the Sound. We keep the enemy guessing."

"Captain," the 7MC crackled.

"Captain, Junior Officer of the Deck, sir," Short Hull said, sounding amazingly steady. Pacino wondered if he himself had sounded anywhere near that solid when he'd first conned out *Vermont* on the *Panther* run. "Request permission to bring aboard the tug on the starboard side, sir."

"JOOD, you have permission to bring aboard the tug to tie up on our starboard side," Captain Seagraves' voice rasped.

Short Hull acknowledged the captain. Pacino handed him the VHF radio.

"Navy tug *Massapequa II*, this is U.S. Navy submarine, permission granted to come alongside and tie up on our starboard side, over."

"Roger U.S. Navy submarine Captain, *Massapequa II*, out."

On the deck, the line handlers accepted the heavy manila ropes tossed over by the tugboat's crew. Soon the tug was made fast to *New Jersey's* starboard side, lashed tight at the tug's bow and stern.

Pacino checked his diver's watch. 1559. The captain had wanted the ship in the channel by 1600. Dammit, they were going to be late.

"Bridge, Pilot," the 7MC blasted. "Captain to the bridge!"

"Pilot, Bridge, aye," Short Hull said into the 7MC mike. Pacino stood aside and lifted up the bridge deck grating. The captain climbed up from the bridge access tunnel.

"Afternoon, sir," Pacino said.

"Afternoon, Captain," Short Hull seconded.

"Good afternoon, gentlemen," Seagraves said. He lowered the grating and climbed the four steps up to the top of the sail, where a temporary set of handrails had been erected, the "flying bridge."

"Mr. Cooper, are we ready to get underway?" Seagraves said, latching his safety lanyard to a D-ring set into the flying bridge's handrails.

"Except for radar, Captain. Navigator requests we raise the radar mast and rotate and radiate."

"No," Seagraves said. "No sense giving listening electronic ears out there our radar pulse rate signature as a newly constructed boat. Let them guess. Tell the navigator to get by with the DynaCorp yacht radar."

"Aye, sir. We're ready to get underway, then, Captain."

"What about the harbor pilot?"

Cooper looked at Pacino, obviously lost.

Pacino reached for the 1JV phone handset and the 7MC mike at the same time, barking into the 7MC, "Pilot, 1JV."

Dankleff's voice answered on the 1JV phone circuit. "Pilot."

"Pilot," Pacino said, "what's the status of the harbor pilot?"

"Officer of the Deck, the harbor pilot is here in control looking at the chart with the Nav. Wait, he is on the way to the upper level and the bridge now."

"Very well," Pacino said and hung up. "Captain, harbor pilot is on the way up."

"Request to lay to the bridge!" an older voice croaked from below.

"Permission to come up," Pacino said. Cooper pulled up the deck grating and a seventy-year-old grizzled sailor climbed up, wearing a high-viz yellow jacket.

"Afternoon, guys," the harbor pilot said. He climbed up the steps to the top of the sail and stood next to the captain, the two talking quietly.

"Check the chart and the tides one last time, Short Hull," Pacino said to Cooper.

"Aye, sir. I mean, yes, Patch."

"Junior Officer of the Deck!" Seagraves barked. "Are we ready to get underway *now*?"

"Captain, yes, sir, *New Jersey* is ready to get underway."

"Well, then, Mr. Cooper, get underway."

"Get underway, aye aye, sir." Cooper glanced at Pacino.

"Take off the brow," Pacino said, referring to the aluminum gangway between the pier and the upper surface of the submarine. He handed Cooper a megaphone he pulled from under the bridge communication box.

"On the pier!" Cooper said into the bullhorn. "Remove the gangway!"

The diesel cherry-picker crane on the pier rumbled to life, its boom pulling the gangway off the hull and rotating to set it back down on the pier. Cooper looked again at Pacino.

"Just order the pier crew to take in all lines," Pacino said. "I'll operate the ship's whistle. And order the pilot to stand by to answer all bells." Cooper nodded. "And be ready to order the lookout to shift colors."

"Pilot," Short Hull said into the 7MC mike, "stand by to answer all bells."

"Stand by to answer all bells, Bridge, Pilot, aye," Dankleff's voice barked.

"On the pier!" Cooper shouted in the bullhorn, "Take in all lines!"

Pacino watched from behind the shorter man, and as the last line was tossed over from the pier, he reached under the bridge cockpit ledge forward and found the ship's air horn lever and pulled it aft. A blasting roar came from the horn, the earsplitting noise sounding like the *Queen Mary* was leaving the pier. Pacino held it for a full eight seconds, the horn notifying all in the river basin that the submarine was getting underway.

"Lookout, shift colors!" Cooper yelled up to the flying bridge. The lookout quickly pulled on the lanyard, and the American flag came up on the mast behind the captain, the flag underneath it the banner of the force, a snarling Jolly Roger skull-and-crossbones on a black field, gothic script stating, "U.S. Submarine Force."

Pacino lifted the VHF to his lips and hit the transmit button. "Navy tug *Massapequa II*, take us to center of channel." The engines of the tug roared as the tug put on ahead turns and maneuvered them to the center of the river. Pacino took a quick look up-river, but the Thames was empty, and there were no vessels down-river either. He looked at Cooper. "Put on ahead one third with a right rudder."

"Pilot, Bridge," Cooper said into the 7MC, "all ahead one third, right full rudder."

"All ahead one third, Bridge, Pilot, aye, right full rudder, and my rudder is right full and Maneuvering answers, all ahead one third."

"Bridge, Navigator," Lewinsky's baritone voice boomed from the 7MC, hold us fifty yards left of center of channel, recommend course one seven five."

"Pilot, Bridge," Cooper said, "come to course one seven five."

"Bridge, Pilot, come to one seven five, aye. Steering course one seven five."

"Pilot, Bridge, aye," Cooper acknowledged. He looked at Pacino. "All good?"

"You're doing a hell of a job," Pacino said, putting the binoculars to his eyes again and scanning down river. The seaway was still empty.

"Bridge, Navigator," Lewinsky said over the bridge box speaker, "turn point at Point Alpha is in one thousand yards, new course one three five."

The submarine and the tug moved slowly down the river, the scenery of the lush Connecticut coastline sliding by, opulent houses lining the river on either side of the nearly mile-wide channel. Eventually the New London Ledge Lighthouse grew large ahead of them and the shorelines to port and starboard were behind them. They'd emerged into the Sound.

"Bridge, Navigator, mark the turn at Point Alpha, new course one three five."

"Pilot, Bridge," Cooper called into the 7MC mike, "left full rudder, steady course one three five."

Dankleff acknowledged. Pacino elbowed Cooper. "Look down channel as we go into and come out of the turn," he ordered. Cooper looked with his naked eyes, then lifted his binoculars.

"Channel is clear," he said.

The harbor pilot shook Seagraves hand, climbed down into the cockpit, excused himself, and vanished down into the vertical trunk to the upper level. Pacino leaned over the starboard side of the sail and saw the harbor pilot walk forward toward the tug. Two of the tug's sailors helped him get back aboard the tug.

Pacino nodded to Cooper.

"Captain, request to shove off the tug," Cooper called up to Seagraves.

"Shove off the tug," Seagraves ordered, his face covered by binoculars as he scanned down the channel.

"Tug *Massapequa II*, when able, shove off," Cooper said into the radio.

"Roger, Navy Submarine. Fair winds, following seas," the VHF speaker squawked.

The deck crew tossed over the tug's lines and the tug's engines roared as she veered off to the right, circling behind them to return to Groton.

"Tell the navigator," Pacino ordered.

"Navigator, Bridge, the tug has shoved off."

"Bridge, Navigator, aye."

"Once the deck is rigged for dive," Pacino said to Cooper. "Increase speed to full."

"Bridge, Pilot," Dankleff called. "Deck is rigged for dive by Chief McGuire, checked by Ensign Cooper."

"Pilot, Bridge, all ahead full."

As the ship sped up, the water climbed up over the nosecone at the bow and splashed up to the leading edge of the sail, breaking on either side and foaming back up over the aft part of the deck. The flags snapped in the wind aft. Pacino smiled to himself. The sounds and sensations of getting a submarine underway always gave him an odd sense of happiness.

"Mr. Cooper, secure the maneuvering watch and station the normal surfaced watch," Seagraves ordered as he climbed down from the flying bridge. "When you can, disassemble the flying bridge." He vanished into the bridge access trunk.

Lewinsky guided the ship through two more turns as Fishers Island faded astern, the new course 090 until Block Island was behind them. At Point Charlie, the navigator had them turn to east-southeast to skirt Martha's Vineyard and Nantucket.

"Bridge, Contact Coordinator," River Styxx's voice came smoothly over the 7MC. "New visual contact, Victor One, bearing one one two, range two thousand yards by radar. Contact bearing rate is right. Sonar reports contact is shut down and drifting."

Pacino trained his binoculars to the bearing. "There he is," he said.

"What is it?" Cooper asked.

"Russian trawler. Or more accurately, a Russian spy ship disguised as a trawler. Lurking just outside our territorial waters."

Cooper scanned it with his binoculars.

"Report it to the captain," Pacino ordered.

Cooper picked up the 7MC and made the report to Seagraves, who simply said, "Captain, aye."

"I see now why the captain decided to keep our radar off."

"We'll rotate and radiate once we turn to the northeast," Pacino said. "The Russian will be well astern by then, and we'll be seeing heavy traffic inbound to Boston Harbor."

As Nantucket grew close, at the hour of 1800, their watch reliefs climbed up to the bridge—Varney and Short Hull—and Pacino and Cooper turned over the watch and climbed back into the submarine.

They hurried down the ladder to the middle level and found the captain seated at the end of the table, digging into the traditional meal he'd called for when the sub got underway, New York strip steak with mashed potatoes.

"Go ahead, Coop," Pacino said to Short Hull.

"Captain, Mr. Pacino and I have been properly relieved of the deck and the conn by Mr. Varney and Mr. Cooper. Ship is steaming at full on course zero nine eight in the channel to the south of Nantucket headed to Point Foxtrot where we will turn northeast. Reactor is natural circulation and the electric plant is in a normal full-power lineup."

Seagraves frowned up at Cooper for a moment, then said, "You did an adequate job up there, Mr. Cooper. Have a seat and get some chow."

Cooper looked disappointed as he pulled up a chair next to Pacino. Pacino smirked at Cooper and said quietly, "The word 'adequate' means 'perfect' in the captain's usage."

"Why?" Cooper asked.

Pacino shrugged. "He worries we'll get cocky and then something would go wrong. It's his sailor's superstition."

"You *Vermont*-ers are fucking weird. No offense, Patch."

Pacino laughed. "None taken."

———————

Vostov knocked on Anya's door and opened it slowly. He found her in Nanny Roksana's lap, being read a story. Her eyes were red and swollen, and when she looked up at him, tears formed and rolled down her cheeks. She jumped to her feet and ran to him and hugged him, her tears wetting his jeans. He sank to a crouch and hugged her tight, glancing up to the nanny and waving her out with his head.

Two SBP security troops in tactical gear stood in the room's corners away from the door, both trying to look inconspicuous and both failing.

"Let's sit down together, okay?" he said gently to her and she nodded, sniffling. He guided her to the overstuffed chair where she liked to have stories read to her before bed. The room was almost identical to her room in the Kremlin complex apartment, which had taken some doing, since the north dacha was much different than the ornate apartment.

The north dacha was a three-story log cabin set in deep woods, with a yard big enough to land a military helicopter, but beyond that, the trees were too thick to see anything beyond the edge of the helipad. Vostov liked this house much better than his gigantic and official presidential retreat fifty kilometers south of Moscow, which was even more ornate than the Kremlin compound, all white marble and soaring halls, as if it had been built by a seventeenth century Tsar. This log lodge had been designed by Vostov personally—perhaps "design" was an exaggeration. He'd sketched on cocktail napkins and a team of architects had given birth to drawings and models, and he'd changed it over and over until it met his approval. Of course, Larisa had always hated it, and usually found an excuse to avoid coming here, but that was fine with Vostov, since it gave him more time to be with Anya by himself.

"I can see that you are very sad about Mommy," Vostov opened.

"Daddy, did *they* shoot her?" She shot a glance at the SBP guards.

"No, Anya. Mommy was in a store and some very bad men came in and took over the store. They tried to get some of their bad men friends sprung out of prison. They threatened to hurt Mommy. But guards like those nice men over there," he nodded his head at one of the SBP men, "went into the store to rescue Mommy, and they did. They shot all the bad men. But the gas they used to put the bad men to sleep, well, that's what hurt Mommy. Mommy had a very weak heart and nobody knew that. They didn't find that out until Mommy was in the hospital. They tried to save her, but her heart was too weak, baby, and—I'm so sorry—but Mommy died."

For the next few minutes Anya just cried and wailed in his lap. What can be said to a six-year-old in the face of death, he wondered. He held her tight and waited for her to calm down.

"Now, in a few minutes, we're going to get dressed in our best clothes and we're going to travel to Mommy's funeral. Do you know what a funeral is?"

"I think so, Daddy. They will put Mommy in a wood box, dig a hole, and put her in the hole, and then they'll put dirt back into the hole. And then there's a stone that goes there."

Vostov nodded. "We'll take Mommy to a big church first, where they will say some things about Mommy's life, and there will be lots of people there, people who loved Mommy and lots of them who love you too, and we'll all be together, we'll all be sad together. And we'll take Mommy in her coffin to a cemetery, which is a very pretty place where we put the people we love after they die. But you have to know that Mommy is not really in that box, sweetheart. Mommy is still alive, she's just alive in Heaven. In the afterlife. Did Mommy ever tell you about Heaven?"

Anya nodded seriously. "She said it was a beautiful place where people go after they die, like my bunny rabbit. Do you think Mommy is there with Bunny?"

Vostov nodded, reaching to the side table for a tissue. He wiped the tears from his cheeks and blew his nose. This was much more difficult than he'd imagined it. But through it all, he noticed, he didn't feel the slightest amount of guilt. Which was strange. He must still be in shock, he thought.

The rest of the morning was something out of a blurred fever dream. Nanny Roksana knocked and brought in a selection of dresses for Anya. One was white, another black, a third a pattern of primary colors. Vostov sank to one knee and asked Anya which one she wanted to wear, but told her, before she chose, that everyone at the funeral would be wearing black, because that was a sad color and a way to show sadness. Anya looked up him, her eyes filled with tears, and said, "Daddy, Mommy would want me to wear bright

happy colors, because Mommy always hated it whenever I was sad."
Vostov nodded at Roksana, feeling a stabbing pain in his chest.

The next thing he knew, he was in the gleaming black
presidential Aurus stretch limo, with Anya, Roksana, and Tonya
Pasternak. He avoided eye contact with them and simply stared at
the floor, only looking up when Tonya reached into the minibar and
poured him a double vodka. He downed it in one gulp. Tonya lifted
an eyebrow to see if he wanted a refill, but he shook his head.

The limo stopped in front of the newly built Cathedral of Christ
the Savior. New, he supposed, in the timeline of cathedrals, the final
touches put on the gold-plated domes in 2000, the year Putin had
come to power. He walked in, Anya's small warm hand in his. They
walked by what seemed a hundred rows of grieving well-wishers
and dignitaries from around the world. He tried mightily to keep his
eyes dry, but when he'd hear Anya sniff, it seemed the wetness came
anew.

The front pew was reserved for him, Anya, and Nanny Roksana.
He waved Pasternak to join them. She'd pinned her hair back in a
prim bun and wore an especially frumpy black dress and flat shoes,
making her seem forty years older, which was a good thing. He
didn't need anyone thinking his beautiful aide was an affair partner.
Not that she ever would be, he thought. With his troubles with
potency in the last decade, it would be something of a relief not to be
expected to perform sexually. He'd heard about pharmaceuticals
that could help with the problem, but that seemed absurd, to take a
pill in order to make love to a woman.

When he realized his mind had drifted inappropriately to sex, he
bit his lip and forced himself to look up at the massive white and
gold coffin made for Larisa, surrounded by flowers piled high
around it, a huge portrait of her hanging in the background, the
photo one of the few Larisa's extreme vanity would allow to be
published. In life, she usually thought that nineteen out of twenty
photos of her made her look ugly or fat, which was insane, since
she'd always been gorgeous.

His mind wandered during the eulogies and prayers. He'd be meeting with a parade of foreign dignitaries after the burial service, all having flown in to offer condolences, which he could do without, but it was all part of the pageantry of being head of state—but it was the part he hated.

He wondered who would be in the American delegation. Carlucci would never come. Vostov's relationship with the American president had had ups and downs, and was currently at a low point after the *Panther* incident. At best, he would send his vice president. What was her name? He went blank for a long moment, then remembered he'd met her at a Kremlin reception last year. Chushi, he thought. Karen Chushi, a pretty, middle-aged slender woman, friendly enough. He wondered what he should say to her, or what she would say to him.

The funeral procession to Novodevichy Cemetery seemed to take hours, then the tiresome graveside service, but finally they were back in the limo for the ride to the Kremlin. The SPB chief had assured him it was now safe to return to the Moscow apartment, but Vostov already knew that. He'd return Anya with Nanny Roksana to the apartment, then go to his palatial Kremlin office suite to meet with the foreign dignitaries. He glanced at his watch, calculating how many hours it would be until his routine could return to normal.

A knock at the door, and Pasternak jumped up to answer. An aide handed in a fresh black suit in plastic. Pasternak took it and handed it to Vostov, who quickly took off his shoes and pants, dumped his jacket on the floor with them, and pulled the freshly pressed identical suit on. The one he'd worn to the funeral was stained with Anya's tears and mucus. He was all for theater on the political stage, but wearing that suit would have gone too far.

As Vostov suited back up, he told Tonya to hold off the first visitor until he had time to talk to her. She took a seat in front of his desk, but he stood and waved her to the more informal setting of the four club chairs clustered around the fireplace. He sat and she put her pad computer on the coffee table and sat stiffly, as if she were at attention. She'd changed out of the loose frock she'd worn to the funeral and now had on a flattering black business suit, a beige blouse under her jacket.

"A few thoughts from our Murmansk trip," he said. She nodded and reached for her pad computer to take notes. "The question the captain of the *Belgorod* had, about the dangers of sailing under the ice with a submarine that big."

"Yes, sir?"

"Have Mikhail make sure they will outfit the submarine with arctic supplies, just in case things go to hell under there. Shelters, generator, heater, parkas, emergency food—hell, snowmobiles. That boat's big, it can store all that stuff inside."

"Got it, sir."

"Also, I want an answer from the Navy about getting one or two nuclear-tipped torpedoes loaded onto her."

"I'll check, sir, but I don't think the Navy has that in their inventory. Let me check." She stroked through the classified search application, arriving finally at an answer. "We haven't manufactured one for twenty years, sir. There was a hundred-centimeter torpedo with a one megaton warhead. We called it the *Gigantskiy*. Apparently NATO named it *Magnum*. It needed a special torpedo tube, it was so big."

"Get the data on it to that Sevmash chief engineer. What was his name?"

"Director Voronin, sir."

"Voronin, right. See if he can either find one or make one. And get it on that sub in the next week."

Tonya scribbled madly for a moment, then looked up at him expectantly. When he stroked his chin and looked at the fireplace, she said to him, "Mr. President, I have to ask. With the time it will take to load all this gear and food and fabricate a new torpedo, plus all the time this journey will take, according to Captain Alexeyev, why don't you just send the sub into the North Atlantic on a direct route to the targets? What is your thinking?"

He nodded, having expected the question, but from Mikhail, not Pasternak.

"What I told Alexeyev, none of that is what I really think. This whole Poseidon or Status-6 project. Have you seen the budget overruns on this program? And the time they've taken? And how much we spent refurbishing an ancient Omega submarine to carry it? And outfitting that deep-diver, *Losharik*, with the capability to place these things? If you haven't, I can tell you, it's billions of rubles. And effort. And time. For a ridiculous weapon that we wouldn't even control. We can't even push a button from here to wake it up and make it explode. We'd have to send a plane with a sonar buoy to ping the sound that makes the thing detonate. Or an underwater commando. What the hell good is that?"

"Mr. Putin seemed to think it would be good for deterrence," Pasternak said. "Plus, you heard the last daily brief's report of the possibility of nuclear munitions placed by the Americans in our ports. If that is true, it would prove that *they* started all this, and our placing the Poseidons will be a good way to force the Americans to remove their bombs."

"Look, Tonya, I'm convinced that these boogeyman bombs in our ports are disinformation—probably planted by the opposition, or the CIA. I'm not taking any action on anything related to these alleged port bombs unless and until FSB or the Navy can find one and show it to me. And as for this ridiculous Poseidon program, I can't just cancel it. That would be a huge admission of failure. Plus, the way the previous administration trumpeted this so-called superweapon, if we canceled it, we might lose support. The *Russkiy Svoboda* Party would call us weak, and they'd pile that on to the evidence from the whole *Panther* mess. Hell, we could lose the election. So the whole program, I can't just let it sit there with even more funding demands rolling in every day. The only real thing I can do is put it on ice. Quite literally. If the sub and torpedoes are out there, supposedly on the way to American targets, we can use that to show that we're strong— hell, we could even leak the plan to NATO. The damned *Svoboda* assholes can't say we're lying down for NATO and the Americans then. Plus, that submarine and those weapons will take months to get in place, if they even make it through the polar icecap at all. This will delay the entire issue until well after the election. How many days?"

"Fifty-six, sir. And by the way, your support jumped three points after Larisa died. But I see what you're doing. It seems to make sense. But why the nuclear torpedo if you really just want to stall the program?"

"I read the file on the loss of the *Kaliningrad*. Once the Americans knew she was going under ice, they sent an attack sub up there after her. *Kaliningrad* had a Gigantskiy torpedo. It might have saved her crew—it busted through thick ice and allowed the escape capsule to surface. I figure, number one, that nuclear torpedo might come in handy in the event there's an emergency and *Belgorod* has to surface and the ice is thick. And number two, if there *is* an American sub shadowing it, the torpedo may come in handy neutralizing it. After all, the way I see it, we get two free shots."

"Free shots?"

"The Americans sank two of our submarines not two months ago and we let it slide for some good reasons, but it still goes without saying that Carlucci owes me two free shots. He can't very well retaliate if he loses a sub under the icecap after sinking two of ours. And the Americans would have trouble blaming us for the loss of their sub under the ice anyway—too many disasters can befall a submarine under the ice. In any case, politically, I can't afford to lose another submarine. If that got out, we'd definitely be moving our personal effects out of the Kremlin."

A knock came at the door. Pasternak hurried over, spoke to the administrative aide, said something quietly and turned to Vostov.

"The American vice president is here, sir. Are you ready to receive her?"

———

Tonya Pasternak opened the door and greeted Vice President Karen Chushi. Vostov stood and smiled at her, shaking her hand. Chushi looked shorter than he remembered her, and her face was newly lined and her complexion seemed almost gray. She didn't look well at all, he thought. God, he hoped she hadn't gotten some kind of food poisoning while visiting Moscow—that's all he needed, accusations that his SVR had attempted to assassinate an American vice president. He made a mental note to take a meeting with SVR's chairwoman, Lana Lilya, to make sure the foreign intelligence service wasn't doing any covert operations he hadn't authorized.

Vostov waved Chushi to a chair at the fireplace. "Madam Vice President," he said, nodding at her, careful to make sure his expression remained somber.

"Please, Mr. President, call me Karen."

"And you should call me Dimmi," he said. "At least when we're behind closed doors, yes?"

"Dimmi it is," she said.

"Do you mind if I have Miss Pasternak translate for us today, Karen? My English, it is a bit weak." And Chushi's harsh, nasal west Texas accent was much too thick for him, Vostov thought.

"That would be fine, sir," she said.

He said something in Russian to Pasternak, who replied with a raised eyebrow, and he nodded at her.

"Madam Vice President," Pasternak said, "President Vostov is asking if you are feeling quite yourself. You look, what is the expression, under the weather?"

Chushi nodded gravely but bit her lip. When she answered, she said, "You're right, but I'm just getting over a stomach flu. I should be fine soon."

After Chushi gave her condolences and the two talked, somewhat awkwardly through Pasternak's translation, of some inconsequential matters, Chushi stood and excused herself, saying she knew Vostov had many other members of the visiting officials to meet.

When she left, Vostov frowned at Pasternak.

"She's seriously ill, isn't she?"

Pasternak nodded. "She looks like my aunt just before she died. Stomach cancer. Metastasized all through her body. Cancer ate her internal organs."

"I wonder, if that's the case, how long she has. Did we have any of the FSB's doctors at the funeral today or the dinner last night?"

"I can check, sir."

"See if any of our physicians agree with your theory. Not that it matters, though. I understand that in American politics, the vice president is just a figurehead. Ceremonial."

Pasternak nodded. "Just waiting around for the death of the president, so she can step in."

"That lady isn't stepping into anything but a chemo chair, if your guess is correct."

"For her sake, I hope we're wrong. She seemed like a nice person."

Vostov smirked. "She's a politician. We all seem nice when you meet us. It's in offices like this, alone with our chiefs of staff, that we're evil sons of bitches."

Pasternak smiled briefly, then went to bring in the British prime minister.

As she did, Vostov made a mental note to have the office swept for bugs when the last of the foreign delegations left. He wouldn't put it beyond any of them to try to plant a listening device in his inner sanctum.

10

He ran south on the smooth packed sand of the beach, almost to the halfway point, his father's black lab Jackson bounding enthusiastically beside him, looking up at him and smiling that euphoric canine smile as if giving thanks for being taken on the run. It didn't seem strange that Jackson, four years before, had made his final trip to the vet to be put to sleep. Today, Jackson was as young and energetic as he'd been as a puppy.

They were almost at the halfway point, three miles from his father's Sandbridge house, where today's workout plan called for him to turn around and run back. But a quarter mile farther on, he saw the figure of a beautiful woman in a bikini strolling in the surf, and there was something about her, something achingly familiar. He decided to continue the run south, knowing Jackson wouldn't mind. As he got closer to the woman, she turned her face up from the waves to look at him and it was *her*. Carrie Alameda, his first love. Dead now, going on two years. He slowed his jog to a walk and approached her slowly.

Her hair blew in the wind and she beamed at him, her lips curving around that gorgeous smile. He could see the constellation of freckles arrayed around her nose and those deep brown almost liquid eyes. He came close enough to touch her, but as he started to reach out to her, he noticed another figure coming from the west, and when he turned, he saw it was Lieutenant Commander Rachel Romanov, clad in starched dress whites with her ceremonial sword, wearing full ribbons, her gold submariner's emblem shining in the bright sun, her long gleaming dirty blonde hair combed down past her shoulders. He looked over at her, then at Carrie, and he realized both women were gazing at him, soft smiles on their faces.

He tried to find his voice. "Why are you here?" he heard himself ask.

"To wake you up, like you *said* you wanted," River Styxx's harsh voice said. He heard the awful sound of his bunk curtain being yanked back suddenly. He blinked in the dim light of stateroom three and saw Styxx's face. She was wearing her at-sea black coveralls, a form-fitting one-piece uniform with the American flag on the left arm, the *New Jersey* patch on the right, embroidered gold dolphins on her left pocket.

"What time is it?"

"Midrats will be out in fifteen. If you hurry, you can get a shower in before you partake in tonight's delicacies of beanie-weenies and cornbread."

Pacino put his legs outside the rack and spun so his back was to Styxx and lowered himself to the deck. Getting out of a top bunk in the crowded stateroom without knocking over Styxx's laptop or smacking her in the face with his foot took acrobatics. He pulled his hand through his tousled hair and rubbed his eyes. He'd gone down after watch relief and dinner, hitting the rack at 1900. If midrats were fifteen minutes away, it was 2315.

The deck was trembling violently, the vibrations coursing through the ship from the power of the propulsor. Evidently the watch section had kicked their speed up to flank, full out with fast speed main coolant pumps, the reactor power meter needle steady at exactly one hundred point zero percent. The deck inclined upward, then dived downward while heeling to port, then starboard, the boat doing slow corkscrews through the water. The sea state must have risen. The swells must be at least five feet high, he thought.

"Didn't you have the afternoon watch for the surface run?" Styxx asked, having taken her seat at her pull-down desk. "You shouldn't be the on-coming officer of the deck until zero six hundred."

"Yeah," he said, grabbing his towel. "XO wants me to take Short Hull under my guidance for the dive. So we both jumped watchsections."

"I take it XO thinks Short Hull has more potential than Long Hull."

Pacino shrugged. "Who can say who will end up being a slug and who will be a hot-runner?"

He looked down, remembering he was only wearing a T-shirt and boxers. Bunking in with Styxx seemed like XO was playing a joke on both of them. He hurried to the officers' head, turned on the water and got wet, then shut off the water, soaped up, shampooed, then turned the water on briefly and rinsed, then took a squeegee and wiped down the stainless steel shower enclosure, finishing the shower in less than ninety seconds. "Submarine showers" like this made a sailor long for home and a "hotel shower" long enough for the hot water to run out. He smirked—they'd been underway less than nine hours, and here he was, already longing for the comforts of home.

He carried his dirty clothes and walked back to stateroom three wearing only his towel, and fortunately Styxx had evacuated the room, presumably for the midnight meal. He dressed quickly in his black coveralls, but he'd brought the ones from Norfolk. They still had the emblem of the USS *Vermont* on the right sleeve. Somehow, he doubted the XO would object.

Aft, in the wardroom, the XO was holding court over the officers seated for midnight rations, sitting in the captain's chair, his habit when the command duty officer watch was stationed. The CDO watch had the executive officer assuming all the functions of the captain so the commanding officer could get some rest, but that seemed odd with them approaching the Point Delta dive point. Pacino had assumed Seagraves would want to be in control for the dive.

Both Engineer Kelly and Weapons Officer Styxx were seated in their usual seats on the outboard side of the table near the captain's end. On the inboard side of the table, the XO's seat was empty with

147

him having commandeered the captain's chair. The navigator's seat next to the XO was empty, probably with Lewinsky in control, supervising the chart for the surface run to the dive point, but Vevera was at his usual inboard seat facing the engineer, with Dankleff on his right. The supply officer's seat was vacant. Varney's chair and Long Hull's were also empty. Pacino crossed behind Quinnivan to take his usual seat next to Communications Officer Eisenhart. Short Hull Cooper hurried into the room and plopped down to Pacino's left. The mess steward came in with a serving tray and served the XO first, then Kelly, then Styxx, going down the table, slopping the thick goo of the beanie-weenies into Pacino's bowl, then serving the other side of the table, serving Vevera, finishing with Dankleff. Pacino grabbed the large bowl of cornbread and passed it to Styxx, who offered it to Kelly and Quinnivan, then gave it back to Pacino, who loaded up on two portions and handed it down to Short Hull.

Quinnivan looked happily down at his plate as if it were Thanksgiving dinner.

"Ah, lads and lassies," Quinnivan noted, "there's nothing quite like the first midrats of a voyage, yeah? And you may not know this, Mr. Short Hull Cooper, but the rules of Quinnivan's midrats are that we can discuss anything openly. This, people, is one of the joys of serving in the submarine force. In this room, during midnight rations, no subject is off limits, and we all leave our ranks behind. At my table, during midrats only, we are all equals. And I would like this team to come together for this operation, yeah? So I thought we would talk about some things that could get us better acquainted. Certainly, the old guard of *Vermont*-ers all know the drill. But you, Madam Engineer, and you, Madam Weapons Officer, are new to us, and we're all new to the Hulls. So let's talk, okay?"

There was an awkward silence in the room for a moment. Pacino saw Vevera and Dankleff smirking at him and looking at Short Hull Cooper, as if to say, *this should be good*. Finally, Eisenhart spoke up.

"XO, with your permission, I think it would do me good to talk about relationships. You know, love and sex and what this submarine force does to relationships."

"Excellent topic, Mr. Easy," Quinnivan said, the laugh lines at his eyes crinkling. "You see, people, the secret to a good Navy relationship is picking out the right person."

"We can't all find people like Shawna Quinnivan," Eisenhart said. "The perfect wife."

Pacino had met Shawna several times, before and after Operation *Panther*. She was a stunning brunette from upper-crust London, and it had been a running joke in the wardroom that she was slumming, having married a rough Irish scrapper like Quinnivan.

"That she is," Quinnivan said. "So you, Mr. Cooper, are you married, engaged, dating?"

Cooper blushed and put down his spoon. "No, sir. I had a girlfriend senior year, but no one since."

"Back to you, Mr. Easy. Word on the street is you've had some trouble along these lines."

"Girlfriend dumped him," Kelly said in a stage whisper to Styxx. "He claims it was because of our long operations, but I think she just woke up to the fact that Easy Eisenhart is a slug." Perhaps the three worst things a submarine sailor could be called were *non-qual, nub* or *slug*.

"Fuck you, Eng," Eisenhart said, but he was smiling.

"Well, then, lass, what about you?" Quinnivan asked Kelly.

"Me? I gave up on the idea of a committed relationship years ago, XO," she said.

"Feel free to call me 'Bullfrog' during midrats," Quinnivan said. "Pass the butter, please."

"Anyway, Bullfrog," Kelly continued, "the fact is, men are at best a mixed bag. I mean, look at you submariners. All pasty white. Not one of you has a tan. You look like you've been hiding in caves. And as men age, pot bellies, male pattern baldness, loss of muscle tone? And that all starts happening at thirty-five. God help you if you stick around another twenty years. And sometime along the road, the main reason for dating a guy pretty much dies unless dosed up on a sex drug. Men smell bad. They're all hairy. And you kiss a guy? You just get enough bristles on your mouth to give you a rash. And we all know, you men are dogs. Acting like they deserve a woman who looks like a centerfold while they're at best a three. And men cheat as often as they breathe. So, what the hell, I crossed the street and started dating women."

Vevera looked at her. "Really, Eng? You? You're gay?"

Kelly shook her head. "Not really. I suppose I'm sort of half-and-half. I mean, the right guy might actually get my blood pumping, but that would be one chance in a thousand. And he'd have to be one hell of a guy. But mostly, sexually, I think women do it for me. But as for romance? It's a myth."

Dankleff swallowed a bit of cornbread and motioned his head for the coffee carafe and poured a cup for himself, looking at Pacino, who nodded and took the carafe and filled his up. The beanie-weenies were not to his liking, but the cornbread and creamy butter had hit the spot.

"So, Eng," Eisenhart asked, "you've never been in love? Had your heart broken?"

Kelly shook her head. "Nope. And I'd just as soon things remain as they are. I've seen the things that people who fall in love do. Very stupid things."

"Hard-hearted Hanna over there," Vevera said. "Hey, maybe we should call you 'Hanna.'"

"So, let me ask you this, Ms. Moose," Quinnivan said, amusement crinkling his features as he poured coffee for himself.

"I fucking hate that callsign," Kelly said.

"Ms. Engineer, then. Say that AI progressed to the point that you could get—let's say—for free, a sex robot. Would it be male or female?"

Kelly pushed her plate away and poured herself coffee. "I'd have to say I'd want one with a selector switch. It could be male on Friday and female on Saturday."

Dankleff chuckled quietly. Pacino looked at Vevera, who seemed more interested in his seconds on beanie-weenies. Perhaps he was hoping the discussion wouldn't turn to him.

"Well, at least we know that you, Ms. River, are definitely into guys." Quinnivan glanced at Pacino. Pacino felt the blood rush to his cheeks.

"That I am, Bullfrog," Styxx said between bites. "And from what I've heard, our esteemed navigator is dating a femme fatale."

"Ah yes, Elvis Lewinsky and The Immortal Redhead," Quinnivan said.

"That Redhead," Dankleff said. "The temperature in the room goes up twenty degrees when *she* walks in."

"Really?" Kelly asked. Vevera reached for his handheld and punched up a photo taken at a wardroom party. He'd managed to get a full-length shot of Redhead alone, her face model-gorgeous, her shining red hair coming below the nipples of her expansive breasts, which were barely restrained in a flowing red gown that had a slit in it up to her upper thigh, revealing a tanned, toned, long leg clad in a black thigh-high stocking, her small feet in tall stiletto pumps. "Holy cow, this chick looks like she was dreamed up by an adolescent male fantasy."

"Here's another one, from her modeling portfolio."

Vevera's pad computer showed Redhead wearing only short-shorts and a revealing halter top, draped across the hood of a fire engine red Ferrari Testarossa.

"Whoa," Eisenhart said. "Squirt Gun Vevera here is stalking the Redhead. You'd better hope Lewinsky doesn't get a whiff of your interest in her. He'd flatten you."

Vevera scoffed. "Any human who has a Y chromosome is interested in that chick." He glanced at Kelly. "And some humans who don't have one."

Kelly looked at the photo for a long time, finally whistling. "Wow, she's all woman, that one."

Eisenhart laughed. "Wait till you meet her."

"Nice car, too," Kelly said, attempting to deflect the junior officers' attention.

"That's not Elvis' Ferrari, but he has one exactly like it," Vevera said. "That's how they met. She saw him climb out of his hot-ass car in Virginia Beach one Saturday afternoon and she swooped in on him like a shark after a tuna," Vevera paused. "I guess sharks eat tuna, don't they?"

"Wait, Lewinsky has a Ferrari like that?"

"Catch up, Ms. Moose," Quinnivan chuckled. "Our young navigator Elvis has a barn full of hot cars. Some he restored himself from rusting wrecks in junkyards, others he bought when his Da' left him some investments, yeah?"

"Let me see that picture again," Kelly asked, her cheeks blushing red. Vevera handed her back the WritePad. "There is simply no way she is faithful to him on our long operations, not a woman like that."

"You kidding?" Pacino said. "Redhead is *obsessed* with Elvis. She'd kill for him. Squirt Gun, show Moose the shot of what she did to his Ferrari."

Vevera took back the handheld and found another photo and showed it to Kelly. In white block letters, the word ASSHOLE was scrawled all over the car. Last time Pacino saw that picture, he counted the epithet at least six times.

"Oh dear God, why did she do this?" Kelly gasped.

Quinnivan took the question. "She somehow got the idea that Elvis had developed a thing for the lovely *Vermont* navigator, Dominatrix Navigatrix. You see, Engineer, jealous obsessed women like Redhead most assuredly do not cheat."

Pacino, on Quinnivan's mention of Rachel Romanov, tried to steer the conversation back to Lewinsky. "Elvis said it had taken a twenty-thousand-dollar repair to fix his Ferrari."

"And they're still together after all that?" Engineer Moose Kelly looked shocked.

Pacino smirked. "The thunderbolt hit them both, Eng. Disproving your assertion that romantic love is a myth." God knew, it was real, he thought, thinking of how stunned he was the first time he'd met Rachel Romanov at Quinnivan's party before the *Panther* run. He couldn't even speak.

"What about you, Squirt Gun?" Quinnivan looked over at Vevera. "Did you ever find a replacement for that young lass you were seeing? The, uh, squirty one?" Vevera had been unwise enough to mention during a midrats session with Quinnivan that his girlfriend was a squirter, which had changed his callsign from Man Mountain to Squirt Gun.

Vevera shook his head sadly. "She evaporated when I got the cancer diagnosis. I never heard from her again. I'm pretty much resigned to having a relationship with my goddamned motorcycle."

"Sorry to hear," Quinnivan said, genuinely sympathetic. "I guess you and Easy Eisenhart should get your asses to the bar at our, shall I say, intermediate destination."

Hoping Quinnivan wouldn't focus his attention on Pacino's ill-fated love life, Pacino asked, "XO, what *is* our destination? And what is this operation?"

"Ah, so can I assume this discussion has wandered away from love and sex and back to tactics, yeah? Well, tomorrow, once we're submerged and headed for Point Foxtrot, we'll have an op brief. For as much as we can, since our orders are pretty vague right now."

"Can't you tell us where we're headed?" Pacino asked.

"I wouldn't want to steal the navigator's thunder, Mr. Lipstick."

"And that's something I wanted to talk to you about, XO," Styxx said, frowning. "Mr. Pacino's nickname, *Lipstick*? I most strenuously object. I find it offensive. Seeing how the lipstick on his face was mine."

There was silence in the room for a moment. Quinnivan became suddenly serious.

"You make a good point, ma'am," he said, addressing Styxx. "Listen up, all you scurvy junior officers. From henceforth, Mr. Pacino will go by the name 'Patch.' No more 'Lipstick.' And tell the others when you see them at watch relief."

Pacino checked his diver's watch. "That reminds me, Short Hull and I need to make a pre-watch tour, XO. By your leave, if we can be excused?"

"Absolutely, Patch. Have a good watch."

Pacino stood. "Thanks, XO."

"And try not to burn the boat down, yeah?"

"Goddammit," Pacino muttered, but Quinnivan was grinning as Pacino and Short Hull Cooper hurried out of the room.

Quinnivan poured coffee for himself while Kelly asked the question, "What about Lip—I mean, Patch? Is there a story about his romantic life?"

Quinnivan leaned back in his chair. "His first girlfriend was Alameda, the engineer from the ill-fated *Piranha*. I assume you've all heard that story. She died suddenly, what, two years ago? Eighteen months ago? From a brain aneurism. Doctors never could figure out whether it was from the stress of the *Piranha* sinking or had just cropped up afterwards. Then, later, young Pacino fell hard for Rachel Romanov, our previous navigator. Turns out, our young Lip—er, Patch, has a thing for older female submarine officers, but I'd warn you off, Moose—the women Patch dates tend to end up dead or in a coma."

"Any word on Romanov, XO?" Dankleff asked.

Quinnivan shook his head solemnly. "So far, the news isn't good. But maybe she'll pull through, yeah?"

Pacino pulled his safety harness on over his foul-weather gear. He must have gotten his sea legs, he thought, since he barely noticed the rocking and rolling of the ship through the waves. He stood at the navigation chart next to Elvis Lewinsky.

"How far to the dive point, Nav?" Pacino asked, reluctant to touch the display or alter the scale when Lewinsky was using it.

"Twenty miles to the hundred fathom curve, another mile to Point Delta," Lewinsky said in his booming baritone voice. Pacino wondered if news of the midrats conversation about him and Redhead had reached his ears.

"Then on to Point Echo on course zero seven zero? Another fifty miles out. What happens then?"

"Then we switch to the top-secret chart."

Short Hull Cooper arrived then, struggling with his safety harness.

"And where are we going, Nav?" Pacino asked. "XO mentioned an intermediate destination. AUTEC, maybe?"

"What's AUTEC?" Short Hull asked.

"AUTEC is the Navy's secret submarine test range," Pacino explained. "Off Andros Island, Bahamas."

"Andros is the wrong direction from our course," Lewinsky said. "Anyway, XO wants to keep things hushed up until we can have an op brief tomorrow. Until then, I'm just going to plot one navigation waypoint ahead of PIM."

Cooper looked at the chart. "What's 'PIM?'" he asked.

"Point of intended motion," Pacino said. "It's a moving point in the sea where the bosses want us. It's set up that way so if a friendly gets a detect on a submarine, they can be made aware that it's us, not a bad guy."

"Yeah, unless a bad guy is trailing us," Lewinsky said.

"So, Short Hull, let's go check out the contact situation." He motioned Cooper to the command console, where Supply Officer Gangbanger Ganghadharan stood behind a large flatpanel display, studying it and training its aim with a hand-held device that resembled a video game controller. "Gangbanger here is contact coordinator. He'll look out for any surface ships that might present trouble. A collision at sea can ruin your entire day. What's it look like, Gang?"

"Three surface ships, gents," Ganghadharan said. "This one here is Visual Twenty." He trained the scope to a view of distant lights, one red, two others white. "Bearing zero four one, angle-on-the-bow port ninety-five, range, let's see," he said as he turned to put his face into the radar scope. Evidently they'd abandoned the yacht radar and energized the ship's BPS-16 radar set. "Range, eight thousand yards, beyond closest point of approach and opening." He trained the scope view to the south. There was a white light and a green light visible. "Visual Seventeen, range seventeen thousand yards, also opening. And over here," again he trained the scope view to look behind them. "Visual Sixteen, a sailboat, meandering toward Nantucket. Other than that, we're clear."

"Did you check infrared?" Pacino asked.

"Yes, but all we have are the three contacts. Visual, radar and infrared all agree. We're pretty much alone out here, off the shipping lanes to Boston, Portsmouth and Halifax."

"Good. Any questions, Mr. Cooper?" Pacino asked Short Hull.

"Can I look?" Gang handed the scope controller to Cooper, who rotated the scope through a slow circle around them. He gave back the device and put his face to the radar scope. Satisfied, he nodded at Pacino.

"Okay, let's lay to the bridge," Pacino said, pulling Cooper over to the pilot's station. "Pilot, to the bridge, relieving watch to the bridge."

The pilot was the chief of the boat, or COB, Master Chief Machinist Mate "Q-Ball" Quartane, the senior enlisted man aboard.

"Wait one," Quartane said. He spoke into his boom microphone. "Bridge, Pilot, oncoming watch relief requests to lay to the bridge."

"Pilot, Bridge," Boozy Varney's voice rasped in the overhead of the pilot's station. "Send them up."

"Let's go," Pacino said, leading Cooper to the ladder to the upper level and to the bridge access tunnel. He climbed the ladder, his safety harness' lanyard over his shoulder. At the top, the officer of the deck had pulled up the grating. "Request to lay to the bridge," Pacino said formally.

"Come up," Varney said.

Pacino climbed up through the grating, stepping aside so Cooper could join them. It was crowded in the cockpit with the four of them there, with Varney standing beside his under-instruction, Long Hull Cooper. Once in the bridge cockpit, the noise from the howling wind and the sea breaking on either side of the sail was deafening. Despite the windshield, Pacino was immediately wet from spray. Up this high, the rocking of the boat seemed severe, the hull rolling far to starboard, hanging up there, then finally rolling to port and pausing there, all the while pitching slowly forward, then pitching back up in the long swells. The deck grating seemed to amplify the vibrations from the propulsor at full power, blasting them through the sea state.

156

The seas were dimly red on the port side and green on the starboard, the ship's running lights trying to shine out through the spray. Ahead of the cockpit windscreen, the radar antenna rotated slowly high over their heads, making a revolution every two seconds.

"JOOD," Varney shouted to Long Hull over the roar of the wind and the bow wave, "Give Mr. Pacino and Mr. Cooper a watch turnover."

"Um," Long Hull said haltingly. "Ship is at all ahead flank on the surface, heading zero seven zero. Three surface contacts." He repeated the information they'd already gotten from Gangbanger. "Approximately eighteen nautical miles to the dive point."

"What's the sounding?" Short Hull asked. Long Hull gulped and grabbed the 7MC mike.

"Pilot, Bridge, report sounding," Long Hull ordered on the microphone.

"Bridge, Pilot, aye...sounding is ... six five fathoms."

"Anything else?" Pacino asked.

"Captain has secured the command duty officer watch. He should be in his stateroom," Varney said.

"Got it," Pacino said. He looked at Short Hull. "Coop? You ready to relieve?"

"Yes, sir. Mr. Cooper, I relieve you as junior officer of the deck."

Pacino addressed Varney. "Mr. Varney, I relieve you as officer of the deck."

"We'll snarf down midrats and relieve you from control in half an hour," Varney shouted.

"Very well," Pacino said formally. "Don't let XO engage you in any bullshit entertaining discussions. Don't be late."

Varney and Long Hull Cooper pulled up the grating and lowered themselves down the bridge access trunk.

"Report our relief to the captain," Pacino ordered Cooper.

Cooper picked up the 7MC and selected the captain's stateroom. "Captain, Junior Officer of the Deck, sir."

"Captain," Seagraves voice responded immediately.

Cooper reported their having assumed the watch. Seagraves sounded bored as he acknowledged.

"Check out the visual contacts with your binoculars," Pacino shouted to Cooper, his voice loud to overcome the hurricane wind of their passage. "Verify where they are and look for any new contacts that the contact coordinator may not have detected. You should have a mental model of the seaway like the radar screen, updating it from time to time from the contact coordinator's reports, verified with your own observation. Radar and sonar both are shit in this sea state, and there might be a trawler ahead that has lights that are out of commission. At this speed, we'd run him over almost before we could react."

"Bridge, Contact," the bridge communication box boomed with Vevera's voice. "Contact coordinator watch relief is complete. Lieutenant Vevera is contact coordinator."

"Contact, Bridge, aye," Cooper answered. "Report all contacts."

Vevera went through the same litany as before, with no new ships out there.

"You're actually pretty good at this," Pacino commented, scanning the horizon for lights as a swell knocked him back against the port bridge coaming. "Captain might even call you 'adequate.'"

"I was JOOD during sea trials," Cooper said from behind his own binoculars.

"What did you think of midrats?" Pacino asked. "And I don't mean the quality of the food."

"It was mind-blowing, sir, I mean, Patch. Shooting the breeze with the executive officer? That would never have happened with our PCU XO. Or the PCU department heads."

"Yeah. Quinnivan's a trip," Pacino said.

"Your old nickname, 'Lipstick.' What happened, if I can ask."

"I heard that Quinnivan saw that I and Navigator Romanov were starting to develop feelings for each other and he wanted to put a stop to it, you know—good order and discipline—so when we pulled into AUTEC, he had our old weapons officer call in a favor from River Styxx. Back then, Styxx was admiral's aide to Catardi, who was commander of the submarine force. So Styxx pulled me onto the dance floor. We were drinking pretty heavily that night. Next thing I know, I'm waking up in her bed in the Q. When I got to the boat, everyone saw my face was smeared with her lipstick from ear-to-ear, nose-to-chin. XO himself christened me 'Lipstick.'"

"Wow, really? You don't remember anything?"

"Nothing. But let me tell you, XO's secret evil plan worked. Romanov was so pissed at me she was spitting nails for most of the *Panther* run after that. Wouldn't even speak to me. It actually turned into a problem."

"Did you two ever get together?"

"Yes and no," Pacino said. "Just before we, the boarding party, departed for the *Panther* takeover, I called her up and told her I was sorry and that I had feelings for her. She eventually forgave me."

"And?"

"Solved one problem, created another one. She was still married at the time. Her divorce was just coming through when the *Vermont* burned. Just before that, she decided it would be more professional for the both of us to remain friends."

"Damn. The cursed 'friend zone.'"

"And now she's in a coma." Pacino pulled out a handkerchief and blew his nose, trying to hide his emotions.

"I'm sorry, Patch."

"Hopefully she recovers and everything's cool. Assuming this mission goes okay."

"What? Why wouldn't it?"

Pacino dropped his binoculars and looked at Cooper. "*New Jersey* is now a top secret codeword project boat. We do things that are more dangerous than the rest of the fleet. We report to the president himself. We do shit that other sailors wouldn't believe, and the operations are so secret that we can't even talk about them among ourselves outside of a SCIF, a special compartmented information facility, and only for a good reason. The battle cry of *Vermont* was, 'it never happened—we were never there.' For all we know, this could be one of those ops where, well, where we don't come back." Like the *Panther* run, Pacino thought.

Pacino could feel Cooper's stare but ignored it as he scanned the horizon in the starlit night.

"Bridge, Control, off-going OOD and JOOD are ready to relieve you in control."

"Let's turn over the watch to Varney and Long Hull, then rig the bridge for dive."

For the next half hour after Varney and Long Hull Cooper took over the watch from control, Pacino and Short Hull rigged the cockpit for dive. The bridge communication box went down first, handed to the waiting messenger of the watch, then the windshield, the hand-held computers, a coffee carafe and two flashlights. Pacino had Cooper search for anything they'd missed, then had him hand down the third flashlight. They took the grating apart and passed it down below, being careful not to fall into the gaping maw of the hatchway. Pacino rigged in the port running light, then turned to supervise Cooper rigging in the starboard light.

"Take a last breath of fresh air, Mr. Cooper. It may be the last real air you breathe for a long time."

Pacino inhaled the sea air deeply, mentally bidding farewell to the surface. He motioned Cooper down the hatch, then reached over and pulled up the port clamshell, then the starboard, then the centerline, the cockpit disappearing, the sail now streamlined for the submerged transit. He lowered himself into the dimly lit access trunk, only two red lights illuminating the space, and pulled the hatch shut and rotated the wheel to engage the dogs.

"Check it," he said to Cooper, who checked the hatch shut. The two climbed all the way down the ladder and emerged into the upper level. Pacino rotated the switch for the tunnel's lights to the off position, then reached up and pulled down the lower access trunk hatch and dogged it, with Cooper checking it, then shut the vent and drain valves, again having Cooper check them. They hurried down to the middle level control room.

"Pilot," Cooper called, "Bridge and access trunk rigged for dive by Mr. Pacino and checked by me."

"Pilot aye," Dankleff said from the pilot's station.

"We'll be right back," Pacino said to Varney. "Coop, go to your stateroom and dump your heavy weather gear, get some dry coveralls and hurry back here." Pacino did the same.

They took the watch back over from Varney and Long Hull. Pacino examined the chart, standing next to Lewinsky, then checked the chronometer. It was one minute before the captain's orders to be ready to submerge.

"Looks like we've arrived, Nav," Pacino said to Lewinsky. The "bug," a lit blue dot on the chart that marked their position, had moved until it was directly over an "X" that marked Point Delta.

"Mark the dive point!" Lewinsky called to the room.

"Sounding!" Pacino called.

Lewinsky's navigation electronics technician replied from aft of the chart table, "One two one fathoms!"

Seagraves baritone voice calmly intoned behind Cooper, "Well, JOOD, your report?"

Cooper swallowed and faced the captain. "Sir, ship is rigged for dive and at the dive point at Point Delta. Sounding is one two one fathoms. We're ready to submerge, sir. Request permission to submerge the ship."

Seagraves glanced at the chart. "I suggest you secure the radar first, JOOD."

Cooper shouted to Dankleff at the pilot station, "Pilot, secure rotating and radiating and lower the radar."

"Rotating and radiating secured, radar mast coming down," Dankleff reported. "Radar mast indicates down."

"We're ready, Captain," Cooper said.

"Very well," Seagraves said. "JOOD, submerge the ship."

"Submerge the ship, aye, sir," Cooper said. "Pilot, submerge the ship to one five zero feet!" Cooper stepped back to the command console's display of the periscope and took the scope controller from

161

Varney, who was automatically secured from his watch at the point of diving.

It was Dankleff's show now, Pacino thought. "Submerge the ship, Pilot, aye!" Dankleff announced, his voice jolly at the prospect of flying the ship into the depths. He selected the 1MC ship-wide announcing circuit and his voice projected throughout the submarine, "Dive! Dive!" He hit a function button on his touch screen and a blaring alarm blasted through the space, *OOOOOOOOO-GAH!* "Dive, dive!" he repeated on the 1MC. "All ahead two thirds, and Maneuvering answers, all ahead two thirds. Rigging out the bow planes, and bow planes indicate deployed. Checking bow planes, and bow plane function checked, checked sat. Opening forward main ballast tank vents. Forward vents indicate open. Opening aft main ballast tank vents, and aft vents indicate open."

"Check the periscope view," Pacino said. "Make sure we're venting."

Cooper had the view trained to directly ahead and rotated the view downward to look at the forward vents. In the view, four geysers of water blasted upward.

"Venting forward," Cooper announced.

"Now aft," Pacino said.

The view aft showed multiple firehose streams of water blasting upward on the aft deck.

"Venting aft."

"Do a surface search," Pacino directed. "Make sure in all this excitement we haven't missed a close surface contact."

"Proceeding to a ten degree down bubble. Depth four zero," Dankleff reported. "Four five."

The deck slowly inclined, still rolling and pitching, until the deck got steep in a forward tilt. The mad vibrations of the deck from their flank speed vanished, the deck now smooth.

"Five zero feet. Five five feet."

"Call 'sail's under,'" Pacino said to Cooper.

"Sail's under."

"Six zero feet. Six five."

The waves grew closer to the periscope view.

"Six nine. Seven zero feet."

Foam blasted up over the periscope display, obscuring the view.

"Scope's awash," Cooper said.

A million bubbles were visible on the display as the view plunged into the waves, until the troughs and crests were above them. The bubbles cleared and the waves overhead could be dimly seen in the view until the view became suddenly black and there was nothing to see.

"Scope's under," Cooper said. "Lowering number one scope." He hit a function lever in the command console until an indicator light flashed on the console. "Scope is retracted."

"Eight five feet. Nine zero. One hundred feet," Dankleff said.

The deck had gotten steeper. Pacino reached for the safety handhold bar at the command console.

"One three zero feet."

The rolling and pitching of the deck seemed to get gentler.

"One five zero feet," Dankleff said. "And steady on depth. Shutting forward vents. Shutting aft vents. And forward and aft main ballast tank vents indicate shut. JOOD, request to obtain a one third trim."

Cooper raised an eyebrow at Pacino, who nodded.

"Pilot, obtain a one third trim."

"One third trim, Pilot aye, and all ahead one third, and Maneuvering answers, all ahead one third."

For fifteen minutes Dankleff operated his console, aided by his copilot, Quartane, flooding some variable ballast tanks with water, pumping some overboard and balancing the boat by transferring water from aft to forward. He had to increase speed back to two thirds at one point, then after more adjustments, slowed back to one third.

"Junior Officer of the Deck," Dankleff said proudly, "the boat has a satisfactory one third trim."

"Very well," Cooper said, then to Pacino, "now what?"

"Take her deep. Five hundred forty-six feet. And chase PIM," Pacino said. "The entire time you were at four knots, the PIM dot kept going northeast at twenty-eight knots."

"Pilot," Cooper barked, "make your depth five four six feet."

"Five four six feet, aye, and going to a down bubble of fifteen degrees."

The deck tilted downward again, the rolling and pitching from the surface gone now. The tilted deck was as steady as the floor of an office building.

"Pilot, all ahead flank," Cooper ordered.

"All ahead flank, Pilot aye, and Maneuvering answers, all ahead flank. Passing two hundred feet."

The frantic vibrations of the deck returned as the speed indicator rose from four knots to thirty-two, their speed submerged eleven knots faster than they could make on the surface. Pacino walked to the chart table and bit his lip. The PIM dot was far ahead of them now, but traveling slower than they were, at the average transit speed of 28 knots.

"Mr. Navigator," Pacino said to Lewinsky, "time to catch up to PIM?"

Lewinsky smiled a crooked smile. "Why don't you get your under-instruction to calculate that?"

"Good idea," Pacino said. "JOOD, get over here."

11

"The news is good, the news is bad," CIA Director Margo Allende said, pouring a black coffee for National Security Advisor Michael Pacino. "In two areas." She glanced at Deputy Director of Operations Angel Menendez. The briefing room adjacent to the White House Situation Room was smaller, the same length as the Situation Room but narrower, most of it taken up with a long table. Both rooms were fully secure SCIFs, allowing Allende to speak freely.

"What do we have?" Pacino asked, sipping the coffee, the brew hot enough to burn his tongue.

"Good news first. The vice president was able to plant our bug in Vostov's office during her visit with him after his wife's funeral."

"Excellent," Pacino said.

"Maybe, maybe not," Allende said. "We expected her to sit in a chair at Vostov's desk, which is how he likes to receive official visitors. It always sounded like a power play to me, like a senior person addressing a subordinate sitting in the seat in front of his big desk. But instead, he took the meeting in a set of club chairs by his massive fireplace. A much more intimate setting, but we think we'll only harvest a fraction of the intelligence we wanted."

"Wouldn't a bug sweep locate that in a day?" Pacino asked.

"New tech," Menendez said. The deputy director favored colorful Hawaiian shirts under a dark blazer with his habitual dark fedora hat, which he'd placed on the table, which irritated Pacino.

U.S. Navy unwritten rules, dating back to the 1700s, strictly prohibited hats on tables—unless the owner of the hat had been to the north pole. On that basis, Pacino had always casually tossed his officers' cover onto whatever table he'd sat at, since he'd been to the pole twice. But he sincerely doubted Menendez had. The rule had been crafted with the thought in mind that no one in the Navy had been or would ever go to the north pole, and then submariners who'd returned from "ICE-EXs" started tossing caps on tables.

"The Russians might find it in a month," Allende said. "By then they won't know who placed it. They could blame the British or French."

"They always blame us," Pacino mused. "So the intel will be less, but who knows, maybe Vostov conducts his most sensitive conversations in those club chairs."

"I guess we'll see," Allende said.

"You said there were two areas," Pacino said.

"Yes. The modified special purpose sub, the Omega II, the *Belgorod*. We still think it's headed up north under the icecap. And it's delayed by at least a week, maybe two."

"Well, that's definitely good news," Pacino said. "That gives us time to get our project submarine up there." He tried to keep his expression neutral, but he was apprehensive about Anthony being assigned to *New Jersey*, which would be ordered to get into position to trail the *Belgorod* and find out what the hell it would be doing. At least this wouldn't be as dangerous as the *Panther* mission, he consoled himself.

"Oh, there's more, Patch," Menendez said, smiling, seeming pleased with himself. "*Belgorod* is taking aboard four comfort women. Must be a long mission they're anticipating."

"That sounds odd," Pacino said. "I know the Russians. When they're forward deployed, they often arrange to bring comfort women in their R&R ships or even on their sub tenders, but comfort women on the boat itself?" Comfort women were essentially prostitutes employed by the Russian Navy, their job to keep male morale from collapsing.

166

"Oh, that's not the good news," Allende said. "The good news is that one of them is ours."

Pacino sat back and stared at Allende. "You've got an asset onboard the *Belgorod*?"

Menendez beamed. "We do indeed."

"That is good news. What's the bad news?"

"We haven't figured out a way for her to communicate with us. We might not be able to get any data from her until *Belgorod* comes back to base."

"Oh," Pacino said. "Perhaps a hack into the radio antenna, like the Blue Hardhat operation you did to the Yasen-M boats?"

Allende shook her head. "We were forced to leak that to the Russians, and now they're absolutely paranoid about their submarine masts and antennae. We don't think we could get away with that now, which is why we're using one of their comfort women. Human intelligence almost always trumps electronic intel, but not if there's no way to pass us a message."

"Well, keep working on it," Pacino said. "The president has taken a personal interest in this operation, like he did with *Panther*." As National Security Advisor, Pacino's rank in the administration was near that of a cabinet officer and Carlucci treated him as if he were Allende's boss. He wondered if the president knew about Pacino's personal relationship with the CIA director. Probably did, Pacino thought. Spying on the spies was big business in Washington.

"I've got to get back to Langley. Good to see you again, Admiral," Menendez said, collecting his hat, standing, and shaking Pacino's hand. After he left the room, Allende poured them more coffee.

"Margo, you said there was something else?" Pacino checked his old, scratched Rolex. "I've got to brief the president in half an hour."

"I don't know how you're going to feel about this one, Patch," Allende said. "The vice president is seriously sick. Late-stage rectal cancer. It's metastasized throughout her abdomen. Looks like all her major organs are affected."

"Oh, no," Pacino said. "She looked terrible at that Status-6 briefing."

"She's been taking some stem cell therapy, but it's terminal and she's only been given a few months. Maybe even less."

"She knows the prognosis?"

"She's the one who told me."

Pacino shook his head. Karen Chushi was not a typical vice president. She was strong-willed, independent, and sometimes even a critic of the president's decisions. Carlucci had brought her onto his ticket as a political move to appease the South, since Chushi was from Texas, and to appease the National Party, since she was friends with the other side of the aisle, so much so that some in the press had called for her to leave the American Party and defect to the National Party. But she'd stubbornly remained on. President Carlucci had tried to keep her contained, only bringing her into the circle when he absolutely had to.

"She's planning on resigning by the week's end," Allende said.

"Any word on her replacement?"

"Carlucci doesn't want new faces in the inner circle. I'm predicting he shuffles the cabinet and elevates a trusted person from within."

"Maybe Hogshead or Klugendorf," Pacino said.

Margo Allende just looked at him with that half-amused look she had when she was keeping a secret.

On behalf of Northern Fleet Commander Admiral Gennady Zhigunov, Captain First Rank Georgy Alexeyev had paid to close the Lamb's Valhalla pub for tonight's meeting, Zhigunov's directive made in defiance of the orders of Admiral Olga Vova, who had placed the establishment off-limits. Zhigunov's armed guards stood watch outside, keeping the regulars at bay. The servers and cooks had been dismissed for the night, more of the admiral's staff sent in to serve their table and bring food.

Alexeyev sat opposite Sergei Kovalov, the *Losharik* captain seeming ill at ease, as he had all week. They'd just come from a long session with Zhigunov at his Northern Fleet headquarters, and the highlights of that meeting had been disappointing.

Kovalov waved over one of the enlisted men to bring a bottle of scotch to the table. The man seemed confused, so Kovalov walked him to the bar and picked out a new bottle of Oban and brought it back himself with two glasses. He poured for the two of them, then looked over at Alexeyev.

"To fallen comrades," Kovalov said, raising his glass.

"Fallen comrades." Alexeyev tossed down a gulp of the scotch, trying to distract his mind from his dead former engineer Matveev. And her ghost.

"This mission just keeps getting better," Kovalov said, pulling over the large ashtray and lighting a cigarette.

"I wonder what the Status-6 delay is all about," Alexeyev said, adjusting his eye patch. The false eye under it sometimes itched, but he was assured it was just allergies, not a return of the herpes that had infected him during the South Atlantic mission, leading to the loss of the eye.

"It wouldn't surprise me if those Status-6 torpedoes don't even work," Kovalov said. "Seriously, a nuclear reactor in an autonomous torpedo, with a ten-megaton warhead? Manufactured by Sevmash? God help us. At best, those things will just be inert. There's a thousand things that can go wrong with an unattended nuclear reactor. The damn things could have a runaway, or worse, they could self-destruct."

"Hopefully, any self-destruct will just be their conventional explosives going off, not a nuclear explosion," Alexeyev said, putting out his hand, and immediately Kovalov shook out a cigarette, handed it and his lighter to Alexeyev, who lit up and blew a cloud at the ceiling.

"That would scatter plutonium over the entire bay where it's placed," Kovalov observed. "And seriously, strategically? Tactically? What the hell good is a weapon that is out of communication with the Kremlin and Defense Ministry? If Vostov decided to push the nuclear button, those torpedoes won't hear him."

Alexeyev shrugged fatalistically. "Supposedly a stealthy team of underwater commandos—hydronauts, yes?—will be dispatched who will locate the weapons with a sonar homing device, then ping a particular sonar signal to program them with detonation directions."

Kovalov scoffed. "Sounds unsophisticated to me. Honestly, what is Vostov's motivation for doing this? Wasn't it just six weeks ago he was playing nice with the Americans? Even after we lost *Kazan*, *Novosibirsk* and *Voronezh*?"

Alexeyev shrugged. Politics were impenetrable. At least their mission and equipment they could understand. Perhaps even control. "Have you seen the schematics and tech manual of the Status-6 units, Sergei?"

Kovalov shook his head and drained his glass. "Still too highly classified. We may not even have them when we sail."

"How the hell—?"

"We'll have an operation manual, Georgy. It'll have knobology. But the inner workings and hidden mechanisms? Probably not in the book." Kovalov pulled the cork on the scotch bottle and poured both of them more scotch. He shook his head. "This is madness. Laying ten megaton bombs in American ports. And carrying them there through the polar icecap?"

"Our ballistic missile subs go up at least once a year per ship," Alexeyev said, trying to sound comforting, but he himself doubted they'd have an easy time of it.

"We're thousands of tons bigger than the Borei-class. And our effective draft with *Losharik* docked to *Belgorod*? Almost thirty-five meters. Talk about a camel through the eye of the needle. One pressure ridge could stop us cold. No pun intended."

"We may have to undock your *Losharik* to get through some narrow or shallow passages at the pressure ridges."

"Great, undocking and re-docking under ice? *Losharik* has no under-ice capability, Georgy. If we get separated, God help us, we'll die down there."

"Well, let's leave that problem for later, Sergei. Besides, the two Gigantskiy torpedoes can be used to break up a closed passage."

"Are you insane, Georgy? Detonating a nuclear torpedo under ice? That would be suicide."

"It's only a one megaton warhead."

"Oh, dear God, *only*?"

"I see your point, Sergei."

"Leave it to the Navy to rehabilitate an old useless Cold War relic for us to take with us," Kovalov said. "The Gigantskiy torpedoes haven't been used since *Kaliningrad* sank. That torpedo design is older than my wife."

"Well, you did rob the cradle, Sergei. Can I borrow another cigarette?"

Kovalov smiled for the first time all day. "Borrow?"

"You know what I mean."

A woman and a man in uniform walked in the front door and took off their greatcoats. The woman was Alexeyev's first officer, Captain Second Rank Ania Lebedev. The other man was Captain Second Rank Ivan Vlasenko, the *Losharik* second-in-command. Alexeyev had only met Vlasenko a few times. He seemed competent enough. Medium height, hair too long out of regulation, slightly overweight, he claimed, due to his wife being a master chef. But it was his sunny disposition that irritated Alexeyev. But then, most optimists did.

Alexeyev glanced at his own first officer, standing and shaking her hand. Lebedev was slender and tall for a woman, with a head of mouse-brown chin-length hair, with no makeup, making her seem washed-out and tired. Lebedev and Alexeyev had sailed halfway around the world for the South Atlantic mission, and Alexeyev and she had literally survived Hell, escaping the burning and exploding wreck of *Kazan* in the crew escape chamber. Before the mission, Alexeyev had had a dim view of Lebedev, having concluded that she was a cold disciplinarian and careerist, who would step on Alexeyev's very face to climb to the rank of commanding officer of a submarine. But the mission had changed her for the better. After facing death and the loss of their comrades from their engineering spaces, Lebedev seemed to gain some kind of deep empathy as if it had fallen upon her from heaven. She was *human* now, Alexeyev thought. And just in time for this ridiculous Status-6 errand. He cautioned himself to show his first officer—and Kovalov's—none of the cynicism and skepticism that had dominated their conversation so far this evening. Pessimism was best confined to the captain's stateroom.

The two first officers sat at the table, Vlasenko next to Kovalov and Lebedev next to Alexeyev, and after an exchange of pleasantries, Lebedev signaled to one of the guards acting as a waiter to bring more scotch, and she and Vlasenko poured, and once again they did the traditional toast to the fallen. Alexeyev glanced quickly at Lebedev, and she looked back, her brown eyes seeming deep, as if she and Alexeyev were both remembering Matveev.

"So, Captain," Vlasenko began, addressing Alexeyev. "Any prediction on when we'll leave on this mission?"

Alexeyev shook his head. "No idea. It could be three days. It could be three weeks. Ania," he said, addressing Lebedev, "how is the equipment loadout going?"

"Sir, food and arctic supplies are aboard and stowed as of this afternoon. All we're missing are the special weapons."

"Have you and the weapons officer reviewed the operation of the Gigantskiy torpedoes?"

"We've had to modify the weapon control software extensively to be able to talk to them and program them for antisubmarine operation. I also reviewed with Sobol the loading procedure. We've brought aboard and installed the roller cradles."

"Roller cradles?" Kovalov asked.

"Sevmash inserted and welded in a chassis of supports and rollers," Lebedev explained, "so the one-meter diameter Gigantskiys could be stable in the two-meter diameter Status-6 tubes. So tubes one, two, and three will be loaded with Status-6 weapons and tubes four and five will house the Gigantskiys. If and when they're launched, the Gigantskiys will depart their tubes in swim-out mode, and the rollers will keep them from scraping on the bottom of the tubes."

"What about the command detonate mode?" Alexeyev asked. "In case we need to punch through a pressure ridge or create a polynya where there is thick ice?"

Lebedev frowned. "We're still working on that, Captain. Sevmash engineers keep saying they have plans A, B and C converging on the problem all at once, but I think they're having trouble."

"I'll talk to Admiral Zhigunov about it tomorrow," Alexeyev said. "Unless he makes a surprise visit tonight."

"You think he's coming?" Kovalov asked.

Alexeyev shrugged. "I don't know. From what I hear, he's getting an earful daily from the chain of command. With the president himself running the mission, the defense ministry and high command of the Navy are all breathing down Zhigunov's neck."

"He may want to escape for a late drink with his crews, though," Vlasenko said, smiling. Alexeyev glared balefully at Vlasenko, who seemed too perpetually cheerful. Perhaps Kovalov's young first officer hadn't yet grasped the gravity of their present circumstances.

"What about *Losharik*, Sergei?" Alexeyev asked. "Are you rigged for sea?"

"Sevmash just replaced the evaporator and the electrical still. Nuclear reactors and steam plants, even tiny ones like mine, go through water like, well, water. We can't test them pier side—the water isn't clean enough. We'll have to wait until we reach open water to fire them up."

"We can feed you deionized water from *Belgorod*," Lebedev offered.

Kovalov nodded. "When you think about it, pure water is mission-limiting. When we're deploying the Status-6 units, we'll be in littoral waters. Shallow, silty, sandy, muddy waters. We'll have to shut down the evaporator and still when we undock to place the Status-6s. We'd better place them damn expeditiously, or we'll run out of water."

"You have steam leaks or primary leaks that are eating your water?" Lebedev asked Kovalov.

Michael DiMercurio

Kovalov shook his head. "Sevmash groomed primary and secondary systems. *Losharik* is tight. As tight as they can make it, anyway."

"While we're on hold, Sergei," Alexeyev said, "perhaps you can take *Losharik* out and test your systems in open water."

Kovalov shook his head. "We'd be out of position if the mission gets ordered to start suddenly. The Status-6 loadout and Gigantskiy load will only take a day. I'd be two days out if I want to do a shakedown."

Alexeyev nodded. "Nothing to do now but wait," he said. "I'm hungry." He checked his wristwatch. "Where the hell are the *zhenshchiny dlya utekh*?"

"We don't call them 'comfort women' anymore, Captain," Lebedev said. "They're *ispytatel'nyye zheny*. Test wives."

"Fine. Test wives. Anyway, while we wait, I'll go to the kitchen and see what they can cook up. I'm sure the fleet guards can't provide the full menu of the Lamb's Valhalla. Which is a shame."

Alexeyev stood to go to the kitchen, deciding to stop at the restroom. He washed up and stepped to the kitchen, where the staff were stirring a large cauldron. A tantalizing aroma filled the kitchen, making Alexeyev even more hungry.

"What is it?"

"Rabbit stew with homemade dumplings, Captain," one of the fleet guards said, wiping a hand on his apron. "Are you ready for us to serve?"

"Not yet, we're missing four people."

Alexeyev left the kitchen and saw the missing four had shown up and were seated. As he approached the table, the newcomers began to stand to greet him, but he waved them back to their seats.

"Captain First Rank Georgy Alexeyev," he said, introducing himself. The woman nearest him shook his hand, her grip soft, her hand warm, and she introduced herself. Alexeyev greeted the other three. They all seemed pretty, but nothing that would tempt him away from his wife, Natalia, he thought, although other married men might not feel their marriages were as solid. He looked over at

174

Kovalov, who seemed to be staring at the oldest of the four. In contrast to the other three, all brunettes, the fourth, the youngest, was a platinum blonde with large blue eyes and puffy apple red lips.

"Have any of you sailed on submarines before?" Lebedev asked the oldest one, who had introduced herself as Captain Third Rank Svetlana Anna.

Anna shook her head. "Our only sea voyages have been on support ships. This will be all new to us."

Kovalov laughed. "You picked one hell of a mission for your first submarine ride."

"Can you tell us about it?" Anna asked.

"That's why we're here," Alexeyev said, putting out his hand to Kovalov for another cigarette.

"Op brief!" Quinnivan bellowed. "Get your arses in here, ye scurvy junior officers! And U-Boat, cut the fookin' crap."

The deck was trembling violently from the power of the flank bell and had been since they'd dived. Pacino had gotten used to it and barely noticed it unless he placed his coffee cup on the table and saw the waves in its surface form from the hull vibrations. But whenever the ship was running flank, blasting through the ocean, U-Boat Dankleff—who absolutely loved hauling ass at flank—would always do his "flankin' it, flankin' it" dance, a ridiculous arm-waving, leg-twisting jig that, to Pacino, just never got old. On Quinnivan's reprimand, Dankleff plopped down in his seat and feigned contrition, but looked up at Pacino and winked.

"Who are we missing?" Quinnivan asked with an angry expression creasing his features. The man, Pacino thought, looked positively jolly most of the time, but absolutely evil when he was mad.

"Electrical officer," Engineer Kelly said, but just then Varney hurried into the room and shut the door behind him.

"Sorry, XO," Varney said, taking his seat. "Watch relief on the conn was delayed."

Pacino reached for the coffee carafe and refilled his cup. Lunch had been sliders with thick steak fries, and he was drowsy from it. That or his scrambled sleep schedule. He'd gotten off the conn with Short Hull at 0600 and had worked out in the torpedo room, intending to catch some sleep after his shower, but Short Hull had wanted several qualification check-outs. It had never occurred to Pacino that giving a system check-out—a verbal test of knowledge— could be as draining to the person giving it as the person requesting it. Cooper had wanted to start big, asking to be checked out on operating the BQQ-10-V6 sonar suite. A sonar check-out like that could involve three or more full watches of questions, answers and "look-ups," when the non-qual was assigned to find the answers to questions that he'd failed. That had taken till noon meal, and when the dishes had been cleared from that, the operation brief had been convened by the XO.

"Well, Nav," Quinnivan said. "Are we here and are we all cleared for this briefing?"

"XO," Lewinsky said, "the supply officer is on the conn and Long Hull Cooper is aft as engineering officer of the watch. We've got everyone else. And, yessir, we're all cleared."

"Very well, then," Quinnivan said. "Madam Engineer, would you be so kind as to call the captain and inform him we're all present and ready for him?"

Kelly reached for the phone set into a small alcove behind her, dialed the captain, murmured a few words, and hung up. "He's on his way."

"Everyone have coffee?" Quinnivan asked, holding the carafe and pouring for himself, then setting a cup in front of the captain's chair and pouring for him.

Seagraves walked into the room from the forward door. "Afternoon, people," he said. In unison the officers returned the greeting. He took his seat, nodded at Lewinsky, and took a sip of his coffee. "Let's proceed."

Lewinsky pointed a remote control at the flatpanel over the missing supply officer's seat and the display came to life. It had two pages projected on it, their orders given to the captain before sailing.

"What we've been ordered so far," Lewinsky said, "is to proceed northeast at flank speed to the U.K. Naval Base, Clyde. Faslane, Scotland. Their submarine base. As you can see on page two, we're to load up arctic supplies, food, and weapons."

Pacino nodded to himself. *New Jersey* had sailed with an empty torpedo room, which was like walking into a war zone without bullets. He would have felt better if they'd at least been loaded with two ADCAP Mark 48 torpedoes as a contingency.

"Also, as you can see, we're to bring on a dry-deck shelter and team of SEALs, the same guys from Task Force Eight Zero who we sailed with on the *Panther* run."

Seagraves spoke up. "The Pentagon is now calling that the Battle of the Arabian Sea."

"Which is odd," Quinnivan said, "seeing as how it wasn't really a battle until the South Atlantic. I note, ladies and gents, it remains top secret SCI codeword-slash-special-handling information that we traded torpedoes with the Russians on that op. As far as the open-source media is concerned, we just hijacked that sub, sailed it to AUTEC, then gave it back. The Russian loss of three subs—well, it never happened. And we were never there."

Pacino glanced at Short Hull Cooper, whose eyes had bugged out at the mention of the details of the *Panther* run. It hadn't been discussed since he'd reported aboard.

"Please continue, Mr. Lewinsky," Seagraves said.

"That's pretty much it, Captain," Lewinsky said. "There's nothing else in the order. And we don't have an operation order for what happens after Faslane. And we don't know how long we'll be in Faslane."

"Is there any context here from a scrub of the open-source news files and the classified intel digest?" Seagraves asked.

Styxx put out her hand. "I did an extensive search, Captain. There's some mention of the Russian Omega II submarine *Belgorod*.

A few articles on the Poseidon torpedoes. A few Russian editorials about Vostov deciding to be more confrontational with NATO and the Americans. But nothing very specific."

"So we're left guessing," Lewinsky said. "Captain, with your permission, may I speculate?"

Seagraves smiled. It was perhaps only the second smile Pacino had seen from the captain. "By all means, Navigator."

"My guess is that we'll be sent to try to trail the Omega II and see what he's doing. The under-ice supplies make me believe the Omega II may try to do an ICE-EX and go to the pole."

"Maybe," Seagraves said. "But why the SEALs?"

"You've got me there, Captain. I can't imagine we'd try to hijack it like we did the Iranian Kilo," Lewinsky said. "The Russians got fooled once. They won't let that happen again."

"Hey," Dankleff said, smirking. "Varney, Pacino and I could conn her to AUTEC if the SEALs got us aboard."

Quinnivan laughed. "I seriously doubt that, DCA. But even if you could, the pole is essentially in Russia's front yard. They'd send a fleet of submarines to get us if we tried."

"Perhaps just a deep contingency," Kelly said. "You know, better to have them and not need them than to need them and not have them."

"Maybe. But we're all guessing here, people," Quinnivan said, looking at the officers sternly. "All we can do is make sure this ship is ready for anything. Eng, what's your material condition looking like? Most of the sea trials issues were in the engineering spaces."

Engineer Kelly cleared her throat. "We're chasing steam leaks, XO. They're overloading the air conditioning plants and chillers and making more demands on the evaporators. We've got a complete inventory of the leaks. Four days, five at most, we'll have them under control."

"See to it, Engineer," Quinnivan said, frowning. "Any other comments? No? Well, people, we're dismissed. Navigator, please brief the supply officer and RC division officer separately since they missed this session."

"Aye, sir."

The room cleared out. Pacino checked his watch and looked at Short Hull Cooper. "You want to continue with your sonar check-out?"

"I think it would help if I took a watch on the sonar stack with Senior Chief Albanese," Cooper said.

Pacino nodded and Cooper left. Pacino opened his pad computer to the classified news files, wondering if there were anything there that Styxx had missed that might shed some light on this operation. A half hour after he'd been into the files, with no results, Elvis Lewinsky came into the room and brewed a fresh pot of coffee, then took his seat at the XO's seat's right side.

"How are you doing, Patch?" he asked. "Coffee?"

"Yes, please, Nav. I'm okay, I guess. I'd be better if we had good news about Romanov."

"Yeah. I heard XO is getting daily status updates about her, but so far, nothing's changed. He did mention Blacky Nygard is out of the burn unit and is doing well."

"That's a relief," Pacino said. "He saw the worst of it."

"He got the flames but not the smoke inhalation."

"Yeah." There was an awkward silence, until Pacino said, "Nav, I bet you have a theory about this op."

"I already did my guessing to the captain," Lewinsky said, scanning his pad computer.

"Come on. I bet you think more than you said to the captain."

Lewinsky looked up. "I do."

"Out with it, Elvis."

"Patch, what if that Omega II—the 'BUFF' as you and Romanov called it—is on the way to deploy some of those Poseidon torpedoes on American shores?"

Pacino sat back in his chair, a frown on his face. "If they were, wouldn't they just go into the Barents Sea, then into the North Atlantic? Why all these preparations to go under ice?"

Lewinsky shook his head. "Maybe the Russians are worried about the SOSUS sonar network tripwires laid down between the

UK, Iceland and Greenland. Maybe they think if they come through the GI-UK gap, they could be detected. Or they're worried that they could be trailed by an American or British sub if they go that route. And they think they can evade a trailing hostile sub by going under the ice."

Pacino shook his head. "The long route? Through the Bering Strait and around South America? That would take months."

"That might be why we're loaded out with months of food."

"It won't matter, Nav. The BUFF is way too big to make it through the icepack."

"It's almost September," Lewinsky said, "so the icepack is at minimum now."

"Hand me the remote," Pacino said. He lit up the projection flatpanel and projected from his WritePad. "This is the BUFF. I superimposed on this image a scale image of a Virginia-class submarine." On the display was a 3D view of the *Belgorod*, with the deep-diver sub *Losharik* docked underneath. Next to it was a Virginia-class boat.

Lewinsky looked at the projection and whistled. "Goddamn, that boat is big. It looks like you could fit five or six of us inside that thing's hull and have room left over."

"Hence, Big Ugly Fat Fucker, Nav. No way that thing gets through the ice."

"Shut the wardroom doors, Patch."

Pacino raised an eyebrow at the navigator, but got up and shut both doors to the room.

"What is it, Nav?"

"This is codeword top secret, so you didn't hear this from me. But this isn't the first time an Omega has gone under the ice. The first unit made it all the way to the pole."

"Really?"

"Sixteen or seventeen years ago or so. In December. Or January. When the icepack was at maximum."

"How do you know this? There's nothing in the classified archive about that."

"Too highly classified. I guess your father never told you about it. Your old man definitely knows how to keep a secret."

"What do you mean?" Pacino stared at Lewinsky.

"I've probably said too much already," Lewinsky said. "But Omega unit one? It never made it home. Your dad put it on the fuckin' bottom. And got the Navy Cross for it."

Pacino stared at Lewinsky with his mouth open, but before he could say a word, the navigator grabbed his pad computer and vanished out the aft door.

12

Weapons Officer Captain Lieutenant Katerina "Ballerina" Sobol frowned from the pier at the weapon loading support ship, tied up at the bow of *Belgorod*. The second Gigantskiy torpedo was finally about to roll into tube five, for the third damned time, she thought. She looked up in time to see First Officer Lebedev walk over from the conning tower access hatch.

"I'll wager you're getting pretty good at this," Lebedev said.

Lebedev was over a head taller than Sobol, who was petite and had a dancer's body, which had contributed to her nickname, although she'd never danced. She'd been more into futbol and track growing up. She'd been fast back then, she thought glumly. She hadn't run more than a kilometer since she had joined this submarine. It was just too busy in port, and all their sea time had been a week here, ten days there, then back into the drydock, then post-drydock sea trials, then back to the pier for repairs, after which they'd repeat the same cycle. It was exhausting. Sobol couldn't remember the last time she'd had a good night's sleep. She touched the back of her head, her habit when frustrated, and grimaced that her hair was greasy. She needed a long hot shower, the kind where it didn't matter how much water she used, she thought. She'd kept her usually shiny raven black hair long, but to conform with uniform expectations, she'd put her hair in a braided ponytail. She couldn't remember the last time she'd taken it out, and she just felt grimy. She could almost hear her mother's voice insisting that a nuclear submarine was no place for a young woman. But if Mother had had her way, Katerina Sobol would be cooking and cleaning at home with four children and a husband, who would probably be an alcoholic like her father, the reason she didn't drink.

"Third time's a charm, Madam First," Sobol said in her soprano voice, which had always irritated her. In college, someone had cruelly said she sounded like a cartoon character. She'd even tried smoking to try to deepen her voice, but the scheme had failed. "I'm hoping this time, they don't find yet another fault that requires them to take it back to Santa's workshop and rewire it or reprogram it."

"Do the Sevmash folks still think the command detonate function problem was inside the torpedoes, not in our battlecontrol system?"

"So they say, ma'am. But they could change their minds again tomorrow. We still have to go through primary testing and then integration to the Second Captain AI."

"What are they saying about the Status-6 weapons?"

"This morning they said they'd be on their way by noon. They're four hours late on that projection."

Lebedev looked at the overcast sky. "You're going to lose daylight." It was late August, which meant they'd have over fifteen hours of daylight, but Sevmash's delivery promises had fallen through three times in the past ten days.

Sobol checked her watch. "Sunset is at 2030 hours, ma'am. It's only 1600 now."

"The last four hours of daylight are dim at best. Sevmash might not get here for another two or three hours."

"I could call for generators and halogen lights," Sobol said.

Lebedev shook her head. "No. Loading a nuclear weapon in less than full daylight isn't safe, I don't care how many lumens you blast at the bow. Bright lights mean shadows. And hell, even at noon, loading weapons is the most dangerous thing we'll do until we approach the icecap. Did I ever tell you about the torpedo loading accident from ten years ago?"

Sobol laughed. She'd heard the story at least a dozen times. Some idiot removed the safety bolts from a UGST torpedo during loading and the weapon engine started. It walked its way out of the tube, armed itself and flashed across the bay and hit a tugboat, about a tenth of its explosive charge detonating, blowing a hole in the tug the size of a turkey platter. The shipyard had had to scramble to save the tug, tying it off to a rail-mounted crane until pontoons could be mobilized and a patch fashioned that would last long enough to get it into a drydock, which had royally messed up the maintenance schedule of the shipyard. It was fortunate for all that the full power of the warhead hadn't gone off, or else the entire pier, rail crane and tugboat would have been destroyed.

"Believe me, Madam First, we are absolutely doing this by the book." She showed Lebedev the dogeared procedure manual, which was opened to the page where the steps were shown that the load crew were executing now.

"Good. Any sign of the captain?"

"No. He's been at Northern Fleet HQ all day."

"Well, let me know if you see him coming down the pier, and let me know when the Status-6 units arrive—if they do arrive. I'll be advising Sevmash that if they're not here by the time you're done loading the Gigantskiy, they'll be waiting until tomorrow for the Status-6 load."

"Understood, ma'am. Can I ask you a question? I can't get a feel for how urgent this mission is. How much of a hurry are we in?"

Lebedev grimaced and shook her head. "If we even make speed-over-ground of four or five knots on average to the Bering Strait, I'd be pleased. That could be a hundred days into the operation. So, another day to load weapons and test them out with the Second Captain won't make a difference."

Sobol nodded. The Gigantskiy was fully inserted into the tube. Now for the next step of shutting the muzzle door. After that, they'd open the breach door, connect the torpedo to the interface to the weapon control system, shut the breach door and flood the tube. With any luck, that wouldn't short out the torpedo, which would force them to start all over again.

"Anyway, I think I'll lay below to see how Michman Yegor is doing with the electronic checks," Lebedev said.

"He should be well along with the tube four Gigantskiy," Sobol said.

"Stay alert up here, Weapons Officer," Lebedev said. "I'll have hot tea sent up."

"Thanks, ma'am." Sobol saluted Lebedev and the first officer returned the salute, turned, and walked back in-hull.

Lieutenant Anthony Pacino leaned over the chart table and glanced at the chronometer in the red-lit control room of the project submarine USS *New Jersey*, which had deeply penetrated Russian territorial waters, which made them all outlaws. It was surreal being submerged in the Zapadnaya Litsa Fjord, barely a nautical mile from the Russian submarine base, not far from the spot that the *Vermont* had been simulated to be when the exercise had gone bad.

New Jersey had been loitering on-station for the past day-and-a-half, rigged for ultraquiet and hovering with one side of the engineroom shut down for sound quieting. The flank run to Faslane had ended a week ago, and their weapon load-out had been done by dark of night in a covered structure they'd been winched into. As expected, the Virginia Payload modules had been loaded with fourteen Tomahawk cruise missiles, twelve of them carrying conventional antisubmarine warfare depth charges, two of them loaded with 250 kiloton nuclear depth charges. Usually, the nukes would be useless, since nuclear release authority had to come from the president himself, and obviously the White House would be out of communication when they would be under ice, but perhaps anticipating the need, the ship had sailed from Faslane with advance nuclear release authority, granting to the captain the decision if and when to deploy nukes, which was a chilling development. Someone in the Pentagon had had a nightmare that *New Jersey* would need to employ nukes. And yet nuclear cruise missiles? They were useless under ice. Big Navy and the upper levels at the Pentagon, Pacino thought, were clueless.

The torpedo room had been filled up with twenty-one ADCAP Mark 48 Mod 9 torpedoes, two SLMM Mark 67 submarine launched mobile mines, and two of the newer swimmer-delivered Mark 80 mines. The dry-deck shelter had been mated to the top of the hull in the same barn, lowered from a bridge crane. Pacino had supervised the shelter being mated to the plug trunk hatch, noting that its height was half the height of the sail. If, when under the ice, they were called on to break through the ice, the vertical surfacing could crush the shelter. They'd been assigned the unit that didn't have the upper surface hardened for ice collisions. Typical Big Navy, Pacino thought, never thinking ahead to contingencies.

The boat had been towed to another building, where the stores load had been accomplished. The 140-day food loadout had been an all-hands evolution, bringing on and storing what fresh food they could—which would run out in two weeks—and canned food and frozen stores. Like they had before the *Panther* run, they'd loaded so many twelve-inch diameter cans of food that they were placed on all walkways forward of the engineering spaces, with plywood laid on top, making the headroom of occupied spaces restricted. More than one sailor had banged his head on a valve, unused to the overhead being closer by a foot. As time went by, the crew would eat their way down to the bare deck plates.

Perhaps most interesting items of the loadout, though, were the arctic supplies, all of them coming down the plug trunk hatch in large cylindrical modules with labels. "Personnel shelter / arctic." "Snowmobile." "Heavy weather gear / arctic." "Diesel heater / arctic." "Diesel generator / arctic." Lewinsky had remarked that they would be ready for anything, but Pacino had doubts. After all, in the South Atlantic, *Vermont* had run out of torpedoes and it had almost proved their downfall.

The crew had been disappointed that there hadn't been time to take in the sights of Scotland or experience the pubs—or the female companionship. They'd been in Faslane less than 24 hours and it was around-the-clock work. By the time they'd shoved off and headed north, the crew was exhausted. Hell of a way to start a mission.

And oddly, the SEALs hadn't arrived until the very last minute, just before Pacino and Short Hull Cooper were ready to remove the gangway. And the SEAL officers had yet to eat a single meal in the wardroom. Wondering why they were so elusive, Pacino had sought out his friends, Commander "Tiny Tim" Fishman and Lieutenant (junior grade) "Grip" Aquatong, who were hiding out in the SEAL accommodations aft of the torpedo room. The SEAL area was self-contained, with a small galley, frozen and refrigerated stores, a conference room that doubled as a movie screening room, and a two-hole head with a shower. With this arrangement, the SEALs could isolate themselves in the thought that a top secret mission would preserve its secrets all the better if they didn't mix with the rest of the crew, but it was a flawed idea, since the SEALs spent hours a day working out in the torpedo room where they rubbed elbows with the crew. That is, until the rig for ultraquiet was imposed, shutting down hot food from the galley and the makeshift torpedo room gym.

Fishman and Aquatong had greeted Pacino warmly enough, but they seemed preoccupied. They probably knew something that they couldn't talk about, he considered. Fishman was Pacino's height and solidly built, the clean-shaven and tough-looking black officer rarely smiling, his serious nature seldom reacting to humor. He was working on his doctorate in philosophy at a different university than the one that had rejected his thesis, a theory about life on earth that resembled a religion, but which had helped Pacino gather his courage to invade the *Panther*. Pacino had hoped Fishman would entertain them at Quinnivan's midrats with his theory.

In contrast to Fishman, the taller and skinnier Grip Aquatong was the comedian of the pair, and he'd grinned at Pacino and delighted in showing him his new pistol, a Desert Eagle .50 cal, the gun heavier than a box of lead. Aquatong had a mop of black hair and still had his closely trimmed beard, which had started to come in gray, which was odd since the junior grade lieutenant was only twenty-three. But like Fishman, Aquatong had seemed somewhere else, cutting the visit short so he could attend a meeting that Fishman had called, which kept Pacino from greeting the SEAL medic, Senior Chief "Scooter" Tucker-Santos, or his right-hand man, Petty Officer

"Swan Creek" Oneida, but Pacino figured the mission had plenty of time for them all to catch up.

Several days out of Faslane, they'd crossed the Arctic Circle and held the traditional Navy "Bluenose" ceremony, but somehow it had lacked the high spirits of the equatorial crossing on the *Panther* mission. The crew's mood seemed somehow subdued, Pacino thought. Somber and serious. It just felt different. Pacino wondered if they were all feeling some darkness arriving from their future. And now, off the Russian submarine base, they were rigged for ultraquiet and tiptoeing. The boat seemed wound tighter than a piano wire.

"Petty Officer Sanders," Pacino called from the chart table to sonarman Walrus Sanders, who had the sonar stack for this watch section. "Anything?"

Sanders had put his hand to his right ear under the headset as if listening hard to something, which had prompted Pacino's question.

"New sonar contact, designate Sierra Seventeen, OOD. Diesel engine. Sounds like the same support ship we've been hearing. Back for another trip."

"Probably delivering something," Pacino said.

"Like what?" Short Hull Cooper asked.

"Weapons, food, personnel. Who knows?"

"Sure would be nice if we had an Apex drone overhead," Cooper complained. "We'd know everything going on. We'd be able to see the BUFF's captain talking to the admiral on the pier. Down to what brand of cigarettes they're smoking."

"You heard the XO," Pacino said, having stepped to behind Sanders' shoulder to see the sonar broadband display. "We're doing this without eyeballs, just using our earballs. Well, hello, you slugs," Pacino said to the arrival of Squirt Gun Vevera and his under-instruction, Long Hull Cooper. "About fucking time."

"Fuck off, Lipstick," Vevera said, smirking. "We're early."

"Oh man, Squirt Gun, don't let XO or Weps hear you call Pacino that," Long Hull said.

"Hey," Vevera said, "when I have the deck and the conn, I'm like a king. And besides, I'm a Vehmontah, I do what I wanta."

188

"Get that off a bumper sticker, did ya, Squirt Gun?" Pacino asked.

"So, what you guys got?" Vevera said, suddenly serious as he looked over the chart.

"BUFF is still dead cold iron," Pacino said. "Sierra Seventeen was just detected, a supply boat, most likely bringing the BUFF more shit for his trip."

"Probably a big load of porno DVDs," Vevera said.

"No way the Russians are as perverted as you, Squirt," Pacino said. "Plus, maybe they're taking along comfort women."

"No way they'd embark hookers," Vevera said. "Sure would be nice if we did, though. You ever wonder what it would be like to take those Rooskie submariners drinking?"

"I spent a few hours with some of them on the *Panther* run. Believe it or not, even after trading torpedoes with us, they seemed like decent guys."

"And girls, right? I heard that blonde Rooskie weapons officer had a crush on you."

"Yeah yeah yeah. You guys got the picture?" Pacino said. "Hurry up, I'm hungry."

"Oh, the XO is in fine form tonight." Vevera rubbed his tummy, smiling.

"What's for midrats?"

"XO ordered hot chili, hot in temperature. He violated the rig for ultraquiet. Said he was tired of cold sandwiches."

"Hey, he does what he wants to also," Pacino said. "Hard to imagine stirring some chili over a gas flame would alert the Russians."

"Anyway, I relieve you, sir," Vevera said.

"I stand relieved. Short Hull?"

"I'm relieved by Mr. Cooper," Short Hull replied.

"Let's hit Quinnivan's midrats," Pacino said.

———————

When Pacino and Short Hull walked into the wardroom, both Executive Officer Quinnivan and Weapons Officer Styxx were laughing.

"Something funny?" Pacino asked.

Quinnivan frowned in reply. "Your report?"

Pacino nodded at Short Hull Cooper.

"Sir, Mr. Pacino and I were properly relieved by Mr. Vevera and Mr. Cooper," Short Hull said formally. "As previously reported, we have a new detect. Sonar thinks it's a supply ship. The BUFF—er, the Omega—is still shut down."

"Have a seat, gentlemen," Quinnivan said, his mirthful expression returning.

Pacino took a seat next to Styxx and put his napkin in his lap while Styxx passed him the bowl of chili. He loaded up on it and grabbed a cornbread from the platter. "You want to share the joke, XO?"

Quinnivan beamed at Pacino. "Some new intelligence from our esteemed weapons officer. Madam Styxx, you want to declassify this for Mr. Pacino?"

"I suppose it's about time, XO." Styxx looked at Pacino, a slight smile on her lips. "So, Patch, that night you spent with me at AUTEC?"

Pacino's spoon froze in mid-air on the way to his mouth. He put it down and looked at Styxx. "Yeah?"

She laughed and said, "We didn't do anything."

"What?"

She nodded. "You were so drunk you passed out at the entrance door to the BOQ. I had to drag you to the elevator and down the hall to my room. And drop you on the bed. And undress you. Have you ever undressed a corpse? You have to roll it to one side, pull off clothes, then roll it back, on and on."

Pacino stared at her. "Really? So how do you explain all the lipstick on my face?" And how would she account for the happy, satisfied look on her face that morning? What had she said to him? *Good morning, tiger.*

Styxx put her face in her hands, laughing and wiping tears from her eyes. "Oh my God, I didn't want you returning to the boat without making it look like you were a conquering hero. Part of my assignment from a certain Royal Navy officer we all know and love."

Quinnivan guffawed, looking pleased with himself.

"But the lipstick stains. You kissed me? When I was out cold?"

"No, dummy," Styxx said. "No way human lips would put that much makeup on your face. I applied it liberally with my lipstick. Took the whole thing. And you bolted out of the room so fast, you didn't even see yourself in the wall mirror."

The other officers were snickering, Dankleff pointing at Pacino and snorting, then coughing as cornbread went down the wrong way.

"And no one even suspected I'd done that," Styxx continued. "You thick-headed males all just assumed Pacino got the lipstick honestly. And no, Bullfrog, that does *not* give you permission to resurrect Pacino's stupid nickname."

It was then the SEAL officers walked in. Pacino felt relief that now the conversation might turn away from him.

"Well, what do you know? Our kick-ass commandos have decided to honor us with their presence," Quinnivan said. "What, did you run out of triple-X rated movies? Everyone, if you haven't met them, this is Commander 'Tiny Tim' Fishman and Lieutenant (j.g.) 'Grip' Aquatong. And speaking of nicknames, Commander Fishman's actual first name is Ebenezer, so, you know. But what about you, Grip?" Quinnivan looked expectantly at Aquatong.

"My actual callsign is 'Autoloader,' except to these assholes I work with. You drop *one* lousy box of grenades, and suddenly—" Aquatong smiled as he took an empty seat. "Anyway, we're here because we heard there was hot food."

"Load up before it's gone," Quinnivan said. "You guys know the old *Vermont* crew, but you may not know Engineer Kelly here or Weapons Officer Styxx. Say hello, people."

Fishman looked over at Kelly and, for the first time in Pacino's memory, smiled. He just said, "Machine. Gun. Kelly."

Engineer Moose Kelly frowned at him. "I hated that nickname. And how did you know it?"

Fishman's smile turned enigmatic. "I had intel, Machine Gun."

Kelly rolled her eyes. "I have to tell you, I like my new name better. Call me Moose."

Fishman raised an eyebrow. "I can't imagine a woman as beautiful as you being called 'Moose,'" he said. "You have a first name?"

Kelly blushed a dark crimson, concentrating on her chili, but she glanced over at Fishman for just a fraction of a second, then just mumbled, "Yeah, my first name is 'Eng.'"

"You are without a doubt the most gorgeous chief engineer I've ever seen."

Lewinsky laughed. "Hey, Tiny Tim. The last chief engineer you saw was *me*."

Kelly's blush got even deeper.

"Wow," Quinnivan said. "I had no idea anyone could make our hard-boiled engineer blush."

The phone handset under the table buzzed, and Quinnivan reached under and pulled it up to his ear. "Command Duty Officer," he said, his voice instantly serious. He listened for a moment. "Very well." He replaced the handset. "Well, people, looks like we're finally seeing some action. The Omega is starting her engineroom."

"XO," Kelly said to Quinnivan, "request to restart our port side."

Quinnivan nodded. "Engineer, you have permission to restart the port side of the engineroom, but get the officer of the deck's order."

"Aye, sir, by your leave, XO." Kelly bolted from her chair and walked out of the room faster than Pacino had ever seen her move.

The phone under the table buzzed again and Quinnivan answered as before. "Junior Officer of the Deck," he said, "restart the port side of the engineroom." He looked at the officers as he hung up. "I'd advise you guys to get some sleep. The Omega will probably be shoving off in the coming hours. I want you all alert when he does."

Back in stateroom three, Pacino took off his coveralls and hung them on his hook as River Styxx walked in and shut the door behind her.

"Sorry about the story, Patch," she said.

Pacino shrugged, trying to act nonchalant. "I guess I should thank you, River," he said.

She just looked at him, a kind expression on her face. "Next time," she said gently, "don't drink so much."

"Good night, Weps," he said as he climbed into his rack, hoping he wasn't blushing as Kelly had.

"Well, I suppose this is farewell and bon voyage," Admiral Gennady Zhigunov said to Captain First Rank Georgy Alexeyev. "Good luck out there."

"Admiral, you're absolutely *sure* you can't send an attack sub to escort us out?" Alexeyev glanced out to the deep water of the fjord. It was very possible that a British or American sub, or even a French nuclear boat, could be lurking off the Kola Peninsula, lying in wait to trail them.

"You know the answer, Georgy. All the Yasen-Ms are in depot-level drydock maintenance for their atmospheric controls troubles. We already lost one submarine from the oxygen generator coming off its foundation just from the vibrations of running flank. And the fix is invasive. It's requiring not one, but two hull cuts. And you know how long it takes to seal a hull cut. The weld quality checks alone take a month."

"But *Arkhangelsk* is out of the drydock. Her atmo mods are complete. You could send her."

Zhigunov shook his head. "*Arkhangelsk* still needs post-drydock sea trials with vibration monitors on all the piping and equipment. We can't lose another sixty-billion-ruble submarine and a trained crew. And even if you forget the human and financial cost—we'd lose the time it takes to build a submarine, Georgy. So you see, yes?"

"An older boat, perhaps? A 971 Shchuka-B? The *Gepard* or *Kuzbass*? Or *Vepr*?"

"That would do you no good. Their sound signatures are many decibels higher than the latest generation American and British subs, and for all we know, the French as well. And their tonal signatures? To modern frequency-filtering sonars, they ring like church bells. Their design was for a decade long past, Georgy. Today, they are only useful as damned expensive training platforms. You and *Losharik* must go out there alone, but don't worry. Sevmash did so many modifications to the *Belgorod* it's almost as stealthy as a new Borei class."

Alexeyev nodded in obedience, but the idea of his crew's lives being in the hands of Sevmash was not a comforting one. "Understood, sir. I just know my crew will ask me the same questions. I needed your answers."

"*Idi s Bogom*," Zhigunov said. "Go with God. Fair winds and following seas, Georgy."

Alexeyev saluted and shook the admiral's hand, then turned and walked over the gangway to the *Belgorod*, saluted the Russian flag aft, glanced at the men removing the shore power cables, and entered the conning tower access hatch.

When Alexeyev had gone below, Admiral Zhigunov lingered on the pier for a long moment, looking at the huge hull of *Belgorod*, her lines singled up, the large yard tugboat already tied up on her seaward side, praying that his words of reassurance to Alexeyev would prove true. Finally, he climbed back into his staff truck and motioned the driver to go.

Alexeyev descended to the upper "zero one" level and emerged through the forward door to the command post, which was full to capacity with watchstanders. He stopped at the chart table and studied it, zooming in to their position at the pier, then zooming back out so he could examine the channel, which skirted the double islands in the fjord. He examined their track out of the fjord, then looked over at the navigator, Captain Third Rank Svetka Maksimov.

"You've laid out the track to the rendezvous?"

"Yes, Captain," Maksimov said. Svetka "*Velikolepnyy*" "Gorgeous" Maksimov was a striking young woman, model-beautiful, even with her hair pulled back in a bun and no makeup on her face. The other officers had been known to tease her about it, but she'd never reacted. As long as Alexeyev had known her, she'd been calm and professional, but quiet. He couldn't remember her ever contributing to the officers' mess conversations.

First Officer Ania Lebedev joined them at the chart table. Alexeyev looked at her and nodded solemnly. For the underway operation, Lebedev would be in the command post, monitoring the watchstanders while Alexeyev and Weapons Officer Sobol would lay to the conning tower's bridge and drive the submarine out on the surface and into the Barents until they reached the dive point.

"It's time, Captain," Lebedev reminded him. She glanced at the captain for a moment. Alexeyev was tall and slender, his formerly black hair now streaked with gray, the gray arriving suddenly on their last mission to the South Atlantic. He was wearing his great coat, his officer's cap clasped under his arm, and still wearing his black eye patch after the loss of his right eye from an infection, also afflicting him in the South Atlantic. He was a strange, quiet officer, Lebedev mused, living deep inside his head, rarely sharing his thoughts with the officers in the mess during meals, only opening up slightly when they were both alone in his stateroom. So far, he had yet to comment on this mission besides the discussion with President Vostov the week before, but Lebedev suspected he might privately have serious doubts about the operation. But as he'd said, they were in business to execute the orders, not formulate them. After what they'd suffered together, Lebedev had gained a deep respect — perhaps bordering on affection — for the enigmatic commanding officer. There was just something about his presence that calmed her, she thought. As long as Alexeyev were here, everything would be okay.

Alexeyev nodded wordlessly and left the command post by the forward door leading to the stairs to the conning tower.

13

Captain First Rank Sergei Kovalov shook out what must be his fifth cigarette in the last fifteen minutes as he stood on the pier waiting for Admiral Zhigunov's staff truck. He looked at his new command, the Project 10831 deep-diving nuclear-powered special salvage submarine AS-31 *Losharik*. It was an eighth the size of his last submarine, the Yasen-M attack submarine *Arkhangelsk*, the boat he'd been pulled off to command *Losharik* for this mission. That had made sense to Admiral Zhigunov, since *Arkhangelsk* was occupied with a long drydock repair availability, which had taken her out of action, and this mission demanded a seasoned submarine commander. But *Losharik* was a freakish submarine, Kovalov thought privately. He'd never give voice to that opinion, not to his crew and not to his wife, but perhaps only to his friend Georgy Alexeyev. The vessel was a deep-diving special purpose boat, designed to dive to 2500 meters and her titanium hull could probably take her several hundreds of meters deeper, to almost three kilometers beneath the surface.

The deep-diving aspect worried Kovalov, giving him recurring nightmares of hull collapse and flooding so far beneath the sea. The boat had no emergency deballasting system, so flooding at depth would likely result in loss of the ship and all hands. And what was perhaps worse was that it carried no weapons. Torpedoes and cruise missiles had always been something of a security blanket for Kovalov. He believed that in an undersea battle, even if he didn't win and went down with the submarine, at least he could fight back. But this boat? Completely unarmed. With the exception of the cradles installed to allow them to carry Status-6 Poseidon torpedoes, the weapons carried on the port and starboard side of the boat, but Poseidons weren't defensive weapons. They were little more than expensive time bombs, Kovalov thought, useless in a fight. He consoled himself that *Losharik* would be docked with *Belgorod*, and *Belgorod* had plenty of defensive and offensive weapons. Thirty Futlyar Fizik-2 torpedoes and ten Kalibr submarine-launched cruise missiles, two of them nuclear-tipped in the hundred kiloton range. The Futlyar units had anti-torpedo settings if needed, and could bring down an incoming American or British torpedo. And, of course, *Belgorod* carried the two Gigantskiy nuclear-tipped torpedoes that had been loaded aboard for this mission, but Kovalov considered them suicide weapons, especially if used under ice. A one megaton warhead? No matter the stand-off range, the shock wave from a weapon that big would deeply damage the firing ship—or sink it outright.

But this mission, not even begun, had impossible challenges. Docking to the submerged *Belgorod* had been attempted twice, and both times had resulted in failure. And unloading an exercise dummy of the Status-6 Poseidon torpedo from *Belgorod* to the carrying cradles of *Losharik* had only been tried once, and they'd dropped the unit to the seafloor of the Barents Sea. At first, it had been thought that *Losharik*, being a deep-diving ship capable of salvage, could retrieve the unit, but her manipulator arms malfunctioned and had to be repaired later by Sevmash. They'd had to abandon the effort, to the extreme disappointment of Northern Fleet Command.

As if reading his thoughts, his first officer, Ivan Vlasenko, strode up on his pre-watch inspection of the ship and said, "Worried about the mission, Captain?" Vlasenko pulled out his own pack and lit a cigarette, some odd French brand his traveling sister-in-law had gotten him.

"I suppose," Kovalov said. "But if there is any good news, it's that sometimes a difficult day in the Navy can distract from a difficult day at home."

Vlasenko nodded seriously, although he himself lived a life without the heavy problems that Kovalov shouldered. "The troubles with Magna?"

"Still giving me the silent treatment. After two years since the, well, the thing." Magna was Kovalov's sixteen-year-old daughter by his first wife Adele. Two years before, when Magna was at the tender age of fourteen, she'd been brought to the apartment by the police, dragged out of a rave party where she had been high on drugs, naked, and having sex with two boys at the same time, a third naked boy watching them. Kovalov's present wife, Ivana, had been apoplectic and panicky over the incident, and they'd applied what discipline they thought appropriate—yelling, grounding her, taking her computer privileges away. But not two weeks later, in the middle of a Saturday night, the police visited again, and again had the same story, except that the drugs were harder, heroin this time, and there were more boys piling on, and Magna didn't care about her parents' disapproval, openly cursing them, waving off any punishment with indifference.

And that had led to what Kovalov mentally called *the grand convening of the wives*. It must be understood, first, that ex-wife Adele and present-wife Ivana absolutely hated each other. Given an advance presidential pardon and a loaded pistol, each would murder the other without a second's reflection. But what had united them was their love for Magna, since Magna was born of Adele but taken care of daily by Ivana. It was Ivana's voice that was the stronger of the two. *How much do you love your daughter, Sergei?* When he'd stated he would do anything for her, Ivana had looked into his eyes with that penetrating look of hers that seemingly could see all the way through him to his back collar and said, *Do you love her enough to hit her?* When he looked confused, Adele had joined in, saying *If she keeps on like this, she'll be in a coffin inside a year. Do you love your daughter enough to beat her to get her attention?* He'd protested that he could never raise a hand to her, but then Ivana doubled down. *We can't do it. We're mothers. We're there to nurture. Shoulders to cry on. You're the father. You're the man. So step up and act like a man. You have to beat her. Hard.* When he had argued that there was no way he could convincingly beat his daughter physically, that he couldn't be an actor, that it would be all over his face that he was reluctant, not angry, the wives had stepped closer to him, pelting him with that weaponized question, *How much do you love your daughter?* He had shut his eyes for five seconds and thought about it. All Magna's life, he had been a gentle father, if anything, being the one who comforted her when she was angry at Adele or Ivana. Magna had always been a daddy's girl, with him as her best friend. There simply was nothing he would not do for his beloved daughter. He'd take a bullet for her. He'd willingly give her both kidneys. And then life had come for him and made this terrible demand. The promiscuity and the drugs, the police had said, all lead to only one future for the girl—she will be found lying in an alley, naked, with needles in her veins, fading away into death or already dead.

How much do you love your daughter, Sergei? Do you love her enough to hit her?

Finally, he had looked at the wives and sadly nodded. "I will do as you ask."

The opportunity had come that weekend while Magna was grounded and against her will was in the truck with Kovalov driving. He started in on her, that her behavior must immediately change. He calculated it would provoke her into cursing at him, and he was correct.

Fuck you, Dad!

As it turned out, feigning anger had not been required. Magna, his adorable little girl, had turned into a possessed demon. *Fuck you, Dad! Fuck you fuck you fuck you*—and he'd felt the anger rise in him, and instead of taming it as he would normally have done, he gave in to it. He made a fist and furiously punched her so hard on the side of her face that her head hit the passenger window, shattering it, glass flying around the car, blood running down her face, and the sound of her pitiful shocked and horrified shrieks sounded like a mortally wounded animal. *How much do you love your daughter, Sergei?* He'd turned the vehicle around and sped her to a clinic, where her scalp beneath her hair had needed a dozen stitches and a large bandage. They'd checked her for a concussion, but other than the cut and the emotional trauma from the punch, she was fine.

But there was nothing fine between him and Magna after that. On returning home with the girl sobbing, half her head shaved, a huge bandage wrapped around her head, both Ivana and Adele had waited for him, both of them in on this little conspiracy, but both had acted shocked and horrified that he had *dared* to lay his hands on Magna. *How could you?* They shot murderous glaring looks at him and shepherded Magna to her room in the back of the apartment. He could hear the wives' low voices comforting her and her wailing loudly, barely able to be calmed. When the wives emerged from her room, their eyes were red and swollen from crying.

"You have to apologize to her," Ivana said.

"What?" he'd said, not believing his ears. "You put me up to this—"

"Shhh!" Ivana hissed. "Never ever mention that this was a plan. This was just something that happened. You got mad and lost your temper. You got that?"

Kovalov nodded seriously. It was never good when his wife's voice sounded like his mother's, he thought. "But is an apology appropriate? Considering what she did?"

"It is now," Adele said. "Trust us. This is the next step."

He walked back to Magna's room, knocked, and went in. She was still sobbing, her shoulders shaking, and she wouldn't look at him. He sat on the bed and tried to touch her arm, but she wailed and retreated to the other side of the bed, crying pitifully.

"Magna," he said sincerely, "I am so sorry I hurt you. I was much more frightened for you than angry, baby. But I will never hurt you again."

She was barely able to be understood as she cried into her pillow, but he made out the words, "Get out! Get away from me!"

Those were the last words his daughter had spoken to him for two years. But the sneaking out, the drugs, the partying, the sex—it all stopped. She went back to studying, her grades rising from failing to exemplary. The clothes she picked out no longer looked suitable for a street hooker, but more of what a serious student would wear. She started to speak to her stepmother about going to the university.

But through it all, there was that black silence. Kovalov's relationship with his daughter was over. He could only interact with her through his wife or his ex-wife, and the pain of it tore his heart out. He tried to console himself that he had *answered* the question, *How much do you love your daughter, Sergei?* He'd saved her, it was true, he thought, but in the same moment he had lost her. She'll come back to you someday, Ivana would say, but he had serious doubts.

And what if this damned mission, this fool's errand, went bad and he didn't return? What would that do to little Magna? Just thinking about it made his eyes moist. He took out a tissue and blew his nose, surreptitiously wiping his eyes.

He looked at Vlasenko, who was on the radio with the yard tug that was tying up to the starboard side of the *Losharik* to tow her out of the bay. Vlasenko put the radio in his belt and shook out another cigarette. "Captain, the reactor is in the power range and the steam plant is started up, keeping the main engine warm by rotating the shaft every few minutes. Systems are nominal and the Second Captain AI has completed all self-checks. We're ready to go as soon as you finish with the admiral."

"How are the hydronauts?" Hydronauts were underwater commandos who reported to GUGI, the Main Directorate of Deep-Sea Research, and would assist outside the hull when it came time to deploy the Status-6 units. Kovalov had met their stand-offish commander, Captain Second Rank Kir Krupkin, a tall, muscular, blonde-haired, blue-eyed, square-jawed officer who had little to say to Kovalov. Kovalov got the impression that Krupkin disapproved of Kovalov's fleshy submariner's body, the rich food and lack of opportunities to exercise leading to a few kilograms around his waist he could well afford to lose. Just another thing to suffer in this mission, Kovalov had thought, and sent Krupkin off with Vlasenko to his and his men's assigned bunks.

"Assholes, as I suppose you'd expect of elite commandos," Vlasenko said. "Once we're aboard *Belgorod*, I imagine we won't be seeing much of them. They'll keep to themselves."

"I'm surprised they didn't just leave port on the *Belgorod*. Why did they want to ship out with us?"

Vlasenko shrugged. "Maybe they just want to get acquainted with the boat."

"They've been training in simulators for a year. Not sure what a ride on the boat gets them at this point. So who's driving us out?" Kovalov should have known the action stations for the underway by heart, but he'd been distracted with all his thoughts about Magna and this operation.

"Systems Officer Trusov will take us out," Vlasenko said.

"Iron Irina," Kovalov said, smiling. Captain Second Rank "Iron Irina" Trusov had been weapons officer of the ill-fated *Novosibirsk*, lost in the Battle of the Arabian Sea, and in her file there had been a citation for her Navy Medal for Distinction in Combat—from her former captain, Yuri Orlov, stating that she'd saved the ship and the crew when everyone had been unconscious. Unfortunately, the ship hadn't stayed saved very long and crew had had to abandon ship in the escape chamber. Yet there was no sign of cockiness, arrogance, or for that matter, trauma, in Trusov's demeanor. She was a serious, calm professional. Unless he'd read her personnel file, he'd never know about the decoration for bravery or the things she'd done on that day of battle. "She'll do a good job."

"Yes, Captain, I know she will," Vlasenko said, glancing down the pier. "Looks like we have company. Sail ho." *Sail ho* was slang for, I detect the approach of a senior officer.

"I'll meet you in the command post," Kovalov said, putting away his cigarettes and stomping on his lit cigarette. He tried to stand straighter as Admiral Zhigunov's staff truck approached, its fender's blue flags with three gold stars flapping in the wind.

Captain First Rank Georgy Alexeyev adjusted his officer's cap, which had been knocked crooked by a sudden breeze. He raised his binoculars to his eyes and glanced down the channel northwest to the unoccupied twin islands at the entrance to *Reika* Zapadnaya Litsa, the fjord that eventually opened into the Barents Sea. The fjord was glassy calm, but if the wind picked up, it wouldn't stay that way long. He looked at the noontime sun, the rays of it making the skin of his face warm, and he took a deep breath, knowing that soon canned air would be the only thing he'd be inhaling, that and his cigarettes. He reminded himself he'd have to kick that habit before they returned home, since Natalia hated the smell of smoke.

"Are we waiting for anything, Deck Officer?" he asked Captain Lieutenant Sobol, the deck officer for the mobilization to sea.

Sobol stood at rigid attention. "*Belgorod* is ready to cast off and leave port, Captain," she said formally in her high-pitched cartoon character voice.

Alexeyev nodded, faintly recalling that she'd already made that report, but he'd been lost in thought, thinking about the icecap. He'd never sailed farther north than the marginal ice zone, but he reassured himself that First Officer Lebedev and Navigator Maksimov had.

"Take us out, Deck Officer," he ordered.

"Aye, Captain," she said, and raised a megaphone to her lips while leaning over the cockpit coaming on the port side, the pier side. "Deck Chief! Cast off all lines!" She watched as Glavny Starshina Maks Alexandr, the auxiliary mechanical systems chief, repeated the order to the line handlers on deck. When the last line was released from its deck cleats and tossed to the pier, Sobol reached under the forward ledge of the cockpit and pulled the air horn lever, and a blasting, booming, earsplitting roar sounded over the slip. She raised the VHF radio to her lips. "Yard Tug Zero Five, take us to center of channel."

The radio blared with the tug captain's reply, "Received, taking you to center of channel and commencing movement to the fjord."

The huge tug's engines throttled up to a growling hum and slowly the massive vessel began to move away from the pier.

"Navigator," Sobol spoke into her microphone connected to the electronics box beneath the windscreen, "Ship is underway, moving to center of channel and commencing tow-out."

"Deck Officer, Navigator, aye," the speaker on the box crackled with Svetka Maksimov's voice.

Alexeyev watched as the piers of the base slowly moved by. Once in the wider part of the channel, south of the twin islands, a second tug, that had been waiting at idle, moved over to their port side.

"Submarine Captain, Tug Five Six, request to tie up to your port side," Sobol's radio blared. Sobol glanced back at Alexeyev and he nodded at her.

"Tug Five Six, tie up on our port side," Sobol ordered on the radio.

With the tugs shepherding *Belgorod* out, there was little to do on the conning tower, Alexeyev thought. He would have preferred to drive the boat out without tugs, but with over thirty-two megatons of nuclear weapons onboard, it made more sense to play it safe and get towed out. It was only ten nautical miles to open water from here. The tugs turned them in the channel when the conning tower moved beyond the twin islands and they proceeded at dead slow on the new northeast course into the deep fjord. The fjord was serpentine, going from northwest at the pier to the twin islands, then northeast past the islands, turning a corner to go due north, then due east, then finally due north. After their dead-slow-ahead journey, taking an hour-and-a-half, the coastline ended and began to fade behind them. After another two miles into open water, they had emerged into the Barents Sea.

"Captain, request to cast off the tugs," Sobol asked Alexeyev.

"Shove off the tugs, Deck Officer," Alexeyev ordered.

"Tug Zero Five and Five Six, take in your lines and clear the submarine, and thank you."

The tug captains acknowledged, *Belgorod*'s deck crew tossing over the lines. The tugs backed away from the hull, each honking their air horns twice in a gesture of farewell, then turned to return to base.

Alexeyev leaned over the side of the cockpit on both sides, checking that the deck crew had rotated all the cleats flush into the hull and had gone below.

"Deck Officer, Navigator," the electronics box's speaker rattled, "deck crew has cleared the deck and gone below. The hatches are shut and dogged. Ship is ready to proceed to the dive point."

"Boatswain," Sobol said into her microphone, "ahead two thirds, steer course zero one five."

The breeze of their passage picked up, the flag raised aft of them starting to flap in the wind.

"Take her to full speed, Deck Officer. I'm laying below," Alexeyev said, taking off his cap before it blew off.

"Full speed, aye, Captain," Sobol said.

Alexeyev entered the command post and found Lebedev.

"Any sonar contacts?" he asked her.

Lebedev shook her head. "We had a good sonar look around when the tugs were clear before the speed increase. No contacts. We're alone in the sea, sir."

Alexeyev nodded. "Good."

———————

When he opened his eyes, he was on his small bed upstairs. The room was lit by a rotating globe that projected small points like stars on the ceiling and walls, but also by a blinking string of Christmas lights that Mommy had placed where the walls met the ceiling.

Mommy was downstairs screaming at Daddy. She was very angry. Daddy was trying to calm her down, speaking to her in a low voice. None of their words could be made out, only their emotions.

He got out of his bed and sat on the floor near the door, his legs crossed underneath him. He could hear better here. Mommy was shouting that it was almost Christmas and Daddy was supposed to stay home.

He heard heavy footfalls on the stair treads and his door opened slowly. Daddy stood there in his officer's uniform, the three gold stripes on his sleeves, his submarine emblem above his ribbons, a circular pin below them that he had explained was given to him because he was the captain of a submarine. He put down a big duffel bag and knelt down.

"Anthony," he said gently. "I have to go away. I'm sorry. I'm going to miss Christmas."

Anthony Pacino looked up at his father, feeling tears fill his six-year-old eyes.

"No. Don't go."

"I have to, Son."

Anthony narrowed his eyes at his father. "Are you going to the North Pole again?"

The elder Pacino hesitated as if he were carefully trying to choose his words. Finally he said, "Yes. I'm going to the North Pole."

"Is there trouble?"

Again his father paused. "It's a bad situation, Anthony. It's very important I go up there with my submarine."

Anthony drilled his eyes into his father's. "It's the Omega, isn't it? Omega unit one?"

Commander Michael Pacino drew back in surprise. "What do *you* know about that? And 'unit one'—there's only one. The Russians named it the Omega because it's the ultimate submarine. There's no unit two."

Anthony nodded. "You're going to sink it, aren't you?"

"I should go," the older man said.

"It has those torpedoes, doesn't it? Nuclear-tipped? One megaton warhead? A meter in diameter, can go sixty knots for an hour, right?"

Michael Pacino stood, crossing his arms over his chest, and Anthony also stood, still looking into his father's eyes.

"We call them 'Magnum' torpedoes," Commander Pacino said haltingly.

"The Russians call them *Gigantskiys*," Anthony said.

"How do you know what the Russians call them?"

"Perestroika," the younger Pacino said. "Means 'openness' in Russian. We don't have to use NATO code names anymore."

"I have to go," Michael Pacino said again.

"Be careful, Daddy. And good hunting."

Michael Pacino stared at his son for a long moment, a look of shock on his face before he withdrew through the door. Again there were footsteps on the stairs, getting fainter. The front door of the house opened and shut. Daddy started the engine of his old Corvette and the engine roared and the tires shrieked as he drove off.

Anthony Pacino stood at the door and slowly opened it. But on the other side of the door, it wasn't the upstairs hallway with the gallery view of the beach house's main level, but the control room of a submarine. Anthony looked down at himself. He was still wearing his favorite pajamas, the ones with the dolphins swimming together. His feet were bare. No one in the room seemed to think it odd that a bare-footed six-year-old in pajamas stood in their control room.

Rachel Romanov noticed him standing beside her and wordlessly passed him a cordless, one-eared headset. He put it on and immediately heard the voice.

"Fire, fire, fire! Fire in forward compartment middle level! We've got a bad fire—"

"I'm going below to take charge at the scene," Romanov said to him, pulling on her emergency air breathing mask.

"No, Rachel, don't go!" Anthony said. But by then she was gone.

As the room filled with thick smoke, he heard himself—as if from a distance—bark words into his boom microphone. "Maneuvering, Conn, report your status!"

As if answering him, he heard the sound of a bunk curtain being jerked aside.

"Why, the reactor is in natural circulation and the electric plant's in a normal full-power lineup," River Styxx's voice said, her face close to his, but it was in shadow in the dim light of the stateroom. "Bad dream, Patch? Again?"

Pacino groaned as he climbed out of his rack. "Oh, damn, I'm so tired."

"Complaints get you nowhere on a submarine," Styxx said. "Now put on your game face. We're manning battlestations. The BUFF is underway. Captain's about to initiate trail ops."

207

The rigged-for-ultraquiet control room was lit by dim red lights and the green glow from the BSY-1 battlecontrol attack center on the starboard side, the sonar stacks on the port side and the array of flatpanels at the pilot and copilot ship control station. Short Hull Cooper stood at the starboard side of the command console and handed Pacino a headset. Forward of the command console, Executive Officer Quinnivan stood, looking over the attack center consoles. To Pacino's left, between the command console and the navigation plot, Captain Seagraves paced between the sonar consoles and the attack center. He saw Pacino and gave him a slight nod. Lieutenant Varney, the off-going officer of the deck, approached and stood between the command console and the captain, facing Pacino.

"Master One, the Omega," Varney said to Pacino, "bears one eight zero and is proceeding north toward our position. Sonar thinks it's being towed by two tugs and thinks its screws are shut down."

"Range to the BUFF?" Pacino asked, looking down at the navigation display that was selected on the command console.

"Mr. Pacino," Quinnivan said over his shoulder. "Refer to the contact as Master One, if you don't mind."

"Sorry, XO," Pacino muttered, rubbing his eyes, still feeling half asleep. The dream had left him like a vapor blown away by the wind, but he remembered screaming out about the status of the propulsion plant before Styxx woke him.

"Fifteen hundred yards, give or take," Varney said. "We don't have a good TMA solution on him, but the channel is only so big, so the contact's bearing and time since the turn led to that estimated range."

"Maneuvering's status?"

"Reactor's in nat circ, normal full-power lineup," Varney said. "Answering bells on both propulsion turbine generators. Main motor is warm."

"Ship status?"

"Hovering at two hundred feet. Both thrusters rigged out to allow us to point south to the contact."

"Our intentions?"

"Let the Omega drive toward us and pass overhead," Varney said. "Once it's out a few hundred yards, put on turns to follow it out of the fjord. Once the tugs are clear, we'll get her sound signature."

"Are there plans to do an underhull?" Pacino asked.

"Captain will decide in a few minutes."

"Weapon status?"

"Tubes one and two powered up, outer doors open. Just waiting for us to send them target information. So, you got the picture?"

"I've got it. I relieve you, sir," Pacino replied.

"I stand relieved," Varney said, then looked at the captain. "Sir, I've been properly relieved as officer of the deck by Mr. Pacino." He stepped over to the Pos Two seat at the attack center and climbed into its seat, his battlestations assignment to determine the magical package of information about the Omega, her range, course, and speed, the data called *the solution*. With a solution of medium quality, they could fire a torpedo at her and be assured of a fairly high probability of a kill. With a good solution, they could count on putting her on the bottom.

Pacino looked at Captain Seagraves and reported, "Captain, I've relieved Mr. Varney as officer of the deck." He looked at Quinnivan, whose battle station was firecontrol coordinator, or just coordinator. "Coordinator, are battlestations manned?"

Quinnivan spun to look at Pacino and bowed. "Officer of the Deck, battlestations are manned."

The sounds came through the hull then, the pulsing whoosh of the tugboat screws and the thrumming of their powerful engines, the noise building up in intensity, getting closer every second. Pacino waited with the battlestations control room crew, holding his breath. The noise reached its peak, moving from dead ahead to directly overhead as the tugs and the colossal submarine sailed over them and continued northward in the channel, now beginning to fade astern.

"Pilot," Pacino said to Dankleff in the ship control station, "take charge of your thrusters and rotate the ship to heading north."

Dankleff acknowledged, reporting a few seconds later, "Officer of the Deck, ship's heading is zero zero zero."

"Pilot, rig in both thrusters. All ahead one third, maintain depth two hundred."

Dankleff acknowledged again. The sounds of the tug screws and engines were diminishing ahead of them.

"Kick up your speed, OOD," Seagraves said. "He's fading."

"Aye, sir. Pilot, all ahead two thirds."

"Master One is drifting right," Senior Chief Sonarman Albanese reported from the number one sonar stack. "He's turning."

"Nav?" Pacino asked, looking at Lewinsky, who stood at the navigation plot.

"One hundred yards to the turn point, OOD," he said. "New course, zero four five."

"Very well," Pacino said, zooming into his chart display to show the northeast portion of the channel.

"Mark the turn to course zero four five," Lewinsky said.

"Pilot, right full rudder, steady course zero four five."

"Eighteen hundred yards on this course, OOD," Lewinsky said. "Next course will be zero nine zero."

"Very well, Nav," Pacino said. "Sonar, any sign of Master One using her own screws?"

"Officer of the Deck, Sonar, no." Albanese said. "Master One bears zero four five. Signal-to-noise ratio is steady."

Pacino nodded. The tug sounds were constant, so they were at the right engine order to match the speed of the tugs and the BUFF, the Omega being towed out at eight knots. Pacino waited impatiently for the turn point.

"Mark the turn to zero nine zero," Lewinsky said. "Three thousand yards on this course."

The navigator guided them through two more turns until they were headed north. The chart showed that they were almost clear of the coastline and that the fjord was fading behind them.

"They should be cutting the tugs loose any time now," Seagraves said.

But for another fifteen minutes, the tugs continued towing the Omega northward out to sea, until finally Albanese reported, "Master One's tugboats have shut down."

"Pilot," Pacino called, "all stop, hover at present depth."

"All stop and hover at two hundred feet, Pilot aye, and Maneuvering answers, all stop."

After five minutes, Albanese spoke again. "Tugs have restarted, bearings diverging from Master One. Tugs are heading back to the barn."

"Very well, Sonar," Pacino said.

The sounds of the tug screws and engines came close again, passed overhead, then faded astern.

"Master One startup," Albanese called. "Master One is making way on two seven-bladed screws."

"Turn count, Sonar?" Pacino asked.

Albanese listened and manipulated his panel. "Master One is making six zero RPM, both screws."

"Captain, do you want a TMA maneuver?" Pacino asked. TMA was target motion analysis, a way to get a contact's range by using passive sonar and parallax geometry by driving the ship back and forth across the line-of-sight to the contact. It was slow and would take at least twelve minutes for an accurate range determination. They couldn't hit the target with an active sonar pulse or it would give away that they were following him, and it would be risky to raise the periscope and use a laser rangefinder, since the Omega's crew might detect the laser. One of the prime directives of the submarine force was, *remain undetected.*

"No time, OOD. Just speed up to eight knots and follow him. We'll keep an eye on his signal-to-noise ratio."

"Aye, Captain. Pilot, all ahead two thirds," Pacino ordered. He checked the bulkhead chronometer. For a long ten minutes, they followed the Omega as he cruised slowly on the surface.

"OOD, Sonar, Master One's turn count is increasing. He's speeding up. I have two one zero turns." Albanese turned to look at Seagraves. "He's bugging out, Captain."

"Take it up to full, OOD," Seagraves said to Pacino.

"Pilot, all ahead full." He looked at Seagraves. "So, no underhull, Captain?"

"Not at this speed, Mr. Pacino. He may be headed to a rendezvous point with his deep-diver sub. Let's see what he does."

"Aye, sir. At least he's loud on the surface, Captain. Signal-to-noise looks good."

"Don't jinx it, Mr. Pacino," Seagraves said, smiling at Pacino.

14

"Good news, Mr. President," Tonya Pasternak said to Dmitri Vostov. "The terrorist attack seems to have created sympathy with the people. Your poll numbers are still growing, now up eight percent since the disaster."

"What's our lead?" he asked, downing the last of the morning's tea.

"About four points, sir."

"I want to see the raw data," Vostov said.

"It's on your desk, sir, let me look." Pasternak stood from the chair in front of Vostov's massive mahogany desk and stood beside his chair, looking through the files she'd placed there that morning, but it was buried in what seemed fifty other files.

"While you do that, I'm going to the restroom," Vostov said. He cursed mentally. It seemed like his bladder got smaller every day. It was down to an endurance of three hours now. It was at the point that he had to visit the men's room just before his official workday began at eight am, then make sure he made another visit before eleven o'clock, or he'd suffer through the pre-lunch meetings. He stood and left Pasternak to rifle through the paperwork on his desk. Vostov hated computers and wouldn't use one himself. He left that to Pasternak. He'd rather read a printout than a glowing computer screen. Pasternak had once chuckled that his love of paper and hatred of screens was a characteristic of people his age.

Vostov made his way to the large side door of the office suite that opened into an ornate bathroom. He stepped up to the urinal and unzipped, shutting his eyes and allowing himself a moment to think about his four-point lead going into the election. What was it, forty-eight days away? Could he maintain that lead, or open it up even further?

In the office suite, Pasternak stood erect at the desk, consternation crossing her features. Where was that report she'd printed out for the president? As if to cover all the bases, she decided to look into his solid gold wastebasket, the rubbish bin a relic of the era of the Tsars. It must weigh twenty kilograms, she thought. Vostov used it for disposal of whatever papers he'd decided he was done with, regardless of their classification. It fell to the SBP guards to empty the trash can and segregate the classified documents for shredding and burning. The can was half full of papers. She reached down for a stack of printouts, careful to keep her hands away from the soggy tissues Vostov had used to blow his nose into earlier.

In the restroom, Vostov had zipped back up and was washing his hands when the booming explosion from his office threw him across the room and into the decorative tile mosaic on the wall. His head hit the tile, and as his body collapsed, he left a blood trail all the way to the floor.

Captain First Rank Sergei Kovalov knocked gently on the stateroom suite door, wondering if he were blushing.

The door was immediately opened by Captain Third Rank Svetlana Anna, who smiled slightly and motioned him in.

"Good evening, Captain. I was pleasantly surprised to get your note."

Svetlana Anna was dressed as he'd requested, wearing a simple skirt and business jacket with a silk blouse underneath, with stylish black pumps. She looked like she could be walking into a conference room at an attorney's office. Her chestnut hair was combed straight, coming down to her shoulders, with the slightest hint of wavy curls. Her face was sculpted, her forehead smooth, her arched brows accentuating her deep brown almond-shaped eyes, her curving nose and strong cheekbones leading to full red lips. Her complexion was clear, a few freckles gracing her nose and cheeks. Her jawline was straight, her throat long and graceful. Kovalov could see how, with her stunning natural beauty, she had succeeded in the ranks of the test wives. Anna was the commander of the test wives and had told him in reply to his note that at her advanced old age of thirty-three, she no longer entertained clients herself, but merely supervised the performance of her younger subordinates and watched out for any problems arising from having comfort women—or the more politically proper term, test wives—embarked onboard a combat vessel. She had written Kovalov that she functioned as the madam or the *mamasan*. But he had repeated his request to just see her.

"I suppose it was an unusual request, Madam Anna."

"Call me Svetlana."

"Svetlana then," Kovalov said, standing awkwardly by the door. "And call me Sergei."

"Please, sit, Sergei." Anna pointed to an area with two large comfortable chairs clustered with a coffee table between them, a small couch on the other side of the coffee table. "May I call for tea?"

Kovalov sank into one of the chairs, thinking this was a small corner of comforting luxury aboard this otherwise all-business naval vessel, as was Svetlana Anna.

"I have no watches to stand until we may need to undock under the ice. So I was imagining something stronger."

Anna smiled at him gently, her teeth small and white. She really had a beautiful smile, Kovalov thought, but again reminded himself that that should come as no surprise, as she was the military's version of a call girl.

"I have Tsarskaya and Beluga Gold," she laughed, "for such special occasions. I've never hosted anyone over the rank of captain lieutenant, so we should celebrate."

"I don't suppose you have scotch, do you?"

Anna smiled. "Would Glenmorangie 1999 do?"

Kovalov raised his eyebrows. "Good God, absolutely." That scotch would cost months of his salary, he thought. Probably reserved for a visiting admiral—or the president himself.

Anna went to a credenza and pulled out a crystal decanter and two crystal glasses and poured for them both.

Kovalov raised his glass to her and said, "to fallen comrades."

She closed her eyes solemnly for a moment, then sipped the scotch and put her glass down. Kovalov kept his glass in his hand.

"I thought we could talk," Kovalov said, haltingly. He felt in the breast pocket of his submarine coveralls. "May I smoke?"

"Of course, Sergei."

Anna put an ornate crystal ash tray on the table, then sat back, crossed her shapely legs, and looked at him with just a trace of amusement on her face as he fumbled to find his lighter. His hand shook as he held the flame to the cigarette.

"Forgive me. I am nervous."

"You can talk to Svetlana. For as long as you need, I am yours." She tried to give him a significant glance, but he'd looked down, concentrating on lighting his cigarette, finally getting it lit. He blew a cloud of smoke to the overhead. She had the impression he was almost trying to hide inside a veil of smoke, but hiding from what?

"I suppose I am here to experience feminine acceptance. Comfort. Encouragement. Affection. Even if those things are manufactured or fake."

"My emotions and reactions are always genuine, Sergei," she said, sipping the scotch. "I don't act. I don't have to. I am never with a man for whom I harbor the slightest distaste. I am only with gentlemen I like. Privilege of rank, I imagine." She smiled at him again, trying to make him feel at ease. "Although it has been two years since I actually hosted a client. My usual function is to find a personality match between the man and one of the test wives reporting to me. But you asked for me specifically. I suppose I should ask you why?"

Sergei nodded, taking a gulp of the scotch. "You're the same age as my second wife. I can't imagine I would gain much comfort from the company of a nineteen-year-old, who is only a little older than my little girl." An expression of agony briefly twisted Kovalov's features.

216

"Tell me, Sergei. Is there trouble between you and your wife? Did she gain weight? Lose her looks?"

"Oh no," Kovalov said. "Ivana is a gorgeous, striking woman." He laughed, but it came out as a bitter kind of noise. "I suppose she has looks that could have served her well if she had wanted to come into your world."

"Go on." Anna gave Sergei an encouraging look, leaning slightly forward in her chair.

"The problem is that she has turned cold to me. I believe she stopped seeing me as a man. She lost respect for me. It came from my parenting of my daughter from my first marriage." He took another sip and coughed as it went down the wrong way. "She thinks I'm easily manipulated by my daughter. I should say she *used* to think that. Something terrible happened."

Slowly, Kovalov told the tale of striking Magna and the agonizing fallout from that single desperate act of fatherly discipline. Svetlana Anna hung on his words, encouraging him when it became overwhelming for him, until finally the story was over.

"So now?" Anna asked. "Your Ivana no longer wants to be with you? Sexually?"

Kovalov nodded. "But it's more than that. She won't speak to me. She won't even look me in the eye. Anyone visiting my house would tell you the marriage is long over."

Anna moved over to the loveseat. "Join me here, Sergei. Allow me to put my arm around you. Would that be acceptable?"

Slowly, Kovalov stood, put out his fifth cigarette and stepped to the small couch and sat beside Svetlana Anna. He could feel the soft warmth of her body. He shut his eyes for a moment, luxuriating in the sensation of feeling the touch of an understanding woman. A woman who had no hatred or contempt for him.

"You know, it wouldn't be so difficult if I'd lost my feelings for Ivana, but I am still deeply in love with her. I know it's over. My relationship with her. And with Magna."

Anna kissed Sergei's neck softly, just for a moment. "Your daughter will come back to you. Little girls always do. I didn't speak to my own father for almost five years. Today we are close." She took Kovalov's hand, interlacing her fingers between his. "Sergei, we can move to the bed if you would like."

"Can we stay like this? Just for a while?"

"Of course." She stroked his shoulder while she held his hand. Kovalov's eyes slowly shut as he felt her touch.

"This is wonderful," he said.

The slight sound of a buzzer came from the wall behind Anna. "Do you mind, Sergei? I have to answer. There could be trouble with one of the test wives."

He opened his eyes and nodded, finding his glass and emptying it.

"Yes, he is," she said quietly into the phone handset. "I'll tell him." She hung up and looked at Kovalov. "It was the command post. Captain Alexeyev requested your presence there."

Kovalov stood. "I suppose it is all for the best that we didn't go any further," he said sadly.

"There's always another time," Anna smiled at him. "Write me on the system and I will clear my schedule for you."

"I will," he said, hoping the scotch wouldn't be detectable on his breath. It was too bad smoking was not allowed in the command post.

Far down the passageway, past the retracted ladder to the escape chamber, he passed the door of the captain's stateroom, then the first officer's. He opened the aft door to the command post and walked in.

Captain Georgy Alexeyev stood at the number one periscope on the starboard side by the tactical console lineup of the battlecontrol system.

"Hello, Georgy," Kovalov said from over Alexeyev's shoulder.

"Ah, Sergei. I thought you might want to see the icepack. We're departing the marginal ice zone and diving under complete ice coverage. One last look at blue sky, yes?"

Kovalov nodded and took the periscope, the rubber eyepieces of the optics warm from Alexeyev's use. He put his hands on the horizontal grips. The left one could change the optical magnification. The right could tilt the view up or down. The deep blue waves of the Arctic Ocean rolled slowly toward the view. In the middle distance was an ice landscape of a thousand colors of white, glinting in the stark sunshine of the cloudless evening, at a latitude where the sun never set in the summer months. A double-peaked mountain range presided over the ice, the valley between them deep but its low point at what seemed at least ten meters higher than the periscope view. Kovalov rotated the scope to look behind them, seeing a few icebergs floating free, most small, two of them fairly large. He returned the view to directly ahead of them.

"Distance to the icepack?" he asked.

Alexeyev said to the watch officer, "configure, energize, and test the under-ice sonar."

Watch Officer Sobol gave the command to Sonar Officer Valerina Palinkova, who stood at the under-ice sonar stack at the forward centerline of the room. As her panel lit up, the large flatpanel displays on the forward bulkhead came on, showing only a deep blue.

Palinkova manipulated her controls and sent out a test pulse. The sound was a pure bell-tone ping for slightly less than a second, the ping a high-pitched sound audible to the naked ear in the room. After a second, another ping sounded, then a third.

"High frequency tested," Palinkova said. "Energizing low frequency."

In between the high-pitched pings, a lower bell-tone sounded, then continued, the high and low tones alternating. On Palinkova's display, repeated on the bulkhead flatpanels, a faint white rectangle appeared at the top of the screen.

"Distance to the icepack, a little over one nautical mile, sir," Palinkova announced.

"Your scope, Georgy," Kovalov said, returning the instrument to Alexeyev. "Did you transmit to Northern Fleet?"

"I did. Admiral Zhigunov knows we're entering total ice coverage. The last he'll hear from us in a long while, if all goes well."

"Let us pray it does."

"Agreed," Alexeyev said, snapping up the periscope grips and reaching for the hydraulic control lever in the overhead. "Watch Officer, lowering number one scope." The optics module silently lowered into the periscope well, the smooth stainless steel pole rolling downward until it stopped with a thump. "Scope retracted. Reduce speed to ahead one third, make revolutions for three knots." He walked forward to the under-ice sonar console, crossing his arms and watching Sonar Officer Palinkova operate the system.

———————

"Make my depth six five feet, Pilot aye," Lieutenant Dankleff reported from the ship control console.

"Look-around number one scope," Lieutenant Pacino said to the room.

"Speed four knots, depth one hundred feet, on the way to six five feet."

"Very well," Pacino answered. "Raising number one scope." The flatpanel on the command console lit up blue, shining brightly in the rigged-for-red control room. Pacino rotated the view while training the scope upward, making sure the Omega hull was not above them, despite sonar believing him to be eight hundred yards in front of them. The display got lighter as Dankleff flew them out of the depths toward periscope depth. Eventually Dankleff called that they were at seventy feet, and the view foamed as it came out of the water and dried off in the sunshine.

"Six five feet, Officer of the Deck," Dankleff barked.

In the distance, the icecap and its twin mountains towered over them. Pacino rotated the view quickly in a circle, but they were alone in the sea with the exception of a few icebergs floating free in the marginal ice zone. "Icecap in sight."

"Take a laser range," Captain Seagraves ordered.

"Laser range aye. Pacino uncovered a toggle switch and flipped it quickly up and back down and replaced the cover. "Range, one thousand eight hundred yards." He looked at Seagraves. "You still want to keep the under-ice sonar set secured, Captain?"

"Lower your scope and take her back to two hundred, Mr. Pacino," Seagraves said.

Back at depth, Seagraves looked over at the sonar stack lineup. "I'm convinced our under-ice sonar could be detected by the Omega's passive sonar. Let's close the distance to him and follow him under the ice. You think you can do that?"

"Yes, Captain," Pacino said. "Our signal-to-noise ratio is strong and we have good contact on his under-ice sonar pings."

"Master One's turn count is slowing," Senior Chief Albanese reported from the number one sonar console. "Looks like he's slowing to three zero RPM."

"Pilot, all ahead one third, turns for three knots," Lieutenant Pacino ordered. He looked at Captain Seagraves. "Sir, request to launch the code three SLOT."

A "SLOT" was a one-way radio transmitter buoy ejected from a signal ejector—a small device resembling a torpedo tube—and would wait the input time delay, then transmit the message in a burst communication to the overhead CommStar satellite, then sink. The message *code three* indicated the Omega was proceeding under the polar icecap and that the USS *New Jersey* remained in trail and was undetected by the Russian.

Seagraves nodded. "Launch the SLOT."

"Nav-E.T., launch the SLOT," Pacino commanded.

"SLOT is away," the navigation electronics technician reported.

"That's the last anyone will hear from us for a while," Pacino remarked, more to himself than Junior Officer of the Deck Cooper.

From the overhead, a strange noise could be heard, getting slightly louder. It was an eerie groan.

"Sounds like a ghost," Pacino said. "An unhappy one."

Seagraves nodded. "We've moved under total ice cover. That's the sounds of the ice shifting. It'll get louder. Mr. Pacino, I want you to bump the number one periscope out of the sail, just enough to expose the optronics," Seagraves said. "Squadron thinks in infrared mode, we can see the hull of the Omega. Or at least his reactor plant components. If that doesn't work, we can switch to visual spectrum and light up the surroundings with the deck and sail under-ice lights."

"Bump up number one, aye," Pacino acknowledged, uncovering the hydraulics toggle switch cover and pushing the hydraulic valve to the UP position for just a half second. The screen came to life, but the view was dim, just the underside of the ice over their heads.

"Mark the bearing to Master One," Pacino called to the sonar operator, Senior Chief Albanese.

"Master One bearing, zero four eight."

"Training the scope to zero four eight," Pacino said. The captain looked over Pacino's shoulder. There was nothing but darkness.

"Light up the infrared," Seagraves ordered.

Pacino hit the IR button and the seascape came into view, ice above them, a pressure ridge to the right of them, and ahead of them in the distance, a heat bloom, showing up on the screen as a series of red shapes. He increased the magnification. Around the red shapes was the slightest indication of a cylindrical envelope around them.

"I have Master One on IR," Pacino said. He hit the switch that projected the view on the control room starboard side's flatpanel display so everyone in the room could see it. He smiled at Short Hull Cooper. "This is turning out to be easier than I thought."

"Don't get cocky, Mr. Pacino," Seagraves said, but he was smiling just slightly.

"Well, people, allow me to gavel this weekly meeting of the Poseidon committee to order," President Vito Paul Carlucci said, taking his end seat in the Situation Room of the White House.

He seemed in a better mood than the last two meetings on the subject, National Security Advisor Michael Pacino noted to himself.

"What do we know?" the president asked, getting right to business.

CIA Director Margo Allende projected her pad computer to the room's large displays, the projection showing the earth from high above the north pole. "The red line shows the path of the Omega II as it left its base near Murmansk in the Kola Peninsula. The red 'X' not far from the coast, in open water, is where the deep-diver sub docked with the Omega when both were submerged. The USS *New Jersey* reported that the docking was conducted with no problems."

Pacino felt a lurch in his stomach whenever Anthony's submarine was mentioned.

"First time," Office of Naval Intelligence Rear Admiral Frieda Sutton said. "They've never been able to do that successfully before. Not with the Omega submerged. They seem to have fixed their artificial intelligence's ability to hover the submarine."

"From there," Allende continued, "the Omega proceeded northward and exited the Barents Sea and entered the Arctic Ocean. She passed under complete ice coverage two hours ago, as reported by the *New Jersey*. It was *New Jersey*'s final transmission before going into radio silence."

"And," Carlucci said, squinting at the display, "what do we think this thing, this Omega, is doing?"

"Her course would seem to take her just slightly wide of the North Pole on the Russian side," Sutton said. "Director Allende, could you plot the extrapolation of her course?"

"If it keeps going like this, Mr. President," Allende said, "its course would bring it to the Bering Strait and into the Pacific."

There was silence in the room for a long moment.

"Now, why the hell would it do that?" Carlucci asked.

"All our intelligence intercepts mentioned carrying the Poseidon weapons to U.S. east coast ports," NSA Director Foster Nickerson said. "So heading to the Pacific is off-script."

"Maybe Vostov is calling an audible," Pacino said. "Maybe he's decided to plant them off our west coast ports."

"Maybe," Allende said. "But who knows what he's thinking at this point? He's survived two assassination attempts in the last month. Those experiences may be warping his judgement."

"Two?" Pacino asked. "I only heard about his office bomb."

"Presidential helicopter was sabotaged," DIA Chief General Rogers said. "Ball bearings were put into the gearbox. But the mechanism to spit them into the works was supposed to wait till the chopper was at a thousand meters. Something went wrong and instead the bearings were injected at an altitude of one meter. Chopper landed safely. The mechanics involved all disappeared. Probably by the FSB."

"Or they were disappeared by whoever led the conspiracy," Allende said. "And as far as the office explosion, we lost our listening devices in Vostov's office. There was no mention of the Pacific Ocean in any of our sound intercepts. Can you confirm that, General Nickerson?"

The NSA director cleared his throat. "That's correct, Madam Director. As of the day of the explosion, we only heard about the Atlantic coast as a potential drop-off point for the Poseidons."

"So now what?" Carlucci said. "Do we do what the cancer doctors call 'watchful waiting'?"

"Sir, if I may?" Pacino said, glancing up and seeing Vice President Karen Chushi entering the room and walking toward her seat at the end opposite the president. She moved slowly with the aid of a cane and was obviously struggling just to make the twenty steps to her seat. She looked so sick he could barely believe that she'd decided to show up for the meeting. Her face was gray and her features were twisted with pain.

"Please, Patch. What's on your mind?"

"Based on the fact that the Omega is carrying offensive nuclear weapons with the intention of placing them inside American territorial waters, and based on the fact that it has transited under complete ice cover, and on the fact that a thousand bad things can happen to a nuclear sub under the ice with no one knowing what happened," Pacino said, coughing and clearing his throat, two thoughts slamming into his mind at the same time, that he himself had gone down under the icecap, and that Anthony was there *right now*. Not a few hundred yards from a killer submarine, an improved version of the one that had defeated Pacino in combat.

"Go on, Admiral." Carlucci said. Pacino imagined the president knew what he'd say next.

224

Panic Switch

"I respectfully recommend we sink the Omega before it emerges from under the ice."

15

Vice President Karen Chushi was shouting while struggling to stand up, leaning heavily on her cane.

"Are you out of your goddamned mind? Seriously?" she screamed at Pacino. "You're going to shoot at a Russian warship during peacetime? Are you aware that's an act of war? Against a goddamned nuclear *superpower*?" Chushi had finally gained her feet. She picked up her cane and pointed it at Admiral Pacino. "You're a goddamned warmonger, Pacino. And *you!*" Her cane pointed to Carlucci, causing his Secret Service detail to flinch, but he waved them to back off. "This is what happens when you bring in a goddamned warmonger to run national security! And you know, there's no need to do every goddamned thing this man says!" Her accusatory cane pointed back at Pacino. "Admiral Pacino, how much of your motivation is driven by revenge for that first Omega sub you shot at under the icecap? And lost to? With the loss of your submarine and every soul onboard except *you*. Yeah, I got access to the goddamned file, Admiral, I know. And how much of your motivation is that your little warmonger son is on that *New Jersey* submarine? Because, if you strike at the Omega now, and let's say you get the drop on it, the Omega sinks, little Pacino Junior won't be in danger anymore, will he? Well, will he?"

Chushi pointed her cane at Allende, who was staring at the vice president with her mouth hanging open in shock. "And *you*, Madam CIA Director, this is ultimately *your* goddamned fault! You and your shady organization did this. Oh, look at the expression on your face, *so* innocent. Yeah, I said it. You nefarious spooks at CIA planted information into the Russian's intelligence agencies that prompted this whole Poseidon mess, didn't you? Isn't it true, Madam Allende, that your double agents, or your electronic so-called 'pipelines,' funneled data to the Russians that was patently false, right? You made the goddamned Russians believe that America had mined all their harbors with two megaton nuclear mines, didn't you? Poor Vostov is called into a meeting and shown a map with little atomic symbols placed in every port, from Murmansk to Rybachiy to Vladivostok to St. Petersburg to goddamned Kaliningrad. How many megatons did you convince the Russians that you'd planted in their territorial waters, Madam Allende? Forty? Fifty? Seventy? And what the hell else was Vostov to do after that provocation, from those lies that *you* planted, which he obviously believed, but deploy his own nuclear munitions?"

"Madam Vice President, we did no such thing," Allende said, stammering.

"And I should believe you? You and your people lie for a living. Oh, I know about your disinformation pipelines, Madam CIA Director Allende. You made the Russians believe in the 80s that the Strategic Defense Initiative missile shield worked and was tested out with a perfect record. You sent fake messages back and forth, messages you knew the Russians were intercepting, that since the missile shield worked, that Star Wars was up and running, that it was time for a first nuclear strike against the Russians, isn't that true? Isn't it true that your deception of the Russian intelligence agencies forced Gorbachev to strike his hammer-and-sickle flag and lay down his guns, surrendering to an America that you'd led him to believe was ready to nuke his country to dust? Isn't that true? No, don't answer, Madam Director, I already know."

She pointed to Brett Hogshead, the Secretary of War, and to Jeremy Shingles, Secretary of the Navy. "And you two," she accused. "Out of the blue you decide to send our frogmen into a Russian Navy port and sabotage their submarine *Kursk*. It goes to sea on an exercise and blows up and kills the entire crew. And for what? Revenge for an American sub they sank thirty-two years before? What was that, your version of revenge served cold?"

She swung her cane to point back at Carlucci. "As for you, you should call Vostov right now and come clean. There are no bombs in his ports. Ask him politely and nicely to call off his Poseidon deployment." She slowly walked toward the entrance to the room, the long voyage on her cane taking place while the room remained in shocked silence. Finally at the door, she said to Carlucci, "Mr. President, please consider this my resignation."

She paused for a moment, just long enough for Carlucci to straighten his tie and say calmly, "Your resignation is accepted."

Chushi shut the door behind her. Carlucci looked up at the meeting's participants, raising his eyebrows. "More coffee, anyone?" When the silence continued, he said, "Well, then, this meeting is adjourned. I'm sure you all have pressing things to take care of. I'd like the room cleared with the exception of the Secretary of War, Secretary of State, CIA director, chairman of the joint chiefs and you, Admiral Pacino. I'm going to take a break for biological reasons. Please feel free to get fresh coffee and then come back."

Pacino followed Allende to the wardroom, where a fresh pot of coffee awaited them. She poured for him first, then herself. Pacino spoke to her in a low tone.

"Is all that stuff Chushi said true?"

Allende waved him back to the Situation Room before answering. She sat and looked at him. "It's all true except for mining Russian harbors with nuclear bombs. We didn't do it and we didn't 'pipeline' fake intelligence to the Russians saying we did do it. I don't know where that's coming from."

"So how had the vice president gotten this information? Could it be she had some contact within Vostov's organization?"

Allende shrugged. "I suppose we could bug her residence at the Naval Observatory and her West Wing office to find out, but I doubt that would bear fruit."

"With her medical condition," Pacino mused, "do you imagine that maybe she just got confused? Mixed up briefing information?

Maybe heard about a potential plan to deploy nuclear mines, a plan rejected? Or an unexecuted scheme to 'pipeline' disinformation into the SVR?"

Allende shook her head. "We never even thought about a plot like that. Maybe one of Hogshead's Pentagon novelists dreamed something up. You know he's had thriller writers on retainer ever since seven-seventeen, charged with brainstorming incoming threats that his admirals and generals wouldn't ever dream up. But if someone did put this idea on a Pentagon whiteboard, we never heard about it. And Hogshead would never embark on a plan like that without involving CIA."

"What about NSA? Those spooks work for the Pentagon. For Hogshead. They could have put this idea into fake message traffic."

"No way," Allende said. "We're tight with NSA and DIA. Hell, we practically live in conference rooms with those guys, and our people are in their task forces and theirs are in mine. NSA can't send out an order for Chinese food without my people knowing about it. That goes for DIA as well. And no one is going rogue in our agencies. Ever since Snowden? Everyone with a clearance over top secret has as much surveillance on them as we put on the FSB or SVR."

When Hogshead wandered back in with Shingles, Allende stopped talking. Once the smaller group was reassembled in the room again, Carlucci walked in, sat down, and poured fresh coffee for himself, then looked at Pacino.

"Well, Patch, let's talk about this option you've proposed. Sinking the Omega."

"It makes the most sense, Mr. President," Pacino said. "Waiting for the Omega to drop off these bombs in American ports, even if he's just making some kind of a statement, could go horribly wrong. What if, while being placed, a circuit shorts or the weapon's AI wakes up and decides the detonation protocols are correct and just blows a ten megaton hole in Norfolk Harbor? Shooting down the Omega might not be a good idea in open water, but under the polar icecap? No satellites can see or hear it, no overhead aircraft will detect it with their sonar buoys or magnetic anomaly detectors, no helicopters with dipping sonars will find it, no antisubmarine warfare ships will detect it on sonar. The water under the icecap is the most isolated location on the planet. And we have an asset a few football fields away from him with armed weapons, ready to take him out. If you give the order, this miserable crisis ends."

"From a practical point of view, how would this happen?" Carlucci asked. "I was made to understand that subs under the ice are out of radio communication."

"Not completely, Mr. President," Jeremy Shingles, the Secretary of the Navy said. "The Navy implemented a four-letter code group for communications with the *New Jersey* while she's under ice. These letters are transmitted in extremely low frequency, Mr. President, so they take a long time to receive, but these radio waves are powerful enough to be received by a submerged submarine. Even under the ice. The transmitters require antennae the height of skyscrapers and take power from dedicated power plants, each of which could light up a small town. It takes up to twenty minutes for a single alphanumeric character to be transmitted and received aboard. The four-letter code group would be preceded by that day's two letter callsign for the *New Jersey*. So six letters in total. Two hours to receive the directive, which is a long time, unfortunately, but the transit under the ice will take weeks, or longer."

"What are these pre-arranged messages?" Carlucci asked.

"There's an entire codebook of possible messages. For example, one was to break contact and come home. A second was to try to provoke the Omega—bang into its hull or ping at it with active sonar. A third was to order the deployment of swimmer-delivered mines to the hull of the Omega, mines that could be detonated by an algorithm like with the attack on the *Kursk*, or by a particular sonar signal. A fourth code to shoot at the Omega with torpedoes and take her down."

"Wait, you can set off a mine placed on the Russian's hull with a sonar sound?" Carlucci asked.

"Sure," Allende said. "That's how we detonated the munitions on the Russian Nordstream pipeline. We placed the explosives under the cover of a Baltic NATO naval exercise with a detonator programmed to go off on receipt of a particular sonar sound. Then, a month or so later, a P-8 antisubmarine plane was sent by Norway to drop a single sonar buoy with a one-hour time delay before it pinged the detonate command. By the time the P-8 landed, boom. Pipeline blew up with none of our fingerprints on it."

"Ah, I remember now," Carlucci said. "I was briefed on that. But still, Admiral Pacino, shooting at a Russian submarine carrying all those megatons of nuclear weapons, it's a little disturbing. Couldn't they go off? Or scatter radioactive plutonium all over God's green earth? And the explosion from your torpedoes, particularly if they cause the Omega's own weapons to blow up, won't that be detected by seismologists? And won't the Russians become aware that we killed their submarine? What will they do then?"

"I believe the Russians will stand down," Pacino said. "Anything else would be a crazy overreaction. Vostov won't send nuclear missiles over the pole because we put his submarine on the bottom. A submarine that was on a nefarious mission to sneak nuclear munitions to the American coast."

"How do you know?"

"Because the Russians didn't do anything in retaliation when we sank the first Omega under the icecap. Nor did they take action when we sank three of their Yasen-M attack submarines this summer."

Carlucci paused. "Unless losing a fourth submarine is the last straw for Vostov. Secretary Hogshead, what say you?"

The Secretary of War cleared his throat. "Mr. President, I understand the clear driving motivation for taking this offensive submarine torpedo system out, but we've had a dozen debates about things like this in the past. We were threatened by, for example, an anti-ballistic missile radar installation outside Moscow, the station bristling with anti-aircraft and anti-missile defenses, which would make Moscow impervious to a nuclear attack, and the station itself was immune to a strike to take it out. It was sort of a miniature version of our own Strategic Defense Initiative. Discussion went to sending in a highly modified B-52 bomber cloaked with anti-radar material, jets with heat signature masking and a new bomb-homing system and a precision laser-guided bunker-busting bomb. I believe the plane had a codename, the 'Old Dog.' 'Allow us to take out the ABM site,' the Air Force pleaded. 'The Old Dog can fly in and out without being detected and the bomb will eliminate the radar installation.' We decided against the plan. It was just too overt and provocative. Plus, if the Russians were to shoot down the Old Dog and capture the crew, it would be a foreign relations nightmare. Instead, we just had CIA and Mossad agents go underground and sabotage it from the inside. Turns out, Madam Director Allende's methods work better than ours in situations like this."

"So, what do *you* think, Madam Director?" Carlucci asked Allende.

Margo Allende swallowed. Pacino realized her loyalty to him and her loyalty to CIA were in conflict. He'd once told her, if that situation arose, to be the CIA director first and his girlfriend last, and she'd looked at him like he was an idiot and said, of course she would. But in reality, he knew she wouldn't want to pollute their relationship by calling his proposal stupid or ill-advised in front of the president.

"Mr. President, I like the idea of placing mines on the Omega's hull that we can detonate remotely if we have to. A mine would make the sinking—if we determine the Omega must be put on the bottom—look like a torpedo room accident, like *Kursk*."

"*Kursk*," Carlucci said. "Refresh my memory, please. *Kursk* was that Russian sub that sank, what, twenty-five years ago from its own torpedo exploding in its torpedo room. Right?"

"Actually, no, sir," Allende said. "The news all trumpeted that version. In actuality, when *Kursk* was in port, our Navy SEALs placed two shaped-charge mines on either side of its torpedo room, programmed with an algorithm. It would wait for depth excursions, time from leaving port, periscope depth trips, the sound of exercise weapons being fired. Then when the algorithm on the master mine was satisfied, it sent a signal to the slave mine and both blew up at the same time. The weapons in the *Kursk*'s torpedo room blew up in sympathy, with sufficient force to vaporize the entire compartment. The Russians had no wreckage or forensic evidence of the torpedo compartment they could use to put the puzzle pieces together."

"I had no idea," Carlucci said, fascinated. "Why did we do that?"

"Retaliation for our submarine USS *Stingray*, which the Russians sank under the polar icecap. With the loss of all hands." Allende gave Pacino a significant look. Pacino wondered if Carlucci knew that *Stingray*'s captain was Commander Anthony Pacino, his father.

"Wait, why would the Russians sink our sub, *Stingray*, under the ice?" Carlucci frowned in confusion.

"Their reason, Mr. President," Allende explained, "was that they thought one of our submarines sank their boat, *K-129*, off Hawaii."

"Dear God, this just goes on and on, doesn't it?" Carlucci said in frustration. "What happens when the Russians decide we sank this Omega? We lose another one of our boats? Or they target the *New Jersey* when it leaves the Arctic Ocean?" Carlucci shook his head. "I'm not ready to shoot down this submarine, people. It's too aggressive. Let's just keep watching it and waiting."

"Sir, are you also rejecting the mine placement plan?" Pacino asked.

"I actually like the mine placement option," Carlucci said. "But let's wait on that too. A bomb that goes off from a sonar sound? Sounds risky." He turned to look at Allende. "And by the way, what about Vostov? How safe is *he*? With all these assassination attempts?"

Allende shook her head. "We think a third attempt is coming. We're trying to find out more. So far, we haven't traced who is responsible for these attacks. And we haven't yet gotten information on what the third attempt will be. Just some communications chatter."

Carlucci nodded. "If you find out in time, I could warn Vostov."

"Why?" Pacino asked. "He's not exactly acting very friendly right now. Not with this Omega and these Poseidons."

Carlucci smiled. "A good faith gesture like that? It might change the calculus of his placing these Poseidons. Besides. Devil you know, Patch. Devil you know."

———————

Margo Allende unlocked her Jaguar and Pacino climbed into the plush leather passenger seat of the slung-back and sleek black sports car.

"Where to, Patch?" she asked, her hand reaching for his.

"I'm thinking the Irish pub," he said.

"Kelly's Irish Times it is." She guided the car out to the street, the way to the pub memorized, as it was practically their watering hole when they were both at the White House.

"How are you?" Pacino asked. "You okay?"

She glanced at him. "Patch, after a day like this, I just want to inhale a big bowl of Irish stew, chug an entire bottle of wine all by myself, then go home, where, if you'll oblige, you'll fuck me hard enough to make me lose consciousness."

"You know, Margo, I've always loved your poetic style of speaking."

"Hey," she smiled for the first time since the meeting, "I'm a delicate fuckin' flower."

———————

They were sitting at the bar while waiting for a table to open up. Pacino had ordered a Macallan 18, double, neat. Allende had opted for a Cabernet from Sonoma. They were just about to start talking about things that weren't classified, when a commotion broke out at the end of the bar, where one of the flat screen displays that wasn't selected to a sports channel was playing the 24-hour SNN news feed. Someone had bellowed, "turn that up!"

The bar quieted down as the announcer came on and went to a reporter pictured outside, where an upside-down Lincoln SUV was lying, its top crushed, its front end smashed flat from a bridge abutment. The scroll at the bottom of the screen read, ...VICE

PRESIDENT KAREN CHUSHI DEAD IN A SINGLE CAR ACCIDENT OFF MARYLAND RT. 50....

Pacino's cell phone began to ring insistently with the White House's ring tone. He picked it up, stated the memorized eight alphanumeric code for the day and the White House operator came on.

"Admiral Pacino, the president wants to see you in his study. There's a car waiting for you."

Pacino hung up and looked at Allende. "You think *we* did this?" He asked quietly as he inclined his head to the screen that was still broadcasting about the vice president's death.

"No telling," Allende said. "If we did, I don't know about it. With one whisper to the Secret Service? Carlucci could have done this."

"Yeah, but Chushi was pretty far gone with cancer, and for all we know, it could have affected her brain, as that outburst in the Situation Room showed. This could be natural causes."

Allende shook her head. "Natural causes don't have convenient timing."

"I guess you're right. Boss wants to see me in his study."

"You can take my Jag," Allende said, searching in her purse for her key fob.

"He's got a car out front waiting for me," Pacino said, smiling. "I guess he knows our habits."

"Your cell has a tracker on it," Allende said.

"So, the big question is, do I drink this scotch or pour it down the bar sink?"

Allende smiled. "For *this* meeting? My recommendation is you drink it."

And Pacino did.

The president's recently remodeled and windowless study next to the Oval Office was a SCIF, a special compartmented information facility, where the most sensitive secrets could be discussed. It featured dark wood paneling, dark tin-patterned ceiling, deep leather club chairs and a massive fireplace. The seating area was arranged at the end away from the door, facing the fireplace. On the door end of the room, a small desk and high-backed chair with smaller chairs in front was placed. For this meeting, the president had called in Navy Secretary Jeremy Shingles and acting Chief of Naval Operations Rob Catardi. Pacino took one of the club chairs opposite the president, a mahogany and marble coffee table between them, Shingles and Catardi sitting on his left. The president had called for one of the stewards to light a fire in the fireplace despite the September heat, the office's air conditioning able to overcome the additional warmth. When the fire was fully stoked and the steward left, Carlucci offered Pacino a cigar. Shingles and Catardi were already puffing smoke, though neither looked comfortable.

"I have Macallan 25," Carlucci said, pouring from a crystal decanter into a rocks glass. "Patch?"

"Yes, please, sir," Pacino said, bringing the Cuban Cohiba to life with Carlucci's torch lighter.

"Well, I wanted to see you all to talk more about this option of placing mines on the hull of the Omega, the kind we can light up with a sonar signal." Carlucci turned to Catardi. "Admiral Catardi, can you describe the nuts and bolts of how this would work?"

"Certainly, Mr. President," the chief of the Navy said, accepting a glass from the president and passing it to Pacino, then accepting one for himself. Catardi wasn't a big drinker, but when the president drank scotch and toked on a cigar, so would the admiral. "The *New Jersey* is outfitted with a dry-deck shelter on her upper hull and there are four SEAL commandos embarked aboard. The SEALs will climb into the shelter with dry suits on and swim to the bow of the *New Jersey* and withdraw the mines. The SEALs have ultraquiet propulsion units that will take them to the Omega hull. They'll attach the mines about forty feet aft of the bow, so that they are adjacent to the storage racks of the Omega's torpedoes, with one mine on each side. Once the mines are in place, they'll connect the mines with a communication wire between them."

"Won't it be tough to swim against the current, with the Omega moving?"

"No, sir," Catardi said. "Under the ice, any speed over about three knots is not safe. A sub can slam into a pressure ridge and damage the bow or sail. This isn't the kind of ice like the stuff that floats in your glass. Polar ice pressure ridges are hard as steel and can rip open a hull and sink a ship. Don't believe me, ask our good friends on the *Titanic*. So this won't be a problem. The propulsion units the SEALs will use are powerful enough to haul the commandos and the mines."

"Will doing this make noise? Won't the Omega hear a clunking sound when the mines are attached?"

"No, Mr. President. They attach first with the suction from a vacuum pump while a powerful electromagnet holds them fast to the hull. A small unit will come out of the body of the mine, cut away any anechoic foam coating on the hull, expose raw steel, and weld itself to the hull. Then the electromagnets and vacuum pump can turn off, conserving battery power."

"How long will the batteries last?"

"In testing, about three months. The mines are in a power-saver mode until awakened by the sonar signal. So then the divers swim back, re-enter the *New Jersey* and they await further instructions."

"Tell me more about the sonar pulse that wakes up the mines and detonates them," Carlucci said.

"The sound won't be anything like a regular sonar pulse. One sonar trigger sound that performed well in testing is the opening bars of Beethoven's *Fifth Symphony*. The ending of the *1812 Overture* worked well also."

Carlucci nodded and refilled his glass, then relit his cigar, which had gone out. "What if we decide to abort the mission? It wouldn't do to have a couple of our mines attached to the Omega's hull when it eventually pulls into port."

"Another sonar signal commands the mines to detach. They torch off the welded lug from the hull and sink to the bottom and self-destruct."

"Good," Carlucci said. "I like it. So, gentlemen, execute this plan. Place the mines on the Omega hull. Give the order immediately, Admiral."

"Right away, Mr. President. By your leave, sir," Catardi said, standing.

"Thanks for coming, Rob," Carlucci said, flashing his politician's smile at the Navy chief.

"You need me anymore, Mr. President?" Shingles asked.

"No, but thank you for coming so late, Jeremy," Carlucci said. He liked informality when the business was over.

Pacino stood and was about to put out his cigar when Carlucci waved him back to his seat. "Stay a moment, will you, Admiral Pacino?"

Interesting, Pacino thought, that there was no informality now, so the business with him must still be ongoing. Pacino sat.

"Yes, Mr. President?"

"Admiral, your swearing in will be at two pm in the Rose Garden. Figure out who you want to hold the Bible or the Koran or the Code of Federal Regulations for you. Supreme Court Chief Justice McDaniel will swear you in."

Pacino stared at Carlucci, momentarily confused. Carlucci just smiled and said, "Welcome to your new role, Mr. Vice President." He stood and offered his hand.

For a moment Pacino was speechless. As he stood, he took a breath to argue with Carlucci that he didn't want the office, but Carlucci seemed to read his mind.

"Don't worry, Patch. You'll retain your national security advisor role and functions, and staff. But now I'll have a VP I can trust. And you get a bigger West Wing office."

Pacino shook the president's hand. What could he say, Pacino wondered. "Thank you, Mr. President. It's an honor."

When he opened the door to the hallway, four Secret Service agents were waiting for him. One of them spoke to his wrist, saying, "Devilfish is on the move."

Hell of a Secret Service code name they'd christened him with, Pacino thought. The name of two submarines under his command that sank.

BOOK III
COMMAND DETONATE

16

Lieutenant Commander Ebenezer Fishman knocked gently on Executive Officer Quinnivan's stateroom door, then opened it and stood back in the passageway.

"Come on in, Tiny Tim," Quinnivan said, taking off his half-frame reading glasses. He was stationed as command duty officer while Captain Seagraves slept in the neighboring stateroom. He glanced at Fishman, who was wearing blue latex gloves.

"I'd better keep my distance for the moment, XO," Fishman said quietly. "We have a problem. A medical problem."

Fishman was joined by the ship's hospital corpsman, a senior chief named Thornburg, who was also wearing blue gloves. Thornburg was an odd individual, Quinnivan thought. He never wore submarine coveralls, preferring to wear the more formal working khaki uniform. He was short and stocky, his arms muscular from hours of weightlifting in the torpedo room. He was old for submarine service, perhaps forty-five, and as such the oldest man of ship's company. His gray hair was cut into a severe-looking flattop haircut. Thornburg interacted minimally with the crew. A serious sailor, he had never been known to smile, not that Quinnivan recalled. The crew had aptly nicknamed him "Grim," and only the yeomen knew his real first name. He was a board-certified internal medicine physician, but had refused the officer accession program and insisted on enlisting, since, according to him, that would allow him to serve in submarines.

"Doc," Quinnivan said. "Are you going to stand out there too? What's going on? And what's with the rubber gloves?"

"XO, we have an outbreak of viral gastroenteritis," Senior Chief Thornburg said quietly. "Three of the SEALs are affected. I've put them in quarantine in the SEALs' quarters."

"Viral what?" Quinnivan narrowed his eyes at the corpsman.

"Stomach flu, XO," Thornburg said. "Senior Chief Tucker-Santos, the SEALs' corpsman, called me to their quarters and told me what he believed was the diagnosis. I've confirmed it. I have the three running IVs for hydration. They all have fevers over a hundred and four, sir. They barely have the strength to make it to their bathroom."

"It's coming out of both ends," Fishman said. "So far, I seem to be okay, but I should self-quarantine just in case."

Quinnivan consulted his pad computer. "Mr. Fishman, move your accommodations to the aft half-sixpack berthing. It's empty. Meanwhile, we'll have your meals brought to you, until we're more sure of what we're facing." He looked at Thornburg. "Doc, tell me what symptoms they have."

"As Lieutenant Commander Fishman said, sir, severe diarrhea, complicated by losing blood in the watery stool. Weakness, nausea, vomiting. Cramps. Whole body pain. Inability to keep down any liquids. That's why they're on intravenous fluids."

"It's bad, XO," Fishman added.

"This is contagious, right?" Quinnivan frowned. "How contagious? How is it transmitted?"

"Well, sir, by sharing liquids or direct touch on a wet surface touched by one of the infected. It's not airborne. But the quarantine is a precaution just in case."

"How did they get it in the first fookin' place?" Quinnivan asked.

"Contaminated food or water," Thornburg said.

"For fook's sake, Doc, are you saying our potable water could be contaminated? Or our food?"

Thornburg looked at Fishman, who nodded and said, "Since no else in the crew is affected, Doc and Tucker-Santos think it's something brought onboard by my people. We brought protein bars and a case of some of those energy drinks with protein."

"The cans of that shit that Aquatong is always slamming down?" Quinnivan asked. "What is that stuff, 'Vulcan Werewolf?'"

"'Vulcan Vampire,'" Fishman said. "I've confiscated the protein bars and cans of energy drinks. We should dispose of them all at the next opportunity to dump trash."

"Make sure that stuff is wrapped up and taped so no one in the TDU room is tempted to try an energy drink or a protein bar." The TDU was the trash disposal unit, a vertical torpedo tube to eject trash. With the rig for ultraquiet, the trash compactor was secured, but the trash room was filling up to overflowing and Quinnivan planned to suggest to the captain that they fade back from the Omega and dispose of their trash. Probably the same time they did a steam generator blowdown, an even louder evolution, but without it, the boiler level detectors would eventually go berserk and they could lose the reactor, and a reactor scram under ice would place the entire crew—and mission—in mortal peril. With total ice coverage overhead, there was no way to run the emergency diesel, and the battery could only stay alive for half a day before there would be a total loss of power.

"How long till the boys get over this stomach bug?" Quinnivan asked.

"Three days is the usual duration, XO," Thornburg said. "But the illness has been known to go on for up to two weeks."

"Well, Mr. Fishman," Quinnivan said, "Looks like your men are out of commission for the time being. Fortunately for you, you won't be called on to do anything."

Quinnivan's tactical 1JV phone circuit buzzed. He held up a finger to interrupt the discussion, put the handset to his ear and said, "Command Duty Officer." He listened for a moment, nodded and said, "Very well, Officer of the Deck."

"Well lads," Quinnivan said, "I need to get to the radio room. We're getting a signal on the VLF loop. Odds are, our overlords are trying to send us a preformatted message. Doc, see to it that Mr. Fishman gets a meal sent to his berthing, and bottles of water."

"Thank you, XO," Fishman said, and he and Thornburg left down the passageway.

Quinnivan debated with himself whether to wake the captain. If they were receiving a signal on the VLF loop, it would take two hours to get it onboard, and the stomach flu situation wouldn't change in that time. But Seagraves was a light sleeper and he'd probably want to know. Quinnivan went to the head between his stateroom and the captain's and knocked on the door to Seagraves' stateroom.

———————————

Captain Seagraves and XO Quinnivan stood in the crowded radio room. Seagraves yawned, then frowned at Communications Officer Eisenhart.

"Communicator, what do we have so far?"

"Two letters, Captain," Lieutenant Don Easy Eisenhart said to Seagraves. He stood behind the console that was occupied by Chief Bernadette Goreliki, the radio chief. "They're our call sign for today, letters alpha delta."

"Let me see the codebook," Quinnivan said, accepting the red binder from Eisenhart. He looked at the column with the date. For today, *New Jersey*'s call sign was the letters A D. He looked at Seagraves. "They're talking to *us*, Captain."

"Well, nothing to do but wait for the word," Seagraves said. "Care to join me in the wardroom? Fresh coffee would go down nicely about now."

The senior officers walked aft to the wardroom, where Navigator Lewinsky, Engineer Kelly, and Weapons Officer Styxx were playing cards. When they saw the captain and the XO, they dropped their cards and stood.

"At ease," Seagraves said. "We're just here for coffee and conversation."

"Something going on, Captain?" Styxx asked.

"We just got a hit from the VLF loop," Seagraves said. "Pentagon is calling our name."

"Whoa," Kelly said. "That could mean we're in for action."

"Or orders to break trail and come home," Lewinsky said. He looked at Styxx and Kelly. "We have time to make a betting pool on what the message will be."

"That could be bad luck, yeah?" Quinnivan said. "No betting pool."

On the conn, Ensign Eli Short Hull Cooper stared over Chief Albanese's shoulder at the number one sonar stack displays, which were crowded with indications of the Omega II. It had a strong trace on broadband, bearing 045, directly ahead of them, with several tonals tracking from its 50 Hz electrical generators. On the transient plot, the Omega's under-ice sonar high frequency pings showed up on a graph of intensity versus time, the .75 second pulses going up like a square wave, then the sound going to zero, then sounding again, making another rectangular shape on the plot. A second plot, identical to it, showed the low frequency pulses, which alternated in time with the high frequency graph bars.

Lieutenant Pacino walked up to Albanese's stack. "Can I listen?" Pacino asked the sonar chief. Albanese handed him a headset without taking his eyes away from the complex screen displays. Pacino handed his tactical headset to Cooper and put on the sonar headset. The sonar pulses from Master One's under-ice sonar were loud in his ears, but there was more than just the high and low frequency pulses now. A faint sound began in the bass register and slowly ramped up to a high-pitched shriek, then descended suddenly to the lower note. "You've got a new sonar signal on that under-ice sonar," Pacino said.

Albanese nodded. "They turn that on every few minutes with no repeating pattern. Seems to be activated randomly."

"What do you think it is?"

"Probably a three-dimensional sonar enhancement of what's in front of them."

"Damn," Pacino said. "I'd like to stand a watch at *their* under-ice console. What's that?" The indications showed a pulse unlike the others, at a different frequency, pinging for a shorter time and happening only once.

"That's their secure bottom-sounder. Fathometer. They've been steady at thirty RPM," Albanese said. "No trouble so far and they haven't had to change course more than five degrees this entire watch."

"Icepack is at minimum," Pacino said. As if answering his comment, a groaning shriek came through the hull as the ice shifted overhead. He glanced at Cooper, but the junior officer of the deck had stepped over to the command console. Pacino looked up at the periscope display flatpanel in the forward overhead, which still showed the heat blooms from the Omega's reactor compartment and engineroom. He became aware of Lieutenant Vevera standing next to him. Without a word, Pacino handed him the sonar headset and put his own tactical headset back on. After listening for a minute, Vevera handed the sonar headset to his oncoming junior officer of the deck, Long Hull Cooper.

At the command console, the periscope view was trained on the Omega. Vevera joined him. "You think the laser range finder would work underwater?" he asked Pacino.

"No way. You'd probably break it," Pacino said.

"You think the BUFF has an optronic scope like ours? If he does, and he's running infrared, he might see us."

"Doubt it. The intel on the *Belgorod* shows it with conventional optical units. The old fashioned kind."

Vevera smiled. "I always think of U-Boat captains spinning their officer caps backward as they peer through the scope."

"It was kind of cool using an old-fashioned optical scope. *Panther* had one. It's actually tough to go back to just looking at a damned TV screen."

"I can imagine. So, what do you have for us?" Vevera asked.

Pacino gave him the briefing on what had gone on for the previous six hours.

"When will the message be onboard?" Vevera asked.

"About an hour after midrats," Pacino said. "Captain and XO will probably convene an op-brief in the wardroom soon after."

"I can't wait to see what the brass has to say," Vevera said. "Pretty strange to think we can't talk back to them."

"Yeah," Pacino said. "You ready to relieve me?"

"I relieve you as officer of the deck, sir," Vevera said formally.

"I stand relieved," Pacino said, then announced to the room, "Lieutenant Vevera has the deck and the conn." He looked at Short Hull Cooper. "JOOD relief?"

Short Hull nodded. "I've been relieved by Mr. Cooper."

"Awesome. What's for midrats, Squirt Gun?"

Vevera smiled. "Pizza," he said, rubbing his belly.

"It don't get no better than this," Pacino said. "Have a good watch."

Pacino and Cooper walked aft to the wardroom. The captain was in his command chair seat with XO Quinnivan on his right side. The navigator, weapons officer and engineer were there, munching on pizza.

Pacino walked near the captain, came to attention, and said, "Captain, I've been properly relieved of the deck and the conn by Mr. Vevera. Master One still bears zero four five and is operating his under-ice sonar. We have strong contact on him on broadband and narrowband, and on the optronic unit in IR. Message traffic on the VLF loops should be received by zero one thirty."

"Very well, Mr. Pacino," Seagraves said seriously. "I have to say, you're doing a barely adequate job up there."

Pacino smiled. "Why, thank you, sir." He sat in his seat and took the platter from Styxx and took a slice of pizza, famished for hot food after a day of cold cuts and peanut butter.

———————

The central command post of the *Belgorod* was whisper quiet except for the pinging and groaning from the under-ice sonar and the occasional sound of the ice shifting overhead. Senior Watch Officer Captain Third Rank Svetka Maksimov, the navigator, was seated at the command console in the captain's seat, the far left seat of the three-seat console where the senior officers of the submarine would guide the actions of the submarine during tactical action stations. During normal under-ice steaming, a department head like Maksimov would be stationed as senior watch officer, her duties mostly supervising the actions of the watch officer, who on this watch was Communications Officer Captain Lieutenant Vilen Shvets. Shvets took the far starboard seat of the command console, but he would often walk around the room or sit at the attack center console. Also stationed was the under-ice sonar operator, which on this watch was Sonar Officer Senior Lieutenant Valerina Palinkova.

On the forward starboard ship control console, two senior enlisted men, the boatswains, manned the panel that controlled the movement of the ship—its ballast systems, the operation of the bow planes and stern planes and rudder, and the engine order telegraph that communicated the ordered speed to the reactor control room watchstanders aft.

On the starboard side of the command console, the attack center console was a long row of four operator stations, each with three display screens with a tabletop with a keyboard and trackball. The attack center was manned by a senior enlisted firecontrol technician. The attack center was designed to program and fire weapons at targets based on information coming from the sonar and sensor consoles.

Forward in the room, on the centerline, was the under-ice sonar, a large one-person console with three display screens and a joystick, with its displays projected to the large flatpanel screens mounted on the bulkhead on either side of the console. The display showed a three-dimensional look at the ice ahead. So far, other than a few deep pressure ridges, the ice overhead had been well-behaved.

"Ice thickness overhead?" Maksimov called to the under-ice operator, Palinkova.

"Eleven meters, madam, and steady," Palinkova replied.

"Sounding?" What was the depth below them to the bottom, Maksimov wanted to know.

"Four hundred seventy meters, madam."

Maksimov decided to stretch her legs and got up to go to the navigation plot table on the aft port side of the room. She saw their position in the center of the display, a bright red dot in a field of blue. Their past path was lit up in a dimmer red, their intended course ahead plotted in bright blue. Maksimov put two fingers on the display and shrank the view, the scale of the plot changing to show a greater area of the sea around them. She continued to adjust the scale until the entire Arctic Ocean was shown on the plot, the blue intended course continuing northeast, then passing south of the pole and continuing in a great circle route to the Bering Strait. She took a deep breath. This transit was going to take months at this speed. What the hell were the bosses thinking, sending them this way into the Pacific, and the all the way around North America and South America to reach the American east coast? There had to be some logic to this, she thought. But whatever it was, the bosses were keeping quiet about it.

Maksimov walked forward to the port side of the room, where the long four-position console was the sonar and sensor center, manned by another senior enlisted petty officer.

"Any detects on anything hostile?" she asked.

"We're alone in the sea, madam," the watchstander said, pulling off one headset ear and turning to look up at her.

"Remain vigilant," she said.

Although what they'd do if they detected another submarine following them had never been made clear by Captain Alexeyev. There was no way to perform evasive maneuvers here under ice without risking a collision with a pressure ridge. And Maksimov seriously doubted they'd ever shoot at another submarine even if they did detect one.

She glanced at the chronometer. Five hours until watch relief. And breakfast. She was hungry and contemplated having some bread and butter brought up from the galley.

Michael Pacino lay in bed next to the warm, naked body of Margo Allende and stared at the ceiling. He checked his phone for the time.

It was one in the morning. He'd gotten back from the White House after ten and had arrived to find a note from Margo that she'd gone to bed, but had brought him a shepherd's pie from the Irish pub. He'd heated up the dish and poked at it in her vast shining kitchen while scanning his phone for new emails or texts. It was too early for communications to come in for his new role as vice president, but by week's end, he thought, he'd be buried in administrative business. And he'd have to set up shop in his new West Wing office and establish residence at the Naval Observatory, the traditional home of the vice president. Finally he'd poured a scotch and drank it while watching the SNN news on Margo's big flatpanel in the media room. There were a few reports on the Russian Kremlin attack on President Vostov, but no other news out of Russia.

Pacino decided to try to sleep, but as he lay next to Margo, who was snoring quietly next to him, all he could think about was Anthony on the *New Jersey*. Was he safe? Pacino tried to convince himself that *New Jersey* was just on a milk run. A simple operation to trail the mammoth Russian submarine. After all, what could possibly go wrong? And then his mind listed the thousand things that could go wrong on a nuclear submarine under the polar icecap a football field away from an Omega II carrying tactical nuclear torpedoes on a mission to deliver death.

He shut his eyes and tried to relax enough to fall asleep. His swearing-in ceremony was thirteen hours from now. He had to sleep. He needed to sleep. There'd be no time for a nap after the ceremony. He wondered for a moment about the *Belgorod*, the Omega II submarine. What was the captain of that submarine thinking? Had he detected the submarine trailing him? And if he did, what would he do?

Captain First Rank Georgy Alexeyev sat in his oversized, high-backed leather command chair at his desk in his stateroom. He spun his pen in his hand, an expensive piece given to him by his wife Natalia. He glanced at her photograph bolted to the bulkhead. Damn, he missed her. She belonged to a very small group of people on this earth who understood him. It was an exclusive club he thought, the other members only Sergei Kovalov and his first officer, Ania Lebedev. It was late and Sergei was probably asleep. No sense waking him up to come to the stateroom and just talk. But Alexeyev was worried about his old friend. Kovalov's depression seemed to be getting worse.

On impulse, Alexeyev picked up his inter-ship phone circuit and dialed up the VIP stateroom, where the commander of the test wives was berthed, Captain Third Rank Svetlana Anna. She answered on the first ring.

"Yes, Captain," she said, her silky feminine voice alert.

"Madam Anna, I know it's late. But I wondered if you might have a few minutes for me in my stateroom."

"Of course, Captain. I'll be right there."

While he waited, he called the central command post on the tactical phone circuit. Captain Third Rank Maksimov answered.

"Central," she said. "Senior Watch Officer."

"Status?" he asked.

"Same as before, Captain."

"Ice thickness and sounding?"

"Ice is at eleven meters. Sounding is over four hundred meters, sir. No pressure ridges. Steaming as before."

"Very well. Do you need tea service for the central watchstanders?"

"I've already called for it, Captain," Maksimov said.

"Have a good watch, Navigator," he said, and hung up just as a knock sounded on his door.

"Come in," he called.

Svetlana Anna came in and shut the door behind her. She was wearing regulation blue submarine coveralls and black sneakers, her shining long hair pulled back into a ponytail.

"Have a seat and relax," he said.

She settled into a seat across his desk and looked up expectantly into his eyes. "Yes, Captain?"

253

"This is about Captain Kovalov. I'm concerned about him. I'm aware he spent time with you recently."

Svetlana Anna met his eyes, but her expression was unreadable. Neither surprise nor indignation. Finally she spoke.

"Relations and conversations between test wives and crewmembers are confidential, Captain, as I'm sure you're aware, by fleet regulations." Her tone was neutral as she said it.

"Not on a combat vessel on a combat mission," Alexeyev said. "You might want to read this." He slid his pad computer across the desk to her. She scanned it for a moment. It stated, in military legalese, that on a combat mission, discussions between a crewman and a test wife could be disclosed to the unit commander.

"Can you send this to me?"

"Certainly," Alexeyev said.

"One thing, Captain, this isn't a combat mission."

"Perhaps you should read this as well," Alexeyev said, taking the pad computer back, finding the operation order from Admiral Zhigunov and sliding it back to Anna. She read it for a long moment. Through all the dry military language, replete with acronyms, abbreviations, and coordinates, the central theme was that the voyage of the *Belgorod* was a combat mission. She sat back and stared at Alexeyev.

"Does this mean that the Status-6 weapons are to be detonated? We're starting a war?"

"No," Alexeyev said, waving his hand in a gesture of dismissal. "Think of it as being similar to a mission on enemy territory to stockpile weaponry in a secret cache, just in case of future need. Placing these Status-6 weapons gives the Kremlin options and perhaps bargaining strength later. Perhaps much later."

Anna nodded. "So, fine, it's a combat mission. Why do you need to know about Kovalov?"

"Captain Kovalov is a vital part of the mission. He and his *Losharik* will place the Poseidons."

"Do you have a specific question about my sessions with Captain Kovalov?" she asked.

"Very specific," Alexeyev said, feeling a cold discomfort that he was looking into the life of his best friend. It was a betrayal, certainly, but Alexeyev's loyalty had to be to Russia first, the mission second, the submarine and crew third, and then and only then, to his friendship with Kovalov. Moreover, he knew Kovalov understood that. Kovalov had once commented, "Where in this Navy-mandated hierarchy of loyalty is loyalty to God? And family?" Alexeyev was a committed agnostic. Who, really, knew anything about God? Those who claimed to speak to Him seemed insane, no matter how reasonable they might sound. No matter how ornate the cathedrals built to honor God, he thought, no one in them had any better idea about God than he himself did.

His thoughts wandered for a moment to that terrifying instant in the central command post of the doomed *Kazan* as she was busy bursting into flames, exploding and sinking at the hands of the Americans. Had he prayed to God then? When he remembered those moments, whether in daylight or dreams, he knew all he thought about was getting the crew to abandon ship before it became too late. Time had expanded so that every second was an hour, and in all that time, there had been no thought of God or praying. Nor of death. Because death was an idea much like God—who could really say what happened after one died? Better to keep one's concentration on the present moment, on the present mission. He looked at Svetlana Anna, who was looking back at him expectantly. He realized in his reverie she'd asked a question. Perhaps Ania Lebedev was right about him, he thought, that he lived deep inside his head, almost as if he were somewhere on the autistic scale more than a few clicks away from normal.

"You were saying, Captain, that you had a specific question about Captain Kovalov?"

He nodded, remembering. "Has Sergei ever made any indications that he is thinking about harming himself? Any suicidal ideation?" The psychological screening that submarine captains were subjected to by Northern Fleet command, with occasional update sessions, habitually asked these questions. A suicidal sub commander with nuclear weapons under his control was a nightmare scenario.

"No, Captain," Anna said, seeming sincere. Alexeyev looked into her eyes, seeking any "tell" of her lying, but she impressed him as being forthright. Of course, he barely knew her, and perhaps the inventory of talents test wives had been selected for, beyond the obvious ones, might include training that would allow them to prevaricate while passing a lie-detector test.

"Was there any expression by Captain Kovalov of doubt about the mission?" *Did Kovalov think this mission was as stupid as Alexeyev himself thought it was?*

"No, Captain. None."

Alexeyev stared at Anna's eyes again, wondering for a moment if he'd have been more perceptive if he hadn't lost one eye.

"Any hint at all that he would sabotage the mission?"

"Why, no, Captain, not at all."

Alexeyev nodded. "Very well, then, Madam Anna."

"Anything else, sir?" she asked.

"That's all."

She stood to go, obviously uncomfortable, and moved toward the door to the passageway.

"And Madam Anna?"

"Yes, Captain?" She turned at the door before opening it.

"I expect you to come to me if you hear any such sentiments expressed to you. That also goes to all your team, if coming from anyone they service during this trip."

Anna frowned. "Of course, Captain," she said, then vanished from the room.

When she was gone, he wondered, if he had the sympathetic ear of a comfort woman, would he confess his own feelings about this odd mission?

He reopened the operation order, going back over the contingency rules of engagement, looking up the directive for the event that they detected an enemy submarine following them. The rules were clear. Evade and escape. Take no hostile actions unless fired upon. Which was nonsensical, he thought. There could be no evading a trailing submarine under the ice, in these restricted passages, with pressure ridges diving down to the sea floor all around them. As if to emphasize the danger of the ice above, a moaning, shrieking groan came through the hull.

"Goddamned ice," Alexeyev said aloud, and closed the file. "Goddamned Vostov."

There was light applause scattered through the sunswept Rose Garden as Vice President Michael Pacino's swearing-in completed. A phalanx of reporters crowded around him, all shouting questions, some about Chushi and what happened to her, and what his new role entailed, and would there be a replacement national security advisor, and if so, did he have a say in who he or she might be, and would he still be involved in the forging of military and national security policy.

He was trying to walk back into the West Wing, promising he'd be available for questions at a later time, when he saw on the other side of the crowd President Carlucci taking CIA Director Margo Allende aside, with Deputy Director of Operations Angel Menendez at Allende's side. He saw Margo shoot a look back at him and nod to the president.

Allende hurried up to him as he stepped into the West Wing. He raised an eyebrow at her.

"Lower level SCIF," she said.

"Okay," he said. "Let's go."

They walked to the lower level and past the Situation Room to the secure conference room next door to it. Pacino found the coffee machine and brewed a cup, loaded it with cream and sugar and handed it to Allende, then made a black-and-bitter for himself. He was taking a seat opposite the CIA director when Angel Menendez joined them and shut the door behind him.

"Air Force Two is waiting for you at Joint Base Andrews," Allende said. "A Secret Service motorcade will take you there.

Carlucci decided against loading you into the presidential helicopter. It would raise questions."

"Okay," Pacino said. "Where am I going?"

"Moscow," Allende said. "I'm having a bag packed for you from my townhouse and having it delivered to the aircraft now."

"You're sending me to Russia? What's going on?"

"Carlucci wants you to warn Vostov." Allende produced a shiny gold object and pressed it into Pacino's palm. "Make him review this."

Pacino looked at what appeared to be an exact duplicate of his Naval Academy class ring. "What's this?"

"Give me your real ring," Allende said. "I'll hold on to it for you. You'll wear this ring instead. When you meet Vostov, give it to him. It's a flash drive. Put it on now and give me your real ring."

Pacino pulled off his Annapolis ring and handed it to Allende and put on the duplicate. It felt the same weight as his authentic ring. "What's on this drive?"

"Details of the next assassination plot," Menendez said.

"Are you going to tell me what that plot entails?"

Allende and Menendez shook their heads at the same time.

"Patch, Carlucci wants this to be strictly between him and Vostov. But I'm authorized to tell you to tell Vostov to delay any speeches he's planning on making in public."

"I assume this drive has a password? Are you going to let me know what that is?"

"Tell him the password is the last name of the Russian admiral who was embarked on the Omega submarine you fought under the polar icecap. He'll know."

Pacino nodded and looked down into his cooling coffee cup. "Is there a pretext for this meeting? Vostov will include me in his schedule?"

"It's labeled as a purely diplomatic gesture. The world sees you as militarily confrontational. And anti-Russian. Chushi had a good relationship with Vostov. Carlucci sent her to Moscow several times."

Yeah, Pacino thought, mostly to get her out of Carlucci's hair on meaningless diplomatic errands.

"Vostov will see you, if only to satisfy his curiosity."

"Did Carlucci give any indication of how friendly—or hostile—I'm supposed to appear to Vostov? Does he want a confrontation about these Poseidons?"

"He wants you to make friends with Vostov, and don't mention the Poseidons. Do you think you can do that?"

Pacino laughed. "Margo, I may be a straight shooter, but in the service of my country, I could have dinner with the Devil himself and convince him I'm his friend."

She smiled. "Imagine—Michael Pacino, a diplomat."

"I'm a man of many talents," he remarked, then hoped that didn't sound to Allende like a double meaning. But she just stood up and walked to the door with Menendez.

"Good luck, Patch," she said.

On the ride to Andrews, Pacino thought about all the questions he should have asked. Wouldn't Vostov think this flash drive might be another virus to attack their systems? Or might explode in his face? But then he considered he was being paranoid and anxious. He wondered whether he'd be able to sleep on the plane.

But as Air Force Two climbed out of the lush Maryland countryside, he decided to lie down on the couch in the presidential office. Before the jet had reached cruising altitude, Pacino was asleep.

17

Lieutenant Anthony Pacino poured fresh coffee and passed the carafe down the table. Despite it being in the midwatch an hour after midrats, the wardroom was filled to capacity with all the officers not on watch. Executive Officer Quinnivan had ordered Long Hull Cooper to take the watch as engineering officer of the watch with Supply Officer Ganghadharan on the conn. The air was thick with expectation, since the communications officer would be arriving with the decoded message they'd received on the VLF loop antenna.

Lieutenant Eisenhart hurried into the room and handed the message pad to Captain Seagraves, who wordlessly passed it to Quinnivan, who put on his reading glasses and read the message over twice, then passed it to Navigator Lewinsky.

"Share the message with the room, Nav," Quinnivan said.

Lewinsky looked up from the message pad and said, "We're ordered to deploy the two swimmer-delivered mines to the hull of the Omega and place them on either side of their torpedo room with acoustic detonation orders programmed in. That is, they'll only go off if we ping at them with an active sonar signal that we should program in now."

"Weps, you'll need to tag out and lock out the active sonar gear," Quinnivan said.

"Understood, sir," Styxx said. "I'll lay to control now and see to it personally."

"Good idea."

Styxx got up and rushed out of the room through the forward door.

"Captain? XO?" Pacino said, looking at the senior officers. "This is going to be a problem. The SEALS are sick as dogs."

"My thoughts exactly, Mr. Pacino. XO, get the doc in here," Seagraves said to Quinnivan. The XO grabbed the inter-ship phone and dialed the chiefs' quarters, speaking quietly into it.

There was a subdued buzz of conversation while they waited. Dankleff leaned over to Pacino. "Patch," he said quietly, "the *Panther* team could place these on the BUFF's hull while the SEALs are puking and shitting their brains out."

"No way, U-Boat," Pacino replied. "That's a mixed-gas tech dive in twenty-eight degree water. Using propulsion equipment we've never even seen. We'd have to train for six months to do that." That, and the fact that the idea was terrifying, Pacino thought. He thought about the panic attack he'd suffered just before they'd locked out of the *Vermont* hatch to go invade the *Panther*. Dankleff, who had been officer-in-charge of the boarding party, had almost pulled Pacino off the detail when he saw Pacino freaking out in the airlock.

The aft door cracked open and Senior Chief Grim Thornburg poked his head in. "You called for me, XO?"

"Come on in, Doc," Seagraves said, and when the senior chief entered and stood at rigid attention, Seagraves said, "Stand easy, Doc. We've got a few questions for you."

Thornburg came to a military parade-rest position. "Yes, Captain."

"First, doc, how are the three sick SEALs? Any idea of when they can return to full duty?"

"The news is not good, Captain, XO. They're still in the midst of this. I doubt they'll be up and walking three days from now."

"Will they be cleared for duty then?"

"Unfortunately, Captain, there's no telling. They could be well tomorrow, or day-after-tomorrow, but they might still be sick a week from today or even two weeks."

"How is Lieutenant Commander Fishman?" Quinnivan asked.

"He seems to be unaffected, XO. I was going to ask you if we can release him from his self-quarantine in the half-sixpack room. He should still sleep there, but he should be fine to eat meals in the wardroom."

Quinnivan looked at Seagraves, who nodded.

"Release him now, Doc," Quinnivan said. "And send him here."

"By your leave, Captain, XO?" Thornburg asked formally.

"Dismissed, Doc," Quinnivan said.

Thornburg withdrew out the aft door as Quinnivan whispered something to Seagraves.

"Well, people," Seagraves said, addressing the officers, "it looks like we may have to wait some days before we can execute this order. Unless there's a contingency plan."

Dankleff spoke up. "Captain, if Fishman's okay with the idea, the *Panther* team can deploy these mines under his supervision. Pacino, Varney, and I could do it."

Seagraves frowned. "I don't think there's any way in hell that would work, Mr. Dankleff, but thank you for volunteering. And for volunteering Mr. Pacino and Mr. Varney without their input."

Fishman knocked on the aft door and came into the room.

"How are you feeling, Mr. Fishman?" Seagraves asked. "And please, have a seat."

Fishman sat opposite Pacino and put his water bottle on the table. "I'm fine, Captain," he said simply, his jaw muscles clenching slightly as if he were trying to look tough.

"Commander Fishman," Quinnivan said formally, looking into Fishman's eyes, "we've been ordered to deploy the swimmer-delivered mines to the hull of the Omega."

Fishman, as if to delay his response, took a long pull from his water bottle. "Captain, XO, we'll have to wait until my team is over this bug."

"There was a suggestion that you might be able to deputize the *Panther* boarding party officers and use them to help you deliver this payload," Seagraves said.

Fishman shook his head. "That's a terrible idea, Captain. We've trained for years on dives like this. It's a mixed gas dive, sir, to depths down to as low as three hundred feet in freezing water, maneuvering a heavy propulsion unit and carrying the mines. We have to decompress afterwards, and that takes some extreme physical conditioning. No offense to you guys," he said, looking at Dankleff and Pacino, then at Varney. "If we tried this, we'd likely not only lose the mines but the divers as well."

"You're certain of that, Commander?" Seagraves said.

"Absolutely, Captain. This dive is for professionals. I recommend we wait, sir, until my guys are released for duty."

Seagraves put his chin in his hand and looked down at the table. When he looked up, he said, "I want to see the XO, navigator, and Mr. Fishman in my stateroom."

The three officers filed out of the wardroom. Pacino turned to Dankleff and Varney. "He's right, you know."

"Any idea how urgent this order is?" Dankleff asked Eisenhart.

The communicator shrugged. "Nothing in the message saying how long we have to execute it. I can only imagine the bosses wouldn't want any delays. But taking the three of you slugs out of the dry-deck shelter to deploy mines? Hell, you should leave behind your last will and testament before you do. And a check made out to the Navy for the cost of the mines."

Dankleff considered, then nodded. "You're probably right." He poured more coffee and looked up at the other officers. "Still, we've proved we can accomplish the impossible mission. Maybe we can do it again."

"I fucking hope not," Varney said. "Dying under the polar icecap in a drysuit ain't my idea of how I want my career to go."

"What about you, Patch?" Dankleff said.

Pacino smiled. "I'm with Boozy Varney on this one, U-Boat."

———

"So, Commander Fishman," Seagraves began when he, the XO, the navigator and the SEAL commander were all seated at the conference table in his stateroom. "Let me ask you a hypothetical question."

"Go ahead, Captain," Fishman replied, frowning.

"If this were a do-or-die combat situation, could you conduct enough training over, say, two days, to bring the *Panther* officers up to speed on the intricacies of this dive?"

Fishman crossed his arms over his chest. "Do-or-die, Skipper? The answer is yes. If you were to ask the next question, what the probability of success would be? I'd have to say maybe one chance in twenty that we get it done. The odds say we'll all die out there and drop the mines. It's a complex evolution, sir."

"Walk us through it, if you wouldn't mind," Seagraves said.

"We start with your torpedo room loading two torpedo tubes, each with a Mark 80 swimmer-delivered mine, pre-programmed for sonar signal detonation. Each mine will be outfitted with cables that will allow it to be towed. Both torpedo tube muzzle doors would be opened. A four-man diver team would lock out of the dry-deck shelter with Mark 76 swimmer-propulsion units, each one powerful enough to bring the diver and the mine to the intended target. The divers would break up into two-man teams and each would maneuver to the bow to retrieve the Mark 80 mines. The divers in each team would have a communication wire between them so they can talk. Ideally, there would be a wire between each team leader, which presents problems, since the mine cables and communication wires can get fouled."

Fishman took another pull of his water bottle, then continued. "The diver teams would swim to the target. Towing a heavy mine like the Mark 80 is extremely taxing—if it's too heavy, it will drag a swimmer to the bottom. Too light, it'll pop to the bottom of the ice overhead or to the bottom of the Omega. So managing the ballast bladder of the mine is a full-time job, and it's a constant adjustment for water temperature and salinity. The mine can be heavy one minute and a balloon the next.

"So, getting to the Omega. Already there's a problem, because you'd have to drive the *New Jersey* very close to the Omega—and we all know there are tactical problems doing that. You could bump into the Omega or your closer noise could alert him, revealing that you're trailing him. If he took evasive action, it could kill the divers. A mine cable could get fouled in his sail and the team could be helpless if he dives deep. Or worse, a cable could get fouled in one of his screws and pull the divers into it, chopping them into fish food. Assuming that the divers can find the Omega, they'd have to maneuver close enough to place the mines in the right place. An exploding mine in the wrong location would do nothing except blow a harmless hole in the Omega's ballast tank. They have to be placed at the point in the Omega's hull where his weapons are stowed."

"Go on, Mr. Fishman," Quinnivan encouraged.

"Bear in mind, during this whole time, the divers are fighting the relative current of the Omega's motion. If he's going three knots, that's a three-knot current that they will have to fight. Not easy even if there's no payload to tow. It takes extreme training. We've practiced this with submerged submarines, over and over. Anyway, let's say that problem is overcome. We'd then have to attach the mines to a hull covered in rubber coating. The mine is opened up at that point. It's a cylinder for stowage in a torpedo tube, but here we'd open it up on its longitudinal axis. Like slicing a banana in half lengthwise. That exposes the vacuum pump of the mine. Fighting the current the whole time, one diver uses the propulsion unit to keep the mine at the right location while the other opens the mine, places it against the target's hull and engages the vacuum pump. If that works, all is well. The mine will cut through the anechoic coating and light off an electromagnet for a temporary connection to the hull. At that point, the mine will weld itself to the Omega hull. If the coating is too thick and the vacuum pump can't keep the mine attached, a diver will have to cut through the coating and expose enough steel that the vacuum pump can get attached. Once the divers are satisfied that the mine is safely attached, they'll activate the mine's electronics, then they have to connect the two mines with a communication cable, wrapping it under the hull and gluing it to the hull surface so it won't flap in the current of the submarine's passage. Then, finally, they have to do a system check and make sure the mines are okay and programmed correctly and talking to each other.

"Then there's the next problem—making it back to the *New Jersey*. And that presents the same issues as finding the Omega in the first place. Very easy to get lost underwater, but under ice? Assuming they find their way back. Based on the depth shown on the diver's wrist computers, they'll decompress in the dry-deck shelter."

Quinnivan smiled. "Is that all? It's a walk in the park."

"Very funny, XO." Fishman frowned.

"Based on what Mr. Fishman has said, gentlemen," Seagraves said, "I think it's safe to say we'll wait for the SEAL team members to heal."

"There is one exception to what I said, Captain," Fishman said haltingly, as if he were regretting what he was about to say. "If the Omega, for whatever reason, decides to surface through the ice, this becomes much easier. No trouble finding him. He'd be visible. The water would be shallow. You could bring *New Jersey* up right under him. And there'd be no relative current. In that event, even if one team had trouble, the other could swim around the Omega hull and help the first team. It wouldn't be a milk run, but I could do it with your men. That assumes I can conduct training with them for a day or two."

Seagraves looked at Quinnivan, then Lewinsky. "What do you think, XO?"

"I doubt the Omega will surface, but we could have Mr. Fishman conduct the training anyway, just in case," the XO said.

"So ordered," Seagraves said. "Mr. Fishman, over the next four or five watches, I want you in the wardroom with Varney, Dankleff and Pacino conducting training."

"I'll need to make an entry into the dry-deck shelter to familiarize them with the Mark 76 propulsion systems," Fishman said. "And your torpedo room will need to move weapons so I can familiarize them with the Mark 80 mines."

"We can accommodate you, Mr. Fishman," Quinnivan said.

"By your leave, Captain?" Fishman said.

"Thanks for educating us," Seagraves said. "You can go. XO, Nav, stay behind if you would."

When Fishman was gone, Seagraves said, "Well, men, what do you think?"

Quinnivan shrugged. "I sincerely doubt the Omega will surface. It can't hurt to train the boys for the possibility. And in the time we get them trained, hopefully by then the SEALs will be well again."

"What about you, Nav?" Seagraves looked at Lewinsky. "You've been awful quiet through this whole discussion. Care to grace us with your thoughts?"

Lewinsky pursed his lips. "No way this will work, Captain. Odds are, we lose the mines *and* the divers. I wouldn't want to be at the board of inquiry for *that* mission failure."

"I worry about it working even if the SEALs are healthy," Quinnivan said. "Fishman's description? Jaysus, I'd rather just fire a fookin' torpedo at the bloke and be done with it. This whole mine scheme was thought up by an academic in a Pentagon basement cubicle. It's nuts."

"He said they'd practiced it on submerged submarines," Lewinsky said.

"He didn't tell us how many times they failed in practice," Quinnivan noted. "I'm going to call the *Panther* lads to my stateroom and break the news to them, that they're a backup contingency."

"Dankleff will be happy to hear that," Seagraves said. "Mr. Pacino and Mr. Varney? Not so much."

"Hey, Skipper," Quinnivan said, grinning, "what does your American Coast Guard say? *You have to go out. You don't have to come back.*"

Seagraves laughed. "I'm sure that expression will be a great comfort to Pacino and Varney."

———

Vice President Michael Pacino climbed down the stairs from the forward hatch of the massive 747, Air Force Two. The bright sunshine of Moscow in September at noon was blinding. One of the Secret Service agents asked if Pacino wanted sunglasses, but he shook his head. There was a minimal greeting party at the airstrip. The American ambassador, Alphonse Captiva, was there to shake Pacino's hand. Captiva was a holdover from the previous administration whom Carlucci kept on because the Russians liked him. He was a former senator from New York who always had been surrounded by whispered rumors of his connection to the New York City mob families, but there had never been any solid evidence of any wrongdoing. The Russian prime minister turned out, a dull functionary named Platon Melnik, who had been briefly president of Russia when Vostov's first two terms ended, the constitution at the time mandating that he step down. During Melnik's four years as president, Vostov had had the constitution amended to allow for longer presidential terms. When Vostov had won the next election, he'd put his crony Melnik into the prime minister seat and used him as a mouthpiece for Vostov's policies.

Pacino shook Melnik's hand, and Melnik told him in accented English that Vostov was waiting for him at the Kremlin. The motorcade consisted of the armored and bulletproof limousines the U.S. president used, flown in alongside Air Force Two in the cargo hold of a C17 Globemaster II Air Force freighter. Pacino climbed into the presidential limo and looked out the window at the scenery of Moscow from the airport Vostov had recently commissioned. The ride was short. Pacino yawned, the ride from D.C. to Moscow exhausting despite the luxury of the jet, his jetlag not helping.

The journey from the entrance to the Kremlin gates to Vostov's temporary office was a blur. To Pacino, it felt like he was falling down a tunnel of dark paneled high-ceilinged hallways, some walls painted hunter green, massive paintings of former Russian officials on the walls, dozens of curious suit-clad aides greeting him. He nodded and smiled as he passed. *Be a diplomat*, he reminded himself. Finally, the procession of Pacino, his Secret Service guards and the Kremlin's SBP guards, arrived at Vostov's office suite. Pacino had read that Vostov had commandeered it from Melnik, the offices belonging to the prime minister, but Vostov's office would be under construction for the next year to repair the damage from the assassin's bomb, and to upgrade its security and make it invulnerable to electronic eavesdropping.

Finally, the last heavy mahogany door opened and Pacino found himself in Vostov's office, face-to-face with the Russian president. Vostov was nondescript, neither handsome nor ugly, Pacino thought. He could have been cast by Hollywood as an aging accountant. He was slightly shorter than Pacino, but outweighed him by at least fifty pounds, much of it gathered around his middle. He was jowly, mostly balding, but had an expressive face that had curled into an appearance of bright happiness. Of course his face was expressive, Pacino thought—he was, after all, a politician at the top rung of a superpower.

"Mr. President," Pacino said, smiling and stretching out his hand, "thank you for meeting me. It's a pleasure to meet you in person."

Vostov smiled even wider and gripped Pacino's hand in a firm, dry handshake. "Vice President Pacino, the pleasure is all mine. Please forgive my English if I stumble or search for words." Vostov's English was perfect, Pacino noted. "I arranged for us to meet alone, one-on-one, man-to-man. I thought we could achieve an understanding this way. Normally my chief of staff would be in here with us, but she unfortunately died in the explosion. Not a week after my wife passed away in the terrorist incident." Vostov's face fell as he said the last remarks.

Pacino looked solemnly at Vostov. "I came to convey my—and President Carlucci's—deep condolences on the loss of your wife, sir, and your chief of staff. I sympathize, Mr. President. My late wife Eileen was suddenly killed in an interstate accident. I felt like I was in a walking coma for a year afterward."

"Please, Mr. Vice President, have a seat," Vostov said, gesturing to a grouping of deep leather club chairs near a fireplace. "May I offer you a drink? We have the best vodka on the planet, but also the best scotch outside Scotland, and the finest bourbon outside your province of Kentucky."

"Sir, I'll have what you're having," Pacino said, smiling as he sat. Vostov poured two glasses of vodka and handed one to Pacino.

"A toast," Vostov said, "to fallen comrades."

Pacino and Vostov drank. Vostov refilled the glasses. "And another toast, to new friendships, yes?"

"Yes, Mr. President, absolutely," Pacino said, taking a second sip.

"When we're here together, alone, please call me Dimmi," Vostov said.

"As for me, please call me Patch," Pacino replied.

Vostov smiled. "So be it, Patch. Your wife Eileen, I'm sorry for your loss. That happened just before your East China Sea war, didn't it? I was made to believe you were in supreme command of United States forces for that conflict, yes?"

"That's correct, Dimmi. I was."

"Well, one thing about losing your wife in a sudden accident, Patch. At least you didn't find yourself in the situation of having to make decisions that would lead to her death. With Lorena? I had to decide whether to send in my counterterrorist troops and risk her dying in the crossfire, or trying to negotiate with the terrorists who took her. I lie awake at night and wonder what would have happened if I'd made the second decision. Maybe my Lorena would still be with me."

"You know, Dimmi, my son Anthony told me a story that might give you some consolation. I wonder if I could take a moment to tell it."

"Your boy is quite a hero, if I remember my briefing," Vostov said. "Won the Navy Cross in that nasty *Piranha* sinking. I imagine you're very proud of him."

Interesting, Pacino thought, that Vostov left out mention of Anthony's role in the *Panther* operation. Certainly, the Russian president must know about that. "Yes, sir, I am," Pacino said. "He's quite an officer."

"Well, please, tell me the story he had." Vostov refilled their glasses again. Pacino wondered if he'd get so drunk he'd be on the floor after an hour.

"This story was told to my son by this tough-guy commando, a man named Fishman. According to Fishman, our lives change dramatically with every major decision. Whether to go to college. Whether to join the military. To marry this woman or that. To take this job or that. In Fishman's view, when a decision is made, a new universe is created with the new reality formed by the aftermath of the decision. But also, a *second* universe is created at the same time, where the *other* decision is made. And both lives continue on in those separate worlds. And over a lifetime, there might be a hundred thousand separate worlds formed by different major decisions. Fishman told my son to imagine what he called a 'base life.' In that base life, the person makes very safe decisions with no risk, and the person lives to a ripe old age, dies and goes on to the afterlife. And in Fishman's version of the afterlife, that man who lived the base life wonders what would have happened to his life if he had made different decisions, and he looks over the results of all the other life realities and he sees which life turned out to be the best. And by seeing all those other lives, all those other realities, he learns everything to be learned by the experiences arising from all those other decisions, and he comes to know peace and to grow. The person's soul is reunited with all the personalities who made different decisions. In the view of Fishman, the very universe you are living in right now is only *one* universe out of thousands in the story of your lifetime. So in another reality, a reality that is happening right now, there is another *you* that made the other decision. You can't know how that turned out until you find yourself in the afterlife, but at that point you will know. And for all we know, *that* reality could have turned out much worse."

Vostov thought for a minute, taking a pull of his vodka. "Patch, that's the most profound thing anyone has said to me in ten years. That gives me great comfort at a difficult time. I thank you for telling me that. And please thank your son as well. And ask him to thank his friend, this commando Fishman."

Pacino smiled. "I'll see to it, Dimmi. Sir, I know you're extremely busy and, as for me, I have to get back to Washington. But before I go, there's a second thing I've been asked to tell you. And something to give you."

Vostov looked at him attentively. "Yes, Patch, please go on."

Pacino pulled off his gold Annapolis class ring and handed it to Vostov, who took it, withdrew reading glasses from his inner jacket pocket and examined the ring under the light of a side lamp. "Your Naval Academy class ring?"

"It's a copy of my ring, sir. It's actually a computer flash drive. It has information on it that President Carlucci is convinced is important and that you need to know. Most urgently, sir. It will synch up to any computer you tie it to. I know we both had problems with our computer networks being infected by combatant viruses, so you may want to connect it to a disposable air-gapped computer, one that isn't tied into the internet or to your network. But I guarantee you, it isn't a virus, just information."

Vostov turned the ring in his hand, then looked up at Pacino.

"What is it? What's the information about?"

Pacino shook his head. "President Carlucci wanted this to be for your eyes only. He did authorize me to tell you to avoid making any speeches in public until you can digest the information in that drive." Pacino gave Vostov a significant look.

Vostov stared at Pacino. "Information about another assassination attempt?"

"I think that's a reasonable guess, sir. It has a password."

"What's the password?"

"The last name of the admiral who was embarked aboard your first Omega submarine that was lost under the polar icecap. I believe your Navy called it the Project 949 Granit submarine." Pacino wondered if Vostov knew that Pacino had been the captain of the submarine that sank it.

Vostov seemed startled and at a loss for words for a moment. "The *Kaliningrad*." He paused, thinking. "I'm not much good at computers, Patch," he said. "I'll have to find someone who can help me open the files."

"Just please make sure whoever you enlist to help you is someone you have absolute trust in, Mr. President," Pacino said, standing. Vostov stood as well and walked with Pacino to the door to his office, turning and shaking Pacino's hand.

"Thank you for this," Vostov said. "And please relay my thanks to President Carlucci. Oh, and thanks again for that story. I shall think about what you said for a long time."

"Goodbye, Mr. President, and thank you for seeing me."

"Anytime, Mr. Vice President. Please stay in touch. And come back soon."

Pacino nodded solemnly as Vostov opened the door. Pacino was immediately surrounded by the Secret Service men and Vostov's SBP security guards. Within twenty minutes, the vice president was strapped into a leather seat in the presidential office of Air Force Two as the 747 climbed out of Moscow and headed westward back to Washington.

Major Grigory Arkov, a GRU sniper assigned to President Vostov's SBP security detail, tried to fall asleep next to the redheaded call girl he'd invited to sleep over. But as it had been for the last two weeks, the insomnia held him in its grip, leaving him staring at the ceiling, thinking and remembering.

Arkov was—or more accurately, had been—a loyal and committed GRU officer with excellent prospects for advancement. He'd been assigned for the last year to the platoon of snipers who took the high ground around any speech to be given by the president, their mission to shoot any threat to the president. During that year, the platoon had only experienced one incident requiring deadly force: a man from a crowd who had broken through the throng of Vostov supporters during a presidential speech in St. Petersburg. As the man was raising his gun to shoot Vostov, two sniper bullets hit the would-be assassin and killed him instantly. One bullet had been from Arkov's rifle, the second from one of the other platoon members. They'd never been told whose bullet had been the kill shot, since one had gone wide and hit the gunman's shoulder, but the other round pierced the man's heart. Arkov maintained that it was *his* bullet that had been the heart shot, but it was an ongoing good-natured argument.

After the killing of the gunman threatening Vostov, Arkov had been told he would be promoted to lieutenant colonel early as a reward for his skillful protection of the president.

But then two weeks ago, Arkov's younger brother Anatoliy, a GRU cadet, had been killed in a training accident. Anatoliy had gone down in a fiery helicopter crash and the human remains were burned beyond recognition and comingled. There was a memorial service, but no caskets, since there were no bodies. A large urn that contained the combined ashes of the cadets and helicopter pilots was all that remained, and it was consigned to a grave honoring the men who had died.

But that had turned out to be a lie, as the FSB officer, Roza Elizaveta, had told him in the bar where she'd found him drinking to try to bury his grief. She'd told him the hard truth that there had *been* no helicopter crash, but that Anatoliy had been a crisis actor in the GUM department store terrorist incident, playing the role of a terrorist, and had been deliberately killed by the SBP. Of course, Arkov hadn't believed her. But she'd convinced him to take her to his apartment, where she showed him the helmet-cam footage from all the SBP troops who'd invaded the boutique and shot the terrorists. From multiple cameras and multiple angles, he saw the hood removed from the corpse of his brother Anatoliy. The SBP invading men had used lethal force, despite the "terrorists" acting under orders of the GRU, and Cadet Anatoliy Arkov had been gunned down, taking two bullets, one to his chest and one to his head. Elizaveta told him that the SBP troops had *orders* to shoot to kill, and that it had been no mistake, but part of their operation order, so that none of the actors playing terrorists could ever tell the real story. That Vostov had used the cadets to cover up a staged and fake terrorist plot as a way to liquidate his own wife.

Then Elizaveta had pointed out the obvious. As one of Vostov's trusted snipers, Arkov had a unique opportunity to avenge the death of his brother at the hands of the president. It had an elegant simplicity. As a sniper, at Vostov's next public speaking engagement, Arkov would be stationed in position where he could shoot anyone threatening the president, but he would also be in a position to shoot the president himself. One shot, and Vostov would lie in a pool of his own blood.

He'd looked into the eyes of the pretty FSB officer and asked what her motivation was. She said she had her own sad story of Vostov's betrayal and was part of a cell of people dedicated to assassinating Vostov.

"You know that one second after I shoot Vostov," he'd said, "either I'll be shot or taken for interrogation. They'll ask how I came to know about the GUM department store plot. They'll torture me until they get me to tell them about you."

"Are you ready to die for what you believe in, Grigory?" she'd asked. "For vengeance for what Vostov did to your brother?"

"Yes," he'd said simply. "I'd rather they kill me on the spot. But being interrogated and tortured? I don't want that. I won't take the chance."

She'd pressed a card into his hand. "This is a dentist's business card," he said, confused.

"The dentist will fit you with a false tooth containing a suicide pill," she'd offered. "He'll train you on how to open it to get the pill. You bite it. It's a cyanide capsule with about five times the dose required to kill you in ten seconds. It won't be an easy death, Grigory, but it will only last a few heartbeats."

He'd looked at her and said, "I sincerely hope they just shoot me on the spot. But if not, I guarantee I'll take the pill."

She'd left him then and he'd kept the dentist appointment. The tooth felt odd in his mouth, a smooth plastic feel to it. Whenever his tongue ran over the capsule, he thought about how it would feel to die from its poison, but then he turned his mind to memories of growing up with Anatoliy.

There was a noise coming from the entrance hall to his apartment. Arkov threw off the covers and was standing up from the bed when the front door crashed open and a dozen black-clad commandos in tactical gear and rifles burst in. Before he could react they grabbed him and put on zip-ties over his wrists and his ankles, duct-taped his mouth and roughly rushed him to his apartment door, down the apartment stairs to a waiting black van.

This was it, he thought, the moment he'd confessed he feared to the FSB turncoat officer. He had told her the truth that he feared capture, interrogation and torture far more than death, and he found the tooth with his tongue, praying to God that it would work. He felt the capsule released from the tooth just as he hit the floor of the van. He bit the capsule hard, the bitter taste in his mouth, and then the horrible pain of the poison killing him.

As his vision got darker, he consoled himself that there would be no torture in his future, only the end. In his last seconds, he thought of Anatoliy, and one thought of regret, that he'd never been able to kill Vostov.

After that, there was nothing.

18

Weapons Officer Captain Lieutenant Katerina Sobol, the senior watch officer in the central command post, stood behind the under-ice sonar console, which was manned by Sonar Officer Senior Lieutenant Valerina Palinkova. Sobol frowned, her arms crossed across her chest.

"Watch Officer, get over here," Sobol called to Captain Lieutenant Vilen Shvets, the communications officer. Shvets bolted up from the seat he'd occupied on the starboard side attack console and joined Sobol at the under-ice station, glancing up at the large flatpanel screen that displayed the output of the under-ice sonar.

"Oh, that's not good," he said.

On the display, a looming wall of ice was coming closer.

"Order all stop," Sobol said.

"Boatswain," Shvets barked, "all stop!"

"All stop, Boatswain, aye, and engineroom answers all stop."

"Report speed zero knots," Shvets called.

"Aye, sir, ship's speed one knot," the boatswain at the ship control console called. "Ship's speed, zero, sir."

"Engage the hovering system," Shvets ordered, "and rig out forward and aft thrusters."

Sobol picked up the tactical phone circuit handset from her station back at the command console and pushed the button for the captain's stateroom. It took the captain a long moment to pick up.

"Captain," Alexeyev's voice buzzed in Sobol's ear.

"Sir, I think you need to come to central."

"On my way."

A few seconds later Alexeyev stood next to Sobol and Shvets behind the under-ice sonar console.

"Looks like pressure ridges have collided here, Captain," Shvets said. "We've got a brick wall dead ahead."

"Train the under-ice view to the port beam," Alexeyev said.

Palinkova turned her joystick to the port side. The view darkened as the wall of ice receded into the distance.

"Twist the ship to the port side," Alexeyev ordered. "Let's see if there's a passage on the north side of this wall. If not, we can look to starboard."

"Boatswain," Shvets ordered, "take charge of your thrusters and twist the ship to the left to heading three five zero."

Lieutenant Duke Squirt Gun Vevera leaned over the number one sonar stack manned by Sonarman First Class Jay Snowman Mercer. Vevera wore his Indian Motorcycle leather jacket over his coveralls, with the control room temperature in the low 60s. He wore his customary wrap-around sunglasses, which he claimed helped him see the displays, and which Captain Seagraves had ordered him to throw away. Mercer shook his head and turned back to look at Vevera, alarm on his face.

"Master One's screws have stopped and his signal-to-noise ratio is climbing. He's stopped."

"Pilot, all stop!" Vevera shouted to Chief McGuire at the ship control station.

"Too close, you need to back down," Mercer said.

"Pilot, all back two thirds." Vevera stepped to stand behind the ship control station. "Mark speed zero."

Vevera turned to the command console and grabbed the 7MC phone and buzzed the captain.

"Speed zero, sir!" McGuire called.

"All stop," Vevera ordered. "Hover at present depth."

"Depth two one zero feet, sir, and engaging hovering."

"Captain," Seagraves baritone crackled in Vevera's ear. "I'm on my way." The captain must have heard Vevera's frantic orders.

Back at the command console, Vevera looked down at the display from the periscope. Master One was alarmingly close. If they'd steamed on for too much longer, they would have driven right into his screws.

"Officer of the Deck, I've got a detect on a new sound signature," Mercer said. "Sounds like small screws."

Seagraves arrived, zipping up his coveralls, his hair wet from the shower. "That could be thrusters," he said. "OOD, get a sounding, fast."

"Nav-E.T., take a sounding," Vevera shouted at the navigation electronics technician.

"Aye, sir, and sounding is one seven eight fathoms. One thousand seventy feet, sir."

"Captain, are you thinking of taking us to the bottom?" Vevera asked.

Seagraves nodded, squinting at the periscope view, but it was too crude to determine the angle of the Omega. "If the Omega turns to look backwards at his past path, his under-ice sonar will be pointing straight at us, and depending on its resolution, he's going to see us. I can't have us be counterdetected."

"Sir, that would take us slightly below test depth. We're at two hundred feet now."

"It should be fine, Mr. Vevera," Seagraves said. "And if it's not, McDermott Aerospace and Shipbuilding will get a very harsh letter. Take us down to the bottom as quietly as possible."

"Bottom us out, aye, sir. Pilot, insert a negative twenty feet per second depth rate."

"Faster than that, Officer of the Deck," Seagraves said as Quinnivan entered the room.

"Pilot," Vevera said, "negative depth rate four zero."

"Trouble?" the XO asked Seagraves.

"Master One is turning to look around. He might see us," Seagraves said.

"Oh, fuck," Quinnivan muttered to himself, looking at the periscope display.

"Negative depth rate, forty feet per second," the pilot announced. "Depth four eight zero feet, passing five hundred."

The hull above groaned suddenly, then emitted several sharp pops like shotgun blasts as the increasing pressure of the deep caused the hull to compress. As if in sympathy, the ice above them joined the cacophony.

"Hopefully the ice noise masks our hull pops. OOD, ease your negative rate as you get closer to the bottom," Seagraves said. "No sense slamming us down on the rocks. Could be bad for business. And make noise."

"Aye, sir, understood. Pilot, mark depth!"

"Nine hundred feet, OOD."

"Ease your depth rate to negative twenty," Vevera ordered.

"Depth, eleven hundred."

"Ease depth rate to negative five," Vevera said.

There was complete silence in the control room as the watchstanders and senior officers waited for the hull to hit the bottom.

"Steady on three five zero, Watch Officer," the boatswain called.

"What do we have?" Alexeyev asked, staring at the under-ice sonar display.

"Sir, the pressure ridge wall continues on, fairly straight," Palinkova said. "I'm not seeing an opening in that wall."

"Watch Officer," Alexeyev said to Shvets, "spin us to the reciprocal bearing."

"Boatswain, turn the ship to the right to bearing one seven zero," Shvets ordered.

A slight vibration came through the deck as the thrusters engaged. The pressure ridge wall scrolled slowly by on the under-ice sonar as the ship turned. As it had on the other heading, the pressure ridge wall continued fairly straight but ended at a corner, where a second wall intersected with it.

"Captain, going south isn't an option," Sobol said to Alexeyev. "It's just another wall."

The shifting ice overhead picked that moment to shriek and groan, the noise continuing for a good thirty seconds.

"Fucking ice," Alexeyev said, looking over and seeing that First Officer Ania Lebedev had joined them behind the under-ice console.

"I recommend we spin back to three five zero and follow the wall that way, Captain," Lebedev said.

"I concur," Alexeyev said. "Watch Officer, take us to three five zero and put on revolutions to take us dead slow, parallel to the wall."

"Boatswain, twist the ship to the left and steady on heading three five zero," Shvets ordered.

The central command post was quiet but for the low roar of the ventilation ducts and shrill whine of the electronics feeding the consoles.

"Watch Officer, turning past heading north, now heading three five zero."

"All ahead one third," Shvets commanded. "Make revolutions for two knots. Maintain present depth."

The officers waited tensely, watching the wall of ice, looking for an opening that would allow them to continue northeastward.

"Sir, the wall continues," Palinkova reported.

For endless minutes, the ship moved along the ice wall, the pressure ridge showing no openings.

After half an hour, Palinkova looked back to Alexeyev. "Captain, I have something to the left. I have thin ice."

The deck jumped as *New Jersey*'s hull hit the rocky bottom of the Arctic Ocean. The deck heeled over five degrees in a port list and tilted upward by ten degrees.

"Bottomed out, Officer of the Deck," McGuire reported from the ship control console. "Depth, thirteen hundred and five feet."

"What is Master One doing?" Seagraves asked Sonarman Mercer.

"Looks he was spinning around to check out the ice, Captain."

281

"Good thing we got out of the way of his under-ice sonar," Vevera said.

"Ask yourself, Mr. Vevera, would we even know if he counterdetected us on his under-ice unit?"

"He'd probably have hit us with his active sonar, Captain," Quinnivan said. "Just to distinguish us from a chunk of ice or a near-field sonar blur."

Seagraves nodded. "Still, you should put yourself into the shoes of the Omega captain. Always be thinking about what *he's* thinking."

"Master One has started back up," Mercer said. "He's making twenty-five RPM on both screws. I have bearing rate left and diminishing SNR. Bearing three five one."

"We still have him on the scope?" Seagraves asked Vevera.

"He's fading, Captain."

"Get us off the bottom and put on turns to follow him," Seagraves ordered. "And close the range. We can't lose him amid all this ice noise."

"Pilot, insert a positive depth rate, forty feet per second and mark depth twelve hundred."

The list and incline came off the deck as the ship lifted off.

"Twelve hundred feet, sir," McGuire called.

"All ahead one third, turns for six knots, steer course three five one, and make your depth two hundred feet," Vevera ordered. To himself he muttered, "Follow that fuckin' BUFF."

———

"Watch Officer, stop here and spin us left to three zero zero," Alexeyev ordered.

Alexeyev looked at Lebedev. "Pressure ridge must have shifted and opened up the ice canopy."

"Sonar Officer, what's the ice thickness at the thin ice?" Alexeyev asked.

"Less than one meter, Captain."

Lebedev murmured in Alexeyev's ear. "Sir, if that ice wall continues, we could hit it with a Gigantskiy torpedo. We don't know how thick it is. There might be a passage on the other side of it."

"We don't have nuclear release authority on the Gigantskiy units," Alexeyev said. God alone knew why they'd been sent with the nuclear units, if not to break through an ice wall like the one they faced. But that was in keeping with the rest of the stupidity of this mission, he thought.

"I know, but that's the reason they loaded us up with them," Lebedev said. "I suppose we could try a Futlyar torpedo or two. See if that does anything."

"I have another idea," Alexeyev said. "Watch Officer, drive us to the thin ice and prepare to vertical surface. Sonar Officer, light up the upward-looking under-ice sonar and chart the size of the thin ice. Let's make sure it's big enough to allow us to surface." Alexeyev stepped back to the command console and motioned Lebedev to join him there. In a quiet voice, he said to her, "Let's call home and see if we can get nuclear weapon release authority. If they say no, we can throw Futlyar units at the wall. But that pressure ridge? I'm guessing we could toss the whole torpedo room at it and it would just laugh at us. One megaton blast on direct contact? It will open up like a door."

"We could still backtrack, Captain," Lebedev said. "Turn around and find another way through the ice."

"I'm not interested in going backwards," Alexeyev said, a tone of annoyance in his voice. "Besides, if we radio Northern Fleet HQ, maybe they've got new orders for us." Maybe, he thought, they might have called off this fool's errand.

"Master One is shut down again, Officer of the Deck," Mercer reported from the number one sonar stack. "Turn count zero."

"All stop," Vevera ordered. "Now what the hell is he doing? Sonar, do you have thruster noises again?"

"No, sir, but he's stopped. He's dead in the water. Wait. Wait. Officer of the Deck, I have blowing noises. He's blowing variable ballast or even main ballast. I'm showing D/E getting higher." D/E was deflection / elevation, the angle to the contact. Mercer was seeing the Omega rising out of the sea. "I've got a loud collision noise. Master One has hit the ice overhead."

"He's surfacing," Seagraves said, glancing at the periscope view. "We're under thin ice. Mr. Vevera, close Master One slowly. Mind your periscope. See if you can drive us underneath him, but take us down to three hundred." He looked at Quinnivan. "This is it, XO. Mobilize Mr. Fishman and the *Panther* team and prepare to place the mines on the hull of the Omega. Officer of the Deck, man silent battlestations."

Lieutenant Anthony Pacino climbed into the dry-deck shelter, waiting to put on his mask over his drysuit hood. The Mark 16 Draeger closed circuit mixed gas rebreather was heavy, heavier than the twin-80 bottles he'd used to invade the *Panther*. He glanced at U-Boat Dankleff, who shot him a thumbs-up gesture. This was the worst part, Pacino thought, remembering his panic attack when the *Vermont*'s escape trunk was flooded before that mission. This time, he intended to keep his eyes clamped shut when the flooding started. Once he'd been completely under water last time, four or five breaths in, he'd been fine.

The shelter was crowded with all four of them inside with the Mark 76 propulsion units, which were also a lot fatter and longer than the ones they'd used on *Panther*, and reduced the space inside available for human occupation. Pacino's earpiece crackled with Dankleff's voice.

"Let's gear up, Patch. Time to flood. Your favorite part of the dive."

Pacino nodded and put on his mask over his drysuit hood, then clamped his double-fed regulator into his mouth and took an experimental breath. The air was dry, but not as dry as the conventional SCUBA air he'd breathed before. Or like the emergency air mask during the *Vermont* fire, he thought. His mind drifted momentarily to Rachel, and he wondered how she was. Maybe the captain would pop up the comms mast at the thin ice after the Omega dived again, and they could get an update on her. He bit his lip and commanded himself to get his head into the mission. This would not be an easy dive.

"Commencing flooding," Dankleff said. For the dive, Pacino and Dankleff were teamed up. Fishman would be diving with Muhammad Varney as his partner. Each team had a communication wire between them, but not between the separate teams. It would have been better if all four of them could be on the same comm circuit. Pacino and Dankleff were amateurs.

The water level rose past Pacino's waist. Even in the drysuit, he could feel the coldness of the water. When the water came up to Pacino's chest, he turned away from Dankleff and clamped his eyes shut. The vision of water rising over his mask was too frightening to bear. But he could feel through his gloved hand that the water level was over his head, and he opened his eyes and turned back to Dankleff and shot him a thumbs-up.

"Opening the shelter door now," Dankleff said. Pacino nodded.

The shelter door opened, the door the diameter of the shelter, almost twelve feet wide. Fishman grabbed his Mark 76 and motored out of the shelter, Varney holding on to a handhold bar on its flank. Pacino clipped his safety harness to the Mark 76 and tested it. No sense falling off the damned thing at depth. Dankleff started their Mark 76 and Pacino grabbed onto the passenger handhold.

As they maneuvered out of the shelter, Pacino looked up to see if the target were visible. The water was much clearer than he'd expected, and as he looked up he could see the dark underside of the Omega, and it was simply enormous.

"Dear God," he said aloud involuntarily.

"Yeah. Big, ugly and fat," Dankleff said. "Fishman's headed to the port side. I'm driving us to starboard. Watch for the torpedo tube door opening."

As Dankleff drove them down the *New Jersey* hull, its curvature changing from horizontal to vertical, Pacino looked down, but below the hull of the *New Jersey*, the water was black. He looked up again to see the ice above and the surfaced Omega. He could make out its bow and could see far back to its aft end, but the rudder, scoops and screws weren't visible, vanishing in a blue blur.

The faint buzzing feeling of the Mark 76's motor stopped as Dankleff piloted them to the *New Jersey*'s starboard side torpedo tube muzzle doors, the elliptical shape of them caused by the cylinder of the tube meeting the curving hull near the bow. Pacino touched the opening of the open upper tube, the steel of the hull cold to the touch. His job was to pull the Mark 80 mine out of the tube by its nose cable. He grabbed the cable with both gloved hands and pulled, using his flipper-clad feet for leverage. The mine moved smoothly and easily out of the tube, as if the torpedo room crew had greased it. Pacino attached the mine's cable to the Mark 76 propulsion unit and continued to pull out the mine, until finally the mine was fully out of the tube. Pacino hurried to its operator panel, ready to adjust its buoyancy. He tested to see if it would sink or pop upward, but the mine was fairly trimmed to neutral buoyancy.

"I've got good trim on the mine," Pacino said to Dankleff. "The mine is secured to the Mark 76. Let's go."

"We've got the BUFF's starboard side," Dankleff said. "Let's get this thing next to the BUFF and get shallow. If we can see its sail, we mount the mine at a position of its trailing edge. If not, we'll have to feel for the torpedo tube door and move aft by twenty feet or so."

"Okay, let's hurry."

Dankleff piloted them upward to the flank of the Omega, perhaps eighty feet over their heads. As he approached the hull, Pacino could see the deep-diver submarine docked to the underside of the Omega's hull. It was much bigger than in his imagination. It had to be over 250 feet long, he thought. He could see it had small but thick portholes in its bow. He hoped no one was in there peering out at them. No one had thought that could be a problem. Pacino kept his eyes on the Russian submarine's exterior where it had curved to be vertical.

"Hey, U-Boat, I think I have the torpedo tube door, drive us aft."

In the shallower water, with the pressure less on the mine, it had begun to get buoyant. Pacino hit the fixed function key on its operator panel to flood its variable ballast bladder until it behaved again. He wondered if there were some way to automate this, but the control system would add volume and weight—taking away payload for explosives. Still, it seemed a risk that the mine could get away from them.

"I don't see it, Patch."

"There, above you about five feet. There's three of them. See them?"

"Oh, yeah, you're right. Let me drive us about twenty or twenty-five feet farther aft."

"Position us at the elevation of the middle tube."

"We're here. Now's the hard part of the day. Open up the mine," Dankleff said.

Pacino manipulated the operator panel's fixed function key for opening up the mine, the software asking him if he were sure he wanted to do that. He hit the "YES" button and the mine slowly opened up so that its cylindrical shape became two half-cylinders. He maneuvered the mine to touch the rubbery coating of the hull, hoping it would be able to attach. While Pacino operated the mine, Dankleff's job was to keep control of the propulsion unit. Pacino could hear the Mark 76 engine occasionally buzz as Dankleff kept it at their depth. Pacino touched the control panel's "ATTACH" protocol section, and energized the "AUTO ATTACH" button. If the unit were able to cut through the rubber hull coating and weld itself to the hull, it would be an easy day.

The mine vibrated as the vacuum pump came on and the unit seemed stuck to the hull. It groaned as the mechanicals tried to cut through the anechoic coating. The sound changed as the welding rig went to work. The status panel read "COMMENCING WELD OP." Eventually the noise quieted and the panel read "ELECTROMAGNET ON" and "VACUUM PUMP OFF." Pacino tried gently budging the mine, and fortunately, it seemed to be holding fast to the Omega hull. The status panel changed to read, "ELECTROMAGNET OFF." The mine still seemed to be holding.

"Arm it, Patch," Dankleff said from behind Pacino. Pacino went to the control panel's arming section and selected "ARM FOR SONAR SIGNAL." He pressed the "YES" key and the unit again asked whether he were sure he wanted to do that, and again he pressed "YES." In a moment the panel flashed green, the text reading "ARMED FOR SONAR SIGNAL."

"Well, U-Boat, our work here is done. I'm disconnecting the mine's cable from the Mark 76. Fishman should be showing up by now," Pacino said. "Maybe he and Boozy ran into trouble. Think we should swim over to them and see how they're doing?"

"May as well. You sure this thing is attached well enough?"

"Yeah. This thing ain't going anywhere," Pacino said. "Take us under the hull to the port side, and watch out for any seawater suction grates."

———

Captain First Rank Georgy Alexeyev motioned First Officer Ania Lebedev to a seat at his stateroom's conference table.

"I'm thinking we get the *Losharik* captain and first officer in here as well," he said. "And send for the navigator and communications officer. We'll dictate the message to them."

"Yes, sir."

While Lebedev called in the other officers, Alexeyev's tactical circuit phone buzzed. He answered it. "Captain."

"Sir, Watch Officer. The engineer requests to conduct a steam generator blowdown and the supply officer requests permission to dump trash."

"Very well. Conduct steam generator blowdowns and dump trash. Any other shallow operations you need?"

"No, sir. We have a good navigation fix and we've downloaded our intel files. No messages for us."

"Fine. We'll be generating the message to Northern Fleet Command in the next few minutes. Have the radiomen ready to transmit it."

"Aye, sir, understood."

Alexeyev looked up to find Sergei Kovalov and his second-in-command Vlasenko coming into the room. Alexeyev waved them to seats as Navigator Maksimov and Communications Officer Shvets came in. Shvets shut the stateroom door.

"Shvets, you get our position from central?" Alexeyev asked the comms officer.

"Sir, yes, sir."

"Have a seat, people, and let's get this message drafted." Alexeyev reached for the ash tray and found his last pack of cigarettes and lit up, wondering if anyone on board had cigarettes for sale. He looked at Lebedev, who was preparing to write onto the message pad. Alexeyev dictated, "From K-329 *Belgorod* to Commander, Northern Fleet. Item one. *Belgorod* surfaced-at-ice at position—" Alexeyev looked expectantly at Shvets.

"Longitude one zero two degrees thirty minutes east, latitude eighty-five degrees forty-five minutes north."

"You got that, Madam First?"

"Yes, Captain. Continue." Lebedev was typing on a detached keyboard paired to the electronic pad computer for the message. She looked up at Alexeyev.

"Item two," he dictated. "*Belgorod* has encountered ice obstructions over many nautical miles that impede movement along the intended track on great circle route to the Bering Strait. The ice walls were mapped and *Belgorod* commanding officer believes there is no viable path to continue."

"Say 'severe ice obstructions consisting of multiple pressure ridges extending from icecap to ocean bottom,'" Kovalov said.

Alexeyev noticed that Kovalov seemed annoyed. Obviously something was bothering him.

"Yes, put that in. It must read that we did everything possible to get by the ice wall," Alexeyev said. Add that after the words 'Bering Strait.'"

"Got it, sir," Lebedev said.

"Item three," Alexeyev continued, "*Belgorod* requests nuclear release authority to employ Gigantskiy torpedoes one and two to attempt to break through ice walls." He paused. "They're never going to grant us that," he said. *Damned fool's errand*, he thought.

Through the hull, the blasting noise of the steam generator blowdowns roared, going on for half a minute, then quieting. There would be four of those noises, Alexeyev thought, as they blew out the contaminants from the steam generators and adjusted their chemistry. Suddenly five-hundred-degree boiler water was ejected into twenty-eight-degree seawater, and it made a hell of a racket. It was a shame they didn't have the sound quieting technology for blowdowns that the new Yasen-M submarines had, like his *Kazan*. But that was an expensive retrofit, and Sevmash had decided to postpone it. Or cancel it altogether. Budget problems, he thought.

"Item four. Alternative to use conventional torpedoes against the ice walls rejected based on ice thickness. Conventional torpedo use will only deplete *Belgorod's* weapons loadout."

He puffed the cigarette and put it out. "Everyone okay with that? On to the next. Item five. One possible alternative is to attempt to drive south to the Russian northern coastline in the marginal ice zone. This option is considered to have the potential for more ice obstacles until more open water is reached, and the path will consume time and ship's resources." *Food*, he thought. Running out of it was a non-starter.

"Add that any delay on the southern route will require mid-mission replenishment," Kovalov said. "No way our food supplies last if we spend an additional month or two fucking about on the southern route."

Alexeyev nodded. "Add that in. Item six. *Belgorod* believes backtracking westward toward the Kola Peninsula and the entrance to the North Atlantic presents a better option than continuing eastward. *Belgorod* requests Northern Fleet Command consider the westward route and advise." He looked around the room. "Anything else to add? No? Okay, Madam First, read back what we have."

When Lebedev finished, Alexeyev said, "Add item seven, that *Belgorod* will wait at this polynya until a response is received from

Northern Fleet Command or until the open water is closed in by pressure ridge movement."

"Add in, Northern Fleet Command is requested to reply most urgently," Kovalov said. "Just in case a duty officer lets it sit in his in-basket."

"Add it, and make the message priority coded as 'immediate.'"

"Yes, Captain," Lebedev said.

"Read it back again," Alexeyev ordered. When she was done, he said to the room, "everyone in agreement? Good. Mr. Shvets, send the message immediately. You're all dismissed. Captain Kovalov, can you remain behind?"

———————

Dankleff drove them under the hull and up the opposite side, aiming for where Fishman and Varney were working with the port side mine. When they arrived, Dankleff took a communication cable and handed it to Fishman so all four could be tied into the same circuit.

"What's holding you slugs up?" Dankleff asked. "Patch and I had ours done in record time."

"Coating gave us trouble," Varney said.

"I'm only now arming the unit," Fishman said. "It's time to deploy the inter-mine comms cable. Dankleff, you and Pacino get back to *New Jersey*. Varney and I will join you in the shelter when we've connected the comms cable."

———————

"Yes? You wanted to talk to me?" Sergei Kovalov said in an annoyed tone.

"Yes, Sergei," Alexeyev said. "What is going on with you? You've disappeared from sight for over a week. You're not in the guest stateroom but sleeping in your cramped and smelly group sleeping quarters on *Losharik*. And when we were collaborating on the message to fleet headquarters, you were openly hostile to me. I want to know why."

291

"I'm surprised," Kovalov said, his tone pugnacious. "Smart officer like you, given command of the super-secret special project submarine *Belgorod*, can't figure it out."

Alexeyev smirked. "First, this boat is a pile of junk, rescued from a 1990s drydock and refurbished ten times, the refurbs stopping every time the Navy ran out of money. It's 1980s design. Hell, 1970s, modified in the 1980s. We're probably louder than a freight train with its last car derailed. The combat control system? Patched together with the old unit overlaid with the new Second Captain AI. This boat has never tested its combat systems with any success. Sergei, I promise you. My assignment to this boat is *not* a promotion. It's a punishment tour. Punishment for losing *Kazan* and a third of her crew. So just cut the attitude, will you? Now, look me in the eye and tell me what the hell is bothering you."

"You really don't know?"

Alexeyev shook his head. "I really don't know."

Kovalov sighed heavily and got out of the table's seat four down from Alexeyev's end and moved to the seat to Alexeyev's immediate right. He withdrew a cigarette pack and offered one to Alexeyev, who smiled and took it. Alexeyev pulled over the ash tray and lit up with Kovalov.

"You asked Svetlana Anna about my private conversations with her."

Alexeyev nodded. "Did she tell you what my inquiry was limited to?"

"No," Kovalov said, looking down at the table.

"I only asked her specifically if you were suicidal. If you'd said anything about hurting yourself."

"What? What are you talking about?" Kovalov said. He seemed genuinely surprised, Alexeyev noted.

Alexeyev shrugged. "You don't talk to me anymore. Just to your comfort woman."

"Test wife," Kovalov said, peeved.

"Fine. Test wife. Forgive my political incorrectness. I also asked Anna if you'd said anything about this mission. Specifically, any opposition to it."

Kovalov started to smile slowly. "I leave those sentiments to my conversations with *you* only, comrade."

Alexeyev smiled back at him. They lit two more cigarettes in silence, when Alexeyev's tactical phone circuit buzzed.

"Captain," he said and listened. "Very well. Send the message pad to my stateroom." He looked up at Kovalov. "Fleet headquarters wrote us back."

"Already?"

"Yes. They must have reflexively said 'no' to our request," Alexeyev said.

A soft knock came at the door. "Enter," Alexeyev said. Captain Lieutenant Shvets stood in the doorway and handed Alexeyev the radio message pad computer. "Mr. Shvets," Alexeyev said as the communications officer was about to shut the door behind him, "please have the watch officer send in Madam Lebedev and Mr. Vlasenko. You should also get Navigator Maksimov and bring her, and come yourself."

"Right away, Captain," Shvets said and left.

"He's a quiet lad," Kovalov observed.

"Keeps to himself. People who do that make me nervous. As our talk today demonstrated," Alexeyev said to Kovalov, smiling at him.

Alexeyev read the message, his eyebrows lifting. He slid the pad over to Kovalov, who inhaled, his hand over his mouth.

"*Yebena mat'*," Kovalev said. "Holy shit."

19

"Excuse me, Captain?" Lieutenant Commander Ebenezer Fishman said, knocking on the door jamb of the captain's stateroom.

"Come on in," Captain Seagraves said. "Wait, before you do, could you grab the XO from his stateroom?"

A moment later, Seagraves, Quinnivan, and Fishman were seated at the captain's stateroom table.

"Your report, Mr. Fishman?" Seagraves asked.

Fishman pursed his lips. "It went smoothly, Captain, XO. Mines were both deployed and programmed. Inter-mine comms cable installed and glued to *Belgorod's* hull. All self-checks performed. Tested, tested sat. We're good to go."

"How did the officers perform?" Seagraves asked.

"Flawlessly. I can't believe I'm saying this, Captain, XO, but it was a textbook operation. I'm actually thinking of recruiting them into the SEAL program."

"Bite your tongue, Tiny Tim," Seagraves said, chuckling. "Those officers belong to me until I release them."

"I suppose that's the only duty we'll have on this run," Fishman said, sounding disappointed.

"Not necessarily," Seagraves said. "There's some discussion about using you guys to interfere with the Status-6 placement. Nothing definite. Just a message back when we were in open water to think about what we could do."

"I'll tell ye what ya can fookin' do, Skipper," Quinnivan said, leaning back in his chair. "You can torpedo the fookin' BUFF right here, right now."

"Why stoop to such a brutal, ungentlemanly, impolite way to neutralize the *Belgorod*, XO?" Seagraves asked, smiling. "When we could just elegantly play the sonar signal to light off the mines?"

"Just out of curiosity, Captain," Fishman asked. "What *is* the sonar signal to command detonate? Some random combination of tones and chords?"

"Don't laugh, Mr. Fishman," Seagraves said. "It's twelve seconds of the climactic ending of the *1812 Overture* by Pyotr Ilyich Tchaikovsky, with the cannons firing and the trumpets wailing. At the final cannon blast, the mines explode."

"Fitting, I suppose," Fishman said. "A Russian composer for an attack on a Russian sub. And cannons blasting just as we're busting open his hull."

"My thoughts as well. How are your men now?" Seagraves looked expectantly at Fishman.

"They're coming out of it, sir. Oddly, Grip Aquatong is the strongest at the moment, which is strange, since he had much more of the energy drink we think caused all this."

"He developed some limited immunity, I suppose," Quinnivan said.

The 7MC circuit from the conn buzzed. Seagraves picked up the handset and put it to his ear. "Captain." He listened, then said, "Very well, pass the word to station silent battlestations." Seagraves looked at Quinnivan. "The Omega is doing some strange maneuvers. I'm manning battlestations just in case."

"Good move, Captain," Quinnivan said. "After all, why does an armadillo have armor? Just. In. Case."

"That joke got old in the War of 1812," Seagraves chuckled.

"You know, we Brits almost won that one," Quinnivan smiled.

"What do you make of this, Madam First?" Alexeyev asked Ania Lebedev, leaning back in his command chair at the end of the table in his stateroom. Lebedev looked vaguely disturbed. Sergei Kovalov was absorbed in reading and rereading the reply message from Northern Fleet HQ.

She looked up at Alexeyev. "We're to employ Gigantskiy unit one against the ice wall. They gave us the unlock codes. Then they said to reserve unit two in case of tactical contingencies and they gave us *unit two's* unlock codes. And they authorized use of unit two as required by *Belgorod*'s commanding officer. What the hell does HQ mean by, quote, tactical contingencies, unquote?"

"Sergei?" Alexeyev said. "What do you think?"

Kovalov nodded. "They think we may have to shoot at someone," he said.

"I notice they said nothing about the alternative course to hug the Russian coastline," Lebedev said. "Or about reversing course to the west."

"I imagine Zhigunov wants to see how we do with the assault on the ice wall," Alexeyev said. "Madam First, pass the word for action stations for tactical launch. I'll meet you in central."

When the officers left but for Kovalov, Alexeyev put out his cigarette and said, "How far do you think safe standoff is for shooting a nuke at the ice?"

"Did Northern Fleet and Sevmash ever figure out how far *Voronezh* and *Novosibirsk* were from the ground zero of the American nuclear detonations?"

"No, they didn't," Alexeyev said. "They guessed the blast was probably five kilometers from *Novosibirsk*. Less for *Voronezh*—she was vaporized. One of the depth charges must have gone off right on top of her. But the depth of the blast was different and the yield of the weapon different. Our ice target is shallower but our nuclear yield is four or five times bigger than the American tactical nukes. So we're going to have to guess."

"The weapon safety settings for standoff are ten nautical miles," Kovalov said. "Any closer and we'll have to switch off that safety. So I guess I'd say anything less than ten miles is risky."

"You actually read the Gigantskiy torpedo operation manual, Sergei?"

"I was bored."

Alexeyev laughed. "Our standoff distance is going to have to depend on the maximum straight-line distance we can get from the ice wall target point. The torpedo will have to go straight. It can't be maneuvered around ice obstacles on the way. And it's not smart enough to navigate itself through an ice maze."

"Are you setting it up for a contact detonation or a command detonate at a point in space?"

"Both. Whichever comes first."

"You know, to find the best and longest straight-line path from the ice target point," Kovalov said. "You will have to survey the sea with active sonar. The under-ice unit is for close-in obstacles."

"Agreed. Will you come to central for this war shot launch?"

"I wouldn't miss it, Georgy," Kovalov said.

"Master One is shut down again," Sonarman Senior Chief Albanese reported. "I've got thruster noise, Officer of the Deck."

"Very well, Sonar," Lieutenant Anthony Pacino replied from the command console. "Pilot, all stop. Hover at present depth."

"All stop, Pilot, aye," Dankleff said. "Speed two knots, depth two one zero, speed one knot."

Pacino squinted at the command console display. Master One, the BUFF, was visible on IR on the periscope display—or more accurately, his reactor and engineroom components were. The rest of his outline was a blurry cloud generated by the slight difference in his skin temperature from the surrounding icy waters.

"Speed zero, hovering, depth two one zero feet," Dankleff called.

"What the hell is he doing?" Seagraves asked Pacino and Quinnivan. Lieutenant Commander Lewinsky joined them as they crowded the command console. Lieutenant Commander Styxx at the weapon control console to starboard was listening intently to their conversation.

297

"He's spinning, sir," Pacino said. "I'd say to his left. He'll be seeing us soon on his under-ice sonar."

"Range guess, Coordinator?" Seagraves asked Quinnivan, who at battlestations was the firecontrol coordinator.

"Close, Captain. Inside five hundred yards."

"Do you want to take her to the bottom again, Captain?" Pacino asked.

"Sounding?" Seagraves seemed deep in thought.

"Nav-E.T., take a secure sounding," Pacino called.

"Sir, ninety fathoms. Five hundred forty feet," the navigation electronics technician reported.

"Take us down slowly, Officer of the Deck," Seagraves said. "I want to minimize our transients from the depth excursion."

"Pilot, negative rate, twenty feet per second," Pacino ordered.

"Negative twenty, Pilot, aye."

"Sonar, is he still thrusting?" Pacino asked Albanese. He stared at his periscope display, trying to make sense of the red shapes of the hotspots of the *Belgorod*'s interior.

"Thrusters still on, OOD."

"Report the second his thrusters shut down," Pacino said.

"Depth four hundred," Dankleff reported.

"OOD, thrusters have stopped. Master One may be hovering," Albanese reported.

It was then the piercing shriek blasted through the hull.

"Captain, ship's heading now two seven zero, west," the boatswain reported from the ship control console.

"Boatswain, secure thrusters and hover," Alexeyev said. "Sonar, do you have any obstructions directly in front of us on this bearing?"

"No, Captain," Sonar Officer Palinkova said, still intensely staring at her under-ice sonar display.

"Weapons Officer," Alexeyev said to Captain Lieutenant Sobol at the port side sonar console, "are you lined up for an active sonar ping?" With the sonar officer at the under-ice sonar set, it fell to the weapons officer to run the active sonar suite with her senior enlisted technician.

"Active sonar is ready, Captain," Sobol said in her high-pitched cartoon character voice. Alexeyev shared a momentary glance with Kovalov, who smirked. Behind closed doors, they'd both marveled at that odd voice.

"Transmit active," Alexeyev ordered. "High frequency first, then low."

"Ping active, aye, sir, high frequency first, then low."

Sobol lifted a protective cover over the sonar mode selector switch for the spherical array and twisted it to the "ACTIVE" position. She lifted a second protective cover over the transmit button for high frequency, then one over the low frequency button. She mashed the high frequency button, and a piercing high-pitched scream reverberated through the room. The high frequency radar-style circular plot of bearing versus range glowed green, a bright green circle growing outward from the center. She hit the low frequency key, and a roaring low-pitched growl shook the room. As she released her finger, the noise stopped. A similar plot for the low frequency sonar lit up, a blue circle growing from the center and moving outward.

"Captain!" Sobol squealed. "I have a submerged contact! Bearing west, range close, a quarter nautical mile!"

"What?" Alexeyev said, hurrying to the active sonar display in front of Sobol. The contact flashed in both high frequency and low frequency plots. "Do you have broadband contact?"

"No, Captain, but we've been searching all through the azimuth. I can train the spherical array beam to center on west with a narrow search cone."

"Do it. Do you have narrowband contact?"

"No tonals, Captain."

"Focus your narrowband search in the westward cone," Alexeyev said.

"Weapons Officer, line up your transient module," Lebedev said, standing to Alexeyev's right.

"Understood, Madam First, and the transient module is engaged, also narrow cone at bearing two seven zero."

"Weapons Officer, send the contact bearing and range to the navigation plot and battlecontrol. Navigator," Lebedev said, glancing at Navigator Maksimov. "Plot the contact on your nav plot and show our past course and the target ice position."

"I've got transients," Sobol reported. "Sounds like his hull is compressing. He must be going deep. Hull pops and water noise, maybe flooding a tank. I have a thump, Captain. Water noise stopped, hull popping is stopped. He may have hit the bottom."

"Depth here?" Lebedev asked.

"Shallow. Two hundred fifteen meters, Madam First," Maksimov said.

"He's got to be hiding on the bottom," Alexeyev said to Lebedev. Alexeyev glanced over Lebedev's shoulder at Kovalov, who had crossed his arms over his chest, frowning deeply. "How long do you think he's been following us?" he asked.

"He had to have picked us up as we left Zapadnaya Litsa," Lebedev said quietly. "No way he's just randomly patrolling the Arctic Ocean just in case he finds a Russian submarine."

"Any chance it's one of our own? Maybe Zhigunov sent a Yasen-M sub to escort us out?" Alexeyev tapped his wedding ring on the back of Sobol's seat.

"And make sure we perform the mission?" Lebedev seemed deep in thought. "There's no way to tell without narrowband contact on him. Or until he transmits active. Or we hear a torpedo sonar that allows us to classify him."

"If he were Russian, after hearing that sonar ping, he'd reply on Bolshoi-Feniks and identify himself," Alexeyev said. "Not sneak to the bottom to hide."

"Sonar Officer, you have any contact on Bolshoi-Feniks?" Lebedev asked Palinkova. The Bolshoi unit functioned as an underwater communication device between them and other Russian submarines. It transmitted pulses that would resemble the sound version of a bar code, unable to be interpreted by a foreign sub.

"No contact on Bolshoi-Feniks, sir," Palinkova reported.

"So, here's what we know," Alexeyev said to Lebedev and Kovalov. "He's under ice. That means he's nuclear powered. So, American or British or French. Or Russian, but without contact on Bolshoi, and with him evading us, I suggest we drop the idea he's Russian. I think we can safely rule out the Red Chinese. And the Indians."

"I think the odds favor this sub being an American, Captain," Lebedev said. "They have many more nuclear attack subs than the British or French. Plus, unlike the British or French, they have a stake in keeping an eye on this mission. What is their expression? Yes, they would say they have a dog in this fight. Plus, he's so ghostly quiet, we didn't detect him until we pinged at him. He's state-of-the-art, late flight. I think it's reasonable to assume this is an American sub. Virginia-class."

"I agree," Alexeyev said, his mind drifting back to the last time he had faced an American Virginia-class. That episode had ended very badly, he thought. He forced the memory from his mind and looked at the central command posts' watchstanders. "Attention in central command. Designate this contact as 'Hostile One.' Now, Madam First, what do you suggest we do about this?" Alexeyev stared at the sonar plot.

Lebedev bit her lip and glanced at the active display, the contact still lit from the returned sonar ping. "We won't see him on active sonar with him on the bottom, Captain. We have his position charted. So one option is to keep going with the plan to open up the ice with a Gigantskiy. The other option, Captain," she paused and looked into Alexeyev's eyes, "is to use the Gigantskiy in command detonate mode and shoot him."

———————

Senior Chief Sonarman Albanese dropped his headphones to the deck and clamped his hands over his ears, muttering, "Oh fuck." He looked up at Seagraves. "I'm okay, sir, just got my bell rung by Master One's first sonar ping."

Pacino looked at Seagraves. "He's lit us up with active," he said. "It's a fair bet he knows we're out here."

"Depth seven hundred," Dankleff called.

"Ease your depth rate to negative three," Pacino replied.

"Negative three, aye."

"Coordinator, Navigator, recommendations?" Seagraves said.

Quinnivan shook his head. "We're awfully close to him, Captain. We might be inside minimum range. If his sonar is like ours, it will screen out anything closer than a few hundred yards to avoid near field reverberations." An active pulse could actually boil water at the sonar dome, and the rising bubbles could interfere with interpreting an active signal, and even if there were no bubbles, the near-field effect of the impurities in the water close to the transmitting sonar would make interpreting a close contact unlikely. "He might not have seen us."

The hull settled on the bottom with a lurch, the deck inclining slowly to a slight starboard list.

"Bottomed out, OOD," Dankleff said. "Depth seven one five feet."

"I say we play possum and just hide here on the bottom," Lewinsky said. "If he snapped us up, he'll hit us with active again."

"Or shoot at us," Quinnivan said.

"No," Seagraves said. "No way he has rules of engagement to fire on a trailing submarine. And if he transmits active again, we're invisible. He won't make us out down here. He can't distinguish us from a bounce off the bottom."

"He's on a war mission, Captain," Quinnivan said. "Based on a good sonar detect, he wouldn't have to hear us on active again. He could just shoot with a command detonate at our position. If he used a Gigantskiy torpedo, a one megaton blast wouldn't have to be accurate. We should spin up two torpedoes in countermeasure mode and open outer doors. And spin up two in offensive mode."

"Opening a muzzle door—if he hears that—is like drawing down on him," Seagraves said, looking down at the deck, his chin in his hand. "That might justify him shooting at us. Let's not provoke him."

"Can we at least spin up the torpedoes?" Quinnivan asked.

Seagraves nodded. "Spin up Mark 48 ADCAPs in countermeasure mode in tubes three and four and flood down and equalize. Spin up Mark 48 ADCAPs in offense mode in tubes one and two, and flood them down and equalize."

"Let's hope he doesn't pick up transients from us doing that," Pacino said. "He's still hovering in place, barely four or five hundred yards out. It's been a couple of minutes since he pinged."

"Recommend firing point procedures," Quinnivan said. "Just in case."

"Wait on that, XO." Seagraves shook his head. "If he decided to launch a Magnum torpedo—I can't bring myself to call it a 'Gigantskiy'—he'd have to clear datum by miles before firing. Let's just stand pat and wait here on the bottom. Everybody just calm down. No need to hit the panic switch. Let's just hold our breath and see what he does."

Lewinsky looked at Seagraves. "We could go to absolute sound quieting, Captain. We could scram the reactor."

"Scramming the fookin' reactor? Under ice? Have you lost your mind, Nav?" Quinnivan said, his eyebrows raised.

Seagraves shook his head, deep in thought. "What is he *doing*?" he asked, more to himself than to his officers.

"No further contact on Hostile One, Captain," Sobol said to Alexeyev.

"What now, Captain?" Lebedev asked. "Are we still going to target the ice with a Gigantskiy?"

Alexeyev shrugged. "We pretty much have to. We got the order from Northern Fleet."

"It's not safe now, Captain," Lebedev said. "Shooting that torpedo, if Hostile One is between us and the ice target, he could interpret that as us shooting at *him*. And then he'd have cause to shoot at *us*. Or the blast could destroy him unintentionally. If the American sinks, it should be because we targeted him."

"Captain Alexeyev," Sergei Kovalov said, speaking up for the first time since the sonar detection. "If I may be so bold as to make an observation."

"Go ahead, Captain Kovalov," Alexeyev said formally.

"It occurs to me," Kovalov said, "that if we've been detected and trailed by a hostile American submarine, our stealth is gone. And evading American knowledge of our mission was the reason to go to the Pacific by way of the Arctic Ocean, yes? And if our secrecy is compromised, we no longer have to go all around North America and South America to get to the Status-6 placement points on the American east coast, right? Which means we can abandon this whole eastward path and just go westward past Great Britain and Iceland into the North Atlantic, their sonar trip wires be damned. It would shorten the mission by months."

"He makes a good point, Captain," Lebedev said.

Alexeyev thought for a long moment. "We could still lose him in the sonar blue-out from the nuclear detonation. He might lose contact on us."

"And we'll lose contact on *him* for the same reason, Captain," Kovalov said. "Once you blow a one megaton hole in the ice, sonar will be useless for hours. We'll have to wait hours for it to calm down enough to see if there's a viable path through the ice, if we made a hole big enough."

"True. Let's do this for now," Alexeyev said. "Let's put on revolutions and keep driving west to establish a maximum straight line path to the ice target. Odds are, Hostile One will come off the bottom and follow us. When we're at the maximum straight line distance from the ice target or ten miles, whichever comes first, we'll hover and spin back to the east and prepare to fire the Gigantskiy at the ice wall. We'll pulse active again and see if we can pick up Hostile One. We'll attempt to get him to bottom out again. When he does, we'll drive farther east until he's behind us. Once we're fairly certain he's behind us, we can shoot the Gigantskiy at the ice target, and Hostile One won't interpret it as an incoming torpedo. It'll be outbound from both of us."

"It will work if he behaves the way you think, Captain," Lebedev said. "Why do you think he'll do that?"

Alexeyev shrugged. "It's what I'd do."

"Master One has started up again," Albanese reported from the sonar stack. "Increasing revolutions, speeding up."

Pacino looked at the periscope display. It was at maximum elevation and the optronics could only look up to an eighty-degree angle from horizontal. He rotated the view, but Master One was not visible. He must be directly overhead, Pacino thought.

"Master One is at three zero RPM," Albanese said. "I hold him at maximum D/E but D/E is decreasing. SNR is fading. I hold Master One at bearing two seven five."

"Captain, I recommend we come off the bottom and follow him," Pacino said.

"He could be messing with us," Quinnivan said. "Seeing if we come back up. Then he spins around and hits us with active again."

"Signal-to-noise is fading," Albanese said.

"I hold Master One on the scope," Pacino said. "He's bugging out heading west. But my image is fading. We follow him now or lose him, Captain," Pacino said.

"Officer of the Deck," Seagraves said. "Take us up and get back in trail of Master One."

"Pilot," Pacino commanded, "take us up, forty feet per second positive rate, report depth six five zero feet."

As Dankleff acknowledged, Pacino looked at the periscope display. He could barely make out the hot spot of the Omega.

"Depth six five zero feet, sir," Dankleff said.

"Pilot, all ahead two thirds, turns for six, steer course two seven five."

For ten long minutes the *New Jersey* pursued the receding contact on the Omega. Finally, Master One was back on the periscope's display, though still distant.

"Sonar Officer, what's the path ahead westward look like?" Alexeyev asked.

"I have a clear path ahead," Palinkova reported.

"Calculated range to the ice target?" Alexeyev asked the Navigator Maksimov at the chart.

"Four point six nautical miles behind us, Captain."

"Keep going west, Watch Officer," Alexeyev said to Captain Lieutenant Shvets.

They waited tensely, the range to the ice pressure ridge opening up as they steamed away from it.

"Five nautical miles from ice target, Captain," Maksimov said.

"Do you think we're good at this range?" Alexeyev said quietly to Kovalov.

Kovalov shook his head. "The hull might survive, but we'd be in bad shape."

"At least the explosion will open up a polynya overhead. There'd be open water. We could surface if we had to," Alexeyev said. "Ping active, Weapons Officer. Let's see how much room we have ahead."

The dual blasting active sonar pings sounded.

"I've got pressure ridges ahead, Captain," Sobol said, sounding disappointed.

"Range to the pressure ridges?" Alexeyev was annoyed. Sobol should have reported that automatically.

"Two nautical miles, Captain."

"Watch Officer, slow to two knots and approach the pressure ridge ahead of us," Alexeyev said. The room was silent for several minutes as the ice ridge became closer.

"Pressure ridge ahead is at half a nautical mile," Palinkova finally said.

"Watch Officer, when under-ice sonar has us three hundred meters from the ice wall, stop, hover and spin us back to the east." Alexeyev looked at Kovalov, who was frowning over the navigation display.

"Boatswain, all stop. Slowing, Captain," Shvets said. "Boatswain, hover at this depth, take control of your thrusters and twist the ship to the right to heading zero nine zero."

After a long moment, the boatswain reported the ship hovering at the new heading of due east.

"Range to the ice target, Navigator?" Alexeyev asked.

"Six point nine nautical miles, Captain," Maksimov reported.

Alexeyev looked at Kovalov and Lebedev. "Almost seven miles. Do you two think this is safe standoff?"

Lebedev took a deep breath. "It's close, sir. It's a risk."

"Captain Kovalov?"

"I don't like it, Captain," Kovalov said. "The shock is going to be severe."

"I guess we'll find out how well Sevmash Shipbuilding did their job," Alexeyev said. "Weapons Officer, ping active."

Back on the bottom for the third time, the USS *New Jersey*'s control room crew waited tensely for what would happen next.

Albanese spoke up from the sonar stack. "Master One's hovering and his thrusters are back. He's spinning. Definite aspect change."

"What's your interpretation of the periscope image, OOD?" Seagraves asked Pacino.

"He's turning to face us again. This time we got to the bottom before he could catch us with a sonar ping."

"This is turning into a PCO waltz," Seagraves said to Quinnivan.

"What's that, Captain?" Quinnivan said.

"I forget, you haven't attended the U.S. Navy's Prospective Commanding Officer school. A 'PCO waltz' is when two submarines are engaged, both know the other guy is out there, and the simulated battle turns into a chaotic melee. There's no such thing as a dogfight between submarines—too much information on the opposition's location, course and speed is unknown, and it changes too fast to get a hit with a torpedo. You shoot a torpedo into that fog of war? Odds are, the weapon will come back to hit *you*. So, in technical terms, a PCO waltz is a cluster fuck."

307

Quinnivan smiled. "Why, Captain, I don't believe I've ever heard you swear. It sounds good coming from you."

Seagraves smirked and nodded.

The high-pitched sonar ping shrieked again, followed seconds later by a low frequency ping. Pacino's ears were still ringing when Albanese said, "Master One's thrusters are shut down, and he's started back up. Revolutions increasing, Captain. He's at two zero RPM."

"Bearing?" Pacino asked.

"Two seven zero but I've got near-field effect. He must be right on top of us. Bearing is shifting rapidly. Contact is in our baffles now, Captain. I only have him on the rear-facing sonar on the rudder and he's faint. He's now bearing...zero eight five."

"He's going east again," Pacino said.

"But why?" Seagraves asked.

"Captain, OOD, I have a torpedo tube door opening transient and a high frequency tonal that wasn't present before," Albanese said, his voice half an octave higher than usual.

"He's going east, drives right past us and opens up a tube door," Quinnivan said. "He's going to shoot at an ice wall."

"With a Gigantskiy torpedo?" Seagraves stepped to the navigation plot. "How far are we from when he stopped and spun around to the west in the first place, Navigator?"

"About thirteen thousand yards, Captain," Lewinsky said, measuring on the electronic surface of the chart.

"That's way too close to shoot a nuke, Skipper," Quinnivan said.

"I have a torpedo in the water!" Albanese shouted. "Torpedo in the water, rough bearing from rear-facing, zero eight five!"

Pacino looked at Seagraves and Quinnivan. "We're on the bottom, facing away from him. If he's launching at an ice wall thirteen thousand yards out, we're about to be next door to a hell of a shock wave. Is it safe to be on the bottom? Is it safe to have the shock wave hit our stern first?"

Seagraves bit his lip. "Which do you want more, Mr. Pacino? Propulsion or sonar?"

"One's pretty much useless without the other, sir."

"Let's stay put," Seagraves said. "But pass the word in all spaces, rig for shock."

"Aye, sir," Pacino said. "Pilot, pass the word to all spaces, rig ship for collision."

"Torpedo is receding," Albanese said, regaining his calm, his voice normal again. "I've lost the signal to Master One and torpedo is faint on the rear-facing."

"Very well, Sonar," Pacino said. "Any idea the speed that Gigantskiy goes?"

"Sixty knots," Quinnivan said. "In about four minutes, we're going to know how our day is going to end."

"Or our week or month," Seagraves said.

"Safety settings?" Alexeyev asked Weapons Officer Sobol, who had left the sonar and sensor console lineup and returned to the starboard side's battlecontrol console.

"Anti-circular run is in. Standoff range is out," she said. "We're closer than ten miles, so I've defeated the interlock."

"Unlock codes inserted?"

"Yes, Captain. Weapon status on nuclear arming is green."

"Attention in central," Alexeyev said. "Prepare to fire on the ice wall, large bore tube one, Gigantskiy unit one, weapon course zero eight five, weapon departure in swim-out mode, direct contact mode enabled, command detonate at six point five nautical miles enabled, run-to-enable one thousand meters."

"Ship is ready, Captain," Shvets said.

"Weapon is ready, Captain," Sobol said.

"Battlecontrol targeting ready," Senior Lieutenant Pavlovsky said from the battlecontrol console.

"Fire Gigantskiy unit one," Alexeyev ordered.

"Fire Gigantskiy unit one, aye, Captain, and I have torpedo engine ignition," Sobol said. "I have torpedo rollout. And torpedo is clear of the tube, Captain."

"Sonar?"

"Weapon is steady on course zero eight five, Captain," Palinkova reported from the sonar and sensor console, where she'd taken over for Sobol. "It's a good shoot."

"It's not good till we see if it gets all the way there and detonates as it's supposed to," Alexeyev said, glancing at Kovalov, who shook his head slowly.

"Attention in central command," Alexeyev said. "All hands strap in. Seat belts on and tight."

20

Gigantskiy Unit One Central Processor Log

1343:03.96 Unit One CPU energized.

1343:04.50 Nuclear unlock codes received, unlock codes Verified correct.

1343:05.88 Target parameters loaded. Unit safety settings loaded. Nuclear yield selected.

1344:12.39 Unit receives signal to start engine.

1344:13.42 Unit's engine started.

1344:14.58 Rollout from torpedo tube commenced.

1344:15.69 Rollout from torpedo tube complete. Unit is in open water. Unit speed, 5 knots.

1344:20.11 Unit steady on course 085. Unit speed, 20 knots.

1345:10.23 Unit steady on course 085. Unit speed, 40 knots.

1345:12.56 Unit steady on course 085. Unit speed, 60 knots. Spooled

cable distance from launching ship, 130 meters.

1350:00.00 Spooled cable distance from launching ship, 10,450 meters.

1352:07.09 Spooled cable distance from launching ship, 11,667 meters. Unit is at point of command detonation. Unit spins arming plate, lining up low explosives with high explosives.

1352:07.10 Unit's CPU provides signal to low explosive to detonate. Low explosives detonate. Flame path to

311

high explosives operational. High explosives begin detonation.

1352.07.11   High explosives compress two halves of plutonium sphere. Plutonium becomes completely spherical. Plutonium neutron level cascades to runaway. Nuclear detonation expected in approximately –

The fission bomb explosion of Gigantskiy unit one formed a plasma that expanded from the close confines of the weapon's plutonium compartment into the heavy water compartment. Up to that point, the nuclear explosion was generating energy from the elimination of mass from the heavy plutonium nuclei splitting into two lighter atoms, with the product atoms weighing less than the original plutonium. The missing mass was converted to energy in the form of explosive heat. As the plasma blew outward, it enveloped the heavy water cans, the heavy water able to fuse together to form helium atoms, and again, the resulting products were lighter than the heavy water at the start of the reaction, the difference in mass converted to pure energy, and the fission bomb became a fusion bomb, also known as a hydrogen bomb.

The plasma expanded outward from the central point and quickly devoured the weapon. Fifty meters to the east, a monolithic ice wall extended from the sea floor to an ice ridge range above. The plasma expanded and reached out to the wall. The surface of the ice wall began to vaporize and become a plasma itself, the electrons of the water molecules flying off into space.

One second after detonation, a half mile hole was blown into the ice wall and the ice overhead opened up into open water, the explosion blowing high into the atmosphere. On the other side of the explosion from the ice wall, the detonation caused a pressure wave to extend outward, at first spherically, but when it hit the shallow bottom and the ice overhead, it reinforced itself into a solid wave spreading out cylindrically.

Six-and-a-half nautical miles from the torpedo explosion, the shock wave hit the Russian submarine *Belgorod*. A half mile farther out to the west, the shock wave encountered the bottomed hull of the American submarine *New Jersey*.

The shock wave was violent and merciless to both submarines.

———

One moment, Captain First Rank Georgy Alexeyev was strapped into his seat at the port side of *Belgorod*'s command console, his seat belt tight, a five-point harness clamped into a central point on his chest.

The next moment the central command post was hit by a high speed freight train and the compartment was thrown to the left until the deck became a wall, and Alexeyev lost consciousness.

In the long moments before he came to, there was nothing but darkness. But then, when he did emerge from unconsciousness, he was still in darkness. Darkness with the smell of smoke.

That same instant, Lieutenant Anthony Pacino was standing at the USS *New Jersey*'s command console. The next, he was flying through space until he hit the aft bulkhead. He faded out into unconsciousness before his body slid down the wall and onto the deck. As he lay in a heap on the deck, blood from a head wound ran down his face.

———

Midshipman Third Class Anthony Pacino felt himself becoming drowsy in the huge amphitheater in Michelson Hall, the physics lecture not only boring, but exactly repeating what was in chapter seven. Why couldn't they just let him read the book and take the exams, he thought. It was his last thought before he fell into a light slumber.

Until he felt a hand shaking him awake by his shoulder. He opened his eyes to see a full lieutenant in service dress blues waking him. Pacino bolted upright in his chair. At the Naval Academy, first class midshipmen were like gods, but if they were gods, the officers appointed over them were some celestial beings from even higher above. Pacino reminded himself that his own father was an admiral, and not just any admiral, but the CNO, the admiral in command of the entire Navy, and he told himself that officers were not beings to be feared, and yet, here, in this cloistered enclave, they were. An officer could put him on report, confine him to Bancroft Hall for ninety days, force him into formal uniform inspections daily, and the conduct report could snowball. A deficiency in a uniform inspection could add demerits to the original batch. And too many demerits and he'd be automatically kicked out of the Academy. Separated from the naval service.

Pacino was already perilously close to being kicked out. He'd been caught "going over the wall" last month. It was really just a rite of passage, to get up from his room at two in the morning, sneak out of Bancroft Hall, skulk out to the closest wall of the Academy, vault over it, and walk to a diner named Chicks that served breakfast around the clock. It was discouraged to graduate without going over the wall, and yet, getting caught was a major conduct violation. The insane cops-and-robbers game at the Academy was woven into its very fabric, and everyone who attended had played it, but play it poorly? That midshipman would find himself a civilian.

So it was that when he felt the hand shake him awake, Pacino's heart slammed in his chest, his pulse instantly racing. He gasped for breath as if he were running hundred-yard dashes. He looked up at the lieutenant. Sleeping in class, he thought. How many demerits was that? Then the lieutenant spoke.

"Midshipman Pacino? The superintendent wants to see you in his office."

Those words had to be the most terrifying of Pacino's life. The only reason the superintendent—the admiral-in-command of the Academy—would want to see him would be to discharge Pacino from the Navy. Dear God, Pacino thought, how the hell would he explain this to his father? Dad was going to kill him.

The walk to the superintendent's office in Leahy Hall seemed like a walk to the gallows. Pacino's knees felt so weak it was like they'd turned to liquid. The passage through the door of Leahy Hall to the admiral's office was like falling through a blurry tunnel, all luxurious walls and fixtures, paintings of past commanding admirals on the walls, elaborate models of ships in glass display cases, until finally the double door of Admiral Murphy's inner office was opened.

Murphy came up to Pacino, but his expression wasn't what Pacino had expected. Instead of harshness, the admiral's face was a mask of pain and sympathy.

"Sit down, Mr. Pacino, please," Murphy said, pointing to a chair in front of his desk. Murphy leaned on his desk in front of Pacino. "Anthony, I hate to be the one to bring this news to you. But your father's cruise ship, the *Princess Dragon*, was torpedoed eighty miles outside of Norfolk harbor and went down with all hands. Your father is presumed to be among the dead. I'm so sorry, Anthony."

Pacino felt the hot tears wet his eyes and trace their way down his face. He put his face in his hands, the tears, unwelcome and unbidden, shaking his entire upper body.

He felt a soft washcloth on his forehead and strong fingers touching the back of his skull. He decided to risk opening his eyes and when he did, he was no longer in Admiral Murphy's office but seated at a table in the crew's mess. A crew's mess completely black but for the uneven lights of several battle lanterns, one of them shining on the back of his head. Even in the dimness, he could see over his left shoulder a large framed photo depicting the World War II battleship *New Jersey* firing all her guns at once, flames and billowing smoke blowing out over the seascape.

Pacino blinked and saw that the hands on his skull belonged to Chief Grim Thornburg, the hospital corpsman assigned to the submarine *New Jersey*. He looked over, his neck shooting pain as he did, and he saw that next to him sat River Styxx in her dark blue coveralls. The damp washcloth was in her hands, wiping away what must have been blood. And the tears on his cheeks. Her eyes were liquid with sympathy.

Dieter U-Boat Dankleff stood behind him, shining the battle lantern on Pacino's head. Pacino felt a sharp stab and he flinched involuntarily.

"Easy, Lieutenant," Thornburg said. "You need twenty stitches at least. A scalp wound bleeds profusely. And the cut went an inch

315

below your hairline toward your right eye. You took a pretty hard hit to your skull."

"Does he have a concussion, Doc?" Styxx asked.

Thornburg shined a penlight into Pacino's right eye, then his left. "He seems to be okay, but keep an eye on him, and don't let him sleep. Mr. Patch, you'll need to consult a plastic surgeon to see about that scar."

"What happened?" Pacino croaked. "I can't be the only one hurt."

"What's the count, Doc?" Dankleff asked, setting down the battle lantern.

"Three crewmen with broken bones," Thornburg said seriously. "Lacerations and contusions affecting another thirty. Mr. Pacino is the only one who lost consciousness, though."

"That's because he's a lazy slacker," Dankleff grinned.

"Fuck you, U-Boat," Pacino managed to say. "How's the boat? Are we damaged? How bad is it?"

"You might tell by the lack of lights, the reactor scrammed," Dankleff said. "Shock opened every electrical breaker aboard."

From aft in the space, the voice of the compartment phone talker spoke. "From Maneuvering, the reactor is critical!"

Dankleff half shook his head once. "We should be self-sustaining and in the power range in sixty seconds and back in a normal full-power lineup in two minutes."

"What's going on with the BUFF?"

"No idea. Until we get sonar back and come off the bottom, we're in the dark."

After another minute of being stitched and bandaged by Thornburg, the phone talker aft called out again. "The electric plant is in a normal full-power lineup. Secure rig for reduced electrical."

The overhead lamps of the space, all of them red for the rig-for-ultraquiet, clicked on.

Pacino waved away Thornburg and Styxx. "Let me up. I need to get to control."

"Reactor trip! Both reactors tripped," the phone circuit rasped with the voice of the chief engineer, Captain Third Rank Virve "Cobalt" Ausra, whose excited voice was an octave higher than her normal mezzo soprano.

Captain First Rank Georgy Alexeyev blinked, momentarily stunned by the jarring impact of the nuclear shock wave. His shoulders and hips ached where the safety belt had kept him tight in his command seat. He tried to shake his head, a stabbing headache making his vision blur. It was completely dark in the space. The usual sound of ventilation ducts was quiet, and the other customary sound in the room, whining hum of the electronic consoles was also gone, which meant the electrical grid in the entire submarine was a casualty of the blast.

"Engineer," Alexeyev said into his boom microphone on the tactical circuit, "report status of reactor and electric plant recovery!"

There was a pause, which would be bad news, he thought. But the chief engineer's voice finally answered.

"Central, Nuclear Control, we are closing the battery breakers. Expect reactor fast recovery in five minutes. Stand by."

The lights in the overhead flashed for a moment, then went out, then flashed again, the third time holding. The ventilation ducts started blowing again, but at a third speed. The ship control consoles came back to life first, then the command consoles, the sonar and sensor lineup and finally the battlecontrol consoles.

"Watch Officer," Alexeyev said to a stunned Captain Lieutenant Vilen Shvets, "get to ship control and attempt to hover, and keep us level."

The engineer's voice returned. "Reactor number one is critical."

The smell of smoke in the room made Alexeyev cough. He looked at First Officer Lebedev. "Do you smell that?"

She sniffed the air. "It's not electrical, Captain. That's not burning insulation. It's something else."

"All spaces, report status," Alexeyev said into the announcing microphone.

"Reactor number one is in the power range," Ausra's voice rasped. "Reactor number two is critical. Recovering the electric plant, but we have steam coming out of the port propulsion turbine casing—" Ausra's announcement was interrupted.

"Fire in the first compartment! Fire in the torpedo room!" the safety announcing circuit blared in Alexeyev's headset.

Alexeyev found the general announcing circuit microphone and toggled the circuit breaker to make it operational again. It had been disengaged for sound quieting, but this was a ship-threatening emergency.

"Fire in the first compartment, fire in the torpedo room," he said into the mike as he consciously tried to keep his voice calm despite his rising panic. His voice was broadcast through the ship like the voice of God. "Emergency support team, report to the second compartment upper level door to the first compartment. All hands, rig ship for fire." He put the microphone back in its cradle, found his emergency air breathing mask, pulled it over his head and looked through its facemask at Lebedev. "Madam First, I want you on-scene. That is the worst place to have a fire."

The sound of the ventilation ducts died again as ventilation systems were shut down for the rig for fire.

Kovalov looked at Alexeyev. "I'll go with her."

"No, Captain Kovalov, you stay in central with me," Alexeyev barked.

"Electric plant is nominal," Ausra reported on the phone circuit. "Reactor number two is in the power range. Ready to answer bells on the starboard propulsion turbine, propulsion limited to ahead standard."

Alexeyev unbuckled from his seat. Kovalov released his own seatbelt at the battlecontrol console and walked to Alexeyev.

"If that's a weapon fuel fire," Kovalov said quietly to Alexeyev, "we have a real problem."

"We need to get back to open water," Alexeyev took the three steps to the navigation console. "Navigator, plot a course to the ice target. The Gigantskiy must have opened up a large polynya there. We can surface and ventilate there."

Maksimov was already ready with the answer. "Course zero eight seven, Captain."

"Watch Officer, proceed at four knots to the open water at the ice target, course zero eight seven," Alexeyev ordered.

The smell of the smoke was stronger now, and central command was getting hazy. With the ventilation systems shut down with the rig for fire, the fact he could smell smoke through his mask was very bad news.

————————

Captain Second Rank Ania Lebedev arrived at the compartment door to the first compartment, which was open. It should have been dogged shut, she thought, for the rig for fire. She unplugged her emergency mask's air hose and stepped over the hatch coaming into the first compartment, which was black with smoke. She plugged her air hose into the manifold in the overhead of the first compartment and saw the senior enlisted weapons chief, Glavny Starshina Semion Yeger, who looked at her through his mask, his expression one of panic.

"Chief, what's the status?" Lebedev shouted through her mask.

"There's a ruptured weapon, middle rack, farthest to starboard," Yeger shouted back. "We're attempting a patch with a high-pressure hose on it, but the fire is in the bilges now."

"Evacuate the compartment, Chief," Lebedev yelled. "I'm activating the liquid nitrogen."

"But Madam First, that will put out the fire but likely rupture more weapons!"

"I don't care, Chief, I intend to auto-jettison."

"All hands, evacuate the first compartment," Yeger ordered in the phone's tactical circuit.

Three enlisted men and one enlisted woman came hurriedly through the smoke, stepped through the hatch and plugged in their air hoses at the second compartment upper-level manifold. Lebedev pushed Yeger out of the first compartment, then stepped through the hatch herself.

"Help me shut it," she yelled to the gathered weapons technicians.

The hatch shut and Lebedev dogged it and locked it. "Chief, call central and inform them I'm activating liquid nitrogen and that I'll auto-jettison afterward."

"Yes, ma'am," Yeger said. He spoke into the circuit for a moment while Lebedev lifted a large warning cover off the emergency liquid nitrogen deluge system. She latched the cover open, exposing a large red mushroom button. She pressed the button, saying a silent prayer that the system would work. If she survived this, she thought, she'd find the Sevmash Shipyard supervisor whose people installed and tested the system and present him with the most expensive bottle of vodka she could get her hands on.

For a long, endless second, nothing happened. Then the sound of flow noise came from above and became deafeningly loud. For a long minute, the liquid nitrogen deluge sprayed into the room on the other side of the hatch, finally exhausting the nitrogen tanks.

"Chief, commence auto-jettison of all weapons," she ordered Yeger.

"Understood, Madam First," he said. "We have a tube-loaded VA-111 Shkval in tube six. It's probably undamaged. Can we keep that?"

"Yes, for now, Chief. I'll advise the captain and see if he wants it jettisoned. Report to central as each weapon leaves the ship." She looked at the weapons technicians. "You're all contaminated with weapon fuel—get to the safety showers, dump your clothes in the sealed hoppers and decontaminate. Chief, I'm going back to central."

As Lebedev hurried aft, Yeger looked at his senior technician. "I don't know if she saved the ship or doomed it. Without weapons? We're helpless."

"We still have the Shkval and a Gigantskiy left," she said.

————————————

"Mr. Pacino, nice of you to return to your watch," Quinnivan said.

"How are you, Lieutenant?" Seagraves asked.

"I'm okay, Captain. A few stitches is all. I'm ready to relieve Mr. Vevera."

"Very well, relieve Mr. Vevera."

Pacino looked at Vevera. "What's the latest?"

"We're back in a normal full-power lineup, main motor ready to answer all bells. Sonar and battlecontrol are restarted with self-checks ongoing for battlecontrol. I've come off the bottom and hovered at three hundred feet. Master One bears zero eight five and he's hovering also. Sonar reported sounds of him starting up his engineroom. He must have scrammed out like we did."

"Damage reports?" Pacino asked.

"No flooding," Vevera said. "So that's good news. Engineer says some of her steam leaks have returned, but all systems are nominal otherwise."

"Torpedo room?"

"All nominal also, as far as we can tell. Short Hull Cooper, the COB and Chief Fleshman are checking all weapons for any fuel leaks. Fleshman will start on torpedo self-checks after he's sure the fish are physically okay."

"Sonar self-checks okay?"

"Albanese says the wide-app arrays are good, the conformal array is good, sphere is good on passive with a few hydrophones out. The active self-check is ongoing. No report on that yet. But the number one scope is tits-up. And we haven't been able to get number two to come out of the sail, so it's broke-dick as well. Gone are the days we could count on seeing Master One on infrared."

"What about the radio circuits?" Pacino asked.

"Radio says their self-checks are okay, but we haven't tried to raise any comms masts. It's a fair bet that if the number two scope won't bump up, there may be hydraulic problems in the sail."

"We good on the VLF loop?" If the VLF loop were a casualty, Pacino thought, the Pentagon and White House couldn't give them any under-ice orders.

"VLF loop checks out. But we won't really know unless we pick up another message on it."

"Good, I'm ready to relieve you, sir," Pacino said formally.

"I'm ready to be relieved."

"I relieve you, sir," Pacino said.

"I stand relieved," Vevera said. "Captain, I've been relieved of the deck and the conn by Mr. Pacino."

"Very well," Seagraves said, not looking up from the navigation plot.

"Captain," Senior Chief Albanese said, "Master One screw noises at low revolutions, increasing, but he's only making way on one screw. The other one seems to be idle."

"Maybe he had a wee bit more trouble than we did," Quinnivan said.

"I have a loud transient from Master One," Albanese called. "Very loud flow noise. Almost like a steam generator blowdown, but it's muted. Maybe inside his hull."

"He could be flooding," Quinnivan said.

"If he were flooding, we would have had the flow noise right after the shock wave," Seagraves said.

"The flow noise transient is dying down, Captain, but now I've got torpedo tube doors opening," Albanese said, his voice excited. "I've got torpedo tube ejection transients, multiple doors opening. Multiple torpedo ejections."

"Recommend firing point procedures, Captain," Quinnivan said, looking at Seagraves. "We need to open tube doors one and two."

Seagraves nodded. "Attention in the firecontrol party. Master One is opening doors and firing torpedoes. Firing point procedures, Master One, tubes one through four, three and four in countermeasure mode, tubes one and two in offensive mode. Coordinator, open doors to tubes one and two. Sonar, are you calling 'torpedo in the water'?"

Albanese held his headphones to his ears as if he were straining to hear. "No, Captain, I hold no torpedo engines. But more door operations and more torpedo ejections."

"What the hell is he doing?" Seagraves asked.

"He must be jettisoning torpedoes," Pacino said. "Maybe he had a weapon fuel fire."

"I didn't think the Omega II-class had an auto-jettison capability," Quinnivan said. "Nothing in the intel literature about that."

"They must have retrofitted that. Nice little feature," Seagraves mused. "The flow noise transient could have been a fire suppression system. Sonar, you're sure none of these weapons have engine starts?"

"No engine noises, Captain. Just tube noises and ejection mechanisms."

"Let's get back in trail, Mr. Pacino."

"You might have asked central command permission to deluge and eject all my weapons, Madam First," Alexeyev said to Lebedev as she rejoined the crew in the central command post.

"I'm sorry, Captain. I honestly thought I was saving the ship."

"Fortunately, I agree with you, Madam First," Alexeyev said. "But our lack of weapons is going to impact this mission. As is our loss of the number two screw."

"What happened to the number two screw, Captain?"

"Ausra's working on it," Alexeyev replied. "But the number two propulsion turbine may have thrown a turbine blade, and if it did, it's dead until we can get into a drydock."

"As to weapons, sir, we still have a Shkval loaded in tube six, Captain, but you might want to consider jettisoning it as well. Shkval's are notorious for fuel leaks, and they're catastrophic."

"Leave it for now," Alexeyev said. "Watch Officer, recover from the rig for fire and get ventilation restarted."

"Yes, sir," Shvets said, his voice sounding shaky.

"Madam First," Alexeyev said, "please stop me if I ever want to fire a Gigantskiy at something closer than ten miles out. Preferably twenty. We got lucky this time."

"Do we have any contact on Hostile One?" Lebedev asked. "The American submarine?"

"Sonar, status of Hostile One?" Alexeyev asked.

"We hold Hostile One on rudder pod sonar behind us, broadband, sir, a repeating transient," Sobol reported from the port side sonar lineup. "Seems to be a screw noise every revolution."

Alexeyev looked at Kovalov. "A screw rub? Virginia-class doesn't have a screw. He has a water turbine propulsor."

"Could be a bearing problem inside his hull or the shaft seals," Kovalov said. "Just accept the good news. Now we have the American even on the weak beam of the rear-facing rudder pod sonar. Which means if we're facing him, we'll have him on the conformal and the sphere. We no longer need to ping active at him."

"We won't have a range on him, though," Lebedev said. "Not without a passive parallax maneuver. Which isn't easy under ice."

"We'll have to judge his range by his signal strength on the shaft rub, or whatever that noise is," Alexeyev said. "If I have to fire on him, I'll hit him with an active sonar pulse to confirm range."

"If he's outside ten miles, sir," Lebedev said, smirking.

"As you said, Madam First, we still have a Shkval. I know from experience, they are quiet effective," Alexeyev said absently, leaning over the navigation plot. "Navigator, distance to the ice target?"

Vice President Michael Pacino arrived at the secure SCIF conference room adjacent to the White House Situation Room. He placed his pad computer on the table and grabbed a coffee cup from the sideboard and filled it up and glanced at CIA Director Margo Allende, raising an eyebrow.

"No coffee for me, Mr. Vice President," she said formally. "I've had about six cups by now."

"Let's start," Pacino said, taking his seat. He took his presidential daily briefing from CIA alone, rather than with Carlucci, who liked to rush through it, usually multitasking by reading memoranda when CIA was trying to brief him on overnight developments, but Pacino wanted all the details and the opportunity to ask questions.

"Any news from up north since the nuclear explosion?" He'd been startled to learn that a nuclear detonation had been detected near the north pole. Startled and filled with a sudden anxiety about Anthony. Was he okay? Had the Omega fired at the *New Jersey*?

"It happened four hours ago, Mr. Vice President," Allende said.

"Call me Patch down here," Pacino said.

"Yes, sir," Allende replied. "Anyway, the blast created a complete loss of sonar at its target point. A million bubbles from the explosion, so no submarine can approach it using active sonar to feel their way. They call it a 'blue-out.' Navy thinks the Omega was probably firing at the ice, trying to break through an ice pressure ridge, but they won't be able to see if they can get through for another few hours. Admiral Catardi says the explosion also opened up the ice above it to open water, and if that's the case, the *New Jersey* can be expected to send us a situation report by a secure radio buoy when they follow the Omega toward the impact point."

Pacino took a sip of his coffee, wondering what they could do if there were silence from the *New Jersey*.

"Okay, we'll revisit this at the Poseidon committee meeting at sixteen hundred," he said. "What else is in the news?"

"Most of today's briefing is about the rapprochement of Red China and White China. After the civil wars, Red China became a commercial colossus, with a positive trade balance with every nation it trades with. At the same time, White China developed some of the world's foremost technology. The White Chinese semiconductor industry is in high gear, and their advancements in AI rival what our Silicon Valley can do. With a new generation of leadership on both sides, much of the memory of the bloody fighting of their civil wars is largely faded. Diplomatic initiatives began in earnest two years ago, and there are rumors coming out of Shanghai and Beijing of a conference on the idea of reunification. They're setting up a monthlong set of meetings in Geneva, to start next week."

"Good God," Pacino said. "That's all we need, a reunited and monolithic China. But how will they reconcile the communists in Red China with the democracy of White China?"

"Decades later? The communists became less ideological and more capitalistic. Meanwhile, the democracy of the White Chinese became more socialistic. They're not as far apart as they were twenty years ago. With the Red's commercial prowess and the White's technology, they decided they had deep mutual interests."

"Okay," Pacino said. "I want the daily brief to highlight any developments. And I want weekly special sessions with me, CIA, and the State Department to go over this. Our diplomacy needs to be in front of this. And invite the Secretary of War as well. A rising unified China will be formidable."

"Yes, sir," Allende said.

"What's next?"

"The Iranians, Patch. That submarine we stole this summer with the fast reactor, the *Panther*? The Iranians have it in a drydock. They're fitting it out with a new compartment. We think they're turning it into a ballistic missile submarine."

"That's bad news," Pacino said, finishing his coffee and putting the mug back on the sideboard. "But that boat, according to Admiral Catardi, was loud as a garbage truck dragging chains. We'd have no problem keeping tabs on it."

"You're not going to like this, Mr. Vice—I mean, Patch. There are a swarm of Russian technicians there. From what we can tell, they're tearing apart the machinery spaces for sound quieting with the latest technology. It'll be quiet. Sorry to disappoint you."

Pacino smirked. "Maybe we should have kept it."

"We tried to convince the president. But he would hear none of it," she said.

"So, what's next on your list?"

"North Korea," Allende said. "Guess who's started to build an aircraft carrier?"

"I wouldn't worry about that," Pacino said. "It would take them ten years to pull that off."

Allende shook her head. "They built modules, Patch, and assembled them inside buildings away from prying satellite eyes. They built a very large covered drydock where they're assembling the modules. We and Defense Intelligence agree, and so does ONI, that we're less than a year away from a North Korean super-carrier."

The door to the room burst open and six Secret Service agents rushed in and pulled Pacino to his feet.

"Sir, please come with us to the Situation Room," the senior man said.

"Margo, come with us," Pacino said to Allende, and when it looked like the agents would object, Pacino glared at the senior man who waved her along with them. "What's going on?" Pacino asked as they hustled him into the neighboring room.

"President Carlucci's been shot, sir."

21

The fund-raising luncheon for American Party Senator Michaela Everett, the chairman of the Armed Services Committee, broke up later than scheduled. Everett was under challenge from Governor Leann Meadow of the National Party, and the polls showed them in a near tie. President Carlucci's speech in support of Everett had been legendary, or at least he thought it had been. His outpouring of support for Everett had surprised the pundits, since he and Everett had clashed several times during his term, most recently over what Everett considered an irresponsible stunt of Carlucci to hijack and steal the Iranian nuclear submarine *Panther*, but apparently they had had several private sessions and horse-traded, and to the outside world, were now fast friends.

Everett walked with Carlucci as the event broke up, intending to walk him to his presidential limo, nicknamed "The Beast" by the Secret Service. They took a back service entrance to the Watergate Hotel, surrounded by Carlucci's Secret Service agents, and despite trying to keep their exit point a secret, the press and political supporters lined the sidewalks. The D.C. police had set up a barricade, but it was barely a car length on the other side of The Beast.

As Carlucci emerged into the September sunshine, the crowd erupted in applause and shouts of greeting. Carlucci smiled his brilliant politician's smile and lifted his arm high over his head to wave at the crowd. It was then the gunshots rang out from Carlucci's right, and two Secret Service agents tackled the president and threw

him into the open doorway of The Beast while two other agents targeted the shooter and fired into his chest. The assassin was dead before he hit the concrete of the sidewalk and by then, The Beast was accelerating toward George Washington University Hospital.

The agents placed Carlucci carefully up on the bench seat, examining him to see how badly he was hit.

"How bad is it?" Carlucci asked.

"Mr. President, you're shot twice, both chest shots," the agent said. "Stay with us."

"Oh, I wouldn't think of going anywhere," Carlucci said, trying to smile.

The Beast screeched to a halt at the emergency portico of the hospital, sirens wailing and beacons flashing from the escort motorcycles and police cars. A gurney waited for him and the doctors and nurses quickly pulled Carlucci out of the limo and onto the gurney. Once in the elevator, an ER nurse initiated an intravenous feed, puncturing the flesh of his right hand and hanging the bottle on a post above the president's body. The nurse looked at him with deep concern.

"We're taking you to surgery now, sir," she said. The elevator rose on the ride to the surgical suite. When the doors opened, Carlucci found himself in the outer chamber of the operating room, surrounded by doctors.

One of them leaned over him. "I'm Dr. Dan Evans," he said. "I'll be doing the operation, Mr. President. Hang on, we're going to get you through this, sir."

Carlucci smiled. "Dr. Evans, I hope you're a member of the American Party."

The surgeon looked seriously at the president. "Mr. President, today we are *all* members of the American Party."

———

Deputy Chairman of the FSB, Colonel General Avdey Ozols, glumly surveyed the large crowd in the courtyard of the Kremlin, the afternoon shadows of the Annunciation Cathedral and the Cathedral of the Archangel growing across the sand-colored bricks. Against

Ozols' emphatic warning, and the warning of the SBP security detail chief, President Vostov insisted on giving his traditional state of the union speech outside. Vostov insisted that the danger was gone now that the traitorous SBP sniper had been dispatched to the next world, and he desperately wanted to show his strength to the Russian people. What better way, he'd asked, than to give the speech outside in a large supportive crowd? Of course, the members of that crowd were vetted, a large number of them working for FSB and SBP, some of them armed, others not, but all wearing discreet communications gear with tiny, flesh-colored earpieces and microphones on their collars with battery packs worn in the small of their backs.

Suddenly there was a loud chopping and buzzing sound.

What—

Ozols lunged his right hand into his jacket to expose the holster of his MP-443 Grach, the weapon small enough to avoid bulging out of his jacket, but in 9 mm caliber for stopping power. His fingers closed on the grip.

the fuck—

Ozols pulled the weapon out of its holster and cleared the fabric of his suit coat and began to bring it to point upward.

is that fucking –

Ozols brought his left hand to the grip to meet the right, his right index finger inside the trigger guard. He aimed.

thing?

Ozols pulled the trigger once, then a second time, the weapon recoil making it jump in his hands.

And where the hell did it come from?

As he began to pull the trigger on his third round, the SBP sniper rifles joined his attack, their bullets slamming into the thing.

Is that thing down yet?

It fell to the bricks, its rotors smashing into fragments, its right-side gun still firing. Ozols ran toward it, continuing to shoot at it until his magazine was empty, and the thing lay there on the courtyard bricks, smoking, its right-side gun finally stopping.

What the fuck is this thing?

Ozols reached the helicopter drone, the unit's bulbous front end two meters long and a meter tall. It had a tail rotor and tail boom like a normal helicopter, but was miniaturized and robotically driven. Where a helicopter would have skids to land on, this had struts that held the right-side and left-side rifles. The right-side weapon was a 9 mm automatic rifle, fed by a large magazine. The left-side unit lay under the wreckage, but Ozols could see it was a belt-fed machine gun. By the look of it, it must have jammed before it could get any rounds off.

Get the fuck away from it before it —

The helicopter drone's self-destruct explosives lit off, scattering pieces of the drone in an orange ball of flames that turned to billowing black smoke. Ozols had been blown backward into the crowd, several bodies breaking his fall. He regained his feet, checking that he had no broken bones, but there was a piece of shrapnel that had penetrated his left cheek and he was pouring blood onto his suit and shirt.

He turned toward President Vostov's lectern to see what damage the drone had managed to do. A crowd was bending over a place a few meters away from the lectern. It had to be Vostov, Ozols thought. He made his way through the crowd and got to Vostov just as the sirens of the ambulances wailed from their staging area at the Ivanovskaya Square. The president had been hit, what looked like twice in the chest, but he was still alive, grimacing and putting his hands to his bloody chest's right side. Three of Vostov's aides were hit as well, one of them taking a bullet in the forehead.

Ozols looked back at the wreckage of the helicopter drone. It must have flown in from the Moskva River side and hidden itself in the glare of the sun, obscured by Taymitskaya Tower until the last second of its flight. He shook his head. It was damned lucky only the magazine-fed rifle had functioned. If the belt-fed machine gun had fired, it would likely have torn Vostov's body in half.

The rest of the afternoon seemed to pass in slow motion, then blur to a fast-forwarded film, then slow to a crawl again. Ozols found himself in the prime minister's conference room, his cheek bandaged and stitched, a new suit and shirt replacing the bloody garments. He was seated with the council of ministers and other senior members of Vostov's staff.

Prime Minister Platon Melnik called for quiet in the room. As Vostov's nominal second-in-command, Melnik would step in as the Russian president until such a time as they knew Vostov's medical condition. Melnik wasted no time in barraging the men in the room with questions.

"What's the president's status?" he barked.

"Sir, President Vostov is in the VIP facility of Moscow Central Clinical Hospital," FSB Chairman, General Gennadi Sevastyan, said quickly. "He's been shot twice. Nine millimeter rounds. One in his upper right lung, the other just below his heart. He'll be in surgery for hours."

"What was this thing, Sevastyan?" Melnik asked, annoyed.

"Our Science Directorate believes this is a Chinese-designed and manufactured drone."

"Red China or White China?"

"Sir, that's the thing. We and SVR's Science Directorate both think it was designed by the White Chinese and fabricated by the Reds. They cooperated on this unholy thing."

"How the hell did it penetrate Moscow airspace? And get over the Kremlin wall without being detected?"

Sevastyan took a deep breath. "Our radars are tuned for bigger and faster things, sir. Remember when that kid landed a Cessna in Red Square in the 80s? Since then we screen for slower aircraft—and lower altitude aircraft—but this is even smaller than our radars would seek. Plus, it was assembled somewhere close. We think its entire flight was only a few hundred meters."

The door to the room swung open and an FSB aide to Sevastyan hurried into the room, to Sevastyan's seat. She handed him a pad computer, whispered something in his ear and rushed back out of the room.

"Mr. Prime Minister," Sevastyan said, "we have captured an individual who had in her possession a controller. It looks like it could be the one that controlled the flight of this drone."

"Did you get her alive?"

"Yes, sir. We're bringing her to the Lubyanka now. Her name is Jingmai Lin."

"Is she from White China or Red?"

"She had Shanghai identification on her, making her from White China," Sevastyan said, putting on his reading glasses and peering at the pad computer. "But she has identification to enter Zhongnanhai, the central headquarters of the Chinese Communist Party and the State Council of Red China."

Melnik sat back in his seat for a moment. "The Reds and Whites are really cooperating? To assassinate the president of a superpower?"

"That would seem to be the case, sir," Sevastyan said.

Melnik turned to Lana Lilya, the acerbic head of the SVR, the foreign intelligence branch of what used to be the KGB. Lilya was in her mid-forties, with straight, sleek, dirty blonde hair cut in a chin-length bob. She had a pretty oval face with piercing blue eyes, and she was unusually tall, often towering over the other ministers. She crossed her arms over her chest and pursed her lips, her expression a deep intimidating scowl.

"Mr. Prime Minister, we at SVR are becoming convinced the Red Chinese and White Chinese are making moves toward reunification. We have no timeline on this, but conferences are scheduled in Geneva in the upcoming weeks."

"I'm surprised," Melnik said. "How many millions of people died in their first civil war? How many tens of millions in their second one?"

"That was a generation ago, sir," Lilya said. "Those wars were fought by the fathers and grandfathers of those in power now. Their senior government officials are liaising with each other. And we know their intelligence agencies have begun to collaborate. As can be seen with today's problem."

Melnik nodded. He looked at Kuzma Zima, the former prime minister before Melnik, who was now the foreign minister.

"Minister Zima," Melnik said, "I want to see the ambassadors of Red China and White China in my office in three hours. And I want an emergency session convened in front of the U.N. Security Council by the end of the week." He looked back at Lana Lilya. "Madam Lilya, I want a special meeting convened this evening to go over covert options for a counterstrike at both Beijing and Shanghai."

"Yes, sir," Lilya said. "We'll be prepared."

"Now, I want to go over where we are with the Omega submarine and the Poseidon torpedoes. Minister Konstantinov, what can you tell me?"

Defense Minister Marshal Radoslav Mikhail Konstantinov sat up straight in his chair. "Mr. Prime Minister," he said, his voice gravelly, his hand shaking as he poured tea for himself, "The *Belgorod* fired a Gigantskiy nuclear torpedo at the ice wall obstructing her progress eastward toward the Bering Strait."

"That was six hours ago," Melnik said, anger in his voice. "What's happened since then?"

"The nuclear detonation created a very large bubble field, sir, which is impenetrable to *Belgorod*'s onboard sonars. She had to wait for it all to calm down. She then proceeded to the ice wall and found open water on the near side from the explosion. The target of the torpedo was blown up, but the ice structure continues, perhaps for miles. So continuing on the previous path is not possible. Her captain surfaced at the open water and transmitted a status report. Apparently, the explosion caused some ship damage. Only one side of his engineroom is working, so he's maneuvering on one screw. He reported a fire in his torpedo room compartment, requiring him to jettison all his conventional torpedoes. He still has one supercavitating Shkval torpedo and one Gigantskiy nuclear torpedo, but that is all he has left. He said he sees no viability in continuing his present track. He requested to take a path south to the Russian coast, outside the icecap and marginal ice zones, and proceed east that way, or preferably, to abandon the eastward passage and simply turn around and return west to the Arctic Circle of the North Atlantic Ocean and go to the American east coast that way."

Melnik glared at the defense minister. "I thought the Navy was worried that going that way into the North Atlantic would alert the Americans with their sonar tripwires laid on the ocean floor between Iceland and England."

"They were, sir, but *Belgorod* reported that they have been followed into the Arctic Ocean by an American submarine. So their stealth is already lost. The secrecy of the mission is compromised."

"This whole scheme was ridiculous," Melnik said. He shook his head in disgust. "If President Vostov asks, I never said that. Minister Konstantinov, aren't these Poseidon torpedoes self-guided? They're autonomous? Isn't that why we spent billions on the program?"

"Yes, sir, that is correct."

"So why do we need our giant sub and its mini-sub to deploy them?"

"Well, sir, they are autonomous, but not all that smart. They may deploy themselves in locations that won't have optimal results."

"No one is talking about blowing up American harbors," Melnik said sharply. "This was all sold to us on the basis of it just being a bargaining chip with the Americans, and to show strength domestically. So who the hell cares if they are in the quote, non-optimal, unquote locations?"

"There's another factor, sir, which is, if they self-deploy, we won't know their exact location if we need to withdraw them. Or God help us all if we have to detonate them."

"You're telling me you might lose these things?"

"Well, they do have a way to respond to a sonar signal that is seeking their location. If hit with a particular sonar signal, they can ping back to indicate their location. We'd use that module if we needed to withdraw them. If we needed to detonate them, we'd just broadcast the command detonate sonar signal until the Poseidon heard it. Not very reliable, and the commandos pinging the weapon could be apprehended by the American Coast Guard or Navy."

"Gentlemen, it's time to end this madness," Melnik said. "Transmit a message to the *Belgorod* to launch the Poseidons from where they are now."

"What about the American submarine following them?"

"Didn't the Americans just sink three of our submarines this summer? They wouldn't have much of a leg to stand on, diplomatically, if we were to sink *their* submarine. Tell the *Belgorod* captain to sink the goddamned American. Then transmit a message when the Poseidons are launched at their targets and the American submarine is destroyed, and when he does, tell him to return to base." Melnik looked at Lana Lilya. "I'm so tired of this stupid operation. God alone knows what Vostov was thinking." He looked at Defense Minister Konstantinov. "You got that directive, Minister?"

"Yes, Mr. Prime Minister," Mikhail Konstantinov said, frowning. "But I am not sure now is the time to hit this *panica knopka*—this panic switch. I believe we can continue the mission without engaging in the act of war of sinking an American submarine. All they have done is snoop on us. They show no hostile intentions. The *Belgorod* can turn to the west and prepare to enter the North Atlantic to shoot their Status-6 torpedoes. The Status-6 transit speed is much higher than any American or NATO sub. So, there is no need to engage the American submarine."

Melnik's face got beet red. He stood, pointed at the defense minister and he raised his voice. "Minister Konstantinov, as acting president of the Russian Federation, I gave you a direct goddamned order. You will follow my order or I will have you placed under arrest and give the order to your deputy. Am I fully understood?"

"Yes, Mr. Prime Minister," Konstantinov said, his face suddenly red. "I will be calling Admiral Zhigunov as soon as we adjourn here."

"Very well. This meeting is adjourned," Melnik said. "I'd like the foreign minister to stay behind."

———

Vice President Michael Pacino frowned at the gathered military and civilian officials in the Situation Room. Four hours before, the twenty-fifth amendment to the U.S. Constitution had been invoked. The attorney general had handed him the official document that officially installed Pacino as head of state until Carlucci was well enough to take over, and the chief justice had sworn him in as president, but he'd be damned if anyone would address him as "Mr. President." The first time that had happened, he had glared and said that he was only keeping Carlucci's seat warm and ordered the staffer to call him the vice president. After that, he'd convened what Carlucci called the "Poseidon Committee," but he'd added the secretary of state to the attendance list.

"What's new since the nuclear explosion?" he asked. He looked at Margo Allende, who had deep, dark circles under her eyes. It was likely she hadn't slept in two days, he thought, but then, neither had he.

"We received a situation report from the *New Jersey*," Allende said, "which she transmitted by secure radio buoy at the open water formed by the explosion."

"Let me see it," Pacino said, glancing down at his pad computer. He read the message, then reread it. "So the Omega shot a nuke at the ice, then jettisoned his weapons, at least the ones inside his hull. He surfaced in open water. Probably to radio home to report on his damage. Maybe to ask if he should continue on with this odd mission. *New Jersey* says their periscopes are out of commission and the radio masts won't come out of the sail. They think their VLF receiver is still functional. But they reported they themselves are making noise now with every shaft revolution. Damage from the explosion. Their own-ship noise reportedly got worse with time." He paused, thinking some unpleasant and dark thoughts. *New Jersey* must have taken a bad hit to their thrust bearing, and not only was that something that couldn't be fixed at sea, it could prove catastrophic by immobilizing the sub under thick ice. "Admiral Catardi, let's consider options. One is to order the *New Jersey* to break trail and return to the UK base at Faslane."

"Mr. Vice President," Rob Catardi said, "if we do that, we lose sight of the position of the *Belgorod*. If *New Jersey* can manage, I'd like her to try to stay in trail of the Omega until we can get her relieved on-station by one or more relief submarines. We no longer can count on President Carlucci's – and your – relationship with Vostov. This new guy, Melnik, he's a hotheaded hawk. He could order *Belgorod* to turn around and take the short route to the east coast and deploy these Poseidons much sooner than we've previously estimated."

"Admiral," Pacino said, frowning, "seeing as how these Poseidons are vicious weapons of war, on their way to American shores, a second option is if I were to order the Navy to just shoot down the Omega. How would that scenario play out?"

Catardi's jaw clenched. "Mr. Vice President, before the Magnum explosion, I would have advised you to make the order to shoot down *Belgorod*, but that nuclear bomb changes everything. Sir, my worry is for the safety of the *New Jersey*. Shooting torpedoes under ice is risky business on a good day, and we don't know if all *New Jersey*'s systems are fully functional. We're not even sure her VLF loop radio will receive an ELF order to shoot the Omega. And we don't even know if *New Jersey*'s torpedoes are okay – the Magnum detonation could have damaged them, in a way the crew can't detect, and one of them could blow up in the torpedo tube or in the torpedo room, or even circle back on the *New Jersey*. Those scenarios are catastrophic. And even if we're successful shooting a torpedo at *Belgorod*, the Russians will hear it and react with a Magnum counterfire. We're fairly certain the weapon jettison operation only ejected conventional torpedoes, so we believe the Omega has one more Magnum. After the damage of the first Magnum, *New Jersey* simply can't survive a second detonation. It would be a ship-killer. I'm sorry, Mr. Vice President." Catardi looked down at the table, obviously miserable. "I know we were all gung-ho to sink the *Belgorod*, but with the *New Jersey* so damaged, it's too risky. We need to dispatch other submarines to the ice to sink the Omega."

"Admiral, what do you think about the idea to have *New Jersey* send the sonar signal to detonate the mines that the SEALs placed?"

"Those mines probably fell off and are on the bottom, sir," Catardi said. "I doubt the shock wave from a nuke was something they could survive."

"We could try."

"Sir, if *New Jersey* pings on the *Belgorod* with the mine detonation signal, the *Belgorod* would definitely counterdetect her. Same problem as if *New Jersey* shoots a torpedo."

"*New Jersey*'s shaft rub problem has probably already given them away. You remember what a 'PCO waltz' is, Rob?"

"Yes, Mr. Vice President."

Pacino cursed to himself. If only President Carlucci had accepted his recommendation to sink the Omega before, they wouldn't be in this situation. He was still tempted to force the Navy to order *New Jersey* to fire on and sink the Omega, but Admiral Catardi's words rang in his ears. *New Jersey* was limping and barely alive. She couldn't be counted on to survive an attack on *Belgorod*. At least, he thought, he'd be saving Anthony by holding back on ordering a torpedo attack on the Russians.

"Okay, people let's reconvene this meeting in four hours," Pacino said. "Between now and then, Admiral Catardi, I want you to equip and mobilize two attack submarines and send them to the Arctic Ocean, to the last known position of the *New Jersey*. And get Navy and Air Force search-and-rescue aircraft overflying the area of the *Belgorod* and *New Jersey* positions twenty-four hours a day until further notice. That's all people. I'd like the CIA director to remain behind."

As the crowd left the room, Pacino buzzed the wardroom for a carafe of fresh coffee. When the coffee came, he looked across the table at Allende.

"Do we know anything about Carlucci's would-be assassin?"

"Red Chinese national," Allende said. "It's unfortunate he died, but even if we hadn't hit him with bullets, he'd be dead. We found a broken ampule of potassium cyanide in his mouth."

"I'll be talking to Red China's ambassador with Klugendorf tomorrow," Pacino said, but he had doubts about the secretary of state, who seemed too conciliatory.

"My people are working on options for something to even up the score on the Red Chinese. When would you like that presented to you?"

"Any time tomorrow," Pacino said. "But a tit-for-tat on this is a waste of time. I know, we have to do *something*. Let's just see what your options look like. Meanwhile, what do you know about the hit attempt on Vostov?"

"It's not good, Patch. A helicopter drone was employed, engineered by Shanghai and manufactured by Beijing, also operated by a White Chinese national whom the Russians captured—alive, if our intel is correct."

"That's not good."

"The drone's AI system was driven by human brain cells," Allende continued. "Organic AI. Didn't you try doing that with that Tigershark torpedo?"

Pacino shook his head. "We didn't use human brain cells. We used canine neurons. The resulting Tigershark brain couldn't be controlled. A Tigershark torpedo just tries to kill anything in its seeker window. It was a suicide weapon."

"Probably the Chinese drone was controlled with conventional AI to get it in position, or just by human control, and then the organic system kicked in to target Vostov and kill him. But one of the two guns on the drone jammed. If it had worked, we'd be living in a different reality."

"Talk about a different reality. Tell me what you think about the idea of attacking the Omega, even with the *New Jersey* damaged."

"Patch," Allende said, putting her hand on his forearm, "if it were my decision and my son were on the *New Jersey*, I'd go with Catardi's recommendation. Let the *New Jersey* linger there and keep an eye on what the Omega is doing until a relief submarine arrives on-station. I know you want that Russian sub on the bottom, but the cost is too high. He's far away from where he'd need to be to deploy the Poseidons. We have time. We can get other subs there before this crisis gets any worse. We just need to hope the *New Jersey* can hold out until the cavalry arrives."

"Yeah," Pacino said. "You're probably right." His stomach growled. "Crisis or no crisis, I'm hungry. Are you?"

"Too bad we can't go to the Irish pub," Allende said.

"But we can order takeout," he said.

Colonel Vanya Nika, GRU, on detached duty to the FSB, the officer who'd been in tactical command of the raid on the GUM mall hostage situation, cinched up his red tie and examined himself in the full-length mirror. He decided it looked good with the dark gray suit. He glanced at his shoes, and they were flawlessly gleaming and shiny.

He walked from the bedroom to the loud sounds of the kitchen at breakfast. His son was arguing with his older sister, and the baby babbled in her highchair. He smiled at his wife Katyusha and kissed her on her cheek. She gave him a flustered smile in return.

"Will you be on time tonight?" she asked.

"It will probably be late," Nika said. "The boys want to meet out for a drink, which will lead to food, and more drink."

"Be careful, darling," Katy said. "I don't like you out on the streets late at night."

"It'll be fine," Nika said. "I'll have my driver standing by."

"I'll wait up for you," she said. "You can tell me all the awful things you and your boys said and did."

Nika knew there was no sense arguing with her, that she was a tired young mother who needed her sleep. She always told him she'd rather talk to him than sleep. And she was enthusiastic for more than just conversation, he thought, with the three children as proof.

He kissed his older daughter, ruffled his son's hair, and waved a kiss at his messy infant daughter, who would have ruined his suit had he gotten within kissing range. He left the apartment by the front door, descended the steps from the second floor, and left the building by the front entrance. A black town car was parked at the curb, his driver, a young junior sergeant, standing at the door handle, waiting for him.

The driver came to attention and saluted. "Good morning, Colonel."

"Good morning, Sasha," Nika said, smiling at the youth. "Lubyanka, please."

It was a pleasant ride through the city, the warmth of September not yet giving way to the coming cold of October in Moscow. The traffic was light, and they arrived at the Lubyanka before 0750.

Nika left the car, entered the wide entrance doors and submitted his identification to the biometric scan of his index finger's fingerprint and his right retina. He was waved on to an elevator lobby, where he entered an elevator car to the subbasement. Once there, he walked down a cinderblock walled corridor to a door to the locker room, where he carefully removed his suit, stripping down to his underwear and socks, and donned the freshly washed and pressed coveralls left in his locker for him. He put on his heavy black boots, zipped up the coveralls and checked his reflection at the sinks, nodding at himself.

He left the locker room and walked down a long hallway until he reached Room 101, where again he put his index finger on the print reader and stared into the retinal scanner. The door clicked and whooshed open. Nika walked into the anteroom of the interrogation facility, past rows of tools and implements. He could already hear the screaming from the other side of what was supposed to be a sound-proof door twenty feet away. He opened the door and quickly shut it behind him.

A Chinese woman was in the center of the room, strapped into a heavy wooden chair. The arms of the chair flattened to small tables, where her hands were immobilized by finger-holds. He could see that all her fingernails had been removed. The screaming was intense, he thought, reaching to a bin on a sideboard and finding ear plugs. He put them in and looked up to see the night watch officer, Major Yevgeny Borislav.

"Good morning, Yevgeny," Nika said, speaking loudly to be heard over the screaming. "Any progress?"

"Nothing yet," Borislav said. "We finally stopped asking questions. We let her marinate in her pain. She should be closer to breaking soon."

"I've got it from here, Yevgeny. Thanks."

Nika made tea for himself while he waited for his technician to arrive. GRU Senior Sergeant Felix Sanya arrived a few minutes later. Nika asked about how things were at home for the younger man, whose wife had just given birth, and neither one of them had had more than two hours of uninterrupted sleep for the last month. Nika sympathized, laughing at the craziness of parenting. Finally they were ready to get to business.

"Let's try dunking her," Nika said.

The seat Jingmai Lin was strapped into was multifunctional. It could be lifted up by a small bridge crane and the mechanism could turn the chair completely upside down. The crane would then bring Lin to a large sink where the chair could be lowered, immersing Lin in the water up to her chest.

Sergeant Sanya operated the chair and brought the inverted chair over the water. Nika leaned in close to her, but rather than make eye contact, she clamped her eyes shut.

"Who is your controller?" Nika asked. "Who is your contact in Russia? Or contacts?"

Jingmai Lin kept her eyes clamped shut.

"Take her down, Sergeant," Nika said, glancing at his watch, figuring thirty seconds should be a good starting point.

The chair lowered and Lin's head submerged into the water up to her waist. Nika looked at his watch, and at thirty seconds after he'd ordered her dunked, he gave Sanya a thumbs-up signal. Sanya hauled the chair out of the water.

Nika looked at Lin's face, dismayed to find her unconscious. Usually, losing consciousness wouldn't happen until the dunking lasted ninety seconds, or two minutes. He felt her throat for a pulse, but there was none.

"What the hell?" he shouted to Sanya, who brought the chair back to its starting position. Nika slapped Lin several times, but she didn't respond. He checked her mouth, and a broken glass ampule fell out.

"I'll be goddamned, she took a suicide dose. Didn't the night shift check her mouth for suicide pills in her teeth?"

"We thought they did, Colonel," Sanya said. "It could have been back in her cheek or under her tongue. Can we revive her?"

Nika sniffed at Lin's mouth. "It's cyanide. So no. It's over. I'll make the report to the third floor," he said. "Take her to the morgue and have her cleaned up. There might be some value in her body. The White Chinese might give us some concession in exchange for it."

It had been a long shot, Nika thought, as he discarded his coveralls in the laundry bin and dressed himself in his suit. Still, it would have been career enhancing to have gotten a confession from the White Chinese woman. They could have broken open the Chinese cell operating in Moscow. But at least her attempt to kill Vostov had failed. The news was that Vostov had come through surgery and was resting comfortably. Nika approved. He wasn't much of a fan of that creep Melnik, he thought.

President Dmitri Vostov operated the switch to raise his hospital bed to sit up straighter. His new staffer, Irina Kovak, handed him the phone.

"The White House switchboard is putting you through to President Carlucci," she said.

He waited a moment, the line clicking softly for some time. "What time is it in Washington?" he asked.

"It's 1930 there, sir. 0330 here."

"Let's hope he's awake and not taking a nap," Vostov said.

"Mr. President?" Vito Paul Carlucci's voice came over the connection. He sounded tired and weak, Vostov thought.

"Mr. President," Vostov said. "I was glad to hear you survived and that your surgery went well."

"Thank you, Dimmi. And I was greatly encouraged that you came through your own surgery."

"In a manner of speaking, Paul, we both dodged a bullet. Although in a literal sense, we didn't dodge them at all."

"I think we have a mutual problem, Dimmi," Carlucci said.

"Yes, we do, Paul. When things return to normal," Vostov said, "we should talk about our good friends in White and Red China." Vostov coughed, and waved over his aide to give him water.

"We will, Dimmi. We definitely will."

"But Paul, I wasn't calling about China. I was calling to give you, what do you Americans call it, a 'head's up,' I believe."

"Yes? Go ahead, Dimmi."

"I heard from my defense minister that Prime Minister Melnik just gave an order to the Navy to relay to our Omega class submarine *Belgorod* under the polar icecap. *Belgorod* reported that they were being followed by an American submarine. Melnik ordered *Belgorod* to attack and sink the American submarine."

There was silence on the connection for a moment. When Carlucci spoke, his voice was choked with emotion. "Mr. President, I thank you will all my heart for this information."

"Paul, I owed you a favor. You saved my life." Vostov chuckled. "That was an assassination attempt ago. Plus, your vice president— I heard his son is on the American submarine that followed my *Belgorod* under the ice. I don't want the vice president's son hurt or killed."

"I guarantee I am conveying Vice President Pacino's deepest thanks as well," Carlucci said. "I should let you rest, Dimmi."

"It has been a pleasure to speak to you, Mr. President," Vostov concluded formally. "Good-bye and I leave you with my best wishes for your return to full health."

"And my wishes for your health, Mr. President," Carlucci said. "Good-bye."

The connection ended and Vostov handed the phone back to Irina, wondering if he had just doomed his own submarine *Belgorod* with this phone call. He shook his head. Probably not, he thought.

Belgorod was armed with a one-megaton Gigantskiy torpedo. The American submarine would just turn tail and run home, he thought. It was, after all, the only logical thing to do.

Vice President Michael Pacino paced the Oval Office as the early evening's emergent domestic policy session continued, becoming impatient with the agenda of internal problems that were paraded in front of him. He had developed a newfound respect for Carlucci and his ability to deal with the minutiae of domestic policy. The infighting between cabinet members was akin to kindergarten, Pacino mused. The office politics were intense. In the middle of a debate about funding for an education initiative, a senior military aide entered the room and hurried up to Pacino.

"Secure phone call from President Carlucci," he said, handing Pacino a secure phone.

Pacino took the phone and left the Oval Office, shutting the door to the president's study.

"Sir," Pacino said. "Mr. President. How are you feeling?"

"Good, Patch, on the mend, but I called you urgently because I just got off with Vostov."

Pacino listened for a moment, his expression a deepening fury. "I understand, Mr. President. If you'll excuse me, I need to get to the joint chiefs and the Navy." He hung up on Carlucci and lunged for the phone on the massive desk.

"White House operator, sir," the female voice said instantly.

"Get me Admiral Catardi immediately, and if you can, patch General Zaka in with us, but don't delay getting me with Catardi while you look for Zaka."

"Please stand by, sir," the operator said.

Pacino leaned on the desk, his eyes shut, thinking of Anthony.

"Admiral Catardi," Rob Catardi said into the phone.

"Admiral Catardi, it's Pacino."

"General Zaka is here with you both," Zaka's voice rasped.

"Yes, Mr. Vice President," Catardi said.

"Admiral, Vostov just told Carlucci that *Belgorod* got orders to sink the *New Jersey*. I know what we discussed before, but now we have no choice but to take the risk. Now we have to hope that *New Jersey* can survive shooting torpedoes at the Omega. Admiral, I'm ordering you to radio the *New Jersey* to attack and sink the *Belgorod* by any means necessary. That includes employment of nuclear weapons, if there's a situation that can make good use of them. Does *New Jersey* already have nuclear release authority?"

There was a second's silence as Catardi wrapped his mind around what the vice president had ordered.

"Yes, sir," he said. "*New Jersey* was sent from Faslane with full nuclear release authority. I will radio *New Jersey* immediately with orders to sink the *Belgorod*."

"Once that's done, you and General Zaka report to the Situation Room. We're going to watch this operation from there."

347

BOOK IV
DAMAGE CONTROL

22

The shipwide announcing circuit clicked with the voice of Captain First Rank Georgy Alexeyev. "All senior officers not actually on watch, report to the captain's stateroom."

"You know, sir," Captain Second Rank Ania Lebedev said, "back in the South Atlantic, you made all the tactical decisions yourself, brushing off all advice from anyone else. Including advice from me." Lebedev stood a meter away from Alexeyev, who was seated in his command chair at the end of the table.

"I know," he said quietly. "You want to know what keeps me up at night, Madam First? What if I had taken your advice instead of doing it my way? Would that have turned the battle? I decided, if we fail in this mission, it won't be from my ignoring advice."

Lebedev nodded in sympathy. "You've changed, Captain. In my way of thinking, for the better."

"You have too, Ania," he said, looking up at her. "You were a cold, calculating careerist when we left for the South Atlantic. You have empathy now. You can see into people. Into me, even."

She smiled. "I hope I remain calculating, Captain. We may need that, with *these* orders." Despite her previous brain-storming suggestion that they could preemptively take out the American submarine, her tone now betrayed that she thought these orders were foolish, but then, hadn't this entire mission been foolish, conceived by politicians who had no idea about the intricacies of operating submarines? Especially submarines under ice?

The officers began to file into the room, Navigator Maksimov first, then Weapons Officer Sobol, Chief Engineer Ausra, then Kovalov and his crew—First Officer Vlasenko, Navigator Dobryvnik, Chief Engineer Chernobrovin and Systems Officer Trusov. When they were all seated, Lebedev shut the door.

"Madam Navigator, would you project your tactical ice plot on the displays for us?" Alexeyev asked.

Maksimov manipulated her pad computer and her display of the nav plot flashed up. "In this scale, the display is roughly fifteen nautical miles wide. You can see the ice wall on the right side—the east side—with the superimposed blast zone at the ice target in the upper right corner of this box of clear water. In orange, I've identified the approximate boundary of the polynya created by the blast, which is about two to three miles wide, east-to-west and perhaps half that north-to-south. You can see that the ice wall didn't open up at the target area but for a thousand or so meters into the ice pressure ridge, so continuing on our previous course is not feasible. To the west on the left side of the screen, you can see the other wall that bounds this rectangle of clear water, approximately seven miles from the ice target. The southern edge of that wall is the passage where we entered into the seven-mile-wide rectangle. Farther to the west, we took a serpentine path around ice ridges to get here. About thirty miles farther west, the ice ridges mostly stopped, and the water depth increased. Average water depth here is between a hundred and three hundred meters, which is probably why we encountered so many ice walls. Our present situation is that we are surfaced here, near the original ice target, at the open water of the polynya, where we transmitted our request for a change of routing, and where we received our new orders."

Alexeyev stared at the plot on the large display. "Can you show our previous track's history?"

"Yes, Captain," Maksimov said, sweeping a lock of raven black hair out of her face. "You can see we entered the seven-mile rectangle here, transited to the southern part of the ice pressure ridge, then ran north until we ran into this corner at the northeast. About fifty meters south of the corner is where we established the ice target. We surfaced at open water, got permission to shoot a Gigantskiy at the ice target, then submerged and ran west until we hit this ice wall. Here, near the west wall, is where we fired the nuclear torpedo, and you can see at this point, I've marked the place where the first compartment fire started and we jettisoned weapons. We'll need that position to be exact, because we'll need to salvage them to avoid the Americans pulling them off the sea floor and examining our technology."

Alexeyev waved his hand in dismissal. "The only thing truly secret about those weapons is their AI software, and that's been compromised by seawater and the liquid nitrogen deluge. Nothing there worth salvaging."

Lebedev parted her lips. "Fleet command may disagree, Captain, or they may want to play it safe."

"Safe? Salvaging torpedoes under ice like this? Captain Kovalov, could you salvage these torpedoes?"

Kovalov nodded. "Sure. I'd need something to put them in after plucking each one off the bottom. A big sled or sunken barge with a bladder or ballast system to get them towed out under ice. We can carry two torpedoes in the external cradles. But an operation like that? I'd need a lot more fuel."

"Fuel? You're nuclear powered, Sergei," Alexeyev said.

"I am, but *Losharik* is at the end of her EFPH and ready for a refuel." EFPH stood for effective full-power hours, the nuclear equivalent of gallons of diesel or tons of coal. "I doubt I have enough fuel to make a voyage of fifty miles. Or even twenty."

"That's cutting it close for our original mission," Alexeyev observed.

"Not really. Deploying the Status-6 units is fairly quick work. We'd only be critical for a few hours for each deployment."

"Navigator, can you show us where the American submarine's track is, and make it correspond to our own? Start at the moment of the Gigantskiy launch."

"I'll erase all track data for a moment, sir," Maksimov said. "We were traveling slowly eastward with our position close to the western wall of the rectangle when we fired, and the American was behind us. We're fairly certain he was on the bottom. At this point, we lost contact on the American, but then we were busy with the fire in the first compartment and the weapon jettison operation. At the point that the fire was out and the weapon jettison was complete, we were here, about halfway across the rectangle on the way to the original ice target. We picked up the American with a bad shaft rub or mechanical noise with his every shaft revolution. His noise got progressively worse, but he followed us to the ice target and the open water. While we were surfaced at open water, we think he was hovering under us or back on the bottom. I expect we will hear him again as soon as we resume motion."

"That's going to be a tactical problem," Weapons Officer Sobol said in her squeaky voice. Alexeyev consciously kept his face neutral, forcing himself not to look at Kovalov for fear of laughing. "If the American follows us as he has up to now, shaft noise or not, we can't execute these orders."

"Let's talk about the orders," Alexeyev said. "Item one, we're ordered to launch the Status-6 torpedoes now rather than deploy them with *Losharik*."

"Right. That's impossible, Captain," Lebedev said, frowning.

"The Status-6 can only navigate on a great circle route," Sobol said. "It can't maneuver through a maze of ice pressure ridges like we've done to get here using under-ice sonar. And active sonar."

"So they aren't smart enough to be launched now," Alexeyev said. "So we're unable to follow that order. We'd need to emerge from the icepack into open water and then launch them, am I correct?"

"That's right, sir," Sobol said.

"That brings up the question of whether we retransmit a new message to Northern Fleet that the orders they gave us are impossible to execute?" Alexeyev frowned in frustration.

"Captain, if I may?" Kovalov said. All eyes on the room turned to the *Losharik* captain.

"By all means," Alexeyev said.

"I would urge you not to send a message to Northern Fleet saying that they are idiots for ordering the Status-6 launch now. For all we know, by the word 'now' they meant 'as soon as feasible.' Which means we have full permission to turn back west to leave the icecap and get to where we are able to launch the Status-6 weapons. At that point, we can advise Northern Fleet that we've followed their orders." Kovalov reached for a cigarette. Sobol passed him an ashtray. He lit up, blew a smoke ring into the overhead and looked back at Alexeyev. "The other important point to note is that when we do send the next message to Northern Fleet, we'd better be able to report to them that the American submarine is destroyed."

"Good points, both, Captain Kovalov," Alexeyev said. "So unless anyone disagrees, we will interpret these orders to be read that we are to launch Status-6 weapons when feasible, and since they want to fly a straight route to the target, they will need to be launched toward the North Atlantic, and we will go from here back west to open water and the North Atlantic. Do I have a consensus on this?"

All the officers nodded assent or said, "Yes, sir."

"Good. Do I also have agreement that we will wait to radio Northern Fleet HQ until we've successfully killed the American?"

Again, nods all around the table.

"Good. So now, let's turn to the matter of sinking the American," Alexeyev said. "How do we do that if he's following us within half a ship length?"

The room was silent for a moment. Finally, *Losharik* Systems Officer Trusov raised her hand. Alexeyev looked at Trusov, realizing this was the first he'd seen her this mission. She hadn't taken meals in the officers' mess with the other *Losharik* officers, which had seemed strange. She insisted on eating in the tiny *Losharik* messroom and making her own meals, and sleeping in the crowded bunkroom, despite the special purpose deep-diver submarine being much colder than the spaces of the *Belgorod*. Trusov's file had crossed Alexeyev's desk early in the mission. She'd been elevated in rank to Captain Second Rank as a result of her heroics on the *Novosibirsk* in the Arabian Sea. According to the file, Trusov had saved the ship when the crew were unconscious and the ship was sinking. In addition to early promotion, she'd been awarded the Medal for Distinction in Combat, one of the highest decorations an officer could receive. But she didn't behave with any swagger, Alexeyev thought.

Trusov was physically stunning. She was short with a curvy feminine figure. She had shining platinum blonde hair and big, bright blue eyes, but her hair was pulled back in a tight bun and she wore no makeup. Someone meeting her for the first time might arrive at the conclusion that her own beauty annoyed her, and that she wanted to downplay it. But her reclusiveness seemed odd, almost alarming to Alexeyev. He'd meant to ask Kovalev his thoughts, but had never gotten to it.

She had something in common with Alexeyev, he thought. Both had been rescued by the Americans who sank them, in separate incidents, his in the South Atlantic, hers in the Arabian Sea. They'd both been interviewed by the same American officer, a young lieutenant named Pacino, who Alexeyev had later learned was the son of the vice president. Alexeyev had been impressed with the young man, who had shown him a deep respect even in the face of Alexeyev's defeat. And according to Kovalov, the same lieutenant had seemingly changed Trusov from a rabid anti-American to someone almost sympathetic to them. Alexeyev wondered if that might have something to do with her self-imposed exile on this operation. Could it be that she was a conscientious objector to the Status-6 mission?

"Go ahead, Madam Systems Officer," Alexeyev said to Trusov.

"Captain, I'm by education a mechanical engineer. I believe the noises we've heard from Hostile One are possibly catastrophic for them." Her voice was smooth, with an almost lilting east-of-the-Urals accent, which was odd for a woman who spent her life on the Kola Peninsula but for education in Moscow. Perhaps the accent came from her mother's side. Her file had indicated she was the daughter of Volodya Trusov, the storied captain of Alexeyev's first submarine *Tambov*. Alexeyev searched his memory of meeting her almost two decades before, when as a junior officer, he'd been invited to the captain's house for dinner, but he came up blank. Perhaps on those occasions, she'd stayed with relatives.

"The noises are catastrophic for them—why?" Alexeyev asked.

"Sir, when we spun around to face east to launch the Gigantskiy torpedo at the ice target, the American—Hostile One—was behind us, but he had been following us headed west when we launched, which means he was stern-on to the shock wave. And if he were facing away from the shock wave, it would have slammed his propulsor shaft into his engineroom. I believe the noise he's been making is from his thrust bearing. And I would predict that it is on the verge of failure. Which means the American will lose propulsion."

"Officer of the Deck," Lieutenant Anthony Pacino said into the 1JV phone circuit after it buzzed from maneuvering back aft.

"This is the engineer," Lieutenant Commander Alyssa Kelly said. "We have a serious problem. I want you to send the captain and XO to the aft compartment at the main motor."

"Captain will want to know why. What's up?"

"The thrust bearing just shit the bed. Now get the captain and XO."

"Right away." Pacino hung up. "Captain, XO, Eng wants you both back aft at the main motor. Eng reports we have a serious problem with the thrust bearing."

Captain Seagraves and XO Quinnivan left the room in a half run. Pacino looked over at Navigator Lewinsky.

"What do you think is going on back there?" Pacino asked.

"If there's trouble with the thrust bearing, this mission is over," Lewinsky said.

"Officer of the Deck, we're making a bad screeching sound every revolution," Sonar Senior Chief Albanese said, breaking into the conversation. "And it got worse with every rev. Fairly well screaming that we're out here. The BUFF has to know we're here."

"On the bottom, right underneath him while he's surfaced at the open water," Pacino said.

In the aft compartment, Seagraves and Quinnivan found Engineer Kelly at the thrust bearing, a cube of metal a meter on a side. It was glowing dark red and smoking. The chief mechanic, Chief Sammy "Sam-I-Am" MacHinery, supervised as two mechanics held firehoses on the thrust bearing to keep it from melting or setting the nearby equipment on fire.

"What do we have?" Seagraves asked.

"It's bad, Captain," Kelly said. "It's seized. It's not coming back."

"Forgive me, Eng," Quinnivan said. "But I came up through the tactical ranks, not the engineering side. What the hell is a thrust bearing and how does it work?"

Kelly looked at him and said solemnly, "The main motor turns the shaft, which rotates the turbine blades of the propulsor, XO, which generates thrust, a pushing force on the ship. This unit here, the thrust bearing, absorbs that thrust and transfers it to the hull to push the boat forward, and it's no small task, because the shaft is rotating and the hull isn't. So the forward part of the thrust bearing, the stationary part mounted to the boat's frame, is just a flat plate of soft metal held in place by a foundation of hard steel. The aft part on the shaft, the part that rotates, has segments of soft metal—also mounted on a hard steel baseplate—that are tilted. Those soft metal tilted segments—just imagine a pizza with each slice at an angle so as the shaft spins, the leading edge of the moving pizza slice is angled away relative to the stationary flat plate and the trailing edge comes closer to the flat plate. The whole thing is filled with oil, and as the pizza slices rotate, they are actually gliding on a thin film of oil. Pizza slices push on the oil, oil pushes on the forward flat plate, flat plate pushes on the boat. Now, all that makes the oil hot, and the soft metal—over time—slowly disintegrates, putting metal particles into the oil. So we pull the oil out, send it to a purifier, which is just a big centrifuge where we pull the pure oil off the center of the centrifuge and shitcan the metal particles on the outside rim. Then we put the oil into a cooler and send it back to the thrust bearing. This thing will work for years if maintained.

"But when we took that shock wave from the nuke? It slammed the shaft into the forward bearing plate. It essentially flattened out the pizza slices. So instead of gliding on a few molecules of oil? We got metal-to-metal contact, and eventually the soft metals wore off from the friction, and only the harder metals of the retaining plates were left. The heat of the friction welded the rotating plate and the stationary plate together. And then the oil got hot enough to catch fire." Kelly looked from Seagraves to Quinnivan. "It's gone, sir. We don't have propulsion on the main motor any longer."

Seagraves nodded. "We'll have to unclutch from the main motor and shift propulsion to the emergency propulsion motor."

Kelly nodded. "I'll have the engineering officer of the watch request to control that we shift propulsion to the EPM. But we'll barely make three knots, Captain. Maybe less."

"We may not be able to keep up with the *Belgorod* at that speed," Seagraves said to Quinnivan.

"Maybe only under the ice, Skipper," Quinnivan said.

"All that assumes the EPM holds up and that its thrust bearing is okay," Kelly said.

"Once he reaches open water," Quinnivan said, "we'll need another submarine to take over this mission."

"To get someone to take over?" Seagraves mused. "That's not easy with no radios."

"We got off the SLOT buoy message. That'll have to be how we'd hand off," Quinnivan said.

"Captain," the engineroom upper level watchstander said, "the officer of the deck reports the first letter of our call sign has been received aboard on the VLF loop. Also, he requests to shift propulsion to the emergency propulsion motor."

Seagraves nodded. "Tell the OOD, permission granted to shift propulsion to the EPM." He looked at Kelly. "Eng, keep a close eye on the EPM. If it fails, we'll have a very long swim home." To

Quinnivan, he said, "in only two hours we'll know what the message says."

"Only two things they could say," Quinnivan said. "Either break trail and come home to Mommy. Or shoot the fookin' BUFF out of the ocean and kill his ass."

"The essential problem of under-ice combat," Alexeyev said to the room of gathered senior officers, "is to establish enough straight-line distance from the target to be able to shoot at him without sustaining damage to our own submarine." The words of his dead engineer came to him then—*distance*. Could this be what she was talking about? "And if Hostile One keeps as close to us as he has been, that won't be possible. We'll have to withdraw from the icecap the way we came in, retracing our steps, and monitoring Hostile One. If Madam Trusov is correct that the American has a propulsion problem, he'll lose the ability to move underwater. If he bottoms out or comes up to a polynya, we would be able to arrange enough distance to shoot him."

"But if he loses that thrust bearing, Captain," Trusov said, "he's not going anywhere. He'll be dead in the water. Plus, he won't be making the noise that's allowed us to track him."

"If we don't hear him," Sobol said, "we can hit that direction with active sonar and get his position. If he's a few hundred meters out, we can shoot him with the Shkval torpedo."

"If that fails, all we have left is a nuclear Gigantskiy," Alexeyev said. "And as we've demonstrated, we need more than ten miles range to avoid damage to us. And we won't get ten miles under ice, not until we're much closer to the marginal ice zone."

"Sir?" Trusov said hesitantly.

"Go ahead," Alexeyev said.

"Sir, if the Americans lose propulsion, they'll be trapped under the ice."

There was silence in the room for a long moment. Finally, Lebedev spoke, her voice harsh.

"Trusov, we're under orders to *destroy* the American. That means we shoot him no matter what's going on with his goddamned engineroom."

"Madam First," Trusov said, frowning, "the Americans are fellow submariners. We can't shoot them if they're helpless. And we can't leave them to die under the ice."

Alexeyev stood up abruptly. "This meeting is over," he said, acid in his voice. "Clear the room except for Madam Lebedev and Captain Kovalov."

When the more junior of the officers had left, Alexeyev looked at Kovalov. "Your systems officer is out of line. But she's also correct."

"Sir," Lebedev said, "we have clear orders concerning the hostile submarine. Shoot to kill. I recommend we discuss the 'how' of those orders, not the 'why.'"

"Let me humor you, Madam First," Alexeyev said. He looked at the projection left on-screen by Maksimov. "We're here, surfaced at the original ice target—open water. The ice walls roughly form a box, seven miles wide east-to-west, perhaps half of that in the north-south direction. Presumably, Hostile One is hovering underneath us or on the bottom, waiting for our next move. Also, I presume he will follow us no matter what we do. So, imagine this. We vertical dive to a hundred meters. Then we follow our course line that got us into this box back to the corner opening into the ice maze farther west of us. But we do that at flank speed."

"Flank speed?" Lebedev said, color draining from her face. "If we do that, we could hit a pressure ridge and rupture the hull. Or shear off the conning tower—or the rudder."

"It's the only way to establish stand-off distance to the American," Alexeyev said. "When we're at the entrance to the box, seven miles from open water, we spin the ship, ping active to get a data package on the American and open fire with a Shkval torpedo. Nominal depth, one hundred to two hundred meters. But we fire it whether or not we have reestablished contact on the American."

"Shooting a Shkval blind means throwing it away," Kovalov said, shaking his head. "If Hostile One is surfaced at the open water after we leave—probably to get or send radio messages, you won't get a return on active sonar. And the probability of a hit on a target not acquired by sonar? You would essentially be jettisoning it."

"So what?" Alexeyev said. "Better to return from this mission with no torpedoes, yes? Which brings me to the next tactic. If we can't confirm a kill on Hostile One after shooting a Shkval at him, we'll fire the last Gigantskiy at him."

Lebedev's eyes grew wide. Alexeyev could see the whites of her eyes above and below her irises. "Sir, the box—as you described it— is only seven miles wide, and the last time we shot a Gigantskiy, we almost lost the entire first compartment to fire and explosions. That could have sunk us. We'll be too close, Captain. The next time we may not be as lucky. Plus, we might have latent damage from the first detonation that we haven't discovered yet. A second explosion could cause a catastrophic failure from a hundred systems."

"My plan is to shoot the Gigantskiy, then spin the ship and sprint northward back the way we came. We'll have a thick ice wall between us and the detonation."

Kovalov looked unhappy. "It's an awful risk, Captain. And still no guarantee this will kill the American. He survived the first detonation."

"Do we care?" Alexeyev asked. "We need to return to Zapadnaya Litsa with no weapons, Sergei. Our patrol report will claim a kill unless we absolutely have proof he survived. And even if the American boat *does* survive, we'll have no more weapons, so there's nothing we can do about the hostile submarine."

"Let me make a suggestion, then, Captain," Kovalov said. "While you are spinning the ship, my crew and I will undock the *Losharik* and maneuver away from you."

"What? Why?" Alexeyev held out his hand for a cigarette, pulled over the ash tray, and sat at one of the seats of the table. Kovalov and Lebedev also sat. Alexeyev lit up and looked at Kovalov through the smoke.

"Just in case, Captain. If something goes wrong and *Belgorod* lies on the bottom, *Losharik* would be helpless with your bulk lying on top of us. You'll be a crushing weight above us. We'll be useless. But if we're free of *Belgorod*, *Losharik* can rescue your crew from the upper hatch of the escape chamber and drive us all back to open water, where we can call for help. And while we wait, we can keep everyone warm and fed—assuming our reactor survives."

Alexeyev nodded. "What do you think, Madam First?"

Lebedev exhaled hard, her cheeks blowing out momentarily. "I don't know, Captain. *Losharik* isn't equipped for operation under the ice. I think she'd have trouble finding open water. And what if the nuclear explosion damages her? How well will *Losharik* survive a shock event?"

"A damned sight better than *Belgorod*," Kovalov said. "Our pressure hulls are spherical titanium, good down to twenty-five hundred meters. That's five times the depth of *Belgorod*'s test depth. We can stand a shock wave better than *Belgorod* can. And if we're under ice without you, I'll use the side-scan sonar to feel out the ice field. I'll have to do a lot of thrusting and spinning, but I can find open water."

"Madam First?" Alexeyev asked.

"I guess it will work, Captain. I'll feel a lot better when that goddamned Gigantskiy is gone and we're still okay."

Alexeyev reached over and clapped Lebedev on the shoulder. "Madam First, we'll be home safe in two weeks."

Lebedev and Kovalov stood. "I'd better start up *Losharik*," Kovalov said.

"I'll brief the central command post crew," Lebedev said. As she left the captain's stateroom, once Kovalov had walked down the passageway, she unzipped her coveralls slightly and pulled out a small, silver crucifix she secretly wore around her neck. She kissed it, her eyes shut, then put it back in her coveralls, looking around to make sure no one had seen her.

The watch officer's voice crackled through the ship on the shipwide announcing speakers. "All *Losharik* personnel, report to the *Losharik*."

"Captain, Officer of the Deck, Master One has started back up. I've got flooding noises. I think he's vertical diving from the open water overhead." Senior Chief Albanese looked over his shoulder. "I recommend we set up to follow him."

"Bring her off the bottom, Mr. Pacino," Captain Seagraves said, "and hover at four hundred while we figure out what he's doing."

"Pilot, insert a positive rate and hover at depth four hundred," Pacino ordered Dankleff.

"Insert a positive rate and commence hovering at four hundred feet, Pilot, aye," Dankleff acknowledged.

"OOD," Albanese called, "Master One is putting on fast revs. I'm getting him over a hundred RPM on one seven-bladed screw, bearing two five five. One-twenty RPM now and still increasing. One-fifty. One-eighty. Two hundred RPM."

"Jaysus," Quinnivan said, leaning over Albanese's sonar stack. "He's hauling ass. What the fook is he doing?"

"Two hundred forty RPM, sir, and now steady on two-fifty."

"He must be going flank on that one screw," Pacino said to Seagraves and Quinnivan.

"Probably backtracking on his original course on his way here," Lewinsky said, "so he can avoid hitting an ice wall. He knows his previous path is safe."

"But what's the hurry?" Quinnivan mused.

"Put on turns on the EPM," Seagraves ordered Pacino. "We'll do what we can to follow him."

"Pilot, all ahead one third," Pacino ordered Dankleff. "Steer course two five five."

"All ahead one third, Pilot, aye, steer two five five, and Maneuvering answers, all ahead one third." Dankleff paused a moment, listening to his tactical circuit from the maneuvering room. "OOD, Maneuvering reports only three knots possible on the emergency propulsion motor."

"Very well," Pacino said. His face suddenly drained of color and he looked at Seagraves. "Something's up, Captain. Something very bad."

"What's on your mind, Mr. Pacino?" Seagraves asked. "You've got that 'someone walked on your grave' look that Mr. Dankleff told me about on the *Panther* run."

"Sir, I can only think of one reason Master One would want to go to flank under ice in a situation like this. He's trying to establish stand-off distance. He's about to shoot us."

"What's the status of the message on the fookin' VLF loop?" Quinnivan asked.

Pacino dialed radio on the 1JV and spoke into it, then looked up at the XO. "Three letters aboard, three to go. The first two are our callsign, so it's definitely a message for us. But it will be another full hour before we can decode the message." He looked at Captain Seagraves. "Captain, if we're about to get shot at, we should turn around and head back to the polynya. If we sustain damage, we could vertical surface."

"Another good thing about Mr. Pacino's recommendation, Skipper," Quinnivan said. "We could get our message traffic instantaneously if we pop up the sail from open water. That'll save us an hour. Plus, we could see if our radios are working."

"Mr. Pacino," Seagraves said, "turn us around and bring us to the open water, and write a draft situation report we can try to transmit on the HDR or COMM antenna. Once I approve it, load it into the buffer and into a SLOT buoy—just in case the antennae are broken. And as important, if we can get the sail out of the water, we can get a precise navigation fix and collapse the SINS fix error circle."

"Understood, Captain," Pacino said. "Pilot, right full rudder, steady course zero eight zero. Navigator, confirm a course back to the open water. Then get ready to get a satellite fix aboard, then transcribe our exact position for the radio SITREP."

Captain First Rank Sergei Kovalov climbed into the left-hand commander's seat in *Losharik*'s cockpit. To his right, Captain Second Rank Iron Irina Trusov buckled into the pilot-in-command's seat. Behind Kovalov, the navigator, Captain Third Rank Misha Dobryvnik occupied the navigation console, and to his right, First

Officer Ivan Vlasenko manned the mission-control console. In the fourth titanium spherical compartment aft, Chief Engineer Kiril Chernobrovin manned the reactor control room. The sixth spherical compartment contained the reactor and steam equipment, the seventh the main engine.

Kovalov strapped on his wireless headset and keyed the microphone on the tactical circuit. "Reactor Control, Captain, status of reactor startup?"

Chernobrovin's voice was dull as he answered, disappointment in his tone. "Captain, I'm executing a pull-and-wait startup. We've been shut down too long. We're non-visible, sir, with nothing showing up on startup range neutron level. I have no idea how much reactivity I've inserted into the core."

"Engineer, this is a tactical situation," Kovalov said sternly. "I need that reactor online and I need it now."

"Sir, I might put too much reactivity into the core before it reads out on instruments. We could go supercritical. We could go prompt critical. It could run away, explode and rupture the hull."

Kovalov sighed. "What's your pull and wait interval?"

"Sir, I'm shimming out for five seconds and waiting for fifty-five."

"Engineer," Kovalov said, peeved, "that'll have us in the power range in a week. I need power now. So I'm ordering you to pull for ten seconds and wait for twenty. You got that?"

"Yes, Captain, pull ten, wait twenty." Chernobrovin's voice was just this side of panic, Kovalov thought.

"How many amp-hours do we have on the battery?"

"At present discharge, sir, the battery has six hours, but if you use the thruster, that'll drain us a lot faster."

"Fine. Reactor Control, disconnect power umbilical from *Belgorod* and take us to internal power on the battery. Prepare to undock on *Belgorod*'s signal."

Kovalov looked at Trusov. "Hope you can hold your breath," he said. "No atmospheric controls until the engineer gets this reactor started. Let's go over the undock checklist."

As Kovalov and Trusov went over the checklist, the ship began to tremble with the vibrations from *Belgorod*'s starboard screw taking them up to flank speed. Kovalov turned to look back at Vlasenko. "We'd better hope the ice hasn't shifted since we covered that ground."

"If it does, Captain," Trusov said, "we should be prepared to emergency undock."

"I'm sure it will be fine," Kovalov said, but he had deep doubts.

23

Captain Third Rank Svetlana Anna, the commander of the test wives, peeked out from the doorway of her VIP stateroom suite down the passageway toward the captain's stateroom. When the last senior officer entered the room, she walked aft to the ladder to the zero two deck, continuing down to the zero three deck, where the weapon control electronics were kept. She arrived at the forward bulkhead, where the door to the electronics room was shut, a primitive push-button lock on the door. With the expertise gained from her recent practice, she withdrew a package from her pocket the size of pack of cigarettes, placed it on the lock's keypad, and pushed an authorization button, then an activation button.

The keypad sparked and briefly burst into flames. Anna waved her hand at the flames, which died out, leaving it smoking slightly. She operated the door handle and the door opened. She looked around, saw no one, and shut the door behind her. She walked down the rows of weapon control electronics, each a modular part of the larger "second captain" AI system that was woven into the fabric of the entire ship, from ship control to reactor control to battlecontrol to sensors. She found the cabinets that she had been seeking, one that controlled the large-bore tubes for the Gigantskiys, the other two for the 53-centimeter torpedo tube banks. She needed to open all three cabinets, even though one would prove useless since the torpedoes were gone but for the VA-111 Shkval supercavitating torpedo loaded in one of the tubes. But Anna had not been able to find out which torpedo bank the Shkval was in, so she would have to make her modifications to both port and starboard bank small-bore tube controllers.

She opened all three cabinet doors and withdrew her wire-cutting and crimping tool from her other coverall pocket. She knew which circuit she was looking for, but her knowledge came from memorized schematics, not physical drawings. She had to identify the major electronics cards first, then the wires connecting them. She found the first module and its signal wire, cut it, removed the insulation, then prepared it to be terminated on the device she withdrew from her left sock.

The device was a white phosphorus grenade, slightly smaller than the size of a can of sardines. She turned the wire around the first termination lug of the grenade, tightened the termination lug, then wound the other end of the wire at the second lug. She tucked the grenade into a void between racks of computer card modules, then performed the same operation on the other two panels. If this had been correctly implemented, a command to launch a weapon would put a small current through the wire that now included the grenade in the circuit, and when it did, the casing of the grenade would rupture and expose the tetraphosphorus to the air of the ship. The white phosphorus was highly flammable and pyrophoric—that is, self-igniting—upon exposure to air. When the casing was cracked, it would explode into toxic flames and ruin the entire cabinet. There would be no weapons leaving the ship after that.

Or, at least, so Anna hoped. She inserted the next two grenades, then closed the cabinet doors, stepped back to make sure it looked like they hadn't been tampered with, then cracked the electronics room door. The space was empty. Anna slipped back through the door, wiped soot off the door keypad with her sleeve, then quickly withdrew the way she had come. She shut the door of her stateroom behind her and breathed in a sigh of relief.

"Pilot, vertical surface the ship," Pacino ordered Dankleff at the ship control station.

"Vertical surface, Pilot, aye." Dankleff hit the diving alarm, since the rig for ultraquiet had been secured after the thrust bearing failed. The shrill and loud OOOOOO-GAAAAAH roared from the speakers. "Surface, surface, surface!" Dankleff announced on the 1MC. "Three hundred feet. Two-fifty. Two hundred. One-fifty. Easing positive rate to five feet per second. One hundred feet. Eighty. Seventy feet. Sixty, and sail's broached. Fifty, forty-five, forty, thirty-nine feet. Ship is surfaced, sir. Recommend starting a low-pressure blow on all main ballast tanks."

"Prepare to low pressure blow all main ballast tanks," Pacino said.

"Officer of the Deck, I have trouble here," Dankleff said. Pacino hurried to Dankleff's seat to look over his shoulder at his flatpanels.

"What's up, Pilot?"

"Main induction failure. Head valve is stuck shut."

"Is it possible it's just an indication problem? A failed instrument?"

Dankleff looked over his shoulder at Pacino. "We'll need to get on top of the sail to find out."

"Conn, Radio!" the overhead speaker rasped. "We have flash traffic off of COMM-1."

"Bring it to control," Pacino said to the overhead, but the radioman was already there with a pad computer, thrusting it into Captain Seagraves' hands. Seagraves read it and passed it to Quinnivan, who pulled his reading glasses out of his pocket and read the message. By then, Seagraves had pulled the 1MC shipwide announcing system's microphone out of the overhead.

"Attention all hands," Seagraves voice boomed throughout the ship. "This is the captain. We have immediate and urgent orders to fire upon and sink the *Belgorod*. Man battlestations."

Pacino traded glances with Lewinsky. This operation had transitioned from surveillance to combat in a single one-sentence radio message.

"Attention in the firecontrol party," Seagraves said to the room as the additional watchstanders rushed in to take over from the section tracking party's watchstanders. "My intention is to open torpedo tube door number one to a Mark 48 ADCAP in offense mode and torpedo tube door number four to a Mark 48 in countermeasure torpedo mode. We will dial in an assumed solution for Master One. I believe Master One is withdrawing to the narrow entrance of this closed-in region of ice and he will fire on us from there. Once we're in position, we will fire the offensive weapon, and if we detect a counterfire, we'll shoot the CMT weapon." Seagraves looked at Pacino. "Officer of the Deck, vertical dive to two hundred feet and spin the ship to face west."

As Pacino executed Seagraves' order, Quinnivan turned to the captain. "Should we try to detonate the mines, Captain?"

"The SEALs seem to think they didn't survive the shock wave of the Gigantskiy torpedo," Seagraves said.

"Can't hurt to try, sir."

"It's an active sonar pulse, XO. It would give away our exact bearing. When we're hovering, we're not making enough noise to be detected."

"We'll make noise once that torpedo leaves the ship."

"True, XO. We can try the sonar pulse after we fire tube one."

"Good plan, Captain."

"Ship is in position, Captain," Watch Officer Vilen Shvets announced from his starboard side seat at the command console. "We've hovered and spun to heading zero eight seven. Request permission to hit Hostile One with an active sonar ping to identify his range."

Captain First Rank Georgy Alexeyev was strapped into his portside seat at the command console with his five-point seatbelt cinched up tight.

"Attention in central command," he said to the room. "My intentions are to fire the Shkval in tube six at Hostile One. We will ping active on him first to get a target data package to insert into the Shkval. We expect only a one-in-three chance of a kill with that weapon. If we are unable to confirm target destruction, we will launch the second Gigantskiy torpedo in ultraslow speed mode, and withdraw rapidly, put distance between us and the detonation point, getting ice walls between us and the point of detonation. Everyone clear?"

The room was silent. He looked at Lebedev, who nodded solemnly. Her reminders on the last mission to announce his intentions—and to seek, and take, advice—had improved his performance, he thought. Perhaps he did live inside his own head a little too much.

"Status of the Shkval in tube six?" he asked.

"Outer door is open, sir," Captain Lieutenant Katerina Sobol reported. "Weapon is on internal power. We need a target data package to be inserted. Bearing, range and speed, or failing that, simply the bearing."

"Status of the Gigantskiy?"

"Large bore tube five's outer door is open. Weapon power is applied from the ship, but all systems are started up and nominal. Gigantskiy unit two also needs a target data package."

"Very good," Alexeyev said, glancing to his right, where First Officer Ania Lebedev occupied the command console's center seat. "You ready?"

"Captain," Shvets said, "*Losharik* requests permission to undock and shove off."

Alexeyev nodded and turned toward Shvets. "Watch Officer, to *Losharik*, undock and shove off."

"I'm ready, Captain," Lebedev said quietly. "I hope we made the right decision about the *Losharik*. I'd hate to lose her up here."

"I'm sure it will be fine, Madam First," Alexeyev said, hoping his voice sounded credible. "Sonar Officer, line up to transmit active sonar and ping at Hostile One's assumed position."

Sonar Officer Valerina Palinkova operated the switch-protector on the sonar sphere's mode selector switch and rotated it from "PASSIVE" to "ACTIVE." She uncovered a second protective cover over the ping buttons, selected high frequency and pushed it.

Nothing happened.

Frowning, Palinkova put her finger on the low frequency active transmit button and pushed it.

Still nothing.

"Captain, I have a serious malfunction," Palinkova said. "Active sonar is not responding." Weapons Officer Sobol jogged to the sonar and sensor console, looking over Palinkova's shoulder.

"I concur, Captain," Sobol said in her squeaky high-pitched voice. "Sonar passed all self-checks, but the hydrophones aren't transmitting."

Alexeyev shook his head in disgust. This damned mission, he thought. "What do you think, First?" he asked quietly to Lebedev.

"Let's input an assumed range and bearing to Hostile One at the open water, Captain, but set it to immediate enable in case he's closer."

"Weapons Officer, input a target package, bearing zero eight seven, range seven miles, but program in immediate enable."

"Any depth selection, Captain?"

"Leave it at the default presets," Alexeyev said, then said to Lebedev. "If he's surfaced or on the bottom, the Shkval will miss."

"If he's hovering under the polynya, we'll hit him," she said.

"Procedures for firing the Shkval," Alexeyev announced loudly to the room.

"Ship is ready, Captain," Shvets said.

"Weapon is ready, sir," Sobol reported. "Assumed target data package inserted. Weapon on internal power."

"Weapons Officer, fire tube six!" Alexeyev barked.

Nothing happened.

"Firing point procedures," Captain Seagraves announced to the room. "Master One, tube one, offense mode, medium-to-medium active snake, one mile enable."

"Ship ready, sir," Pacino said in his boom mike.

"Weapon ready, Captain," Lieutenant Commander Styxx reported.

"Solution ready," Quinnivan said.

"Shoot on generated bearing," Seagraves ordered.

"Set," Lieutenant Vevera said from the battlecontrol console, sending the final target solution to the torpedo in tube one.

"*Stand*-by," Styxx said, taking the large trigger lever on the far aft weapon control console from the twelve o'clock position to the nine o'clock stand-by position, which instructed the weapon that launch would be immediate.

"*Shoot!*" Seagraves barked.

"*Fire!*" Styxx said, taking the trigger lever all the way to the three o'clock firing position.

A booming roar sounded in the room, the thunderclap smashing the eardrums of the battlestations crew as the ejection mechanism boomed.

"Tube one fired electrically," Styxx reported.

"Own-ship's unit, normal launch," Senior Chief Albanese called from the sonar stack.

Seagraves shared a glance with Pacino and Quinnivan. "And now we wait." As if an officer from an old World War II U-boat movie, Quinnivan had clicked an old-fashioned stopwatch.

"Twenty-five knot transit speed for medium speed search," Quinnivan said. "Seventeen minutes, Captain. Maybe we should have set it to high-speed transit. We could update it through the wire if you want, Skipper," Quinnivan said.

"Let's wait and see what happens," Seagraves said. He looked at Quinnivan. "Did you read Mr. Dankleff's patrol report from his *Panther* run?"

"I may have given it a quick read-through, Captain, yeah?" Quinnivan said. "Why do ye ask?"

"And did you ever get access to the top secret codeword patrol report of the first *Devilfish*?"

"No, sir. ComSubCom wouldn't release it to me. I'm a Brit, or as you Americans would say, a foreign national, and some secrets have to stay in the house."

"Navigator," Seagraves said to Lieutenant Commander Lewinsky, "get over here."

"Yes, Captain," Lewinsky said, glancing at the display on the command console, which Pacino had set to the same display as Pos Three of the battlecontrol lineup, a God's eye view of the battle area, with superimposed lines where the ice walls were estimated to be. A blinking red diamond symbolized Master One, the BUFF, situated just at the western opening of the box-like walled-in area.

"You read the *Devilfish* report, didn't you?"

"I did, Captain," Lewinsky said, raising his eyebrows.

"And Dankleff's *Panther* report?"

"I did, sir."

"Notice any similarities?" Seagraves asked.

Lewinsky shook his head. "No, sir, not at all."

Seagraves half-smiled and nodded. "Keep thinking about it, Navigator. Let me know your thoughts if you think you've solved the riddle."

"Time to ping active on the mine command detonation signal, yeah, Captain?" Quinnivan prompted.

Seagraves took a deep breath. "Yes, XO. Senior Chief Albanese, line up to ping active with the mine command detonate signal."

"Aye, Captain," Albanese said. "Request to replace fuses in the active sonar circuit."

"Replace fuses as needed, Senior," Seagraves said, eyeing the repeated display on the command console. He turned toward the weapon control console. "Anything, Weps?"

"Nothing yet, sir," Styxx said. "I've still got wire-guide continuity. Weapon is past point of enable and searching using active pinging."

"Good," Seagraves said.

"Sonar is ready, Captain," Albanese said.

"Sonar, ping active at Master One, signal for the command detonate of the mines."

From forward, the loud sound could be heard in the room, almost as deafening as the torpedo launch, fifteen seconds of the roaring climax of Tchaikovsky's *1812 Overture*, starting with a cannon blast, a wailing trumpet battle call, another cannon blast, the trumpet call repeating, the sequence repeating a second time, ending with a final loud cannon firing.

Seagraves looked at Quinnivan. "What do you think our good friends on the *Belgorod* will think of that?" he asked.

"Depends if it works," Quinnivan replied.

"Anything?" Pacino asked Albanese, leaning over his sonar stack's seatback.

Senior Chief Albanese held his headset to his ear as if listening hard, but he shook his head and looked back at Pacino, then Seagraves. "Nothing, nothing at all. The mines must have either fallen off or went tits-up from the nuke's shock wave."

"All that work for nothing," Pacino said to himself.

"Torpedo run time, eleven minutes, Captain," Quinnivan said. "Six to go."

"Makes you miss the old Vortex missiles, doesn't it, XO?" Seagraves said. "A supercavitating underwater missile would have reached Master One in about two minutes."

"They just tended to blow up the firing ship until they came up with the Mod Echo," Quinnivan said. "But you're right, it would have been nice."

"Captain," Styxx said from the weapon control panel, "I've lost wire guide continuity on own-ship's unit."

"Sonar," Seagraves called. "Is our torpedo still pinging?"

"Yes, Captain," Albanese said. "The pinging sounds are rising and falling in volume and pitch. The weapon must be circling, sir."

"Reattack mode," Pacino said to Cooper. "It can't see the target. So it cut its wire and is just circling around, hoping it finds something."

"How much fuel do you think it has left, Weps?" Quinnivan asked Styxx.

"Somewhere between five minutes and ten," Styxx replied. "Without wire continuity, I have no data."

"Master One must be hiding himself behind an ice wall," Pacino said.

Quinnivan frowned. "We'd better hope that fookin' weapon finds him and takes him out before he shoots another nuke, this time, with a note on it that says, 'Dear *New Jersey*, with love from your good friends aboard the *Belgorod*.'"

"Captain," Albanese said from the sonar stack, "own-ship's unit, pinging has shut down."

"Ran out of fuel, sir," Styxx said sadly.

Pacino glanced at Short Hull Cooper, whose eyes were as wide as hard boiled eggs. "You okay?" Pacino asked him.

Cooper swallowed hard. "I'm fine," he said, but Pacino could tell he was frightened.

"What the hell do you mean, Weapons Officer?" Captain Alexeyev asked harshly.

"I've got a weapons control trouble light," Weapons Officer Sobol said. "I'm showing an open circuit on the weapon control panel, sir."

"Can we take local control and bypass the panel?"

"Yes, Captain, but I'll have to program the weapon at the tube control panel station."

"Well, get down there," Alexeyev ordered.

"Wait, Captain," Lebedev interjected. "If we're having trouble shooting the Shkval, let's switch to shooting the Gigantskiy. Let's see if that works. We were planning on launching it anyway."

Alexeyev nodded. "Stay at your station, Weapons Officer, and line up the Gigantskiy in large bore tube five. Slow speed transit. Enable it at two miles. Active search. Full one megaton yield. Set for proximity detonation with contact detonation as a backup in case it hits the ice wall at open water. Same target data package as for the Shkval, bearing zero eight seven, range seven miles." Alexeyev paused, then announced to the room's watchstanders, "Procedures for firing the Gigantskiy."

"Ship is ready, Captain," Shvets said.

"Weapon is ready, sir," Sobol reported. "Assumed target data package inserted. Your presets inserted. Weapon on internal power."

377

"Weapons Officer, fire large-bore tube five!" Alexeyev barked. And again, nothing happened.

"Goddammit, Weapons Officer, what *now*?"

"Captain, same indications as for the Shkval. I've got a weapons control trouble light," Weapons Officer Sobol said. "Another open circuit on the weapon control panel."

"Get down there and sort this out with Glavny Starshina Yeger. Insert the presets locally and try to get the tube to fire."

"Sir," Sobol said, "do you still want the Shkval first? Then the Gigantskiy?"

"Yes," Alexeyev said. He rubbed his bad eye, which was itching through the eye patch. This fucking mission, he thought. What the hell else could go wrong?

The sonar ping came through the hull, audible to the naked ear, lasting a long fifteen seconds, which was long for a pulse. Sonar pulses generally tended to be short, so the sender would shut up and listen for a return ping. The surface navy used long pulses that rose and fell in pitch like a police siren, but they had large equipment capable of transmitting and receiving at the same time. *Belgorod* was not similarly equipped. But the oddest thing about the pulse wasn't just its length, it was the content.

"Did you hear that, Captain?" Lebedev asked Alexeyev.

"What the hell is it, First?"

"It's the ending of the *1812 Overture*," Lebedev said. "By Tchaikovsky."

"A Russian composer," Alexeyev said. "Why the hell do you think they're transmitting music from a Russian composer?"

"Maybe they're trying to communicate with us, sir. Maybe they are saying they're friendly."

"Begging us not to shoot them?" Alexeyev shook his head. "No, it can't be that. Damned if I know what they're doing."

Lebedev blew her lips out for a moment. "Who knows what the crazy Americans are thinking at any given time?" she asked. "At best it's a trick."

"Yeah," Alexeyev said, glancing at his watch. "This is taking too long. Madam First, get down to the torpedo control console and see if you can help."

"Right away, sir," Lebedev said, unbuckling her seatbelt and vaulting out of her chair to rush to the first compartment.

Lebedev hurried down the steep stairways to the zero three deck, jogged forward through the narrow passageway, emerging into an equipment room. The door to the weapon control electronics room was open and Chief Yeger and Sobol were standing inside staring at the inside of a cabinet. Lebedev entered, noting it was a tight squeeze with all three of them in the space between the racks of electronics.

"What was wrong?"

Three tube bank control cabinets were opened. Two of them were unrecognizable, both ravaged by fire, black fused wires and control panels still emitting thick noxious smoke to the overhead.

"Look at this, Madam First," Glavny Starshina Semion Yeger said. He pointed to a package slightly smaller than a cigarette pack, the unit nestled into the wiring harness cableway inside the port tube bank's controller cabinet, which was undamaged.

"What is it?"

"An explosive device," Yeger said. "Wired to go off when you gave a weapon launch signal. So the large bore cabinet and starboard cabinet are destroyed. The port cabinet survived since we didn't try to launch anything out of it."

"Is there a selector switch that would allow us to take manual control of the tubes? Weapons Officer Sobol said we could do a local launch."

Yeger looked up from the undamaged port tube bank cabinet. "That is correct, we could, but it will be faster to wire the starboard tube bank to the undamaged port tube panel. I'm almost done wiring it, I just need to remove this bomb or whatever it is and jump the wires. When I give you the word, tell the central command post to give a signal to fire tube six, which will actually launch tube five."

"What about the Gigantskiy?"

Michael DiMercurio

"Once the Shkval is away, I'll do the same thing with the large bore tube cabinet."

"Hurry up," Lebedev said.

"Captain, XO?" Pacino said. "If I could make a suggestion?"

"You have an idea, Mr. Pacino?" Seagraves put his chin in his hand, his tell when he was deep in thought.

"Yes, Captain. Let's do what you did in the Arabian Sea. Fire two nuke SUBROCs at Master One. One set at the other side of the box opening. The other, say, another five miles north—the direction he entered from. We set for maximum yield. Two hundred and fifty kilotons. We'll set the depth charges to go off at depth zero."

"Wouldn't they just bounce on the icepack?" Quinnivan asked. "Especially if it's thick ice above a pressure ridge?"

"Possibly, XO, but I think it'll work. If the ice where the depth charge comes down isn't too thick, maybe one of the depth charges will see something close to depth zero and detonate. Even if we're not close, it could damage the Omega. Maybe fatally."

Seagraves looked at Quinnivan and Pacino. "Mr. Pacino, coordinate with the navigator and weapons officer to set presets on the SUBROCs in VPT tubes eleven and twelve, report when ready to open the VPT door."

Quinnivan grinned and rubbed his hands together. "A couple of nuclear explosions ought to end this mission nicely."

"For us," Seagraves said. "Not for them." He raised his voice. "Attention in the firecontrol party. My intention is to fire two nuclear tipped Tomahawk SUBROCs at positions input by the navigator and weapons officer, intended to bracket Master One, even if he runs from our first-fired unit. We will hover at one hundred feet and when ready, open the aft Virginia Payload Door, spin up tubes eleven and twelve, and launch the SUBROCs."

"Central," Watch Officer Shvets said into the phone at his seat at the starboard side of the command console. "Understood," he said.

380

"Captain, if we select small-bore tube six and fire it from here, the weapons officer has wired it into tube five. That will shoot the Shkval."

"Very well," Alexeyev said. "Watch Officer, you man the weapon control station in the absence of the weapons officer."

"Yes, sir." Shvets unbuckled and switched seats, to a seat in the center of the starboard side battlecontrol lineup.

"Attention in central command," Alexeyev said. "Let's try this again. Procedures for firing the Shkval."

"Ship is ready, Captain," Shvets said, then added, "Weapon is ready."

"Watch Officer, fire large-bore tube six to launch the Shkval in tube five!" Alexeyev barked.

Shvets hit the fixed function key on the weapon control panel.

Finally, Alexeyev thought, something worked, as the sound of the tube firing rumbled the deck for a fraction of a second before the roar of the Shkval's rocket motor ignition shook the room.

"Captain, *I have a rocket motor ignition!*" Senior Chief Albanese yelled from the sonar stack. "Possible supercavitating torpedo! Bearing two six five!"

"Captain, we need to get out of this hover," Pacino said, his voice louder than he'd intended. "We need to emergency blow to open water, we need to surface!"

"We can shoot a CMT at it," Seagraves said.

"No, Captain, you can't," Pacino said, trying mightily to keep his voice even and level despite the adrenaline burst into his system. "It's going two hundred knots, a torpedo will never acquire it, much less speed up to hit it, and the Russian weapon is searching for something at a depth between fifty meters and a hundred and fifty meters. If we blow to the surface, it won't see us."

"How do you know all this, Mr. Pacino?"

"I read the Shkval tech manual," Pacino said. "Originally in Russian, translated to Farsi, then to English. That missile saved my life."

381

Seagraves nodded. "Officer of the Deck, emergency blow to the surface."

The VA-111 Shkval torpedo lay quietly in small-bore tube five, on internal power, waiting patiently for the acceleration of the tube launch. All self-checks were nominal. The fuel tank pressure was holding, its pressure pressing up against the ball valve that would, when opened, admit the self-oxidizing fuel to the combustion chamber. The rocket engine nozzle gimbals were free and lubricated. The computer control was crawling through its lines of code, going over the target data package, the torpedo instructed to fly off to the east to a target point near the first explosion point of the Gigantskiy torpedo fired earlier. If there were a submarine target in the bracketed depth, the torpedo would aim for it. If not, it would detonate on contact with the ice wall.

Then, suddenly, there it was, the tremendous three-G acceleration as the torpedo tube forced the unit out of the tube like a bullet from a gun. As the acceleration passed 1.5-Gs, the unit checked the input from the blue laser seeker, which—if dark—would indicate a malfunction and that it was still in the torpedo tube, but if were lit, indicated the torpedo was in free water.

The blue laser seeker was lit up. With the acceleration now easing off with the torpedo in open water, the block valve at the fuel tank opened and fuel flowed into the combustion chamber. The spark unit lit off the peroxide fuel and the pressure in the combustion chamber soared to over eleven thousand kilopascal, the super-pressurized combustion gases needing to escape. The gases were routed to the rocket engine nozzle and flew out of the aft end of the torpedo at supersonic speed.

The accelerometer registered the thrust on the unit climbing and the electromagnetic log speed sensor showed the torpedo climbing in speed. Fifty knots, one hundred, one-fifty, one-eighty, finally steadying at two hundred knots. At two hundred knots, the torpedo armed the warhead, a small 250-kilogram conventional high-density explosive in a shaped charge, which, while small, was additive to the tremendous ton-and-a-half mass of the torpedo, which at two hundred knots, would present formidable kinetic energy to blast through a hull even if it were titanium.

The blue laser seeker ahead scanned for a target, but so far, at time-of-flight at thirty seconds, the sea ahead was clear. The fuel would last for a time of flight of a little less than three minutes.

At flight time of one minute, all systems remained nominal. No contact on the sea ahead.

Time of flight, ninety seconds, and all systems were still nominal. No target detected.

Time of flight, two minutes, and all systems remained nominal. Still no target ahead.

Time of flight, two minutes, six seconds. With no target in sight, the unit slammed hard into the ice wall. The contact shut a deceleration activated relay, which sent the signal to the explosive to detonate.

The explosion raged against the ice wall, but did little more than create a cave ten meters deep and five meters wide.

Watch Officer Vilen Shvets looked at Captain Alexeyev. "Captain, *Losharik* has shoved off per our indications in the docking bay. *Losharik* is out of communication unless we activate the Bolshoi-Feniks system."

"Very well. Sonar, do you hold *Losharik* on sonar?" *Losharik*, as a deep-diver submarine constructed for deep sea salvage, was not sound-quieted. If she were within a mile or two, she should be detectable on broadband, not just from her screw, but pump and turbine noises from her reactor and machinery space.

"Yes, Captain, she's moved ahead northward down the ice corridor."

"Good. Sonar, do you still hold the Shkval engine?"

"Yes, Captain, no, wait, I have a detonation at bearing zero eight seven. The Shkval warhead has exploded. No rocket engine noises."

"How loud was the impact? Any secondary detonations? Hull creaking noises? Bubbles?"

Senior Lieutenant Valerina Palinkova spun at her seat at the sonar and sensor console to look at the captain. "Sorry, sir, no."

"Dammit," Alexeyev breathed to First Officer Lebedev. "Attention in central command, prepare for firing of Gigantskiy unit two."

24

It was two months ago that Captain Third Rank Svetlana Anna was led by a male secretary into the outer office of the Chief of Staff and First Deputy Commander of the Navy, Vice Admiral Pavel Zhabin. Her heart raced and she imagined that other people could tell that it was about to jump out of her chest. Flustered, she ran her hand through her long chestnut colored hair, hoping it was in place to meet the number three officer in the entire Navy, although the admiral-in-command, Anatoly Stanislav was gravely ill, and his deputy, Mikhail Myshkin, had recently died, leaving Zhabin as the heir apparent.

She'd been flown out from Murmansk to Moscow in a Navy private jet, with her as the only passenger, for this meeting late yesterday, arriving at almost midnight at the hotel, with this morning's meeting starting before many Muscovites had even awakened. The cryptic orders sending her here had said nothing except where to meet the plane, where to check into the hotel, and what time to meet the driver who would bring her to the Admiralty building.

The large mahogany doors of Zhabin's office opened with a majestic creak, revealing the admiral himself and another person, a woman in a well-tailored business suit. Zhabin was in his sixties, balding, going to fat, but with a face so fierce that it was rumored in the fleet that he could stare a man to death. His nickname—and it was unknown whether he himself knew it—was *Litso Smerti*. Death Face. The woman with him was beautiful, tall, slender and elegant, with long legs, a small waist, an expansive chest somewhat disguised by her navy blue business suit. She had dirty blonde hair—probably dyed, Anna thought—cut into a chin-length bob. She looked like she'd stepped out of the society pages of *Russkaya Zhizn'* magazine. Her age seemed indeterminate. She could be a mature-looking thirty-eight or a youthful-looking forty-eight. But she carried the same air of authority that Zhabin did.

"Please, Captain Anna," Admiral Zhabin said, attempting to be gracious, which came off false with his snarling expression. "Have a seat with us here." He waved Anna to a wing chair that faced a couch across the coffee table, on which was an elaborate sterling silver tea service. "How do you like your tea?"

"One sugar, two creams, sir," she said. Zhabin poured and sat on the couch next to the elegant woman.

"Allow me to introduce you to SVR Chairman Lana Lilya," Zhabin said.

Anna rose to stand to greet the director of the foreign intelligence service, but Lilya waved her back to her seat. "Please," Lilya said in a honey-smooth voice with an elegant central Moscow accent. "Let's be informal here, Captain. Do you mind if I call you Svetlana?"

"That's fine, Madam Chairwoman," Anna said.

"Please call me Lana," Lilya said, smiling at her with movie-star perfect white teeth.

"And you can call me 'admiral,'" Zhabin said, chuckling. "But let us proceed to business, Svetlana. I'm sure you have important matters waiting for you up at Northern Fleet."

Anna adjusted her posture in her chair, taking a sip of tea to be polite, but she had no desire for it. Her pulse had slowed, but she still felt as if she were in deep water.

"Yes, Admiral?"

"We brought you here to brief you on a mission so secret that no one can or will commit it to writing. You and your group of 'test wives'—that is the proper term, yes?"

Anna nodded.

"We will be ordering you to put to sea with the *Belgorod*. The submarine will be executing a top-secret mission that will take it around the globe, eventually to the United States east coast, to drop off and activate three Status-6 hydrogen bombs, hidden in the bays and waterways offshore of American Navy ports."

"Sir, we've never deployed on submarines before."

"Relax, Svetlana. It is not so different than a Navy surface ship sailing at night. No sunshine." Zhabin smiled at her, or tried to, but his eyes remained cold.

"Understood, then, sir. How long is the mission?"

"Svetlana, it could be months. President Vostov has ordered that the submarine transit to the Pacific by way of the polar icecap to avoid detection by the Americans' sonar trip wires in the North Atlantic. Then around South America. So it could take as long as four months to get in position."

"I'll brief my troops," Anna said, thinking that now the meeting might end, although she wondered why the head of the foreign intelligence service was here for this somewhat unusual but otherwise straightforward mission.

"There's more," Chairman Lilya said. "President Vostov's intention to hide hydrogen bombs in American territorial waters is no different than if he were to launch intercontinental ballistic missiles at American targets. It's an act of war. More subtle than ICBMs, certainly, but no less an attack. The senior ranks of the military and intelligence agencies oppose this mission. We have all gone through channels and the chain of command. Our arguments have met President Vostov's brick wall. So it is our intent to sabotage this mission. And this submarine. And you're the one who has been chosen to do it."

Anna sat back in her chair, exhaling as the wind seemed knocked out of her. Her own Navy, intent on sabotaging their own ship?

"I know," Lilya continued. "This seems incredibly desperate and irresponsible. But we have a multi-pronged set of missions designed to stop this Status-6 deployment from happening. For obvious reasons, I can't tell you what they are. Well, I can disclose one of them, I suppose. At the highest levels of our intelligence agencies, we've reached out to our opposite numbers at the American CIA and Defense Intelligence Agency—we've informed them about this mission and the possible date of *Belgorod*'s departure, and that *Belgorod* will be transiting under the polar icecap. And that we will place a human 'asset' aboard to sabotage the plan from within. That would be you, Svetlana. What the Americans do with that information is up to them, but I imagine they will send an American submarine to follow the *Belgorod*, quietly, to see what it is doing. In the worst case, the Americans may decide to attack it."

Lilya filled a teacup and spooned sugar into it and drank a sip, then looked up at Anna.

"As I said, there are other plans in place that will make that eventuality unnecessary. We believe that with our other scenarios, *Belgorod* will be ordered to abandon the mission and return home. But, as a deep contingency, you will be aboard to stop the deployment of these Status-6 weapons."

"Svetlana," Admiral Zhabin said, "are you able to accept this mission? For the good of Mother Russia? And, in fact, for the fate of the world?"

"Admiral, I am an officer in the Russian Republic Navy," Anna said. "I will follow my orders, no matter how unpleasant or dangerous."

"Well, Svetlana," Zhabin said, "we deeply hope that if it comes for you to do your work, it will be something that you will survive—along with the rest of the crew of *Belgorod*. It may come to it that the situation will degrade, and the only way to accomplish your—and our—aim is to execute progressively more radical means. In the ultimate case, you will have to cause damage so severe to the submarine that it will sink." Zhabin paused to stare into Anna's eyes.

"Sir, I'm not eager to die," Anna said haltingly. "But if that is the only way to fulfil the orders, well, there is always the next life, yes?"

Zhabin smiled, with his eyes also, this time. "Excellent, Svetlana. I will be recommending you for advancement to Captain Second

Rank when this is over, and a decoration for bravery in service to the republic."

Assuming she lived, she thought.

"What are the specifics?" Anna asked.

Lilya leaned forward, putting her elbows on her knees, drilling her blue eyes into Anna's eyes. "There will be a contact waiting for you in Severomorsk at Northern Fleet Headquarters. Over the coming weeks, you'll meet with her. She will educate you as to each task. The specifics are sensitive, so you will be required to memorize all technical information. You'll be given various tools to accomplish the work, all disguised as normal items—toiletries—or tools of your trade—sex toys, yes?"

Anna nodded. "What if my baggage is searched?"

"All the items will pass a normal security inspection. No one could find them unless he knew exactly what he was seeking."

Anna exhaled, blowing out her cheeks. "I understand."

"Again, Svetlana, we can't emphasize enough the importance of your mission," Lilya said. "The placement of these so-called Poseidon torpedoes *must* be stopped. By any means at our disposal."

"There's a driver waiting for you now," Zhabin said, standing and extending his hand to Anna. She stood up and shook the admiral's hand. "He'll take you to the airport. Your plane is waiting for you."

"Thank you, Admiral," Anna said to Zhabin. She turned to shake Lilya's hand. "Madam Chairwoman. I'll not disappoint you."

"I know you'll do fine," Zhabin said, shutting the office door behind her.

The flight in the jet with her, once again, as the only passenger, seemed to take longer than the flight to Moscow. As she stared out the window, holding a rocks glass of vodka, she reflected that her career had started strangely and was progressing even more strangely. She'd been a young psychology student at the prestigious M.V. Lomonosov Moscow State University, concentrating on human sexuality and sexual dysfunction. It was a field of study that had few students, which was good for her, since it meant less competition for coveted post-graduate assignments. After completing one course concentrating on sex workers, her professor asked her to his office after the final exam. She'd been worried that there might be something wrong, but he was all smiles and poured them drinks as he waved her to a seat opposite his desk. He told her she'd gotten a perfect score on the final exam and that her term paper was the best he'd ever read, and that he wanted to collaborate with her over the summer to write a paper for publication.

As she'd worked with him, he eventually disclosed that as a sideline, he worked for the FSB, the internal security branch of Russia's intelligence agencies. He recruited her to the Brigade of the *Testovaya Zhena*, the test wives. She had been repelled and intrigued at the same time. Her professor had said this would be a perfect way to study sex workers in the military and help shape policy for decades to come. For example, he'd said, what about the females in the military? There were no sex workers for them, presumably because they could be satisfied with relations with male members of the military, but didn't that impede morale and good discipline? And what of people who were homosexual? Would test wives service lesbians? What about male homosexuals? The questions were numerous and the issues heavy, he'd said.

And so it was that Svetlana Anna, after graduate school graduation, had joined the Navy's test wives. At first, she thought the work would be disgusting. After all, one thing was clear, that in the Navy, in a combat vessel, forward deployed, water was rationed, and people routinely went days without showering. Would this lack of personal hygiene make the work awful? But Anna had always had a strong sex drive, and growing up, it had threatened to get her in trouble numerous times. Could that be harnessed in the service of the country?

The answer was that it indeed could. The first few years were actually pleasant, but as Anna got older, she was less sought out as a companion. But the Navy had seen leadership skills in her, and had promoted her to the rank of captain third rank and put her in command of a group of test wives and requested she keep working.

Panic Switch

It had gone well until the meeting with Admiral Zhabin and Chairwoman Lilya.

And now it was time to execute the next plan, since the sabotaging of the torpedo control cabinets had failed, which she'd found out when the ship launched the supercavitating torpedo.

In Anna's coveralls pocket was a 5.45 mm PSM pistol, a weapon barely bigger than her palm, though it was heavy. In the other pocket was a package of Semtex plastic explosive, over a kilogram of it, the bulk of it making her pocket bulge. This wasn't the watered-down Semtex of the 2020s, it was the good stuff from the Cold War, 1980s vintage plastic explosive. A kilogram would be sufficient to blow up the entire atmospheric control machinery room, but she wasn't relying on that alone. The atmospheric controls would assist in this particular task.

Anna made her way down two sets of steep stairs—ladders, the Navy called them—to the zero three deck, until she emerged into the same space where she'd walked forward to the weapon electronics room. Instead, she walked aft down a narrow passageway, passing doors to other electronics rooms—sonar, battlecontrol, the second captain AI system—until at the end of the passageway she reached the machinery room marked with a sign reading, *MASHINNOYE OTDELENIYE KONTROLYA ATMOSFERY*—atmospheric controls machinery room. This room didn't have a combination pad lock, she noted. She turned the knob and let herself in.

She'd expected the room to be empty. She'd made her way below easily, unobserved, since the ship was at action stations, and every person on board had a place to stand his or her watch to shoot torpedoes—or evade them. But a watchstander stood next to the oxygen generator, or the *bombit'*, which meant "bomb."

From Anna's studies with her SVR contact in Severomorsk, she'd learned that the "bomb" was so named because it made hydrogen and oxygen in the exact molecular mix to explode with enough power to destroy everything in the machinery room, maybe even breach the hull. The bomb took distilled pure water into its two meter by two meter box of steel and placed it between high voltage direct current anode and cathode, the process called electrolysis, which caused the water to split into hydrogen and oxygen. Separate compressors took the products, the hydrogen put into a high-pressure bank for later discharge, since it was hazardous and there was no use for it, and submarines could be tracked by the stream of hydrogen emitted if it weren't stored. The oxygen was compressed and put into the oxygen banks, huge high-pressure stainless steel bottles outside the hull that contained all the oxygen the crew would need for two days if the bomb decided to stop working.

An explosive device placed on the large-bore oxygen manifold at the top of the bomb, if detonated, would vent hydrogen and oxygen into the room, adding to the explosive power of the Semtex. Odds were, it would destroy half the zero three deck, she thought.

What gave her pause was that this particular task could lead to her own death. But she'd believed in her mission. *For Mother Russia,* she told herself, knowing how silly that would sound to a civilian.

The watchstander was surprised to see her. "Captain Anna," he said, smiling. "What are you doing here?"

"It gets boring when all you boys are at action stations," she said, smiling seductively. At least she hoped she looked seductive. "I thought maybe you could explain to me how we keep the air breathable down under the water."

The mechanic smiled. "I'd love to."

Anna waited through his overly technical explanation until he turned his back to her for a moment to point out the oxygen and hydrogen piping above the unit. As he did, she pulled the PSM pistol out of her right pocket, put the barrel to back of his skull and fired twice. The mechanic was dead before he fell to the deck. The report from the weapon was loud, but she doubted anyone would be near enough to hear it. It was academic anyway, she thought. The next loud sound from here would eliminate any other thoughts from the minds of the crew. And the damage would eradicate the evidence of what happened. The mechanic's body would only be a vapor of blood and shards of bone by the time Anna's task was complete.

She climbed up on the steps set into the side of the bomb, found the oxygen manifold, a pipe as big around as her head. She pulled the package from her left pocket—it's bulge never noticed by the now-dead mechanic—tore the backing from the adhesive on the device and pressed it hard against the warm pipe. From her inner left sleeve, she pulled off a quarter-meter length of fiber-reinforced adhesive tape and wrapped it around the device and the pipe. She pulled another length off her right sleeve, double wrapping the device to the pipe. She uncovered the electronics package, turned the time delay to three minutes and armed the device.

Three minutes, she thought. Would that be enough to get outside the blast radius of the atmospheric controls room?

She knew she didn't have long to wait. She hurried down the passageway, took the steps of the ladder back to the zero one deck and walked quickly to her room. She'd barely had time to hide the PSM pistol before the Semtex—and the bomb—exploded.

"Sonar, do we still have contact on Master One?" Seagraves asked.

"Master One has faded," Albanese said. "He might have decided to bug out after firing that supercavitating torpedo."

Pacino looked at Vevera. "We may have to blow off this mission and limp home. We can only fight the ship as well as McDermott Aerospace and Shipbuilding designed and built it. If they'd hardened that thrust bearing against shock, we'd still be in the fight."

Vevera nodded, his face downcast. "Maybe mention that to your dad when we get home. He's got the juice to tune up those goddamned drydock rats."

Captain First Rank Georgy Alexeyev bit his lip and tugged on his uncomfortable five-point seatbelt. He needed to stand, he thought, but with the nuclear-tipped torpedo to be fired in the coming moments, programmed to detonate only seven or eight nautical miles out, he knew the ship would soon be taking another hard shock. He shifted his display to the navigation plot, with the overlaid ice walls drawn in by the navigator along with their track in and out of the ice wall rectangle where they'd shot the first Gigantskiy and later, the Shkval. Navigator Maksimov had drawn in what she thought the boundaries of the open water were, at the original ice target and the Shkval impact point.

They'd lost contact on the American—Hostile One—but it was a good bet that he was at the open water location, either surfaced or hovering beneath it. There were no longer any of the noises that had accompanied his movement in the water. Perhaps, Alexeyev thought, he'd shifted to an emergency propulsion system, but he could only guess based on what he knew about Russian submarines.

He'd positioned the *Belgorod* at the opening of the ice wall box, hovering and facing east. According to the chart, he had almost six nautical miles northward clear before he'd have to maneuver once he headed north. There was no doubt, trying to drive a big submarine like *Belgorod* through these ice obstacles at flank speed would be like driving a city bus though downtown Moscow at 150 clicks while blindfolded. And hitting an ice wall at speed could rupture the hull easily. Alexeyev had decided to withdraw north for the six-mile run at fifteen knots, which would get him to the turning point to proceed due west in a little over twenty minutes, which meant he'd only be halfway to where he could turn west ten minutes after the explosion.

He'd debated with Lebedev the idea of increasing the northward speed, but the risks of impact to ice were just too high. He had to rely on the seven-mile distance from the impact point of the Gigantskiy and the thickness of the ice pressure ridge separating him from the box-shaped area.

"Procedures for Gigantskiy unit two launch," Alexeyev announced to the central command post watchstanders.

After the litany of readiness reports, Alexeyev ordered the Gigantskiy to launch in swim-away mode, since its diameter was much smaller than the diameter of the Status-6 tube it lay in. After engine start, it would roll out on the chassis with the rollers inserted into the tube. Sonar would be able to monitor it to make sure it had a normal launch.

He realized the room was silent, and that the watchstanders were waiting for him to make the order. "Fire tube five, Gigantskiy unit two," he called.

"Firing five," Weapons Officer Sobol replied, hitting her trigger fixed function key.

The sound of the Gigantskiy leaving was faint. Alexeyev wondered if he were really hearing it, or simply imagining it.

"Sonar Officer?" he barked at Senior Lieutenant Palinkova.

"Torpedo is away, Captain, and nominal engine start. Unit is speeding up to approach speed, forty-five knots."

"Let's get the hell out of here," Alexeyev said to Lebedev. "Mark the time. Watch Officer, spin the ship to course north and when on course, put on fifteen knots."

He got out of his seat—he promised himself, just for a moment, while the Gigantskiy sailed off on its long run to the target—and stood at the navigation chart display and watched while Navigator Maksimov, buckled into her jump seat at the navigation console, traced out the estimated location of the Gigantskiy torpedo, updating its position every fifteen seconds.

"Ship is on heading north," the boatswain reported from the ship control console.

"All ahead standard, turns for fifteen knots," Captain Lieutenant Shvets ordered.

Alexeyev looked forward to the under-ice sonar, which Palinkova had started up, leaving her post at the sonar console to Captain Lieutenant Sobol, who was no longer needed at the weapons control console. Alexeyev glanced at Lebedev, who was tugging at her own safety belt. She must have had the same thoughts Alexeyev had, debating standing up from the console.

"Sonar Officer, make sure you are calling out if ice ahead is clear," Lebedev snapped at Palinkova.

"Yes, Madam First. Ice ahead is clear, five hundred meters, ma'am."

The violent explosion roared through the compartment. Alexeyev grabbed a safety handhold on the navigation console and managed to keep his feet. The lights went out and the room started to fill with smoke. For thirty long painful seconds, Alexeyev felt an odd paralysis, like in a nightmare when he couldn't move his arms or legs. Finally his central nervous system seemed to snap out of it. He heard his own voice croak out, "What the hell was *that*?"

The emergency phone circuit clicked, the emergency phone piped into the ship's general announcing speakers, although raspy and faint. But it was still unmistakably clear this time. "Central Command, this is Glavny Starshina Yeger, in the zero three deck. There's been a fire and explosion in the auxiliary machinery room. The entire room is gone and there's smoke and fire. It's an oxygen fire!"

"All hands," Alexeyev barked into the general announcing speakers, "fire in auxiliary machinery room. All personnel, don emergency air breathing masks. Rig ship for fire in the second compartment. Fire-fighting teams, muster in the zero two level with Chief Yeger."

Alexeyev looked at Lebedev after he'd strapped on his mask. "You know what the procedure calls for," he said quietly.

She nodded. "We don't have a choice, Captain."

"Watch Officer," Alexeyev said, "set up to jettison oxygen banks overboard."

"Sir?" Shvets said, astonished. "Captain, if we do that, we'll not only have no atmo control but no oxygen. And we're under thick ice, sir!"

"I know, Shvets. Now follow your goddamned orders."

Alexeyev didn't blame young Captain Lieutenant Vilen Shvets for his outburst. The younger generation of officers were taught not to take orders blindly, but to think and contribute. Except in emergencies where "immediate actions" were called for. And ice or no ice, the immediate action for an oxygen fire submerged was to dump the oxygen overboard. No oxygen, no fire.

"Sir, we're set up to blow oxygen overboard," Shvets said hesitantly.

"Watch Officer, jettison oxygen," Alexeyev said. He turned to Lebedev and leaned in close to her. "Well, that's it," he said quietly. "That's the end of the mission."

"Commencing O2 blow overboard, Captain," Shvets said. The sound of rushing gas could be heard in the room, the sound continuing for half a minute. Alexeyev felt a mourning for all that life-giving oxygen leaving the ship. That meant he'd need to return to open water, where the first Gigantskiy had detonated and opened up a polynya, and where the second one was headed. But making turns toward open water would take him closer to the second Gigantskiy's detonation point. But it couldn't be helped. If the hull could hold up to the second detonation and maintain some kind propulsion, he could radio for help and save the crew.

All that assumed, of course, that the American—Hostile One— was on the bottom in pieces.

It was quiet in the control room of the USS *New Jersey*. It was also crowded, with watchstanders at every console. Captain Seagraves stood between the command console and the navigation plot. Not far from him, XO Quinnivan stood behind the attack center of the BSY-1 battlecontrol system. At the end of the row, the weapon control console was manned by Weapons Officer Styxx. Behind the command console, Officer of the Deck Pacino stood, rotating the display from navigation to weapons control to sonar. On the sonar screen for broadband, there was no sign of Master One. They could no longer hear him on narrowband and there'd been no transients. The Omega had disappeared.

"Attention in the firecontrol party," Seagraves announced. "Firing point procedures, aim point number one for Master One, VPT door two, tube eleven, Tomahawk SUBROC, depth zero detonation."

"Ship ready," Pacino reported.

"Weapon ready," Styxx called.

"Solution ready and input as aim point number one," Quinnivan said.

Michael DiMercurio

Aim point number one was the opening of the rectangular ice wall area where Master One had withdrawn to, and from where he'd fired the supercavitating torpedo. Odds were, he was no longer there, Pacino thought, and had driven out the way he'd come, on a northward path, but aim point number two was ahead of him by five miles. Between the two detonations, they'd definitely do some damage.

"Shoot on generated aim point," Seagraves ordered.

"Tube eleven, *fire!*" Styxx shouted as she rotated the trigger lever from the nine o'clock position to the three o'clock position.

The sound of the tube firing vibrated the deck, but wasn't the ear-slamming explosion of a torpedo tube firing. A few moments later, the sound of the rocket motor ignition could be heard faintly from above them.

"I have Tomahawk SUBROC normal launch," Senior Chief Albanese called from the sonar stack.

"Firing point procedures," Seagraves announced, "aim point number *two* for Master One, VPT door two, tube twelve, Tomahawk SUBROC, depth zero detonation."

The launch reports and actions were repeated, until the second Tomahawk SUBROC had lifted off from the open water overhead.

Pacino walked to the navigation chart and joined Navigator Lewinsky. "You have aim points one and two drawn in?"

"Inputting them now," he said. A red circle appeared at the entrance to the ice-wall box. Lewinsky drew it to be a quarter mile in diameter. The blast damage zone would be bigger, certainly. A second red circle appeared five miles north of aim point one, also a quarter mile in diameter.

"Time of flight, XO?" Seagraves asked.

"Two minutes thirty seconds, Captain," Quinnivan said. "Two minutes to go for unit eleven."

"*Torpedo in the water! Bearing two six one!*" Albanese's voice cracked as he made the announcement.

Pacino turned his command console display to sonar's transient module, then to the broadband display. Streaking down the

398

broadband waterfall was a loud trace, at constant bearing 261. Which meant it was coming right for them.

"Classify the torpedo, Sonar," Seagraves snapped.

"It's another Magnum, sir. A Gigantskiy."

"Fuck," Quinnivan said.

"Snapshot tube three in countermeasure mode, bearing two six one, immediate enable, high-to-medium active snake!" Seagraves ordered.

A *snapshot* was a quick reaction torpedo launch and usually ejected a torpedo with no firecontrol solution, just shot it out on a bearing line and hoped for the best. Ironically, it was a tactic picked up from the Soviet submarine force in the Cold War.

"Weapon ready!" Styxx said.

"*Fire!*" Seagraves ordered.

The deck jumped and Pacino's ears slammed. He glanced at Lewinsky, then at Short Hull Cooper. A one megaton torpedo was inbound, and based on how badly they'd fared from the Gigantskiy detonation six miles away, if this one got closer than that, this mission was definitely over. Hell, the ship itself might be destroyed, he thought. For Pacino, there was no fear of death, not after the *Piranha* sinking and his near-death experience. He knew down to the marrow of his bones that life and consciousness didn't end. But still, there was regret, regret at failure. At failing to win in battle against the *Belgorod*. And sadness at the thought of never seeing his father again. Or Rachel Romanov. Or his friends from the crew. And about Rachel, did she ever come out of the coma? Would she live? And if Pacino died, how would she react to the news?

"Snapshot tube four in countermeasure mode, bearing two six one, immediate enable, high-to-medium *passive* snake!" Seagraves ordered.

"Weapon ready!" Styxx said.

"*Fire!*" Seagraves ordered.

The deck jumped again, and again Pacino's eardrums slammed.

"Line up tube three and four in CMT mode," Seagraves ordered Styxx.

"Tube three is ready, Captain," she replied.

"Snapshot tube three!"

The torpedo firing in countermeasure mode continued with tube three fired, then a second torpedo fired from tube four, when the sudden *bang* sound came from the west, the direction the ship was pointed. It was loud and abrupt, but there was silence afterward. Was it from outside the ship or from their own bow?

Quinnivan looked at Seagraves, his eyes wide. "Was that from *us?*"

Albanese turned to face the captain. "That was from the west," he said. "Not our SUBROC, obviously. I'm guessing it was from Master One. Maybe something happened to him."

"Isn't it time for the SUBROC detonation, XO?" Seagraves asked Quinnivan.

Gigantskiy unit two experienced the signal from central command to start its engine and proceed on its assigned path to seek out the submarine target.

The engine started and the turbine spun up, the propulsor's revolutions increasing until the build-up of thrust pushed it forward. The walls of the oversized torpedo tube rolled by the sonar seeker in the nosecone as the unit surged ahead, the open water cooler than the heated up water in the tube. The unit sped up to the ordered transit speed of forty-five knots, headed toward the estimated target's position seven miles to the east-northeast. A few ship lengths from the launching point, the unit enabled and armed the one megaton nuclear warhead, the safety plate rotated to establish a clear and open channel between the low explosives and the high explosives, which would collapse the segmented plutonium into a dense sphere and start the fission explosion, which was the trigger for the thermonuclear reaction.

The sonar set for the active search went through a self-check, and when it showed all circuits and systems nominal, it lit up the active pinger, seeking forward for the submarine target. In case the target were closer, the weapon would detonate upon driving up to a close range of a hundred meters. If not, and there were no submarine target detected, the unit would proceed to the aim point. If there were no target in the sonar seeker window by the time it approached the far side ice wall, the unit would execute what was called a default detonation, the logic behind it that a one megaton blast didn't need to get close to destroy a target.

But the sonar seeker, instead of hearing a pulse return from a target, heard a ping at a much higher frequency from something else. It was faint at first, but then louder as it got closer. The weapon was confused. It had no protocol for hearing this oddly insistent pinging sound.

At a distance from launching point of two miles, that pinging sound got extremely loud and a sudden impact cut the Gigantskiy torpedo in two, and an explosion started from aft of the warhead and the computer controls. There *was* a protocol for something like this happening. When the accelerometers registered over one G in any direction, a default detonation command would be programmed, the thinking that a countermeasure torpedo would not prevent the weapon from exploding. Rather, it would just explode early.

The low explosives lit off as the back half of the Gigantskiy vaporized in the explosion of the Mark 48 ADCAP countermeasure torpedo, and the high explosives detonated, compressing the plutonium fragments into a sphere, and nanoseconds later, the plutonium exploded, its plasma sphere engulfing the heavy water canisters, which started the fusion reaction, and the full one megaton yield of the torpedo lit the previously coal mine darkness under the ice into bright daylight. The explosion blew upward into thick ice, but the ten meter thickness of the ice canopy was unequal to the tremendous force of the explosion, the entire ice canopy blowing into splinters and shards and flying upward for a radius of three hundred meters, the violent expulsion of water vapor of the explosion rising to over a mile over the surface. The pressure wave from the blast hit the bottom and reflected upward, the shock wave becoming a cylinder around the blast zone and traveling away at sonic speed in all directions, until it encountered an ice wall to the west, blowing the ice wall to fragments.

On the other side of the ice wall was the huge hull of the launching ship, the *Belgorod*, and the deep-diver submarine, the *Losharik*. *Belgorod* was at a depth of 150 meters, with *Losharik* bottomed out at 470 meters. The shock wave slammed into *Belgorod* like the punch of a fist, but it passed over *Losharik*, only rolling the deep-diver submarine over. The flooding of the *Belgorod* started immediately after the impact.

25

Tomahawk SUBROC unit one, in tube eleven of the aft Virginia Payload Tube, lay snug in its waterproof capsule, nestled in the vertical tube. It was connected to the BSY-1 battlecontrol system by a signal wire leading to the flank of the capsule and penetrating it and connected to the weapon's electronics. The target location was programmed in and accepted, as well as the present position of the weapon. The warhead yield was dialed in at maximum, 250 kilotons of thermonuclear power. The signal wire from the battlecontrol system disconnected. The missile was on its own now, its battery keeping it alive until the turbine could start up in the near future.

The weapon felt the sudden intense acceleration upward as the launching system ejected it, a rocket motor directed into a reservoir of pure water at the base of the tube, flashing the water to high-pressure steam that acted like the gunpowder explosion of a cannon ejecting a cannonball. The cannister flew out of the tube, accelerating more as it rose out of the tube, but as the stern of the capsule cleared the tube, the pressure of the steam eased and the acceleration became negative as the weapon slowed. The steam created a bubble around the capsule and the steam and the cannister rose quickly toward the surface a hundred feet above, to the open water of the polynya formed by the first Gigantskiy detonation.

The weapon continued rising until the nosecone of it broached into the cold arctic air. As it did, a wet-dry sensor at the tip of the cannister detected dry air, and it activated twenty-four explosive bolts around the circumference of the cannister, blowing the nosecone cleanly off, the fiberglass of it tumbling end over end high in the air. As the nosecone reached the apex of its flight and started falling back toward the water, the missile's first stage rocket engine ignited, and the missile roared out of the waterproof cannister and blasted out of the water, rising vertically up over the icy landscape. Behind it, the polynya grew smaller as the rocket motor roared, lifting the missile to a height of a thousand feet.

As suddenly as it had begun, the rocket thrust stopped, the solid rocket fuel exhausted. By then, an air inlet scoop had popped out, the scoop sucking in air. Another two dozen explosive bolts blew the rocket motor off the aft end of the weapon, the first stage tumbling back down toward the polynya, and as it did, the explosive blast of steam could be seen below as a second missile's cannister broached into the open water.

The missile's winglets popped out into the airflow and directed the missile to dive downward straight toward the ice below. As the missile flew downward in a glide, its speed rising as it fell, the air coming in through the scoop spun the turbomachinery, the compressor on the forward end and the turbine on the aft end beginning to spool up to operating speed, and as the compressor blades rotated, they compressed the incoming cold air and the pressure in the combustion chamber rose, as well as the temperature, until the combustion chamber was super-pressurized and red hot. The missile's computer opened the valve to the pressurized fuel tank and jet fuel flowed into the combustion chamber and the spark plugs lit the atomized fuel and air mixture, the chemical reaction causing temperature and pressure to soar far over what they'd been to start. The hot combustion gases sought the relief of a lower pressure and first blasted through the turbine blades, some of their energy going to spinning the turbine harder and faster, which kept the compressor spinning up forward. The remainder of the hot, high-energy gases flowed aft through the missile's exhaust nozzle, the thrust of them propelling the missile, but by then, the missile was approaching the solid ice below.

At an altitude of seven meters above the ice, the winglets pulled the missile out of the dive and it flew west-northwest toward the aim point, hugging the terrain of the ice, following the rises and valleys, until it was a mere thousand feet from the aim point.

Behind the missile, the second-launched unit was climbing to the height of its rocket-driven flight, jettisoning the rocket motor stage and diving for the ice canopy. The first-launched unit rotated its winglets and climbed vertically in its pop-up maneuver, until at a thousand feet over the ice, it again arced over and down until the nosecone was pointed straight down at the aim point. The time for powered flight was ended, and explosive bolts blew the payload module away from the missile body, which pulled away, flew on to the north and then self-destructed.

The payload, the hydrogen bomb mounted in a depth charge, armed itself and prepared for detonation. When the altimeter indicated it was at sea level, it would detonate the nuclear warhead.

The aim point got closer and closer as the warhead fell. A drogue parachute blew out one end, stabilizing the depth charge long enough for the main chute to deploy, which slowed the depth charge down to walking speed as it fell lower to the ice.

The ice approached from below and the depth charge impacted against a steep cliff and bounced off it, then came to an abrupt stop in an ice valley. The altimeter read twenty-four feet above sea level. The warhead's protocol for detonation was unsatisfied. It was programmed to detonate at between twenty and zero feet, not twenty-four. The depth charge rolled to a halt, its computer system kept alive by a small battery, but battery endurance would be measured only in minutes.

As the depth charge's battery died, the second-fired missile streaked overhead, five nautical miles to the north, its winglets rotating to bring it to the vertical flight path of its pop-up maneuver. It arced downward and the missile body blew off and the second depth charge descended, its descent masked by the ice ridge that the first depth charge had hit.

Thirty seconds after the death of the first-fired depth charge, the second one detonated, the 250-kiloton hydrogen bomb's explosion sixteen times as powerful as the atomic bomb dropped on Hiroshima. The explosion pounded downward into the ice and blew two pressure ridges aside. The ice under the depth charge vaporized, the water below with it.

Five miles to the south, the shock wave of the second-fired depth charge hit the *Belgorod* and the *Losharik,* and like the explosion of the second Gigantskiy, the cruel shock wave showed no mercy.

Captain Second Rank Iron Irina Trusov removed her headset and hung it on a hook on the starboard side of her pilot-in-command console in the cockpit of the *Losharik*. She looked at Captain Sergei Kovalov to her left, in the mission commander's seat.

"All sonar systems deactivated, Captain," she said in a dead voice. "We're bottomed out at four hundred seventy meters, thrusted snug against the west ice wall of the north-south passage. All water-tight doors are shut and ship is prepared for shock impact."

Kovalov nodded. "Not much we can do now except wait for the Gigantskiy detonation," he said.

Trusov pursed her lips in annoyance. A combat operation was happening just outside the ship and she was trapped in a research vessel when she should be the one shooting torpedoes in anger. She'd been preparing for undersea combat her entire life.

When Trusov was ten years old, she and her father, Captain First Rank Volodya Trusov, had built a huge model of the submarine he commanded, the Shchuka-class submarine B-448 *Tambov,* the model carved from a soft wood and fully a meter-and-a-half long. The submarine's flank could be removed to show the interior, that she and her father had carefully crafted, carving each feature out of wood and painting them, then inserting them into the hull. All three decks of the submarine were shown up forward, with the second compartment's central command post, electronics rooms, officer berthing, the middle level mess facilities and crew's berthing, and the lower-level machinery spaces with atmospheric control. The first compartment was shown, with the torpedoes in their cradles, the tubes running forward to the nosecone, even the sonar array below the torpedo tubes. Aft, the model depicted the reactor compartment and the machinery compartments. At a party her father gave for his officers, she had proudly displayed the model, to the astonishment and delight of the guests, who lauded her for her detailed work. They had laughed that other little girls played with dollhouses, but Irina played with nuclear attack submarines. One of the visitors, her father's second-in-command, had cautioned Captain Trusov against running afoul of the GRU and KGB for a military security violation, so accurate was the model. That had been the happiest day of Irina Trusov's life.

It was less than a month later that her father lay quietly in his grave, dead of a heart attack at the age of forty-one. Irina's mother was a classic beauty, with long, shining platinum blonde hair—just as her daughter had—and big, bright blue eyes—also exactly as her daughter had. It came as no surprise to anyone when her mother remarried, but no one could ever replace Daddy. Worse was that Irina's alcoholic stepfather, Borya Feodor, was a sloppy, bald, fat, supply logistics manager in the closed city of Severomorsk, where they'd lived when Daddy was alive. By then, Irina was thirteen and blooming from girlhood to womanhood, a fact that greatly interested her stepfather, who had taken to sneaking into the bathroom whenever Irina showered. The first time that had happened, Irina pitched a fit to her mother, but her mother ignored the implications and insisted that Father Borya was merely trying to be friendly. Friendly, right, Irina had argued, standing next to her in the shower naked, insisting on touching her to wash her back or her hair, and lately he'd begun to become excited as he did so, his disgusting male organ swelling, sometimes tapping her hip or buttocks as he washed her. Her mother dismissed the allegations, saying that Irina was exaggerating.

Irina tried everything to forestall the bathroom visitations, locking the door and putting a chair against the knob or showering in the middle of the night. She had gone so far as to shorten her shower duration by chopping off her shining platinum hair, cutting it almost as short as a boy's, thinking it would have the added advantage of making her look less feminine to the boorish Borya, but nothing seemed to stop her stepfather.

No matter her protestations to her mother, the shower invasions continued, and Irina feared that her stepfather would progress to even more overt harassment, perhaps even rape. Finally, Irina had planned to run away from home to get away from the pervert. On a Sunday afternoon, she'd decided to take one last shower before escaping—with all that was going on, she felt constantly dirty and greasy. No amount of soap or shampoo seemed to ease the dirty feeling. She was rubbing shampoo into her hair when Borya, as usual, opened the shower curtain from behind her and slipped into the shower, naked and aroused.

It was all too much and the rage filled her in a tenth of a second, and without even rinsing the shampoo out of her eyes, she grabbed Borya by his head with both her hands and with all her strength, rammed his head into the water fixture as hard as she could. Borya fell to the floor, the warm water washing over him. Irina cleared her eyes of the shampoo and leaned over his prone body. Blood was flooding the floor of the shower, but when she felt his neck, she could feel a pulse. He was only unconscious, and for how long, Irina couldn't guess. She crouched down over him and clamped one hand over his mouth, sealing it, and with the other, pinched his nostrils. She shut her eyes and counted to two hundred, and by then the water had gone cold, but she didn't care. When she reached the end of her count, she checked for a pulse again, and there was none. Borya was gone.

She rinsed, then turned off the water and got out, finding her bath sheet and drying herself. She wrapped the towel around herself and left the bathroom to find her mother, who was calmly reading the newspaper in the kitchen.

"I think something's wrong with Father Borya," Irina said calmly. "He fell in the shower."

She could still hear her mother's plaintive wailing all these years later. Irina had moved in with her father's former first officer's family, who were childless and lonely, and they finished raising her with affection, dealing with her lingering anger as best they could. Fortunately for Irina, she was the number one student in her school, and with that and the legacy of her father, she was accepted into the M.V. Frunze Military Academy in Moscow for undergraduate studies, then continuing her education at the Komsomol Submarine Navigation Higher Naval School, graduating first in her class.

At the age of 27, Trusov was still a virgin, the nastiness with her stepfather poisoning any chance of successful dating. At Frunze Academy, when she was a second-year cadet, she'd gone out for drinks with three other female cadets, and a first-year male had tried to slip something into her drink. When he wasn't looking, she'd dumped it into the bar sink and gotten a fresh one, but she wondered what would have happened if he'd been successful in drugging her. Her mind had danced with the fantasy of dispatching him as she had with Borya, but she had walked away, and never seen a man romantically since. Some of the male cadets labeled her a man-hater, others frigid, and still others insisted she was a lesbian. She wasn't, she knew, she just wanted to meet a man like her father.

She'd been assigned to the Project 971 Shchuka-B submarine K-154 *Tigr* as the sonar officer. Three years later, after a successful assignment, she turned down a shore duty teaching assignment at N.G. Kuznetsov Naval Academy to join the crew of the Pacific Fleet's new Yasen-M class attack submarine K-573 *Novosibirsk*, reporting aboard as the weapons officer.

On *Novosibirsk*, she'd avoided the advances of the other officers, who obviously considered her beautiful—she'd grown out her hair again, but usually kept it tied up in a bun or a ponytail. There was not much she could do about her expansive chest or her bright blue eyes, but she avoided makeup and kept her mannerisms all business, shutting down all romantic approaches.

For a time she'd had a romantic admiration for *Novosibirsk*'s commanding officer, Captain First Rank Yuri Orlov, a trim, tall and handsome officer, but he was on the rebound from another woman, and hadn't returned her feelings. It didn't matter, since *Novosibirsk's* mission became a horrible maritime disaster in the Arabian Sea in a freak confrontation with an American Virginia-class submarine that was hijacking the Iranian nuclear submarine *Panther*, which *Novosibirsk* had been charged with guarding and escorting, and had failed. An American cruise missile had nearly destroyed the ship, knocking out the entire crew, and the vessel was sinking. Trusov had been the first to wake, and had taken action to save the ship, bringing it to the surface, starting the emergency diesel generator, and ventilating out the smoke, but though the ship had limped on for a few hours, it was doomed. Eventually Captain Orlov had ordered the crew to abandon ship, and that was when the mission became surreal.

The escape chamber of the *Novosibirsk*, big enough to allow rescue of the entire crew, had successfully detached from the hull of the sinking submarine, and had rolled sickeningly in the swells of the Arabian Sea. To Trusov's terror, the Americans had surfaced the stolen submarine *Panther* right alongside and taken them aboard, hostages and prisoners. Irina noted that before the sinking of the *Novosibirsk*, she had been as anti-American as anyone she knew. Captain Orlov had even scolded her for it at one point, saying that rage and hatred were illogical. She wondered how he would see her rage and hatred toward Father Borya, because that was certainly logical in her mind.

But as it turned out, the crew of *Novosibirsk* weren't hostages or prisoners of the Americans. The Americans—dreaded and hated for decades—fed and clothed the Russians and repatriated them at the first opportunity, not even interrogating them. There was one officer in particular, an American Navy lieutenant, a stunningly handsome young man named Pacino, who had patiently spoken to Irina and calmed her down, insisting they weren't taking the Russians prisoner, and who had fed them and escorted each of them to the showers and given them fresh coveralls and called for a hospital ship to treat their radiation-sickened engineering personnel, and to evacuate them.

Counter to their expectations, upon returning to Moscow, the Navy had treated them as heroes, despite losing the battle and the submarine. For her quick thinking and action to save the ship, Trusov had been decorated with the Medal for Distinction in Combat, Type 2 Award. She had inwardly considered it ridiculous. Certainly, she'd saved the ship, but only for an hour or two. If one of the other officers had awakened first, he would have won the award, not Trusov. Other officers considered her humble, but she knew that she'd acted out of instinct and training, not some grand heroics.

From time to time, Irina Trusov's mind returned to that young man she'd met on the *Panther*. If she were honest, she thought about Lieutenant Anthony Pacino a lot. He reminded her of her father. Intense, but so very kind. Kind and caring, even though, as American submariners, they had been out to sink and kill the Russians. Trusov's opinions about the Americans changed that day. If life had been different, and Pacino had been born Russian or Trusov had been born American, she could easily see them being together.

But things were radically different now. Because here they were again, on a mission to deploy President Vostov's Status-6 torpedoes, when an American attack submarine intervened and intended to stop them. When presidential orders came into the *Belgorod* to attack and sink the American, Trusov was of two minds. On the one hand, she wanted to *win* this engagement. The loss to the Americans in the Arabian Sea had been humiliating. On the other, she hoped their adversary weren't the same Virginia-class sub they'd lost to in the Arabian Sea, not because she feared them, but because their crew had included Anthony Pacino.

As she waited for the detonation of the Gigantskiy torpedo, Captain Second Rank Trusov wondered what Anthony Pacino was doing at that very moment.

The blood had soaked through Anthony Pacino's shirt. He followed Rachel Dominatrix Navigatrix Romanov into the master bathroom in the upstairs level of Jeremiah Seamus Bullfrog Quinnivan's Virginia Beach house. The noise of the party roared from the basement, two levels down, the crew raucously celebrating the conclusion of the *Panther* mission. At the awards ceremony that morning, Pacino had been pinned with the silver star, but far more importantly, awarded his gold dolphins, the coveted emblem indicating that he was qualified in submarines, the dolphins pinned on by Rob Catardi, the commander of the submarine force. In the audience that day, Pacino had seen his father standing tall in a dark suit, sending him a rigid salute. It was the best day of Pacino's life, and it was only the beginning, he thought.

The officers had all kidded Pacino that his dolphins were a gift, that he hadn't been onboard the *Vermont* long enough to have earned them legitimately, but XO Quinnivan had shut down the teasing by promising that anyone who chose to could take a punch at Pacino's dolphin emblem with the backing tabs removed, so that the sharp pins of it were all that kept them on his shirt. Pacino's fellow officers and friends lined up to punch his dolphins, the hardest coming from Captain Seagraves. When Rachel came up to take her swing, she had just gently caressed his chest instead, and whispered in his ear that now that he was qualified, she couldn't torment him anymore about him being a non-qual air-breathing puke, but that she'd find something else to tease him about. Squirt Gun Vevera stepped up to take his turn to punch Pacino's dolphins, and Rachel had said, laughing, "Be gentle with him, Squirt Gun, he has delicate feelings."

By then, with all the punches, the pins of the dolphins had made twin deep puncture wounds in Pacino's chest, and Rachel had taken him by the hand upstairs to clean him up, borrowing a first aid kit and a shirt of Bullfrog's from Quinnivan's wife. She shut and locked the bathroom door behind them, pulled off his shirt, sat him down on the toilet lid, found a washcloth, and washed away the blood. She dried him off, then carefully disinfected and bandaged the wounds, putting Quinnivan's shirt on him when she was done, leaving the long-sleeved shirt unbuttoned. She rinsed Pacino's bloody shirt in the sink and cleaned the dolphins, handing them to Pacino. She sat on the rim of the bathtub opposite him and told him the news that she and her husband Bruno had broken up, that it had been a long time coming, but that the marriage was finally over. She wiped a tear out of her eye then, and stood from the tub edge and straddled him, her soft thighs warm on Pacino's.

Her left hand stroked his hair and her right hand touched his cheek, her slim fingers soft and cool on his skin. He looked up at her, and she came close. He shut his eyes as her lips met his, her silky, soft, warm tongue in his mouth, making slow circles around his.

When she finally pulled back, she looked at him, her eyes shining brightly.

"Let's get out of here," she said. "Take me to your apartment and make me glad I'm a woman."

He smiled at her. They stood and she buttoned his shirt. They emerged from the upstairs, and without a word to any of the revelers, walked out to his old Corvette, parked in the driveway next to Feng Lewinsky's Ferrari. Pacino opened the door for her and Rachel climbed in, folding her long legs into the car. He smiled to himself as he climbed into the driver's side and clicked the ignition, the supercharger whining as he gunned the engine.

"My place, right?" he said.

She smiled. "Yes, but first—don't laugh—I am dying for a cheeseburger, with huge steak fries and a regular, old-fashioned, sugary Coca Cola."

"Hell with Coke," Pacino said. "After a run like this, I need an ice-cold beer."

"Take us out of the subdivision and turn right toward the beach," Rachel said. "I know a place."

Pacino drove the five miles to a tumbledown diner that had seen better days during the Ford administration.

"Here? You sure?"

"This place has the most amazing cheeseburger you will ever taste."

At the table, the waitress brought the plates. If she thought it odd that Pacino and Romanov were sitting on the same side of the table, she didn't show it. Rachel's hand on his thigh was heaven on earth.

"Coke for the lady. Corona with lime for the gentleman," the waitress said, handing the drinks to them.

But mysteriously, as Pacino looked up at the server, she flashed in and out of an odd reality for a few fractions of a second. One instant she was simply a waitress in a diner. Then, for just a tenth of a second, she was a skeleton. Then she snapped back to being a waitress. Then, click, she was a skeleton.

He looked at Rachel to see if she'd noticed the strange phenomenon of the waitress. Rachel was wearing a tight red sweater, tight jeans, and tall brown boots. Which was a good thing, he thought. That meant she was real. In his dreams about her, she was always in starched high-collar service dress whites, with full medals. He looked up at the waitress, who still had her hand on his beer bottle, but now there was no sign of her as a normal person. Now she stayed a skeleton. In alarm, he looked over at Rachel, but now Rachel was wearing starched choker whites with her medals, her ceremonial sword, and officers' cap on the table. He was opening his mouth to speak when she picked up the ketchup bottle and held it over his head while smiling at him. She flipped its lid and started pouring ketchup on his head, and strangely, it wasn't room temperature, but warm. The skeleton server put down the beer and picked up another bottle of warm ketchup and started pouring it on his head as well.

Pacino spat to get the ketchup out of his nose and mouth, and it was in his eyes. He wiped his eyes and blinked, and he was in the dark. The diner was gone. The skeleton waitress was gone. And Rachel Romanov was gone. He coughed into the silent darkness, wiping what must be blood out of his eyes.

Then he heard Rachel's voice. *Here, baby. You're gonna need this.* And suddenly a heavy weight of a solid object dropped from a height and hit him in the stomach. He flinched, wondering what the object was. It was too dark to see it, but he could tell by feel it was a battle-lantern. If a car battery had a bulb, a lens, and an on-off switch, all

414

wrapped in a rubbery yellow case, it became a Navy battle-lantern. He felt the on switch and clicked it on. By the strong light of the lantern, he could see he was sitting in the dark, silent control room of the submarine *New Jersey*, leaning against the navigation console. He shone the light around the room. He could see Dankleff in the pilot's seat, still strapped in, but he was out cold, his head resting on his right shoulder. Pacino looked around the rest of the room. There were bodies piled up forward, some aft, but they were all unconscious, some bloody, one with a compound fracture of the leg.

"Hello?" he called. "Anyone awake?"

He struggled to his feet, feeling a dizziness threatening to toss him back down again, but he grabbed the safety bar of the command console, then noticed that the deck was tilted steeply downhill, and it wasn't just the dizziness. They were pitched forward, at a crazy thirty-degree angle downward.

He was blinded by a renewed stream of blood in his eyes, and he wiped it away with his sleeve, then felt his forehead. A gash had opened up above his right eye and it hurt when he touched it. He grabbed a box resembling a box of tissues, but filled with paper towels—"Kim Wipes." He wiped his head and face, dropping the soaking wipe to the deck while he pulled out a fresh one. He stuffed his pockets with the wipes. There was no time to deal with his head wound now. He staggered over to Dankleff's panel, slipping on a blood trail that he was fairly certain had come from him. He grabbed Dankleff's shoulder, shaking it.

"U-Boat! Wake up! Dankleff!"

But Dankleff was out cold. Pacino shone the light on the panels, all of them dark. He found the old manual bourdon tube pressure gauge off to the port side of the wrap-around displays, the U-boat era gauge not needing electricity or computers to provide its indication. Pacino squinted at the gauge. The needle pointed to 600 and was rotating toward 650.

The bottom, as Pacino remembered it, was about 700 feet, well above crush depth, but the bottom wasn't safe. If the ship were sinking, with the reactor shut down and no power, they'd need to surface and get to open water. Otherwise they'd die down here. They'd been directly below a polynya of open water formed by the first Gigantskiy detonation when the second one had exploded. Assuming the boat hadn't been moved away by the explosion, the open water should still be overhead.

By now, the deck was tilted downward by 35 degrees. Pacino shone his light on the bubble-type inclinometer, another relic of World War II submarining, and it showed the deck going to a 40 degree down angle.

Pacino took a deep breath. "Let's hope this works," he muttered to himself. He found the big stainless steel levers of the emergency ballast tank blow system outboard of the copilot's seat. The one on the right was the forward system. He pulled down the interlock device and rotated the large lever from straight down to straight up.

Immediately a roaring, blasting sound slammed Pacino's eardrums, and the room filled with thick fog, the condensation from the super-cold emergency blow manifold. He shined the light back up to the inclinometer, which was now showing a twenty-five-degree dive, easing to fifteen. Pacino operated the aft main ballast tank emergency blow lever, and the fog in the room got denser and the blasting noise louder, if that were possible. He checked the depth gauge—now showing 400 feet and trending upward.

Soon the roaring noise got quieter and the fog cleared. Pacino rotated both blow levers back down and watched the depth gauge, the needle climbing up past 200 to 150. Finally it stopped at thirty-five, and the deck rolled to starboard, then port, then steadied. They were on the surface. The inclinometer showed a slight up angle, by two degrees. Pacino hoped that wasn't bad news. If they were flooding aft, the up angle would increase and the day would end early.

Pacino called out to the room. "Anyone awake? Hello?"

He shone the battle lantern light around the room, slower this time. Everyone was out cold. His light fell onto River Styxx, whose head had impacted the weapon control console, shattering the display and deeply cutting her face. He felt her neck, but there was no pulse and her flesh was cold. At the Pos Two console, Easy Eisenhart sat, his head completely turned around so that it faced backwards, a look of terror frozen on his face. His flesh was also cold, although Pacino knew it was useless to verify it.

Dammit, he cursed to himself. He had to stop worrying about the crew and hurry aft and get the battery online. The nuclear explosion must have opened every electrical breaker onboard. He carefully stepped aft, trying to avoid slipping from the blood on the deck, until he left control and was in the central passageway, then down the ladder to the middle level of the crew's mess. There were bodies on the deck, none of them conscious. His light shone on the form of Senior Chief Corpsman Grim Thornburg. Pacino tried to shake him awake, but there was no response. He felt his neck for a pulse. The skin was warm and there was a pulse, but he was nonresponsive.

Beside Thornburg was the body of Chief McGuire, the A-gang chief, whose head was only connected to his bloody neck by a few fibers of flesh, the blood puddle surrounding him.

Pacino hurried to the dogged-shut hatch to the shielded tunnel of the reactor compartment. He held the handle of the battle lantern in his teeth while he undogged the hatch, opened it and set it on the latch, then stepped through. He jogged down the tunnel, since there was no blood and no bodies, got to the aft hatch and undogged it and latched it open, then emerged into the aft compartment's engineroom.

He sniffed the air for smoke, but it just smelled like steam, lube oil, and atmospheric control amines. But the deck seemed to be tilting, just slightly, aft. He forced himself to ignore the deck's tilt and found what he was looking for in the long rows of cabinets of the motor control center. The battery breaker cabinet was memorized by every sailor onboard as part of qualifying in submarines. Pacino could have found it in the dark, he thought. He put down the battle lantern, reached down to the breaker handle—a large tongue of tough black plastic—and pulled it upward with all his strength. As it came to rest in the closed position, it made a loud thump, and almost instantly the overhead lights flickered on, just for an instant,

417

then went out, then flickered back on, then out again, but the third time they came on and held. In the circle of light between the panels, the electrical division chief, Senior Chief McGraceland, could be seen, face down. Pacino felt for a pulse, but McGraceland's skin was cold and he was obviously dead. Pacino turned off the battle-lantern and jogged farther aft to maneuvering, the nuclear control room.

He shook his head in dismay. Lieutenant Commander Moose Kelly was on the deck, the body of Ensign Long Hull Cooper on top of her. The electrical and reactor operators were on the deck beneath their panels. Pacino crouched down and verified that none of the prone crewmen had a pulse. *So much goddamned death*, he thought. He stepped to the right-side console, the electric plant control panel. Now that the battery was online, he could use its electricity to operate the other breakers. He looked at the battery amp-hour meter, which was clicking very slowly.

"Mr. Patch!" a voice from the door to maneuvering called. Pacino turned. It was the mechanical division chief, Chief Sam-I-Am MacHinery, his face covered in grease and blood.

"Help me, Chief!" Pacino said. "I can operate the electric plant but I need help starting up the engineroom."

"Can you get the reactor restarted?"

Pacino looked at the reactor plant control panel. Unlike the electric plant, it was like the ship-control station—all flatpanel displays driven by computers.

"I don't know. We may need the diesel if we can get the head valve opened. But let me try."

Pacino reached to the electric plant control panel and snapped shut the breaker from the battery breaker to the port side motor-generator. The motor-generator was a caveman means of converting DC power to AC power, by having the DC electricity drive a motor, connected by a shaft to an AC generator, which then powered the AC buses in the absence of a steam turbine generator. Pacino scanned the voltage at the DC end, then the AC end and the AC frequency, which had stabilized at 60 Hertz. So far, so good. He snapped shut the MG output breaker, energizing the port AC vital bus. He listened and sniffed. No sound of any electrical explosions and no smoke.

The flatpanels at the reactor control panel flashed to life, going from their default screen to a startup display, finally stabilizing with all the normal reactor control indications. *Thank God*, Pacino thought. Now, if he could get the inverter breakers shut, they'd be able to restart.

He left maneuvering, MacHinery following him, back to the motor control center, where he found the reactor control rod inverter cabinets.

"Shutting inverter A breaker," he said, and pulled up a thick black plastic tab much like the battery breaker's operator. The breaker shut. "No fireballs. It's a good day, Chief." He found inverter B. "Shutting the breaker for inverter Bravo." He pulled it up, the inverter humming with power. "Inverter Charlie now." He pulled that breaker up and sighed in relief. All three breakers held and there were no electrical shorts.

He stepped out to the row between the cabinets and checked RCP-5, the master reactor control remote cabinet. He opened the plexiglass cover and checked the protection circuits and the instrumentation circuit breakers. Everything was nominal.

"We're good to go, Chief," Pacino said. He walked back into maneuvering, found the curled microphone cord for the 1MC general announcing circuit and spoke into it, his voice booming through the ship.

"This is Lieutenant Pacino. Any personnel who are awake and able, report to maneuvering. Commencing fast recovery startup."

On the touchscreen, he selected the control area for the nuclear instrumentation, selected the source range channel selector switch, and put it into the mode labeled "startup range." He selected the rod group control function area on the touchscreen and selected group one rods to inverter A. He reached down to the panel for the pistol grip for the control rods. "Latching group one rods," he said to MacHinery as he pulled out the pistol grip and rotated it to the nine o'clock position. He got a light on the display. He rotated the grip to the three o'clock position to withdraw rods. "Pulling out group one to the top of the core."

It took thirty seconds to get group one rods out. The last time he'd been in maneuvering, group one was fully withdrawn and the reactor was controlled by group two, with group three halfway withdrawn. He selected inverter C to group three rods, then latched them as before. "Pulling group three to forty inches," he said, again rotating the pistol grip to three o'clock. Fifteen seconds later, he selected group two rods to inverter B, latched them and started pulling.

"Pulling group two to criticality." On the display, he monitored the source range nuclear instrument, the power level slowly climbing out of the startup range. He looked at the startup rate meter, which was climbing up from two decades per minute to three. Each decade was an increase in the neutron flux power level by a factor of ten. Startup rate climbed. Seven, eight, nine decades per minute, a rate fast enough to make a civilian nuclear operator faint dead away, and in fact, the procedure was so dangerous that the ship was required to be more than fifty miles from land to execute it.

Pacino released the pistol grip, the rods holding at eighteen inches from the bottom. At nine decades per minute, the reactor power was screaming out of the startup range and headed for the intermediate range. He reached to the touch screen and deactivated the source range nuclear instrument, which would be burned out by the flux of the intermediate range. The intermediate startup rate meter came alive and showed a startup rate of eight decades per minute. Pacino shimmed out until the needle was steady at nine decades per minute.

Thirty seconds later, the reactor power level had reached the power range, that level of neutron flux where additional reactivity insertion into the core could heat up the water of the primary loop.

Pacino clicked the 1MC mike. "The reactor...is *critical.*"

Pacino pulled rods out and watched reactor average temperature. Normally, the heat-up rate was required to be slow, to avoid blowing up the reactor vessel from thermal stress, but this was an emergency. The core temperature came up from 300 to 350, then 400. Soon average core temperature was 500 degrees. It was time for the reactor to take over from the battery.

"Reactor is in the power range," he announced on the 1MC. "Your show, Chief," he shouted to MacHinery. "Start up the engineroom."

"Give me main seawater pumps one and two, aux feedwater pump one and engineroom freshwater pump two," he said. Pacino spun around to the aft panel and hit the toggle switches for the pumps. As he did, MacHinery left to start the steam plant.

The faint hiss of steam could be heard in the piping overhead. On the display panel, Pacino watched the steam generator levels. The trick was to get a steam turbine generator online before the boilers went dry, and since the main feed pump to the boilers couldn't be started on the battery, there was a huge hurry to get a steam turbine on the grid. Failure at this would mean the reactor plant would die.

The steam sound was roaring and screaming now as the steam headers dumped out the condensation and warmed up. Chief MacHinery skidded to a halt at the door to maneuvering.

"I've got full vacuum on the port condenser. I'm gonna crank the port SSTG now," he said, then disappeared. Aft of maneuvering, on the port side, the sound of a turbine rolling could be heard. Soon it was loud in the space, the sound a bass whining, then starting a soprano scream, almost as if a jet engine were roaring up to full throttle right outside the maneuvering room. Finally, the shrieking scream steadied on pitch, and a moment later MacHinery put his head into the room.

"Port turbine generator is on the governor and ready for loading! I'm going to the feed station! Get that SSTG on the bus!"

Pacino selected the ship's service turbine generator frequency meter and touched the function to parallel it into the AC bus, whose frequency was managed by the motor-generator. It would be disastrous if the steam turbine came online out of synchronization — it could jump right off its steel foundation. But the auto-synch function worked perfectly. Pacino loaded up the turbine generator, taking the load off the battery.

He clicked the 1MC mike. "Electric plant is in a half power lineup on the port SSTG," he announced. That was MacHinery's cue to start one of the massive feed pumps to put water into the almost dry boilers.

He saw the pump energized indication and watched as boiler water levels climbed off the bottom.

There was a damage control saying in the submarine force, Pacino thought. *First, save the mission.* Obviously, *that* was no longer possible. *Second, save the ship.* For the moment, the ship was safe, but that deck tilting aft had to be looked into. It had gotten a little worse. *Third, save the reactor.* Done, Pacino thought. *Fourth, save the crew.*

"Chief, can you take over here?" Pacino called.

"I got it, L.T.," MacHinery said. "Good job, sir."

"Chief, we're taking on water aft," Pacino said. "Deck is tilting since I emergency blew. See if you can find where the flooding is. I'll call you from forward and maybe I can get the drain pump running."

As Pacino passed through the forward hatch of the reactor compartment tunnel, he almost ran into Senior Chief Corpsman Thornburg.

"Doc," Pacino said. "How are we doing?"

Thornburg shook his head solemnly. "I'm setting up triage in the crew's mess," he said. "Some folks are walking wounded, but we've lost some people."

"Keep working, Doc," Pacino said, clapping the chief's shoulder. "I'll be in control."

26

Weapons Officer Captain Lieutenant Ballerina Katerina Sobol lay face down in the central command post, unconscious. Her breathing was slow and deep, her pulse likewise slow. She lay like that for a long time until the pool of blood reached the level of her mouth and nostrils, and she began to inhale blood.

She woke suddenly, spitting and coughing. She tried to sit up, but the vertigo of her sudden movement made her fall back down again, back into that bloody pond. She pulled her face out, wiping off the blood with her sleeve, and blinked in the light of the emergency lanterns at the four corners of the room. They were weak and trying to illuminate the space through a light haze of smoke. Sobol took in a breath but couldn't smell anything burning. She reached up to her head and found the bleeding gash. It hurt, but it was superficial. She reached up to a handhold at the attack center console, where she had been strapped in by a five-point harness to her seat, but the seat had been ripped from the deck and the seatbelts had broken off, dumping her to the deck. She pulled herself up, noticing for the first time the distinct list to starboard. At least an alarming ten degrees, in an environment where even one degree of tilt was noticeable. She looked around the space. The watchstanders, the captain, and the first officer were all still buckled into their seats, but no one seemed awake.

She stepped to the command console and felt Captain Alexeyev's cheeks. His eyepatch had flown off in the high-G shockwave and it

423

was nowhere to be seen. His skin was warm. She felt his neck for a pulse, and it was strong and slow. She lightly slapped his face.

"Captain. *Captain!* Captain?"

There was no response. She tried to awaken the first officer. "Madam First! Madam Lebedev! *Wake up,* madam!"

Nothing. The right-hand seat of the command console was the watch officer's chair. Captain Lieutenant Vilen Shvets, the communications officer, was out cold. She tried to rouse him, with the same result. She looked down at the console displays, but they were all black. She looked around the room, and every console was dark.

"Second Captain," she said loudly to the AI system. "Second Captain, respond!"

There was no answer.

She forced herself to recognize the good news. She seemed to be the only one conscious after the nuclear explosion. And no one seemed to be dead, at least not yet. But the ship, she thought. The ship was dying.

She left the central command post by the aft door and hurried aft to the dogged-shut hatch to the third compartment with its shielded deck over the reactor. She realized she was panting like a sprinter. The oxygen level had fallen since the machinery room exploded and with atmo control gone, the carbon dioxide levels were climbing, but it seemed too early to be this winded. Perhaps it was just adrenaline, she thought. She was forced to slow down on her way aft. She opened the hatch and shut it behind her. The emergency lights were out in the space, and it was coal mine black. She felt for a flashlight on the bulkhead, and it was where she'd expected it, hopefully fully charged. She clicked it on, then made her way to the compartment's aft hatch, going through it to the darkened fourth compartment with its electronic cabinets, and main breaker bank, through its aft hatch to the fifth compartment, the steam machinery room, where far aft, the nuclear control room was situated. Nuclear control was an enclosed space with its own air conditioning, cooling it in the environment with a hundred steam leaks, which even in arctic waters, made the compartment hot and humid. One would erupt in sweat just in the walk from the fourth compartment to nuclear control, but not now. The space was eerily cool, which was a very bad sign. Cool and dark. She stopped just outside nuclear control when she heard something. It was the rush of water flowing. She shone her light aft, to the narrow passageway to the hatch to the sixth compartment.

She went to the hatch with its circular window and shone her light into the window. She could see a water level halfway up the window and climbing. Which meant the sixth compartment was almost completely flooded. The sixth compartment contained the engineering plant's battery, and if it had flooded, there would be no power without the reactor, but the reactor needed power to start, to run all the pumps and controls for the plant's systems.

She wondered if there were a way to connect the forward battery in the first compartment to the engineering space's systems, but she was a tactical officer and not qualified in the propulsion plant systems. She had to find someone who was. She returned to the door to nuclear control and tried to open it, but it would only come open a few centimeters. There was a body lying against the door. She shoved on it mightily, moving the body of the chief engineer out of the way. Sobol stepped over the body of the chief. On the deck the body of Chief Engineer Captain Third Rank Cobalt Ausra was nearly decapitated and lying in a hideous pool of blood, her head connected to her torso by a few blood vessels, a large bloody binder on the deck next to Ausra's head the probable culprit. The book must have flown off a shelf and hit the chief engineer right in her throat. The book was labeled, *RUKOVODSTVO PO REAKTORNOY USTANOVKE—* REACTOR PLANT MANUAL. The Sevmash engineers still insisted on paper procedures rather than switching to pad computer documents, and this was the result, Sobol thought.

Sobol stepped away from the dead chief engineer toward the seat of the engineering watch officer, Senior Lieutenant Anatoly Blackbeard Pavlovsky. She felt his throat for a pulse, and it was weak but present. She slapped his cheeks, but there was no response. In a cupholder was a covered cup of tea that had remained in the holder despite the massive shock wave. Sobol picked it up and felt it—the tea was cold. She removed the top and splashed it into Pavlovsky's face. He sputtered and spit, opening one eye, then the second and peered at Sobol as if he were in a dream. His eyes stared into the distance without focus. Sobol slapped his cheek again, harder this time.

"Pavlovsky! *Blackbeard!* Wake the hell up!" She shouted into his face and he shook his head, then put his hand on his neck. He must have suffered whiplash, she thought, hoping he hadn't broken his neck.

"Blackbeard. I know you can hear me. Wake up!"

"What?" he said slowly. "What the hell happened?"

"Nothing," Sobol said, her voice pitch even higher than normal. "Just a goddamned nuclear explosion. Come on, we're the only two awake. There's flooding in the sixth. The aft battery's gone. We need to see if we can get power from the forward battery and restart the reactor!"

Pavlovsky slowly unbuckled himself from his seat and tried to stand. Sobol helped him stay upright.

"Are you hurt badly?" she asked.

"I think I'm okay," he said. He sniffed the air. "Smoke," he said. "And it's stuffy. Hard to breathe." He took Sobol's flashlight from her and shone it toward the door and saw the body of Ausra. "Oh hell," he said. "Without her, I don't think we're coming back from this."

"Can't you restart the reactor?"

"I don't know. I don't think so. And there are systems in the sixth we'd need. There's no training drill for something like this."

"Well, hell," Sobol said. "Let's find anyone still alive from the spaces and get them forward then. Maybe we can evacuate the ship."

"Evacuate? How are you going to abandon ship under thick ice? The escape chamber will just clunk into the bottom of the ice cover."

"Maybe the Gigantskiy explosion opened up a polynya overhead."

"You can't count on that, Weapons Officer."

"Maybe we can call for the *Losharik* to pull us out. That's why they undocked before we shot the Gigantskiy."

"They did? I didn't know," Pavlovsky said. "But you'll have to communicate with it."

"If we can get the central command post power, we can light off the Bolshoi-Feniks sonar communications system."

"Didn't the first detonation kill our active sonar?"

"Wow, you *are* paying attention to goings-on in the central command post. It did, but Bolshoi-Feniks can be switched over to an emergency sonar array with its own hydrophones. If we can connect it to the forward battery, we'll be in business. Come on."

Sobol led a limping Pavlovsky through the upper level of the compartment, trying to collect the other engineering watchstanders, pausing to try to wake them up. Three crewmen were able to regain their feet, but four couldn't get off the deck and another two were dead.

There was no doubt, Sobol thought. This was going to be a very long day.

As she opened the hatch to the fourth compartment, a loud ripping noise slammed her ears, followed by a roaring like a mighty waterfall. Sobol turned around and saw the stream of seawater flooding the space, presumably from the main seawater piping rupturing. She pulled the hatch shut behind her and dogged it, peering through the high-pressure glass window into the space as its lights went out and it filled with seawater.

Goddammit, she thought. This day just kept getting worse.

———

Georgy Alexeyev sat at a table on the sun swept sidewalk in front of the UDC Café on Moscow's Kamergersky Lane, a pedestrian-only area decorated year-round with hanging lights, the sounds of a street musician's guitar playing soulfully a block away. Alexeyev smiled, happily sipping a double espresso, waiting for his wife Natalia to join him after a leisurely Saturday afternoon of shopping. He glanced down at the pad computer's article he'd been reading, about

President Vostov and his five-year program for the Navy. Fortunately, the president was a true believer in the power of the Navy of the Russian Republic. Alexeyev was halfway through the article when his cell phone buzzed. He pulled it out of his sports jacket's inner pocket. The caller was unidentified, but he decided to answer it.

"Go for Alexeyev," he said, which was a better and more concise way to answer than Captain First Rank Alexeyev. It worked for strangers, subordinates, and superiors alike.

It's me, Captain, the unmistakable voice of Chief Engineer Alesya Matveev said. The dead chief engineer.

"Chief," he said, pulling the phone from his ear and staring at it as if it had turned into a toad. Slowly, he put the phone back to his ear. "How are you calling me?"

Look to the south, she said.

Alexeyev looked to his right, and a few tables over, Chief Engineer Matveev sat, a cup of coffee in front of her. As if in a dream, Alexeyev hung up the phone, placed it in his pocket, stood and walked slowly to her table. She was dressed exactly as she had been on the Kazan—in her powder blue coveralls with high-visibility yellow stripes running across the torso beneath her throat and on her sleeves. Her hair was shining and clean, pulled back into a ponytail. Her face shone with good health, but still bereft of any sort of makeup. In life, she'd seemed plain to Alexeyev, but in death, she had an inner beauty that was reflected in her face. Hesitantly, he sat down opposite her.

"I miss you," he said, not intending to say it.

I miss you too, Captain, she said without speaking, her voice in his mind. She smiled slightly with that enigmatic unreadable expression. But you didn't listen to me. She found her pack of rancid cigarettes, pulled one out and lit it with a lighter with the emblem of the sunken K-561 *Kazan.* The smoke was distinctive, but not entirely unpleasant, Alexeyev thought, because now it reminded him of his dead friend. *You didn't take my advice,* her voice said.

"What do you mean?" he asked.

I told you the one word to bear in mind. Distance. *You got too close. Now your ship is dying. If it's not already dead.*

Alexeyev looked down forlornly at the table surface. He picked up her lighter and looked at the *Kazan* emblem, sad for days gone by. How good had he had it in the time before the South Atlantic run, he thought, when his crew were all alive? And his submarine was in one piece? He looked back up at Matveev, but she wasn't finished talking.

I blame myself. Perhaps I was too cryptic. So today I shall try to be more...specific. So you can understand. Understand, and live.

"What happens now?"

She half-smiled at him with an air of mystery. *You have a long walk ahead of you in your very near future. Bundle up. It will be very cold. Make sure you tell the crew to walk with you or else they'll die.*

"What?" he said. "A long walk? And the crew dies if they don't come with me?"

Yes, she said. *Walk east-northeast for eight kilometers. Remember, Captain. East-northeast. Eight kilometers.*

"What do you mean by that?"

She just looked at him, that same half-smile on her face, but then her expression turned serious. She frowned and said suddenly, in a loud voice, *You have to wake up.*

"Wake up? From what?"

Matveev leaned forward, opened her mouth wider and shouted, *Captain, you have to wake up!*

He felt a stinging slap on his face and he blinked, and as he did, the Moscow bistro evaporated, and with it, Chief Engineer Matveev, and he was staring into the panicked face of his weapons officer, Katerina Sobol.

"What happened?" he asked weakly, coughing in the darkened room filled with a slight dark haze of smoke, Matveev's words haunting him even as reality returned. *A long walk,* he thought. *East-northeast. Eight kilometers. Bundle up. Bring the crew.*

"I can't say for sure, sir," Sobol said in her ridiculously high-pitched voice, "but I think the Gigantskiy blew up too close. We didn't have enough distance. Or it went off prematurely."

Alexeyev rubbed his head. He had the worst headache of his life, worse even than during the fire onboard *Kazan* as that submarine died. He reached for his right eye, since it felt different. His eye patch was gone. Blown off in the shock, he thought.

"Do you know the status of the ship?" he asked.

"It's bad, Captain. Sixth is flooded and the fifth started flooding, and it looked catastrophic, probably from a double-ended main seawater shear or loss of the hull valve. The aft battery is gone. The reactor is gone. And the explosion in the machinery room blew away our atmo control, and with the oxygen jettisoned, we're slowly suffocating. I'm so sorry, Captain, but *Belgorod* is gone and it isn't coming back. The mission is over. We need to abandon ship, sir, but we're under thick ice."

Alexeyev unbuckled from his seat. "We need to energize the Bolshoi-Feniks and call for *Losharik*," he said. "*Losharik* will have to rescue us through the upper hatch of the escape chamber. Prepare the crew to abandon ship. And try to wake up the sonar officer, Palinkova. We're going to need her, or her senior enlisted."

"Sir," Sobol said, "do you think the *Losharik* came through this okay?"

Alexeyev shook his head. "If it didn't, this day will end very badly," he said, wondering how Sergei Kovalov had taken the nuclear detonation.

Irina Trusov was playing in her room when her father came in after smoking his pipe and having his after-dinner drink with Mommy. He habitually spent an hour at the end of the day with Irina, talking, reading stories, teaching her to play chess, or working on the submarine model.

"Daddy, look," Irina said, "I made a figure of you for when you are driving the boat on the surface." She showed him the carving she'd made, the size of a fingernail, of a man in a heavy black coat with a fur cap on, the detail of the tiny character exquisite.

This is great work, Irina, he said, the pride in his voice filling her with pleasure. Carefully, he placed the figure in the conning tower of the large submarine model.

"I want to make one of you for the central command post," she said. "Like you're standing at the periscope. Show me how you'd stand at the periscope, Daddy."

He stood from the bed and crouched slightly down, extending his hands out as if holding on to periscope grips. *I'd be wearing my blue submarine coveralls*, he said. Irina took a mental picture and smiled at him.

But then he stood erect, his smile vanishing, a serious expression crossing his face. *Nizkiy uroven' kisloroda*, he said loudly, frowning. Daddy's alarm clock started blaring from the other room. His face took on a look of fear. He said it again. *Nizkiy uroven' kisloroda...oxygen level...low.*

"What?" she said, staring at him. "Why is your alarm clock going off?" The sound of the alarm clock's blaring alarm got louder, as if it were being held against her head.

There was terror in Daddy's expression. *Oxygen level...LOW!*

Captain Second Rank Iron Irina Trusov, the systems officer and pilot-in-command of the deep-diving submarine *Losharik*, blinked and coughed, realizing she was having trouble getting her breath, then tried to focus her eyes on the console in front of her. The master alarm was blaring and the Second Captain AI system kept repeating, *OXYGEN LEVEL...LOW.* Trusov silenced the alarm and coughed again, trying to make sense of her surroundings. Something was deeply wrong. Instead of the usual brightly lit panel, it was dark. And the space, the cockpit, usually so well lit, was also dark. Dark and cold. Trusov shivered, exhaling, her breath visible in the space lit only by dual emergency lamps placed aft in the cockpit compartment.

But perhaps the strangest thing was that she hung from her seatbelt. She turned her head, trying to ignore the dizziness. There was something very wrong, in addition to the space being ice cold and dark. *The room was completely on its side.* Tilted an entire ninety degrees to starboard.

Carefully, Trusov unbuckled her five-point belt and lowered herself to the surface that used to be the bulkhead to her right, but was now a deck below her boots. She climbed away from her seat and console and found a battlelantern on a bracket of the deck — which used to be the bulkhead. She hit the on-switch and shone the light around the compartment. The other three—Captain Kovalov, First Officer Vlasenko and Navigator Dobryvnik—were all still strapped in, but hanging from their seatbelts. She reached up to try to rouse Kovalov, but although he was breathing, he wouldn't respond. She tried the first officer and navigator, but their skin was cold and neither had a pulse. The shock must have hit them harder, or they weren't as strong as she and Kovalov, she thought. She headed aft slowly, carefully, climbing over manuals that had fallen from their bookshelves, pad computers, teacups and other gear. She stared at the heavy hatch to the second compartment, but fortunately, the hinge was on the deck — if the boat had tilted to port, she would have been trapped in the cockpit compartment, unable to lift the two-hundred-kilogram hatch. She undogged the hatch, hit the opening lever, and it fell toward her with a loud slam just as she jumped away.

The second compartment was a complete wreck. Normally, the galley compartment, it was littered with cooking implements, pots, pans and stored food. It took a long time for her to reach the hatch to the third compartment, but when she got there, she opened it the same way she had with the last hatch. If the second compartment were messy, the third compartment looked like a huge bomb had detonated there. The hydronauts, the divers, should have been in this compartment, but there was no sign of them. The compartment housed the hotel quarters. Bunks, lockers, and bathrooms. With all the contents heaped up on the deck as high as a mountain, she had no idea how she'd get to the fourth compartment, but after ten minutes of climbing over debris, she made it to the fourth compartment hatch.

Beyond, the fourth compartment housed a large airlock for the hydronauts' lock-out chamber, plus the atmospheric control equipment. The divers' gear was strewn all over the deck, but it was less of an obstacle than the third compartment's mess. She made it to the hatch to the fifth compartment, where nuclear control was situated. The sixth and seventh compartments were unoccupied, housing the nuclear reactor and steam machinery. Trusov opened the hatch, jumped away as it clanged open, and stepped through, a large puddle of blood below her boots. She looked down and saw the body of *Starshina Statji* Roman Leonty, the engineering senior chief petty officer. On the opposite end of the compartment, the chief engineer, Captain Third Rank Chernobrovin, lay on the deck covered in heavy books and manuals. She pulled the debris off his body and tried to sit him up.

His color was good, there was no blood, and he had a pulse. Trusov slapped him, but he didn't respond. She considered for a moment that if she were the sole survivor, she would die when the air ran out. Or when the battery died, or the vessel started flooding. Or caught fire.

"Chernobrovin!" she screamed. "*Chief!* Wake the fuck *up!*"

She kept that up until, finally, the chief engineer's left eye opened into a slit.

"Fuck," he said.

"Yeah, fuck is right," Trusov said. "Now wake the hell up and help me recover."

"What happened?"

"The hell you *think* happened? We took a nuclear explosion. We're on our side. We need to get the ship on an even keel and restart the reactor."

The engineer put his head in both hands and moaned.

"No time to whine now, Chief," Trusov said. "How do we right the ship?"

"Propulsion," Chernobrovin said.

433

"What? Talk like it matters, Chief. What did you say?"

"The screw," he said. "It's a ducted propulsor but it has a large range of motion, up to forty-five degrees from the long axis of the ship. If I can get propulsion, you can aim the propulsor to get us off the bottom and get the list off the ship."

"Well, then restart the reactor and do it," she said.

"I can't," Chernobrovin said. "The reactor won't work unless it's oriented correctly. Too many gravity systems. Even coolant through the core needs the correct gravity vector, because it's natural circulation. It won't work on its side. And the condensers won't drain so no steam will happen. Hell, the boilers won't even work on their sides. And the turbine bearings need gravity to drain them."

Trusov took a deep breath. What was it about engineers, she fumed. Always the thing that had to be done was impossible.

"So connect up the battery and use it to operate the propulsor," she said, hoping that would be possible.

"Help me," he said. "We need to get to the compartment's lower level by this hatch." He pointed to a hatch that should have been on the deck, but instead was on the bulkhead. "You can take local control there."

Together they pulled on the hatch opening mechanism until it finally budged and came down, almost hitting her.

"I've got to get in there and reset the breakers. Shock makes them open circuit."

"Well, do it, for God's sake," she said. He climbed into the space that was beneath nuclear control but was now a room to port. She climbed in after him and there was barely room for one person. There was a small jump seat at the aft end with a joystick, throttle, and small control panel. Trusov heard thumping as Chernobrovin shut breakers. With one thump, half the lights came back on. With another one, they all lit up. Trusov wasn't sure what was worse—operating in the darkened hull, or seeing all the crazy damage with the lights on, the disorientation of the ship lying on its side inspiring raw fright.

She took a deep breath and made her way to the jump seat and tried to strap in. She had to stretch and reach up, since the seat was on the ship's centerline and she was standing on what was the far starboard bulkhead.

"Help me into this seat," she told the engineer. He pushed while she pulled, and he held her in place long enough for her to fasten the seat belt.

"You should have power to the propulsor," he said. "If you put on what would be a left turn and backing revolutions, the propulsor should pull us off the bottom into clear water. As you feel it, straighten out, but keep the backing turns on and the propulsor angled upward so it pulls up at an angle off the bottom. Once you get the boat in clear water, it should right itself on its own. At least I hope it does. Just bear in mind, battery amp-hours are a limited resource, so just use enough power to get this done, then stop when we're level, but don't be timid, or the suction from the bottom will keep us there."

"Fine, yes, I have it," Trusov said impatiently. Goddamned engineers, she thought. She was tempted to let him do it himself, but she was the systems officer and pilot-in-command, and driving the ship was her responsibility. "Turning the prop now," she said, putting the joystick in her right hand over hard to port. "Backing down now." Her left hand closed on the throttle and she smoothly but quickly moved it from its central detent to far aft.

The ship vibrated as the propulsor spun up. She monitored RPM on the small control panel. The prop speed went from 30 to 40 to 60, the vessel vibrating harder, but nothing was happening. Trusov pulled the throttle back to full astern. Revolutions climbed to 120, then steadied at 150, and the whole ship shook so hard it jarred her teeth. She clamped her eyes shut for just a half second, hearing her own voice in her mind: *help me, Daddy, please help me.*

With a sudden jarring motion, the ship angled upward, and slowly the list came off, the wall once again becoming a floor. Trusov pulled the joystick back to rotate the thrust upward to get them off the bottom. A loud scraping noise sounded beneath them, and she could feel it vibrating through the mounting of the joy seat.

435

"Good," Chernobrovin said. "Now straighten out the prop and keep backing down. You can ease it to 60 RPM."

"Wish we had a depth gauge here," she mumbled.

"That should do it," the engineer said. "Can you get forward to the cockpit and hover the boat before we sink back to the bottom?"

"On my way."

By the time Trusov got to the first compartment and the cockpit, she was wheezing and short of breath. She strapped herself into her seat and pulled on her tactical comms headset.

"Chief, once you get the reactor back, you need to restart atmo control, or else we'll faint before anything else happens."

Chernobrovin was silent for a long, frightening moment, but then came on, "Pilot, the reactor is back online. You have full propulsion. I am restarting atmo controls."

"About time," Trusov said under her breath. Her panel had come back to life. She rotated through the displays, examining ship systems' status, then putting up the navigation display. She needed to get the boat to open water.

"Pilot, Engineer," Chernobrovin said as Trusov was flying the boat southward to the entrance to the box-shaped area where *Belgorod* had fired its torpedoes at the American.

"Go ahead," Trusov said.

"Be advised," Chernobrovin said, his voice heavy, "we are severely nuclear fuel-limited."

"I know," Trusov said. *Losharik* had been overdue for a core refueling, but it had been postponed until after this operation. The mission profile had called for it to use minimal power to withdraw the Status-6 torpedoes from *Belgorod* and place them in the harbor bottoms, so it was judged that they could accomplish the mission with less than a hundred EFPH, or effective full-power hours, which was Sevmash's estimate of the useable fuel level remaining in the core. "We need to find out what's going on with *Belgorod*, then make our way to open water," she said. "If the second-fired Gigantskiy blew up prematurely, there will be a close polynya in the box-shaped area."

"Incoming message on Bolshoi-Feniks," the Second Captain announced in that emotionless female computerized voice everyone hated.

"Read the message," Trusov said, concentrating on the nav display and on power level to the propulsor. At 150 meters depth, she should avoid the bottom and pressure ridges. The side-scan sonar was no substitute for the under-ice sonar systems of submarines like *Belgorod*, but it was functional enough to get them through this ice maze back to open water.

"Message reads, '*Belgorod* damaged beyond repair and *Belgorod* crew requests immediate rescue from upper hatch of the escape chamber. *Losharik* requested to respond.' The message is repeated over and over. Do you want me to read it again?"

"No," Trusov said. "Prepare an outgoing message on Bolshoi-Feniks to *Belgorod*," she said.

"Ready," the Second Captain said.

"*Losharik* en route to *Belgorod*'s position. Stand by for rescue."

"Bolshoi-Feniks fault," the Second Captain said.

"What do you mean?" Trusov asked. "Specify."

"Bolshoi-Feniks is not transmitting," the Second Captain said.

"Are any circuit breakers open in the system?" Trusov asked. If the damned Second Captain were on its game, it would already have reported on the status of the system's circuit breakers.

"All breakers are nominal," the Second Captain said, maddeningly emotionless. "All Bolshoi-Feniks system self-checks nominal."

"Well, obviously not," Trusov said, "or else the fucking system would work." But it was futile arguing with AI, she thought. She trained the side scan sonar to the right, then the left, then forward, seeking the hull of the *Belgorod*.

"Well, Mr. Pacino," Captain Seagraves said, a bloody bandage on his head, "Good of you to join us. Where have you been?"

"Starting the reactor," Pacino said.

"Who helped?" Vevera asked.

"Chief MacHinery."

"You mean the chief started the reactor and steam plants and you watched?" Vevera said, standing near his firecontrol watch station.

"I guess you didn't hear about what young Patch did at nuclear prototype," Dankleff said.

"What?"

Dankleff grinned. "The entire place put down hundred-dollar bets young Pacino couldn't start the reactor and steam plants all by himself. Then he actually did it. Then, no one believed he really succeeded, they all wanted him to do it again, double-or-nothing. So he did. Those hundred-dollar bets? They paid for his new crate engine for the Corvette, the supercharger, the transmission, and the new computer controls, with something left over for tires, since his new engine tended to shred them after a few months."

"Dear Heavenly Father, was Naval Reactors aware of this?" Vevera said. Short Hull Cooper was staring with his eyes wide. Naval Reactors was the Navy's version of the Nuclear Regulatory Agency, and more than one career had been torpedoed by the safety Nazis.

"Not in real time," Pacino said, "but they heard about it eventually. I took a slap on the wrist, but the commander of prototype got a severe talking-to."

"So we're in the power range," Quinnivan said, grinning.

"Half-power lineup on the port turbine generator," Pacino said, "but there's trouble with the starboard motor-generator. And we have bigger problems."

"What?" Dankleff asked.

"Chief MacHinery thinks we're flooding from the shaft seals," Pacino said. "If that's true, the aft compartment is going to flood, get heavy and drag us to the bottom. We need to dewater with the drain pump, and we need to do it now."

Dankleff vaulted back into his pilot seat, brought up his displays, adjusted the valving to the drain pump to take a suction on the aft compartment bilges, then hit the function key to start the drain pump.

Instead of starting, a large blinking red light lit up his panel.

"Drain pump trouble light," he said. "Dammit, do we have power available? Is the breaker shut?"

Pacino picked up the 1MC general announcing circuit mike. "Chief MacHinery, 1JV," he said, then reached for the 1JV tactical phone and put the handset to his ear.

"MacHinery," the chief's voice said.

"Chief, check the drain pump breaker," Pacino said. "And while you're at it, check the trim pump breaker."

"Stand by," MacHinery said.

Pacino waited, impatiently. He looked up at the inclinometer mounted over the portside sonar lineup, and the angle had moved from two degrees up to five. The aft end of the ship was sinking.

"Control, MacHinery," a breathless voice intoned over the phone circuit.

"Go ahead, Chief," Pacino said.

"Both drain pump and trim pump breakers are shut. They both have power."

"Thanks, Chief," Pacino said, hanging up. "Drain pump and trim pump have power," he said to Dankleff.

"Let's try again," Dankleff said, trying again to start the drain pump, but the trouble light flashed red again. "Drain pump trouble light. I'm cross-connecting the trim pump to the drain system." Dankleff manipulated his panel, opening some valves, shutting others. "Cross-connection complete. Starting the trim pump to drain the aft compartment bilges." Dankleff mashed the function key. The trim pump's red pump trouble light lit. "Goddammit," he said. "The trim pump has shit the bed."

The 1MC announcing circuit lit up with MacHinery's panicked voice. "Flooding from aux seawater in the aft compartment! Chicken switches have failed, they're not shutting the hull or backup valves! I've got—" MacHinery paused, then shouted, "I've got a fire in the motor control center and RCP-5 is in flames! Reactor scram! I'm evacuating forward."

The overhead lights flickered.

Pacino looked at Captain Seagraves. "Captain, we're going down. We need to evacuate to the ice and get all the arctic gear out of the hull. We only have ten to fifteen minutes, maybe less."

Seagraves grabbed the 1MC mike. "This is the captain," his voice boomed throughout the ship. "All hands, listen up. We are going to offload all arctic gear to the ice and set up an ice camp. Once we've gotten the crates off the ship, we will be evacuating to the ice camp and abandoning ship. Permission is granted to attempt to open forward and plug trunk hatches. That is all." He replaced the mike in the overhead cradle and looked at XO Quinnivan. "Let's get the torpedoman chief up here."

"Torpedoman? Why, Skipper?"

"We're losing the boat in shallow water where the Russians can salvage it." He glanced up at the inclinometer on the port side, which was showing a seven degree up angle. "I'll need him to rig up some explosive charges."

A half minute later, Torpedoman Chief Gordon "Fleshy" Fleshman arrived in control. "You wanted me, Captain?"

"Chief," Seagraves said, "can you pull two warheads out of the Mark 48s to use as demolition charges? With a detonator rigged to a long wire and a switch?"

Fleshman's eyes widened. He nodded. "I can, sir. I'm not sure how long it will take. Why two?"

"One for the torpedo room. That will take out the forward half of the boat when the other torpedo warheads go off in sympathetic detonation. One for the reactor compartment."

"I'll get on it, Captain."

"Sir, Short Hull and I can help," Pacino said.

"Go with the chief," Seagraves said. "XO, make sure we're organized on the arctic gear offload."

"Captain," Quinnivan said, putting down a phone, "A-gang Leading Petty Officer Naughtright opened the plug trunk hatch. He reports the dry-deck shelter has been completely blown off, but the upper hatch is operational. He requests we try to thrust over to port to get closer to the edge of the polynya. Otherwise we can't cross over to thick ice to offload material—or personnel."

Dankleff vaulted into his pilot seat. "Rigging out fore and aft thrusters," he said. "Thrusters trained to two seven zero. Starting thrusters."

"XO," Seagraves said, "Go supervise and let us know when we can knock off the thrusters. When the battery goes, we're going to lose the lights."

27

Systems Officer and Pilot-in-Command Irina Trusov had driven the *Losharik* south toward the corner entrance to the box-shaped area where the American hostile submarine had been targeted, but on the side scan sonar, there was no trace of the *Belgorod*. Nor were their passive broadband sonar systems hearing anything, but they were crude, so that wasn't news. If there were good news, it was that if *Belgorod* had been destroyed, the passive broadband would be full of noise. Flooding, crushing bulkheads, water boiling from broken reactor piping.

She was turning the ship back to the north, hoping she could find *Belgorod* before the boat's low fuel status turned them to dead cold iron. A minute into the northern run, Captain Kovalov came awake with a tremor, sputtered, coughed, shook his head, winced, and looked over at Trusov.

"What happened?" he said.

Trusov was concentrating too hard to give him much of an answer. "We took a hit from *Belgorod*'s Gigantskiy going off too soon. They sent a message on secure Bolshoi-Feniks asking for rescue. I'm trying to find them now."

"Did you reply?"

"Our set is out-of-commission. They don't know we're coming for them."

Kovalov would normally have pelted her with questions, orders, and demands. But today he seemed twenty years older than his biological age, weak, and seemingly resigned. Trusov didn't have time to worry about his feelings.

"I've got something," she said.

"Energize your bow lamps and camera," Kovalov said. "We may pick them up that way better than side scan."

"Hitting the bow lights and camera. Can you put your display on the readout? I'm still on side scan."

"Bringing it up now," Kovalov said, trying to concentrate on the camera's murky field of view forward.

For several tense minutes, Trusov drove the boat toward the *Belgorod*, its signature getting more distinct on side scan sonar.

"I've got *Belgorod* on visual," Kovalov said.

"Switching to visual," Trusov said.

"Energize your lower hatch lamps and camera," Kovalov said.

"Lower hatch lamps and cam coming on."

Trusov watched as the colossal hull of *Belgorod* appeared slowly out of the darkness of the ocean, the vessel seeming intact, but it lay at a ten-degree list on the bottom. If she hadn't received the Bolshoi-Feniks message, she would be convinced that it was a sunken wreck.

"Can you find the hatch of their escape chamber?"

"Nothing on the lower hatch cam yet," she said. "Wait, I have the forward edge of the conning tower. I have mast opening hatches visible."

"A little more aft," Kovalov said. "Just a few more meters."

"I think I have it," Trusov said.

The sound of a banging, clanging noise came through the hull from below.

"They're pounding on the hull for rescue," Kovalov said.

"They didn't get a response to their message," Trusov said. "Lowering the skirt to their hatch." She reached into the overhead and hit a toggle switch. "Energizing vacuum pump. Skirt pump-down progressing. Opening high-pressure air to the skirt. Skirt draining, and I have a dry skirt."

Kovalov unbuckled. "I'll go to the lower hatch and organize getting the survivors onboard."

"Phone me with progress, Captain," Trusov said, glancing at her watch.

It was urgent they got the personnel off the wreck of the *Belgorod* and made their way to open water before the reactor breathed its last.

Captain First Rank Georgy Alexeyev hoisted the sledgehammer and took a hard swing at the hull at a spot where he'd had the insulation removed. A reverberating clang slammed the eardrums of the survivors in the escape chamber. He hit the hull a second time, then a third, handing the heavy tool to Communications Officer Vilen Shvets, who took over and started banging on the hull.

Alexeyev looked around the escape chamber and counted heads. He had the crew from the central command post and most of the engineering personnel. Two of the test wives had been found and brought to the upper level to climb into the escape chamber, but their commander and first officer, Svetlana Anna and Selena Laura, hadn't been found—probably dead from the atmospheric control machinery room's explosion, he thought. The machinery room's destruction had taken out the entire emergency assistance team that had their action stations in the crew's messroom, waiting there to be directed to whatever damage control emergency needed them, and then the emergency ended up killing them all, some three dozen crewmen. Alexeyev counted twenty-five survivors including himself, out of a crew of seventy. Forty-one of the crew were confirmed dead, with nine missing. The lead test wife was one of the missing. Other than those nine, they'd identified the dead, with Lebedev noting the names for later, assuming they lived to tell the tale. Alexeyev shook his head. It had been a bad day, he thought, and it would get worse if *Losharik* didn't hear them banging on the hull.

Captain Lieutenant Shvets had grown exhausted after a dozen hard slams of the sledgehammer, and he'd sat, sweating, the tool between his knees, when the sound of a banging noise came through the hull at the upper hatch. Alexeyev looked at Lebedev.

"Did you hear that?" he said. "Or am I dreaming?"

Shvets vaulted back to his feet and smacked the hull again with the sledgehammer. He was answered with a bang from outside.

"Open the upper hatch," Alexeyev said, looking again at Lebedev. "If there's no one there, he won't be able to get the hatch opened because of the sea pressure. If the hatch opens? We're rescued."

He watched, holding his breath, as Shvets operated the circular hatch opening mechanism and pushed on the hatch.

The hatch came open.

Shvets blinked in the glare of a battlelantern from above.

It was Kovalov.

"Anybody awake in here?" Kovalov asked. "Can I interest anyone in a ride in a deep-diver submarine?"

Alexeyev smiled and laughed with Lebedev. He wiped a tear out of his eye.

They were rescued.

Captain Third Rank Svetlana Anna opened her closet door from the inside and peeked into her stateroom. Three times, crewmembers had opened the door and called for her, searching the room and her bathroom, but had finally given up. The noise of the crew abandoning ship had been loud for some time, as they marshaled heavy weather gear, emergency transmitters and rations and loaded the equipment and themselves into the escape chamber. Captain Alexeyev had called multiple times on the ship's general announcing circuit for any survivors to muster at the ladder to the escape chamber hatch, which was close to the door to Anna's stateroom.

When the noise of the crew's evacuation was finally quiet, she'd waited another ten minutes, finally emerging into her stateroom. There were still lights, although they'd been flickering since the crew's evacuation. There was probably not much time, Anna thought. The air was stuffy and hazy with smoke. It had been hard to breathe, just sitting in the closet. Anna imagined she'd get severely winded doing the next part of her mission.

The ship had been crippled and abandoned as a wreck. But the Status-6 Poseidon torpedoes had survived, the three of them nestled securely in their two-meter diameter torpedo tubes in the bow. With them intact, Anna's mission was incomplete. The Navy could send *Losharik* or another deep-diver sub back here and pull the Status-6 units out of the wreckage and still use them. Her mission could only end, she thought, when those Poseidons were gone.

She stood and reached for the handle to the large rollaway bag. The black bag weighed over fifty kilograms and had taken two men to lug into the hatch and down to her stateroom. Northern Fleet security, on scanning their luggage for this run, had singled the bag out for a visual inspection, just as her FSB contact in Severomorsk had said they would, and she had fed the security inspector a cover story.

"It's a hydrotherapy rig, Senior Lieutenant," she'd said with a smile. "For high colonics."

"Hydrotherapy? High colonics? What is that?" the security officer had asked.

Anna had pulled out a special nozzle connected to a thick black tube that snaked into the guts of the mechanicals inside the suitcase.

"It's for a special kind of warm water enema. This nozzle gets special lubrication, and when the subject is sufficiently relaxed, this tube goes up into—"

The security officer had stopped her. "Ugh. That's just disgusting. Please put it away." He'd waved her on, and two enlisted personnel from *Belgorod* had muscled the heavy bag into her stateroom. She'd asked them to put it in the closet, hoping she'd never need it. But today, it would fulfil its destiny, she thought. Assuming it would work.

She hoped she'd be able to get it to the torpedo room without falling down the steep stairs. It was probably too delicate to survive a tumble down the stairs.

As she rolled it to the forward stairs, she could hear a banging noise from up above. She paused for a moment, and the noise came again. Probably someone banging on the hull, hoping for rescue, she thought.

She lined the bag up to the top of the stairs, climbing down four steps, pulling the handle of the bag down with her. The bag rotated until it was horizontal, then tilted downward. Anna pulled it slowly and it made a thump as it came down one step. She was breathing heavily, but she nodded to herself. She'd managed to keep control of the bag. Only fifteen more steps to go, she thought. With painstaking caution, she lowered the bag down each step, until finally it came to rest at the middle level landing. She pulled the handle and the bag was vertical again.

Anna was soaked in sweat and becoming exhausted, but there was just a little more to do, she thought. She pulled the bag with determination until she reached the hatchway to the first compartment. She undogged the hatch and opened it on the latch, then with a gigantic effort, pulled the bag up over the hatch coaming and into the first compartment. She pulled the rolling bag down the catwalks between the empty torpedo racks until she finally reached the forward bulkhead, where the door to the electronics room was located, where she'd come before to sabotage the tube launching mechanisms. She leaned the bag against the bulkhead and sank down to sit on the deck next to it, huffing, puffing, and sweating like she'd run a marathon.

The hammering and pounding had continued during her voyage to the forward bulkhead of the first compartment, but it had finally stopped. Either the crew had given up the attempt, she thought, or they'd been rescued by the *Losharik*. The latter seemed unlikely. A nuclear explosion violent enough to destroy *Belgorod* had to have been merciless on *Losharik*, but she imagined that it depended on the deep-diver sub's distance to the detonation.

Still, she waited, just in case the *Losharik* was pulling crewmembers out of the escape chamber. After twenty minutes, with the air so unbreathable that Anna knew she was barely clinging to consciousness and could wait no more, she admitted to herself it was time. She unzipped the bag and discarded the hose and nozzle,

447

which had been attached to the plumbing of the mechanism for show. She opened the latches of the door of the unit, exposing the arming controls. She rotated a switch from SAFE to ARMED. She rolled the TIME DELAY selector to its lowest setting, 5 minutes. She pressed the TIMED DETONATE button and watched the timer start rolling downward. Four minutes and fifty seconds.

Anna shut her eyes and tried to breathe deeply. In a few short minutes, the mission would be accomplished.

The bomb, a suitcase nuclear demolition explosive, was a compact hydrogen bomb designed to generate a twelve-kiloton thermonuclear explosion. The plasma from initial detonation would consume the front half of *Belgorod*, including the Poseidon torpedoes. They would be nothing but atoms after the detonation. The aft half of the boat might still exist, but would be mostly splinters and small pieces. The heavy components like the reactor vessels might survive, and the boilers, maybe the pumps, but the remaining wreckage would be unrecognizable as having belonged to a submarine.

And there would be nothing left of Svetlana Anna.

While she waited for the timer to roll down, the sweat rolling down her forehead, she tried to think about her happiest memory. It was the communal farm where she lived with her aunt and uncle when she was a little girl. They had owned an adorable Siberian Husky puppy named Baku, and Anna had delighted in playing with him. Baku, all his life, had had this unusual and funny bark, sort of a high-pitched *rough-raow* sound, that she would imitate and bark back at him, which would make him smile and bounce on his front paws and bark even louder at her. She'd been inseparable from Baku all through school and college, but Baku had gotten old and one summer day he stopped eating and just lay on his bed, whining. Anna wouldn't leave his side, putting blankets down next to him to try to keep him company during the night, and the last night, while she held him, his whining gave way to wheezing, and finally, the wheezing got quieter and shallower, and Baku breathed his last. As Anna remembered, a tear leaked out of her eye.

Panic Switch

The timer of the bomb ran out. There was a loud click, and then Anna's vision was filled with a blindingly bright light that faded to a deep black, but oddly, the blackness had a texture to it, almost as if it were made of dark thunderclouds, and the clouds were rotating around her and seemed to form a sort of tunnel, and a lightness grew at the center of the tunnel, at what seemed a tremendous distance, until the light grew brighter and warmer and then the strangest thing happened.

Svetlana Anna could hear a noise.

It was a happy noise.

Rough-raow, the sound came. *Rough-raow!*

It was Baku!

The memory of that trip was so vivid, it seemed like it happened yesterday, despite it having been over a month ago.

"Can I get you a drink, ma'am?"

"After a day like this? I think a vodka martini with a twist, chilled and up," CIA Director Margo Allende said to the steward.

The Gulfstream SS-12A jet had lifted off from Ronald Reagan International at 1800, climbing swiftly east-northeast toward the Atlantic.

She looked across the aisle at Chief of Naval Operations Admiral Rob Catardi, who had asked for an old fashioned. The steward came by with a tray and handed her a drink, then set down Catardi's.

"Do you think this has any chance of success?" she asked Catardi.

Catardi shrugged. "Who knows what the crazy Russians will do at any moment," he said. "I'm just surprised they accepted your invitation."

She nodded, then opened her tablet computer and scanned through the intelligence updates. The Status-6 torpedoes were late being loaded onto *Belgorod*. The intel brief suspected that there were technical problems with them, and the shipyard at Sevmash had recalled them for modifications. But Allende knew the truth, that CIA's assets within the shipyard had been sabotaging the torpedoes. Unfortunately, the Status-6 units had been placed under more rigid security—perhaps someone suspecting sabotage—and the units left Sevmash fully functional.

Meanwhile, the submarine USS *New Jersey* was being prepared for its run north to linger outside the Kola Peninsula submarine bases, to trail the *Belgorod*, and if need be, put it on the bottom. The raging debate was how to provide the new submarine with a crew, since her crew had spent three years building her, with only a few weeks of sea trials, and were considered incapable of a top-secret special operation.

In other news, the previous project submarine USS *Vermont* was considered a wreck after a disastrous fire in the forward compartment while in drydock, and plans were being drawn up to mate *Vermont*'s aft compartment to the new USS *Massachusetts'* forward compartment, restoring the *Vermont* to operational status in six months or less. *Vermont* would be renamed, according to the article, since it was soon to be half *Massachusetts*. The Navy announced plans to rename it to be the USS *New England*, in honor of the two states forming her hull. That left the aft portion of the former *Massachusetts*, to be mated to a repaired *Vermont* front end, and which so far hadn't been renamed. American Party Senator Michaela Everett had floated the idea of naming the submarine the USS *Michael A. Pacino*. Allende smiled at that, wondering what Pacino would think of that. He'd probably hate it, she thought, smiling to herself.

After the drinks were carried away, she and Catardi were served a light dinner. Allende took a sleeping pill, downing it with a sparkling water, put on a sleeping mask, leaned her leather seat far back, and tried to sleep. It was insane, she thought, how when she needed to sleep, sleep evaded her. But when she needed to stay awake? She could sleep ten hours.

Finally she fell into an uneasy slumber, seeing the imagined scene of the chalet and the Russians they'd be meeting, and in the craziness of the dream, she, Rob and the two Russians were trying to decide how to get rid of a dead body.

She finally woke when shaken gently awake by the steward. "We're descending into Geneva, ma'am," he said.

Catardi looked at her with amusement. "You talked in your sleep," he said, smirking. "Probably not the best thing for the CIA director to be sleep-talking."

"Oh God, what did I say?" she asked.

"You kept saying 'Michael, I have the body.' There are several interpretations one could make of that," he laughed.

Allende rubbed her forehead. "Now I have a headache."

They landed gently at Cointrin Geneva Airport, taxied to the general aviation building, and climbed out. On the tarmac, a black SUV waited. The steward loaded their luggage in the back and handed Allende a heavy parka. "May as well have this with you in the car, ma'am. It will be chilly on the way to the chalet."

The drive to the chalet went quickly, although it was a hundred kilometers from the airport, through a winding mountain road. At the higher altitude, the ground became snow-covered, blinding from the glare of the morning sunshine.

Eventually they arrived at the chalet, a huge log affair overlooking a wide and deep valley. The roof and grounds were under several feet of snow, and the air was crisp and cold. The front door opened and a hostess smiled and invited them in, taking their coats while the driver brought in their luggage. Allende looked at her overnight bag, thinking that if this went the way she hoped, she'd never need it, and they could return to the airport that same day.

"Are the other guests here yet?" Allende asked.

"They phoned from the road, ma'am," the hostess said. "You can set up in the living room if you'd like. We've had a fire built for you, per your request."

"No conference room?" Catardi asked Allende.

Allende shook her head. "I figured the less formal this meeting, the better."

The hostess served coffee and set up a tea service on the coffee table for the Russians, with two bottles of Jewel of Russia vodka and four glasses. Allende could hear noise from the foyer, the arrival of the Russians.

They walked into the room then, the tall, slender and well-built figure of the SVR Chairman Lana Lilya and behind her, Vice Admiral Pavel Zhabin, the chief of staff and first deputy commander of the Russian Navy, technically their number three man, but the deputy commander, Mikhail Myshkin, had died the week before and the chief commander of the Navy, Admiral Anatoly Stanislav, was fighting pancreatic cancer—unsuccessfully—and had just been admitted to hospice care in Moscow. With Stanislav sick and Myshkin dead, Zhabin was by default the commanding admiral of the Russian Navy. If Admiral Zhabin was Catardi's equivalent, SVR Chairman Lana Lilya, as head of the foreign intelligence service, was Allende's.

They shook hands and introduced themselves, finally sitting around the coffee table. Catardi spoke first.

"Admiral Zhabin, I'm sorry to hear about Admirals Stanislav and Myshkin," Catardi opened.

Zhabin nodded but smiled. "I'm sorry as well. Admiral Stanislav was brilliant, but a harsh taskmaster. A screamer, as you Americans would say. Many in the fleet are happy to see him go. But to me, he was sort of a second father. And Myshkin, well, Myshkin was just an overgrown aide de camp to Stanislav, and he and I never got along, God rest his soul."

"Funny how office politics are embedded in all human activity," Allende said.

"That they are, Madam Allende."

"Call me Margo, Admiral," she said.

"And I'm just Rob," Catardi said.

Zhabin grinned. "Pavel is fine for me. You can always use the nickname the fleet has for me. *Litso Smerti.* 'Death Face.'"

"I think Pavel works." Allende smiled at Zhabin.

"Of course, call me Lana," Lilya said, not smiling.

"Would you care for tea?" Allende offered. "Coffee?"

Zhabin eyed the vodka bottle, his eyes twinkling. "For a secret covert meeting like this, may I suggest something stronger?"

Catardi grabbed the glasses and filled each with the vodka, handing them out, then sitting again. Zhabin raised his glass. "A toast. To fallen comrades." They toasted, and then Lilya said, "And a second toast, to cooperation between the intelligence agencies and navies of the world's superpowers."

Allende smiled and drank. She knew the business of the meeting was about to start, and she'd debated with herself how to present the matter to the Russians. She opened her pad computer and selected an image of the Status-6 weapon.

"We wanted to talk to you about the Poseidon torpedoes," she said, changing the image to an overhead view of the east coast of the United States. "Or Status-6 units. We've gotten word that your president has ordered them deployed off our Navy bases, here, here, and here." Red circles glowed at New London, Connecticut; Norfolk, Virginia; and Kings Bay, Georgia. "We know that your special project submarine *Belgorod* is getting ready to put to sea with three of the Status-6 torpedoes. Meanwhile, one of our own submarines is preparing to go to the Barents Sea and shadow the *Belgorod*. And as you both know, armed warships in a tense situation like this, well, bad things can happen."

There was silence in the room for a moment. Allende expected the Russians to deny her assertions, to tell her that she was very much mistaken, but to her surprise, Lana Lilya's face softened. She put down her glass and looked at Allende, then Catardi.

"There are many of us in the president's administration who virulently disagree with the invention of this weapon. And with its deployment. We've voiced our concerns to President Vostov, but he has turned a deaf ear to us. We have been looking for a way to prevent this disastrous mission. We even had Sevmash engineers sabotage the three weapons earmarked for *Belgorod*, hoping they would be loaded onto the vessel, and only many weeks later, be shown to be defective and inert. But a self-test audit by the *Belgorod*'s weapons officer in the factory showed the defect, and Sevmash engineers were forced to fix the weapons under her supervision. There was no further opportunity to sabotage the Poseidons before they were loaded onto *Belgorod*."

So that was why the torpedoes were late to be loaded, Allende thought, with the sabotage detected.

"But we have another means of stopping this deployment," Zhabin said. "We have an agent in place on the submarine." He withdrew an envelope from his briefcase and pulled out a photo of a beautiful woman in a Navy uniform. "Captain Third Rank Svetlana Anna. She's a test wife. Previously known as a comfort woman."

Allende nodded.

"Captain Anna has a number of methods to stop this mission," Zhabin continued. "We are hoping that we can end this with no loss of life to the *Belgorod* crew, but that is not assured. We'd ask that you avoid ordering your submarine to attack *Belgorod*. For one thing, she is armed with nuclear-tipped torpedoes, and President Vostov has gotten very permissive with nuclear release authority since your use of them this summer. I guarantee, if your submarine tangles with *Belgorod*, it will go poorly for them."

"Which means, your deployment of the Status-6 units would succeed," Catardi said. "This agent, what is she planning on doing?"

"She'll monitor the tactical situation," Lilya said. "She is prepared to take out the torpedo-launching capabilities of the torpedo tubes. If that fails, she can sabotage atmospheric controls, forcing the *Belgorod* to abandon the mission and return home. In the ultimate case, where nothing succeeds, she is equipped with a nuclear demolition munition. That would destroy these Status-6 torpedoes for good, although it would be deleterious to the crew."

Deleterious indeed, Allende thought.

"For our part, Admiral and Chairwoman, we'll insist on rules of engagement for our submarine that will keep them from firing on *Belgorod*," Allende said.

"But we can't guarantee anything if *Belgorod* fires on our sub first," Catardi said, frowning, his expression suddenly fierce. "Our submariners are trained to return fire, and they won't stop until there's nothing left of *Belgorod*. Our rules of engagement will specify to only fire when fired upon, but if fired upon, rest assured, our submarine will unleash the fires of Hell itself on the *Belgorod*."

"Understood, Admiral," Zhabin said, smiling. "I would make the same orders in your position."

"Is there anything we can do on our end to help you?" Allende asked.

Lilya answered. "Tell your president that these weapons are opposed by much of Vostov's own government. But ask him to let us solve the problem ourselves."

Allende nodded. "Admiral Catardi? Anything to add?"

"Not from my end. I want to thank you for meeting us," Catardi said.

Zhabin smiled. "Another toast, Admiral and Madam Director. To success with no loss of life."

Catardi and Allende drank. By the time the farewells had been said, Allende was getting fuzzy from the vodka. She and Catardi watched as the Russian's vehicle vanished down the mountain road, then climbed into their SUV for the trip to the airport.

Back in the Gulfstream, as it lined up to take off, Catardi looked over at Allende.

"How'd you know the Russians would be open to a talk about this? How'd you know they didn't agree with Vostov's placement of Poseidon torpedoes?"

Margo Allende tilted her head and grinned at Catardi. "I'm CIA. We know everything."

But since that meeting, the situation had gone to holy hell.

———————————

"Margo," Vice President Pacino said harshly to the Situation Room full of admirals, generals, and intelligence agency senior officers. "What the bloody hell is going *on* up there?"

"Admiral Sutton, ONI, has an analysis for us, Mr. Vice President," Allende said.

Frieda Sutton walked to the large display of the chart of the Arctic Ocean. "Our seismic and sonar sensors output their data, that was examined using triangulation from widely separated sensors to come up with this analysis, but be aware, this is by no means definitive. Mr. Vice President, this is our best guess."

"Skip the goddamned fine print," Pacino barked. "Just get to it."

"Yes, sir. Starting yesterday at 1320 Zulu time, the first nuclear detonation was detected here, in the range of one megaton. We believe this was a Russian Magnum torpedo, or, as the Russians call it, a Gigantskiy." The plot zoomed into a space on the map, at latitude 85 north. "For ninety minutes, there was nothing heard but the aftermath of the explosion, but when that calmed down, there was a very small explosion, probably an impact of a conventional torpedo, which was triangulated to the same place as the Magnum detonation. A few minutes later, at 1458 Zulu, a rocket launch was detected from approximately the same location. We believe this to be a Tomahawk SUBROC lifting off. At 1459, a second rocket launch was registered. Two minutes later, a second Magnum torpedo exploded, this one a few miles west of the original detonation. Very soon after, one of the SUBROCs exploded, perhaps ten or twelve miles north-northwest of the Magnum explosion, registering about 250 kilotons. We only recorded one SUBROC depth charge detonation. The other one must have been a dud."

"Has there been any communication from the *New Jersey?*" Pacino asked.

A third-class petty officer in crackerjack blues knocked and was admitted. He rushed a pad computer over to Admiral Sutton, who scanned it quickly, then passed it to Admiral Catardi.

"Sir," Sutton said, "we just got a detect of an emergency locator beacon, an ELB, coming from the zone of the first Magnum detonation."

"Is there a situation report?" Pacino asked.

"There was a faint transmission," Sutton said. "It was garbled. All we have is the ELB, which is just a dumb SOS transmitter that tries to upload its latitude and longitude."

Pacino turned to Air Force General Abdul Zaka, the chairman of the joint chiefs. "General, what's the status of search and rescue aircraft being dispatched to this ELB site?"

"Sir," Zaka started, glancing at the table, a sure sign the news was bad. "SAR was terminated an hour ago. There's a 'once in a generation' storm equivalent to a Category 4 hurricane brewing out of north Canada that's headed to the pole." He projected his display, and Sutton's map disappeared, a weather map taking its place over the north pole, the circulation of the massive storm showing it approaching the pole within the next hour. "Mr. Vice President, we're grounded, from Alaska to the Baffin Bay."

"Can we ask the Russians for help?" Pacino asked.

Zaka shook his head. "By the time they put together aircraft and crews, sir, the storm will have overtaken the ELB location. In a few hours, the entire Arctic Ocean will be socked in."

"How long will this persist?" Pacino demanded.

"At best, three days. At worst, two weeks," Zaka said.

"Admiral Catardi," Pacino said, "What's the status of the rescue submarines?"

"Sir, the *Hyman G. Rickover* and the *Montana* left a week ago per your orders. They've departed the marginal ice zone north of the Kola Peninsula and have proceeded under total ice cover, but as you know, it's a slow slog once under ice, and our ability to communicate with them is limited."

Pacino stood. "Send them the location of the ELB, and tell them to hurry," he said. He looked at Allende. "I want to see the CIA director and the CNO in my study."

Allende glanced at Catardi. She'd never seen Pacino this furious before.

457

28

Captain Seagraves paused outside the plug trunk hatch. "What was that?"

A bright flash suddenly lit the landscape from the west. He climbed out of the hatch to the deck above. On the ice on the ship's port side, what looked like a thousand packages, parcels and equipment containers were piled, with the crewmen opening them and carrying them up the slight incline to a flat spot a ship length away from the rapidly freezing spot of open water. They'd nailed together half a dozen wood crate lids to form a makeshift gangway between the hull and the thick ice.

A few seconds after the flash, the shock wave hit, knocking Seagraves and the other crewman to the deck or the ice. Far to the west, a bright orange mushroom cloud appeared and rose slowly, angrily toward the sky. The roaring blast was so loud that Seagraves lost all hearing for a moment. He forced himself to look away from the blast.

"Don't look at the mushroom cloud!" he screamed out, his own voice sounding muted in his ears. He pulled himself to his feet, the ringing loud in his ears. When the flash had darkened, he turned around to glance at the explosion, then back away. His eyes met Quinnivan's.

"What the hell did that, Captain?" XO Quinnivan said, lifting his goggles up to his forehead. The fur-lined hood of his arctic parka blew in the slight breeze. Seagraves looked over to the west, where the mushroom cloud had bloomed.

"I wonder if that was the position of the *Belgorod*," Seagraves wondered aloud.

Lieutenant Anthony Pacino emerged from the hatch after pushing a parcel up to the deck. He stood on the deck and shaded his eyes and looked west. "Maybe a nuclear self-destruct charge, XO," he said. "That couldn't be *Belgorod*'s torpedo room going up. We're fairly sure they jettisoned all their conventional torpedoes. And that detonation was way more explosive power than a conventional charge."

"It was too small for a Magnum warhead detonation," Seagraves said, steadfast in his practice not to call the Russian nuclear-tipped torpedo a Gigantskiy. "A one megaton blast would have knocked us a hundred feet from the boat and likely burned our exposed skin off."

"Why would they need a demolition charge?" Lieutenant Vevera asked, joining the group.

Lieutenant Commander Lewinsky stepped over. "Maybe trying to create open water," he said. "When the first Omega went down, their escape chamber detached and got trapped under the ice canopy. Maybe this Omega decided to blow a nice hole of open water overhead before ejecting the escape chamber."

"How do we even know what happened to the first Omega, if the chamber got trapped under ice?" Pacino asked.

"Because the U.S. sub trailing that Omega—your dad's boat—emergency blew through the ice and the impact opened up a polynya," Lewinsky said. "And as it turned out, our guys rescued their guys."

"Jaysus," Quinnivan said. "Still, an explosive to open up a polynya wouldn't be nuclear, or if it were, it wouldn't be that big. That blast had to be the size of the Hiroshima bomb."

"We should investigate," Pacino said. "If that was an attempt to make open water for an escape chamber, the Russians could have survived. They'd be there, on the ice."

"I doubt an escape chamber would have survived *that* blast," Quinnivan said. "The wind's picking up. The broadcast called for a massive arctic storm, Mr. Pacino. No one's going out in that."

"When does it get here?" Pacino asked.

"The storm is two to four hours out, Mr. Pacino," Quinnivan said. "Even if you started now, you'd get caught in it by the time you got to the detonation location, which, I'd remind you, is a high radiation zone."

"Maybe it was closer, Captain, XO," Pacino said. "We could set off that way and turn back when the wind picks up."

"Absolutely not," Quinnivan said. "You'd be in a whiteout. Hell, I don't even know if we have a compass in our survival gear capable of functioning this close to the north pole. Be thankful you just survived the universe's latest attempt to kill you, young Pacino. So stay put. Help putting up the shelter. We need it urgently, before the storm gets here."

"Aye, sir," Pacino said, grimacing and setting off with Vevera, Dankleff, and Lewinsky to lug gear up the hill to the shelter taking shape.

When they'd walked away, Seagraves looked at Quinnivan. "You know, XO, I would have let them go."

"And lose the son of the vice president in a storm?" Quinnivan said. "Or to radiation? Are you insane?"

"I could have kept him behind and sent Vevera and Dankleff."

"Good luck with that, Skipper. Pacino would howl like a wolf with his paw cut off if you tried to keep him from a mission like that."

Seagraves looked over at the damaged hull of the USS *New Jersey*. The sail had a large dent on the port side, as if a giant fist had hit it, and it was leaking hydraulic fluid, the hull below the sail covered with oil. The hull's anechoic coating was blown off all over the deck and the towed array fairing was gone. The boat was settling into the water, its up-angle even more alarming than it was ten minutes before from the shaft seal flooding and the flooding from auxiliary seawater in the aft compartment.

"Do you think anyone heard our distress call or our situation report?" Seagraves asked.

"Doubtful, Captain," Quinnivan replied. "The antennae are, to use the technical term, tits-up. Almost to the point of being, to use another technical term, broke-dick."

"Yeah," Seagraves said. "Any luck with the SLOT buoy encoder?" They'd salvaged half a dozen radio buoys, but the laptops used to encode messages into them were hopelessly out-of-commission.

"The encoders are even worse, Skipper. They've—to use another technical term—shit the bed."

"I hate when that happens, XO." Seagraves sniffed the air. The occasional breeze had picked up, a gentle wind blowing in from the south. "What about the emergency locater beacons?"

"We lit off all three at intervals," Quinnivan said. "We can't verify they worked. But they looked okay. Our hopes rest on them, at the moment."

"Let's get the strobe beacon going, XO," Seagraves ordered. "Visible light and infrared, full azimuth and inclination. If the clouds get too thick for aircraft to see us, maybe a satellite can detect our position."

"You want the strobe programmed to do 'S.O.S.' in Morse code?" Quinnivan asked.

Seagraves shook his head. "Do we know today's call sign for the *New Jersey*? The two letter group for ELF radio signals?"

"I'll bet the radio guys know, Skipper, although their chief, Gory Goreliki, didn't make it. You want that programmed into the strobe?"

"Do this, XO. Have the strobe give off our call sign, then pause and transmit 'S.O.S.,' in case someone else can get a visual on us. Drones, satellites, or SAR aircraft."

"Done, sir. I'll see to it."

Chief Torpedoman Fleshy Fleshman climbed out of the hull and approached Seagraves and Quinnivan, stepping carefully on the makeshift wooden gangplank. He froze for a moment, glancing at the smoke that had risen from the mushroom cloud to the west.

Fleshy's callsign was a misnomer, as he was skinny as a prisoner on a hunger strike. Even in his thick arctic parka, he looked like a waif.

"Captain. XO," Fleshman said, saluting the two men, who returned the gesture. Submariners rarely saluted when surfaced at the ice, but Fleshman was old school, having been raised by three proud generations of chief petty officers, all torpedomen, his great-grandfather serving on the original *Nautilus*, his grandfather on the Cold War boat *Piranha* and his father on the East China Sea War 688-class boat *Olympia*. "I've opened up two torpedo warheads and removed them for use as demolition charges. I've got one ready in the reactor compartment's shielded tunnel and the second nestled in with the Mark 48s in the torpedo room. My guys are rigging up the wires and the detonation triggers now."

"How is the battery?"

"It's almost dead, Captain. Battery compartment hasn't taken on water yet, but it's just a matter of time. It won't be long now, sir."

"Chief, get your men out and bring those triggers. Get on the 1MC and order the ship evacuated, no exceptions."

"Aye, aye, sir," Fleshman said, saluting again and turning to hurry into the doomed hull.

"The water will reach the plug trunk hatch soon," Seagraves said sadly. "I'm going to be damned sad to see the great submarine USS *New Jersey* sink."

"We didn't have much time with this old girl," Quinnivan said. "But in a few short months, the *Vermont* will be hammered back together. Or I guess I should say, the *New England*."

"You think they'll let us have her back?" Seagraves asked wistfully.

"After losing *New Jersey*? Probably not, Skipper."

"Yeah. That's what I was thinking."

"There's still time if you want to go back aboard and say good-bye, Captain. Just be quick about it."

"No, XO. I'll say good-bye from up here."

"Prudent decision, sir. Sir, while we wait, perhaps you can read off the names of our dead to honor them."

Seagraves nodded. "Attention all hands," he called, his voice projecting out over the ice. "I want to take this moment to commemorate our dead friends and shipmates. Lieutenant Commander Alyssa Kelly. Lieutenant Commander Wanda Styxx. Lieutenant Don Eisenhart."

Seagraves continued, until all twenty-four names of the dead were read off.

Finally, Fleshy Fleshman climbed out of the plug truck, two engineering watchstanders helping him with the wire coils, another three emerging after Fleshman. They unwound the wire spools along the gangway, which was splintering and disintegrating. Fleshman approached and saluted again. "Everyone's out of the hull, sir."

Seagraves and Quinnivan returned the salute. "Very well, Chief," Seagraves said, his voice cracking. He sniffed, then blew his nose into a handkerchief.

Fleshman took a knee at Seagraves feet, stripped the wires on the spools and terminated them onto the detonation triggers he pulled out of his oversize parka pockets.

"Hurry up, Chief," Quinnivan said, looking at the *New Jersey*. The hull had settled to the point that water was about to pour into the open plug trunk hatch. "She's about to go down."

Fleshman finished with the wires and handed the two switches to Seagraves. "The T-switch rotates ninety degrees clockwise, Captain. That will detonate the charges. You'll want to start with this one, which is the reactor compartment. Then, immediately after, the torpedo room."

The crew had abandoned their chores of hauling equipment and material up the hill to the shelter and assembled in a large group behind Seagraves and Quinnivan. In the front row, Pacino rubbed his fingers together with his gloves half-off, the cold starting to soak into his bones the minute physical activity stopped. A gust of wind blew off his hood. He shivered and pulled it back on, tightening it with the strings on either side.

"You should say some words, Skipper," Quinnivan said to Seagraves, noting the crowd of the crew behind them, all there to witness the death throes of the *New Jersey*.

"I'm not much of a man for speeches," Seagraves said. "But I'll try." He cleared his throat and turned toward the crowd, then glanced back at the *New Jersey* hull, which had begun to ship water into the plug trunk. "Crew," he said loudly. "At this time, I commit the United States submarine *New Jersey* to the depths of the Arctic Ocean. I know I speak for all of you when I say to this sacred collection of steel, cables, and electronics, *thank you* for safeguarding us to this point in our lives. We will all go on with those lives, but none of us will ever forget you, and the immortal spirit of the USS *New Jersey* will perpetually be in our hearts and in our souls for the rest of our days."

Seagraves twisted the first T-handle and a resounding thump came from the hull, and the ship seemed to rise slightly from the water for just an instant. Seagraves looked back at the crowd.

"All hands, back up twenty yards," he ordered as he dropped the first detonator to the ice. "This one's going to be a bit more violent. You too, XO."

When the crew had backed up, Seagraves twisted the second detonator, and a similar loud thump sounded, the bow lifting slightly out of the water, and then the secondary detonations started, and a tremendous explosion blew the bow wide open, shrapnel blowing over the ice and what was left of the open water, a huge billowing orange mushroom cloud rising over the ice and into the heavens.

After that, it only took the USS *New Jersey* four seconds to depart the surface. What was left of her hull hit the bottom seven hundred feet below less than two minutes later.

Seagraves wiped dust and soot off his parka, his hood, and his face, dropping the second detonator to the ice. Twenty yards up the slope of the hill, Pacino could swear he saw a tear streaking down the captain's sooty face.

"Pilot, Engineer," Chief Engineer Chernobrovin said in Systems Officer Trusov's headphones. "We've lost the reactor."

Trusov's voice was biting over the intercom. "What do you mean, you *lost* it? Did it wander off somewhere?"

"Pilot, all reactor control rods are fully withdrawn from the core, but reactor coolant temperature is dropping, as is steam pressure to the turbines. We're thirty seconds from reactor plant shutdown due to fuel exhaustion."

Trusov looked over at Captain Sergei Kovalov. "Why the hell did they send us out with three percent fuel, Captain? Why?"

Kovalov looked at Trusov, frowning. "Continue on with battery power," he said, as he vaulted out of his mission commander seat to the space behind his and Trusov's seats, but in front of Vlasenko's and Dobryvnik's seat.

"Engineer, Pilot," Trusov said over the intercom, "continue propulsion on the battery."

"I'm raising the periscope," Kovalov said. "I might be able to find open water from the Gigantskiy detonation from the light filtering down from above."

The sudden and violent explosion from behind them shook the ship hard, the vessel heeling over thirty degrees, then slowly returning to an even keel. The overhead lights flickered, but mercifully, they stayed lit.

"Captain, what was that?" Trusov asked, even though she knew Kovalov knew as little as she did. "What bearing was it?"

"It was to the west," Kovalov said, training the periscope to look behind them. "I've got nothing visually. No surprise," he said, training the scope forward again.

Trusov turned her display to the navigation plot, which had been overlaid with ice thicknesses, showing where they'd been and the ice pressure ridges forming walls of this box-shaped area. The position of the *Belgorod* was plotted as a blood-red dot. The explosion had to have come from *Belgorod*, four miles aft of them. Perhaps one of the Status-6 units cooking off, but at a partial yield. If it had blown up at full strength of ten megatons, *Losharik* would have been blown to bits at this distance.

"Pilot, Engineer," the intercom clicked. "Four percent battery life. I've got leakage in the sixth and seventh compartments from whatever that explosion was. I'm not starting the drain pumps since they would draw the battery all the way down."

"Engineer, Pilot, concur," Trusov snapped into her boom microphone. "We're taking on water, Captain," she said to Kovalov. "I hope you've got something on the scope."

"Nothing yet," Kovalov said.

"Pilot, Engineer, three percent battery and the boat's taking on an up-angle from the leakage."

"More like flooding," Trusov muttered. "Understood," she said into the intercom. "Maintain propulsion on the battery."

It occurred to Trusov then that this was the day. This was *the day.* The last in her life. She, the *Losharik* crew and the rescued personnel from *Belgorod* would all die down here. She couldn't think of a more desolate place to die than a cold, dark, drifting nuclear submarine trapped under polar ice. Whenever she considered the idea of her own mortality, she figured she would eventually die in some kind of battle, a conflict, perhaps, with the Americans. But never of old age. She'd always felt like a young soul, she thought. If she'd had previous lives, she imagined that she had died young in all of them. And now she would die young in this one.

"Two percent battery," Engineer Chernobrovin announced on the intercom.

"Captain, it's now or never," Trusov said.

"Bring us five degrees to the left," Kovalov ordered.

"You have something?" Trusov asked, as she pushed the joystick control of the rudder over, changing course by five degrees.

"Pilot, Engineer, one percent battery."

"Captain, please tell us you have good news," Trusov said, her voice too loud in the cramped cockpit.

"Pilot, Engineer, circuits are shutting down. Battery power is gone."

"Blow all ballast!" Kovalov yelled.

Trusov hit the twin toggle switches to open the large-bore valves admitting high-pressure air from the main air banks to the forward and aft ballast tanks.

Two seconds later, the lights went out, the panel displays went out and the *Losharik* became a derelict, drifting collection of titanium, steel, cables, and electronics.

But in the room, Trusov could hear the sound of high-pressure air blowing into the ballast tanks. She took off her headset and leaned back in her pilot's seat, pulling her hair out of her eyes. She shut her eyes. When she opened them, the dim light of battle lanterns lit the space in an eerie, shadowy semidarkness.

Maybe today wasn't the day after all, she thought with relief, and as she did, she realized it seemed almost like a prayer giving thanks.

Captain Second Rank Irina Trusov grabbed her arctic parka and climbed out of the main egress hatch. She reached down and helped up *Belgorod* Captain Georgy Alexeyev, who looked around at the icescape around them.

Losharik had surfaced through a large polynya. If Trusov's nav plot had been correct, this was on the path that the second Gigantskiy had taken on the way to the Americans, but it had blown up way too early. Off in the distance, she could see the rise of the pressure ridge that had been the target of the Gigantskiy. It had to be at least five nautical miles out.

She stepped to the aft part of the hull that was closest to thick ice and stepped off. The crew and the *Belgorod* rescued personnel were offloading whatever supplies they could grab. Battlelanterns, blankets, rations. But the boat's up-angle had gotten worse and the upper rudder was no longer visible as the hull settled into the sea. There were only minutes left before the boat sank to the point that the water came in the egress hatch.

"Captain," Trusov said to Kovalov, "should we shut the egress hatch and seal the boat? With the inter-compartment hatches shut, perhaps only the sixth and seventh compartments will be fully flooded. The boat could be salvaged."

"Possibly," Kovalov said, "but perhaps not by us. Leave the egress hatch open. We'll let her flood. The water is too shallow here to crush her hull, but seawater will degrade any systems the Americans could use."

The survivors of *Belgorod* and the *Losharik* crew stood among the offloaded gear and watched as the deep-diver submarine began taking on water through the open egress hatch.

"Good-bye, *Losharik*," Captain Kovalov said, his voice trembling, his hand over his heart.

"It was a good boat," Alexeyev said to Kovalov. "It saved our lives."

"Imagine if we'd had a full load of nuclear fuel," Kovalov said. "We could have sailed right into Kola Submarine Base."

As they watched, the bow angled up, the hatch went under, and eventually the conning tower lowered into the dark water, the boat standing straight up, the bow pointing at the sky, until it settled lower in the water, and after a long moment of the bow hanging there, the hull gave up and sank out of sight, with nothing but a thousand bubbles rising to the surface to mark her departure.

Georgy Alexeyev listened to see if he'd hear the sound of the hull hitting the bottom, but it was no longer quiet on the icecap. The wind had risen steadily and it began to snow. At first, the flakes were almost microscopic, but then began to grow. He looked over at Kovalov.

"We need to walk," he said. "East-northeast. Eight kilometers."

"What are you talking about?" Kovalov said.

Alexeyev pulled Kovalov away from the crowd. "Remember the ghost of Matveev?" he said.

"Oh no. Another revelation?"

"She returned. She was more specific this time. She said east-northeast. Eight kilometers. She said we had a long walk in front of us."

"But, Georgy, there's nothing to the east-northeast," Kovalov said.

"Yes, there is," Alexeyev said. "The Americans have a camp."

Kovalov shook his head. "Georgy, you are mistaken. The Americans are no more."

There was the sound of a loud thump from the east-northeast, then the sight of a bright orange flash, the sound of the explosion coming a few seconds later, the force of it shaking the ice beneath their feet. A mushroom cloud of orange flames rose up into the sky, shrouded by dark smoke.

Kovalov stared at the mushroom cloud, which had calmed down and was no longer orange flames, but only dark smoke wafting upward.

"Maybe the Americans *were* there," Kovalov said. "But after *that*, they probably aren't any longer."

"They just blew up their weapons to avoid salvage of their submarine," Alexeyev said. "Just as we would have if we'd had the means."

"You seem convinced the Americans are still alive," Kovalov said, looking at Alexeyev as if he'd escaped from a psychiatric hospital.

"I know they are," Alexeyev said, his hand rubbing his right eye, missing his eye patch. "Engineer Matveev *knew* they would be. Come on. Let's get this crowd moving. Walk toward the smoke of that explosion."

The wind howled and the quarter-sized snowflakes blew horizontally, illuminated by the ghostly strobe light that lit up the polar night, the lamps of it broadcasting at all points of the compass and straight up, the Morse code spelling "D.X....S.O.S." and repeating over and over.

Lieutenant Anthony Pacino pulled his fur-lined hood close to his face, the mask beneath it ineffective against the wind and snow. Above the mask, his clear goggles kept fogging up. He'd put them on top of his inner hood beneath the parka hood, but then his eyes felt like they were freezing and he'd have to put the goggles back on.

He paced back and forth in front of the entrance vestibule of the high density polyethylene bubble of the shelter, the bubble round and plump, the shape designed to avoid being blown over by high winds, the shelter's corners and mid-walls secured into the ice by thirty-six-inch drilled steel foundations. Pacino could hear the rumbling of the diesel heater and diesel generator, barely audible over the roaring noise of the wind.

The vestibule outer door of the shelter opened and shut behind Captain Seagraves. He walked toward Pacino, who stood at attention, cradling his high-powered rifle.

"How are you doing, Mr. Pacino?" Seagraves asked, shouting over the noise of the wind.

"I was colder than I've ever been in my life two hours ago," Pacino said, shouting back. "Now I'm used to it. That or I'm just numb."

"Can you go on another hour?" Seagraves said, idly looking around the ice beyond the camp, but visibility was less than a hundred feet.

"Yes, Captain. No problem."

"I brought you this," Seagraves said, pulling a military helmet out of a fabric bag. "It has night vision and infrared. Strap it on under your parka hood. Use it occasionally."

"What's this for, Captain?"

"Polar bears," Seagraves said. "The people in the shelter would be quite the meal for a hungry polar bear."

Pacino nodded and pulled on the helmet, trying the night vision and infrared. If he pointed the monocular away from the strobe, he could see much farther. Not that there was anything to see.

"Captain, I'm thinking that if there is a polar bear, *we* should be eating *him*. How long will the rations last?"

Seagraves shook his head. "There's a problem. They should have been good for four days, but anything with chicken in it is contaminated. Probably salmonella. We've got forty hands sick of food poisoning. I'm having the bad rations brought out of the shelter."

"Are the other rations good?" Pacino hadn't partaken of any of the emergency food supplies. He hadn't been hungry over the last day. Who could be, he thought, with this shitshow going on?

"So far, the other meals seem okay, but the chicken was over half of our rations."

"So, we're down below two days," Pacino said. "Maybe we could use the bad chicken rations for a polar bear trap."

"I've read about polar bear meat," Seagraves said. "It's said to have worms in the flesh that would infect humans, to the point of fatality, that resist cooking unless you burn the hell out of the meat."

"Well-done bear meat, even if it's shoe leather, is better than nothing, Captain," Pacino said.

"That assumes you can get a fire started out here, and with this wind, even if you could get it lit, how would you keep it lit?"

"I'll work on it, Captain. A wind break, something to burn, some fuel and a lighter. Something to use as a grill or a spit."

Seagraves clapped Pacino on the shoulder. "Try not to freeze solid out here, Mr. Pacino. I haven't had much sleep over the last five days, so I'm going to try to shut my eyes in the shelter, but if there's anything unusual, call for me."

"Only thing I can think of that would be worth disturbing you is if our good friend Mr. Polar Bear shows up," Pacino said.

Seagraves smiled. "Have a good remainder of your watch, Mr. Pacino. I'll send the relieving section out a half-hour early. I'm doubling up on this watch. We need one man to make sure the other doesn't fall asleep and die in the snow."

"Good night, sir," Pacino said, deciding to try the infrared monocular and the night vision. It was no better than regular human vision, he decided. There was just nothing to see.

"Just a little while longer," Captain First Rank Georgy Alexeyev said to Captain Second Rank Irina Trusov, who was falling behind the

471

group of people hiking toward the east-northeast, where they'd seen the explosion.

"I'm tired, Captain Alexeyev," Trusov said over the hurricane wind of the storm. "I'm losing strength."

"Do you want me to carry you?" Alexeyev asked.

Trusov looked at him in horror. "Dear God, *no*, sir. I'll die in my boots before someone carries me."

Alexeyev laughed, putting his arm around Trusov to help her walk. "Come on, we're almost there."

"Captain! What is that!" Trusov pointed out in front of them.

Alexeyev looked up. It was a flashing light, a strobe light. Were they both hallucinating it?

He shouted to the crowd. "Does anyone know Morse code and English letters?"

Captain Third Rank Chernobrovin, the engineer of the *Losharik*, held up his hand. "I know Morse, but not English letters."

"What about 'SOS,' the international standard for distress?"

Chernobrovin nodded. "Yes, Captain, I know it."

"Can you see the strobe?"

"I see it. Let me observe it for a moment." Chernobrovin stared off into the distance. "There is definitely an SOS, but there are other letters I don't know."

"Let's keep walking," Alexeyev said. "Sergei, join me at the head of the column, we will need to approach the American camp carefully. No sense getting shot by a sentry."

Pacino supervised as Chief Albanese emptied the tins of chicken entrees onto the ice about fifty feet away from the shelter and the distress strobe light.

"How's this, Mr. Patch?"

"That should do it, Chief. Keep a weather eye out for polar bears, but if you see one, two to the central mass, then two to the head."

"L.T., I'm going to empty the entire goddamned magazine into any polar bears happening by," Albanese said. "But don't you think they're sheltering from this storm?"

"Even bears are too smart to be out in this storm," Pacino said, but just in case, he pulled off his goggles and turned on the night vision, then put the infrared scope to his eye. "I'll be dipped in shit," he said in disbelief.

"Polar bear?" Albanese said, training his rifle the direction that Pacino had looked.

Pacino put his arm out to Albanese's barrel, lowering it.

"It's *people*," Pacino said. "The Russians! Get to the shelter. Get the captain and XO."

29

Sonarman Chief Albanese bolted for the shelter as the column of people slowly approached. The lead figures looked like two tall men supporting a limping, smaller female.

The captain, XO and navigator hurried out of the shelter, then the other junior officers, until the driving curiosity brought out all the crew but for the three dozen who were still deathly ill from the food poisoning. The *New Jersey* crew stood there in the driving winds and blinding snow until the approaching people could be made out in the light of the strobe lamp of the emergency beacon.

Pacino looked to his right at the captain. "Do you want the helmet, sir?" The column of people was a hundred yards long, maybe fifty of them. Seagraves took the helmet from Pacino, put it on and adjusted the infrared and night vision scopes. "Can you get a count, Captain?"

"I think so. Looks like twenty-four or twenty-five."

The leaders of the column came closer, until their features could be made out. Pacino squinted in the blizzard, his mind filling with disbelief.

"Captain...Captain Alexeyev? Irina? Irina Trusov?"

One of the men holding up the near unconscious female was unmistakably Captain First Rank Georgy Alexeyev.

Alexeyev looked at Pacino, recognition dawning on his face.

"Lieutenant—Lieutenant Pacino, right?" Alexeyev's voice was a weak croak, barely audible over the wind.

"You two know each other?" Seagraves asked.

"Captain," Pacino said to Seagraves, "this is Captain Alexeyev of the Yasen-M submarine *Kazan*. And now presumably, captain of the *Belgorod*, right? Captain Alexeyev, this my commanding officer, Commander Tim Seagraves and my executive officer, Commander Jeremiah Seamus Quinnivan, Royal Navy. You remember Lieutenant Dankleff? And our SEAL officers?"

Alexeyev dropped to one knee, exhausted, the female kneeling with him, the other burly man looking at Seagraves.

"I'm Captain Kovalov of the submarine *Losharik*," Kovalov said over the howling noise of the wind, "the deep-diver submarine assigned on this mission with *Belgorod*. May I ask if we can join you in your shelter? We are all exhausted and near frozen."

"Where are my manners?" Seagraves said, smiling. "Come on, please, this way. XO, get everyone inside." He looked at Senior Chief Thornburg. "Doc, help get these people warmed up, some hot tea all around, and coffee. And see if anyone needs first aid."

"Yes, Captain." The corpsman led in the two men and the nearly unconscious female. When all twenty-five of the Russian survivors were inside the shelter, the *New Jersey* crew followed them in. Pacino handed his rifle to Dankleff, who would stand the next two hours of polar bear watch.

"Now we *really* need to shoot a polar bear," Pacino said. "I hear we're out of rations."

"With the chicken gone, the rest went fast. So it's a polar bear or cannibalism," Dankleff said over the blasting wind.

"I could use some hot coffee right about now," Pacino said, watching as the last of the crew and the Russians entered the shelter.

Dankleff coughed. "I could use some good scotch right about now. Hell, forget good scotch, I'll take that rotgut we found in Faslane."

Pacino pulled open the heavy outer door of the shelter, entered the vestibule, shut the door behind him, then went through the door flap of the inner door. The oppressive, stuffy, dry heat of the shelter hit him like a fist in the chest.

"Oh my God, it's like Hell in here," Pacino said, pulling off his parka and hanging it with the others in the corner of the shelter. He looked over at one of the picnic tables, where the hurt female sat, the Russian submarine captains on either side of her. One of them held a cup of hot tea to her lips. She looked up from the tea, saw Pacino, handed her cup to Alexeyev, took two big steps to Pacino and slapped him hard in the face. Both the Russians and Americans stared. Pacino could feel the stinging welt on his cheek, his other cheek feeling hot from blushing in embarrassment.

"You fucking asshole!" she screamed, her accent thicker than he remembered. "You fucking did it again!"

Pacino rubbed his face while Alexeyev and Kovalov pulled Irina Trusov off him.

"What's she talking about, Georgy?" Kovalov asked, mystified.

"Mr. Pacino here," Alexeyev said, trying not to smile, "commanded the hijacked Iranian submarine I told you about. In the melee of trying to escape, with us trying to keep him from escaping, he got lucky and sank the *Kazan*. But then he came back and pulled us out of our escape chamber."

"I was just the second-in-command of that mission, Captain," Pacino said, turning to see Seagraves and Quinnivan looking on from over his shoulder.

"Were you here in the same submarine as in that conflict, Lieutenant?" Alexeyev said, having calmed down Trusov and sitting her back down to drink her tea. "What was it, named after one of your provinces—*Vermont*? *Vermont*, yes?"

Pacino glanced at the deck. "No. *Vermont* is in the drydock. There was a bad fire. We drove her replacement up here." Pacino decided not to name the *New Jersey*. No sense being accused of giving the Russians intel.

"Well, if I must be shipwrecked in a polar storm with my enemy, I'd prefer it be you, Lieutenant." Alexeyev looked at Kovalov. "Mr. Pacino not only rescued us, he was very kind to us. I suppose this is two favors I owe you, Lieutenant. Do you have food here?"

"I'm afraid the news is bad, Captain," Pacino said. "We're as out of food in this shelter as we were on the *Panther*. Most of it had gone bad. Half the crew is sick, the other half is starving."

"This storm will die down soon," Alexeyev said. "I expect airborne search-and-rescue will come for us soon enough. Both yours and ours. With all the explosions, Northern Fleet Command must have heard all the events."

"Captain Alexeyev, did you have a radio to call for help?" Seagraves asked. "A distress call?"

Alexeyev shook his head. "Unfortunately no. *Belgorod* was immobilized by the Gigantskiy explosion. There were many deaths. We survivors were pulled out by *Losharik*, which we'd undocked before the battle. Also unfortunately, Northern Fleet sent *Losharik* here with almost no nuclear fuel left. She was barely able to glide to a halt under the polynya formed by the Gigantskiy detonation. By the time *Losharik* was able to surface, she had no power to use for the radios. That's why we had to walk from where we surfaced to here."

"How did you know we were here?" Quinnivan asked.

"We saw an explosion," Kovalov said. "Your self-destruct charges?"

"Yes. They were improvised," Seagraves said. "They turned out to be a bit bigger than I'd anticipated. But speaking of self-destruct, is that what that last nuclear explosion was? From the direction to *Belgorod*? *Your* self-destruct charge?"

Alexeyev shook his head, accepting a cup of tea from Doc Thornburg and cradling it in his hands. "We don't know *what* that was," he admitted.

"Maybe one of the Status-6 weapons going off?" Pacino asked. "In a partial yield?"

Alexeyev shook his head a second time. "No way. With a Status-6, it is all or nothing. The full ten megatons or zero. We thought that blast was from you."

Seagraves glanced at Quinnivan, then back at Alexeyev. "We shot a 250 kiloton depth charge at you, but it went wide and long.

Too far away from you. It blew up a few seconds after the Magnum. Or, Gigantskiy, as you would say."

"You did?" Alexeyev said, genuinely surprised. "We didn't know. The shock wave from it must have hit us about the same time as the Gigantskiy shock wave. The Gigantskiy detonated nearly five miles too close. Was that because of you?"

Seagraves nodded. "We hit it with half a dozen countermeasure torpedoes. They found your torpedo, but I suppose it had some programming to blow up if it thought it would be destroyed."

"We call it a default detonation," Alexeyev said. "But all it did was kill *us*."

"It sank us as well," Seagraves said. "It just took a while. We stayed operational long enough to surface here and get the survival gear out. Then the boat—with our dead inside it—went down."

"I'm sorry, Captain Seagraves," Alexeyev said. "How many did you lose?"

"We're still tallying, but about twenty-four or twenty-five. What about you?"

"We lost fifty, Captain."

"Bad day at sea, Captain Alexeyev. I assume your search-and-rescue planes and ours will be buzzing around here soon. We had three emergency locator beacons. I hope they worked."

"Everything depends on this storm easing up," Alexeyev said.

There was silence for a moment, and then Navigator Lewinsky pulled Captain Seagraves aside.

"What is it, Nav?" Seagraves asked.

"I think I figured out your riddle, sir, about what the *Panther* op and the *Devilfish* mission had in common."

"Go ahead, then, Nav," Seagraves said, an expression of amusement crossing his face.

"In both operations," Lewinsky said, "the good guys rescued the bad guys. And now a third mission is ending the same way."

"Let's hope this doesn't end up like the *Devilfish* scenario," Seagraves said, serious again. "Everyone died. Except for the Russian admiral and Pacino's dad."

"Yeah," Lewinsky said, looking down at the deck.

Anthony Pacino warmed his hands near the diesel heater and looked up to see that Irina Trusov had gotten to her feet and limped to the far end of the shelter, dropping down and leaning against the insulated shelter wall. He left the heater and knelt in front of Trusov.

"Irina. Why did you hit me?"

She looked up at him, her big blue liquid eyes drilling into him, tears suddenly leaking out of them. "You just *had* to ruin another Russian mission. You just had to sink *another* Russian submarine."

"Not my choice, Irina. It wasn't personal. It was just business. You had your orders. We had ours. We were just following them."

She shut her eyes and the tears ran down her face. "Two failed missions for me now, Lieutenant Pacino. My career is obviously over. The stink of this won't leave me, not ever. My poor father is probably rolling in his grave."

"I'm sorry," Pacino said. "Do you mind if I sit next to you?" He didn't wait for her to answer, but sat next to her, leaning against the insulated wall, the dull hum of the diesel heater just slightly louder than the blowing, howling wind outside. He thought Trusov would slide away from him, but she moved closer, until he could feel the warmth of her body touching his arm and thigh, and her touch seemed electric. He shook off the feelings, reminding himself that he hadn't seen an eligible female in weeks, and that comatose Rachel Romanov waited for him in a hospital bed in Norfolk.

"Coffee, Mr. Pacino?" Short Hull Cooper asked, holding out a fresh cup of coffee. Pacino nodded and took the cup. "For you, ma'am?" Cooper handed a cup to Trusov and took her cold cup, then went back to the coffee pot.

"Have you ever had coffee?" Pacino asked.

She nodded, sipping the broiling hot brew. "In Havana a few years ago. This is weaker, but I think I like it better, Patch. Do you mind if I call you Patch?"

"Yes, please call me Patch." Pacino said.

Michael DiMercurio

She looked at him closely for a moment, and she put her hand on his forehead. "What happened here?" She gently touched the bandage on his forehead and the top of his skull.

"I cut my scalp. I got tossed pretty hard into a bulkhead after the first Gigantskiy explosion."

"Let me look," she said, pulling the bandage aside. "Oh, it's deep. That will leave a red scar on your forehead."

"Our corpsman says I can have plastic surgery to make it go away." Pacino shrugged. "I'll see how it looks after we get home."

"Patch, what was that sonar signal you pinged at us? It was music. From the *1812 Overture*. Why did you do that? Were you trying to say you knew we were Russian? I mean, that was obvious. Or were you trying to say you were friendly?"

Pacino laughed. "That sonar ping was trying to send a detonation command to two mines we'd placed on *Belgorod*'s hull when it was surfaced at the polynya before you launched the first Gigantskiy. Later, we got orders to fire upon you but I think you got the same orders first. We pinged the command detonate signal, but obviously the mines either failed or were blown off by shock waves and nothing happened. The signal itself was just a happy coincidence — the cannon fire and trumpets make for a lot of acoustic contrast and the sound is unmistakable. No way the mines would hear that particular twelve or fifteen seconds of sound from nature or your own pings. No sense having mines detonating due to some random noise source."

"You planted mines on *Belgorod* before there were hostilities ordered? How could you do that?" Trusov sounded hurt, as if she were taking it personally.

Pacino shrugged. "It was just a contingency. Just in case. At the time, our leadership showed no intentions of us engaging with you. Something must have changed or happened. Suddenly our orders became much more aggressive. I don't know the whole story. Not yet, anyway."

For a long time she was silent, staring at the deck of the shelter, as if she were pouting. He tried to change the subject.

480

"So, Irina, how much trouble do you think we'll both be in with our bosses after we're rescued?"

She looked at him. Those deep blue eyes again, he thought, blinking and looking away. At least her crying had stopped, but there were still the tracks of her tears on her dirty face. "We need rescue first. For all we know, this is our last stand."

"Don't let yourself think like that," Pacino said. "Think positive thoughts. The universe will listen. At least, that's what my friend Fishman, a professional bad-ass frogman, says."

"I'm cold," she said. "Do you think you could hold my hand?"

Pacino blushed. "Of course," he said, putting her small, soft, ice-cold hand in his. She squeezed his hand. He could feel his pulse race for a moment.

And suddenly, the sound of the roaring wind stopped.

"Mr. Vice President? The Virginia delegation is here," President Carlucci's secretary announced. Eve LaBelle was seventy-two years old and couldn't weigh more than eighty-five pounds, Michael Pacino thought, with a big head of hairsprayed gray hair.

"Please show them in, Eve," Pacino said, slapping down the folder he'd been scanning on the huge desk, the label on it reading TOP SECRET / SCI / SPECIAL HANDLNG / RELEASE 12 / OPERATION POSEIDON. As he did, Carlucci's chief of staff, Remi O'Keefe, scooped up the dossier and left by the door to the presidential study.

Pacino smiled at the two women from Virginia. So far, everyone had learned that Pacino did not have a politician's smile, and that if he smiled, it was genuine.

"Madame Senator. Madam Governor, please come in. I'm honored by your visit. And a little stunned by your cross-aisle cooperation. Please sit," he said, waving to the floral-patterned couch facing the coffee table, and taking the wing chair opposite. He looked at the pattern on the couch, thinking that Carlucci's taste was odd — the couch looked like it had been upholstered using Great Aunt Maude's curtains from the 1940s. Same décor as Carlucci's cabin at

481

Camp David, Pacino thought. It probably reminded the president of comforting times in his childhood.

The women seated themselves. Pacino paid attention to how closely they sat—close enough to hold hands if they'd wanted to—and their tense body language, which was formal, both sitting up straight on the couch, on the front five inches of the cushions, their feet on the floor rather than crossed, their hands on their knees. He judged they were here to ask for a favor.

"Can I offer you anything?" Pacino asked. "The coffee here is Navy coffee. Beans grown in Colombia on a Navy-owned plantation outside Bogota. Best cup of coffee you will ever have, with the notable exception of the coffee in a nuclear submarine. I also have some good tea. And, of course, scotch and bourbon. I note the sun isn't over the yardarm yet, but it must be somewhere." Pacino smiled, realizing he was babbling. These two women made him nervous, all the more so since they waved off any beverage.

Virginia's American Party Senator Michaela Everett was a populist and in her first term, and though she was only a freshman senator, she was a media superstar, a firebrand, and a loud party partisan. Which made it all the more odd that she'd come today with Virginia Governor Leann Meadow, a staunch National Party icon, revered and feared both inside and outside her party, and who would be running against Everett in the next election. Both women were in their early fifties, very slender—one could even say slinky—and had long, straight blonde hair, blue eyes, red lips and clear alabaster complexions. Despite their vast political differences, they looked like they could be sisters.

Senator Everett spoke first. "Mr. Vice President—"

"Call me Patch, please," Pacino said.

Everett smiled. "Patch, then. I'll get right to business. Paul Carlucci's term is up soon, and no one knows if he will run again. Or if his health will hold out after the assassination attempt."

"I heard he was recovering nicely," Pacino said, frowning.

"What I mean," Everett said, "is that in the case where Mr. Carlucci decides not to run, we'd like to draft you as the American

Party candidate for president. And if he does run, we'd like you to stay on as vice president and focus on running four years later."

The governor smiled, her eyes crinkling. "And if the American Party doesn't want you, the National Party certainly does."

Pacino sat back heavily in his seat. This was unexpected, he thought. In his mind, he was the worst fill-in president in the past 150 years. He was impatient with domestic issues, irritated at partisan politics, erupting at aides and congressman that their issues were ridiculous and not meaningful to the continued survival of the United States. On more than one occasion, he'd scolded powerful members of the opposition, and his own party, for lacking patriotism, and feeding like hogs at the troughs of corrupt Washington. He'd made an impassioned impromptu speech at one of the meetings that they were *all* Americans, and the political class had lost sight of that vital fact. Someone, an aide, or maybe even Carlucci's secretary, had secretly filmed the ass-chewing and posted it on the internet, and it had gone viral, making the national news for days. Pacino had been embarrassed, mad at himself for forgetting what a public figure he was. Yelling at politicians was not his job, and probably reflected poorly on Carlucci, but the country—both American Party faithful and National Party devotees—lauded and applauded Pacino's instinctive, stirring, blazing rhetoric. He was later told that no one since Kennedy or Reagan could speak like he could.

He'd dismissed the hero worship. People loved the idea of an outsider, someone who wasn't a career politician, taking office. But as time had proved over and over again, those outsiders eventually became insiders, and forgot about the American people, seemingly only caring about their power and continuation of government. They were the politicians he'd hated the most, remembering how his mission to rescue the *Tampa* had been handcuffed by the then-president's wife, that bitch who thought she was the power behind the throne.

It occurred to him that Everett and Meadow were looking at him expectantly, waiting for his answer. As he opened his mouth to speak—not knowing what he'd say—he was saved by the main entrance door suddenly opening and Chief of Staff O'Keefe dashing in, coming up to Pacino and whispering in his ear.

"There are developments in Operation *Poseidon*, sir. We need you in the Situation Room immediately."

Pacino stood. "Madam Governor, Madam Senator, I'm afraid I have to leave you. But I will consider what you said. Very seriously. Please excuse me."

Pacino followed O'Keefe out of the Oval Office, the chief of staff nearly jogging, Pacino struggling to keep up while acting calm.

As he and his Secret Service detail entered the already crowded Situation Room, Pacino said a silent prayer that Anthony was okay. How many times had he said that same prayer during Operation *Panther*, he wondered. Too many to count.

When the wind stopped, everyone who wasn't sick rose to their feet, grabbed their parkas and walked out into the polar dawn. The thick clouds had cleared, blown south. To the southeast, the sun rose over an ice ridge.

Pacino had grabbed a rifle. It occurred to him that with all the people on the ice, a polar bear might find the gathering too interesting to pass up. He checked the magazine, loaded it into the rifle and shouldered the weapon. As he did, he could hear the powerful roar of jet engines. He looked over at U-Boat Dankleff and smiled.

"I hope whoever that is has food onboard," Pacino said.

"Whoever that is? They're probably Russians," Dankleff said dully. "The weather cleared from the south, the Russian side. The Canadian side is probably still socked in."

"No matter," Pacino said. "I'd sooner grab a ride with the Russians than stay here, freezing when the diesel heater runs out of fuel, with no food."

"Except for polar bears."

"Polar bears who have been avoiding us," Pacino said. "Look, it's visible." He pointed to the huge four-engine jet that flew overhead, making a low altitude pass, perhaps to determine if it could land.

"I can see a flag on its tail," Dankleff said. "White over blue over red. It's Russian."

"You think it can land on ice?" Pacino asked.

"I think we're about to find out."

The jet transport flew over again, turned, flew away, then from the far distance to the east, came lower in altitude and sailed in, its large wingspan sprouting flaps, the jet engine noises escalating, quieting, then rising again.

"It's got skis," Pacino said. "Definitely landing."

The jet transport came closer to the ice and then set down, the ice splintering behind it into a huge fog of ice and snow. The jet's engines roared with reverse thrust as it slowed, until it came to a stop some fifty feet from the shelter.

"Now that's some precision flying," Dankleff said.

Pacino nodded. "Well, the Russians live up here in the arctic, so landing on ice is probably what they call a Tuesday."

The rear ramp door of the jet transport slowly opened. Pacino noticed that the Russian survivors had moved off to the right side, all of them gathered together. He sidestepped to Captain Seagraves and XO Quinnivan.

"Captain, why am I getting a bad feeling about this?" Pacino asked.

————————————

"What do we know?" Vice President Michael Pacino said curtly, taking his seat at the end of the table. The Situation Room was crowded to full capacity with admirals, generals, cabinet secretaries and their aides. On the wall opposite the end seat, an aerial view was projected.

"Sir," Secretary of War Bret Hogshead said crisply, "we were able to get an Apex drone launched out of Alaska and overhead over the north pole. The distance to the loitering position was great, so we may only have twenty or thirty minutes on-station before we run out of fuel. When the fuel goes, the Apex will self-destruct. The image you're seeing is the ice near the nuclear explosions detected by our seismologists. You can see four sites of open water where we think the explosions were located. At the far east site, we've detected an arctic survival shelter. It correlates to the gear that was loaded onto the USS *New Jersey*."

Pacino smiled in relief as he saw the video play out on the screen. He could see the black expanse of open water and the large arctic shelter erected north of it. On the ice, there were what looked like a hundred people standing, looking at a huge four-engine jet transport that had landed and taxied to a halt near the shelter.

"So, the rescue forces arrived," Pacino said.

"Sir, the news isn't good," CIA Director Margo Allende said. Pacino looked at her. She was being completely professional. Their relationship had been suspended by his rising to be the acting president. He hoped she understood. When all this was over, he thought, maybe he could make it up to her.

"What do you mean?" Pacino asked.

"Sir, NSA Director Nickerson should explain this," she said.

National Security Agency commander General Nick Nickerson cleared his throat and looked over at Pacino. "Mr. Vice President, we've been hearing a lot of chatter from the Russians as they launched this particular aircraft. It's a Russian Ilyushin IL-76, a four-engine cargo jet, capable of arctic operations. And search-and-rescue operations. But this particular plane is run by the GRU, the Russian military intelligence organization."

"What was the 'chatter' you intercepted?"

Nickerson cleared his throat again. "Sir, the Russians have been talking about taking the crew of the *New Jersey* back to Russia as prisoners of war. And prosecuting them as murderers of the lost crewmen of the *Belgorod* and the deep-diver submarine."

The room broke out in muffled conversation.

"Quiet, everyone," Pacino said. "Secretary Hogshead, is the Apex drone armed?"

"Yes, Mr. Vice President," Hogshead said. "It has two Brimstone missiles."

"Are we in range?" Pacino asked.

"Yes, sir."

"Mr. Vice President, if you attack that jet," CIA Director Margo Allende said, her hand out, "you'll be giving away that our intel agencies were able to determine the Russians' intentions."

"I don't care," Pacino said. "Mr. Secretary," Pacino said to Hogshead, pointing at him, "fire both missiles at the Il-76. Do it now."

———————

"That thing," Lieutenant Dieter U-Boat Dankleff said, pointing to the huge four-engine jet transport, "is the BUFF of airplanes."

When the rear loading ramp came all the way down, three men in green arctic parkas walked out, the leader with an automatic rifle in his hands. The second carried a heavy machine gun, the third a device that unfolded into a tripod, a large ammo can in his other hand. The second man put the machine gun on the tripod and the third produced a belt of ammunition from the can and latched it to the feeder mechanism of the large gun. He checked it, then aimed the machine gun at the gathered Americans. The leader walked closer to Seagraves, Quinnivan, and Pacino. Pacino lifted his rifle and aimed at the Russian's chest, a fact the Russian evidently disapproved of, as evidenced by him lifting and aiming his own rifle at Pacino.

"Lower your rifle, young man," the leader commanded in English, in a hard, gravelly voice with a thick Russian accent. "Or you will find the consequences severe for yourself and your shipmates."

"The hell I will," Pacino said, putting his trigger finger into the trigger guard and sighting in at the Russian. For the moment, the Russian commander decided to ignore the threat.

"Who is in command here?" the leader asked, looking at Seagraves and Quinnivan.

"I am," Seagraves said in his baritone, no-nonsense command voice. "Commander Tim Seagraves, United States Navy."

The Russian bowed and smiled, but Pacino noticed the smile didn't reach the man's hard eyes. "I am Vanya Nika, Colonel, GRU, and I am in command of this rescue mission."

"Good of you to come," Quinnivan quipped. "Perhaps you and your men should lower their weapons. We're not a threat to you."

"And *you* are? You sound English," Nika said.

"*English*, my white pimpled Irish ass," Quinnivan said, an edge in his voice. "I'm fookin' Irish. The name is Jeremiah Seamus Quinnivan, Commander, Royal Navy."

"Well, then, Commanders Seagraves and Quinnivan, please be so good as to inform your men—and women—that you are now prisoners of the Russian Federation, and under arrest for the very serious crimes of interfering with an official Russian Navy mission. Your crimes include sinking our submarines *Belgorod* and *Losharik* and for murdering many members of those submarines' crews. So, Commander Seagraves, order your man here—" he pointed to Pacino—"to put his rifle on the ground."

"No. I'll do no such thing," Seagraves said, crossing his arms, but as he did, a blinding bright streak angled down from the heavens and a sudden violent explosion blew the jet transport apart, the blinding white fireball turning orange and red, with black smoke as the fuel ignited, the explosion sending pieces of the airplane flying. A second after the first explosion, a second streak of light came down from above and hit the already flaming transport.

The explosion blew everyone standing onto the ice, and as Pacino fell, his trigger finger twitched on the trigger and his rifle barked as a single round was fired. Pacino landed flat on his back. He sat up quickly, worried he'd hit one of the Americans with his stray bullet. Once he sat up, he saw a bright red stain growing on the green parka of Colonel Nika, who was prone and raising his own weapon to aim at Pacino. Pacino quickly flipped the rifle's mode selector switch from semi-automatic to full automatic and pulled the trigger, firehosing Nika with bullets, then the two men who had been standing at the machine gun but who had also been blown to the surface of the ice. Pacino stopped firing when it became clear the three Russians were dead, either from the blast of the missiles hitting the jet, the jet's exploding jet fuel, or his bullets.

In the next moment the jet's cockpit door flew open and three of the flight crew jumped out of what was left of the airframe, gained their feet and raised their sidearms at the Americans. Pacino sighted in on the one farthest to the left and, in full automatic, emptied his magazine as he swept right, and the three pilots went down, cut in half by Pacino's rifle fire.

"That was adequate shooting, Mr. Pacino," Seagraves said as he regained his feet. "But that's enough for now."

"I'm out of ammo anyway, Captain," Pacino said, standing up, his vision suddenly clouded by a stream of blood from the top of his head. Dankleff pulled off his own inner hood and put it to Pacino's head and face as a bandage.

"You got another gash, this one from flying airplane debris," Dankleff said. "This one's worse. You're going to have another nasty scar from this—it goes from your hairline to your left eye, then down to your cheekbone. Does it hurt?"

"I'm so pumped with adrenaline I can't feel anything," Pacino said. "Not even the cold."

Quinnivan turned to the captain. "Well, Skipper, unfortunately, that plane was our ticket out of here."

"Yeah, a ticket to a Russian gulag," Seagraves said. "No thank you. I'll wait for the next plane."

A loud crashing noise came from behind them and down the slope to what used to be open water, but had now frozen over in the storm and the cold. Pacino turned and saw ice bulging, then foot-thick blocks of ice being moved aside. A black shape slowly rose from between the blocks of ice, the shape rectangular. Pacino waited to see if the shape would be that of an American conning tower—or a Russian one. But twenty seconds later the shape could be made out to be the sail of an American Virginia-class nuclear submarine. The comms masts emerged from the sail, extending to the heavens, then both periscopes. Finally a man could be made out emerging from the top of the sail.

"Ahoy there!" he yelled into a megaphone. "Someone call for a rescue?"

Pacino smiled at U-Boat Dankleff and Squirt Gun Vevera, then at Short Hull Cooper. "Well, boys, I imagine we'll be having steak for dinner tonight."

A hundred feet farther to the south, a second black sail emerged from the ice, the hump of ice behind the sail revealing an ice-hardened dry-deck shelter. That sail also sprouted communications antennae and periscopes.

Pacino felt a tugging on his sleeve. It was Irina Trusov. Pacino gulped, wondering if she would be angry at him for killing the Russians.

"I'm glad you won't be prisoners of war, Patch," she said gently, looking up at him with her liquid blue eyes. "But now I fear *we* will be."

Pacino shook his head. "We don't operate that way, Irina. You know that." He pointed to the submarine conning towers. "Right now, they're calling for another Russian arctic transport to come get you guys. We'll resupply our shelter with fuel and food—and rifles and ammo—and leave it to you while you wait for your second plane."

"Are you sure? How do you know?"

"I don't," Pacino said. "I have to sell it to the captain first." He smiled at her and walked down the slope to where Seagraves, Quinnivan, and Lewinsky were conferring with the commanding officers and executive officers of the two rescue submarines. Pacino pulled Seagraves aside and proposed to him what he'd promised Trusov. Seagraves merely nodded and went back to his conversation.

Pacino returned to Trusov's side. "Captain agrees, Irina. You and your countrymen will remain here, warm, fed, safe and resupplied. But first, let's go to the shelter. I need to get this second gash bandaged up. And change the dressing on the first one."

"Thank you, Patch. I will help you."

Inside the shelter, Irina pulled off Dankleff's inner hood, which had stuck to Pacino's forehead from coagulated and frozen blood, tenderly cleaned the wound, then disinfected it and put a gauze bandage on it. She changed the other wound, cleaned it, bandaged it, and wrapped tape around his head to hold both bandages. Pacino was suddenly reminded of Rachel Romanov cleaning his chest wound from when the officers had punched his dolphin emblem, an ancient ritual, that drove the pins of the device deep into his chest and made him bleed. And he thought of River Styxx helping to bandage his first gash. When Trusov was done, she stepped back to look at her handiwork. She nodded, satisfied.

"You know, Patch," she said, "I am going to miss you. It is a shame you and I never get a normal situation to share."

"Come to Virginia when you get your next leave," Pacino smiled. "I'll show you around."

"I would love that, Patch." She looked at the entrance to the shelter. "I should join Captains Alexeyev and Kovalov now." She came close and hugged him, but before he could wrap his arms around her, she had broken the embrace and rushed out of the shelter to join the Russian crews. Pacino left the shelter, taking a quick look back, then walked down the slope to where the other junior officers were standing.

"What happens now, Mr. Patch?" Short Hull Cooper asked.

Pacino looked toward the closest submarine, where the senior officers were deep in conversation. "The bosses are deciding if we're riding back with the rescue subs or waiting for one of our own search-and-rescue aircraft to land here. Seagraves or Quinnivan will let us know in the next few minutes. If they give you a choice, Short Hull, I recommend you ride back with a rescue boat and keep working on your qualifications for dolphins."

"If they give *you* a choice? What would you do?"

Pacino took a deep breath. "I imagine I'd fly home and check on Rachel Romanov."

"Yeah," Cooper said. "And debrief with your dad."

Quinnivan walked to them, the other junior officers crowding over to see what was going to happen.

491

"Gents, I have news from home about Commander Romanov," Quinnivan said, his expression unreadable.

"What's the latest, XO?" Pacino asked.

"Good news first, lad. Physically, she's almost fully recovered. The hospital released her last week. She's resting at Bruno's house. Bruno's taking care of her."

Pacino inwardly winced at the thought of Bruno Romanov, Rachel's ex-husband, nursing her back to health. "And the bad news, XO?"

"She's got partial amnesia," Quinnivan said. "They're calling it 'retrograde amnesia'—which usually means the patient loses memory of events before a traumatic brain injury. In Rachel's case, she's lost the last six or seven months."

"Dear God," U-Boat Dankleff said. "That means she's lost the entire *Panther* run."

"And it means she won't remember *me*," Pacino said, trying to keep his voice level and emotionless, but failing.

"Take heart, laddie," Quinnivan said, clapping Pacino on the shoulder. "They say familiar sights or aromas can bring the memories crashing back. Maybe if she sees you, it will all return. Or if she smells the inside of a submarine again."

"Yeah, maybe," Pacino said. "So, XO, what's the plan for getting us back to Norfolk?"

"Everyone, gather around," Quinnivan said in a loud voice. The crew surrounded him, standing close to hear what he had to say, the SEAL officers and enlisted, with their white parkas, among the crowd. "The SEALs will embark aboard the USS *Hyman G. Rickover*, the sub with the dry-deck shelter. They'll dive the wreck of the *New Jersey* and make sure it can't be salvaged. Then they'll go out and dive the wrecks of the Russian deep-diver sub and the *Belgorod* to do a post-action damage assessment. And to see if the Status-6 torpedoes are destroyed. If not, they'll take care of *that* little problem.

"The other sub, the USS *Montana*, has called for a C130 arctic transport out of Joint Base Thule in Greenland. The plane should be in the air as we speak. The *Montana* will loiter here until we're all safely embarked and in the air flying back to Thule. However, anyone among the crew who doesn't have dolphins will be joining the *Montana* for the trip back, so you can continue to work on qualifications without interruption. And finally, *Montana* will radio SubCom to dispatch a second Russian rescue aircraft to pick up our good friends from the *Belgorod* and *Losharik*."

Pacino looked at Short Hull Cooper. "Looks like you're riding home on the *Montana*," he said.

Squirt Gun Vevera pulled Pacino aside, away from the crowd. "Patch, if Rachel's moved back in with Bruno, that leaves her room in the Snake Ranch available. You want to invite Short Hull to join us? We need the rent money. And he seems like a good guy."

"Let's wait till *Montana* pulls into Norfolk," Pacino said. "There's still a chance Rachel may regain her memory."

"I'll light a candle to that as soon as there's a convenient church," Vevera said.

Pacino laughed. "Squirt Gun, if you darkened the door of a church, the roof would cave in."

"Which is why God will listen," Vevera smiled back.

The sound of turboprops could be heard in the distance. Pacino shaded his eyes and looked for the plane. Eventually he could make it out. It circled the area, then slowed, made its approach, lowered skids, and landed on the ice, coming to a stop a hundred feet from the shelter. Pacino saw the star and stripes on the tail and the block letters on the fuselage spelling U.S. AIR FORCE and breathed a deep sigh of relief.

"Guys," Pacino said to his friends. "Let's get the hell out of here."

30

"Mr. Vice President," Presidential Secretary Eve LaBelle said from the side entrance door to the Oval Office, "the president and attorney general are here to see you."

Vice President Michael Pacino stood up from the desk, pushing back the monstrous leather chair and smiling as Paul Carlucci was wheeled in, looking annoyed at being in a wheelchair, but smiling back at Pacino.

"I'm glad you're back, Mr. President," Pacino said, reaching out and shaking Carlucci's hand. Carlucci's handshake was strong, but nothing like the politician's grip he'd had before the shooting. "How do you feel?"

"Like hell, Patch. Being shot is *not* an experience I'd recommend. Zero stars."

Pacino laughed and looked at the attorney general. Madilynn Campbell was immediately recognizable, her gigantic figure regularly the subject of biting satire on social media. Carlucci had confided to Pacino that he had wanted to replace her, but she was embedded with the party faithful, he'd said, and he couldn't spend the political capital to fire her. How much damage, he had wondered, could an attorney general really do?

"Good morning, Madam Attorney General," Pacino said, reaching for her hand, but instead she slapped a folder into his hand.

"I hope you'll sign this without any drama, Mr. Vice President," she said, getting straight to business.

Pacino opened the folder. It was a one-page document signed by the president and the cabinet revoking Pacino's interim appointment as acting president under the 25th Amendment. There was a space at the bottom for him to sign. Campbell handed him a pen, and he signed the document and returned it and the pen to her. Without a word, the beefy attorney general turned and left the room.

"She's a real sweetheart, isn't she?" Carlucci quipped.

"I suppose that job would bring out the dark side of anyone, sir," Pacino said.

"Can you imagine what she would have done if you'd refused to sign that? I might have advised you to do that just to see the look on her face," Carlucci chuckled. "Anyway, have a seat, Patch," Carlucci said, waving to the floral-patterned couch. "I need to talk to you."

"Why do I feel like I did whenever one of my wives used to say, 'we need to talk'?" Pacino said, taking a seat on the couch so he could face Carlucci's wheelchair.

"Exactly," Carlucci said, his expression turning grim. "Patch, there's no easy way to say this, so I'm just gonna say it. You're fired. I need you out of the building in the next thirty minutes."

Pacino stood and offered his hand to Carlucci. He smiled and said, "it was an honor working for you, Mr. President."

"Wait, Patch, what the hell? Sit back down," Carlucci said in exasperation. "Don't you want to know why I'm firing you?"

"Reasons for being fired never matter, Mr. President. Only the decision matters. Besides, as to reasons to fire me? I probably know a dozen reasons that haven't even occurred to *you* yet."

"Maybe, Patch, but you'll need to know in case the media asks. And they *will* ask. What you will say affects us both. So let's get our story straight."

Pacino sat back down. "Go ahead, then, sir," he said.

"First, you *didn't* get fired. You *resigned*. Getting fired as the VP would stain your reputation. But you're walking out of here by your own choice. That way, politically, you live to fight another day. And I don't look like a jerk for firing a popular vice president."

Carlucci's chief of staff, Remi O'Keefe stuck his head in the side door. "Should I wait, Mr. President?" he asked.

"No, Remi, come on in."

Chief of Staff Remi O'Keefe strode in, all six foot four inches of him. He was a African-American attorney who'd been a college basketball star at LSU and almost played for the NBA before a bad knee changed his career to law. He'd recovered nicely, Pacino thought, Harvard Law and a career as a Manhattan prosecutor, even being recruited to run for district attorney, but sometime during his travels, he'd sat on an airplane seat next to Carlucci, who at the time was running for mayor of Cleveland, and the two had become friends. O'Keefe had left Manhattan to become Carlucci's chief of staff when Carlucci had been elected to the Senate, and had been by his side ever since.

Oddly, O'Keefe had been completely absent during Operation *Panther*, Pacino thought, as well as this op, Operation *Poseidon*, until the bitter end. Carlucci had hinted that O'Keefe was a staunch pacifist, hated all things military, and would object to being in any room that had Pacino in it. O'Keefe kept to domestic affairs, leaving international issues and national security to the president and national security advisor. Odds were, Pacino thought, O'Keefe had objected to Carlucci hiring a former admiral-in-command of a war fleet as his national security advisor, but Carlucci kept his own counsel when it came to hiring and firing.

O'Keefe took a seat on the wing chair near Carlucci, facing Pacino. He nodded at Pacino. "Morning, Mr. Vice President," he said respectfully.

"Anyway, Remi, I was just talking to the vice president about his sudden decision to resign, which is a serious problem." Carlucci winked at Pacino as he said, "Hell, Patch could run against me in the primaries, and who knows, with his recent popularity, he might knock me out of my party's nomination."

"That won't happen, Mr. President," Pacino said.

"Never say never, Patch," Carlucci said. "Anyway, we were speaking about reasons? I thought I'd let Remi fill you in on that on your way to clear out the vice president's office."

"Good-bye, Mr. President," Pacino said, standing and shaking Carlucci's hand. "I hope you feel better."

"I hope I can call on you for advice, Patch," Carlucci said.

Pacino smiled. "Any time, Mr. President," he said, and turned and walked toward the main Oval Office entrance, the most direct route to the vice president's office. O'Keefe paused to pick up something in his office, across from Pacino's. Once in Pacino's VP office, O'Keefe shut the door.

"Something about reasons?" Pacino asked.

O'Keefe nodded solemnly. "You did something that Carlucci would never have allowed. You attacked that Russian rescue airplane."

Pacino nodded. "I did. And I'd do it again."

"Having a son on the ice that day, well, that presents a conflict-of-interest. It could be construed that you attacked that plane just to save your son."

"I did," Pacino said. "But I'd still do it if my son were safe at his home in Virginia Beach. Besides, shooting the Russian rescue aircraft that could have saved my son? That's acting *against* any conflict of interest."

"Sir, you gave away to the Russians that we'd successfully spied for the intel, the information that they were planning to take our survivors hostage."

"For all we know," Pacino said, "the Russians dangled that in front of us *intentionally* to see what we would do. If we let them take our survivors as prisoners of war, they'd know we were weak. And that would make dealing with them in the future that much more difficult."

O'Keefe considered for a moment and nodded. "You make a good point. What did the CIA director think of that idea? Or the director of the NSA?"

"I didn't ask," Pacino said.

"See, that's another of Carlucci's reasons," O'Keefe said. "You don't consult experts. You just act. One day that could get you into trouble."

"I'll take that under advisement, Remi," Pacino said, finding a book that had gotten buried under papers, then putting a framed photo of him and young Anthony on top of the book. There was little else to remove from the office. "But I'm returning to retirement, so I don't think your advice will get used."

"I doubt that," O'Keefe said, smiling.

"Are there any more reasons?" Pacino asked. "I should get going."

"Chopper isn't here yet," O'Keefe said, glancing out the office's south window. "The president wants you to take Marine One to wherever you want to go. Also, he needs a little time to gather up the press."

"That's considerate of the president," Pacino said. "But he could have arranged a limo. I'm just going back to Annapolis."

"Listen...Admiral," O'Keefe said, searching for the proper title to call Pacino, since he was no longer the vice president. "President Carlucci wants you to run against him in the primaries."

Pacino stopped searching his desk for any other things to bring with him and stared at O'Keefe.

"What?"

"You heard me right. Carlucci wants you to run for the American Party nomination next spring and win it."

"Why? If he's done, why doesn't he just resign? Or announce that he won't run?"

"He's definitely done, Admiral, but he believes it's better to lose to *you* in the primaries than quit. I think his exact words were, 'winners never quit and quitters never win, but you can always lose the primaries and go home with your dignity intact.' He says once he loses, he will endorse you and throw his full political weight in your favor so you win the general election."

Pacino inhaled. "That's a lot to take in," he said after a moment.

O'Keefe smiled. "Can I tell the president you didn't reject the idea?"

Pacino nodded. "As you said, I need to confer with the experts. So I will consult them."

"Excellent, Admiral. Here, let me take your photo and book. I'll have a Marine bring this to the chopper with your briefcase."

"I don't have a briefcase here," Pacino said.

"You do now. It will contain a tablet computer with information Carlucci wants you to have with access to his files and his database. It's highly classified, so—"

"I'll take good care of it, Remi," Pacino said, smiling.

He felt a thousand pounds lighter as he walked out of the office, wondering what he'd say to the reporters gathering on the south lawn.

The rotors and engines of the gigantic helicopter, Marine One, had been shut down, presumably, Pacino thought, so that the crowd of reporters could hear what he had to say.

He stepped to the podium that had been set up and looked out over the crowd. "Good morning, everyone," he said, the crowd quieting. "You may have already heard that I tendered my resignation as vice president to President Carlucci this morning. I'll be returning to private life and retirement. Other than that, I have no further comment."

He walked from the podium but the reporters mobbed him, four Secret Service agents pushing them aside and forming a corridor allowing Pacino to walk to the helicopter, which had started its engines.

"Did you resign, Admiral, or did you get fired?" one reporter shouted.

"Did you have disagreements with Carlucci?" another asked.

"Are you running for president next year?"

"Did the Russians contact the White House about your order to attack their rescue aircraft?"

Pacino frowned at that last question. He'd ordered Operation *Poseidon* to be classified so highly no one would know about it for a decade, but maybe Carlucci had leaked the information or even declassified it. It would make sense, Pacino thought. Firing on the Russian aircraft would gain Pacino points with a lot of voters, he thought, although it would lose him others.

The helicopter's jets had spun up to idle, the loud whine of them drowning out the other questions from the crowd. Pacino approached the chopper. A Marine guard in dress blues saluted him. Pacino stopped, turned to face the Marine, and rigidly returned the salute. The Marine couldn't help smiling as Pacino turned at the top of the steps and waved toward the White House, wondering if Carlucci could see him, and ducked into the helicopter as the rotors started spinning.

"Welcome, sir," a Marine officer said, saluting him. Pacino saluted back. "Destination, sir? Your Annapolis house?"

"Yes. Annapolis," Pacino said, and buckled into a seat. He looked up as someone brushed past him and took the seat opposite his.

It was CIA Director Margo Allende, who smiled at him as she buckled in.

"What do I call you now, sir?" she asked. "Mr. Vice President? Or Admiral?"

Pacino smiled back. "How about 'honey' or 'sweetie'?"

"How about babe?" she asked, smiling at him.

He winked at her. "That works."

The helicopter lifted off the south lawn and flew out toward the Washington Monument, then turned toward the southeast.

The Air Force C130 had landed at Joint Base Thule in northern Greenland. Off to the side of the runway, there had been half a dozen Gulfstream SS-12s at idle, their hatches open. Captain Seagraves and XO Quinnivan had directed that their jet's passengers should also include Pacino, Lewinsky, Dankleff and Vevera.

As soon as Lieutenant Anthony Pacino climbed out of the cargo turboprop and stepped to the SS-12, he felt exhaustion overtake him.

He'd taken his seat behind Quinnivan's and opposite Dankleff's, strapped in and shut his eyes. He'd fallen into a deep sleep when an attendant in the blue uniform of an Air Force sergeant nudged him awake and asked if he'd like a drink.

"I'd love a scotch, double, neat, Macallan if you have it," Pacino said, his hand going up to his head to feel his bandages. The wounds throbbed. He wondered how frightful his face would look when the wounds healed.

"Yes, sir," she said, returning with drinks on a tray, delivering Seagraves' and Quinnivan's drinks first, then Lewinsky's, then Dankleff's, then Vevera's and Pacino's.

Pacino looked solemnly at Dankleff and Vevera. "A toast, U-Boat and Squirt Gun. To our fallen. To Moose Kelly. To River Styxx. To Easy Eisenhart. To Gangbanger Ganghadharan. And our non-qual, Long Hull Cooper."

"And to our lost friends in the goat locker," Dankleff said, referring to the chief petty officers of the submarine. "To the COB, Q-Ball Quartane. Fancy McGraceland, E-div. Drive Shaft McGuire, A-gang. And Gory Goreliki, radio, and K-Squared Kim, firecontrol, both fellow pirates from Operation *Panther*."

"All on eternal patrol," Pacino said, his eyes getting moist as he thought of Lieutenant Commander Wanda River Styxx. What was the last thing she'd said to him before the shitshow started? *Next time, don't drink so much.* Hinting that there would *be* a next time. But not now, Pacino thought. Her body had been placed in the *New Jersey*'s frozen stores locker with the other dead. Had the locker survived the torpedo room explosion? Did she lie quietly at the bottom of the Arctic Ocean? Or was she blown to smithereens?

Pacino downed half the whisky in one gulp, putting the glass down on the table between his and Dankleff's seat and looking out the window. There was nothing to see, just sky above and clouds below. The sun was harsh, so Pacino shut the window blind. He drained the glass and the sergeant came back with a second whisky. He was about to take a sip when XO Quinnivan stood up and shouted.

"Lads, take a look at this," Quinnivan said, then sat back down.

The television flatpanels at the forward and aft bulkheads of the jet, which had previously been showing a projection of their route from Greenland to Washington, and their progress on that route, switched to a Satellite News Network news segment, the reporter standing on the White House south lawn as the Marine One helicopter lifted off and sailed away. The scroll at the bottom of the screen read, *...VICE PRESIDENT PACINO RESIGNS AND DEPARTS WHITE HOUSE...*

"Vice President Michael Pacino's resignation leaves the White House with the decision of whom to replace him with, with many suggesting that Secretary of War Bret Hogshead is first in line for the position, since President Carlucci likes having a military expert as his number two person. When asked if he would run for president against Carlucci, Vice President Pacino refused to comment. Back to you in the studio, Freddy. Monica Eddlestien, SNN News, the White House."

"Wow," Dankleff said. "Looks like Patch here just lost all his juice."

Quinnivan turned off the news clip and the screen returned to showing their route progress. The copilot of the flight, an Air Force major with her blonde hair pulled back into a ponytail, came into the cabin, stepped up to Captain Seagraves and quietly said something in his ear, then turned and returned to the flight deck. Seagraves stood, putting one hand on Dankleff's seatback and one on Vevera's across the aisle.

"Gentlemen, our destination has been changed," Seagraves said. "We're apparently no longer invited to the White House to meet the vice president and debrief at CIA headquarters. We've been rerouted to Norfolk. Our debriefings will be held at ComSubCom headquarters Wednesday morning." With that, Seagraves sat back down.

Dankleff and Vevera were staring at Pacino.

"What?" Pacino said.

"The hell happened with your dad?" Dankleff asked. "You think he got fired by Carlucci for shooting missiles at that Russian rescue plane? Which, by the way, was an act of war."

Pacino frowned. "I'll ask him when I see him," he said. "As to an act of war, shooting at the *Belgorod* was an act of war too, I'd remind you."

Dankleff shrugged. "That happened under the polar icecap," he said.

"So what?" Pacino asked.

"Patch," Dankleff said, "every submariner knows that what happens under the ice…*never happened.*"

————————————

Captain Second Rank Iron Irina Trusov carefully carried the long submarine model to the headstone, then kneeled down and laid the model on the ledge of the stone. The black granite stone's engraved text read:

Volodya Trusov

Captain First Rank

Navy of the Soviet Union, Red Banner Northern Fleet

Commanding Officer, B-448 *Tambov*

Medal for Military Valor, 2nd Class

Medal for Distinguished Military Service, 1st Class

Trusov stood, taking a mental image of the submarine model laid at her father's gravestone. She decided to sit on the granite bench a few feet uphill from the headstone and keep her father company for a little while. Her thoughts were interrupted by a familiar voice from over her shoulder.

"Anything you leave on a grave gets collected for the museum, you know." The tall man reached into a pocket of his greatcoat and

503

pulled out a cigarette and lit it, blowing smoke from his nostrils. He nodded at the gravestone. "He was a good man, your father. I served with him on *Tambov*. It was my first submarine. I like to think he taught me all he knew about underwater combat."

Trusov stared. It was Georgy Alexeyev, with a new black eye patch over his right eye, wearing a black uniform greatcoat, but his shoulder boards were new. Gone were the two gold stripes and three gold stars of a captain first rank, replaced with shoulder boards with two gold stars. He was a vice admiral now.

She stood. "Admiral? Admiral Alexeyev? You got promoted?"

He nodded and smiled. "Do you mind if I sit with you here for a little while?"

"Please, sir, go ahead." Once he took a seat on the bench, she sat next to him, uncomfortable that the bench was only long enough for two people if they sat close together.

"Admiral Zhigunov retired," Alexeyev said. "He said this operation aged him another five years and he feels he doesn't have that long left. Meanwhile, Admiral Zhabin was promoted to Chief Commander of the Navy after that asshole Stanislav passed away, and Zhabin and I go way back. Funny thing, *Litso Smerti*—Death Face—Zhabin was the first officer of *Tambov* when I reported aboard. He's an old friend. He insisted I take command of the Northern Fleet."

"I see," Trusov said dully. "I'm glad the polar mission of the *Belgorod* didn't hurt your career."

Alexeyev smiled. "It didn't hurt *yours* either, Irina. There's an awards ceremony Wednesday immediately after the memorial service for our fallen comrades. You're being awarded the Medal for Distinction in Combat, second award. And you're out of uniform." Alexeyev reached into his greatcoat pocket and pulled out a clear package containing the shoulder boards of a captain first rank.

Her eyes grew wide. "Really? But I'm so young, Cap—I mean, Admiral."

"You're wise and brilliant beyond your years," Alexeyev said. "And that is not all. I have a project for you. I'm putting you in charge of building a new special-purpose submarine. Not something cobbled together from old spare parts like *Belgorod*, but planned from the keel up. It will be magnificent." He smirked. "And hardened against nuclear shock. Once it's constructed, *you* will be the captain. Here, let me help you." She stood to face the admiral, and he removed the new shoulder boards from the packaging, took her captain second rank boards off and replaced them with the new boards of captain first rank. "It looks great on you, Irina."

He stubbed out the cigarette butt on his shoe, put it in his pocket, and lit a second one. "I want to invite you to my house this weekend to meet my wife Natalia. We'll cook up something delicious and talk about the new submarine. Just promise not to tell her I've started smoking again." He laughed. "When she smells smoke on me, I tell her it's from that degenerate, Kovalov."

"Admiral," Trusov said, glancing for a moment at the model sub on the gravestone. "This new submarine. Does it have a name yet?"

Alexeyev shook his head. "Only a project number, why?"

"Admiral, I want to be the one to name it."

Alexeyev smiled. "Do you have anything in mind, Irina?"

She answered immediately. "*Mest*."

"*Revenge*," Alexeyev said. "I like it already."

———

Lieutenant Commander Tiny Tim Fishman slowly and carefully lowered himself through the open plug trunk hatch of the wreck of the USS *New Jersey*, switched on his helmet camera, then turned to wait for Grip Aquatong, Scooter Tucker-Santos and Swan Oneida to swim in after him. Once his crew were all inside, Fishman swam through the side hatch into what had once been the forward compartment upper level. He accepted the light unit from Aquatong, set it in place, and turned it on, the strong illumination able to show the entire interior of the forward compartment, or what was left of it. The compartment was only partially a compartment—anything forward of Frame 40 had been blown to shards by the weapons explosion, and the middle third of the compartment was almost unrecognizable, just piles of rubble. The aft third of the compartment seemed to be less damaged, its three decks visible and still standing, and might yield what they were seeking.

Fishman swam down to the blown apart middle level, shining his flashlight left and right, eventually finding an intact passageway aft of what had been the control room, which no longer existed. Down the passageway, he found what he was looking for—the safe in the captain's stateroom. He accepted the torch handed him by Aquatong, lit it and began torching through the metal of the safe. It wouldn't matter if the torch destroyed the contents—that was the mission, to destroy the top secret and higher material to save it from any Russian salvage.

A few minutes later, Fishman and Aquatong had pulled the contents of the captain's safe and the XO's safe into a bag. The control room safe no longer existed, nor did the wardroom's safe, but there was a double safe in the sonar equipment space and another in radio. It didn't take long to see that the radio room and SES were blown to splinters by the torpedo room explosion. It was possible the safes had survived and had just been blown out into the surrounding ocean, but finding them would be for a later mission. This dive was for the low hanging fruit of the intact safes, and tablet computers, if any were visible in the rubble of the wreckage. And there was one other reason passed down from Admiral Catardi, the chief of naval operations.

Fishman and Aquatong swam aft into what had been the crew's mess and the galley. It was pure chaos, debris scattered everywhere. Then they saw what they were looking for. The door to the frozen stores locker, normally a huge space the size of half a railroad boxcar, storing the food for 120 people for four months. Fishman tried the handle, but it was stuck. He called for the torch and torched off the latching mechanism, then opened the door and shined his light inside. The interior had minimal damage, he noted, just a ruptured area at the top port side.

To the right of the door, Fishman found the bodies, neatly stacked, each in a body bag. He counted twenty-four bodies. He pulled out the body on top and floated it over to Aquatong, who in turn passed it to Tucker-Santos and Oneida. It took ten minutes to pull all the bodies out. Oneida and Tucker-Santos lashed the bodies into a long line so they could be withdrawn from the plug trunk hatch without losing anyone or jamming up the hatch.

Tucker-Santos and Oneida left the hull and received the bodies up above as Fishman and Aquatong handed them up. All four SEALs then grabbed their propulsion units, making sure the bodies would stay tethered, and propelled over to the hull of the *Hyman G. Rickover* for the trip to the next dive site. Assuming good luck in locating the wreck, the next dive would be to the Russian deep-diver *Losharik*, then on to *Belgorod* to see if any of the Poseidon torpedoes had survived. If they did, *Rickover*'s mission was to bring them to AUTEC for dismantlement and study.

There had been debate about whether to bury *New Jersey*'s dead at sea, but Admiral Catardi's directives were to bring them home. He didn't want any of *New Jersey*'s dead to lie under polar ice, he'd said.

Inside the dry-deck shelter's decompression chamber, Fishman pulled off his dive mask.

"Tough day at sea," he said to Aquatong, who just stared glumly at the deck.

"Yeah, boss. Makes you wish you'd never become a diver in the first place."

Fishman clapped Aquatong on the shoulder. "We did a good thing today. An important thing. The spirits of our dead watch us right now and I know they approve."

"I hope so, boss. I hope so."

Anthony Pacino shut off the engine of the old Corvette, the supercharger still emitting a high-pitched whine for a long minute after engine cut-off. Pacino got out and shut the door, pocketing his phone.

He walked up the front walkway to the door of the suburban Virginia Beach house, the two-story center-hall Colonial identical to what seemed ten thousand others in the beachside village. He knocked and waited, and after a short wait, the door opened and

Bruno Romanov's large, shaved head appeared. He smiled in genuine pleasure.

"Patch Pacino. Come in, come in. Can I get you a drink?"

It was Saturday at two in the afternoon. A little early to drink, Pacino thought, but he looked at Bruno and said, "is there any good scotch in the house?"

Bruno laughed. "Of course! Let me go get us a round. Double, right? Three fingers?"

Pacino smiled. "Three fat fingers," he said.

"Rachel!" Bruno called up the stairs. "There's a visitor here for you. A certain Lieutenant Patch Pacino."

Rachel Romanov came down the stairs, her shining and partly curled dirty blonde hair down past her nipples, dressed in a form-fitting red sweater—which Pacino thought might be the same one she'd worn when he first met her at the XO's party a million years ago—with tight jeans and tall brown boots. She smiled, showing her even, white, perfect teeth, but there was no recognition in her smile.

"Hello. I'm sorry, I didn't catch your name. Patch, is it?"

"Anthony Pacino," he said, taking Rachel's outstretched hand. "My callsign is Patch, but some people used to call me Lipstick." He watched her face for any sign of her remembering, but her face was blank.

"Did I know you before?" she asked.

"Yes, Rachel," Pacino said, as Bruno handed him a rocks glass with three fingers of scotch in it and Rachel a glass of red wine.

"A toast," Bruno said in his booming, deep voice with his slight eastern European accent. "To old friends, even if we don't remember who they are."

Pacino took a sip of the whisky, the liquid burning down his throat. "Dear God, Bruno, what is this?"

Bruno laughed. "I'm told you and your guys in Faslane liked it. Anyway, come over to the living room. Let's sit down and talk."

Rachel sat on a wing chair facing the couch. Pacino put his drink down on a coaster on the coffee table and looked at Rachel, but her face was still blank.

"Rachel," Pacino said, "you and I were in the control room of the *Vermont* when the fire started. You went aft to take charge at the scene."

She shook her hair off her shoulders and pursed her lips. "I'm sorry, Patch. Patch, right? I'm sorry, I just don't remember."

"Did someone show you the video of the control room before and during the accident?" Pacino asked.

She nodded. "Bruno got it for me. I watched it." She shrugged. "It was like watching strangers."

Pacino nodded and took another sip of the whisky. "I get that. What is the last thing you do remember?"

"I was getting off a limo bus and walking up to Quinnivan's house for a ship's party."

Pacino looked down at the carpeting. She had remembered up to ten minutes before the moment when she'd met him for the first time. If her memory had only gone one hour longer, he thought, she'd know who he was.

"I wanted to ask you and Bruno something," Pacino said.

"Go ahead, Patch," Bruno said.

"Commander Quinnivan, our XO, made arrangements with the captain and XO of SSN-778, USS *New Hampshire*, out of Norfolk's Squadron Six, to give Rachel a classified tour including the control room. The doctors I talked to said the sights, sounds, and smells of the submarine might bring back your memory."

Rachel shook her head. "I don't want a tour. I'm not sure I *want* my memory back," she said. "I heard the fire on the *Vermont* was awful. And I'm not sure if I'm staying in the Navy or if I stay, whether I'll stay in the submarine force."

"Oh," Pacino said, his face and tone giving away his disappointment.

"Listen, Patch. Anthony. I'd just as soon forget about my experiences on the *Vermont*."

"I should be going," Pacino said, draining his scotch and standing.

"You sure you won't stay for dinner?" Rachel said, smiling brightly. "Bruno's grilling steaks and I'm making salad and sides."

"No, I'll leave it to you two," Pacino said.

The conversation at the front door seemed endless, and Pacino just wanted to go. Finally, they said their last good-bye and he walked out to the Corvette.

He knew what he needed, he thought. He programmed the destination into his phone and followed the app's turn-by-turn directions toward the north.

Toward Annapolis.

31

It was early evening when Anthony Pacino cut the engine of the Corvette on the wide driveway of his father's Annapolis house. The house looked like every light had been turned on inside, with the exterior lights making the driveway look like daylight. He'd texted his father that he'd be driving up, but he wasn't sure if the old man would be there, or still in D.C. — or perhaps at the Sandbridge beach house.

His father had only replied "OK" to the text message, probably worried about the younger Pacino texting and driving. Pacino walked up to the front door, and looked back at the car, wondering if he should pull out his "go bag" of spare clothes and toiletries, but he had kept a week's worth of clothes at the Annapolis house.

The house was a huge three-story log structure built on an artificial peninsula jutting into the Severn River, with sweeping views of the Maryland Route 2 bridge over the river and the northernmost grounds of the United States Naval Academy, the green-tinted copper dome of the chapel in the background. Back when his father was the admiral-in-command of the Navy, his direct reports had named the estate "Pacino Peninsula." Pacino looked up to the second floor's western deck, where he and his father had had happy hour every night in the month after Carrie Alameda died. He shook his head. Carrie's death had slammed him hard, but losing Rachel to amnesia seemed almost as bad. She walked and talked, yet had no idea who he was or what she'd meant to him. Perhaps his father would have some advice, he thought.

He tried the front door and it was unlocked.

"Anthony?" his father called down the stairs.

"It's me," Pacino said, taking the stairs two at a time. He grinned as he saw his father. The old man wore a NAVY 90 sweatshirt, still grease-stained from when he'd wear it to work on his sailboat, which he'd sold after his divorce.

"Damn, it's so good to see you, Son," the elder Pacino said, pulling Anthony into a bear hug. He pulled back and looked at Anthony's bandages.

"We need to change these dressings," Michael said. "I know a good plastic surgeon, Son. Not to worry."

"Hey, the scars might look cool."

Michael shook his head. "I guarantee you they won't. Anyway, you're back and safe, finally."

"Well, it got close a couple times, Dad. Four nuclear explosions, an arctic storm, and the Russian GRU trying to take us all prisoner." Anthony bit his lip. "We lost five officers and five chiefs. And fourteen of the enlisted, one of them Snowman Mercer, the sonarman who first detected the *Panther* in the Gulf of Oman."

"I heard the USS *Rickover* is bringing their bodies home," Michael Pacino said solemnly. "There will be a service at Arlington National Cemetery." The admiral picked up the crystal carafe from the bar. "Let's grab a drink on the east deck." He tossed Anthony a black sweatshirt with the emblem of a skull and crossbones. "It's a little chilly but it's a nice night." He handed the scotch carafe to Anthony and grabbed two glasses and strode to the deck's sliding glass door. He waved Anthony to a chair and poured for them both, then sat.

"A toast," Michael Pacino said. "To your safe return and knowing that your mission was accomplished."

"And to our fallen friends," Anthony said. He drank, then looked at his father. "What did you mean the mission was accomplished?"

"Your SEAL friends did a dive on the *Belgorod* wreckage. The entire forward two thirds of the boat were blown to atoms. Those Poseidon torpedoes were vaporized."

"Well, nice to know. I guess. Dad, I wanted to thank you for, you know, blowing up that Russian rescue plane. I really didn't want to spend the next ten years in a Russian prison."

"My pleasure," Michael smiled. "Any time."

"So, Dad, did you really resign? Or did Carlucci fire you?"

Pacino took a sip of his drink as if weighing his words. "You know, Anthony, when you eventually leave the military and have a job, you'll realize that there's the moment in your mind when you resign, and then there's a later moment when you tell your *boss* you resigned. As for me, I resigned mentally ten seconds before giving the order to launch Brimstone missiles at that Russian Il-76."

"Why?"

"Because I knew all of D.C. would have a complete meltdown about it. Carlucci would never have allowed that. 'An act of war,' all that pacifist horseshit. Carlucci would have let you get captured, then negotiated for your release as the more prudent, responsible, statesmanlike thing to do. Hell with that. I blasted that goddamned plane to Hell, naysayers be damned. And the intelligence community, the signals intelligence spooks, were *outraged* that I acted on intel that revealed that we'd broken the Russian codes and were translating their radio traffic in real time. The damage from that, they say, could take years to fix. I even heard that ball-busting attorney general tried to get Carlucci to agree to having the Justice Department put me up on criminal charges. Fortunately for me, he told her to pound sand."

"Wow," Anthony said. "Now for the hard question, Dad. If I hadn't been on the crew of the *New Jersey*, would you still have fired those missiles?" Anthony expected his father to use his usual explanation, that no man can say what he'd do in any given situation until he was actually *in* the situation.

But Michael Pacino put down his whisky glass, looked Anthony in the eye and said seriously, "You're goddamned right I would have."

Anthony smiled. "I actually came for advice," he said.

Michael refilled his glass and then Anthony's. "Go ahead."

"It's about my friend Rachel Romanov. My former navigator."

Michael nodded. "You two were involved."

"Almost, Dad. Just not quite yet. She wanted to keep it platonic for a while longer, but I could tell that was about to change. I had it bad for her. I still do. Just as I thought she might be ready to agree to a relationship, the fire happened. And now? 'Retrograde amnesia'? Her memory stops an hour before she met me."

Michael considered, his hand on his chin. "And you think there's something meaningful about the timing of that."

"Yeah. I think she's blocking my memory out. If she remembers me, she has to remember that she'd gotten a divorce from her husband Bruno."

"She was living with you junior officers in that Virginia Beach rental house, right?"

"The Snake Ranch. Yeah. She had the big master bedroom after she pulled rank on all of us." Anthony smiled for a moment at the memory of Rachel strong-arming them all when it came time to pick rooms.

"Where is she living now?"

"She's back at her former marital residence. She's with Bruno. Which, I've got to tell you, cuts my fucking heart out."

"Yeah," Michael said. "I could see that."

"I went to see her hoping it would jog her memory, but nothing."

"And you want to know if you should keep pushing," Michael said.

"Yeah. The doctors said familiar sights, sounds and smells might jar the memories loose. I was thinking about taking her down to an operational Virginia-class boat, maybe walking her into the control room, you know, and stand there next to her like I did during Operation *Panther*."

"Well, if you *don't* do that, you'll always wonder what would have happened if you did. And if you do take her to the submarine, and she still doesn't remember you, well, you can move on with no regrets. You did all you could. But you don't control the situation.

Rachel could decide to say 'no' to your request to take her down to the boat."

"She already said no. I pitched the idea to her. She refused. She said she's not even sure she *wants* her memory back."

"Is there anyone else who has influence on her, who could convince her?"

Anthony considered for a moment. "Yeah. Her ex-husband Bruno. They were still friends. But Bruno would have to act against his best interest. If he convinces her to go down to the submarine, he could lose her to me."

"So talk to Bruno," Michael said. "Man to man. Tell him that you and he both need to 'draw the box' around Rachel—that is, you should both care enough about her to do what's best for *her*, not for either of you."

"And then, if he says no, or if she still says no, I did everything I could."

"Right. And I know you can live with the loss after that."

Anthony nodded, pointing to the whisky carafe. "I'll take one more. Then I'm going to hit the rack. All this has been emotionally exhausting."

"I can imagine," Michael said.

"So, Dad, there's a lot of press speculation about you running in the primaries against Carlucci. Are you *really* running for president?"

Michael laughed dismissively. "A presidential election campaign costs about seven billion dollars. We could build a Virginia-class submarine for that amount."

Anthony laughed. "I noticed, Dad, you didn't answer a yes-or-no question. I think you may have turned into a politician in spite of yourself."

When Anthony had turned in, Michael Pacino picked up his phone and dialed the number for Captain Scotch Seagraves. Seagraves answered on the first ring.

"Mr. Vice President?" he said.

"It's just 'Patch' now, Captain. Listen, I know it's late and you're busy, but I wanted to ask you for a favor."

"Let's get these bandages off," Dr. Gupta said. The plastic surgery had wrapped a week before. Anthony Pacino wondered how the result would look. Would he resemble someone who'd survived a knife fight? Would the scars make him look tough? Or would there be those hideous red streaks on his skin like he'd had before Gupta took the knife to him? It occurred to Pacino that maybe the bandages and scars had made Rachel fail to recognize him. If Gupta had been able to return Pacino to his previous appearance sooner, maybe that might have brought her back.

When Gupta had cut off the bandages, he held a large hand-held mirror up to Pacino's face.

"It looks the same as it always did, before the...before the thing," Pacino said, rotating the mirror slightly, hoping his voice sounded happy rather than disappointed. A nice scar would have made his tale of piracy on the high seas more believable.

"You can just see the faintest ghost of the scars, Lieutenant Pacino," Gupta said, smiling. "In the right light, you can convince a lady that you are indeed a tough guy. Too bad that nightclub lighting won't do. You may have to carry a bright flashlight with you."

Pacino laughed. "I've already got the lady, Doc, but thanks."

But did he? Or was Rachel Romanov lost to him forever?

Lieutenant Anthony Pacino leaned on the handrail of the platform overlooking Graving Dock Number One, where the hull of the USS *New England* was coming together after the aft end of the *Vermont* had been welded to the forward end of the *Massachusetts*. The boat was so surrounded by scaffolding, it could barely be made out to be a submarine, the scaffolding extending all the way up the sail. The metal of the hull was a dull anti-rust green from the inorganic zinc primer sprayed on her. The intermediate and final paint coats would wait for the ship to be closer to leaving the drydock.

Despite the boat being far from ready, the crew of the *New Jersey* had been reassigned to the *New England,* assisting the shipyard in bringing her back to life. It was Monday, and Pacino was the off-going duty officer. The XO had made a new policy that after standing duty, an officer could take the next day off. Standing duty for a ship in the dock seemed stupid to Pacino, since there was not much for the duty officer to do in the shipyard. He looked at his watch, and it was 1045. He was about to cross the street and get in the car for the ride back to the Snake Ranch when a car glided to a halt behind him.

The driver's window rolled down. It was Commander Quinnivan in a black Lincoln town car. Quinnivan grinned at Pacino.

"Get in, loser. We have a lunch date at Squadron Six."

Pacino walked to the passenger side, but Quinnivan waved at him to get into the backseat. As he climbed in, he saw there was another passenger. It was Rachel Romanov, in uniform. She wore oversize sunglasses and her uniform ballcap, the cap featureless rather than the blue one with dolphins and the embroidery spelling USS NEW ENGLAND. Pacino looked at her.

"Hi, Rachel," he said. He wondered, now that his head wounds were healed, would she recognize him? Would his face return her memory? But so far, she hadn't reacted.

"Hello Patch," she said without looking back at him, her voice neutral. Was there a coldness in her voice, he wondered, or was he just being too sensitive?

"What's going down, XO?" Pacino asked.

"I got a phone call from Balaclava Driscoll, my opposite number on the *New Hampshire*. He and his captain, Gray Wolf Austin, agreed to bring you and Rachel down for a tour of their boat."

Pacino stared at Rachel. "Really?"

"Captain Seagraves thinks it's important that Madam Romanov reacquaint herself with the Virginia-class. I'll be there to remind her of what's what. *You're* coming, young Pacino, since XO Driscoll and Captain Austin want to talk to you. They've got a slot in their wardroom opening up."

"If it's all the same to you, XO, I'd prefer to stay with the old *Vermont* crew on the *New England*."

"Ah, but young Pacino, the *New England* will take months to get out of the dock. I figured you'd be craving action and want to get back to sea pronto."

"Well, normally, yeah, XO, but I'm still coming down from our most recent action. I could use a nice boring month or two."

"It may not be up to you, Patch, but let's see what happens."

The hull of SSN-778, the USS *New Hampshire*, looked exactly like the *Vermont* before the fire, or like the *New Jersey* before the battle with the Russians. Commander Jeremiah Seamus Quinnivan seemed almost out of place, one of the few people on the crowded pier not wearing the Navy's two-piece organizational clothing uniform, an ill-conceived, baggy-looking outfit that resembled pajamas tucked into black combat boots. By contrast, Quinnivan wore his sharp Royal Navy-issued blue uniform, his tailored long-sleeved shirt smartly tucked into starched pants, with gleaming leather black shoes, wearing a black beret with the emblem of the Royal Navy's submarine force, his rank displayed on the center of his chest, the emblem showing three broad gold stripes, the uppermost stripe forming a circular loop at the top.

Quinnivan, Pacino, and Romanov walked up to the topside sentry, who was wearing a set of crisp, dark blue crackerjacks. The sentry came to attention and saluted, and the three officers saluted back.

"Ahoy, lass, I'm Quinnivan, XO of the *New England*," the Irishman said to the topside watchstander, his brogue suddenly becoming comically thick. "I'm here to see your XO and Captain."

"I'll call down, sir," the topside petty officer said, reaching into a comms box and dialing a number on the phone inside.

"They're not using VHF radios with the repeaters anymore?" Romanov asked Quinnivan.

"Nah," Quinnivan said. "They're a security risk. A Pentagon 'red team' of hackers was able to use the VHF repeaters, in-hull radios and exterior system to eavesdrop on conversations inside the boats.

So we're back to what worked from forty years ago. It may be old, but it works just fine, and it's secure."

The topside sentry put the phone back in the box and turned to Quinnivan. "XO will be right up, sir."

"So, lassie, how long have you been assigned to this bucket o'bolts?" Quinnivan smiled at the sentry.

"A year, Commander," she replied, obviously uncomfortable with the question.

"No submarine dolphins yet? These qualified lads not taking care of you, gettin' ya trained?"

"Oh, no, sir, nothing like that. I'm just delinquent in my qualifications."

"Is it studyin' ya need to do, or do ya need practical experience at sea?"

"Sea experience, Commander. *New Hampshire* has been tied to the pier for a month."

Quinnivan nodded, filing the information away, Pacino noted, probably to use in conversation with the *New Hampshire* exec.

"Well, Petty Officer Schwarzengruber," Quinnivan said, stumbling over her name, "as soon as the *New England* is waterborne, you can join our crew any time and leave these *New Hampshire* pikers in the rearview mirror."

The petty officer blushed. "Thank you, sir. I'll bear that in mind."

A man wearing the khaki two-piece working uniform emerged from a canvas doghouse that had been erected over the plug trunk hatch. He was extremely tall and thin, with closely cropped black hair showing a receding hairline, his face long, his cheeks hollow. He wore wire-rimmed glasses and his expression was grave, as if he were walking into court as a handcuffed criminal. Pacino stared—he had thought Quinnivan and this officer, Lieutenant Commander Oliver Balaclava Driscoll, were friends. Apparently not.

Driscoll approached, frowned deeply at Quinnivan and snarled, "You've got some nerve coming here, Bullfrog."

"I came to return your mother's panties, Lurch—at least I *was*," Quinnivan said in hostility, "but the stench was just too great, so I tossed them in the Elizabeth River and got written up for causing an environmental disaster."

Driscoll flushed, his expression murderous. "Oh yeah? Well, *your* mother smells like a dumpster baking in the August sunshine that hasn't been emptied in a month and just got vomited on by a homeless guy and shit on by a flock of seagulls."

"Oh yeah? Well, fuck you, Lurch."

"Oh yeah? Well, fuck your mother, Bullfrog."

"Come here, ya skinny-ass fart-breath," Quinnivan said, bursting into a grin, and Driscoll came up and hugged the Irishman, the two men laughing and smiling. "Goddamn, Lurch, how long has it been?"

"At least a year," Driscoll said. "I meant to call you when we got back from being forward deployed for six months, but you know how it is. The in-port time is busier than the sea duty."

"Yeah, I get you. You've got to come to the house before I leave for my new assignment," Quinnivan said. "Shawna will whip up something. And I'll break out the good scotch."

"What's the new assignment, Bullfrog?" Driscoll asked.

"Shh. Top secret, lad," Quinnivan said, grinning and glancing at Pacino and Romanov. "Not in front of the children." He turned toward Pacino and Romanov. "Patch, Silky, this is Lieutenant Commander Lurch Driscoll, my old roommate and stateroom mate on the HMS *Astute* back home. I was the navigator. Lurch isn't smart enough to navigate, so they put him in charge of the weapons department. He never could figure out that Spearfish torpedo, though. Damn near blew us up doing maintenance one day. Lurch, this is Rachel Silky Romanov—you've heard of iron fist, velvet glove? Well, Lieutenant Commander Romanov here has a titanium fist in a *silk* glove. And this youngster here is Lieutenant Anthony Patch Pacino. We're particularly proud of this young'un."

Driscoll shook Rachel's hand, then Pacino's.

"The name is actually '*Balaclava*' Driscoll,'" he said to Pacino. "I convene a captain's mast for anyone calling me 'Lurch.' But some assholes are just too stupid to be retrained," he said, winking at

Quinnivan. "And you, Mister Pacino. I was informed your callsign is actually '*Death Toll.*' How many Russians have you killed in the last two ops?"

Pacino smirked. *Death Toll Pacino.* He supposed anything was better than his old callsign, Lipstick.

"Come on down, you three," Driscoll said, smiling. "Let me introduce you to the captain, and then you can wander around as needed."

Pacino followed Romanov and Quinnivan down the gangway to the hull, all three of them saluting the American flag mounted aft, then across to the doghouse overlooking the maw of the plug trunk hatch. When Pacino's turn came to enter the submarine, that unique and powerful smell of the boat filled his nostrils, an unmistakable witch's brew of atmo control amines, ozone, diesel fuel, diesel exhaust, cooking grease, seasoned with a touch of raw sewage. Wives of submariners often made husbands take off their boat uniforms before entering the house, the smell soaking into fabric and only a strong detergent able to eliminate it. It could get worse on a long run, Pacino thought, especially in the tropics, when stale human sweat was added to the mix, sometimes exacerbated by the laundry being shut down if there were trouble with the evaporators. Clean water was reserved for the oxygen generator, the reactor, the steam plant, and only after that for cooking and drinking, and dead last, for laundry. Pacino realized he hadn't smelled that scent since climbing out of the *New Jersey,* and the strong aroma brought him back to the moments before the sub sank.

He wondered if the smell would hit Rachel the same way it was hitting him. Would that crazy smell wake her up? Or would her amnesia persist? The trouble was, the smell had been present in her memories of her year on the *Vermont* before Pacino had shown up. He followed the other officers down the steep staircase to the middle level and forward to the door to the captain's stateroom. When Romanov turned to face Pacino at the door, he could tell from her blank stare that nothing had changed for her. The amnesia was continuing, he thought, his stomach dropping a few floors.

The man in the captain's stateroom stood. He seemed way too young to be a sub captain, Pacino thought. He stood barely over five feet tall, with a shock of red hair and a red five o'clock shadow. His face was open and friendly. He grinned in pleasure at Quinnivan.

"The mad Irishman cometh," he said, shaking Quinnivan's hand. "How the hell are ya, Bullfrog?"

"Great, great," Quinnivan said. "I'm just about done destroying American submarines."

"Tour coming to an end? Is the exchange program continuing?" The captain looked at Driscoll. "I hope so. Maybe I could get a British XO who would actually be competent instead of *this* loafer."

"Fuck you, Skipper," Driscoll said, smiling. "Gentlemen and lady, this is Captain Grey 'Gray Wolf' Austin, commanding officer of the legendary submarine USS *New Hampshire*. Captain, this is Rachel Silky Romanov, *Vermont's* former navigator, and their sonar officer, Anthony Patch Pacino."

Austin smiled. "Pleased to meet you guys," he said, reaching out to shake Rachel's hand, then Pacino's. "Your XO is correct about this being a legendary submarine. The *New Hampshire* is here to save Western civilization, as we have done many times already." He looked sympathetically at Rachel. "I heard there was, as Bullfrog would say, a spot of bother on the *Vermont* in drydock. You're all healed up now?"

"Yes, Captain," Rachel said, her voice neutral, almost dead sounding. She obviously was not happy with this errand. Pacino wondered if Bruno had convinced her to visit the sub or if Quinnivan or Seagraves had demanded the trip. "I've just lost a few months of my memory. There is the valid concern that what I do remember is complete enough to return me to submarine duty, or if I need to be retrained. Hopefully I haven't suffered so much brain trauma that I've lost what I know about operating a submarine."

"Good, good, well, you've come to the right place. *New Hampshire* is the best submarine in the fleet," Austin said, smiling. "With the finest officers, chiefs and enlisted personnel. Not like those blithering idiots on the *New England*."

"Hey now," Quinnivan said, striking a boxing pose. "Captain, Lieutenant Pacino here, you may have heard stories about him. Disregard them. They're all lies."

Austin laughed. "What, are you saying he *didn't* machine gun down a platoon of Russians about to take you hostage? Or launch a Russian supercavitating torpedo to sink a Yasen-M class Russian boat? After sneaking aboard an Iranian nuke sub and hijacking it?"

"And not only that," Quinnivan said, "he's the son of Admiral Pacino."

"Wow, that's your dad? He's running for president against Carlucci," Austin said.

"No, I don't think so," Pacino said.

"He just announced his candidacy this morning," Austin said, finding his tablet computer, putting on his reading glasses and handing the unit to Pacino. Pacino squinted at it and scanned it. Austin was right. Dad was running for president. Pacino blinked, feeling disoriented, like he'd stepped into an alternate universe, one where his father had become a politician and his woman had no idea who he was.

"Anyway, you guys go wherever you want," Austin said. "If you're going aft, get set up with the engineer first with dosimeters. Eng is in stateroom two. Come to the wardroom at 1145. We're having an amazing meal today."

"What's for lunch, Captain?" Quinnivan asked.

"Sliders," Austin grinned. "With steak fries and my favorite, cornbread. No one makes cornbread like my mess cooks. They make my old Aunt Martha from Waycross, Georgia, look like an amateur."

"We'll be there, Captain," Quinnivan said. "I'm hungry already." He looked at Pacino and Romanov. "Come on, let's go hang out in control first."

The three of them spent a half hour in the control room, which was cold and quiet, all the electronics shut down when in port, the air conditioning tuned for when every console would be operational and hot. Pacino kept stealing glances at Romanov to see if she'd recognize him, but she just stood there, silent as a statue. He'd moved close to her to get her to move to the space aft of the command console and he took the position to her immediate left, where they had stood for the early parts of Operation *Panther*, but still nothing seemed to penetrate the fog of her memory loss.

Eventually, the supply chief came for them, announcing that lunch would be dished up in the next few minutes. They all walked aft to the wardroom. Pacino stood behind the seat he used to sit in on the *Vermont*, on the outboard side, facing Rachel when she sat in the traditional seat of the navigator, to the right of the XO, who would sit to the right of the captain's seat at the end of the table. As tradition demanded, they stood behind their chairs until the captain's arrival.

The captain entered the room with Driscoll and they all took their seats. Pacino unfolded a guest linen napkin and placed it in his lap. A messcook came by and put two hamburger buns on each officer's plate, the buns full size. Submarine sliders weren't the same as what civilians called sliders. A submarine slider was simply a grilled hamburger, but so greasy that it would slide down one's throat. The onions, tomatoes, and pickles came next, then the hamburger patties.

"Where are your officers, Captain Austin?" Rachel asked.

"I told them to eat in the crew's mess today, Madam Romanov," Austin said. "I wanted to talk to you three without my junior officers misbehaving, those ill-mannered scurvy youngsters."

Quinnivan, Driscoll and Austin soon became deeply engaged in conversation. Old stories about former senior officers, former junior officers, their exploits on former submarines. The buzz of them talking soon faded in Pacino's mind, and his focus narrowed to Rachel, looking at her while trying to appear that he wasn't staring at her.

She slowly assembled a hamburger and took a bite. Pacino waited, hopeful, that the taste of the slider would bring her back, but there was still no recognition.

"So, Patch," Austin said, his voice penetrating Pacino's trance. "Or do you prefer 'Death Toll'? Tell us the whole story of Operation *Panther*. Now that's it's declassified, we want to hear it from you, not some stale patrol report—that's probably just filled with Bullfrog Quinnivan's lies."

Pacino put down his burger and looked to the end of the table toward the senior officers.

"Not much to tell," he said.

"Come on. Modesty is *not* allowed at my table," Austin said. "You've heard me bragging all morning about the USS *New Hampshire*. Let's give those fighter pilots a run for their money when it comes to cockiness. Tell the whole story, Patch. All the details. Leave out nothing."

"Well, it all started with us trying to hijack a Colombian narco-sub as a dry run," Pacino began. He told the tale of the narco-sub being run by AI, then the *Vermont's* sprint to AUTEC to get new orders from Admiral Catardi. To provoke Rachel, Pacino decided to throw in the story of how he'd returned from a night of liberty at AUTEC and his face was covered with Wanda River Styxx's makeup, earning him the embarrassing epithet 'Lipstick,' after which Quinnivan told how Pacino had looked walking into the wardroom that morning, Driscoll and Austin howling with laughter at the image of Pacino wearing what had resembled clown makeup.

Pacino mentioned that the incident had enraged Rachel and that all during the flank run to the Indian Ocean and the Arabian Sea, she'd given him the smoldering silent treatment. He told how they had arrived in the Gulf of Oman, slowed down and rigged for ultraquiet. Pacino took small bites of his lunch as Quinnivan would add color commentary or answer questions from Driscoll and Austin. Then Pacino told the long tale of how he'd been part of the boarding party that had taken the sub. He decided to say how, just before it was time to lock out of the *Vermont* and swim to the Iranian submarine, he'd called Rachel on the conn and apologized for the lipstick incident, and how that seemed to break her stony silence.

Engaged in his story, Pacino went on to describe what happened after they'd captured the Iranian submarine, but a few minutes into it, he was startled to see that Rachel had put down her hamburger and was staring intensely at him, her hands in her lap, and as Pacino reached the end of the story, he could see her eyes flooding with moisture. She wiped her face with her napkin, asked Austin if she could be excused, vaulted out of her chair and ran to the officers' bathroom at the end of the passageway.

Pacino was at the end of the story, so he asked if he could also be excused and left the wardroom and hurried to the officers' head to talk to Rachel. The door was shut and locked.

"Rachel? It's me, Anthony," he said, knocking. "Can you open the door? I need to talk to you."

He heard the door unlock and it opened slowly. Rachel's face was red, her cheeks were wet from tears and her mascara had run down her face. She pulled Pacino into the room, shut the door behind him, locked it and pulled him into a hug. He could feel sparks all along his body where her warm, soft body touched his. He hugged her so hard she pulled back to be able to breathe. She looked at him, her eyes liquid and threatening to leak tears again.

"Oh my God, Pacino," she said, her voice trembling. "I remember! I remember everything. I'm so sorry, I was gone somewhere, and then suddenly, it all came back! God, I miss you so much!"

Pacino looked at her. Her eyes moved from looking at his left eye to his right. He started to smile at her.

"What was it that brought you back?" he asked. "The slider?"

She shook her head, her blonde hair falling into her face for a moment before she shook her hair back.

"It was your voice. Or your story. Or both. You put me right back in that control room at the moment you apologized to me, and right then, everything just returned."

Pacino breathed a sigh of relief and hugged her tight again.

"Pacino?" she said, almost in a little girl's voice.

"Yes, Rachel?"

"You know I love you, don't you?"

He pulled back and grinned at her. "Actually, no," he said. "I don't. Why don't you tell me all about it?"

He felt the impact of her punching his arm in mock anger and he looked at her and laughed.

"Ow," he said. "But you already know I love *you*."

"I want to thank you, Pacino."

"For what?" he asked.

"For fighting so hard to bring my memory back. It was *your* idea to get me on another sub, wasn't it?"

"Yeah. I was upset when you said you didn't want the tour."

"Seagraves gave me a direct order," she said. "You must have called him."

Pacino shook his head. "I didn't have a chance to bring it up to him. I guess he just decided on his own. You know, great minds think alike." He looked at the door. "So what happens now?"

"Now," Rachel said, "we try to act professional and finish lunch, then go back to the *New England* admin building and finish the work day."

"And then?"

"And then, you're taking me to the Snake Ranch and moving your stuff into my master bedroom. And after that? You're going to make me glad I'm a woman. Preferably, twice."

"I can do that," Pacino grinned. "I can definitely do that."

———————————

The officers and chief petty officers of the submarine *New England* were gathered on the pier, watching the USS *Hyman G. Rickover* coast to a halt in the Elizabeth River Reach. Two tugboats spun her around so her bow was facing outward, then backed her into the slip so she could tie up, port-side-to.

Once she was tied up, the watchstanders in their informal two-piece working uniforms disappeared below, replaced by sailors wearing dress blues, the crackerjack uniforms made famous by recruiting posters and World War II movies.

The first body bag was lifted out of the hull. The topside sailors put it on a waiting stretcher, covered it with an American flag, and slowly walked it off the deck, up the slope of the gangway and into a waiting black truck. The *New England*'s officers and chiefs stood at attention, and as the body went by, the captain called for them to render a hand salute, and all of them rigidly saluted until the body was placed in the truck. When the second body came out, the ritual was repeated, until all twenty-four of the dead were placed in the back of the truck.

After the truck drove off, the group on the pier broke up. Anthony Pacino walked down the pier toward officers' parking, Rachel Romanov by his side.

"It's hard to believe Styxx and Kelly are gone," she said. "And Easy Eisy, and Gangbanger." She sniffed and pulled out a tissue and wiped her eyes and blew her nose.

"And the COB," Pacino said. "And Gory Goreliki and K-Squared Kim from the *Panther* op. And Snowman Mercer, who first found the *Panther*. And we lost our new nub, Long Hull Cooper. Goddamned bad day at sea."

Romanov sighed. "Let's get back to the Snake Ranch and do something fun. Grill out some steaks, maybe. I want a happy memory to replace this one."

"XO made this a long weekend for us all," Pacino said. "We have no work duties until the funeral on Tuesday. We'll have to roll out super early that day. Rush hour traffic out of Norfolk and on the way to D.C. will be murderous."

"Let's find a five-star hotel in D.C. and stay over Monday night," Rachel said. She smiled at Pacino as he opened the Corvette's door for her. "We'll stay in bed and have scrumptious room service."

"And some scrumptious *other* things?" Pacino smirked at her as he started the car, the supercharger's high-pitched whine and the deep throbbing notes of the powerful engine making him feel better already.

"Maybe," she said, jutting out her lower lip as if considering the idea, then shrugging. "Depends on my mood."

"Oh, no problem. I can get you in the mood in two minutes," Pacino said, grinning at her.

"You're just lucky you're with a hot-blooded girl, Pacino," she said. "I'm *always* in the mood when you're around. With the exception of this hour, today."

"Yeah," Pacino said solemnly. "And the entire time that you had amnesia. It was almost like you were robotic, like your soul wasn't in your body. I gotta tell ya, it was unnerving."

"It felt like a walking nightmare to me," she said. "One second it was six months ago, then suddenly I'm in a hospital room with Bruno, painful bandaged burns on my legs and abdomen, with Bruno telling me we were divorced, and that I had a new boyfriend and that the boyfriend was this hot-running hero-slash-pirate from an operation where *Vermont* stole an Iranian submarine. Can you imagine? The U.S. Navy just walking up and stealing the submarine of another sovereign nation? And now I have a *boyfriend?* And then I meet you, and you're all handsome and swashbuckling, enough to make a poor girl swoon, but I was *sure* I had to stay away from you."

"Why?"

"I didn't know you. For all I knew, the new Rachel might not even *like* you."

"Rachel Romanov not liking me?" Pacino laughed. "Impossible. And did you really think I was, quote, swashbuckling, unquote?"

"You're a real-life pirate, Pacino," she said, looking out the window at the industrial side of Norfolk giving way to the bayside high-priced real estate, then to the suburbs of Virginia Beach. "Pacino?" she asked. He noticed that since she came back from her amnesia, she no longer called him 'Anthony' or 'Patch.' Just 'Pacino.' He liked it, he thought. No one else addressed him that way. "Where do you think our dead shipmates are right now?"

"Well, if Tiny Tim Fishman were here, he'd say they all went to the afterlife to contemplate what their lives would have been like had they made different decisions. In some of the multiple universes Fishman believes in, many of them are still alive, so I imagine they watch themselves living out those lives in real time. In essence, they would be haunting themselves."

"Do you believe all that?"

Pacino shrugged. "In my near-death experience, I only made it into the tunnel, not all the way to the afterlife. But before the tunnel vacuumed me into it, I had the thought that I could just stick around earth and watch things. Maybe haunt people. If that's true, I think the *New Jersey* dead are probably still with us, maybe even sitting in this car, listening to us talk. I think they'll attend the funeral Tuesday. Then they'll feel free to leave and go on to the next world."

"You know, that's kind of freaky, the idea of them in this tiny car with us."

"We have nothing but fond memories of them," Pacino said. "I'm sure they find that comforting. I just hope they withdraw when you and I are, you know, in a 'tactical situation.'"

"Oh man, Pacino, now I'm definitely *not* in the mood."

Later, much later, the day would just be a blur of intense images in Pacino's memory.

The mournful sound of a bugle in the crisp, clean, sunny autumn morning.

The clop of hoofbeats of the horses carrying the twenty-four caissons to the twenty-four freshly dug graves.

The caskets covered with bright American flags.

The color guard firing off three shots for each deceased person.

The solemn announcement of each person's name, rank and job function on the USS *New Jersey*.

The chaplain, standing in the middle of the two dozen graves, an open Bible in his hands, reading a passage from the Old Testament—

The righteous perish and no one takes it to heart;
The devout are taken away, and no one understands
That the righteous are taken away to be spared from evil.
Those who walk uprightly enter into peace.
They find rest as they lie in death.

The inconsolable wives, husbands, and children, all of them crying.

530

The survivors saluting on cue, all of them dressed in service dress blues with full medals and white gloves.

The honor guard taking American flags off coffins, folding them into triangles and presenting them to widows and widowers, children or parents, or just close friends.

The chaplain's concluding prayer.

The bugle call at the end of the ceremony.

Pacino's eyes teared up as he and Rachel Romanov walked back to his car. He sniffed and looked at Rachel, who looked back adoringly at him.

32

"*Ahoy there!* Attention all hands. Listen up," XO Quinnivan shouted, "all you rowdy, misfit, criminal pirates, we have a lot to go over, so shut the fook up, yeah?" Quinnivan's brogue was more pronounced than normal, a sure sign he'd been drinking.

The officers and some of the chiefs of the USS *New England* stood or sat in the great room of the Snake Ranch, the Virginia Beach rental house occupied by Pacino, Romanov, Dankleff and Vevera. With Quinnivan's upcoming relocation back to the UK, his house was a wreck from packing. He'd donated his gigantic television, the Sony "Wall," to the Snake Ranch as a parting gift. Dankleff and Vevera had spent the entire day getting the monstrous TV set up.

Pacino looked around, noting half a dozen new faces. The replacements for the dead officers, he thought. He took a sip of the scotch Quinnivan had brought over, the Irishman showing up with two plastic milk crates full of alcohol that he didn't want to move back to England. After emptying one of the crates, he now stood on top of it to address the crowded room.

Pacino leaned over and whispered to Rachel, "you think the new captain is here?"

"He could only be that older guy standing next to Seagraves."

"Yeah. You're probably right."

"Okay, so first off," Quinnivan said, "I want to introduce one of Captain Seagraves' buddies, one Commander Mikey 'Headlock' 'Side-Eye' Cydice from Pearl Harbor. He's got temporary duty here at ComSubCom, so I brought him over to see if he could rent the spare room at the Snake Ranch for the next month. Mikey, say a few words to this crowd. Just speak slowly, they're all mentally challenged."

Commander Cydice laughed as he stepped up on top of Quinnivan's milk crate. He was a few inches taller than Quinnivan but several inches shorter than Seagraves. He was of a slight build, a runner perhaps. His black hair was short on the sides, longer on top. He had pronounced cheekbones and a strong jawline. He wore a gray button-down shirt under a black sportscoat over black jeans, with black harness boots. He could almost be a biker, Pacino thought, if he traded out his jacket to a leather vest.

"Thank you, Bullfrog," Cydice said, his voice deep and sonorous. "And thank you all for allowing me to attend your magnificent party. As Bullfrog says, Scotch Seagraves and I go way back. We were roommates at the Academy and I was constantly bailing him out of trouble. I was his best man back in the day." He looked at Seagraves solemnly. "I was sad to hear, Scotch. Anyway, I have a month here before I go back to Pearl Harbor. Until recently, I was the executive officer of the Virginia-class battle-E-winning boat USS *Mississippi*, SSN-782. I have to say, with all the chatter about what's going on with Red and White China reuniting, it looks like the Pacific theater is going to heat up even more than it is now. You junior officers, I recommend you blow off this sissy east coast shit and come out west, because nothing ever happens on the Atlantic side—you Atlantic guys are a bunch of pussies on vacation compared to us Pacific submariners."

The room booed the commander, a few empty cups flying his way, which he gleefully ducked.

"I'm just kidding, you guys know that. After your last hairy mission, we all know you did a great job. I do have a message for you from ComSubCom. Admiral Stiletto Patton sends his regards and respectfully requests that you refrain from *destroying* any more of his submarines."

"You ever wonder how it would turn out if we did a sub-*versus*-sub exercise, us against a Pac Fleet boat?" Pacino said to Rachel. "We could put money on the outcome."

"Or a couple of milk crates of alcohol," she said.

"Back to you, Commander Quinnivan," Cydice said. "But you Snake Ranch guys, what do you say? Can I bunk in with you pirates?"

"You have to buy all the beer for that month!" Vevera shouted.

Cydice grinned. "Done!"

"Okay, next," Quinnivan announced. "We all know our beloved commanding officer is moving on to bigger and better things, but we're all fortunate that he will still be local. Captain, can you tell us what's in your future?"

Seagraves nodded and stepped up on the milk crate. "Well, everyone, first, tonight I will have the honor of drinking my eagles." He was referring to the time-honored and strictly prohibited practice of an officer dropping new collar devices in a tall glass of whiskey and drinking his way down to the emblems. That was how the whole lipstick incident had happened, Pacino thought, when he drank down to his lieutenant bars. And by "eagles," it meant Commander Seagraves was being promoted from the rank of commander to the rank of captain. "I'd like Commander Quinnivan and Commander Cydice to pin them on me now, so I can unpin them, put them into the whiskey, and get started."

The junior officers applauded. "Congratulations, Skipper," Romanov shouted.

"Just don't fuck up, Scotch," Cydice said to Seagraves, smiling. Cydice and Quinnivan pinned eagle captain emblems on Seagraves shirt and handed him a nearly full tumbler of bourbon. Seagraves removed the eagles and dropped them into the whiskey. He took a sip, then looked up at the crowd.

"There's more news, ladies and gents," he said. "My new orders call for me to report as the new commodore of Squadron Six."

"Nice," Lewinsky said. "You'll still be the boss. Make sure the *New England* gets the best of squadron resources!" Navigator

Lewinsky stood next to his clingy girlfriend, Redhead, who had her arms wrapped around his arm as if he'd wander off. The woman was a caricature of a crooning nightclub singer, wearing a tight red pencil skirt, slit up the sides showing her long legs, the dress clinging to her narrow waist, then expanding greatly in an attempt to restrain her melon-sized round breasts, the dress' neckline plunging daringly between them. Her copper auburn hair cascaded in gentle curls down to her nipples.

"What is it with that goddamned Redhead," Rachel commented quietly to Pacino, her tone acid.

"She's like a fourteen-year-old boy's fantasy," Pacino whispered. "Just like Lewinsky's car. I mean, really, who the hell drives a V-12 Ferrari?"

Rachel laughed. "Every one of you boys just wishes you could wake up and be Elvis Lewinsky."

"No way," Pacino said. "I've heard his midrats stories of how crazy Redhead is. I half expected Elvis to show up with a black eye." He looked at Romanov. "Makes me feel lucky I know you."

She smirked. "You *are* lucky. Make sure you treat me right."

"Not to worry, Elvis," Seagraves said. "I'll make sure the USS *New England* gets the best of the best. Just try to keep an eye on Pacino, that he doesn't set it on fire."

"Oh hell," Pacino said. "I was hoping people would forget that."

"So, XO," Seagraves said to Quinnivan while stepping down from the crate, "why don't you tell the room what your next assignment is?"

"Wait a minute, Skipper," Lewinsky said. "Who is going to be the new captain?"

Seagraves shrugged. "A first round draft pick to be named later. Sometime before *New England* leaves the drydock. Until then, the new XO will be acting captain. And don't ask who the new XO is yet. We'll have that info for you in a minute. So, Commander Quinnivan, your next assignment?" Seagraves prompted.

Quinnivan took his spot on the crate and smiled. "Well, first I'm going to do some house hunting. Shawna over there, say hello, babe." His wife smiled and waved. "My wife is impossible to please when it comes to houses, so that phase could take a while. I'm going to the next Perisher course, which is what you lads and lassies would call Prospective Commanding Officer School. No guarantee that I'll pass, but if I do, I'll be taking command of the Astute-class submarine S120 *Ambush*. See, the Brits know how to name a submarine, yeah? None of this sissy *New England* crap. New England, isn't that a football team that wanted more market share than just Boston?"

"He makes a good point," Pacino said.

"Now I'd like to introduce a new officer reportin' aboard, Lieutenant Commander Christopher Prettyboy Byrehind, who will be our new chief engineer. Step on up here, Eng," Quinnivan said.

Byrehind was short with a mop of fine dirty blonde hair and a baby face, looking far too young to be a department head. He smiled at the crowd.

"Good to be aboard your—our—fine submarine," he said, smiling. "I look forward to getting to know all of you," he said.

"Tell the crowd something about yourself, lad, yeah?" Quinnivan said.

"Well, like Commander Cydice over there, I'm also from Pearl Harbor, from the USS *Texas*, where I was main propulsion assistant. Where's my MPA in this crowd?"

"That would be me!" Vevera shouted from the rear of the room.

"What's his name?" he asked Quinnivan.

"That there be Squirt Gun Vevera."

"Ah, yes, the one for whom Commander Cydice has to buy all that beer. Squirt Gun—I'm sure your handle has a story behind it?"

Vevera blushed. Quinnivan said something in Byrehind's ear, who grinned and laughed.

"Oh, okay, the XO informs me that the story is unsuitable for mixed company. My callsign, Prettyboy, was given to me by my older brother when I was three and it stuck hard. He's pushing fighter jets off the USS *Ronald Reagan* somewhere. Anyway, I went to Dartmouth and Northwestern for physics, I'm married to lovely

Linda—where are you, Linda? There she is, wave to the boys and girls, honey. We have two kids and I plan to spend long hours on the boat to keep away from them, they are absolute terrors. Linda's genes, you know. Anyway, that's about it."

"Is that true, Linda?" Quinnivan asked.

A female voice from the rear answered. "It's a lie, XO," she said, smiling. "Those boys are just Prettyboy clones. There's nothing of me in them at all."

"For our next guest," Quinnivan said, "I'd like to have our new weapons officer step up."

A tall, slender woman with streaky blonde hair stepped up to the crate. She was pretty, wearing light makeup, with a long-sleeved silk blouse and bell-bottom jeans, which had inexplicably come back into fashion.

"I'm Lieutenant Commander Alexis D'Assault. My callsign? The original one was 'Allen Wrench,' since I was good at working on engines."

"You'll enjoy working with Pacino, then," Quinnivan said, pointing to Pacino. "That young man replaced a Corvette engine and transmission himself, put in computer control and a supercharger. How many horses does that beast have, Patch?"

"Six hundred and forty," Pacino called. "But who's counting?"

"But there's a more recent callsign, isn't there, Madam Weapons Officer?" Quinnivan said, prompting her.

She sighed and smiled, her face flushing red. "I graduated from Kings Point, the Merchant Marine Academy, and I was a merchant marine sailor, third mate on a container ship and in the Navy reserve. We were off Yemen when a fairly large pirate raider boat came out of nowhere and zoomed up and started tossing grappling hooks up to the deck. I had one of the AR-15 rifles. They were really just for show and the captain wanted us to keep them unloaded and just wave them at any pirates, like that would do anything. I was about to do some recreational shooting, but when I saw the pirates, I just started blasting. Four of the raiders died, four more were wounded, and we had to call a medical helicopter. And yes, that incident got me fired. And it earned me the other callsign, 'Pirate Killer Girl.' Thank God for the Navy," she said. "I doubt I would get hired anywhere, but my dad knew Admiral Patton and made a phone call, and here I am."

"Dear God," Romanov said. "Now the boat has pirates *and* a pirate killer girl. You'd better watch out for her. Do you think she's pretty?"

Pacino stared at Romanov. "All women are ugly compared to *you*, Silky," he said, deadpan, trying not to smile.

"I'd punch you right now if we were alone," she growled. "Tell me the truth."

"Yeah, she's a cute-ass babe," Pacino said. "But Lewinsky should watch out. Redhead will claw his eyes out if he looks at her twice."

"Well, Pirate Killer Girl," Quinnivan said, "there are three no-shit *actual* pirates in this crowd. You should have fun comparing notes. One of them, Mr. Pacino—that lad over there—he's as trigger-happy as you are. You should all get along famously. Thank you, Madam Weps. Now, Mr. Elvis Lewinsky, come on up here." Lewinsky stepped to the front of the room. "Elvis only found this out an hour ago. He's leaving the *New England* and taking over as the XO of the USS *Montana*, also in Squadron Six."

"Congrats, Elvis!" Pacino shouted. The crowd clapped and shot sarcastic remarks at the former navigator.

"Don't be strangers, you guys," Lewinsky said. "Come over to my boat for lunch whenever you want."

"Thank you, Elvis, and now the junior officers. You three get up here."

A tall, slim blonde kid walked up, a stormy look on his face. The second officer was a short, well-built black man. The third was a petite blonde woman with pale skin and hair so fine it looked like a comb would fall through it.

"This tall guy is Ensign Adam 'Cool Hand' Farina. Say a few words for us, Cool Hand."

"Hi everyone," the youth said in a baritone voice, obviously not happy to be speaking publicly. "I was a mechanical engineer out of the University of Vermont. I played baseball. I almost flunked out of nuclear power school, a little bit of trouble with a girlfriend, so I'm trying to make a comeback. I have to tell you, I had to fight to get assigned to this crew. I asked the recruiter for the *New England* specifically, and there was a waiting list, but I got lucky. So it's good to be here."

"Mr. Cool Hand here will be the new communications officer, yeah?" Quinnivan said. "Welcome to the *New England*, lad. Next is Ensign Rupert 'Three Round' Harrington. What say you, Three Round?"

"Hi folks," Harrington said in a gentle, almost feminine soprano voice. "I'm from Louisiana and an electrical engineer from Tulane and Georgia Tech. I boxed in college and had some luck in the third round, so that explains the name. Now I'm into mixed martial arts."

"Mr. Three Round will be our new supply officer," Quinnivan said. "So, Three Round, do you have any experience in felony grand larceny?"

Harrington laughed. "No, sir, sorry."

"Not to worry, lad, we'll teach you. You'll be stealin' parts by dark o'night from the supply depot in no time. And now for our third J.O., Ensign Regina 'Suction Cup' Ingersol. How about sayin' a few words for us, yeah?"

"Hello," Ingersol said, blushing. "I'm from California and a math and physics major from Stanford, master's in political science from Berkeley."

"She almost looks like an albino," Rachel whispered to Pacino.

"Nah, she's just fair."

"Do you think *she's* pretty?"

"Oh my God, would you stop?"

"Poly sci, eh?" Quinnivan said. "Maybe Pacino's da' could use ya. He's runnin' for president, don't ya know? And your callsign?"

She blushed deeper. "Also not suitable for mixed company," she said. "I run marathons and I do ballet. At least I did. I have a knee injury, so I'm nursing it for a few months."

"Madam Ingersol will be our reactor controls division officer. So, okay then, thank you, you new nubs. I want you all qualified in ten months," Quinnivan said. "Or at least the new XO will, maybe even sooner."

"Who *is* the new XO?" Pacino shouted.

"I'm glad you asked that question," Quinnivan said, winking at Seagraves. "Captain?"

Seagraves took the post on the milk crate. "We have an unusual situation," he began. "First of all, we're replacing three officers with no turnover from the previous holders of each position due to their deaths. We have a gapped position of commanding officer with the new XO becoming acting captain. So, with all the turnover and lack of continuity of leadership, ComSubCom had to make some tough decisions. Either to delay my departure—and that of Commander Quinnivan—or propose a flea-flicker play. So here's the deal, guys. You all already know and love your new XO and acting captain. Could I have Lieutenant Commander Rachel Silky Romanov step up to the front of the room?"

Romanov's jaw dropped. "Are you fucking kidding me?" she hissed to Pacino. The room broke out in applause and cheers, Pacino clapping, smiling at her, and patting her on the back. Romanov went to the front of the room and smiled back at the crowd.

"You know," she said, "I think my amnesia is back. Who the hell are all you people and why are you in my house?"

"Speech!" Quinnivan said, clapping.

"What do I say," Romanov began. "Well, Captain and XO, it's an honor to be named to this position. I won't let you down."

"We know," Seagraves said, shaking Romanov's hand, then Quinnivan shook her hand and clapped her on the shoulder.

"Can I ask," Romanov said. "If I'm XO—and acting captain—who is the navigator?"

"Ah," Quinnivan said, "that's the other part of the flea-flicker." He looked at Seagraves. "Should I tell him?"

"I'll tell him," Seagraves said. "Lieutenant Pacino, come on up. You are the new navigator of the USS *New England*."

Pacino stared. The crowd grabbed him and pulled him to the front of the room. "Thanks, Captain, XO," he said.

"This will extend your tour on the submarine, Patch," Seagraves said. "It's an extra year. But somehow I think you'll be okay with that."

"I'm okay with that, Skipper," Pacino said, barely believing how many things had changed in the hour of the party.

"Before we get to the important part of the day, the partying," Seagraves said, "I have one final surprise."

The room grew suddenly quiet.

"Some of you may not know this, but the secretary of the Navy, Jeremy Shingles, was at grad school at Yale and was friends and roommates with a man named Philip Dean Sievers III. Does anyone here know who Sievers is?"

The silence in the room continued.

"Well, I'll tell you who Philip Dean Sievers III is," Seagraves continued. "He's the governor of the great state of Vermont."

"Oh my God," Rachel whispered to Pacino. "They're renaming the boat."

"There was a phone call," Seagraves continued, "and, reportedly, a box of cigars and a case of whisky changed hands, and you've all guessed it. Now hull number SSN-792 will be renamed the USS *Vermont*. The re-christening ceremony is next week. Get your dress blues cleaned and pressed, gang. And that's all I have. Now, let's get this party started."

Captain Seagraves and Commanders Quinnivan and Cydice stood on the back yard deck of the Snake Ranch at sunset, all of them leaning against the deck railing and staring at the pink sky.

"Red sky at night," Quinnivan said. "Sailor's delight. A good omen, yeah?"

Quinnivan passed out cigars, a cutter, and a torch, and they all lit up and blew smoke into the sky for a long moment.

"So, Mikey," Seagraves said to Commander Cydice. "You didn't want us to disclose to the boys and girls that you're nominated to be the *Vermont*'s new commanding officer. Why is that?"

Cydice blew out a cloud of smoke and looked at Seagraves. "It's not official until I pass Prospective Commanding Officer School, which is not a given, since the failure rate is, what, thirty percent? And Admiral Patton at SubCom has been ominously quiet about confirming the assignment. There was a slight incident in Hawaii I need to explain away. So I don't want to jinx it."

"Incident?" Seagraves asked.

Cydice nodded. "I punched out the squadron engineer. While I was submerged, he was diddling my wife and posting sex videos on the internet with him and her in action."

Seagraves shook his head in shock and sympathy. "Man, I would have killed that guy. What's going to happen to him?"

"He's already been given a dishonorable discharge. Fitting, actually, for all his dishonorable discharging into my wife. My soon-to-be ex-wife."

"I'm sorry to hear, Mikey."

"Yeah."

The three men were silent for a moment.

Quinnivan blew a smoke ring and looked at Cydice. "So anyway, in the meantime, you're playin' undercover boss at the Snake Ranch, peekin' in on our scurvy junior officer pirates, yeah?"

Cydice nodded. "I need to wait here for interviews about the thing. I may as well wait while drinking beers with the boys. I have a feeling they'll cheer me up."

"Well," Quinnivan laughed. "Just don't be doin' anything those cutthroats can blackmail ye with, yeah? That would make for a very long tour once Admiral Patton comes to his senses and gives you the *Vermont*."

Cydice grinned. "Me? I'm a Boy Scout, Bullfrog."

———

Lieutenant Anthony Pacino stopped on the way to the parking lot to lean over the observation platform overlooking Graving Dock

Number One. He was usually alone when he visited the platform, but this afternoon, the tall, gaunt figure of Ensign Adam Cool Hand Farina was there, looking at the submarine. The sounds from the dock, though muted by distance, were still loud. Grinding, rail mounted cranes' backing alarms, the shouts of shipyard workers.

Pacino walked up next to Farina and leaned on the rail. For a moment Pacino didn't say anything. Then he spoke first.

"Fancy meeting you here," he said.

Farina snickered. "We've got to stop meeting like this. People will talk."

Pacino smiled. "You know, Cool Hand, I'm surprised you asked to join this crew."

"You are? Why? This is the hottest-running submarine in the fleet."

"No, it's not," Pacino said, his voice solemn. "We've lost the captain. We lost the XO. The navigator's gone. The engineer is dead. The weapons officer is dead. The communicator is dead. Supply officer? Dead. Reactor controls officer? Dead. So are the COB, the E-div chief, radio chief, AI chief and A-gang chief. And a dozen more. The sub we sailed lies on the bottom of the Arctic Ocean. Did you notice that NavPersCom *didn't* assign a commanding officer to this boat? That's because nobody wants the fuckin' job. And *you*, after your trouble at nuke school? You got assigned here, not because you fought to get the billet, but because this is a hardship tour. A punishment tour. And meanwhile, the boat is being Frankensteined together from the halves of two other boats, and God knows if that will work, and the shipyard's rushing it, trying to beat an arbitrary deadline thought up by a pissed-off admiral, and shipyard mistakes cause subs to sink. Don't believe me, ask our good friends on the *Thresher*. Not to mention, it'll be months before this thing gets its hull wet. And all that time will be lost to you for the purpose of qualification progress. It would have been better if you had requested an operating boat where you could work on quals and stand watches instead of waiting here while our boat sits high and dry on the drydock blocks."

Farina looked at Pacino, the color draining from his face. "I'd always heard you were an optimist. That's a pretty downer view of things."

"A military funeral for two dozen of your friends will do that to you. That's another thing. Despite all the levity at the Snake Ranch party, the crew from the old wardroom, before you new guys showed up, all feel the same. The loss. The sadness. The hopelessness of it all. The dead all died for a cause, I suppose. The mission got accomplished, but not by *us*. Sure, we tossed weapons at the bad guys, but in the end, those Poseidons were destroyed by the Russians themselves, and they sank themselves with their own goddamned nuclear-tipped torpedo. We were just along for the ride."

"I know I'm just a non-qual nub," Farina said. "But I see it differently. After all, there's Silky Romanov. Squirt Gun Vevera. U-Boat Dankleff. Boozy Varney. And *you*. The revered-and-feared Death Toll Pacino. You guys are all storied heroes. Combat tested bad-asses. Real life pirates. You've all sailed into harm's way and fired torpedoes in anger. You've all gotten medals for valor that the rest of the Navy just dreams of. You? The silver star, second award. The goddamned Navy Cross? And one of my nuke school buddies sent me a picture of the brass plaque in the Naval Academy's Memorial Hall on the wall right next to your father's plaque. It reads, 'If I have to die on this mission, I intend to die with an empty torpedo room.' Lieutenant Anthony Pacino, USS *Vermont*, Operation *Panther*. So, in what universe would I *not* want to join this crew?"

Pacino smiled, perhaps for the first time that day. "You know, for a non-qual air-breathing puke, you make a good point. Tell you what. Monday, you and I will walk over to the *New Hampshire* at Squadron Six and I'll give you a sonar walkthrough. I'll ask their skipper, Gray Wolf Austin, if he can take you for a few weeks or a month on their next op so you can get some sea time under your belt. And I'll threaten his life if he tries to steal you. Then XO and the yeoman will get temporary duty orders cut for you. You'll come back in a couple months halfway to your dolphins."

"You'd do that for me?" Farina looked at Pacino in gratitude. "Thank you, Patch."

"Any time, Cool Hand. Have a good weekend. Oh, and Cool Hand? Text the photo of that plaque to me. I want to send it to my dad."

Pacino walked slowly to his car, hearing his own words again in his mind that he'd said to Farina. He was reminded of his father, who used to get in dark moods, sitting in his office with the lights out, staring into space, drinking alone, especially after the sinking of the cruise ship. It could take the old man a year to snap out of a funk, Pacino thought. He hoped this heavy hopeless feeling wouldn't last a goddamned year.

He got to the car, tossed his bag in the back, and moved slowly through the lot and wheeled the car to the door of the admin building, where an annoyed Lieutenant Commander Rachel Romanov waited for him. He rolled down the window.

"Get in, loser," he said, grinning in spite of his mood. "We're going to Annapolis."

"Where have you been?" she said. "I've been out here waiting for you for ten minutes."

"I stopped to yell at one of our new nubs. Cool Hand Farina."

"What do you think of him?" she asked, tossing a bag in the back, shutting the passenger door and strapping in.

Pacino tilted his head, considering his answer. "I think we can make him into a submariner."

He drove in silence until they'd left the military complex and headed through Norfolk toward the Chesapeake Bay Bridge, Pacino figuring that a transit up the eastern shore would be faster than battling I-64 traffic toward D.C.

"You're awfully quiet, Pacino," Rachel said.

"Yeah," he said dejectedly. "I'm sad. All the loss just sort of hit me all at once. I think I was in shock until now."

"Pull over here at the diner," she told him.

"You already changed out of your uniform," he said. "Did you want me to change?"

"That's not why I asked," she said. "Park way over there, where the parking lot is deserted. Underneath the tree."

"Yes, ma'am," Pacino said, wheeling the Corvette where she'd pointed.

"Cut the engine and stay there." She got out of the car and walked around to his side and opened his door. Carefully, she climbed on top of him, straddling him in the close confines of the cockpit, then shut the door.

"What are you doing?" Pacino asked.

She wrapped her arms around his neck, came close, and kissed him, the kiss starting slow but building in passion. He could feel one of her soft hands stroking his face, the other's fingers going through his hair and he got an electric charge from it, and in spite of his mood, he could feel himself getting aroused. Finally, as Rachel was starting to disconnect from the kiss, the Corvette's horn honked, loud and long.

"Oh my God," she said, blushing in embarrassment. "Did my fat ass just honk your horn?"

Pacino laughed. "No, your slender, shapely, feminine ass just honked my horn. And I think you honked my horn metaphorically as well."

"Good," she smiled. "Now we can go."

"You're just going to start my engine and leave me hot and bothered?"

"Yup," she said, smirking. "Why don't you go inside the diner and change? I'll wait here." She climbed out of the car, got back in the passenger side, pulled her tablet computer from her bag, and switched it on.

Pacino could feel a bounce in his step as he walked toward the diner with his go-bag. Somehow, Rachel had managed to change his mood in just minutes. There was no doubt. She was definitely a keeper.

———————

Unlike the last time Pacino approached his father's Annapolis house, there was a security fence erected at the entrance to the long driveway, the part of the yard both inside and outside the fence acting as parking lots. A small metal security building had been placed to the left of the new gate, the roof of it sprouting multiple dish antennae. A man in a black suit, white shirt, and black tie, wearing dark shades, came up to the car. He wore a comm unit in his ear, the coiled wire from it snaking into his shirt collar. He looked like a caricature of a Secret Service agent.

"May I help you, sir?" he said formally.

"I'm Lieutenant Pacino," Pacino said, handing the agent his military ID, then passing him Rachel's. "That's Lieutenant Commander Romanov. We're here to see Admiral Pacino. My dad."

The agent scowled at the identifications, then went into the security building. He was still frowning as he came out, then handed Pacino the military IDs.

"Have a nice visit, Lieutenant," he said. "You can drive up to the front door, but leave your keys with an agent there. He'll park your car and another one will go through your things before you enter the house."

Pacino wheeled the car to the house, left the engine running, got his bags and walked to the front door with Rachel. A Secret Service agent got in the Corvette and drove it back to the security building. A second asked him to turn over his bags for a search, then patted Pacino down. A female agent did the same to Rachel. Finally the unsmiling agents waved them into the house, where yet another agent waited inside.

Pacino could see into the great room on the main floor, where what seemed like thirty people in suits were gathered around Admiral Pacino, a spirited debate going on there.

"You can wait in the admiral's office," the inside door agent said.

Pacino took Rachel to his father's office, a large space with heavy wood furniture and leather seating gathered around a huge stone fireplace. The walls were covered with painted scenes of the older Pacino's submarine commands, a painting of the old man as a youth standing by his father in front of the submarine *Stingray*. The corners of the room were taken up with glass encased submarine models.

The first *Devilfish*, the *Seawolf*, the SSNX. There were other photos on the bookshelves, showing Michael Pacino shaking the hands of several presidents. A large oil painting of his father's mentor, Admiral Dick Donchez. Anthony Pacino's Academy graduation photo had a central place of honor, as did a large framed photo of Anthony as a child standing next to his father in front of the hull of the *Seawolf*.

"This is the ultimate man-cave," Rachel said. "It's like a shrine to the submarine force. And to you. Not a single photo of a woman in here."

Pacino shrugged. "Two divorces and one wife lost to a drunk driver," Pacino said. "I think my dad is done with romance."

"I heard he has been seen forehead-to-forehead with that pretty head of the CIA," Romanov said.

Admiral Michael Pacino picked that moment to enter the office, and Rachel blushed crimson.

"Dad!" Pacino said. "What's going on out there?"

"Hi, Son." Michael Pacino hugged Anthony, then looked at Rachel. He smiled and shook her hand. "I'm glad to meet you, Rachel. And I'm particularly pleased you healed from that drydock incident. And that you're friends with my boy. Maybe you can keep him out of trouble."

She smiled back. "I doubt even I can keep him out of trouble, sir. Anthony talks about you every chance he can get," she said. "I feel like I know your whole life story."

The elder Pacino smiled and said, "He doesn't know the classified parts."

"So Dad, how is your campaign going? And who are all those people?"

The admiral rolled his eyes. "Advisors. Press consultants. Representatives of big donors. It's a circus."

"Part of that seven billion dollars, right, Dad?"

"Exactly. Look, this thing has another hour to go, and my lead press consultant wants to talk to you. Rachel can come out and see the craziness with me in the den."

"Your guy wants to talk? To me? Why?"

"You're a big press draw, Anthony. You seem to make the news as often as I do. Reporters, bloggers, and podcasters will want to interview you. And it matters not just what you'll say, but how you'll say it."

"Fine," Anthony said. "Bring him in."

"Her," the admiral said. "Diane Palmer." He opened the door a crack and said something to the agent waiting outside the door.

A thirty-something-year-old woman walked in, so slender her collarbones jutted out. Maybe she was anorexic, Anthony thought. Her hair was a lush mop of blonde curling locks which she swept off her shoulder. She wore a silk beige suit and carried a tablet computer. She smiled at Anthony and Rachel. Introductions over, the admiral and Rachel left and Anthony sat on a club chair opposite the press consultant.

"Anthony, I'll get right to business," she said, her tablet computer in her lap. "About a hundred different people will be asking to interview you. I want to conduct a mock interview and ask the hard questions they'll throw at you and see how you'll answer."

"You're prepping me?"

"No. At least, not yet. I'll listen to your answers first and see what I think. Let's start with a softball. Tell me about yourself."

"I don't really like talking about myself," Pacino said, frowning.

"Look, that question will come at you a few times. Once you answer it, you can go on to other things. Go ahead and try. Hit the high points."

Anthony took a breath and started, mentioning his childhood with his father, the Naval Academy, his disastrous midshipman cruise on the ill-fated *Piranha*, then grad school, his assignment to the *Vermont*, and the mission of Operation *Panther*, then the *New Jersey* and Operation *Poseidon*. When he finished, Palmer was frowning at him.

"No," she said. "*No*. Not like that. You spoke as if all that happened to someone else. It's too deadpan. And there's none of the drama. You didn't even mention what you did to win the *Panther* operation or that you rescued the Russians. We need the kind of details that will make people like you."

"Why?" Pacino said. "I don't give a damn if people like me."

"It's important to your father's campaign."

"*He's* running for president. Not me."

The admiral opened the door and walked in with Rachel. He grinned. "I was listening for a bit of that. I told you exactly how he'd be, Diane."

Palmer sighed. "You two are both hopeless."

"We're patriots, not politicians," Michael Pacino said, smiling. "Diane, let's reconvene the team tomorrow. I want to take these two cool kids to dinner out in town."

"Will the Secret Service let you do that?" Palmer asked.

"Do you think for a moment I care what the Secret Service wants?"

Palmer sighed and shook her head. She imitated someone saying, *"Join Michael Pacino's campaign, they said. It'll be fun, they said.* Dear God. You're going to destroy my career."

She left, exasperated.

Anthony smiled at his father. "You're enjoying this, aren't you?"

Michael Pacino smiled back. "Son, you have no idea."

————————

Prime Minister and Acting President Platon Melnik sat at the gigantic desk and read the article on the tablet computer, his half-frame reading glasses perched on his nose. It was an intelligence summary from the SVR about resurgent China, with it now seeming a certainty that Red China and White China would reunite. They had debated for weeks about what to name the new nation, finally settling on, "the Federated States of the Middle Kingdom," or FSMK.

Melnik detected motion in the room. Two of his SBP security guards put their hands to their ears as if they were listening, then suddenly wordlessly walked out of the room.

"What the hell?"

The door they'd left from remained open and four burly men in black tactical uniforms stormed in, with automatic weapons, full-face helmets and body armor. Their weapons were raised and aimed at Melnik. He stood from his desk, the tablet computer crashing to the carpeting. As he opened his mouth to speak, a man in a suit came into the room, wearing a black suit and red tie, exactly like Melnik's. He was Melnik's height and build and had the same baldness pattern. And as he grew closer, Melnik felt like he was looking into a mirror. The stranger was an exact duplicate of him.

"Who the hell are you?" he demanded.

Another figure walked slowly into the room and shut the door. It was President Dmitri Vostov, in a sweater and jeans, limping in on crutches. He answered Melnik's question, gesturing at the imposter.

"Why, this is Prime Minister and Acting President Platon Melnik. Say hello, Mr. Prime Minister."

The imposter opened his mouth to speak, and Melnik's voice came out. He said, "who is this man, Mr. President?"

"That man, Platon, is a man who violated my trust and almost started a war. He ordered our submarine to attack and destroy an American submarine. He ordered the Status-6 units be launched knowing that their navigation systems would be, at best, approximate, losing us control of the weapons, perhaps placing them in American hands. I do not know if he is incompetent, a traitor, or both." Vostov looked at the tactical team. "Take him away."

"Where am I going?" Melnik asked, watching the imposter calmly pick the computer back up and sit at the desk.

"To a dacha out of town," Vostov said. "Don't worry, it is luxurious. Fully stocked with food and alcohol. Fully staffed by beautiful hostesses. With news and internet and everything you could want, with the exception of a phone or the ability to send emails or digital information. You'll remain under house arrest until I say you can return to society."

Melnik swallowed hard and tried to resist the tactical team manhandling him out the door. They rushed him to the elevator, down the hall and out the building entrance doors. A waiting black panel van waited and he was loaded in the back. The van doors shut, and he was handcuffed into restraint hardware on the van wall. The van drove for hours, until it must have been hundreds of kilometers outside Moscow.

The van finally parked. The engine stopped. The back door opened. It was dark outside. Melnik was marched into a clearing of the woods.

"What's happening?" he asked. "Where are you taking me?"

He felt the pistol barrel on the back of his head.

After that, there was nothing.

The tactical SBP officer behind the body of Melnik picked up his legs and his deputy picked up the body's shoulders. They rolled him into a deep grave. A concrete truck's engine started and it backed up to the grave. A chute came out and the truck driver pulled a lever and cubic meter after cubic meter of concrete flowed down the chute and into the grave. The truck drove off, and the SBP officers scattered topsoil and brush over the concrete, then returned to the van. The van's engine started, and it turned back toward Moscow.

———————

Captain First Rank Sergei Kovalov walked down the jet ramp into the Murmansk terminal and through the doors from the secured area. The terminal waiting hall was filled with people.

He recognized the teenage girl running toward him, her mother smiling behind her.

"Daddy!" Magna Kovalov squealed. "You're alive!"

She ran to him, almost knocking him down, and threw her arms around him. He hugged her back and kissed the top of her head. By then, Kovalov's wife, Ivana, came up to him and hugged both Kovalov and his daughter.

"The news said your boat and *Belgorod* sank under the icecap," Ivana said, sobbing. "They said there were no survivors. What took you so long to come here? Where were you?"

"We had to debrief with President Vostov in Moscow," Kovalov said. "It took longer than anticipated. Vostov had a thousand questions."

"What happens now?" his wife asked. "Your *Losharik* sank, so you don't have a boat."

"We have a meeting with Admiral Alexeyev tomorrow morning. I suppose he will let me know then. I'm hoping he'll put me in command of one of the Yasen-M attack boats coming out of the drydock after atmospheric control modifications."

"I'd be happy if you just had a nice, safe, boring shore duty," Ivana said.

He smiled at her and his daughter, thinking that if there were anything good about this horrible mission, it was that it had returned his daughter to him. And his wife.

EPILOGUE

"Follow me," Anthony Pacino said to Rachel Romanov, leading her to the rear of the Naval Academy chapel, where concrete steps led down to a black brass double door. Pacino tried the knob, but it was locked. He pulled the knob upward and the door groaned. He pulled on the knob and the door slowly opened.

"What are you doing? Are you breaking into the chapel?" Rachel asked.

"This door has been rigged for decades," he said. "A secret that only midshipmen and grads know."

"Why doesn't the admiral-in-command have it fixed? Isn't he a graduate?"

"It's this way on purpose. Sometimes, in the middle of a dark night—or a dark night of the soul—midshipmen need to sneak down here. I used to. All the time. And in fact, once I met Admiral Murphy, the Superintendent, when I was here at three in the morning. Turns out he did the same thing I did."

"What are you talking about?" she asked.

"You'll see." Pacino opened the door and guided her in. She gasped as she entered.

"Oh my God. What is this?"

The beige marble floor led to an octagon formed by eight dark marble columns. In the center of the columns, a massive gleaming black sarcophagus was supported by four marble dolphins, the circle

554

of floor beneath the coffin gleaming black. An inscription was engraved on the floor.

JOHN PAUL JONES, 1747—1792

U.S. NAVY, 1775—1783

HE GAVE OUR NAVY ITS EARLIEST TRADITIONS

OF HEROISM AND VICTORY

ERECTED BY THE CONGRESS, A.D. 1912

"Captain John Paul Jones," Pacino said, "meet Lieutenant Commander Rachel Romanov."

"I'm absolutely speechless," she breathed. "I've never seen anything like this."

"Come over here and sit on this bench. This is where I used to sit when I'd come down here to talk to Captain Jones."

They sat on the marble bench that had a view of the coffin from the side.

"It's beautiful. It's amazing. I can see why you'd come here for inspiration."

"Not only inspiration," Pacino said, "but for luck."

"Luck?"

"I'd come before final exams. Or after I'd typed a term paper. There was a bad semester when I was sure I was going to get kicked out."

"You?"

"Yeah, I was okay in academics but I was a bit of a conduct case. Sneaking out to go to Chick's Diner out in town in the wee hours. Drinking in a Baltimore strip club as a third-class midshipman when a first-class midshipman came in, recognized me, and put me in for a class-A conduct violation. So yeah, Captain John Paul Jones and I talked a lot that semester."

Rachel laughed. "I'd say he gave you lots of luck," she said. "Maybe that's why your submarine operations go so well."

"All that death, Rachel. I don't think this last one went well at all."

"You lived and came back to me, Pacino," she said, looking adoringly into his eyes. She put her hand on his face. "That's all that matters. But why do you need luck *now*?"

"Because I'm going to ask you a question." Pacino stood, pulled something out of his pocket and sank to one knee.

"Oh dear God, no, Pacino, what are you doing?"

He opened the ring box, looked up at her and said, "Rachel Romanov, will you marry me and change your last name to Pacino?"

She'd clamped her hand to her mouth and tears suddenly streamed from her eyes, her cheeks wet with them.

But she looked at him through the tears and started laughing.

"What?" he said, feeling foolish, still kneeling.

"*No way* I'm marrying you, Pacino," she said, laughing. She plucked the ring from the box, admired it, and put it on her left ring finger, held out her hand and stared at it, smiling. "But I'm not an idiot, I'm keeping the ring."

Pacino stood up, his heart sinking. But when Romanov saw how his face fell, she stood and pulled him over to her, hugged him and whispered in his ear, "*Of course* I'll marry you, you idiot. But we can't do it now. They'd send one of us to a different ship or even a different base."

He looked into her wet eyes. "We could get married in secret," he offered.

"What good would that do? The whole purpose of getting married is to announce to the world that we're a couple and not to mess with us. And believe me, I can't wait for my last name to no longer be 'Romanov.' *Rachel Pacino*. Has a nice ring to it, don't you think?"

"What about the ring?" Pacino asked. "You can't wear that."

"I'll get a chain for it tomorrow and wear it around my neck. Next to my heart. Pacino?"

"Yeah?"

"Do you think you can wait?"

"It'll be years," Pacino said.

"I could always quit the Navy to be with you," she said.

"Hell no," Pacino said to her. "Are you kidding me? I'm not an idiot either. I have an executive officer—and acting captain—who dances to my tune. Why would I give *that* up?"

"*Dances to your tune?* Listen, mister, not only do I outrank you, I wear the pants in this family." She pulled a tissue from her purse and wiped her face. "Until you take the pants off me, that is."

Anthony Pacino smiled at Rachel Romanov, touched her face, brought her in to kiss her, then just hugged her hard as they stood silently in the crypt. He looked over at John Paul Jones' sarcophagus and mouthed the words, "Thank you, Captain Jones."

ALSO BY MICHAEL DIMERCURIO

VOYAGE OF THE DEVILFISH
Commander Michael Pacino is ordered on a mission of revenge to sink his father's killer, Admiral Alexi Novskoyy, who is aboard the Russian supersub Omega under the polar icecap about to deliver a surgical strike on the United States. The Russian Magnum nuclear torpedo dooms Pacino's USS *Devilfish*, which is trapped under thick polar ice and sinking fast.

ATTACK OF THE SEAWOLF
Captain Michael Pacino is called out of retirement to command the USS *Seawolf* on a desperate secret rescue mission during the Chinese Civil War when the Red Chinese capture the spying submarine *Tampa* in the Bo Hai Bay outside Beijing. While the SEAL commandos prepare to board the *Tampa*, the Red Chinese Northern Fleet closes in, leaving Pacino no option but surrender.

PHOENIX SUB ZERO
World War III breaks out between the United Islamic Front of God and the Western Coalition, and the Sword of Islam calls on the Japanese-technology super sub *Hegira* to deliver a new weapon to turn the course of a losing war. With the USS *Augusta* down and the *Phoenix* missing, Captain Michael Pacino is given the suicide mission of taking the USS *Seawolf* to sea and stop the Islamic submarine before it can unleash death on Washington.

BARRACUDA FINAL BEARING
When Japan attacks the new state of Greater Manchuria with a nuclear weapon, the U.S. responds with Operation Enlightened Curtain, a blockade around the Home Islands that the Japanese easily break with the highest technology submarine force ever built. The President gives Rear Admiral Michael Pacino the impossible mission

of using his underdog submarine fleet to turn the tide of the war, and Pacino leads the force into the war zone aboard the *Barracuda*.

PIRANHA FIRING POINT

Red China's ambush of breakaway White China could only be accomplished using a fleet of hijacked Japanese Rising Sun-class nuclear submarines, the best in the world. The sinking of the U.S. Rapid Deployment Force kicks off the War of the East China Sea, and the President turns to Vice Admiral Michael Pacino to win the counterattack. Pacino has no choice but to take the untested SSNX submarine to sea on a mission certain to fail.

THREAT VECTOR

Chief of Naval Operations Admiral Michael Pacino plans a stand-down retreat for the senior officers of the U.S. Navy. Eighty miles out of Port Norfolk, their cruise ship *Princess Dragon* is torpedoed by an unknown military terrorist. The SSNX submarine, the winner of the War of the East China Sea, sets out to find the submarine intruder, only to be put on the bottom. It is up to Commander Kelly McKee and the newest Virginia-class submarine in the fleet to find the attacking submarine and destroy it, but the terrorists' submarine *Vepr*, under the control of war criminal Alexi Novskoyy, has other plans.

TERMINAL RUN

One ship could revolutionize submarine warfare as we know it: the USS *Snarc*. A robotic combat sub carrying no crew, the *Snarc* has proven unbeatable in sea trials. And now it has fallen into the hands of an unseen enemy. The *Snarc*'s first casualty: the USS *Piranha*, the nuclear sub carrying Midshipman Anthony Pacino, the son of retired Admiral Michael Pacino. The only man who can match wits with the *Snarc*, Pacino returns to sea in a high-tech underwater battle unlike any that's been fought before, one that could engulf the world in war—and bring him face to face with his most hated nemesis.

EMERGENCY DEEP

U.S. Navy submarine commander Peter Vornado is at the top of his game in underwater warfare when a devastating illness takes him out of the service—and almost to the grave. Without duty, honor, or something to fight for, his life is as good as over. But the CIA needs a man like Vornado. A terrorist cabal has acquired a scrapped Soviet sub from the Cold War—a technologically advanced failure still able to outrun any torpedo or enemy vessel and strike at will. With a nuclear payload, it will enable them to strike directly at Israel—and throw the world into chaos. All that remains is to modernize the sub with the latest technology. Only one man can infiltrate the group, take the helm, and stop a holocaust—a man who has already stared down death, and is ready to do battle once more.

VERTICAL DIVE

As hurricane Helen barrels in toward the Virginia coastline, the U.S. Navy's Commander-in-Chief Atlantic Fleet orders all vessels to scramble to sea, including Burke Dillinger's *Hampton* and Peter Vornado's *Texas*. But this is no mere storm evacuation. There is something sinister going on in the eastern Atlantic. The Navy's eyes are on the ballistic missile submarine force, the "boomer" submarines loaded to the gills with intercontinental nuclear warheads. The French boomer submarine *Le Vigilant* has "gone bad," hijacked by an Algerian terrorist who dreams of completing the circle of revenge and using French nuclear weapons on the French who imprisoned his father. As terrorist Issam Zauabri's forces learn how to employ the nuclear missiles, Vornado's *Texas* and Dillinger's *Hampton* close in on the threat, but Issam knows how to use torpedoes as well as he does the missiles, and *Le Vigilant* is one of the quietest submarines ever built. Once the American subs are on the bottom, his attack can proceed on Paris, but since it was Americans who interfered, Issam will save one missile for New York.

DARK TRANSIT

Lieutenant Junior Grade Anthony Pacino reports aboard the "project boat" USS *Vermont* two years after having survived the catastrophic sinking of the *Piranha*. *Vermont*'s mission: to intercept and steal the Iranian Navy Kilo-class diesel-electric sub *Panther*, which is outfitted with a Russian fast reactor, the Russians using the Iranians for a dangerous test of the revolutionary reactor, a unit so potentially unstable that it could go prompt critical and explode. Anthony Pacino is chosen to be the second-in-command of the mission to hijack the *Panther*. The Russian Republic, expecting to monitor the nuclear reactor test, has sent two frontline Yasen-M-class nuclear fast attack submarines to escort the *Panther* during her test, but realizing the Americans are guilty of piracy on the high seas, the Russians have orders to seek and destroy both the *Panther* and the *Vermont*. The crew of *Vermont* soon realize that escaping with *Panther* has become a near impossibility. At the point that weapons fly, which submarines will survive and which sink is anyone's guess.

THE COMPLETE IDIOT'S GUIDE TO SUBMARINES

For those hungry to understand the technology of the nuclear submarine, this nonfiction guide describes the machinery, operations and personnel of a modern nuke. You'll learn how to make a periscope approach on a "skimmer," sneak up on a submerged target, program and launch a torpedo, scram and recover the reactor, and even flush the toilet at test depth. You'll see why a submarine can submerge without sinking, how nuclear power works, and how the steam plant makes the screw turn. You'll learn the main characters, from the COW to the Eng to the XO. Written in a humorous and engaging fashion, this book is an easy and fun read, yet packs all the information of an official U.S. Navy Submarine School tech manual.

ABOUT THE AUTHOR

Michael DiMercurio is an American veteran of the U.S. Navy Submarine force, engineer, project management and construction expert, bestselling author, commentator, and humorist.

DiMercurio graduated academically first in his U.S. Naval Academy (Annapolis) class with a bachelor's degree in mechanical engineering despite the class-A conduct offense of parking his hotrod in the admiral's space. In the face of Navy misgivings, DiMercurio was a National Science Foundation scholar to the Massachusetts Institute of Technology (MIT), graduating with an S.M. master's degree in mechanical engineering.

DiMercurio joined the crew of the Cold War-winning nuclear fast attack submarine USS *Hammerhead* where he earned the nuclear Navy's coveted "qualified in submarines" gold dolphins, allowing him to stand command watches as officer of the deck submerged. DiMercurio rose to become the "bull lieutenant," the most senior of the eight junior officers aboard and fifth-in-command. *Hammerhead* conducted numerous top secret North Atlantic and Mediterranean Sea operations, including "snapping up" and trailing three Soviet nuclear submarines and crossing the Gulf of Sidra's "Line of Death" to hide under a Russian nuclear cruiser to catch a targeted incoming Soviet attack submarine. While DiMercurio was a rebellious practical joker of an officer, invariably violating the captain's direct orders not to smoke cigars in the control room, he was undisputedly a tactical genius at detecting and trailing Soviet submarines.

After DiMercurio and *Hammerhead* won the Cold War and defeated the Soviet Union's sweeping octopus of world communism, making the world safe for democracy, with liberty and justice for all, amen, DiMercurio left active duty for civilian heavy industry project and construction executive management. DiMercurio built chemical and power plants in sites from Australia, Thailand, Indonesia, South Korea, India, Ontario, and dozens of sites in the USA, experiencing harrowing dealings with Mafia contractors, Rajasthani criminal thugs, and transgender barflies.

DiMercurio authored nine USA Today bestselling Navy submarine fiction novels such as *Dark Transit*, *Vertical Dive*, *Emergency Deep*, *Attack of the Seawolf*, and *Threat Vector* and the satirical non-fiction work, *The Complete Idiot's Guide to Submarines*. He was a commentator on Fox News during the 2005 Russian submersible *AS-28* rescue, personally calling out Vladimir Putin to man up and accept Western rescue efforts rather than deliberately letting his sailors die as he did in 2000 during the *Kursk* sinking. Suitably chastised, Putin gave the green light to British and American rescue divers and equipment, and the sailors lived.

As a commentator and columnist, DiMercurio writes essays on topics as diverse as international politics, conspiracy theories, the humorous side of divorce, military and civilian office politics, modern electronic-aided dating, and even such wildly ambitious topics as grammar and understanding women.

DiMercurio hangs his hardhat in Undisclosed Location, USA, and when he isn't writing, providing incisive content on social media sites, annoying the females in his life, he can be found lazing in a mellow cloud of cigar smoke, sipping Kentucky bourbon, or riding his obnoxiously loud Harley.

DiMercurio's website is www.terminalrun.com and his twitter is twitter.com/MikeyDiMercurio. He can be liked on Facebook at: http://facebook.com/michael.dimercurio.author.

Curious about other Crossroad Press books? Stop by our
website: http://crossroadpress.com
We offer quality writing
in digital, audio, and print formats.

Subscribe to our newsletter on the website homepage and receive a
free eBook.

Made in United States
North Haven, CT
23 November 2023

44450282R00350